Paris

EDWARD RUTHERFURD

HODDER

First published in Great Britain in 2013 by Hodder & Stoughton
An Hachette UK company

First published in paperback in 2013

1

A CIP catalogue record for this title is available from the British Library

A format ISBN 978 1 444 76763 6
B format ISBN 978 1 444 73681 6

Printed and bound by Clays Ltd, St Ives plc

Hodder & Stoughton policy is to use papers that are natural, renewable
and recyclable products and made from wood grown in sustainable
forests. The logging and manufacturing processes are expected to
conform to the environmental regulations of the country of origin.

Hodder & Stoughton Ltd
338 Euston Road
London NW1 3BH

www.hodder.co.uk

This book is dedicated to
the memory of my cousin,
Jean Louis Brizard,
paediatrician at the Beaujon Hospital,
the British Hospital, and the American Hospital in Paris

Contents

Paris

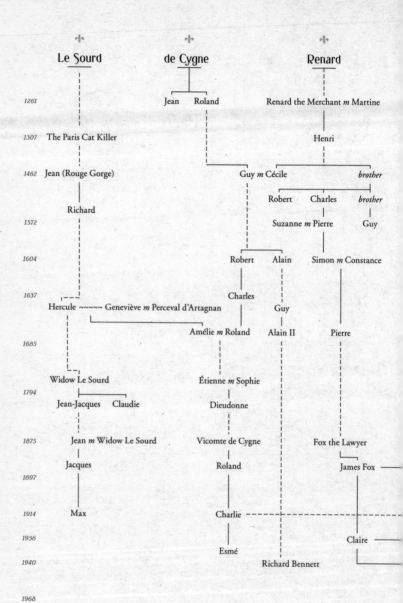

Le Sourd   de Cygne   Renard

1261   Jean   Roland   Renard the Merchant *m* Martine

1307   The Paris Cat Killer   Henri

1462   Jean (Rouge Gorge)   Guy *m* Cécile   *brother*

Richard   Robert   Charles   *brother*

1572   Suzanne *m* Pierre   Guy

1604   Robert   Alain   Simon *m* Constance

1637   Charles

Hercule ~~~~~ Geneviève *m* Perceval d'Artagnan   Guy

Amélie *m* Roland   Alain II   Pierre

1685

Widow Le Sourd   Étienne *m* Sophie

1794   Jean-Jacques   Claudie   Dieudonne

1875   Jean *m* Widow Le Sourd   Vicomte de Cygne   Fox the Lawyer

Jacques   Roland   James Fox ——

1897

1914   Max   Charlie - - - - - - - - - -

1936   Claire ——

1940   Esmé   Richard Bennett

1968

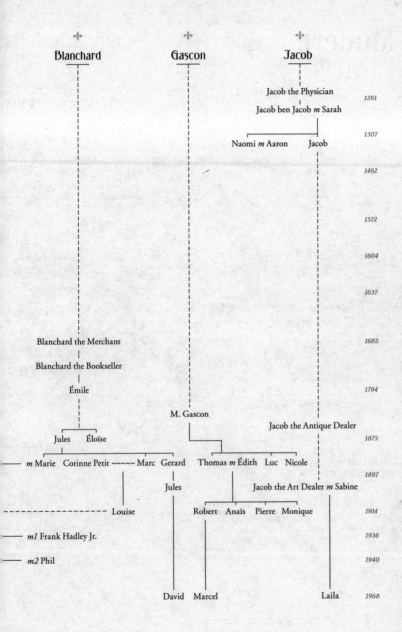

Blanchard   Gascon   Jacob

Jacob the Physician   1261
Jacob ben Jacob *m* Sarah

Naomi *m* Aaron   Jacob   1307

1462

1572

1604

1637

Blanchard the Merchant   1685

Blanchard the Bookseller

Émile   1794

M. Gascon

Jacob the Antique Dealer

Jules   Éloïse   1875

— *m* Marie   Corinne Petit ~~~~~ Marc   Gerard   Thomas *m* Édith   Luc   Nicole   1897

Jules   Jacob the Art Dealer *m* Sabine

---------------------- Louise   Robert   Anaïs   Pierre   Monique   1914

— *m1* Frank Hadley Jr.   1936

— *m2* Phil   1940

David   Marcel   Laila   1968

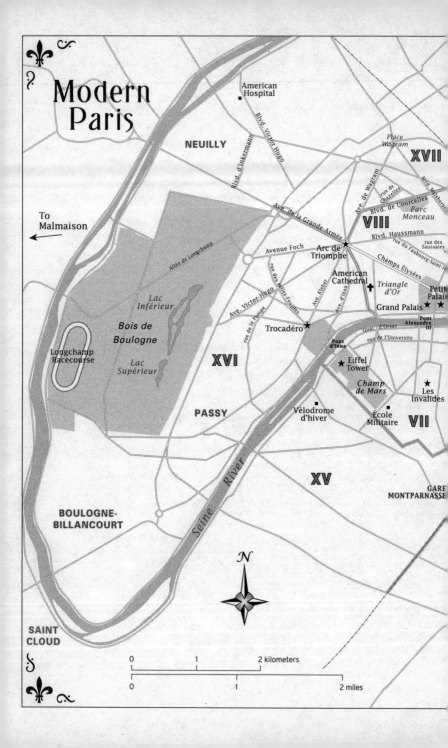

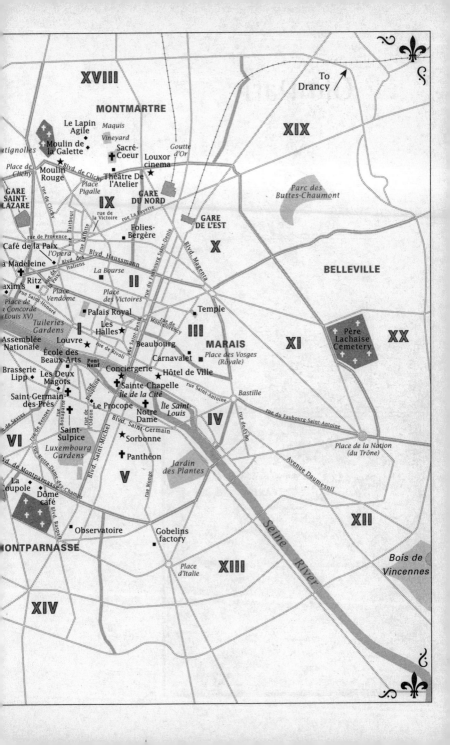

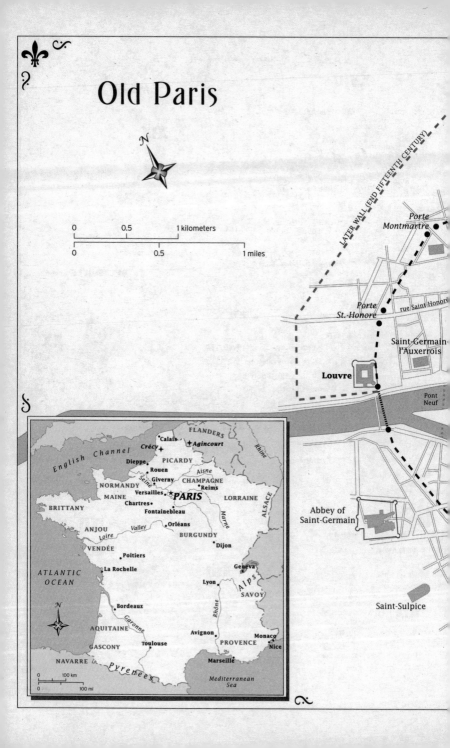

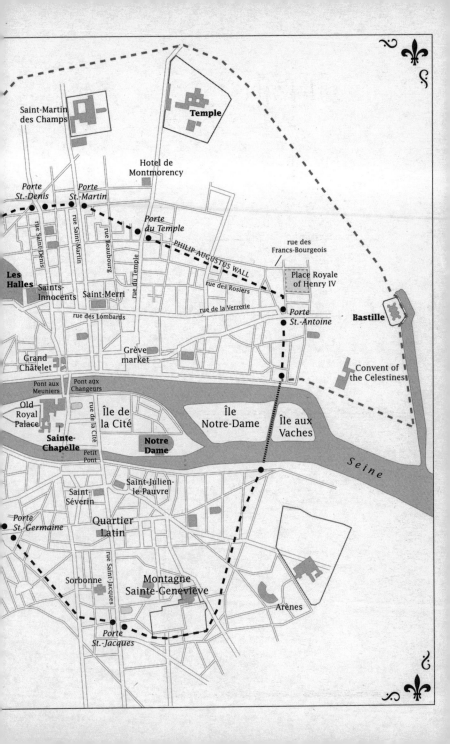

Saint-Martin
des Champs

Temple

Hotel de
Montmorency

*Porte
St.-Denis*   *Porte
St.-Martin*

*Porte
du Temple*

rue des
Francs-Bourgeois

PHILIP AUGUSTUS WALL

rue Saint-Denis

rue Saint-Martin

rue Beaubourg

rue du Temple

**Les
Halles**

Saints-
Innocents

Saint-Merri

rue des Rosiers

Place Royale
of Henry IV

rue de la Verrerie

*Porte
St.-Antoine*

Bastille

rue des Lombards

Grève
market

Convent of
the Celestines

Grand
Châtelet

Pont aux
Meuniers

Pont aux
Changeurs

Old
Royal
Palace

rue de la Cité

Île de
la Cité

Île
Notre-Dame

Île aux
Vaches

**Sainte-
Chapelle**

**Notre
Dame**

S e i n e

Petit
Pont

Saint-Julien-
le-Pauvre

*Porte
St.-Germaine*

Saint-
Séverin

**Quartier
Latin**

Sorbonne

rue Saint-Jacques

**Montagne
Sainte-Geneviève**

Arènes

*Porte
St.-Jacques*

Chapter One

1875

*P*aris. City of love. City of dreams. City of splendour. City of saints and scholars. City of gaiety.

Sink of iniquity.

In two thousand years, Paris had seen it all.

It was Julius Caesar who had first seen the possibilities of the place where the modest Parisii tribe made their home. The Mediterranean lands of southern Gaul had already been Roman provinces for generations at that time; but when Caesar decided to bring the troublesome Celtic tribes of northern Gaul into the empire as well, it hadn't taken him long.

The Romans had quickly seen that this was a logical place for a town. A collecting point for the produce of the huge fertile plains of northern Gaul, the Parisian territory lay on the navigable River Seine. From its headwaters farther south, there was an easy portage to the huge River Rhône, which ran down to the busy ports of the Mediterranean. Northwards, the Seine led to the narrow sea across which the island of Britannia lay. This was the great river system through which the southern and northern worlds were joined. Greek and Phoenician traders had been using it even before the birth of Rome. The site was perfect. The Parisian heartland lay in a wide, shallow valley through which the Seine made a series of graceful loops. In the centre of the valley, on a handsome east-west bend, the river widened and several big mudflats and islands lay, like so many huge barges at anchor, in the stream. On the northern bank, meadows and marshes stretched far and wide until they came to the lip of low, enclosing ridges, from which several small hills and promon tories jutted out, some of them covered with vineyards.

But it was on the southern bank – the left bank as one went downstream – that the ground near the river swelled gently into a low, flat hillock, like a table overlooking the water. And it was here that the Romans had laid out their town, a large forum and the main temple covering the top of the table with an amphitheatre nearby, a grid of streets all around, and a north-south road running straight through the centre, across the water to the largest island, which was now a suburb with a fine temple to Jupiter, and over a farther bridge to the northern bank. They had originally called the town Lutetia. But it was also known, more grandly, as the city of the Parisii.

In the Dark Ages after the Roman Empire fell, the German tribe of Franks had conquered the territory in the Land of the Franks, as it came to be called, or France. Its rich countryside had been invaded by Huns and Viking Norsemen. But the island in the river, with its wooden defences, like some battered old ship, survived. In medieval times, she'd grown into a great city, her maze of Gothic churches, tall timbered houses, dangerous alleys and stinking cellars spread across both sides of the Seine, enclosed by a high stone wall. Stately Notre-Dame Cathedral graced the island. Her university was respected all over Europe. Yet even then, the English came and conquered her. And Paris might have been English if Joan of Arc, the miraculous maid, hadn't appeared and chased them out.

Old Paris: city of bright colours and narrow streets, of carnival and plague.

And then there was new Paris.

The change had come slowly. From the time of the Renaissance, lighter, classical spaces began to appear in her dark medieval mass. Royal palaces and noble squares created a new splendour. Broad boulevards began to carve through the rotting old warrens. Ambitious rulers created vistas worthy of ancient Rome.

Paris had altered her face to suit the magnificence of Louis XIV, and the elegance of Louis XV. The Age of Enlightenment and the new republic of the French Revolution had encouraged classical simplicity, and the age of Napoléon bequeathed imperial grandeur.

Recently, this process of change had been accelerated by a new town planner. Baron Haussmann's great network of boulevards and long, straight streets lined with elegant office and apartment blocks was so thorough that there were quarters of Paris now where the rich mess of the Middle Ages was scarcely to be seen.

Yet old Paris was still there, around almost every corner, with her memories of centuries past, and of lives relived. Memories as haunting as an old, half-forgotten tune that, when played again – in another age, in another key, whether on harp or hurdy-gurdy – is still the same. This was her enduring grace.

Was Paris now at peace with herself? She had suffered and survived, seen empires rise and fall. Chaos and dictatorship, monarchy and republic: Paris had tried them all. And which did she like best? Ah, there was a question . . . For all her age and grace, it seemed she did not know.

Recently, she had suffered another terrible crisis. Four years ago, her people had been eating rats. Humiliated first, starving next. Then they had turned upon each other. It had not been long since the bodies had been buried and the smell of death dispersed by the wind, and the echo of the firing squads departed over the horizon.

Now, in the year 1875, she was recovering. But many great issues remained still to be resolved.

The little boy was only three. A fair-haired, blue-eyed child. Some things he knew already. Others were still kept from him. And then there were the secrets.

Father Xavier gazed at him. How like his mother the child looked. Father Xavier was a priest, but he was in love with a woman, the mother of this child. He admitted his passion to himself, but his self-discipline was complete. No one would have guessed his love. As for the little boy, God surely had a plan for him.

Perhaps that he should be sacrificed.

It was a sunny day in the fashionable Tuileries Gardens in front of the Louvre, where nannies watched their children play, and Father Xavier was taking him for a walk. Father Xavier: family confessor, friend in need, priest.

'What are your names?' he playfully asked the child.

'Roland, D'Artagnan, Dieudonné de Cygne.' He knew them all by heart.

'Bravo, young man.' Father Xavier Parle-Doux was a small, wiry man in his forties. Long ago he'd been a soldier. A fall from a horse had left him with a stabbing pain in his back ever since – though only a handful of people were aware of it.

But his days as a soldier had marked him in another way. He had done his duty. He'd seen killing. He had seen things worse than killing. And in the end, it had seemed to him that there must be something better than this, something more sacred, an undying flame of light and love in the terrible darkness of the world. He'd found it in the heart of the Holy Church.

Also, he was a monarchist.

He'd known the child's family all his life, and now he looked down at him with affection, but also with pity. Roland had no brother or sister. His mother, that beautiful soul, the woman he himself would have liked to marry had he not chosen another calling, suffered with delicate health. The future of the family might rest on little Roland alone: a heavy burden for a boy to bear.

But he knew that as a priest, he must take a larger view. What was it the Jesuits said? 'Give us a boy till he's seven, and he's ours for life.' Whatever God's plan for this child, whether that service led to happiness or not, Father Xavier would lead him towards it.

'And who was Roland?'

'Roland was a hero.' The little boy looked up for approval. 'My mother read me the story. He was my ancestor,' he added solemnly.

The priest smiled. The famous *Song of Roland* was a haunting, romantic tale, from a thousand years ago, about how the emperor Charlemagne's friend was cut off as the army crossed the mountains. How Roland blew on his horn for help, to no avail. How the Saracens slew him, and how the emperor wept for the loss of his friend. The de Cygne family's claim to this ancestor was fanciful, but charming.

'Others of your ancestors were crusading knights.' Father Xavier nodded encouragingly. 'But this is natural. You are of noble birth.' He paused. 'And who was D'Artagnan?'

'The famous Musketeer. He was my ancestor.'

As it happened, the hero of *The Three Musketeers* had been based upon a real man. And Roland's family had married a noblewoman of the same name back in the time of Louis XIV – though whether they had taken much interest in this connection before the novel made the name famous, the priest rather doubted.

'You have the blood of the D'Artagnans in your veins. They were soldiers who served their king.'

'And Dieudonné?' the child asked.

Hardly were the words out before Father Xavier checked himself. He must be careful. Could the child have any idea of the horror of the guillotine that lay behind the last of his names?

'Your grandfather's name is beautiful, you know,' he replied. 'It means "the gift of God".' He thought for a moment. 'The birth of

4

your grandfather was – I do not say a miracle – but a sign. And remember one thing, Roland,' the priest continued. 'Do you know the motto of your family? It is very important. "*Selon la volonté de Dieu*" – "According to God's Will".'

Father Xavier turned his eyes up to survey the landscape all around. To the north rose the hill of Montmartre, where Saint Denis had been martyred by pagan Romans, sixteen centuries ago. To the south-west, behind the towers of Notre-Dame, rose the slope above the Left Bank where, as the old Roman Empire was crumbling, the indefatigable Saint Geneviève had asked God to turn Attila and his Huns away from the city – and her prayers had been answered.

Time and again, thought the priest, God had protected France in her hour of need. When the Moslems had first swept up from Africa and Spain, and might have overrun all Europe, hadn't He sent a great general, the grandfather of Charlemagne, to beat them back? When the English, in their long, medieval struggle with the French kings, had even made themselves masters of Paris, hadn't the good Lord given France the maiden Joan of Arc to lead her armies to victory?

Most important of all, God had given France her royal family, whose Capetian, Valois and Bourbon branches for thirty generations had ruled, reunited and made glorious this sacred land.

And through all those centuries, the de Cygnes had faithfully served those divinely anointed kings.

This was the little boy's heritage. He would understand it in due course.

It was time to go home. Behind them, at the end of the Tuileries Gardens, lay the vast open space of the Place de la Concorde. Beyond that, the magnificent sweep of the Champs-Élysées, for two miles up to the Arc de Triomphe.

The little boy was still too young to know the Place de la Concorde's part in his history. As for the Arc de Triomphe, grand though it was, Father Xavier did not care for republican monuments.

Instead, he gazed again at the hill of Montmartre – that site where once a pagan temple stood; where Saint Denis had been martyred;

and where such terrible scenes had taken place in the recent upheavals in the city. How appropriate that this very year, a new temple should be arising there by the windmills, a temple to Catholic France, its pure, white dome shining like a dove over the city. The basilica of Sacré Coeur, the Sacred Heart.

This was the temple where the little boy should serve. For God had saved his family for a reason. There was shame to be overcome, faith to be restored.

'Could you walk a little way?' he asked. Roland nodded. With a smile, the priest reached down and took the child's hand. 'Shall we sing a song?' he asked. ' "*Frère Jacques*",' perhaps?'

So hand in hand the priest and the little boy, watched by several nannies and their charges, walked out of the gardens, singing.

As Jules Blanchard reached the Louvre end of the Champs-Élysées and walked up towards the church of La Madeleine, he had every reason to be a happy man. He already had two sons, good boys both of them. But he'd always wanted a daughter. And at eight o'clock this morning, his wife had presented him with a baby girl.

There was only one problem. And solving it would require a certain delicacy – which was why, at this moment, he was going to a rendezvous with a lady who was not his wife.

Jules Blanchard was a well-set, vigorous man, with a solid family fortune. The century before, as the charming, rococo monarchy of Louis XV encountered the grand ideas of the Enlightenment, and the French Revolution turned the world upside down, his ancestor had been a bookseller of radical views. The bookseller's son, Jules's grandfather, was a doctor who came to the notice of the rising general, Napoléon Bonaparte, during the Revolution, and never looked back. A fashionable physician under Napoléon's empire and the restored Bourbon monarchy that followed it, he'd finally retired to a handsome house in Fontainebleau, which the family still possessed. His wife was from a merchant family, and in the next generation, Jules's father had gone into business. Specialising in wholesaling grain, by the mid-nineteenth century he had built up a considerable fortune. Jules had joined the business and now, at the age of thirty-five, he was ready to take over from his father, whenever that worthy gentleman chose finally to retire.

At La Madeleine, Jules turned half-right. He liked this boulevard because it led past the city's huge new opera house. The Paris Opéra, designed by Garnier, had been completed only at the start of this year, but already it was a landmark. Besides its many hidden wonders – which included an ingenious artificial lake in the cellars to control the swamp waters below – the Opéra was such a magnificent concoction that, with its great, round roof, it reminded Jules of an enormous, decorated gâteau. It was rich, it was flamboyant, it was the spirit of the age – at least, for lucky fellows like him.

And now he was in sight of his rendezvous. Just a short way past the Opéra, on a corner site, was the Café Anglais. Unlike the Opéra, it was rather plain outside. But inside was another matter. It was lavish enough for princes. A few years ago, the emperors of Russia and Germany had dined there together for a legendary feast that went on for eight hours.

Where else could one meet Joséphine for lunch?

They had opened the big panelled room known as Le Grand Seize for lunch today. As he entered past bowing waiters, gilt mirrors and potted plants, he saw her at once.

Joséphine Tessier was the kind of fashionable woman whom head waiters placed in the centre of the room – unless the lady murmured that she wished to be discreet. Expensive and elegant, she was wearing a pale grey silk gown, a lace ruff at her throat and a jaunty little hat with a feather in it.

He was greeted by a rustle of silk, and an intoxicating scent. He lightly kissed her hand, sat down and told the waiter to bring champagne.

'A celebration?' inquired the lady. 'You have good news?'

'It's a girl.'

'Congratulations.' She smiled. 'I am very happy for you, my dear Jules. It's what you had wanted.'

He had been wonderfully fortunate, Jules considered, to have been Joséphine's lover when they were both young. For all his wealth, he thought, he probably couldn't afford her now. A very rich banker indeed kept her these days. Nonetheless, he counted their relationship as one of the best that a man can have. She was his former mistress, his confidante and his friend.

The champagne arrived. They toasted the baby. Then they ordered, and chatted of this and that. Only with the appearance of a light, clear soup did he broach the subject on his mind.

'There is a problem,' he said. Joséphine waited. His face became gloomy. 'My wife wants to call her Marie,' he said at last.

'Marie.' His friend considered. 'It's not a bad name.'

'I always promised you if I had a daughter, I should call her after you.'

She looked up at him, surprised.

'That was a long time ago, *chéri*. It doesn't matter.'

'But it does matter. I wish to call her Joséphine.'

'And what if your wife associates the name with me?'

'She doesn't know about us. I am certain of it. I mean to insist.' He sipped his champagne moodily. 'You really think there is a danger?'

'I shall not tell her, you may be sure,' Joséphine answered. 'But others might . . .' She shook her head. 'You are playing with fire.'

'I thought I'd say,' he persisted, 'that I want to name her after the empress Joséphine.'

The beautiful wife of Napoléon, the love of the emperor's life. A romantic legend – up to a point.

'But she was notoriously unfaithful to the emperor,' Joséphine pointed out. 'Perhaps not a good example for your daughter.'

'I was hoping you'd come up with something.'

'No.' Joséphine shook her head. 'My friend, this is a very bad idea. Call your daughter Marie, and make your wife happy. That is all I have to say.'

The next course was another speciality of the house: lobster, sliced in aspic. They spoke of old friends, and the opera. It was not until the dessert, a salad of fruits, that Joséphine, after looking at him reflectively for a few moments, took up the subject of his marriage again.

'Do you want to make your wife unhappy, *chéri*? Has she done something bad to you?'

'Not at all.'

'Are you unfaithful?'

'No.'

'Does she satisfy you?'

He shrugged.

'It's fine.'

'You must learn to be happy, Jules,' she said with a sigh. 'You have everything you want, including your wife.'

It had not been a shock, nor even a surprise, to Joséphine when Jules Blanchard had married. His wife was a cousin on his mother's side, and brought a large dowry. As Jules had put it at the time: 'Two parts of a family fortune have found each other again.'

But Jules was still frowning.

Joséphine Tessier had studied many men in her life. It was her profession. In her opinion, men were often discontented because their occupation did not suit them. Of others, one could even say that they had been born at the wrong time – a natural knight in armour, for instance, trapped in a modern world. But Jules Blanchard was perfectly made for nineteenth-century France.

When the French Revolution had broken the power of the king and the aristocracy – the *ancien régime* – it had left the field open to the rich, the haute bourgeoisie. Napoléon had created his personal version of the Roman Empire, with his triumphal arches and his quest for glory, but he had also taken care to appeal to the solid middle classes. And so it had remained after his fall.

True, some conservatives wanted to return to the *ancien régime*, but the only time the restored Bourbon monarchy tried that, in 1830, the Parisians had kicked out the Bourbon king and installed Louis Philippe, a royal cousin of the Orléans line, as their constitutional and very bourgeois monarch.

On the other side, there were radicals, even socialists, who hated the new bourgeois France, and wanted another revolution. But when they took to the streets in 1848, thinking their time had come, it was not a socialist state, but a conservative republic that emerged, followed by an ornately bourgeois empire under Napoléon III – the great emperor's nephew – that again favoured the bankers and stockbrokers, the property men and larger merchants. Men like Jules Blanchard.

These were the men to be seen riding with their beautifully dressed women in the Bois de Boulogne on the city's western edge, or gathering for elegant evenings at the huge new Opéra house, where Jules and his wife liked to be seen. There was no doubt, Joséphine thought, that Jules Blanchard had the best of the present century.

Why, he'd even had her.

'What's the matter, my friend?' she gently inquired.

9

Jules considered. He knew that he was lucky. And he valued what he had. He loved the old family house at Fontainebleau, with its enclosed courtyard, his grandfather's First Empire furniture and leather-bound books. He loved the elegant royal château in the town, older and more modest than the vast palace of Versailles. On Sundays he would walk in the nearby Forest of Fontainebleau, or ride out to the village of Barbizon, where Corot had painted landscapes filled with the haunting light of the River Seine. In Paris, he was happy trading in the great medieval wholesale market of Les Halles, with its brightly coloured stalls, and bustle, and the scents of cheeses, herbs and fruits from every region of France. He was proud of his intimate knowledge of the city's ancient churches, and its ancient inns with their deep wine cellars.

Yet it wasn't enough.

'I'm bored,' he said. 'I want to change my career.'

'To what, my dear Jules?'

'I have a plan,' he confided. 'It will astonish you.' He made a sweeping gesture. 'A new business for the new Paris.'

When Jules Blanchard spoke of the new Paris, he didn't mean only the broad boulevards of Baron Haussmann. Even from the days of France's great Gothic cathedrals, Paris had liked to think of herself – at least in northern Europe – as the leader of fashion. Parisians had not been pleased when, a quarter of a century ago, in a dramatic palace of glass built for the occasion, London had captured international headlines with her Great Exhibition of all that was new and exciting in the world. New York had followed soon after. But by 1855, Paris was ready to fight back, and her new emperor, Napoléon III, had opened her Universal Exposition of industry and the arts, in a stupendous hall of iron, glass and stone on the Champs-Élysées. A dozen years later Paris did it again, this time on the vast parade ground on the Left Bank known as the Champ de Mars. This 1867 exhibition was the biggest the world had ever seen, featuring many marvels, including Siemens's first electric dynamo.

'I want a department store,' said Jules. New York had department stores: Macy's was thriving. London had Whiteleys in the suburbs and a few cooperatives, but nothing dramatic yet. Paris was already ahead in size and style, with Bon Marché and Printemps. 'It's the future,' Jules declared. And he began to describe the store he had in mind, a great palace selling all kinds of merchandise to a huge audience. 'Style, keen prices, right in the centre of the city,' he explained with growing excitement, while Joséphine watched him with fascination.

'I never knew you could be so passionate,' she remarked.

'Oh.'

'I mean, in the head.' She smiled.

'Ah.'

'And what does your father think?'

'He will not hear of it.'

'What will you do?'

'Wait.' He sighed. 'What else can I do?'

'You would not go off on your own?'

'Difficult. He controls the money. And to disrupt the family . . .'

'You love your father, don't you?'

'Of course.'

'Be kind to your father and to your wife, my dear Jules. Be patient.'

'I suppose so.' He was silent for a while. Then he brightened. 'But I still want to call my daughter Joséphine.'

Then, explaining that he must get back to his wife, he got up to go. She laid a restraining hand on him.

'You must not do this, my friend. For my sake, also. Don't do it.'

But without committing himself, he paid the waiter and left.

After he had gone, Joséphine was thoughtful. Did he really mean to call his daughter Joséphine? Or, remembering a foolish promise made long ago, had he just played a pretty scene, putting her in a position where he could be sure she would free him from that promise? She smiled to herself. It didn't matter. Even if the latter, it was kind and clever of him.

She liked clever men. And it amused her that she was still left wondering what he would do.

The tall woman paused. She was gaunt. Beside her stood a dark-haired boy of nine, his hair cut short, his eyes set wide apart. He looked intelligent.

The widow Le Sourd was forty, but whether it was the drab clothes that hung loosely from her angular body, or that her long hair was grey and unkempt, or that she had a stony face, she seemed much older. And if she looked grim, it was for a reason.

The night before, not for the first time, her son had asked her a question. And today she had decided that it was time to tell him the truth.

'Let us go in,' she said.

The great cemetery of Père Lachaise occupied the slopes of a hill about three miles to the east of the Tuileries Gardens, from which Father Xavier and the little Roland had departed an hour before. It was an ancient burial ground, but in recent times it had become famous. All kinds of great men – statesmen, soldiers, artists and composers – were buried there, and visitors often came to admire their tombs. But it was not a grave that the widow Le Sourd had brought her son to see.

They entered by the gateway on the city side, below the hill. In front of them stretched tree-lined alleys and cobbled walks, like little Roman roads, between the sepulchres. It was quiet. Apart from the guardian at the gate, they had the place almost to themselves. The widow knew exactly where she was going. The boy did not.

First, just to the right of the entrance, they paused to view the monument that had made the place famous, the tall shrine of the medieval lovers Abelard and Héloïse. But they did not stay there long. Nor did the widow bother with any of Napoléon's famous marshals, nor Corot the painter's recent grave, nor even the graceful tomb of Chopin the composer. For they would have been distractions. Before she told her son the truth, she had to prepare him.

'Jean Le Sourd was a brave man.'

'I know, Maman.' His father had been a hero. Every night, before he went to sleep, he would go over in his mind everything he could remember about the tall, kindly figure who told him stories and played ball with him. The man who would always bring bread to the table, even when Paris was starving. And if sometimes the memories became a little hazy, there was always the photograph of a handsome man, dark-haired and with eyes set wide apart, like himself. Sometimes he dreamed of him. They would go on adventures together. Once they were even fighting in a street battle, side by side.

For several minutes his mother led him up the slope in silence until, below the crown of the hill, she turned right on to a long alley. Then she spoke again.

'Your father had a noble soul.' She looked down at her son. 'What do you think it means, Jacques, to be noble?'

'I suppose . . .' – the boy considered – 'to be brave, like the knights who fought for honour.'

'No,' she said harshly. 'Those knights in armour were not noble at all. They were thieves, tyrants, who took all the wealth and power they could. They called themselves noble to puff themselves up with pride, and pretend that their blood was better than ours, so they could do what they liked. Aristocrats!' She grimaced. 'A false nobility. And the worst of them all was the king. A filthy conspiracy that went on for centuries.'

Young Jacques knew that his mother revered the French Revolution. But after the death of his father she had always avoided speaking about such things, as though they belonged in some place of darkness that she did not want to enter.

'Why did it last so long, Maman?'

'Because there was a criminal power even worse than the king. Do you know what that was?'

'No, Maman.'

'It was the Church, Jacques. The king and his aristocrats supported the Church, and the priests told the people to obey them. That was the bargain of the *ancien régime*. An enormous lie.'

'Didn't the Revolution change that?'

'The year 1789 was more than a revolution. It was the birth of Freedom itself. Liberty, Equality, Fraternity: these are the noblest ideas that men can have. The *ancien régime* fought against them, so the Revolution cut off their heads. It was absolutely necessary. But more than that. The Revolution released us from the prison that the Church had made. The power of the priests was broken. People were free to deny God, to be free of superstition, and follow reason. It was a great step forward for mankind.'

'What happened to the priests, Maman? Were they killed, too?'

'Some.' She shrugged. 'Not enough.'

'But the priests are still here today.'

'Unfortunately.'

'So were all the men of the Revolution atheists?'

'No. But the best were.'

'You do not believe in God, Maman?' asked Jacques. His mother shook her head. 'Did my father?' he pursued.

'No.'

The boy was thoughtful for a moment.

'Then nor shall I,' he said.

The path was curving towards the east, drawing closer to the outer edge of the cemetery.

'What happened to the Revolution, Maman? Why didn't it last?'

His mother shrugged again.

'There was confusion. Napoléon came to power. He was half revolutionary, and half a Roman emperor. He nearly conquered all Europe before he was defeated.'

'Was he an atheist?'

'Who knows. The Church never got its power back, but he found the priests useful to him – like most rulers.'

'And after him, things went back to how they were before?'

'Not exactly. All the monarchs of Europe were terrified of revolution. For thirty years they managed to hold the forces of freedom down. The conservatives in France – the old monarchists, the rich bourgeois, everyone who feared change – they all supported conservative governments. The people had no power, the poor grew poorer. But the spirit of freedom never died. In 1848, revolutions started breaking out all over Europe, including here. Fat old Louis Philippe, the king of the bourgeois classes, was so frightened that he got in a taxi and disappeared to England. We became a republic again. And we elected the nephew of Napoléon to lead it.'

'But he made himself emperor.'

'He wanted to be like his uncle. After two years leading the republic, he made himself emperor – and since the great Napoléon had left a son who died, he called himself Napoléon III.' She shook her head. 'Oh, he was a good showman. Baron Haussmann rebuilt Paris. There was a splendid new opera house. Huge exhibitions to which half the world came. But the poor were no better off. And then, after ten years, he made a stupid mistake. He started a war with Germany. But he was no general, and he lost it.'

'I remember when the Germans came to Paris.'

'They smashed our armies and surrounded Paris. It went on for months. We nearly starved. You did not know it, but at the end, the little stews I fed you were made of rats. You were only five, but luckily you were strong. Finally, when they bombarded us with heavy artillery, there was nothing more we could do. Paris surrendered.' She sighed. 'The Germans went back to Germany, but they made us give up Alsace and Lorraine – those beautiful regions along our side of the River Rhine, with their vineyards and mountains. France was humiliated.'

'It was after that when my father was killed. You always told me he died fighting. But I never really understood. The teachers in school say –'

'Never mind what they say,' his mother cut in. 'I will tell you what happened.' She paused nonetheless, and upon her face there briefly appeared the ghost of a tender smile.

'You know,' she continued, 'when I wanted to marry, my family were not very happy. We were quite poor, but my father was a school-teacher, and he wanted me to marry an educated man. Jean Le Sourd was the son of a labourer, with little formal schooling. He worked at a printer's, setting type. But he had an enormous curiosity.'

'So what happened?'

'My father decided to educate my future husband. And your father didn't mind. In fact, he was a wonderful student, and soon he was reading everything. In the end, I think he had read more than any man I know. And it was through his study that he came to the beliefs for which he died.'

'He believed in the Revolution.'

'Your father came to understand that even the French Revolution was not enough. By the time you were born, he knew that the only way forward was the absolute rule of the people and the end of private property. And many brave men thought the same thing.'

On their right now, behind some trees, they could see the ceme-tery's outer wall. They were almost at their destination.

'Four years ago,' she continued, 'it seemed the chance had come. Napoléon III was defeated. The government, such as it was, rested in the hands of the National Assembly, which had fled to the country palace of Versailles. The deputies were so conservative, we thought they might decide upon another monarchy. The Assembly feared Paris, you see, because we had our own militia and a lot of cannon up on the hill of Montmartre. They sent troops to take our cannon. But the troops joined us. And suddenly it happened: Paris decided to govern itself. That was the Commune.'

'My teachers say it didn't go well.'

'They lie. It was a wonderful time, that early spring. Everything functioned. The Commune took over Church property. They started giving women equal rights. We flew the Red Flag of the people. Men like your father were organising whole districts like workers' states. The Assembly at Versailles was terrified.'

'Then the Assembly attacked Paris?'

'They were stronger by then. They had army troops. The Germans even returned prisoners of war to strengthen the Versailles army against the people. It was disgusting. We defended the gates of Paris. We put up barricades in the street. The poor of the city fought like heroes. But in the end, they were too strong for us. The final week of May – Bloody Week – was the worst . . .'

The widow Le Sourd stopped speaking now for a few moments. They had come to the south-eastern corner of the cemetery now, where the path rose more steeply as it curved to the left up the central hill. To the right of the cobbled walk, down a slope, stood the blank stone face of the graveyard's outer wall, with a small, empty triangle of ground in front of it. It was a nondescript little corner of the place that had never been given any dignity or name.

'In the end,' the widow went on quietly, 'the last area to hold out was the poor quarter of Belleville just nearby. Some of our people were fighting up there.' She gestured to the tombs on the crown of the hill behind them. 'Finally, it was over. The last hundred or so of the Communards were captured. One of them was your father.'

'You mean, they took him to prison?'

'No. There was an officer in charge of the troops. He ordered them to take the prisoners down there.' She pointed to the blank stretch of wall. 'Then he lined up his troops and ordered them to shoot the prisoners. Just like that. So this is where your father died, and that is how. Now you know.'

Then the tall, gaunt widow Le Sourd suddenly started to weep. And her son watched. But she soon corrected herself and gazed stonily, for a minute or so, at the blank wall where her marriage ended.

'Let us go now,' she said. And they began to walk back.

They were nearly in sight of the entrance to the cemetery when Jacques interrupted her thoughts.

'What happened to the officer who had them shot like that?' he asked.

'Nothing.'

'You know this? You know who it was?'

'I discovered. He is an aristocrat, as you might expect. There are still plenty of them in the army. His name is the Vicomte de Cygne.' She shrugged. 'He has a son, younger than you, called Roland.'

Jacques Le Sourd was silent for a minute.

'Then one day I shall kill his son.' It was said quietly, but it was final.

His mother did not respond. She walked on a dozen paces. Was she going to tell him not to think of vengeance? Not at all. Her love had been passionate, and passion takes no prisoners. The righteous strike down their enemies. It is their destiny.

'Have patience, Jacques,' she answered. 'Wait until the time is right.'

'I shall wait,' the boy said. 'But Roland de Cygne will die.'

Chapter Two

1883

The day started badly. His little brother Luc had disappeared.

Thomas Gascon loved his family. His elder sister, Adèle, had married and moved away; and his younger sister, Nicole, was always with her best friend, Yvette, whose conversation bored him. But Luc was special. He was the baby of the family. The funny little boy whom everybody loved. Thomas had been almost ten when he was born, and had been his guide, philosopher and friend ever since.

In fact, Luc had been absent the evening before. But since his father had assured them that the boy was with his cousins who lived less than a mile away, nobody had worried. Only when Thomas was about to go to work had he overheard his mother's cry.

'You mean you don't *know* he's at your sister's?'

'But of course he's there.' His father's voice from his bed. 'He went there yesterday afternoon. Where else would he be?'

Monsieur Gascon was an easy-going man. He earned his living as a water carrier, but he wasn't very reliable. 'He works exactly as much as he has to,' his wife would say, 'and not a second more.' And he would have agreed with her because, in his mind, this was the only reasonable thing to do. 'Life is for living,' he'd say. 'If you can't sit and have a glass of wine . . .' He'd make a gesture, indicating the futility of all other occupations. Not that he drank so much. But sitting was important to him.

He appeared now, barefoot and unshaven, pulling on his clothes and ready to argue. But his wife cut him off.

'Nicole,' she commanded, 'run to your aunt at once and see if Luc is there.' Then, turning to her husband: 'Ask the neighbours if they have seen your son. To your shame!' she added furiously.

'What shall I do?' Thomas asked.

'Go to work, of course.'

'But . . .' Thomas wasn't happy about leaving without knowing that his brother was safe.

'You want to be late and lose your job?' his mother demanded crossly, then softened. 'You're a good boy, Thomas. Your father is probably right that he's at your aunt's.' And seeing her son still hesitate: 'Don't worry. If there's a problem, I'll send Nicole to find you. I promise.'

So Thomas ran down the hill of Montmartre.

Although he was worried about his little brother, he certainly didn't want to lose his job. Before becoming a water carrier, his father had always been a labourer, in and out of work all the time. But his mother had wanted Thomas to have a skill, and he'd become an ironworker. Just under medium height, Thomas was stocky and strong, and he had a good eye. He'd learned fast, and although he wasn't yet twenty, the older men were always glad to have him on their team, and teach him.

It was a fine morning in late spring. He was wearing an open shirt and a short jacket. His baggy trousers were held up with a broad leather belt; his worker's boots scuffed the powdery dirt in the street. He had only two and a half miles to walk.

The geography of Paris was very simple. Beginning with the ancient oval of settlement on the banks of the Seine around its central island, the city had gradually expanded down the centuries, enclosed by walls that were built in a series of ever-larger concentric ovals. By the late eighteenth century, just before the French Revolution, the city was enclosed by a customs wall, approximately two miles out from the Seine, at whose many gates there were toll booths controlled by hated tax collectors. Outside this large oval lay a huge ring of suburbs and villages, including, to the east, the cemetery of Père Lachaise, and to the north, the hill of Montmartre. Since the Revolution, the hated old customs wall had been dismantled, and just before the recent war with the Germans, a vast line of outer fortifications had enclosed even the outer suburbs. But many of them, especially Montmartre, still looked like the ancient villages they were.

At the bottom of the hill of Montmartre, Thomas crossed the untidy old Place de Clichy, and entered a long boulevard that ran south-west, along the line of the dismantled customs wall, with the streets of the city on his left, and the sprawling suburb of Batignolles village on his right. Occasionally a tram pulled by a team of horses rumbled slowly past him, but like most labouring men he seldom cared to pay the fare to go on the trams and omnibuses whose horses, in any case, hardly went faster than a brisk walk.

After half an hour, he came to a line of smart iron railings on his left, through which one could see the green spaces of the Parc Monceau. Formerly a princely garden, now an elegant public space, the Parc Monceau was the entrance to an exclusive quarter. Gathered around its southern side were the impressive private mansions of the richest bourgeoisie. But its most charming feature lay up here, in the middle of the railings on the northern side.

It looked like a small, round Roman temple. In fact, it was the old toll booth. But in keeping with its aristocratic surroundings, this humdrum function had been served by a perfect, domed rotunda encircled by classical columns. Thomas liked the little temple. It was also the sign that he had reached his destination.

Crossing the boulevard, he walked northwards fifty yards and turned left into the rue de Chazelles.

A generation ago, this had been a modest area of workshops and allotments. Then small, two-storey villas with mansard roofs had begun to appear. And since Baron Haussmann had started carving his great thoroughfares through the quarter, some long, six-storey apartment blocks could be seen nearby. The project that Thomas Gascon was working on lay at number 25 rue de Chazelles, on the north side of the street, rising high above the roofs of the neighbouring villas: a gigantic truncated figure, completed to its midriff, swathed in metal drapery and surrounded by scaffolding. It was so tall that it could be seen from across the Parc Monceau.

It was the Statue of Liberty.

The workshops of Gaget, Gauthier et Cie occupied a large site that ran back to the street behind. There were several big, high sheds, a foundry and a movable crane. In the middle of the site stood the huge torso.

First, Thomas went into the shed on the left. This was the atelier where the craftsmen worked at long tables, making the decorative friezes for the head and the torch. He loved watching them work, but his real reason for entering was because the bald and corpulent foreman was usually here in the early morning, and he liked to say a polite '*Bonjour, monsieur*' to remind that all-powerful figure of his existence.

This morning, however, the foreman was preoccupied. Monsieur Bartholdi was there. The designer of the Statue of Liberty looked every inch the fashionable artist he was, with his handsome, finely drawn face, his broad brow, and his floppy cravat tied in a large bow. He'd been working on the idea for years. Originally he had conceived a similar statue to stand at the entrance to the Suez Canal, the gateway to the East. That project had been abandoned. But then this other, wonderful opportunity had arisen. With a huge public subscription, the people of France would commission a statue as a gift to America, to stand beside New York harbour, the gateway to the West. And now Monsieur Bartholdi had become one of the most famous artists in the world.

Not daring to interrupt them, Thomas went quickly out of the atelier and entered the shed next door.

If Bartholdi had designed a magnificent statue, a huge problem still remained: How the devil to construct it? The original plan, suggested by the great French architect Viollet-le-Duc, had been to build the statue around a huge stone pillar. But then the great man had died without leaving further instructions, and no one knew what to do. Finally, a bridge-builder had said he could construct a framework for the statue, and so he had been brought in as the project's engineer.

The engineer had set about his task almost as if he were building another bridge. The statue was going to be hollow. Instead of a stone pillar, the central core would be a pylon of iron girders. The outer framework would be a huge skeleton of iron. And on to this skeleton the thin copper outer skin would be riveted. Spiral staircases inside would allow people to go up into the viewing platform in the statue's diadem.

The engineer's plans also allowed the statue to be constructed in several pieces at the same time. Liberty's right hand held a great torch up to the sky; but in her left, she would clasp the tablets of the law, on which the date of the Declaration of Independence would be carved. This was the hand upon which Thomas and his crew were working.

There were two others working with him on the hand that day, both bearded, serious men in their forties. They greeted him politely, and one asked if his family was well.

It did not seem appropriate to say that his little brother had gone missing. Indeed, Thomas thought, it might bring bad luck. For if you said a thing, it might happen.

'They're fine,' he said. For now, he'd concentrate on his work.

The hand was huge. A dozen men could have sat on the outstretched palm and fingers. The inner core was a sturdy framework of thick iron bars. But around this framework were wrapped dozens of long, thin metal strips, like so many straps. They were only two inches wide, lay quite close together, and exactly followed the contours of Bartholdi's model, so that, when they were all attached, the resulting hand would look like a limb from some gigantic wicker man.

Fixing them in place was careful and patient labour. For over an hour, the three men worked quietly, speaking little. And they were not interrupted until the foreman's morning visit.

He was still in the company of Monsieur Bartholdi. But they had been joined by a third figure.

Most of the engineering supervision at the workshops was done by the engineer's junior partner. But today the engineer himself had come to pay a visit.

If Bartholdi was every inch an artist, the engineer also looked his part. Where Bartholdi's face was long and poetic, it seemed that the god Vulcan had fashioned the head of the engineer in his forge and compressed it in a vice. Everything about the man was compact and tidy – his close-cropped hair and beard, his clothes, his movements – yet also full of energy. And his eyes, which bulged slightly, had a luminous quality that suggested that he, too, could dream.

For several minutes he and Bartholdi inspected the huge hand, tapping the thin bands of iron, measuring here and there, and eventually nodded with approval to the foreman and cheerfully announced: 'Excellent, messieurs.' They were about to leave when the engineer turned to Thomas and remarked: 'You're new here, aren't you?'

'Yes, monsieur,' said Thomas.

'And what is your name?'

'Thomas Gascon, monsieur.'

'Gascon, eh? Your ancestors came from Gascony, no doubt?'

'I do not know, sir. I suppose so.'

'Gascony.' The engineer considered, then smiled. 'The old Roman province of Aquitania. The warm south. The land of wine. Of brandy too: let us not forget Armagnac.'

'Or *The Three Musketeers*,' Bartholdi chimed in. 'D'Artagnan was a Gascon.'

'*Voilà*. And what can we say of the character of your countrymen, Monsieur Gascon?' the engineer continued playfully. 'Aren't they known for chivalry, and honour?'

'They're supposed to boast a lot,' said the foreman, not to be left out.

'Are you boastful, Monsieur Gascon?' asked the engineer.

'I have nothing to boast about,' answered Thomas simply.

'Ah,' said the engineer. 'Then perhaps I can help you. Why do you think we are constructing the statue in this particular way?'

'I suppose,' said Thomas, 'so that it can be disassembled and taken across the Atlantic.' He knew that after the statue was completed here in the rue de Chazelles, its copper skin attached with temporary rivets, the whole thing could be taken down and reassembled again in New York.

'That is true,' said the engineer. 'But there is another reason. The statue is going to stand beside the open waters of New York harbour, exposed to the winds, which will catch it like a sail. If it is completely static, it will be under enormous stress. Temperature changes will also cause the metal to expand and contract. The copper skin could crack. So firstly, I have constructed the inside like a metal bridge, so that it can move, just enough to relieve the stress. And secondly, I have arranged that the plates of beaten copper that form the skin shall be riveted, each one separately, on to these metal strips – these 'saddles' as you ironworkers call them. The copper plates are attached to the framework, but not to each other. So each plate can slide, just a fraction, against its neighbour. In this way the skin will never crack. You will not see it with the eye, but all the time, the Statue of Liberty will move. This is good engineering. Do you understand?'

Thomas nodded.

'Good,' the engineer went on. 'And now I can tell you why you may boast. Because of its engineering, and your careful work in putting it together, this statue of ours will last for centuries. Countless millions of people will see it. Quite certainly, my young friend, this will be the most famous construction that you, or I, will ever build. That is something we may boast about, don't you think?'

'Yes, Monsieur Eiffel,' said Thomas.

Eiffel smiled at him. Bartholdi smiled at him. Even the foreman smiled, and Thomas Gascon felt very happy.

Just then he saw his sister Nicole standing by the doorway.

She was trying to catch his attention, yet was afraid to come in. She was going through that phase when her legs looked thin as stalks, and with her pale face and her large eyes, she seemed very vulnerable. If their mother had sent her all the way here, it could only mean that Luc was lost. Or worse.

But what a moment to arrive. If she would just wait until the foreman and the visitors were gone. He saw her eyes pleading as he tried to ignore her.

But the foreman missed nothing. Seeing Thomas's momentary distraction, he immediately turned and stared at Nicole.

'Who's that?'

'My sister, sir.' It was no use lying.

'Why is she interrupting you?'

'My little brother vanished this morning, sir. I think he must be . . . I don't know.'

The foreman was not pleased. Staring at Nicole, he motioned her to approach him.

'Well,' he said abruptly. 'What is it?'

'My mother sent me to find Thomas, monsieur. My brother Luc is nowhere to be found. They are fetching the police.'

'Then they have no need of Thomas.' He motioned her to go away.

The little girl's mouth fell open. Involuntarily, Thomas started to move towards her, then checked himself.

He couldn't lose his job. The foreman might be harsh, but he was quite logical. Perhaps if the matter had been brought to him privately . . . But not with Monsieur Bartholdi and Monsieur Eiffel watching. He had to keep discipline.

If only Nicole would go now. Quickly. But she didn't. Her face started to pucker. Was she going to cry? She turned to him.

'What shall I tell Mother?'

And he was just about to say, 'You must go now, Nicole,' when the voice of Monsieur Eiffel interrupted.

'I think that, upon this occasion – and this occasion only – our young friend should go and find his brother. But tomorrow morning, Monsieur Gascon, we shall expect you here to complete this great work.' He turned to the foreman. 'Would you agree?'

The foreman shrugged, but nodded.

'Go,' the foreman said to Thomas, who would have thanked him properly, except that his sister had already fled.

Seen from a distance, the hill of Montmartre hadn't changed so much since Roman times. For centuries old vines had grown there, tended by local nuns in the Middle Ages, though the vineyards nowadays had either been built upon, or lapsed into waste ground. But one pleasant change had occurred. A number of wooden windmills had gathered near the summit, their lumbering sails turning in the wind, giving the hill a picturesque appearance.

Only when one drew closer did it become clear that Montmartre had become a bit of a mess. Too steep and inconvenient for Baron Haussmann to tame, it was still half rural. But in the places where Montmartre had tried to smarten itself, it seemed to have given up, its crooked streets and steep alleys breaking off unfinished, turning into trackways of wooden huts and cabins scattered, higgledy-piggledy, across the hillside.

In all this mess, no part was more disreputable than the shanty town just over the hill on its north-western flank. The Maquis, they called it: the bush, the wilderness, or even skid row. The house in which the Gascons lived was one of the better ones: a simple frame covered with wooden boards and an upstairs balcony that made it look like a shanty version of a Swiss chalet. An outside staircase led to the upper floor that the family occupied.

'Where have you looked?' Thomas asked, as soon as he got there.

'*Partout.*' Everywhere, said his mother. 'The police came.' Her shrug indicated that she had no faith in them. Monsieur Gascon was sitting in the corner. The yoke he put across his shoulders to carry the water buckets lay on the floor beside him. He was staring at the floor in guilty silence. 'You should go to work,' his wife said to him quietly.

'Let them do without their water,' he said defiantly, 'until my son is found.' And Thomas guessed his father thought that little Luc was dead.

'Your aunt gave him a balloon yesterday afternoon, and sent him home,' his mother continued to Thomas, 'but he never got here. None of the children at the school have seen him. One boy said he had, but then he changed his mind. If anyone knows anything, they're not telling.'

'I'm going out to search,' said Thomas. 'What colour was the balloon?'

'Blue,' said his mother.

Once outside, Thomas paused. Could he find his brother? He told himself he could. There seemed little point in searching the Maquis again. Down the hill, the city outskirts spread northwards to the suburb called Saint-Denis. But so far as Thomas knew, his little brother never went out there. The small free school his mother made him attend, and most of the places Luc knew, lay up the hill. Thomas started to climb.

The Moulin de la Galette stood on the ridge just above the Maquis. It was one of a pair of windmills owned by an enterprising family who had set up a *guinguette* bar with a little dance floor there. People came out from the city to enjoy some cheap drink and rustic charm, and Luc haunted the place. He'd sing songs for the customers, who'd give him tips.

The barman was sweeping the floor.

'The police have been here already,' he said. 'Luc never came last night.'

'He may have had a blue balloon.'

'No balloon.'

Thomas went along several streets after that, stopping here and there to ask if anyone remembered a boy with a balloon the day before. Nobody did. It was hard not to feel discouraged, but he pressed on. After half an hour of wandering about like this, he came out on to the great platform of ground overlooking the city where, behind a high wooden fence, they were building the huge basilica of Sacré Coeur.

Thomas had been seven years old during the German siege. He remembered the big cannon up on the hill, and the fighting over

26

them, and the terrible shooting of Communards when the government troops arrived from Versailles. His father had been careful to stay out of trouble – or perhaps he was just too lazy – but like most working men, he had no liking for this vast, triumphant monument to Catholic order that the conservative new republic was placing on the hill to stare over the city. Thomas, however, had been fascinated: not by the church's meaning, but by how the huge thing was built.

And for that reason, as he gazed at the sacred site on the hill of Montmartre, he began to feel a sense of dread.

The hill was mainly composed of the soft stone material known as gypsum, which possessed two qualities. First, it would slowly dissolve in water, and was thus a poor foundation for any large building. Second, when heated, after giving off steam, it could easily be ground to the powder from which white plaster was made. For that reason, men had been burrowing into the hill of Montmartre for centuries to extract the gypsum. And so famous had these quarryings become that now, even across the oceans, white plaster had come to be known as plaster of Paris.

When the builders of Sacré Coeur began their task, therefore, they found that the underlying terrain was not only soft, but so honeycombed with mine shafts and tunnels that, had the great building been placed directly upon it, the entire hill would surely have collapsed, leaving the church in a stupendous sinkhole.

The solution had been very French: a combination of elegant logic and vast ambition. Eighty-three gigantic shafts were dug, each over a hundred feet deep, filled with concrete. Upon these mighty columns, like a huge box almost as deep as the church above, the crypt was constructed as a platform. This work alone had taken almost a decade, and by the end of it, even those who hated the project would remark with wry amusement: 'Montmartre isn't holding up the church. It's the church that's holding up Montmartre.'

Every week, Thomas had gone to the site to gaze. Sometimes a friendly workman would take him to see the cavernous excavations and giant masonry up close. Even when the work on the church itself had begun, the site was still a muddy mess, cratered with pits and trenches. And now, as he stared at the high boards of the fence, the thought came to him, with a horrible urgency: What if his poor little brother's body had been dumped somewhere on that site? It might be days before it was noticed, if it hadn't already been covered over. Or what if it had been dragged into the maze of tunnels and shafts below? There were ways into that labyrinth, but once inside it was easy to get lost. Was Luc down there, in the dark and secret chambers of the hill?

No, he told himself, no. He mustn't think like this. Luc was alive. Just waiting to be found. All he had to do was think. Where might he be?

He walked forward to the corner of the street below and paused. All Paris lay before him. Here and there a golden dome could be seen, or a church steeple rising above the rooftops. On the main island in the Seine, the towers of Notre-Dame Cathedral rose higher than all. And above them, the blue sky still reigned, uninterrupted. And telling him nothing.

He tried to pray. But God and His angels were silent as well.

So after a while, he started along the street that led westward along the contour of the hill. There were some houses here, of the better sort, with small gardens. The lane began to descend. On his right a steep bank of land appeared, with a garden wall above it. The bank was covered with bushes.

'Psst. Thomas.' A whisper from above. He stopped. His heart leaped. He looked up into the bushes. He couldn't see anyone. 'Are you alone? Is anybody in the lane?' It was Luc's voice.

'Nobody,' said Thomas.

'I'm coming down.' Moments later, Luc was at his side.

They both had the same soft brown eyes. But where Thomas Gascon was thickset and sturdy, his brother Luc, at the age of nine, was a thin little boy. The features of the young workman's sunburned face were short and straight, and his close-cropped brown hair was already showing the first, faint signs of thinning. His brother's skin was paler, his hair was dark and long, his nose more aquiline. He might have been a young Italian boy – looks he inherited from his father's mother, who had come to Paris from Toulon.

He was dirty and his hair was a mess, but apart from that he didn't look too bad.

'I'm hungry,' he said. He'd been hiding there all night. 'I was going to wait until this evening and go down the hill, so I could meet you coming back from work,' he explained.

'Why didn't you go home? Mother and Father are sick with worry.'

Luc shook his head.

'They said they'd be waiting for me. They said they'd kill me.'

'Who?'

'The Dalou boys.'

'Oh.' This was serious. There were several gangs of boys in the Maquis, but the Dalou boys were vicious. If they told Luc they'd kill him, he could expect to be hurt badly. And they were quite capable of waiting up for him all night. 'What did you do to them?' Thomas asked.

'Aunt Lilly gave me a balloon. I met them in the street and Antoine Dalou said he wanted it. But I said no. Then Jean Dalou knocked me down and took it.'

'And then?'

'I was unhappy. I wept.'

'So?'

'As they were going away, I threw a broken bottle at the balloon, and it burst.'

'Why did you do that?'

'So that they shouldn't have it, either.'

Thomas shook his head.

'That was stupid.'

'Then they came after me, and Antoine Dalou picked up some big stones to throw at me, and I ran. He hit me once, in the back. And I got away. But they didn't give up. And Jean Dalou shouted that they were going to kill me, and that I'd never get home alive. So I stayed away. They won't attack you, though. They'll be afraid of you.'

'I can get you home,' said Thomas. 'But what then?'

'I don't know. Can I go and live in America?'

'No.' Thomas took his hand. 'Let's go.'

As soon as Luc was safely home, Thomas went out again.

It didn't take him long to find the Dalou boys. They were hanging out near their shack on the other side of the Maquis. Most of the little gang seemed to be there: Antoine, the same age as Luc, with a narrow face like a ferret; Jean Dalou, a bit better looking, and a couple of years older, who led the gang; Guy, one of the Noir family, their cousin, a woebegone-looking boy, with a vicious bite; and two or three others. Thomas came straight to the point.

'My brother shouldn't have burst the balloon,' he said to Jean Dalou. 'But it wasn't kind of you to take it.'

Nobody said anything.

'Anyway,' Thomas continued, 'it's over. But leave my brother alone, or I shall be angry.'

Jean Dalou didn't reply. Then Antoine Dalou spoke.

'I kept the broken bottle he threw. He's going to get it back in his face.'

Instinctively, Thomas made a move towards him. As he did so, Jean Dalou shouted, 'Bertrand!' And a moment later the door of the shack burst open and a young man rushed out. Thomas silently cursed. He'd forgotten about Jean's elder brother.

Bertrand Dalou was about the same age as Thomas. He worked, sporadically, on construction sites. He had a great mop of shaggy brown hair that was both greasy and dusty, since he seldom washed. He looked furiously at Thomas, while Jean Dalou shouted: 'His brother threw a broken bottle at Antoine, and now he's come to beat Antoine up.'

'Liar!' cried Thomas. 'My brother was out all night, with the police looking for him, because these boys said they'd kill him. I came to tell them to leave him alone. You want the police instead?'

Bertrand Dalou spat. It didn't matter what the truth was, and they both knew it. Honour was at stake. And there was only one way to deal with that, in the Maquis. He began to circle, and Thomas did the same.

Thomas had never fought Bertrand before, but since he was a Dalou, he'd be fighting as dirty as he knew. The question was, how much did he know?

His first move wasn't subtle. He rushed as though to close, swung his fist towards Thomas's face, to make him draw his head back, and launched a savage kick to his groin. But instead of blocking with his leg, Thomas leaped back, caught Bertrand's leg on the swing and wrenched it upward so that Bertrand crashed to the ground. Dalou was quick though. Thomas hardly got one kick in before he was up again.

A moment later they were grappling. Bertrand tried to throw him, but Thomas kept his balance and got in a short, hard punch just below the heart that shook Dalou up enough for Thomas to get him in a throttle hold. He squeezed. He wasn't careful enough, though, and the Dalou boy punched him so hard in the eye that he let go.

Again they circled. Thomas's eye was throbbing, and soon it would start to close up. The fight had better not last too long.

Dalou's next move was cunning. Putting his tousled head down, he made another rush towards Thomas, as if to butt him in the midriff and knock him over. Only at the last instant did Thomas see the hand come up in a two-fingered eye gouge that could have blinded him. Quick as a flash, he whipped his fist up in front of his nose so that Bertrand's fingers smashed into his knuckles.

Watching his opponent recoil, Thomas wondered what was coming next. He didn't have to wait long. Bertrand's hand suddenly clapped down to his pocket. Thomas saw the hand starting to come out again, and knew what it meant. If things weren't going to get really ugly, he had one second, and he must not miss. The hand was out. The razor was opening.

He kicked. Thank God he was fast. Dalou's hand jerked violently up as the razor flew into the air. With a cry of pain Dalou looked up, to see where his razor would fall. And that was his mistake.

It was time to end the fight. One more kick. A big one. With perfect speed and balance, Thomas struck. His heavy workman's boot swung up into Bertrand's groin with such a mighty impact that it lifted the eldest Dalou brother clean off the ground so that he seemed to hang in the air, like a rag doll, before falling to the ground.

Thomas circled him, looking down, ready to strike again, but there was no need. Bertrand Dalou was staying down.

It was over. Order, such as it was in the Maquis, had been restored. The Dalou gang wouldn't be bothering his little brother any more.

The Gascon family were happy that night. When Thomas had returned earlier in the day, his mother had fussed over his eye, which was rapidly turning black, but his father had understood. 'It's done?' he had inquired, and after Thomas had nodded, his father had said no more. Then his mother had informed them that she would be

31

cooking a large meal for that evening, and disappeared with Nicole to the market. Luc had fallen asleep for a couple of hours.

By late afternoon, the rich smell of a ragout was filling their lodgings, and long before sundown they were sitting down to a feast. Onion soup was the food of the poor, but delicious for all that. Fresh baguettes from the bakers. Madame Gascon's ragout would usually consist of pig's trotters, vegetables and whatever seasoning she had, food that was as cheap as it was healthy. But today there were morsels of beef swimming in a sauce that was thicker than they had tasted in a long while. Then there was a Camembert, and a goat cheese, and a hard Gruyère, all washed down with cheap red wine.

Luc had quite got over his ordeal, and gave them an imitation of Antoine Dalou that had them all in stitches. Thomas told them about his encounter with Monsieur Eiffel, and what he had said about the Statue of Liberty. And then Luc suddenly piped up again.

'I want to live in America.'

This was met with protests.

'Will you leave us all behind?' asked his mother.

'I want you to come too,' said Luc. But nobody wanted to go.

'America is a fine country. No question,' said Monsieur Gascon expansively. 'They have everything there. Big cities – not like Paris, of course. But great lakes, and mountains and prairies as far as the eye can see. If your own country is not so good – if you're English, or German, or Italian – unless you're rich ... *Alors* ... it's probably better in America. But in France, we have everything. We have mountains – the Alps and the Pyrenees; we have great rivers like the Seine and the Rhône; we have huge farmlands, and forests. We have cities, and cathedrals, and Roman ruins in the south. We have every kind of climate. We have the greatest wines in the world. And we have three hundred cheeses. What more do you want?'

'We haven't any deserts, Papa,' said Nicole.

'*Mais oui*, my little one. We have.' Monsieur Gascon puffed his chest out as though he had accomplished the feat himself. 'When I was your age, France went to Africa and conquered Algeria. We have all the desert we want, right there.'

'This is true,' laughed Thomas.

'But people don't fight each other in America,' said Luc, with feeling.

'What do you mean?' his father cried. 'They're always fighting in America. First they fought the English. Then the Indians. Then they fought each other. They're worse than us.'

'You stay here and be grateful,' said his mother affectionately.

'As long as Thomas protects me,' said Luc.

'Ah,' said Monsieur Gascon, looking proudly at his elder son, 'let us all drink to that.' And they did.

The next morning when Thomas got up, he went to his little brother.

'You know,' he said, 'you're very funny. You should stick to that. Make people laugh. Then even the Dalou boys will like you.'

When he got to work, the foreman was looking out for him.

'You found your brother?'

'*Oui, monsieur.*'

The foreman stared at his eye for a moment.

'Can you see to work?'

'*Oui, monsieur.*'

The foreman nodded. One didn't ask questions when people came from the Maquis.

So Thomas worked quietly all day. Monsieur Eiffel didn't come by.

On the following Saturday morning, Aunt Éloïse stood in the big open space known as the parvis of Notre-Dame Cathedral, looked at the three Blanchard children standing in a row in front of her, and thought that her brother Jules and his wife had not done badly.

Gérard, at sixteen the eldest, was a solid, determined fellow, with a square, hard face, who would undoubtedly become his father's partner one day. She had to confess, she preferred his younger brother, Marc. He was going to be tall and handsome like his father, though of a more slender build, and being an intellectual and imaginative boy, he was closer to her in spirit. True, his schoolwork was a little erratic, and he was inclined to daydream. 'But you shouldn't worry about him,' she'd told Jules when he'd been concerned. 'Thirteen-year-old boys are often a little dreamy. And who knows, perhaps he will do something in the arts or literature one day that will make our name famous.'

And then there was little Marie. At eight years old, thought Aunt Éloïse, one could only say a little about her character. But she was sweet and kind – that was certain. And how was it possible not to love those blue eyes, and that mass of golden curls, and the charming plumpness that might easily turn, one day, into an excellent figure?

Yet in one of the three children, it seemed to Aunt Éloïse that she had detected a character flaw. Not too serious, but concerning. She kept her own counsel about this, however. Even if she was right, it might be corrected. And besides, she reminded herself, nobody was perfect.

Meanwhile, her own task in the family, as she saw it, was to bring them whatever gifts of the spirit she could. That was why this morning, on their visit to the Île de la Cité, she had first taken them to the exquisite Sainte-Chapelle.

Marc liked his aunt's tall elegance, and the fact that she knew so many things. They had stood in the high, painted chapel, bathed in the warm light from its great windows, and gazed up at the tall Gothic vaults of blue and gold, and he had felt moved by the beauty of the place.

'It's like a jewelled casket, isn't it?' said Aunt Éloïse quietly. 'That's because when King Louis IX, whom we call Saint Louis, went on crusade six hundred years ago, the emperor in Byzantium – who you can be sure needed the money – sold him some of the most important relics in Christendom, including a piece of the Cross, and the Crown of Thorns itself. Then Saint Louis built this chapel, like a great reliquary, to house these sacred treasures. Cathedrals like Notre-Dame, as you know, often took centuries to build, but the Sainte-Chapelle was finished in just five years, all in one style. That's why it is so perfect.'

'What were the other relics?' Marc had asked.

'A nail from the Cross, a miraculous robe worn by the infant Jesus, the spear that pierced His side, some drops of His blood, some milk from the Blessed Virgin Mary. And also the rod of Moses.'

'You think they were genuine?'

'I couldn't say. But the chapel was the most beautiful in the world.' She had paused for a moment. 'However,' she continued, 'I am sorry to say that at the Revolution this wonderful place was completely destroyed. The revolutionaries – who were not at all religious – stripped it bare . . . The Sainte-Chapelle was absolutely ruined.

There are many things about the Revolution that were fine, but the destruction of this chapel was not one of them.' She had turned to Marc and held up her finger. 'This is why, Marc, it is important that – especially at times of war and upheaval – there should be people of culture and humanity to protect our heritage.'

Why did she always address these remarks to him, and not to his brother? He'd seen Gérard turn his eyes up to the sky in boredom. But his brother wasn't really bored, Marc thought. He was jealous that Aunt Éloïse so clearly had a higher opinion of Marc than she did of him.

Aunt Éloïse was in full flood.

'Fortunately, things of beauty are not so easily destroyed – at least, not in France. And Viollet-le-Duc, the architect, completely restored the Sainte-Chapelle to its former glory, as we see it now. It's wonderful, almost a miracle.' She looked approvingly at Marc again. 'So you see, my dear Marc, no matter how bad things seem, we must never give up. As long as there are artists and architects, and patrons – you might be any of these – even miracles can be accomplished.'

And now they were standing in front of the mighty towers of Notre-Dame. Beside them was a huge equestrian statue of the emperor Charlemagne. Aunt Éloïse, feeling she hadn't paid enough attention to Gérard in the Sainte-Chapelle, remarked that it was only just before his own birth that the medieval buildings of old Paris had been swept away from the place. 'Until then, Gérard, Notre-Dame was surrounded with gabled houses and dark alleys – just like in *The Hunchback of Notre-Dame*,' she added pleasantly.

'I'm glad they were destroyed,' he said in a surly voice.

Aunt Éloïse considered. Was there something challenging in his tone? Did she imagine she must be in love with every picturesque reminder of the Middle Ages? Was he letting her know that he'd be happy to smash down her own sensibilities, like Baron Haussmann with his demolition gangs?

'I quite agree with you, Gérard,' she said, with a charming smile. 'First of all, there was only a tiny space in front of the cathedral, and that was filled with disreputable stalls. And second, by the time they were demolished, the old houses were rotting where they stood, and the people in them lived like rats. Whereas now' – she gestured around the parvis – 'we have this magnificent space to enjoy.'

That seemed to shut him up. It was time to pay attention to little Marie. But as she turned her gaze towards the little girl, Aunt Éloïse noticed she was looking unhappy. 'Is something wrong, *chérie*?' she asked.

'No, Aunt Éloïse,' said Marie.

It had been just after breakfast that the terrible thing had happened. Marie supposed that it had been her own fault, for stupidly leaving her diary on the table in her bedroom. Normally she kept it locked in a drawer. But all the same, did Gérard have to come into her room when she wasn't there and read it?

Even that wouldn't have been so bad if she hadn't just confided to it a secret that she wouldn't for all the world want anyone to know. She was in love. With a school friend of Marc's.

'So, little sister,' he'd said cruelly, 'I see that you have secrets in your life.'

'That's none of your business,' she'd cried, going scarlet with embarrassment.

'We all have secrets,' he said, handing her the book contemptuously. 'But yours aren't very interesting. Perhaps there'll be something better to read when you're older.'

'You're not to tell,' she wailed.

'Who would I tell?' he'd asked coolly. 'Who would care?'

'Get out! I hate you!' She'd only just stopped weeping with mortification and rage an hour later, when Aunt Éloïse had come to collect them.

Aunt Éloïse cast about in her mind for something that might interest Marie. One story occurred to her, not quite appropriate for a nicely brought-up girl of eight, but with a slight alteration . . .

'There's a wonderful story, Marie, a true romance that belongs to this very place. Do you know the tale of Abelard and Héloïse?' Marie shook her head. 'Very well.' Aunt Éloïse gave the two boys a hard stare. 'I shall tell the story, Gérard and Marc, and you will not interrupt or add anything at all. Do you understand?' She turned back to Marie.

'Long ago, Marie,' she began, 'in the Middle Ages, just before this great cathedral of Notre-Dame was built, there was a big old church, not nearly so beautiful, upon the site. And there was something else very important that was here. Does anyone know what that was?'

'The university,' said Marc.

'Exactly. Before it moved across to the Left Bank – to the area we now call the Sorbonne – the University of Paris, which was really a school for priests, occupied some houses here on the Île de la Cité by the old cathedral. And at the university there was a philosopher called Abelard whose lectures were so brilliant that students came from all over Europe to hear him.'

'How old was he?' asked Marie.

'Not old.' Aunt Éloïse smiled. 'He was lodging in the house of an important priest named Fulbert. And Fulbert's young niece, Héloïse, was also living there.'

'Was she pretty?' Marie wanted to know.

'Without a doubt. But more important, this Héloïse was a most remarkable and intelligent girl. She could read Latin, and Greek, and even Hebrew. She took lessons from Abelard. And we should not be surprised that these two extraordinary people fell in love. They secretly married, and they had a son, named Astrolabe.'

'Astrolabe?'

'An instrument for showing the position of the stars. I admit the name is a little strange, but it shows that their love was absolutely cosmic. But Héloïse's uncle Fulbert was very angry, and he punished Abelard, and made them part. Abelard went away, though he continued to be a famous philosopher. And Héloïse became a nun, and finally a famous abbess. And she and Abelard wrote extraordinary letters to each other. She was one of the most remarkable women of her age.'

'And were they still in love?' Marie asked.

'With time, Abelard became a little cold. Men are not always kind.'

'No, they are not,' the child said furiously, with a glance at Gérard.

'But the lovers were buried together, and they are now in Père Lachaise.'

'And were you named after Héloïse? Are you like her?'

'No, I was named after my grandmother Éloïse.' Aunt Éloïse smiled. 'And my life has been quite different. But the story is famous,

37

and it shows that even if we cannot be happy all the time, we can still have a life that is rich in every way.'

Marc watched his aunt carefully. He had been amused by the way she had altered the story. Fulbert's punishment of Abelard had been far more terrible: he'd hired thugs to castrate the great philosopher. But such things were not for the ears of little Marie.

He also knew that something else Aunt Éloïse had said was not quite true. A year ago, his father had told him: 'Your aunt wanted to marry a man who's quite a famous author now; but unfortunately he married someone else. Don't tell her I told you. She had other offers, but she never found anyone who interested her enough.' His father had shrugged. 'She's an attractive woman, but too independent.'

Marc knew his aunt had friends who were writers and artists. When he'd shown some talent for drawing at school, it was always her opinion he wanted on his efforts. He could easily imagine Aunt Éloïse as an abbess in the Middle Ages, or as one of those eighteenth-century women who held salons where the great men of the Enlightenment would come. Had she had lovers? If she had, no one in the respectable Blanchard family had ever breathed a word.

It was only a moment's walk to the Petit Pont bridge, where they stared over the water to the Left Bank. Aunt Éloïse tried to engage Gérard in conversation again.

'The Île de la Cité is just like a boat in the river, isn't it?'

'I suppose so.'

'You know, Gérard, that on its coat of arms, Paris is pictured as a ship. Do you remember the city's Latin motto? "*Surgit nec mergitur*": "Whatever the storm, the ship sails on". It never sinks. That's exactly the story of Paris.'

Gérard shrugged. Most Parisians were proud of their city and its treasures. People came from all over the world to see them. But the truth was, he didn't really care. He knew Aunt Éloïse and Marc despised him for it. No doubt little Marie would as well, one day. Well, let them. He knew what he was going to do with his life. He was going to run the family business.

No one else in the family could do it. His grandfather had seen it, right from the start: 'Gérard's the one with the sound head,' he'd told the family, when Gérard was only ten. Marc was no use. He was like Aunt Éloïse: full of useless ideas and distractions. Little Marie, as a girl, didn't need to be considered. Even his father, Gérard privately considered, was a poor custodian.

Jules Blanchard had waited until his father's death before he had fulfilled his dream. Three years ago, his elegant department store had opened. Cheekily, he had chosen a site on the boulevard Haussmann behind the Paris Opéra and only a stone's throw from the great Printemps store. Like Printemps, he offered high-quality clothing at fixed prices that the middle classes could afford, including some lines for which he'd signed exclusive deals. He'd called the store Joséphine.

Why Joséphine, his family had asked? After the empress Joséphine, of course, he'd explained. She'd been the wife of Napoléon, she was exotic and, if she had faults of character, she was always elegant. It was the perfect name, he'd told them.

Jules had borrowed hugely to finance it. It had to be confessed, he'd had the devil's own luck. Just a year after Joséphine opened, the mighty Printemps emporium had burned down, and was still being rebuilt. With the main competition temporarily removed, Joséphine's business had surged. 'Make hay while the sun shines,' Jules had remarked cheerfully.

But Gérard wasn't impressed. He hated retail. The wholesale business, which thank God his father had kept, produced cash; the retail business ate the cash. Wholesalers could lend money. Retailers borrowed. A wholesale premises was a simple, functional building that lasted a lifetime. A department store was like a stage set. His brother, Marc, loved the glamorous store, and Gérard's secret dread was that he might want to run it one day. At all costs that must be prevented.

For Gérard's plan was simple. One day, when his father retired or died, if the department store hadn't ruined them in the meantime, he was going to get rid of it. Sell it if possible; if not, close it.

Chapter Three

1261

It was spring in the year of Our Lord 1261, saintly King Louis IX was on the throne of France, and day was dawning. The young woman rose from the mattress on the floor.

Martine could see a thin slit of light between the wooden shutters at the window. There was no sound from the yard below; but from across it came the noise of her uncle's loud, rhythmical snores, like the rattle of a portcullis being raised at one of the city gates.

Still naked, she went to the shutters and pushed. They opened with a crack. Her uncle's snores faltered, and she held her breath. Then the rattle resumed, thank God.

She had to be careful. She mustn't get caught.

Martine looked back at the mattress. The young man lying there was asleep.

Until last year, Martine had been married to a rich merchant's son. When her husband had caught a fever and died, she'd been left a widow at the age of twenty. Soon, no doubt, she'd marry again. But until then, she thought, she might as well enjoy herself – so long as nobody found out.

If she got caught, she supposed her uncle might give her a whipping and throw her out – she really didn't know. But not only did she need the protection of his roof: if she wanted a rich new husband, she had to keep her reputation.

The young man on the mattress was poor. He was also vain. And he had a great deal to learn about making love. So why had she picked him up?

In fact it was he who'd approached her, ten days ago, in Notre-Dame. After a century of building, the new cathedral was almost complete. But to beautify it further, the transept crossings near the centre were being remodelled in the latest style, their walls turned into great curtains of stained glass, like those of the king's new chapel. She'd been gazing up at the huge rose window in the north transept when he appeared, wearing a student's gown and, like all the students, the crown of his head was shaved in a clerical tonsure.

'Isn't it admirable?' he had remarked pleasantly, as though he'd known her all his life.

'Monsieur?' She'd given him a disapproving look. He was a good height, slim, dark-haired. Pale skin, without blemishes, a long, thin nose. Not bad looking at all. A year or two younger than she was, she thought.

'Forgive me. Roland de Cygne, at your service.' He bowed politely. 'I mean that, like a beautiful woman, Notre-Dame is growing even more lovely in her maturity.'

She felt she had to say something in return.

'And when she grows old, monsieur, what then?'

'Ah.' He paused. 'I will tell you a secret about this lady. At the eastern end just now, I detected tiny cracks, a slight sagging in the walls, which tells me that one day this lady will need some discreet support. They will give her flying buttresses, as they call them.'

'You are an expert in the needs of women, monsieur?'

For just a second, she saw him tempted to boast. Then he thought better of it.

'I am only a student, madame,' he said modestly.

Martine had to admit that there was something quite seductive in this combination of flirtation and respectful formality. The young man certainly had an elegant way of talking. She was impressed.

It wouldn't have impressed her uncle. 'Talk,' he'd say contemptuously, 'that's all these cursed students do – when they're not getting drunk and assaulting people. Most of them would be sentenced to a whipping,' he'd add, 'if the king and the Church didn't protect them.'

Since the university was run by the Church, a bunch of students who smashed up a tavern had only to answer to the Church court, which would probably let them off with a penance. It was hardly surprising if ordinary Parisians resented this privilege. And as for pious King Louis IX, while the holy relics he'd placed in his gorgeous new chapel had added sanctity to his capital and his dynasty, he knew that the real prestige of Paris came from its university. A century ago, the castrated Abelard might have had his faults, but nowadays he was

remembered as the greatest philosopher of his age, and young scholars eagerly came from all over Europe to the university where he had
taught.

'And where do you go after this?' he inquired.

'I go home, sir,' she said firmly. Cheeky monkey.

'Let me accompany you.' He bowed. 'The streets are not always
safe.'

Since it was broad daylight, and they were in the middle of the
royal quarter, she had found it hard not to laugh.

'It won't do you any good,' she told him.

They walked the short distance to the northern side of the island.
A little farther downstream, a bridge led across to the Right Bank. As
they crossed it, she had asked: 'Your name begins with a "de". Does
that mean you're noble?'

'It does. Beside our little castle was a lake with many swans, so that
the place was called the Lac des Cygnes. Though my family also
claim that it was the swanlike grace and strength of their ancestors
that gave us the name. I am called Roland after my ancestor, the
famous hero of the *Song of Roland*.'

'Oh.' The story had been popular for more than a century, but
Martine had never thought of meeting a real Roland. She was
impressed. 'Yet you have come here as a humble student?'

'My older brother will inherit the estate. So I must study hard and
hope to make a career in the Church.'

As they turned upstream again, he told her about the estate. It lay
to the west, on the lower reaches of the graceful River Loire on its
journey towards the Atlantic Ocean. He spoke of it with obvious
affection, which pleased Martine. Soon, however, they were
approaching a large area of wharfs and a marketplace known as the
Grève.

The broad spaces of the Grève market on the Right Bank were
always busy. Ships and barges carrying wines from Burgundy and
grain from the eastern plains unloaded on the river bank. On the
other side lay the old quarters of the weavers, with the glassmakers a
block farther. Her uncle's house lay on the rue du Temple that ran
northwards between them. Too many people in the market knew
her. She didn't want to start gossip. It was time to get rid of her aristocratic young companion.

'Good-bye, monsieur, and thank you,' she said politely.

'I'm studying tomorrow,' Roland remarked, 'but the day after, I shall visit the Sainte-Chapelle at this hour. Perhaps,' he suggested pleasantly, 'I shall see you there.'

'I doubt it, sir,' she said, and walked away.

But two days later, she'd gone there all the same.

It wasn't long since the saintly King Louis had completed his sumptuous sanctuary for the holy relics. The upper chapel was reserved for the king himself, who had a private entrance from the royal palace next door. But lesser folk could worship in a humbler chapel below. And even this was beautiful. The cryptlike space shimmered by the light of countless candles. As Martine looked at the delicate columns of red and gold and observed how they branched out into the low, blue vaults, so richly spangled with golden fleurs-de-lys, she felt as if she had entered a magical orchard. By coming to meet Roland, she had already opened the way for an intimacy between them. In the glimmering candlelight, with the soft scent of incense in every nook and crevice, it seemed only natural that she should draw close to his side.

And in doing so and leaning, once or twice, close to his body, she noticed something else. Notwithstanding the incense, she could smell him: a faint, pleasant smell of the light sweat on his leather sandals, and something else – was it almonds perhaps, or nutmeg? – that came from his skin.

They had been there some minutes, quietly enjoying the beauty of the place, when a priest came past them, and to her surprise her young student had addressed him.

'I was wondering, *mon Père*, whether I might show this lady the chapel above.'

'The royal chapel is not open, young man,' the priest replied sharply. And that, she thought, was the end of it. But not at all.

'Forgive me, *mon Père*, my name is Roland de Cygne. My father is the lord de Cygne in the valley of the Loire. I am his second son and plan to take Holy Orders.'

The priest paused and looked at him carefully.

'I have heard of your family, monsieur,' he said quietly. 'Please accompany me . . .' And minutes later, they were in the royal chapel. 'We can stay only a moment,' the priest whispered.

43

The sunlight was coming in through the tall windows, filling the high, blue and gold spaces with celestial light. If the lower chapel had seemed like a magical wood, this was the hallway to heaven.

Her young student, who spoke so well and smelled so good, had the power to open the secret gardens of earthly delights and royal sanctuaries. That was the moment when she decided to try him as a lover. Besides, she'd never had an aristocrat before.

As she stared at him now, in the early morning light, he opened his eyes. They were tawny brown.

'It's time to go,' she whispered.

'Not quite.'

'I mustn't get caught.'

'Don't make a sound, then.' He grinned.

'We'll have to be quick,' she said, as she lay down beside him.

Afterwards he told her that he must study the following night, but could come to her the night after that. She told him yes, then led him downstairs into the yard. Like most of the better merchant's houses in Paris, her uncle's house was tall. The front door gave directly on to the street, but behind the house there was a yard with a storehouse, above which she slept, and a gateway to the alley that ran along the back. Drawing the bolts to the gate softly back, she pushed him through, and quickly bolted the gate behind him. From the house, her uncle's snores could still be heard.

As Roland de Cygne made his way along the alley, he felt pretty pleased with himself, and his conquest. Before this, he'd had only brief and fumbling encounters with farm girls and serving wenches, so Martine was a good start to what he hoped would be a fine career as a lover. Of course, she was only a young woman of the bourgeois, merchant class, but good practice. And he supposed that she in turn must be quite excited to have a boy of noble blood for a lover.

He thought he'd handled his first approach to her especially well. As for telling her that he was descended from the hero of the *Song of Roland*, that had been only a slight embroidery on the truth. As a child he'd asked why he was named Roland, and his father had explained: 'When your grandfather went on crusade, he had a wonderful horse called Roland, after the hero of the tale. That horse went with him all the way to the Holy Land and back, and he deserves to be remembered. It's a good name, too. I'd have given it to your brother, but the eldest in our family is always called Jean. So I gave it to you.'

'I'm named after a horse?'

'One of the noblest warhorses ever to go on crusade. What more do you want?'

Roland had understood. But he didn't think he was going to get many girls by telling them he was named after a horse.

He cut through an alley back into the rue du Temple. The sky was brightening over the gabled houses. The city gates were open by now, but there was hardly anyone about. The sound of the dawn chorus was all around, bringing as it always did a little thrill to his heart. He sniffed the air. As usual in the city streets, he could smell urine, dung and woodsmoke; but the delicious smell of baking bread also wafted past him, and the sweet scent of a honeysuckle bush from somewhere nearby.

Roland hadn't wanted to go to Paris. But his father had insisted: 'There's nothing for you here, my son,' he'd said. 'But I think you have more brains than your brother, and that in Paris you could do great things for the honour of your family. Why, you might even surpass your grandfather.' That would be a fine thing indeed.

Roland's grandfather had been favoured by history. After the mighty Charlemagne had died, and his empire crumbled back into provinces and tribal territories built on the ruins of ancient Rome, the kings of the Franks were often masters of little more than the Paris region, known as the Île-de-France, while huge domains, ruled by rich and powerful feudal families, encircled them: Provence and Aquitaine in the south; Celtic Brittany on the northern Atlantic coast; Champagne to the east; and below it, the tribal lands of Burgundy.

And with Charlemagne gone, the terrible Viking Norsemen had begun their raids. On one shameful occasion, Paris had bought them off and sent them to ravage Burgundy – the Burgundians had never forgiven the Parisians for that. Even when, finally, the Norsemen had settled down in Normandy, their rulers were still restless. And when William of Normandy had conquered England in 1066, his family's wealth and power had become greater than that of the French king in Paris.

45

But worst of all – more greedy, ruthless and frankly vicious – were the rulers of a smaller territory below Brittany, on the mouth of the River Loire: the counts of Anjou. Ambition had led the Plantagenets, as they were called, into marriage with the ruling families of Normandy and Aquitaine. Worse still, by outrageous dynastic luck they'd got their hands on the throne of England too.

'By your grandfather's day,' Roland's father had told him, 'the Plantagenets had almost surrounded the Île-de-France and they were ready to squeeze.'

France had been saved by a remarkable man. King Philip Augustus of the Capet dynasty, the grandfather of the present king, had been brave and cunning. He'd gone on crusade with England's Plantagenet king, Richard the Lionheart, but he never missed a chance to set one Plantagenet against another. And when the heroic Lionheart was succeeded by his unpopular brother John, the wily French monarch had soon managed to kick him out of Normandy and even Anjou. Indeed, after John's own English barons rebelled against him, it had looked for a moment as if the French kings might get England as well.

And during all these years of strife, no one was more loyal to the French king than the lord de Cygne. He was only a poor knight. The warhorse Roland was his most valuable possession. But he had gone on crusade with Philip Augustus, and the king called him his friend. So although his small estate lay within Anjou, and the Plantagenets might take it away at any time, he stayed at the side of his king. And when Philip Augustus had triumphed, he was able to reward his modest friend with lands that more than doubled the family's wealth.

But the de Cygnes had not prospered since then. Roland's father had sold some of his lands. Perhaps his brother could marry an heiress. That would be good. But there was something else that Roland could do for his family. He could rise in the Church.

The universal Church was many things: a source of comfort and inspiration, of scholarship and dreams. For the crusading family of de Cygne, it now offered another life-giving support. There was money in the Church – a lot of it.

Those who rose in the Church enjoyed the revenues of its vast estates. A bishop was a powerful man, and lived like a prince. Great churchmen could provide money for their families, and help them in every way. The vow of celibacy didn't appeal to Roland. But fortunately, despite their vows, many a bishop had left illegitimate children. The Church provided the educated class, and the great administrators of the crown. For a clever fellow, the Church was a way to fortune.

Roland was ready to do it. He wanted to be a success. Yet he still had one dream, a crusader's dream, that he supposed could never be realised.

He looked up the street. A quarter of a mile away, between the narrow canyon of wood-beamed, gabled houses, he could see one of the gates in the city wall. Philip Augustus had built that mighty stone wall, enclosing both banks of the Seine in a huge oval. The gate was open. His way led in the opposite direction, but he couldn't resist it. He walked towards the open gate.

As he passed through the gateway, the road continued straight ahead. On his left behind some orchards, he could see the Priory of Saint Martin in the Fields. There were a number of walled sanctuaries both inside and outside the city gates, containing important monasteries and convents. But the great enclave that had drawn him lay a short way ahead on his right. It was built like a fortress. Two castle towers rose fearsomely within. Its mighty doorways were barred, and bolted. Roland stood in the road and stared.

This was the Temple. A country in itself.

It was the Crusades that had created the Knights Templar. They began as security guards, bringing bullion safely across dangerous territories to the armies that needed it. Soon they were the guardians of huge deposits in many lands. From there, it was only a step to being bankers. As a religious order, they paid no taxes. By the reign of Philip Augustus, the Templars were one of the richest and most powerful organisations in Christendom. They answered only to the pope himself, and to God. And within the mighty Templars was a cadre of the most awesome warriors in the world: the Temple Knights.

The noble Knights of the Temple never surrendered. They were never ransomed. They fought, always, to the death they did not fear. To beat them, you had to kill them all.

To join them, you had to undergo an initiation so secret that no detail of it had ever leaked out. But once accepted, you were one of the innermost, sacred circle of the world of the Crusades.

Roland had always dreamed of being a Temple Knight since he was a little boy. It was the only way he could imagine of equalling his crusading grandfather. He'd still dreamed of it before he came to Paris. But his father wouldn't hear of it, for a good and simple reason.

Templars had no money. When the Temple Knights took their vows of poverty, they meant it. The order was rich beyond imagining; but its great men were poor. No use to the family of Roland de Cygne.

So now, as the spring morning light fell on the Temple towers, Roland gazed a little while and then turned away, back into the city. If the Temple had been his boyhood dream, he had to confess that life in the streets of Paris wasn't so bad. He could enjoy Martine, for instance.

He thought of the day ahead, and smiled to himself. He liked Martine. But when he had told her he had to study the coming night, he had lied.

The sinking sun was throwing a huge red light over the rooftops, and the shadows in the streets were lengthening when Roland set out from his lodgings on the Left Bank. They lay just a hundred yards towards the setting sun from the Abbey of Sainte-Geneviève, on the broad top of the hill, where once the Roman Forum had stood. Ruined for centuries, its rubble smoothed over to a gentler slope, the Forum was covered with religious houses now. A Roman street down to the river remained, but had gained a new name: since pilgrims bound for Compostela passed this way, it was called the rue Saint-Jacques.

Roland started down it. There were students everywhere. Recently, as the university shifted from the area of Notre-Dame to the Left Bank, the hillside was becoming covered with the small colleges where the students lived and worked. The college of the king's chaplain, Robert de Sorbon, fifty yards away on his left, was the first; but many others were springing up.

He continued down the long slope, past the Abbot of Cluny's palace, and the parish church of Saint-Séverin until, reaching the river, he prepared to cross the old bridge to the island, where the sunset's rays were turning the western front of Notre-Dame into a molten mass of red and gold.

Roland felt excited. He was going to see another woman.

His story that he must study tonight was easy for Martine to believe. The university students worked hard. For Roland, however, learning had come easily. Even before he came to Paris at the age of fifteen, a local priest had taught him to speak and read Latin thoroughly – for the university courses were almost all taught in Latin. He had completed the traditional trivium, of grammar, logic and rhetoric, Plato and Aristotle – a syllabus that dated back to Roman times – in less than the usual time, and moved swiftly on to the quadrivium of arithmetic, geometry, astronomy and music. He did the work so fast that his fellow students called him Abelard. But Roland was no philosopher, and had no wish to be. He had a quick mind and a wonderful memory, that was all. Soon he'd complete the quadrivium and become a master. After that, he meant to study law.

So tonight he was free to make love to that girl he'd picked up in the rue Saint-Honoré.

He'd met her three days ago. One of the law professors at the university, a man he wished to cultivate, had asked him to take a letter to a priest on the Right Bank.

The great Cemetery of the Innocents lay just west of the city's central line, only three hundred yards from the river, on the rue Saint-Denis. If one followed that street out through the city wall, it led northwards for miles, all the way to the great Abbey of Saint-Denis, where the kings of France were buried. But the occupants of the Innocents were of a much humbler sort. Its ten-foot walls enclosed the mass graves of the poor. Beside those sad walls, however, there was a pleasant church, where Roland found the priest, a small elderly man with a scholarly face, who thanked him most gratefully for his trouble.

On the western side of the cemetery lay a much more cheerful place. The open area of Les Halles was the city's biggest market. As he wasn't in a hurry, Roland had wandered about there for a while, admiring the colourful stalls. He'd just been inspecting a booth selling fine Italian leather when, glancing towards a group of merchants talking together under an archway, he noticed that one of them was staring at him intently. He wasn't large, but he stooped forward in a way that suggested a menacing energy. His face was partly covered by a short, straggly grey beard. He had a beak of a nose, which wasn't quite straight. His eyes were hard. And they were looking at him as though he were a viper to be crushed.

It was Martine's uncle. Roland knew what he looked like because, out of curiosity, he'd waited nearby one morning and watched him leave his house. So far as he knew, the merchant didn't even know of his existence. But still the eyes glared at him.

Did the merchant recognise him? How much did he know? He moved slowly away, trying to take no notice of the dangerous stare. He went behind another stall from where he could observe the merchant unseen. The man's piercing stare had been transferred to another part of the market now. As far as Roland could see, Martine's uncle was looking at that in exactly the same way. He hoped so. But he'd left Les Halles all the same.

That's when he'd gone into the tavern around the corner in the rue Saint-Honoré. The girl had been working in there. She wasn't any relation of the innkeeper, just a servant girl. A bold girl, with a mass of thick black hair, and dark eyes to match, and large white teeth. He noticed one or two men try to flirt with her, and that she cut them off firmly. But from the moment their eyes met, he saw that she was interested in him. He'd stayed there quite a while. She'd told him she'd be free tonight. Her name was Louise.

Now, as the evening sun burnished the face of Notre-Dame, Roland crossed cheerfully to the Île de la Cité. Before continuing over to the Right Bank, he paused for a moment. On the left, downstream, was a bridge supporting a dozen water mills, behind which lay quays where the boats unloaded salt and herring from the Normandy coast. Past that, the narrow western tip of the island divided the Seine's waters, gleaming golden in the sunset. And a little farther downstream, where the stout wall of Philip Augustus reached the riverbank, a small, square, high-turreted fort called the Louvre, equipped with massive chains that could be drawn across the river, stood guardian to the sacred city, protecting her from the rough invaders who might want to ravish her.

Roland gazed westward at the warm sun, and smiled. It struck him as very convenient that Martine lived on the east side of the Right Bank, and Louise on the western side. With luck, he thought, he might be able to go from one to the other for some time.

Martine was quite excited the following night as she waited for her lover to arrive. She had some sweetmeats and a jug of wine on the small table in her room. She had gone to confession the day before, and as always after penance and absolution, she felt a tingling sense of freshness, as if the world had been made anew. Despite the young man's faults, she even found herself trembling a little in anticipation.

She waited until darkness had fallen. Two of the servants slept in the attic of the main house, a third in the kitchen. The kitchen door was locked and bolted now, and the shutters closed. Her uncle would still be in his counting house, but that looked on to the street at the front.

She put on a dark cloak and slipped down to the yard. Trailing clouds covered the moon. She was almost invisible. She went to the gate that gave on to the alley and slipped the bolts.

Roland was waiting. He stepped swiftly into the yard. A moment later they were stealing up the winding stair to her room.

The candle gave a warm light. The room was snug. Roland seemed in a cheerful mood. Quite pleased with himself, in fact. He was delighted with the little meal she'd prepared.

'I went to confession yesterday,' she said with a smile, as she poured him more wine.

'Have you so many sins to confess?'

'Just you.'

'Ah. A mortal sin. Did you receive penance and absolution?'

'Yes.'

'And do you mean to sin again?'

'Perhaps. If you're nice to me.' She looked at him curiously. 'What about you? Do you go to confession?'

'Now and then.'

'Well, I should hope so, Roland,' she teased him gently. 'Don't forget you're tonsured. You're going to be a priest.'

'Perhaps.' He shrugged. 'These sins of the flesh are not so important.'

'Is that what I am, then? A sin of the flesh?'

'According to theology.' He looked away for a moment, and then continued, almost to himself: 'A woman with a husband would be a greater sin. A widow is different. And it's not as if I'd seduced a girl from a noble family.'

'It's all right because I only come from a merchant family. A *bourgeoise*.'

'You know what I mean.'

Oh yes, she knew all right. He was noble, so he considered himself above the rest of humanity. This impoverished, inexperienced, cocky little aristocrat thought he could bed her because his ancestors had been friends of Charlemagne. And he expected her to accept it. Just like that. She had half a mind to throw him out.

But she didn't. She was in the mood to make love. And having gone this far, she thought, she might as well get what she wanted. Two people could play the game of using someone.

He put down his wine, and grinned. She assumed he was about to make a move towards her. But then he paused.

'I didn't tell you last time. But I saw your uncle in the market the other day. He stared at me as if he knew me. It was quite frightening. But then I realised it's just the way he looks. You don't think he knows about me, do you?'

'He has no idea. I promise you.'

'Glad to hear it.'

Now he was ready to make his move. He began kissing her. They rolled on to the straw mattress. Martine was only wearing a shift, but he was still dressed. Young Roland was aroused, and so was she. His hand moved between her legs. She gave a little gasp. Soon afterwards, he was pulling down his hose, entering her.

'Take off your shirt,' she said, pulling at it. Like most people, Roland wore his shirt for a week or more, and it smelled of sweat and the street. But she liked that he washed more than other men she knew. Admittedly, dashing oneself with cold water from a bowl wasn't much of a bath, but it was as good as it usually got in the Paris of the Crusades. 'Ah,' she whispered, 'that feels good.' She could smell his sweat, and that faint scent of almonds on his skin. He was getting more and more excited, thrusting rapidly. She arched her back. He pressed himself close.

And then she frowned. She smelled something else. She thought she must be mistaken. But no, there was no mistake. It was the smell of perfume, but not the kind that she might use. This was the sickly smell of the cheapest kind of perfume that the street girls used to try to hide the fact they hadn't washed for a month.

There was only one way that Roland could have got that smell on his skin. She understood in a flash. That's what he'd been up to last night. Her body went rigid.

He came. Early.

Martine did not move. For a moment, a great sense of hurt engulfed her, like a wave. But it quickly receded. She wasn't in love with him. Then she felt rage. How dare he? She'd offered herself, and he'd run around the corner with some whore he'd picked up God knows where. Had he no respect for her at all? Did he have any idea how lucky he was? She wanted to scream. She wanted to strike him with something hard and heavy. She wanted to make him suffer.

But still she lay quite still. He leaned over. She forced herself to smile. Then she put her head on his chest, and stroked it, closing her eyes as if she were drowsy. After a little time she felt his body relax. He was dozing. She pulled away and lay beside him, thinking.

She gave a small smile of satisfaction. Revenge was a dish best served cold. She was glad, now, that she had kept silent. He would suspect nothing. She closed her eyes.

It was dawn when she awoke. In the faint light from the shuttered window she could see that he was lying on his side, his head raised on one arm, watching her.

'At last,' he said. He reached across.

He kissed her neck and started to move down her body. She let him. It felt good. He wasn't in a hurry, and nor was she.

'I'm a little sleepy,' she said. He was hard, and that was what she wanted, too. She let him enter. He was moving slowly and rhythmically, taking his time.

'You know,' she said softly, 'about what you said last night.'

'You talk when you're making love?'

'Sometimes. I mean about my uncle. You don't have to worry. He has no idea.'

'Good.'

'I'd know at once if he did. He'd beat me.'

'Oh.'

53

'He wants me to make a good marriage. As for any man who slept with me . . . Aiee . . .'

'What?'

'He'd suffer the fate of Abelard.'

He stopped.

'You're not serious.'

'You don't know him.'

'He'd castrate me? Cut off my balls?'

'Oh, he'd have some roughnecks do it. He has the power.'

'But I'm a noble.'

'So was Abelard.' It was true that the great philosopher came from a minor noble family.

She felt him shrink inside her. She pulled him close.

'Don't worry, *mon amour*, he has no idea,' she coaxed. But Roland's manhood was in full retreat. 'Don't leave me now,' she whispered. 'Finish what you came to do.'

He pulled away. He glanced at the sliver of light between the shutters.

'I'd better go,' he said.

'Will you come back tonight?' she asked.

'I have to study tonight,' he said.

'Tomorrow?'

'If I can.'

The day passed quietly, giving her time for further reflection. On the whole, she had to admit, it was probably just as well that things had worked out the way they had. She'd been a fool to run such risks. Her little interlude with Roland, such as it was, had made one thing very clear to her. She needed a man in her life again.

It was time to get married. She could probably get a rich husband. Her uncle would see to that. There were plenty of good men in Paris, so she might as well marry a rich one.

Roland had to go. But that didn't mean she wouldn't punish him.

Could she have been wrong about the other girl? She didn't think so. Every instinct told her she was right, but she wanted to be certain. By the afternoon she was forming another plan.

It was evening and the sun was sinking over the Seine when she made her way along to the bridge that led from the Left Bank to the

Île de la Cité. Of course, it was possible that he had a girl on the Left Bank, but it would be harder for him to escape detection there. It was far more likely that the other girl was on the northern side of the river. She found a convenient spot on a street corner from which she could observe, and she waited.

She didn't have to wait long. He came over the bridge with a jaunty step. So much for studying tonight. She pulled a shawl over her head and followed him at a distance. There were enough people about for her to follow him inconspicuously. Some were standing on the bridge to admire the sunset, and Roland did the same. After that, he continued over to the Right Bank, and went northwards until he turned left into the rue Saint-Honoré. She continued to follow. She saw him go into a tavern. She hesitated. If she went in there, people would turn to look. He'd probably see her, and that would be embarrassing. On the other hand, she wanted to know what he was up to. She stood in the street, wondering what to do.

He obligingly saved her the trouble by coming out again. There was a girl beside him, with a mass of black hair, just the sort of cheap slut, thought Martine, that she'd imagined. She saw him put his arm around the girl, who reached up and pulled his head down to kiss him on the mouth. Martine quickly turned her head so as not to be seen, but they didn't even glance in her direction.

For just a moment, she felt a cold shock that he'd betrayed her. But it was followed by a sense of satisfaction. She'd been right. Her senses and her instincts hadn't let her down. It was time to complete her revenge.

That evening, finding a moment when the kitchen was empty, she stole in and removed a long kitchen knife that was seldom used. Then, while her uncle was in his counting house, she entered the empty parlour, where there was a large oak table, and spent several minutes stooped over it, apparently examining the grain of the wood.

The following morning after breakfast, her uncle went out to the Grève market. The cook and the two other servants were in the kitchen.

Martine stepped into the parlour. She knew exactly what she had to do. She knew it was going to be painful. But she'd worked it out carefully, tried everything out to make sure that it would work as planned. As she took a deep breath and prepared herself, her whole face was screwed up in anticipation of the pain. If it hadn't been needed for her revenge, she couldn't have gone through with it.

So now, involuntarily crossing herself, she took careful aim, twisted her head so that she shouldn't break her nose, and let herself fall, hard, against the edge of the big oak table in the middle of the room.

She didn't need to fake her howl of pain. The servants came running.

'I tripped,' she wailed. She saw drops of blood on the floor. She hadn't meant to break the skin, and hoped it wouldn't leave a scar. But the main thing was that already, she could feel a huge, throbbing pain around her left eye.

While the younger servant girl ran to fetch Martine's uncle home from the market, the cook, a small, vigorous woman, took charge. The cut over the eye wasn't bad. The cook bathed it, held a wad of cloth over it, and staunched the bleeding. Then she put grease on the cut and wrapped a bandage round Martine's head. A cold compress helped the swelling.

'But you're going to have a big, shiny black eye,' the cook informed her cheerfully.

By the time her uncle arrived at the house, Martine was quite composed, sitting in the kitchen and taking a little broth. Her face was swelling up nicely. Once he was satisfied that his niece was neither badly injured nor disfigured, her uncle returned to the market, and Martine told the servants that she was going to rest in her room and would come down again at midday.

Everything was going exactly according to plan.

She waited in her room for a while, until there was no one out in the yard. Then, slipping the long knife she'd stolen into her belt and concealing it under her gown, she slipped unseen out of the back gate into the alley that Roland had used for his night-time visits.

She walked swiftly southward, skirted the Grève marketplace and made towards the river. As she had the evening before, she kept a shawl over her head to hide the bandage.

It was only a quarter of a mile to the bridge that crossed from the Right Bank to the Île de la Cité. Just before she reached it, ahead of her, she caught sight of the high roof of the Grand Châtelet, where the provost of Paris dispensed justice to the people. University students like Roland, who only had to answer to the Church courts, were exempt from the provost's stern rule. Martine smiled to herself. She had a special kind of justice reserved for young Roland de Cygne.

She crossed to the island. Over the rooftops on her right rose the high vault of the Sainte-Chapelle, grey against the sky. The sacred relics concealed within might bring joy to the king, but the royal reliquary looked like a tall, cold barn to her that day. And the memory of her budding passion for the boy, when they'd gone in there together, was as dead as ashes. She crossed the Seine once more, by the narrow bridge to the Left Bank, and started up the long, straight slope of the rue Saint-Jacques.

She didn't often come to the Left Bank. The Latin Quarter, some people were calling it these days, since it had started filling with scholars. She cursed as she almost stepped into a pile of steaming faeces that someone must have tossed from an upper window. That's right, she thought grimly: the scholars could talk Latin and preach in church, but life still came down, in the end, to the same old stink in the street.

She was nearing the top of the hill. She put her hand down and felt the handle of the long knife under her belt. Ahead of her was the gateway in the city wall through which the Compostela pilgrims passed. She knew Roland's lodgings were somewhere here. A student came out of a doorway, and she was about to ask him if he knew Roland, when the young man himself appeared, from another house nearby. He saw her and stopped in surprise. She went quickly to his side.

'We must talk at once,' she said urgently. 'Alone.'

He frowned, but led her a short way along the street and turned into a churchyard. It was quiet there. No one could see them.

'What's the matter?' he asked. 'I was coming to you tonight.'

'You can't,' she said. 'Look.' And she pulled back her shawl.

He stared in surprise at the big red-and-black swelling on her face. 'My God. What happened?'

'My uncle. He beat me. He knows about us.' She watched him go pale. 'I slipped out of the house to warn you.'

'How? He was asleep when I left yesterday. I heard him snoring.'

'The cook saw you. She told him.'

'He knows who I am?'

'Not yet. I wouldn't tell him your name. But he has men out already making inquiries.'

He looked thoughtful.

'No one knows. Did the cook get a good look at me?'

'She gave him a description.'

'God be damned.'

'Oh, Roland.' She looked pitiful. 'He'll beat me again until I tell him your name. I can't hold out much longer.'

Roland looked away for a moment. Cursing his bad luck, no doubt. She felt for the knife in her belt, but she didn't draw it out yet. He turned back at her.

'You don't really think . . . ,' he started.

'Oh, Roland,' she cried, 'you've got to leave Paris. Leave at once.'

'I can't do that.'

'You don't understand. You don't know him. Once he's made up his mind . . . And he has the power.'

'He'd really have me castrated?' He stared at her in horror.

'Nothing will stop him. The king couldn't stop him.'

He was squirming. She watched him. It was perfect.

'I can't leave Paris,' he muttered. 'I've nowhere to go.'

'We could run away together,' she said. 'I have some money. We could run away to Normandy. Or England.'

'That won't do,' he answered, staring at the ground. She knew he'd say that.

'You don't want me,' she wailed. 'I'm lost.'

'No, no. I care for you,' he answered.

There was a long pause.

'He doesn't mean to kill you,' she pointed out. 'That's something. They say that Abelard was a greater philosopher after it happened to him.'

It was clear from Roland's face that philosophy wouldn't console him.

'What can I do?' he cried.

It was time. She reached below her cloak and pulled out the knife. He shrank back.

'Here,' she said. 'It's for you.'

'For me?'

'If they come for you, use it. Don't hesitate. You won't have any time. They'll mean business. But if you can kill them, or wound them, maybe it'll stop him trying again. It's your only hope.'

He took the knife. He weighed it in his hand, and pursed his lips. She saw him glance around.

And suddenly she thought she read his thoughts. The one thing she hadn't allowed for. Could it be so? Was he wondering whether he should use the knife to kill her? To get her out of the way? Nobody had seen them. If she was dead, he could be thinking, her uncle would never discover his identity.

How could she have been so foolish? She'd brought the knife only to make her story seem more convincing. And she'd been so busy plotting her own revenge that she'd overlooked this weakness in the plan. She froze.

But then he shook his head and gave her back the knife.

'I have a weapon of my own,' he said. Though whether she had been wrong, or he had calculated the odds and decided against killing her, or his conscience had intervened, she would never know.

'I must go before I am missed,' she said. 'But take care, my Roland. I fear we may never see each other again. May God protect you.' And pushing the knife back into her girdle, and covering her head with her shawl, she hurried out of the churchyard.

As she went back down the street towards the river, she wondered happily how many sleepless nights and nightmares he would suffer, and whether he would run away from Paris. And oh, the pleasure of watching the cocky little swine while he squirmed.

Revenge was sweet.

The rest of that day did not go well for Roland. He tried to go about his business. He attended a lecture. He went to his usual tavern, where he met some friends. He longed to share his troubles with them, but didn't feel that he could. He bought bread, a little cured meat and some beans, and took them back to his lodgings.

The room where he lodged was up a creaking wooden staircase. The door had a bolt, and he wondered whether to add a second one. But he decided there was no point. A couple of determined men could break it down anyway. There was a heavy oak chest, however.

He could drag it over to the door. If he laid his mattress beside the chest, he'd be sure to wake up instantly as soon as anyone tried to break in.

The window worried him. It was only ten feet above the street. But it was narrow and the shutters were stout. He might be able to defend it.

As for a weapon, he did have a dagger. He wished he had a sword, but a student couldn't walk around the streets with that. The dagger was long and made to be used in battle. It had belonged to his grandfather. He tested the blade. It was sharp. Even if several men battered down the door, he ought to be able to kill one of them, maybe two.

He stayed indoors until evening, ate his food, set up his barricade and prepared for the dangerous night.

But he couldn't sleep. Each creak he heard made him start. Around midnight something outside, a rat probably, disturbed a little pile of faggots, one of which fell with a soft click on the cobbles. In a flash, Roland was up, waiting beside the window, dagger in hand, not daring to signal his presence by opening the shutters but straining every nerve to hear if anyone was in the street, or coming up the stairs. He stayed there almost half an hour before lying down again, still listening.

And as he listened, thoughts chased through his head. Why had he got involved with Martine? If only he'd been chaste. If only he'd been a Temple Knight. And what should he do? Could he return home? How would he explain it to his father? His family would be furious. He was supposed to be helping them and he'd let them all down. He dreaded the thought of facing them almost as much as he dreaded mutilation.

The hours passed. He didn't even doze. At dawn, he started violently again, as someone threw slops from a window down into the street. And by the time the city gates were opening, and people were moving about in the streets, he staggered down the stairs, hollow-eyed, to face the day.

He had to attend his first lecture early that morning. He didn't want to go out unarmed. But a student couldn't wander around with a weapon in his belt. How could he keep it under his hand unseen? After looking around his possessions he hit upon a solution. He had a roll of cheap parchments, mostly rabbit and squirrel, the kind that clerks and merchants used for transactions. Slipping the dagger through the middle, he found that he could carry it quite hidden, but pull it out with ease. Thus armed, he descended into the street to join his fellow students.

Everything seemed normal. He felt some comfort from being in a crowd, but he couldn't help wondering – if he were suddenly attacked, would his fellow students protect him? From some angry townsman with a club, probably. From two or three armed men? Perhaps not. Even as he walked back in their company towards his lodgings after the lectures, he found himself glancing over his shoulder to see if he was being followed.

Another thought also occurred to him. Shouldn't he try to protect his body in some way? Could he wear a leather vest, like a man-at-arms, under his clerical dress? Some of them had metal studs. If he could somehow attach the ends together between his legs, might that give him some protection, or would his assailants just slit it with a knife?

On the western side of the Latin Quarter, there was a gate in the city wall where the road led out to a church in the suburbs called Saint-Germain-des-Prés. Just inside this gate there was an armourer's workshop. He'd never been in there, but he'd heard it was one of the best. In the afternoon, therefore, he paid the place a visit.

The little factory was certainly busy. It had forges like a black-smith. He saw swords, helms, chain armour, all manner of imple-ment and protective clothing for the fighting man. But while every-thing was designed to protect the head and arms, the torso and the legs, there was no individual item to protect a man between his legs. And I can hardly walk around in a suit of body armour, Roland thought.

He asked for the master armourer, and was pointed towards a short, brisk figure with a close-cropped greying beard, who listened carefully as he explained the protection that he wanted.

'Never been asked for that before,' the craftsman remarked. 'Did you get caught with somebody's wife?'

'Something like that.'

'Well, I always say we can make anything. You want something like a chastity belt, only it would have to be bigger. Difficult to make that out of metal. I doubt you could sit down.' The armourer considered. 'To be flexible, it would have to be like a short hose, chain armour over a leather backing, I should think. It'd be quite heavy, you know, and it'll cost you.'

'You could do it?'

'Not for a month, at least, maybe longer. I've orders waiting from some of the greatest nobles in the land.' He looked up at the unhappy young man. 'Can it wait that long?'

'Probably not.'

'Better hang on to yourself, then.' The craftsman grinned.

Roland departed sadly. He probably couldn't afford such a thing, even if he could find anyone to make it.

It was almost a day and a half since he had slept, and he was starting to feel light-headed. He hardly knew what to do with himself. Returning to the rue Saint-Jacques, he turned down towards the river. Soon, on his left, he passed the Church of Saint-Séverin. And in the hope that the place might calm his spirits, he went in there to rest.

There was something very intimate about its strange, old, narrow vaults. Though rebuilt from time to time, the church had already been there for seven hundred years, since the days of the early Frankish kings. As he sat on a stone bench, his back to the wall and his eyes on the door, with his dagger concealed in the roll of parchment across his knees, young Roland reflected on his situation.

The facts were all too obvious. He had sinned, and God was punishing him. He deserved it. That much was clear as day. But what could he do? He must repent. He must beg forgiveness with all his heart, though whether it would be granted was another matter.

A terrible thought occurred to him. Could it be that God actually intended he should be castrated? Was God not only punishing him, but saving him from further temptation? Had God decided to ensure that his life was dedicated to religious service as a celibate priest or monk? Surely it could not be. Wasn't it God's will that he should overcome temptation, more or less, rather than have temptation removed from him? Abelard might have suffered that fate, but Abelard was a great scholar and philosopher. His own place in the world was far more modest. He wasn't worthy of so much attention. Plenty of other men in Holy Orders had done the same as he had, and got away with it. If he dedicated his life to serving the Church, he told himself, that ought to be enough. If he truly repented, forgiveness would be granted.

So Roland tried to pray. He tried very hard indeed, for over an hour. And at the end of that time, he did feel a little calmer. At least he'd made a start, he thought. That was something. He got up, and cautiously went into the street.

If only he didn't feel so tired. He must get sleep. But he didn't want to sleep at his lodgings. He needed to find another place. Somewhere the men searching for him wouldn't think of. Where could he go?

And then, it seemed to him, he had a good idea. What about the girl on the rue Saint-Honoré? What about Louise? Neither Martine nor her uncle knew about her.

Louise had a little room near the tavern. She'd surely let him sleep with her there. And to show that his repentance was sincere, he wouldn't make love to her. That might work. He'd go to the tavern and ask her.

With this new, confused hope in his heart, he crossed over the river, and headed north.

There was only one thing that worried him. Once in bed with her, would he still be able to resist temptation? And would she let him? Still pondering this difficulty, he came to the rue Saint-Honoré and started to turn into it.

A hand closed on his elbow. He leaped in the air. His hand flew to the roll of parchment. He twisted, with a terrified face, towards his assailant.

'My dear young man. Did I startle you?'

It was the priest from the church by the Cemetery of the Innocents. The man to whom he'd delivered the letter the week before.

'Father!' he cried.

'I'm very sorry I made you jump,' said the elderly priest apologetically. 'But I thought I recognised you. You came to my house the other day. Are you all right?' His mild blue eyes were peering at the younger man. 'You look very pale.'

'Yes, *mon Père*, I am well.' Roland stared at the priest with a mixture of relief and embarrassment. 'Thank you. Ah . . . The truth is that . . . I did not sleep well last night.'

'Why was that, my son?'

'Well, you see . . .' Roland searched his mind feverishly. 'There was a fire in my lodgings. Just a small fire. It was put out. But my room is a terrible mess. Black dust everywhere . . .' He was babbling, but the elderly priest continued to look at him kindly.

'And where will you sleep tonight, my son?'

'Oh . . . Well . . . I was going to ask a friend . . .'

'Why don't you sleep at my house? There's plenty of room.'

'Your house?'

'It would be a strange thing if the priest of the Saints Innocents did not help a scholar in need.'

And then it seemed to Roland that he understood. This was a gift from the Almighty. God had sent this priest to save him from temptation in his hour of need. He need not sleep with Louise. He would be safe.

'Thank you, *mon Père*,' he said. 'I accept.'

The priest's house lay almost beside the church. It wasn't large, but it had a pleasant hall with a fireplace and a window, and an area partitioned by a heavy curtain, where a mattress could easily be laid for a guest. An elderly nun from a nearby convent came in each day to act as the priest's housekeeper, and she quietly laid out a meal for them both. After he had eaten a rich stew, and a little cheese, and drunk a goblet of wine, Roland started to feel very much better.

The priest's conversation was pleasant. He asked Roland about his family and his studies, and it was soon clear that he was an excellent scholar himself. He spoke about his parish, and its poor. And it was only towards the end of the meal that he gently inquired: 'Are you in some sort of trouble, my son?'

Roland hesitated. How he would have liked to tell the kindly priest the truth. Should he make his confession and ask for his help? Could the priest perhaps arrange for his protection? The Church was powerful. He wanted to confess.

But he couldn't do it.

'No, *mon Père*,' he lied.

The old man didn't press him. But as the sun was falling he remarked that at the end of each day he went into his church to pray, and suggested that perhaps Roland would like to accompany him.

'I should,' said Roland fervently. And he went to pick up his roll of parchment, so that he'd have his dagger with him, just in case.

'There's no need to bring that with you,' the old man said. 'It will be quite safe here in the house.'

What could he do? Reluctantly he went out unarmed.

The Church of the Saints Innocents was silent. They were alone.

'Each time I pray here,' the priest remarked, 'I like to remember that I am in the presence of all those poor Christian souls, the simple people of Paris without even a name by which to remember them, who lie in the cemetery beside us.' He smiled. 'It makes our own troubles seem very small.'

Then he went to a small side altar, sank to his knees and silently began to pray.

Roland knelt beside him, and did his best to do the same. The old man's presence was comforting. He felt a sense of peace. Surely, he thought, in this quiet sanctuary, he must be under God's protection.

And yet . . . As the time passed, and the church remained silent, he could not help it if his ears were straining for any tiny sound. He wanted to turn his head to look around, to make sure that no shadowy figures were stealing towards them. But he did not dare, for fear of disturbing his companion's prayers.

And then, to his shame, came other thoughts. What if the church door suddenly burst open now, and two or three armed men rushed in? He didn't have his dagger, but the old priest was not heavy. Could he pick him up and use him as a shield? He was just contemplating this possibility when he heard the priest's voice at his side.

'Let us say a *Pater Noster*, my son.'

Pater Noster, qui es in caelis, sanctificetur Nomen tuum . . . the eternal words of the Lord's Prayer, murmured softly in the quiet church.

And when it was done, and they had returned to the priest's house and bolted the door, Roland lay down on the bed prepared, with his roll of parchment beside him, and slept in peace.

The sun was already well up when he awoke. Breakfast was awaiting him on the table. The old priest had already gone out, but had left a message with his housekeeper that he would expect Roland to join him for supper again that evening, and to stay in his house that night.

As he made his way across the river to the Latin Quarter, Roland felt quite refreshed. Whatever the dangers that lurked, he thought, there must be some solution – some way, if he were truly repentant, that God would grant him protection. Perhaps, this evening, he would confess everything to the old priest and ask his advice.

He went up the rue Saint-Jacques. There were plenty of students about. He kept his eyes open, but saw no sign of danger.

He was fifty paces from his lodgings when a student came up to him.

'There's a fellow looking for you,' he said.

Roland froze.

'A man? What sort of man?'

'I don't know. I never saw him before.'

'Just one?' His heart was starting to beat violently. 'Are you sure there weren't several?'

'I saw only one,' the student said. And Roland was just wondering whether to make a run for it when the student waved to a poor-looking young fellow up the street and called out: 'Here he is.'

Roland began to turn and run. But then he stopped.

No. He wouldn't run. He couldn't go on like this. There was only one young man, probably sent as a scout, to check out his whereabouts before the thugs were brought in. If I can just bring him down, he thought, and make him confess . . . take him to the authorities . . . It'd be hard for Martine's uncle to attack me after that.

He reached into the roll of parchment, pulled out the dagger.

And with a shout of rage, he rushed at the stranger, hurling himself upon him. The young man went down. Roland stayed on top of him. He pressed the dagger blade to the fellow's throat.

'Who sent you?' he cried. The young man's eyes were wide with terror.

'The lord de Cygne,' he answered hoarsely. 'Your father, sir.'

'My father?'

'I am Pierre, the miller's son, from your village.'

Roland stared at him. It could be true. He realised that the young fellow's face was vaguely familiar. He hadn't seen him for a few years. He kept the dagger at his throat, in case.

'Why are you here?'

'Your brother. He's had an accident. He is dead. Your father wants you to return home at once. I have a letter for you from the priest.'

'My brother is dead?' That could mean only one thing. He'd have to take his place back at home as the future lord de Cygne.

'Yes, sir. I am sorry.'

And then, without thinking – for in truth he loved his brother – but in sheer relief at such an unexpected way out of his troubles, Roland spoke the words that, for the rest of his life, would cause his villagers behind his back to call him the Black de Cygne:

'Thank God!' he cried.

The letter from the priest explained the details. His brother had suffered a fall from his horse on to a gatepost, had punctured his lungs, and died within the hour. The priest urged Roland to do his father's bidding and return at once, since his presence was greatly needed.

He well knew, the priest wrote, what a sacrifice it would be to give up his studies at the university, and the religious life. And indeed, Roland thought, he might have felt some reluctance to leave Paris, had it not been for this trouble over Martine with the merchant. But, the priest went on, it was not for us to question providence. One must simply bow one's head and do one's duty. It was clearly a sign, the priest explained, that God had decided that Roland should serve Him in another calling.

Roland made the arrangements that very day. He told his teachers that his father required him urgently to go into Normandy, but that he hoped soon to return. He told his friends that he was secretly hoping to study in Italy, at the University of Bologna. To Martine, he sent no message at all. And having, he hoped, left enough confusion to throw her uncle off his track, he spent the night at the house of the kindly old priest and departed the next morning for his home in the valley of the Loire.

Since he made no inquiries, he never knew that, six months later, Martine was married to a merchant named Renard. But had he known, he would have been glad.

Chapter Four

1885

Thomas Gascon found his true love on the first day of June, in the morning. It had rained the day before, and grey clouds were still passing across the open sky above the Arc de Triomphe. But the horse chestnut trees were in their full, white blossom, and the promise of summer was in the air, as the huge crowds gathered.

He had come for a funeral.

Writers were honoured in France. And now that Victor Hugo – beloved author of *Les Misérables*, *The Hunchback of Notre-Dame* and a score of other tales – had died at the age of eighty-three, France was giving him a state funeral.

The entire legislature, senators, deputies, judges and officers of state; the leaders of the universities, the academies and the arts, had arrived at the Arc de Triomphe, where the author had been lying in state. More than two million people lined the route the funeral cortege would take, down the Champs-Élysées to Concorde, over the bridge to the Left Bank and along the boulevard Saint-Germain until, at last, it would climb to the summit of the old Roman hill in the Latin Quarter where the mausoleum of the Panthéon now stood, ready to receive the greatest sons of France.

Paris had never seen such a crowd – not in the days of the Sun King, not during the Revolution, not even under the emperor Napoléon.

And all for a novelist.

Thomas had arrived at dawn to get a good view. Some people had camped out in the street the night before to get a good position, but Thomas had been more cunning. He had inspected the place previously and chosen a spot near the top of the Champs-Élysées, on its southern side, with his back resting against a building.

As the huge avenue rapidly filled, his view was soon blocked, but he didn't mind. He waited patiently until everything was in place, the police and soldiers all busy lining the roadway and the crowd around him so thick that it was impossible to move.

First, he reached down to the rope tied around his waist and unwound the loose end, to which he'd attached a small hook. Just behind him, at shoulder height, a narrow ledge ran along the stone facade of the building, and above that was a window protected on the outside by a metal grille. Skilfully, he tossed the rope up so that the hook caught in the grille.

Then, suddenly grabbing the shoulders of the two people in front of him, he levered himself up quickly. They hardly had time to protest before he was scrambling up their backs, and a moment later, with a foot resting on the head of one of them, he got his other heel firmly on the ledge, reached up, pulled the hook through the grille and tied the rope off. The two men below were now cursing volubly, and one of them tried to punch him, but the crowd was so close that it was hard for the man to get a decent swing. And after Thomas made a motion as though to kick him in the head with his workman's boot, he contented himself with a contemptuous '*Cochon!*' and turned away.

Thanks to this arrangement, tethered safely to the grille behind by the rope around his waist, Thomas could lean out to left or right as he pleased and watch everything over the heads of the people in front of him.

Across the avenue, the balconies were crammed with people; there were heads at every window. Some of these folk had paid large sums of money for these vantage points. But he had a view as good as theirs, for free.

To his left, the wide space around the Arc de Triomphe had been cleared for the dignitaries who were all in deepest mourning dress, or uniform. The great arch itself was an extraordinary sight. Three years ago, a huge sculpture of the goddess Victory in her chariot had been placed on top, making it even more dramatic than before. An enormous drape hung like a scooped curtain over one side of the monument; long banners hung from its corners. And taking up most of the great central arch was the ornate and massive catafalque, sixty feet high, in which Victor Hugo had been lying in state.

It was more than a funeral. It was an apotheosis.

The crowds were all in black. The better-off men wore top hats. Thomas himself had put on a short coat that was dark enough, but he wore a blue working man's cap. He supposed Victor Hugo wouldn't mind.

He was staring towards the arch, where the funeral orations were beginning, when he saw the girl.

She was standing about fifteen yards away, in the front row. He could see only the back of her head, and there was nothing special about that. There was really no reason he should have felt drawn towards this particular head in the sea of people all around. But for some reason it seemed to him to be special.

He could see that she had frizzy brown hair. The skin on the back of her neck looked pale. He couldn't tell what she was wearing, but he thought that she probably belonged to the poorer classes, like himself. He wondered if she would turn round.

The funeral orations were starting. He couldn't hear them properly, but that didn't matter. He was there. He was part of the great event.

And everyone knew what must be said. Victor Hugo wasn't only a great romantic poet and novelist. *Liberty*, *Equality*, *Fraternity* were his watchwords, and he'd lived by them. When Napoléon III had made himself dictator, Hugo had shamed him before all the world, choosing exile in the island of Guernsey, and refusing to come back until democracy was restored. When the Germans invaded France, he'd returned at once, to share starvation with the people of Paris. He'd served as a deputy and a senator too, and taken up residence on one of the splendid avenues that radiated out from the Arc de Triomphe. He was France's greatest patriot, the conscience of the nation, the finest spirit of the age.

A few years ago, as a birthday present, the city had even renamed the avenue where he lived: avenue Victor Hugo.

From time to time, an oration would end, and the echo of applause could be heard before another speech began. Each time, Thomas would watch the young woman carefully, in case she turned her head. But although she shifted her position a little, he never saw her face. Meanwhile, the clouds were departing from the sky, and the Arc de Triomphe was bathed in sunlight.

At last the ceremonies were drawing to a close. He heard a church bell start to sound the hour of noon. And at that moment, the entire sky above Paris seemed to shake as a huge roar of cannon split the air. Gun after gun saluted, each bang and rumble reverberating off the buildings, so that it was hard to guess where the guns were placed.

He saw the girl step forward into the roadway, trying to discover where the sounds were coming from. She turned right around, saw him and stared – which was hardly surprising since, thanks to his rope, he was leaning so far forward that he appeared to be hovering in the air above the heads of the people in front of him. As for Thomas, he was gazing at her as if he'd seen a vision.

She was wearing the plain dress of a simple working girl. Her face was lightly freckled, her nose small, her mouth was not too wide, but generous. Her eyes were hazel, as far as he could see. She looked at him quizzically. And then she smiled.

To his surprise, at that moment, he didn't feel a rush of excitement. In fact, he felt strangely calm, as if everything in the world had suddenly fallen into place.

This was the one. He didn't know how, or why he knew it, but he did. This was the girl he was going to marry. This was his destiny and nothing could change it. He was filled with a sense of lightness, of warmth and peace. He smiled back at her. Had she felt it as well? He thought perhaps she had.

But already the huge cortege was starting to move. A soldier was making her move back. Her head turned, there was a jostling in the crowd and he lost sight of her.

He must get to her side. He reached up and started to undo the knot in the rope. But he had been leaning out for so long that the knot was too tight for even his strong fingers. He felt for the knot where the rope went around his waist. The same thing. He struggled for a minute or two, without success.

'Has anyone got a knife?'

The black coach bearing the casket was passing. All the men were taking their hats off. Nobody even looked at him. He remembered, just too late, to remove his workman's cap. The coach passed. A phalanx of the great men of France walked behind it.

'For the love of God, has anyone got a knife?' he called again. Slowly, the man whose head he'd stepped on turned up to look. Thomas gave him an apologetic smile. 'Pardon, monsieur,' he said politely, 'but as you see, I've been left hanging here.' The man

71

considered him for a long moment. Then he reached into his coat pocket, drew out a pen knife and showed it to him.

'I have a knife,' he said.

'If you could do me the kindness . . .,' Thomas continued, using his best manners.

'It's a pity,' the man remarked pleasantly, 'that the rope is not around your neck.' Then he put the knife back in his pocket, and turned to look at the cortege again.

Thomas thought for half a minute.

'Hey,' he called down. 'Monsieur with the knife.' The man paid no attention. 'I've got to pee. You want it on your head?'

The man looked up furiously. Thomas shrugged, put his hands to his front and started to unbutton his fly. The man tried to move away, but the crowd was pressed so thick he couldn't budge. With a curse, he reached into his pocket again.

'Cut your cock off, then,' he replied. But he handed up the knife.

The knife was quite sharp. It took only a few seconds for Thomas to saw through the rope and release himself. He folded the knife.

'*Merci,* monsieur,' he cried. 'You are very kind.' Then he tossed the knife down so that it fell just behind the man's back, leaving him trying helplessly to pick it up from the ground.

Using the narrow ledge and where necessary the heads of the spectators, he managed to move along the building to the corner, where he found enough space to get down. Worming and discreetly kicking his way forward, he began to work his way towards the street. '*Pardon, madame, pardon, monsieur,* I have to pee,' he cried. Some let him push through. Others resisted. 'Pee in your pants, you little shit,' said one man. But eventually Thomas reached the roadway.

Ducking and weaving behind the soldiers lining the route, he managed to get back to the place where he had seen the girl.

But she wasn't there. He looked right and left. No sign of her. It was impossible, he thought. No one could move far in that crowd – unless they used tactics like he had.

But somehow she had gone.

He managed to get a little farther along the line of spectators, before a soldier stopped him and made him stand still. Detachments of cavalry passed, and important men in top hats, and bands. The cortege seemed endless. Though he continued to crane his head this way and that, he never caught sight of the girl again.

It was mid-afternoon when Thomas arrived back at Montmartre. Monsieur Gascon had declared that he could honour Victor Hugo best by taking a drop of wine at the Moulin de la Galette, and his wife, who'd been suffering lately from a painful vein in her leg, had been glad to go there with him. As for young Luc, he had declared that it was his duty to keep his parents company, though Thomas knew very well that his little brother was just being lazy.

So Thomas joined them at the Moulin, and gave them a general account of the proceedings. It was only later, when they were alone, that he confided to Luc about the girl.

Although Luc was still only twelve years old, it sometimes seemed to Thomas that his little brother was already more worldly than he was. Perhaps it was his constant hanging around places like the Moulin, or perhaps it was just something innate in Luc's character, but Thomas was more likely to confide such information to him than to most adults.

'You had a *touche*,' Luc said. A mutual attraction.

'No,' said Thomas, 'more than that. A *coup de foudre*.' A thunderbolt. Love at first sight.

'How will you find her again?'

'I don't know. It'll happen.'

'You think it's fate?'

'Yes.'

'That's impressive.'

But he didn't find her. He had no information he could use. The city and suburbs of Paris now contained more than three million people, and she could be anywhere. She might even have come from another town.

At first, on days when he wasn't working, he'd go to the spot where he had seen her. He'd go at noon, the exact moment when their eyes had met. Might it be that she was also looking for him? And if so, mightn't she have the same idea and find him there? It was a long shot, but it was the only hope he had.

As the weeks and months went by, in his spare time, he'd go for a walk in a different part of the city, just in case he might catch sight of her. He came to know Paris far better, but he never saw the girl. Only Luc knew about these wanderings.

'You're like a knight in search of the Holy Grail,' he told his older brother, and each time Thomas returned, Luc would quietly ask, 'Did you find the Grail?'

Though he did not find the Holy Grail, these wanderings had another effect upon Thomas that was profoundly to influence his destiny. That spring, he'd been busy at Gaget, Gauthier et Cie. Although the Statue of Liberty had been completed in time for the Fourth of July the previous year, the huge pedestal on which it was to rest in New York had not been ready. It wasn't until the start of 1885 that Thomas had helped dismantle the huge statue, which was finally packed into 214 large crates and shipped across the Atlantic. It had been on its way to New York on the day of Victor Hugo's funeral.

The question then became, what was he to do next?

To his mother's delight, Gaget, Gauthier et Cie were happy to employ him. Evidently his hard work and his good eye had impressed them. 'They tell me that in a few years, I could become one of the skilled men who make the carvings and the ornaments,' he reported. Skilled work. Safe work. It was everything his mother had always hoped for.

The trouble was, he didn't want it.

Was it the long walks in his quest for the girl? Was it the feeling of being cooped up when he was working in the sheds at the foundry? Or the prospect of one day sitting at one of the long work tables with all the craftsmen and being unable to move? Whatever the cause, his strong young body revolted against the idea. He wanted to be out of doors. He wanted to feel the strength of his arm. He scarcely cared about the weather, even when it was cold, or raining, as long as he was physically working.

He was young. He was strong. He rejoiced in the sense of his physical power.

He loved to watch the men on the bridges, the riveters on the building sites. One day, without telling his parents what he had done, he politely explained to the foreman at the rue de Chazelles that he was quitting. A week later, he had joined a gang of ironworkers as the most junior member of a riveting gang, and he was working on the railways.

When his mother discovered, she was distraught.

'You don't understand,' she cried. 'Labouring men get sick. They get injured. You won't always be young and strong. But if you have a skill, you work indoors and you can always find employment.'

But Thomas wasn't listening.

The Gare Saint-Lazare lay only a short walk south-west from the foot of the hill of Montmartre. Its ever-expanding railway lines serviced the many towns of Normandy, and there were always repairs and alterations to be done.

Through the second half of 1885, therefore, and the spring of 1886, Thomas Gascon went about his work quietly. Early each morning he would walk the mile from his home in Montmartre to the Gare Saint-Lazare. On his days off, he continued to trudge around the different quarters of Paris, in the hope of seeing the girl again. By the spring, he admitted the quest was absurd, but he still went out a couple of times a month, out of habit as much as anything.

'Time to look for another woman,' Luc remarked to him one day. 'You're too faithful.'

'One should be faithful,' Thomas answered with a smile.

Young Luc shrugged and said nothing.

It was in May 1886 that the competition was announced. It was not before time. There were only three years to go before the centenary of the French Revolution, which was, as all Frenchmen knew, the most significant event – with the possible exception of the birth of Christ – in the history of humanity. It was imperative therefore that Paris have another great exhibition. And at the gateway, the Republic wanted something dramatic. Nobody knew what, but it had to be a structure that would make the whole world gasp. On the first of May, the city asked for submissions. And they wanted them fast.

The plans soon started coming. Many were banal. Some absurd. Some structurally impossible. One, at least, was dramatic. It proposed a towering replica of the guillotine. This, however, was deemed a little grim. Would the world's visitors really want to walk under a vast, hanging blade? Perhaps not.

And then there was the proposal from Monsieur Eiffel.

He had originally suggested the project some time before, but the city authorities had been uncertain. The huge iron tower he proposed was certainly daring. It was modern. It might be a bit ugly. But as they viewed all the entries now, one thing above all impressed the committee. After the complex construction of the Statue of Liberty, it was clear that Gustave Eiffel the bridge-builder knew what he was doing. If he said the thing could be built, then he'd do it.

All Paris had been following the competition. When the winner was announced, there were many protests. But when Thomas Gascon saw it in the newspaper, he knew at once what he wanted to do.

'I'm going to work with Monsieur Eiffel on his tower,' he told his family.

'But what about your job with the railway?' his mother demanded.

'I don't care.'

They'd need a lot of ironworkers. He intended to be first in line.

Sometimes Thomas worried about Luc's character. Had he been too protective of his little brother?

Luc had taken his advice. At school, he'd become the boy who made the other children laugh. Recently, his face had started to fill out, and together with his dark hair he looked more Italian than ever. He was clever, and worldly-wise. But it seemed to Thomas that Luc was also in danger of getting lazy, and soft. And he privately resolved to do something about this. It was part of his secret programme that, one Sunday that October, he took Luc for a strenuous walk.

The mid-morning sun was on the autumn leaves when they set off. Luc had looked up at the clouds scudding in from the west, and told Thomas that he thought it was going to rain, but Thomas had told him not to be silly, and that he didn't care if it rained anyway.

In fact, when he'd woken up that morning, Thomas had thought he might be starting a cold, but he wasn't going to let a small thing like that distract him from the more important business of toughening up his brother.

'I'll take you somewhere you've never been before,' he promised him.

Descending the hill of Montmartre and walking eastward, they crossed a big, handsome canal that brought water to the city from the edge of the Champagne region, and soon afterwards were walking up the long slope to their destination. The walk made him feel good, and by the time they reached the entrance, he felt he had shaken off his cold.

Though Baron Haussmann had built many handsome boulevards, his most delightful project was not a street at all, but a romantic park on the city's eastern edge. The Buttes-Chaumont was a high, rocky outcrop, about a mile north of the Père Lachaise Cemetery. Formerly it had been a quarry like Montmartre, but Haussmann and his team had transformed it into a rural retreat in keeping with the spirit of the times.

If the formal gardens of Louis XIV's reign had given way to the more natural landscaping of the Age of Reason, the nineteenth century was enjoying a rich duality. On the one hand, it was the age of steam, iron bridges and industry. Yet in the arts it was the high Romantic period. And while Germany had given the world the cosmic themes of Wagner, Romantic France was more intimate and picturesque.

They entered through one of the western gates. The winding paths led through glades planted with all manner of trees and bushes, many of them still richly coloured. In the middle of the park a small artificial lake surrounded a high, rocky promontory on the top of which a little round temple had been built. It looked like a scene out of some lush, Italian landscape painting.

They had brought some bread and cheese to eat in the middle of the day, and a bottle of beer. But before beginning their picnic, they agreed to visit the park's best-known attraction. Crossing to the island by a long, suspended footbridge, it took them little time to find it.

The grotto was a magical spot. Situated just inside a small cave in the rock face, its high chamber was festooned with stalactites. Still more striking, a high waterfall cascaded water from sixty feet above into a pool at the back, from which it flowed away over rocks. If a nymph from classical mythology had suddenly appeared from behind one of the grotto's rocks and started dancing with her companions, it would hardly have seemed surprising.

And most wonderful of all, it was artificial. The cave was the entrance to the old quarry. The stalactites were sculptures. The waterfall was created by hydraulic engineering. It was romantic, certainly. But the romance was not that of forest and cave and majestic mountain. It was theatre.

'Perhaps,' said Luc mischievously, 'the maiden you've been seeking lives here in the grotto. Wait a minute and she'll come out of the waterfall.'

'Let's go and eat,' said Thomas.

They crossed the bridge again and followed another path until they came to a green lawn, where they sat down. High above the island, they could see the craggy peak where the little temple stood. All around them, the leaves on the trees were gleaming gold. They ate their bread and cheese, and drank their beer. Thomas stretched out and looked up at the sky.

There were more grey clouds than before. He watched idly as a large bank of clouds approached the sun, screened it in a haze and then obscured it. He waited for the cloud to break, but it didn't. He felt a draught of colder, damper air and heard a light rustle in the leaves. The leaves weren't golden any more, but had taken on that strange, luminous yellow colour that he'd often noticed when there was electricity in the air. He stood up.

'It's going to rain. We'd better head home,' said Luc.

'Not yet. We'll visit the temple first.'

Luc looked up at the high crag.

'That would take a while,' he said.

'Not long,' answered Thomas. 'Let's go,' he commanded.

They crossed over the bridge to the island again. And then they took the steep path that led them up the hill. It was quite picturesque, like climbing a mountain ravine, and Thomas was happy even if Luc was not.

They were halfway up when, from the west, they heard a distant rumble of thunder.

'Let's go back down,' said Luc.

'Why?' said Thomas.

'Do you want to get caught in a thunderstorm?'

'Why not?' said Thomas. 'Come on.'

So they continued up the steep and winding path until they emerged at the little round temple. And just as they did, they heard the thunder again, and this time it echoed and reverberated all around the huge, broad valley in which Paris lay, so that if he hadn't felt the wind from the west, Thomas would hardly have known where the weather was coming from.

The temple was a small folly, modelled on the famous Temple of Vesta in Rome. From this high vantage point, Thomas could see the broad summit of Montmartre, and looking to his left, between high trees, he glimpsed the towers of Notre-Dame in the distance. He knew there were many strange figures on the top of those towers – Gothic gargoyles and all manner of stone monsters, looking out over Paris – and it pleased him to think that, perched up here on this crag, he might be as high in the sky as they were.

The grey clouds were overhead now, but a few miles to the west was a great line of darker clouds. Beneath it, a curtain of falling rain stretched across the city. Above it rose layers of black cloud banks. As Thomas gazed at these, he saw a flash within, followed by a crack of thunder.

The curtain of rain was advancing up the far side of Montmartre. On the hilltop, the tall scaffolding on the site of the rising Sacré Coeur stood out like a group of gallows. And while Thomas watched, the big site seemed to dissolve, and the hill with it, as the rain swallowed them up.

Then came another flash; and this time, with a tearing crack, a great stanchion of forked lightning snaked down the sky and struck close by the towers of Notre-Dame. And as Thomas imagined the stone figures up there, staring out at the storm while the lightning crashed around them, their faces quite unmoved, he smiled to himself.

The storm was coming swiftly towards them now, over the rooftops, over the canals. Luc called out that they'd better seek shelter, but Thomas didn't want to. Ever since he was a little boy, he had loved the electric excitement of thunderstorms. He didn't know why. The rain began to pour down on them and Luc stood under the temple arches in a futile attempt to keep dry, but Thomas stayed where he was, standing on a slab of rock, letting the rain pound on his head. The rain was coming so hard that he couldn't see the park below. The storm was directly above the park now. A huge bang shook the air as lightning struck a tree not a hundred paces away, but while Luc cringed, Thomas kept his feet planted, testing himself, proving that a poor young man in workman's boots could dare the gods of the storm to strike him down, like a romantic hero.

Ten full minutes passed before the rain slackened a little and Thomas and Luc descended the hill and began their walk home. It was raining all the way, and Luc complained, but Thomas trudged firmly on, knowing that he must make a man of his brother.

So he was quite annoyed when, the next morning, he woke with a sore throat. By noon, he was shivering.

The illness of Thomas Gascon lasted many weeks. At first they thought it was the flu. Then they feared tuberculosis.

When pneumonia finally set in, and a fever racked his body, and he became delirious, the doctor told his parents that he might survive, because he was young and strong.

By November, he was past the worst; by December he was resting. But in January the doctor warned his parents that his lungs were compromised.

It was his father who found an answer: a charcuterie at the bottom of the hill of Montmartre, and run by a widow he knew, named Madame Michel, who had a daughter. It wasn't a bad place. Unwillingly, Thomas worked there through the early months of 1887.

But he still dreamed of working on Monsieur Eiffel's tower, and one February day, when the weather was mild and he had the afternoon off, he decided to go down to look at the site.

The huge rectangle of the Champ de Mars lay about a mile south of the Arc de Triomphe, just across the river on the Left Bank. Until the eighteenth century, it had been a pleasant quarter of market gardens and allotments. But then a big military school was built along its southern edge, and the gardens running from the school to the Seine became a parade ground, and a site for great gatherings after the Revolution. The place had been made even more splendid a few years later when, to celebrate one of his many victories, the emperor Napoléon had ordered a fine bridge, the Pont d'Iéna, to be built across the Seine directly opposite the place. So the Champ de Mars had been an excellent choice for mounting the World's Fair of

1889. People would be able to walk across the Pont d'Iéna to the Left Bank and then directly under Monsieur Eiffel's astounding tower, whose four splayed iron feet would form the colossal entrance arch.

Everything had been set. Except for one thing.

Thomas remembered the day his father had come in with the news.

'Your friend Monsieur Eiffel has a problem,' he'd announced. 'The city has told him to build his tower, but they're giving him only a quarter of the money.'

'So who's paying for it?'

'Eiffel. He's got to pay for the tower himself.'

It was an extraordinary situation. To celebrate the centenary of the French Revolution, the city of Paris had ordered a tower and refused to pay for it.

But if Eiffel was a great and inventive engineer, he now showed that he was an entrepreneur of huge courage and vision. 'Give me the right to the first twenty years of the tower's earnings,' he said, 'and I'll find the money.'

So as Thomas approached the empty building site, he knew that before him lay not only the pride of France, but the financial triumph or ruin of Monsieur Eiffel himself.

In front of Thomas now was a huge field of mud. The great 136-yard square that would be the footprint of the tower was marked by huge trenches at the four corners – north, south, east and west – where crews of labourers were busily digging.

He started to walk on to the site to take a look. A man in an over-coat and bowler hat rushed over and told him sternly that he must leave. But after Thomas explained that he had worked for Monsieur Eiffel on the Statue of Liberty, and that he'd been sick, the man became friendly and offered to conduct him around.

They looked first at the two big excavations at the southern and eastern corners, where one could already see, at the bottom of the pit, a good, dry base where the concrete foundations could be poured. Then they walked over to one of the riverside diggings. And Thomas gasped.

The huge pit in front of him was like a mineshaft. Down at the bottom was a great, open metal box of the kind used to keep out river water when the piers of a bridge are being built. Inside it, the men were using pickaxes and shovels to tear away the ground.

'They're already below the level of the Seine,' his guide explained. 'The committee chose the site, but when Monsieur Eiffel tested it, he found that the ground on the riverside was so wet it wouldn't take the ordinary foundations.' He grinned. 'Paris would have had its own Leaning Tower of Pisa, but five times higher.'

'Can the tower still be built?'

'Oh, yes. It'll have two dry foundations, and two deep ones like this.' He smiled. 'But it's lucky Eiffel knows how to build in rivers.'

For nearly three more months, Thomas continued to work in the store. Madame Michel was kind to him. He also noticed something else.

Her daughter was a sallow, yellow-haired girl named Berthe, of about his own age. She seldom spoke at all, and moved about behind the counter at a languid pace that, secretly, almost drove Thomas mad.

So he was greatly astonished when, in May, his father announced: 'The widow likes you.'

'I'm glad.'

'So does Berthe.' His father smiled. 'She likes you a lot.'

'Are you sure?' And when his father nodded and grinned, he was forced to say: 'The feeling's not mutual.'

'You could do well there,' his father continued, as though Thomas hadn't spoken. 'She'll inherit the store, you know . . . It's a nice little business. Marry her and you'll be set up for life.'

'I'd rather die,' said Thomas.

'A man's got to eat,' said his father. 'Your mother thinks it's a good idea, too.'

It was the last Sunday in May, and he'd gone for a stroll around Montmartre in the afternoon. The sun was out, and as he entered an intimate little square called the Place du Tertre, he saw that several painters had set up their easels there.

Attracted by the cheap rents and picturesque surroundings, artists had taken to living up on Montmartre since about the time he was born. He'd heard tales of Monsieur Renoir up at the Moulin, and it was quite normal to find a few painters out in the open with their easels on a sunny afternoon. Thomas walked through the square glancing at the canvases as he went, but without much interest. Most of the artists were painting the view from the square along the street to the building site of Sacré Coeur, where the scaffolding made a striking outline against the sky. But as he passed one of them, he noticed something different.

The man was a good-looking fellow in his early thirties, with a light brown beard and a pipe. He had two easels, side by side. One held a sketchbook, the other a primed canvas on which he was just starting to work. Thomas stared at the sketch, and stopped.

'Pardon, monsieur,' he said politely, 'but isn't that the Gare Saint-Lazare?'

'It is.' The artist looked up with a pleasant smile. 'It's a sketch I made last winter. A snow scene, but I felt like working it up today.' He shrugged. 'It's nice to sit out in the sun.'

'I worked there last year,' said Thomas, inspecting the sketch. 'I can see the railway lines, the steam from the trains. That's exactly how it looks.'

'Thank you.'

'But why would you paint a railway?'

'Why not? Monet has painted several pictures of the Gare Saint-Lazare.'

'So are you what they call an Impressionist?'

'You can call me that if you like.' The artist smiled. 'The term began as an insult, you know. But nobody really knows what it means. Half the people they call Impressionists don't in fact use the word.'

'You live here, monsieur?'

'Mostly. I was in Holland, in Rotterdam, this spring. I may go back there.'

'What is your name, monsieur?'

'Norbert Goeneutte.'

'You know Monsieur Renoir?'

'Very well. I have modelled for him, in fact.'

'My name is Thomas Gascon. I live here. I am an ironworker. I built the Statue of Liberty.' They shook hands. Thomas continued to inspect the sketch. 'I still can't believe you painted a railway line.'

'You expect artists to paint gods and goddesses in pretty Italian landscapes?'

'I don't know.'

'Plenty of people expect that. But what I try to do, and Monet, and many others, is paint the world around us. Paint what we really see.'

'But a railway station isn't beautiful . . .'

'Are you familiar with any writers?'

'I was at the funeral of Victor Hugo.'

'So was I. Can't think how I missed you.' The artist paused a moment. 'Hugo was a great man. No question. But for myself, I prefer another writer of that generation – and that's Balzac. He tried to depict the exact reality of the world he saw all around him. From the richest aristocrat to the poorest fellow in the street, and all the men and women in between – lawyers, shopkeepers, whores, beggars. We call it realism. That's what some of the people you call Impressionists are doing, too. Renoir painted the people at the Moulin de la Galette. I paint all kinds of things, including railway trains. As for beauty, what does that mean? A railway is beautiful to me. Because we don't live in a world of nymphs and fawns and classical gods. We live in a world of railways, and steam and iron bridges. It's new and exciting. It's the great adventure. It's the spirit of the age.' He grinned at Thomas. 'You build the bridges, my friend, and I'll paint them.'

Thomas stared at him. No one had ever spoken to him like this before. But he understood well enough. And the painter was right. The railways and their bridges were the spirit of the age. He, a humble ironworker, should be part of it. And the greatest iron construction in the history of the world was about to begin, here in Paris.

'I am going to be building Monsieur Eiffel's tower,' he suddenly declared.

Norbert Goeneutte stared at his canvas thoughtfully for a moment, then he looked up and delivered his verdict.

'I congratulate you. That's a big adventure, my friend.'

That Wednesday was the first of June. Luc was surprised when Thomas insisted he accompany him to Madame Michel's emporium in the morning, but he set off with him all the same. It wasn't until they were halfway down the hill of Montmartre that Thomas told him his plan.

'You're mad,' said Luc. 'What will our mother say? And father too.'

'I'm going to do it anyway,' said Thomas.

While Thomas waited, therefore, Luc went through the Place de Clichy to the widow's store and told her: 'My brother is sick today. He sent me to tell you and apologise.' Madame was most concerned, and only when Luc had assured her that Thomas had nothing more than an upset stomach, and that he would certainly be back at work the next day, did she let him go.

It took them over an hour to walk to the Eiffel company work-shops in the north-western suburb of Levallois-Perret. When they got there, they found a hive of activity. The framework of the huge tower was being assembled in fifteen-foot sections that were placed in huge stacks prior to shipment from the factory to the building site. Over a hundred ironworkers were busily engaged in this assembly and riveting work. But when Thomas politely asked if Monsieur Eiffel was there, he was told that the engineer was to be found at the Champ de Mars that day.

Once again therefore the brothers set off, to the south this time, passed by the Arc de Triomphe and finally, towards eleven in the morning, crossed the Pont d'Iéna and entered the huge building site.

The foundations were all but finished now. They looked like four gigantic gun emplacements, ready to fire across each other to the four horizons. In the middle of this great platform a group of engi-neers and other gentlemen clustered around a single figure, like a general with his staff.

'That's him,' said Thomas. 'That's Monsieur Eiffel.' He took a deep breath. 'Come on.'

Since Monsieur Eiffel was deep in conversation, they stood a little way apart. They had to wait half an hour before the group finally broke up, and Eiffel began to walk off the site with just a couple of companions, towards the river.

'Monsieur Eiffel,' Thomas called out, just loud enough for the engineer to hear, as he moved to intercept him. Eiffel turned and looked at the two young people inquiringly. 'Monsieur Eiffel, I am

Thomas Gascon. I worked for you on the Statue of Liberty,' Thomas said, as he came up with him.

'Ah.' Eiffel paused, clearly trying to remember him. Then he smiled. 'Young Monsieur Gascon from Aquitaine, who went to search for his brother, *n'est-ce pas*?'

'Yes, monsieur.'

Eiffel indicated to his companions that they should move on and that he would join them shortly.

'And I forget – did you find your brother?'

'This is him.' Thomas indicated Luc.

'And what can I do for you, Monsieur Gascon?'

'I should like to work for you on the tower, Monsieur Eiffel. Just like I did on the Statue.'

'But my friend, we have a full complement. It would have given me pleasure to employ you on two such notable projects. Why did you not apply at the start, when we were hiring?'

Thomas hesitated only a second.

'My brother here was sick, monsieur, and my family needed me at home.' He glanced at Luc, who managed to cover his astonishment, and continued: 'He is well now, as you see.' And Luc solemnly nodded.

Eiffel looked at him thoughtfully.

'I know you're a good worker,' said Eiffel. 'And as it happens, we are short one man at present. But this is not in the factory. We are short a "flyer", the fellows who go up the tower.'

'That is what I should like best of all, monsieur,' cried Thomas. 'Perhaps this is fate,' he added hopefully.

'Hmm. Have you ever worked on a high bridge? Do you have a head for heights? It would be very dangerous for you if you hadn't.'

'I have a wonderful head for heights, monsieur, I promise you.'

'Very well. Report here on the last Monday of this month. Ask for Monsieur Compagnon. I shall tell him to expect you. The wages aren't huge, but they're fair.' He nodded, to indicate that the interview was over, and set off towards the river.

'Thank you, monsieur,' Thomas called after him.

As Thomas and his brother crossed over the Pont d'Iéna a short time later, Luc turned to him.

'Why did you lie? Why did you tell him I was sick?'

'It was necessary,' Thomas confessed. 'If he'd thought I was sick, he wouldn't have hired me.'

'But you are sick. At least, a bit. Are you strong enough to do this?'

'I'll be fine by the end of the month.'

'Everyone's going to be furious,' Luc reminded him. 'The doctor, our mother, Madame Michel . . . and especially Berthe.'

'I know. We needn't tell them yet.'

'Well, if you don't marry Berthe, maybe you'd better find that mystery girl of yours.'

Thomas laughed.

'To tell you the truth, I can't even remember what she looks like. Do you know, it's two years, to the day, since I saw her at Victor Hugo's funeral.'

They continued a little farther in silence. Then Luc spoke.

'Are you sure you have a head for heights?'

Chapter Five

1887

Jacques Le Sourd watched the entrance of the school. It was the last full day before the lycée closed for the summer.

Nobody took any notice of him. Why would they? As far as any of the people in the rue de Grenelle were concerned, he was just a young man of twenty or so, probably a student, or an artisan.

And nobody knew what he was thinking. That was the wonderful thing. It made him free, and powerful. Thanks to his anonymity, he could wait, undisturbed, for the boy he was going to destroy.

Not that he was going to kill him today. He probably could, but he didn't want to. Not yet. When the right moment came he would do it. That was quite certain. But he was patient and, in his own mind, his patience also gave him power. Power to choose the time. Power because no one would suspect him.

It was amazing, really, he considered, how simple it all was. Discovering where Roland de Cygne lived and where he went to school was easy, of course. And given the school's regular hours, he could come by and watch the boy arrive or leave the school any day he wished. He'd got to know the other places young Roland went to. He observed him like this every month or so.

This small matter had made him realise how most people lived their lives by following very predictable patterns. One knew where they were. With a little further study, one could probably guess what they were thinking. Disrupt their routine and they would panic. Offer them a new routine, and they would take it because it made them feel safe. A skilful planner, he suspected, could make people do almost anything he liked. And that is what he meant to do one day, when he changed the world.

Young de Cygne had to be destroyed, then killed. The punishment was due. The death of Jean Le Sourd had to be avenged. How else could he show his love for the father he'd lost?

But Jacques wasn't just checking on the boy's whereabouts. His purpose was deeper than that. He wanted to get to know him. The things he did, the company he kept. If possible, he would have liked to know young de Cygne's mind, even see into his soul. He wanted to understand exactly the unworthy place that Roland de Cygne occupied in the universe, so that his death should be justified as part of a larger pattern of righteousness.

And how laughably predictable the boy's life had been so far. Where did his family live? In the aristocratic Saint-Germain quarter, of course. Where else? Where did he go to school? In the private, Catholic Lycée Saint-Thomas-d'Aquin, in that same aristocratic quarter. Naturally. Everything was mapped out for him. He would be a perfect little representative of his detestable class.

And here he came, out of the door of the lycée, with a dozen others of his kind. Jacques Le Sourd watched. Young Roland would be walking eastward along the street, towards his home.

But no. He was walking the other way. Very well. Jacques Le Sourd continued to observe. Some of Roland's friends peeled off at the boulevard Raspail, but de Cygne crossed it. A few minutes later, he was alone and still walking westward.

Curious, Jacques followed.

Roland de Cygne missed his mother. He'd been seven when she died. Some boys were sent away to boarding school; but on the advice of Father Xavier, his father had sent him to the Catholic lycée near the family house, and he'd been happy there. For Roland delighted in his home.

The house itself was undeniably grand. Its spirit was that of Louis XIV, the Sun King – large, baroque, powerful. One entered through handsome iron gates into a courtyard with wings, known as *pavillons*, on each side. The hall and broad staircase were of pale, polished stone. In the high, handsome rooms, on parquet floors and Aubusson carpets, Louis XIV formal chairs, lacquered cabinets and heavy boulle desks, their brass inlay softly gleaming, lay like stately ships at anchor. Marble tabletops dimly reflected the sunlight, which entered respectfully into the aristocratic quiet of the house. Ancestral portraits – sad, baroque generals, bland rococo courtiers – reminded today's de Cygnes that not only the deity, but their ancestors, also saw all that they did and expected – whether or not they could be good – that they should at least uphold the family honour.

The grandest family mansions of the aristocracy were known as *hôtels*. And had his title been just a little higher up the ladder of nobility, the vicomte might almost have called his house the Hôtel de Cygne.

And yet, despite the severe, masculine grandeur of the house, Roland was very happy there. From his earliest childhood, the big, silent rooms had the familiar peace of holy places. The stately armchairs with their ornate wooden arms and tapestry seats were like so many ancient aunts and uncles. And the sometimes daunting portraits were his grandparents, his friends, for whom he felt a deep and primitive urge to protect and defend.

Above all, although it was only sparsely populated, his home was full of affection.

His father, who hadn't remarried so far, was always kind. His old nanny had also remained with them, providing an endless fund of warmth, and effectively running the house for his father. There were only a small staff of six required to keep the place going, but most of them had been with the vicomte all their lives, and Roland thought of them as practically his family, too. And there was Father Xavier, like a favourite uncle, who never failed to look in every week or so.

But he often thought of his mother, and kept a little photograph of her on the table by his bed, and kissed it every night after he had said his prayers.

Only one thing worried Roland. He was fifteen now. It was time to be thinking of a career. And he still didn't know what he wanted to do.

'I shan't force you into anything,' his father told him, 'but your position is rather like that of your ancestor Roland, back in the days of Saint Louis. He began life as a younger son, and went to Paris as a student. By all accounts, he was very devout, and lived a life of great purity. Almost a monk. But then his brother died and he had to return home to run the estate, because it was his duty. Since you're the only son, and there's no one else to carry on the line, that's rather your position, too. As you'll be running the estate, it wouldn't be a bad thing for you to study law.'

Yet the law didn't seem a very exciting profession. As the descendant of crusading knights, and even the hero Roland, the boy couldn't help feeling that fate must have some nobler destiny in store for him.

'What about the army?' he'd several times asked his father. But for some reason his father had seemed reluctant to encourage that ambition.

'I was in the army, of course,' he'd say, 'until I resigned my commission. But I don't want it for you.' He never explained why.

Nor was Father Xavier explicit.

'Do you wish to serve God?' he gently inquired.

'Yes, Father.' He truly did. Indeed, if ambition was not a sin of pride, he hoped he might do some great thing for the world, in the Lord's service.

'Then you have nothing to worry about,' the priest assured him. 'If you commit yourself to God, then He will show you the way.' He smiled. 'I know that you desire to do good in the world, Roland, and it does you credit. How pleased your mother would be.'

'Sometimes I dream of her,' the boy confessed. 'Perhaps she will show me the way.'

'Perhaps. But be careful,' Father Xavier counselled. 'It is not for you to choose how God conveys His wishes. He will decide the means, and it may be something quite unexpected.'

Once his school friends had parted from him in the street, Roland unconsciously picked up his pace. He wasn't going on this mission because he wanted to, and he hoped to get it over with as quickly as possible.

After all, he was going to see a horror.

Roland was a conscientious pupil. It didn't come naturally, because he often didn't want to work. It was only because of his mother, really, that he forced himself to do it. 'Promise me, Roland, that you will try your best at school.' It was almost the last thing she'd ever said to him. And to his credit, he had always kept his promise. Other boys in the class might be cleverer, but by working hard, he usually managed to get grades that were only a little behind the leaders.

So when, during a history class that morning, the teacher had asked how many boys had been to visit the horror, and he was the only one not to raise his hand, and the teacher had told him to go to see it, he'd decided to go at once. After all, it wasn't far.

A mile away at the end of the rue de Grenelle lay the great space of the Champ de Mars, with its western sweep down to the river. But Roland had gone only half that way when his object came in sight.

The great military hospital of Les Invalides occupied a huge open space, once known as the Plaine of Grenelle. In the seventeenth century, Louis XIV had built it in a severe, classical style suitable for a military foundation – though in the middle, for magnificence, he'd added a royal chapel with a gilded dome like St Peter's, Rome. From the cold, stern facade of Les Invalides, one could gaze over a long parade of iron-clad lawns, and thence across the Seine to the trees of the Champs-Élysées in the distance. It also housed an artillery museum nowadays, but this was not Roland's object. Entering the first courtyard, he made straight for the central chapel.

And as he gazed upon the horror that lay within, he understood what the teacher had meant when he'd said: 'The chapel of the king has been defiled.'

A square church. Four chapels at the corners made a cross between them. Over the centre of the cross, a circular dome. A classic pattern for Christian worship, from Orthodox Russia to Catholic Spain.

But there was nothing Christian about the chapel now. Instead of finding a nave beneath the dome, one looked down from a circular gallery into a marble pit. Twelve pillars of victory encircled this pagan crypt, and in its centre, upon a massive, green granite pedestal, rested a stupendous sarcophagus of polished red porphyry, bulging with imperial pride.

The tomb of Napoléon, child of the Revolution, conqueror of God's anointed monarchs, emperor of France. This was the horror that Roland had been sent to see.

'That vulgar tomb,' the teacher had declared, 'that infamous, pagan monument. The sepulchre of Napoléon is an insult to Catholic France.'

'And yet, Father,' one of the class had questioned, 'isn't it true that the emperor Napoléon supported the Church?'

'As an opportunist, yes. But only to get the support of the faithful who did not realise that, in truth, he believed in nothing and mocked them behind their backs. When Napoléon was in Egypt, he supported the followers of Muhammad. "If I had a kingdom of Jews," he said, "I would rebuild the temple of Solomon." If' – the teacher warmed to his theme – 'you want proof of the wretched man's impiety, remember that, when he was to be crowned emperor by the pope – like the pious emperor Charlemagne a thousand years ago – and before a crowd of thousands in Notre-Dame, he seized the crown from the hands of the Holy Father and placed it on his head himself.'

Roland had been gazing at the tomb for a minute or two when he noticed an old man arrive. Like Roland, he advanced to the parapet and stared down at the huge red urn, but there the resemblance between them ended. For the old man was behaving in such a strange manner that Roland soon found the visitor more interesting than the monument.

He was old, but how old it was hard to tell. His hair was snowy white, and he had a silky walrus moustache. His skin had a translucence that suggested great age. But he was a good six feet tall and he held himself ramrod straight, as though he were on parade. Indeed, Roland realised, the old man was actually standing to attention, arms by his sides, as though the emperor himself were inspecting him. And he was so concentrated on this business that he seemed quite oblivious to anything else.

It would have been rude to stare, but while he pretended to admire the painted dome above, Roland continued to observe the old man for a good five minutes until, finally, he saw him salute the tomb, and then gravely turn to walk away. As he did so, however, he noticed Roland.

'Well, boy,' he said sharply, like a sergeant addressing a new recruit, 'what are you staring at?'

'*Pardon*, monsieur.' Roland found himself looking into a pair of blue eyes, proud but not unkindly. 'I did not mean to be impolite. I noticed you salute.'

'Certainly, I salute the emperor. So should all those who remember the Glory of France.'

La Gloire. Many nations had known glory in their history, but perhaps none had felt it so keenly as the nation of France: for monarchists, the glory of the Sun King; for republicans, the glory of the Revolution; for soldiers and administrators, the glorious victories of the emperor Napoléon.

'You are a soldier, sir?' Roland dared to inquire.

'I was. And my father before me. He served in the Old Guard.'

'Your father knew the emperor?'

'He did. And so did I. My father survived the Retreat from Moscow. And when the emperor returned for his great final battle and called upon all France to rise to his aid, my father went, and I went with him, though I was hardly older than you. My mother didn't wish it. She was afraid to lose me. But my father said, 'Better my son should die than fail to fight for the honour of France.' So I marched with my father. It was the proudest day of my life.'

'And you did not die.'

'No. It was my father who gave his life. At Waterloo, the emperor's final battle. I was at his side.' The old man paused. 'Ever since, on my father's birthday, I have saluted him, and the emperor, and the honour of France. That's seventy-two years. And for the last twenty-six years, since this tomb has been here, I have come to Les Invalides to pay my respects.'

Napoléon might have died in exile on the island of Saint Helena, but his legend had lived on. To his enemies, he remained an upstart and a tyrant. But to many of Europe's peoples, oppressed under their rigid old monarchies, he remained the republican liberator, the hero of the common man. And to many in France, as well.

Even King Louis Philippe, to make himself more popular, had felt obliged to bring the emperor's body home to Paris; and now, with a magnificence unmatched by any French king, his ashes rested in this mighty mausoleum in the heart of France.

Whatever he thought of the sacrilegious emperor, Roland had to admire the dignity and the nobility of this old soldier, who must be nearly ninety, yet who stood so tall and straight.

The blue eyes under the bushy eyebrows surveyed Roland carefully.

'And who might you be, young monsieur?' he asked.

'My name is Roland de Cygne, monsieur,' Roland answered.

'A noble. Well, there were nobles who served the emperor, too. Promotion was on merit, whoever you were.' He nodded. 'Our country was respected then. Not like now. To think that I should have lived to see the humiliation of Paris and Alsace–Lorraine given to the Germans.'

'Our history master says that we must avenge the dishonour of 1870,' Roland told him. Hardly a week went by without the class getting a lecture on the subject. It was a lesson given in schools all over France. 'He says we must recover Alsace–Lorraine.'

The old man looked at him, perhaps privately measuring whether this new generation was up to the task.

'The honour of France is in your hands now,' he said finally, and glanced towards the doorway to indicate that the interview was over now.

Hardly knowing that he was doing so, Roland stood to attention as the old man walked stiffly away. And he waited a little time after he was gone before heading out himself.

As he did so, he noticed a young man, with dark, close-cropped hair and eyes set wide apart, dispassionately watching him. As he drew level, he couldn't resist sharing what was in his mind.

'Did you see that old soldier?' he asked.

The young man inclined his head.

'He knew the emperor Napoléon,' Roland said.

'No doubt.'

'*C'est quelque chose*,' Roland remarked. 'That's something.'

The stranger didn't reply.

The next day school broke up at noon. When Roland returned home, his father was absent, but had left a message that he'd be returning after lunch and that they were going out.

When his father duly arrived to collect him, however, and Roland asked where they were going, he was only told, 'To see a friend of mine', which made him rather curious.

Was this friend a man, he asked himself, or might this be a lady?

He'd often wondered about his father's romantic life. Though the Vicomte de Cygne was devoted to the memory of his late wife, whom he'd adored, he was no hermit. A good height, elegant, quite rich and certainly aristocratic, his father kept his military bearing and moustache, but he always moved gracefully and knew how to make charming conversation. He must surely, Roland guessed, be attractive to women.

Like most aristocrats, the vicomte would have considered it beneath him to be an intellectual, but it wasn't unfashionable to keep up with the goings-on of the literary and artistic worlds, and he would often go to exhibitions and occasionally put in an appearance at one of the salons where writers and artists could be encountered. A few months ago Roland had found a copy of *Les Fleurs du mal* on his father's library table. He'd heard at school that these poems of Baudelaire were pagan, and indecent. But when he nervously asked his father about them, the vicomte seemed quite unconcerned.

'Baudelaire is a bit of a dandy. But some of his poems are exquisite. Have you heard of the composer Duparc? No? Well, his setting of Baudelaire's 'L'Invitation au voyage' is one of the loveliest things one ever heard. He has perfectly captured the sensuousness of France.'

Such conversations hinted to Roland that there were aspects of his father's life that might be hidden from him. His father's occasional absences, the fact that his nanny would say approvingly, 'The vicomte is a proper man,' his father's jaunty manner, sometimes, when he went out, had made Roland wonder if he kept a mistress somewhere. He understood that his father would never bring his mistress, even if she were a fashionable and aristocratic lady, into the home where his son was living and which was still sacred to the memory of his late wife.

But was it possible, Roland wondered, that his father had decided he was now old enough to encounter such a person? Was this the friend they were going to see? It was a prospect that filled him with curiosity and some excitement.

Or was there another, more serious possibility? Was his father taking him to meet someone he meant to marry? A stepmother? What might that mean for his future?

When they left the house, the vicomte had still given him no clue. And knowing that his father liked to tease him a little, he knew that it was quite useless to ask him for any further information.

The Vicomte de Cygne's favourite coach was a fast, light, covered phaeton. It was drawn by two grey carriage horses – the family had always used greys since the eighteenth century, he assured his son. It was driven by the family's old coachman who, though always immaculately turned out, liked to wear an old-fashioned tricorn hat. It was an equipage combining sportiness, fashion and tradition; and Roland always felt proud to accompany his father on these excursions.

Soon the phaeton's large wheels were bowling along the boulevard Saint-Germain up towards the river. Coming out on the Quai d'Orsay, Roland had only a moment to admire the classical portico of the National Assembly and the handsome Foreign Ministry beyond, before the phaeton was briskly crossing the broad bridge that led across the river to the great open space of the Place de la Concorde.

Roland had been ten years old before his father had told him why his family had no love for that huge square.

'They call it the Place de la Concorde now,' he'd explained, 'but during the Revolution, it was one of the main sites of the guillotine. That's where my own grandfather lost his head.'

Hardly knowing they did so, both father and son now averted their eyes towards the Tuileries Gardens, on their right, rather than survey the tragic place.

Straight ahead, just a short distance back from the square's northern side, lay the Roman columns and wide pediment of La Madeleine. For some reason, the handsome church always seemed cheerful to Roland.

'Did you know,' his father remarked, 'that centuries ago there was a Jewish synagogue on that site?' He smiled. 'Then the Church took it over. It was Napoléon who built the structure you see now, as a sort of pagan temple for his army. And now it's a church again.' He glanced at Roland. 'So you see, nothing is permanent, my son.'

Roland loved and admired his father. For all the rites of passage and initiation for which every father should prepare his son, he knew he could rely on him completely. His father had taught him to ride, and how to hunt. How to behave, how to dress properly. How to kiss a lady's hand. He'd taken him to the races, and taught him how to place his bets. All the things a young man of his class should know to begin his life. And this trust in his father brought him a sense of warmth and comfort. But sometimes, when it came to larger matters, in ways that he could not clearly formulate, he sensed that his father was failing him. It was as if, at times, his father did not believe in things the way he should.

And Roland wanted certainty. Perhaps it was the loss of his mother, or his age, or more likely some innate part of his character, but he needed to believe. Things should be right, or wrong, good, or bad. For if not, how was one to know how to act? What certainty could there be in the world?

And though of course he could not love Father Xavier in the same way that he loved his father, he sometimes preferred the priest's advice. Father Xavier was clever, certainly. Yet even if he could not follow the many turnings of the priest's subtle mind, he always sensed that behind everything Father Xavier said and thought, there lay an absolute certainty. The rules by which the priest lived were fixed and eternal. He might consider carefully how best to make a journey, but at the end of the day, he knew exactly where he was going, and why he was going there. In short, the priest knew the truth. This was the strength of Holy Church.

Roland longed so much for his father to be like that.

The phaeton turned right into the rue de Rivoli. Roland loved that long street's grandeur. On one side lay the Tuileries Gardens and the Louvre Palace. On the other, a seemingly endless line of sonorous, arcaded buildings, begun by Napoléon, with fashionable stores behind the arcades on the street level, and apartments fit for princes on the floors above.

'Did you know that the original Louvre was just a small medieval fort guarding the river, in the corner of the present palace?' his father inquired casually.

'Yes,' Roland replied. 'It was just outside the old city wall of King Philippe Auguste.'

'Good.' His father smiled. 'Glad they teach you something at school.'

They had gone far along the rue de Rivoli when his father called to the coachman to stop, and Roland saw that they were outside the Hôtel Meurice. He knew that this was where the English travellers liked to stay, and immediately wondered with alarm: Was his father going to marry an Englishwoman?

But it was only to leave a letter for a sporting English friend of his father's who was about to arrive in Paris. And Roland was still no wiser about where they were going.

So he told his father about the old soldier he had met at Napoléon's tomb. On the one hand, he had admired the man's simple dignity. Yet he had dedicated his life to serving an evil master. What did his father think?

The vicomte considered.

'A soldier's duty is simple,' he replied. 'It is to obey orders and to serve his country. And that is what the old man did. As for Napoléon, I dare say his soldiers thought they fought for liberty and for France.'

Roland was not very satisfied with this answer.

'But people like us cannot be friends with the followers of the emperor, can we? The priests at the lycée say that Napoléon was a monster, and he didn't really support the Church at all.'

His father sighed.

'We may have different views, but we don't have to be enemies, you know. In any case, it's not always so simple.' He paused. 'Do you follow politics at all, my son?'

'A little.'

'What would you say of the present government of the Republic?'

'It's not very strong. It's not popular.'

'Correct. After the disaster of the Commune, most of the elected deputies, certainly most of rural France, wanted the monarchy restored. They wanted stability, really. And peace. They thought a constitutional monarch, something like the British monarchy, would provide it. And there would have been a restoration, I've little doubt, if the then head of the royal family hadn't insisted that any monarch must have sweeping powers.' The vicomte shook his head. 'Obstinate to the last. So a temporary constitution was made, with a president and legislature. And as time has passed without war or catastrophe, the monarchist cause has grown less popular.

'But I can't say the government has been impressive. And the present crowd are both mediocre and corrupt. There are many people who would still like a monarchy or a dictatorship. Whether that would be any better is open to doubt, perhaps, but that is what they want. And at present those parties have a hero. Who is it?'

'General Boulanger, I suppose.'

'Indeed. He was minister of war until recently. He was able to embarrass the Germans a couple of times. He was fired the other day, but he has a big political following. If there's ever a crisis in the Republic, which is possible, he might be the man to rule France. What do they say in the lycée?'

'That he is a bad man. He does not believe in God.'

'Well, he may, or he may not. But because he said he didn't believe in God, the Republican politicians of France thought he couldn't be a monarchist, and so they trusted him, and made him a minister. Now they have discovered not only that he has a big public following, but he has the backing of both the monarchists, including important members of the royal family, and of the Bonapartists, including members of the emperor's family. So the Catholic monarchists and the followers of Napoléon are all on the same side supporting a man who may or may not believe in God. What do you make of that?'

'I don't know.'

His father smiled.

'Well, nor do I, my boy. I wonder what Father Xavier thinks. We must ask him.' And this thought seemed to amuse the vicomte even more, for he burst out laughing.

Roland wished his father wouldn't mix things up in this way. He tried to get back to something with a simpler answer.

'The old man said we should avenge the dishonour of 1870,' he said. 'Do you agree with that?'

'The War of 1870 was an act of stupidity,' his father answered. 'It was we who started it. Napoléon III was a fool, and the Germans took advantage of it.'

'But shouldn't we avenge our dishonour?'

'Who knows? Probably not.'

Roland gave up. He would never get a simple answer out of his father. At least, not in his present mood. They had passed the Louvre now, and were approaching the old Châtelet. Yet there was something he still wanted to know. Something he'd often wondered, but never asked before.

'Papa,' he said, 'can I ask you a question?'

'Certainly.'

'Why did you leave the army?'

And this time, he could see, his father was not so comfortable answering.

'I'd served for years. And someone had to look after the estate. It needed my care.' He was silent again for a little while. 'The War of 1870 was terrible, you know.'

'You mean, losing to the Germans?'

'Not that so much.' His father fell silent for a minute. 'It was the fighting afterwards, against the Commune . . . A civil war is a terrible thing, my son. May you never live to see one.'

'Father Xavier told me that the Communards did unspeakable things. He says that in the final week, they killed the archbishop of Paris and massacred innocent monks and priests in cold blood. He said they were martyred, just like the priests in the Revolution.'

'It's true.' His father nodded. 'And we killed a lot of Communards, too, you know. Thousands.'

'But they were in the wrong.'

'Probably.' He shook his head. 'I dare say they thought they were fighting for Liberty, Equality and Fraternity.'

'And disorder.'

'That, too, no doubt.'

'Did you kill many Communards?' Roland asked.

There was a silence.

'Let us speak of other things,' the vicomte said.

The rue de Rivoli was long. After a mile and a quarter, it briefly changed its name before ending in the square where the old Bastille had stood. They passed the site of the old Grève market on their right, and Roland was just looking at some workmen refurbishing the huge Hôtel de Ville beside it when the phaeton made a crisp turn to the left and started up the rue du Temple.

'You know how this street got its name?' his father inquired.

'The Knights Templar lived up here.'

'There's hardly a trace of their buildings now, but did you know that for centuries after the Templars were destroyed, the tax exemptions on their land remained? Made it a popular place to live!'

The street seemed to grow narrower as they went northwards, until they reached a dark square. Just off the square was a small street.

'Here we are,' said his father.

The shop had a single window in which, before a dark brown velvet curtain, Roland saw a Louis XIV armchair that needed repair. It seemed a dingy sort of place. His father saw his face and smiled.

'My friend is very discreet,' he remarked. 'That chair, by the way, is a museum piece, and the sort of person who buys it will want to see it unrestored.'

Realising that this visit must be part of his education, Roland stared at the chair and said nothing.

The door of the store was locked. His father rang the bell. And a few moments later, a small, middle-aged man, slightly stooped, dressed, despite the warm weather, in a tightly buttoned black frock coat, and wearing thick glasses, peered through the glass and then let them in.

'Monsieur de Cygne.' The man made a quick bow. 'It is a pleasure to see you.'

'I received your summons, my dear Jacob, and came at once,' the vicomte answered easily. 'This is my son, by the way. Roland, this is Monsieur Jacob.' And to his slight discomfort, Roland found himself shaking a small, proffered hand, aware of only one thing: that his father, an aristocrat and a good Catholic, had apparently answered the summons of a man who was, obviously, a Jew.

The door closed behind them. While his father went through some brief inquiries about the owner's family and general health, Roland allowed his eyes to roam around the long and narrow space. There was the usual clutter of eighteenth-century tables, classical heads and china that one might expect to find in any antique store. Behind this was an open space, and farther back, a door that probably led to a storeroom. There was not a lot of light. He felt confined. But above all, he felt uncomfortable.

He remembered asking Father Xavier, once, what he thought about the Jews.

'They gave us our God, the Old Testament and the prophets,' the priest answered carefully.

'But they killed Christ,' Roland objected.

'This cannot be denied,' Father Xavier agreed.

'So they all go to hell,' Roland continued, because he wanted to get it right.

But here Father Xavier had hesitated for a moment, as if considering what was just and proper.

'We may suppose,' he said finally, 'that in normal circumstances, it is unlikely that a Jew, or indeed a Protestant, will enter Heaven. But we cannot know the mind of God. And in His infinite wisdom, He may make exceptions.'

Roland might have preferred something more definite, but it seemed enough to be going on with. Non-Catholics were in a lot of trouble. And when it came to all the things he heard people say about the Jews, at school and in the homes of his friends, he felt he could assume that most of the evil tales must be based upon something.

He looked at Monsieur Jacob with suspicion, therefore, and wondered why his father was treating him in such a friendly manner.

'So what would you like me to see?' his father was asking.

'A moment, monsieur.' Jacob disappeared through the door at the back, returning shortly with what looked like a rug, which he proceeded to unroll. 'A moment more,' he said, as he lit several lamps around it. '*Voilà*, Monsieur de Cygne, and young Monsieur Roland. Here it is.'

They stepped forward. And his father gasped.

'Where the devil did you find it?' he cried.

'On a friend's recommendation, I bid blind on the entire contents of a house in Rouen,' the dealer explained. 'A month later, to my surprise they told me I'd won the auction. When I went to clear the place out, I found this wrapped up in the basement.' He smiled. 'Then I thought, this might belong in Monsieur de Cygne's château down in the Loire valley. It's the right period. But if it should not be of any interest to you, then I will show it to other customers.'

'My dear Jacob . . .' The vicomte turned to his son. 'Do you know what this is, Roland?'

The tapestry at which Roland was gazing was remarkable in many ways. In the first place, it had no border, and every inch of its luminous blue-green background seemed to be covered in magical flowers and plants, from which birds, animals and humans were emerging. The whole tone of the picture, as well as the dress of the knights and ladies, suggested that it was medieval.

'Because they are so sprinkled with plants, these tapestries are known as *mille fleurs*, a thousand flowers,' his father said.

'It looks magical,' Roland said.

'The glow,' Monsieur Jacob explained – he had a soft voice so that Roland had to strain to listen, which irritated him – 'comes from the fact that the background colour is dark blue, to which the green is added.' He turned to the vicomte. 'As you see, there is a little wear and tear on one corner. This can be repaired if you wish. There is also a little discolouration from damp near the bottom. It may be treatable, or it may not. Overall, however, it is in remarkable condition.'

'It really looks like a painting,' said Roland. It wasn't much of a comment, but he wanted to say something.

'Excellent,' said Monsieur Jacob softly. 'You are more correct than you know. Before a tapestry was made, it was normal for the artist to paint the design separately. This is known as a cartoon. But in the case of these particular tapestries, the artist painted directly on to the canvas backing, through which the needleworkers would pass their wool and silken thread. The colours were matched precisely.' He turned again to Roland's father. 'But it is the figures themselves that we should examine.'

Roland stared. Amid the bright flowers and plants were several trees. Apparently this was meant to be a wood, or perhaps an orchard. There were birds in the trees. Four people, two men and two women, dressed in rich clothes, were walking in a stately way through the scene. They were accompanied by several hunting dogs. Farther off, other animals lurked in the undergrowth. Then he heard his father exclaim.

'My God. A unicorn.'

In the upper right-hand quarter of the scene, leaping away through the trees, where one might have expected to see a deer making its escape, was a pale unicorn. So perfect was the composition that, having spotted it, the eye was led right around the scene before returning to the lovely, haunting presence of the magical creature.

'There are two famous tapestry sets that feature the unicorn,' Jacob said. 'There is the spectacular Lady and the Unicorn series, on its dazzling red background, which was placed on show just five years ago in the Cluny Museum. Do you know this museum, young Monsieur Roland? It's on the site of the old Roman baths on the Left Bank, only a short walk from your father's house. And there is also another set, called the Hunt of the Unicorn, on a green background, that is owned by the Duc de La Rochefoucauld. Both those sets, we are almost certain, were of Flemish origin – made in what, today, we call Belgium. But this tapestry is French. It dates to a little later than those sumptuous masterpieces – to the early fifteen hundreds – and belongs to what we call the Loire School. Perhaps this unicorn was inspired by those famous tapestries, or perhaps it came there by chance. But I like that it is rare, and the work is of very high quality.'

At last, thought Roland, he's finished. When Jacob had called him young Monsieur Roland, and asked if he knew the Cluny Museum, which in truth he'd never entered, although it was close to his home, he'd felt as if the antique dealer's soft voice, in some insinuating way, was rebuking him for his ignorance, and putting him down. He hated Jacob for it.

But his father was gazing at the tapestry with admiration.

'My dear Jacob,' he said at last, 'tell me what you want for it.'

The dealer wrote something on a piece of paper and handed it to him. De Cygne glanced at it and nodded.

'The restoration?' he asked.

'If you will leave it to me . . .' Jacob suggested.

'Of course.'

Roland had seldom seen his father so pleased as when he got into the carriage afterwards.

'It's perfect for the château,' he remarked. 'Exactly the right date, the right spirit. Each generation, my son, should add something of beauty to a house like ours. That will be my contribution.'

They started back down the rue du Temple. His father stared ahead thoughtfully.

'Jacob didn't have to do that, you know,' he suddenly remarked. 'He could have sold it to a dozen rich collectors for more than I paid him.'

'Why did he offer it to you, then?' Roland asked.

'I did him a good turn some years ago, when I recommended him to the Comte de Nogent, who's become one of his most valuable customers. Jacob must have been waiting for an opportunity to return the favour.' He nodded. 'Certainly, his choice couldn't have been better.'

'You think he really bought it the way he said?'

'Why not?'

Roland didn't answer. But he knew exactly what he thought about the soft-voiced dealer who had tried to put him down.

Jacob had probably stolen it.

It wasn't so strange for him to imagine such a thing. Whether seriously or in jest, it was the sort of thing that most of the boys he knew at school would have said. So would their parents. The presumption was general: the Jews were all in league together, and they were all conspiring to cheat the Christians. The first proposition would have come as a surprise to the Jewish community; the second dismissed as absurd.

But it was not a question of logic. It was a question of tribe. The Jews were not of the French tribe, for they had their own. Nor their religion. And therefore, tribal instinct declared, they could not be trusted – not even to obey the Ten Commandments that they themselves had given the world. Roland supposed this was something that everybody knew. And he would have been most surprised if anyone had told him he was prejudiced, it being the nature of a prejudice that those who possess it have no idea that it is prejudice at all.

So, as they drove away in the elegant phaeton, Roland experienced a secret sense of disappointment that his father should, through moral carelessness, have allowed himself to be cheated by Jacob, and indeed, that he should have had any dealings with Jacob at all. It was just one more indication, he thought, that his father, though kind, was shallow and lacked any fixed centre.

In such circumstances, how was he to find any certainty? Whatever his father's shortcomings, he himself was still the descendant of crusaders, and of the heroic friend of Charlemagne himself. What life could he follow that would be worthy of those ancestors, and of his mother, too?

There was the Church, of course. But he also had a duty to provide heirs for the family. It looked as if providence had chosen that he should follow the path of his pious namesake in the reign of Saint Louis, and attend to the estate and his family. But in some way that might make up, perhaps, for the moral laxity of his father.

He was still brooding about this when, as they reached the foot of the rue du Temple, the coachman took another way home and crossed directly over the bridge to the Île de la Cité. And they were just passing in front of the parvis of Notre-Dame when he turned to his father and declared: 'I have decided upon my career, Papa.'

'Ah. The law, perhaps?'

'No, Papa. I wish to join the army.'

Chapter Six

1307, October

Jacob ben Jacob had been out all night and half the next day. He'd searched the main road that led towards the south, asked every farmer and passer-by. Nothing. He'd searched other roads, farther to the east.

Not a sign. Either his daughter had taken some other way, or they were still hiding in the city. Or, just perhaps, it had all been a mistake, and she had come safely home after all. It could be so. He prayed to God that it was so.

But if not, then he faced a huge problem. How to explain her absence? Could he pretend that she had died? He went over the possibility in his mind. He couldn't say that she had fallen sick. Quite apart from the fact that no physician had seen her, the two servants in the house would know it wasn't true. Might she have had an accident outside the city? Could some story be concocted that would satisfy the authorities? Could the little family mourn behind an empty coffin, watch as it was lowered, and bury the memory of his daughter safely in the ground?

But what if she came back again?

Yet somehow the business had to be covered up. No one must know what Naomi had done.

Jacob ben Jacob was a small man with thinning hair and pale, kindly blue eyes, and he loved his daughter Naomi with all his heart. But he also thought of his dear wife Sarah. She had gone grey when Naomi was still a little girl, but for all her loyal and silent suffering, the skin on her face was still as smooth and her eyes as bright as they had been twenty years ago. How much more would she suffer, if the business were discovered? Even her little brother would be implicated – at the very least the object of suspicion for years. As for himself – he tried not to think of what the consequences would be.

And all this Naomi knew very well. He could not help it therefore if, despite his love, he cursed his daughter now.

The sun was already sinking when he crossed the Seine and made his way northwards up the rue Saint-Martin. When he got to his house, he went in quickly. Sarah was standing in the hall.

'Well?' he cried. 'Where is she?'

'I do not know, Jacob.' His wife shook her head sadly. Then she handed him a piece of parchment.

'What's this?'

'A letter. It's from her.'

Jacob slept badly that night. He rose at dawn and decided to go for a walk. Putting the letter in a pouch on his belt, and wrapping his cloak around him, he stepped out into the street. His house in the rue Saint-Martin was not far from one of the northern gates. From the gate, he took the lane that he and Naomi had taken so many times before that led towards the little orchard he owned on the high ground.

It was Friday, the thirteenth of October. A misty morning. As the lane wound its way to the upper slopes, he was greeted by the sight of the sun rising over the eastern horizon into a blue sky, while below, the great walled city and its suburbs were hidden by the mist, except for the towers of Notre-Dame and half a dozen medieval pinnacles, which emerged and seemed to hang, as if by magic, over the silvery carpet. And as Jacob gazed at this lovely sight, he wondered: How could any soul, Jewish or Christian, fail to be uplifted by these exquisite citadels floating in the heavens?

Jacob ben Jacob loved Paris. It was his home, as it had been for his father and grandfather before him. Even as a boy, he'd loved the wide sweep of the Seine, the vineyards on the hills, the aromas in the narrow streets; even the beauties of Notre-Dame and the Sainte-Chapelle, although they belonged to a religion not his own. And he still did. He never wanted to leave it. Yet now, the sight of Paris brought him nothing but despair.

He took out Naomi's letter and read it once more.

There was no doubt about one thing. The letter was clever. Very clever. The huge lie it contained was obvious to him; but she intended anyone else who read it to believe what she wrote. And her trick might work. It might.

But that did not alter the one, awful fact. He had lost his daughter. Perhaps he'd never see her again.

Was it his own fault? Certainly. The Lord was punishing him. He had committed a terrible crime. Now he must pay the price.

Jacob shook his head sadly, and wondered: Had he been making bad judgements all his life? When had he started to go wrong?

Alas, he knew the answer to both these questions all too well.

His childhood had been happy. His father was a scholarly man who made his living as a physician. His standards were high. 'The best Jewish scholars are in Spain and the south,' he liked to say, 'but Paris is not so bad.' He also had a mild disdain for the intellect of the rabbi, of which the rabbi was aware. But to a little child, he was gentleness itself. Each night he would come in to little Jacob as he was going to bed, and say the night-time Shema with him:

Shema Yisrael Adonai eloheinu Adonai ehad.
Hear O Israel: the Lord our God, the Lord is One.

And each morning he would repeat the prayer with his son again. His father also had many friends. And as he treated prominent Christian families as well as Jewish, and was well liked, young Jacob had grown up in an easy-going environment. His best friend, Henri, a handsome boy with dark red hair and alert brown eyes, was from a rich Christian family of merchants called Renard.

As far as Jacob could remember, his destiny had been decided from his birth. He was going to be a physician like his father. His father was quietly proud of the fact. His family and friends all understood it. As a little boy, the thought had been delightful to him. Everyone respected his father. All he had to do was follow in his footsteps, and he'd have a wonderful life.

He was twelve years old when he began to have doubts. He hardly knew why himself. Perhaps it was a talent he had for mathematics that did not find much outlet in the physician's art. Perhaps there were other causes.

And then there were the patients. Sometimes his father would take Jacob on his visits, and let him watch him examining people;

and afterwards he'd explain to him the treatment he was recommending, and why. Jacob became quite good at spotting ailments and suggesting remedies. His father was pleased with his progress, and Jacob was proud.

Yet as time went on, he began to find that he didn't enjoy it. First he was surprised, then concerned. The fact was, he didn't want to spend his life with sick people. He admired his father very much, and he'd always hoped to be like him. But perhaps he wasn't.

What should he do? He had no idea. And since he couldn't explain his feelings in a satisfactory way, he'd felt too embarrassed and guilty to mention them to anyone. Certainly not his father.

So he tried to put the matter out of his mind. He told himself that he was being childish. And this was no time to behave like a child. For very soon he was to become a man.

The bar mitzvah that lay ahead of him was a serious but simple observance. All the Jewish families he knew celebrated it the same way. On the Sabbath following his thirteenth birthday, he would be called in the synagogue to read from the Torah and to recite the blessings. Unlike in some other communities, this would be the first time he'd be allowed to do so. Afterwards, at the family house, there would be a small gathering of family and friends to celebrate the occasion.

Jacob was looking forward to it. He was well prepared for the religious part of the proceedings. He could read Hebrew just as well as he could Latin. From that day, in theory at least, he could be considered an adult. He was determined, therefore, to put aside these foolish uncertainties about his life before the day arrived.

It was a month before his bar mitzvah that he went for a walk with his mother's cousin Baruch.

His father didn't like Baruch. Jacob could see why. Baruch was about his father's age, but there all resemblances ended. Baruch was corpulent, and inclined to be loud and argumentative. He had little respect for scholarship. But he wasn't stupid. Jacob knew that his mother's cousin was richer than his father. Baruch was a moneylender.

He didn't often come to their house, but he'd looked in to see Jacob's mother that day, and as he was leaving he'd said: 'So why don't you walk with me, Jacob?' He'd turned to his cousin. 'Your son never talks to me.'

'I never see you,' replied Jacob.

'Go and walk with your cousin Baruch,' his mother told him.

It was a fine afternoon. They'd walked out through the nearby postern gate and followed a lane that led towards the big compound of the Templars. Trying to make conversation, Jacob had asked Baruch about what he did.

'I lend money,' said Baruch. 'Then I try to get it back.'

'I know this,' said Jacob.

'So what do you want to know?'

'I don't know. How you do it, I suppose.'

'How does your father cure people? He gives them medicines they think they need. Then they get better. He hopes. I give people money they need. Then they get richer. They hope. I hope. Otherwise they can't pay me back. It's obvious.'

Jacob considered.

'So how do you decide whether they're a good risk?'

'That is a good question.' Baruch seemed to soften a bit. 'Maybe you're not so stupid after all.' He paused. 'You need security. The man has to pledge something for the loan, so you have to figure what it's worth, and whether he really owns it. And you need a good head for numbers. If the risk is high, you're going to need a higher interest rate to protect yourself. Are you understanding me?'

'I think so. You have to calculate.'

'Yes. But you know what? It's not just that. It's an art as well. You really have to understand the man's affairs. And you have to judge his character. Sometimes that's the most important thing of all. Character.' He shrugged. 'So maybe it's like being a physician. It's instinct, you know. I'm a money physician. I look after people's lives. It's a terrible occupation.' He looked at Jacob to see how he was taking it.

'I think it's interesting,' said Jacob frankly.

'It's not so bad.'

'The Christians call it usury.'

'The Jews call it usury. It's in the Torah. "Thou shalt not lend money at interest." It says so.' He paused a moment. 'You know something? The Torah is very good at telling you what not to do. But if there is no profit to be had, no interest, then there is no reason for anyone to lend, and so nobody can borrow anything. They can steal it from their grandmother, but they can't borrow it.' He smiled. 'But there is an escape clause. A Jew is not allowed to lend at interest to another Jew. But it doesn't say that you can't lend to someone who is not a Jew. So we can lend to Christians.'

'And the Christians are allowed to borrow from us.'

'By the same logic. They say they mustn't lend at interest, because it says so in the Bible. But if a Jew is prepared to lend, then that's all right. They say the Jew is probably going to hell anyway, so who cares? It's one of the few occupations they allow us to follow, which is very convenient for them.' He made a dismissive motion with his hands. 'They get the money. We go to hell.'

'But the Christians lend money too,' Jacob objected. 'What about the Italian moneylenders, like the Lombards? I heard that they're sanctioned by the pope himself.'

'Ah. But they don't charge interest.'

'So how can they have any profit?'

'They charge a fee instead.'

'What's the difference?'

'Mathematically? There is no difference. But the word is different.'

They were coming close to the huge compound of the Knights Templar now, and they had stopped to gaze at it.

'How is it the Templars are so rich?' Jacob had asked Baruch.

'They had huge land grants. For generations. They don't pay taxes. And they lend money. The king owes them a fortune.'

'They lend for a fee, then,' Jacob said. 'No interest.'

'Of course,' Baruch replied. 'Actually,' he went on, 'the Templars are interesting. They lend money. But that's only part of it. They're brilliant.'

'Why?'

'Look at their building. It's an impregnable fortress. There's probably more gold in there than any other building in France. It all got started when they transported bullion out to the Holy Land for the crusaders to use. They kept the money in fortresses out there, too. But that was just the start. Since then, they've built forti- fied bullion stores all over Christendom. So what's so clever about that?'

'I suppose then they have bullion ready for any purpose, in any country.'

'True, but that's not the point. The point,' said Baruch, 'is that when you travel, you don't have to take a lot of money with you. No armed guards. No fear of getting robbed. You just deposit your bullion with the Templars in London or Paris, get a receipt, and that gives you credit to draw on the Templars' bullion deposits wherever you're going. The Templars will charge you a large fee for the service, but it's worth it. You've saved yourself a fortune in security.'

'Did the Templars invent this?'

'No. The old merchants around the Mediterranean have been holding credit balances with each other since time out of mind. But the scale of the Templars' operations is stupendous. They've got enough stashed in some of their forts to pay for an army.'

'They must have to transport bullion themselves, sometimes,' Jacob said.

'Yes. But who's going to attack a bullion shipment guarded by the Temple Knights? You'd have to be an idiot. Those bastards fight only to the death.' Baruch chuckled. 'Funny, isn't it: the only knights who always fight to the death are the ones protecting the money.'

Jacob had nodded and smiled. Yet his mind was in a whirl.

No doubt his cousin Baruch just thought he was having a chat with a boy who was going to be a physician. But his words were having a much more profound effect than he could have imagined.

As he'd listened to Baruch discourse on the art of moneylending, it had felt to Jacob as if someone were opening a door in front of him. This was an occupation that would use all his talents. This was the challenge he'd always been looking for. He just hadn't known it. And with this realisation came that wonderful sense of peace that comes to everyone when they find their natural metier. I could do that, he thought. That's what I want to do.

And when Baruch had described the huge, international capacity of the Templars' dealings, he had felt a sense not just of affinity, but of inspiration. It wasn't only the scale that was fascinating. The efficiency of the operation, the intellectual economy, struck him forcibly. The endless possibilities of a credit system that spread all over Europe seemed to him one of the most beautiful and exciting ideas he had ever encountered. What could be better, what could be more interesting, than to take part in the workings of the universal world of money, the lifeblood of all enterprise, that knows no foolish boundaries, but can flow unimpeded from kingdom to kingdom? Though he did not quite know how to formulate the idea, he had just been given a glimpse of the wonders of finance.

'Could I come and work for you?' he suddenly asked Baruch.

'I thought you were going to be a physician,' the big man said in surprise.

'I don't think so,' said Jacob.

'You had better talk to your father.'

Jacob promised that he would.

But somehow he couldn't bring himself to do it. He meant to. He was certain what he wanted. But telling his father that he was going to turn his back on his birthright and wanted to work with a man his father didn't like . . . It wasn't so easy.

The next week he met Baruch in the street.

'Did you tell your father?' Baruch asked.

'I'm going to.'

'You can change your mind, you know.'

'No. I want to work for you.'

'I can talk to him if you want.'

'I'll do it.'

'Don't leave it to your bar mitzvah.'

But still he'd put it off. Each time his father smiled at him approvingly, or his mother said 'We're all very proud of you', it grew harder to broach the subject. How could he disappoint them all? And as the days went by he began to think that maybe it would be better to get through the business of the bar mitzvah and talk to his father about it afterwards.

And so he'd let it drift, and drift . . . until the day.

He'd read well in the synagogue. They were all very pleased with him. That evening there were about twenty people in their house. His parents, their closest friends, the rabbi and Baruch had also been invited.

Baruch had looked at him questioningly, but Jacob had whispered, 'I decided to talk to him after this is over.'

And everyone was congratulating him, and one of the neighbours' wives said, 'Just look at Jacob's eyes. You have wonderful eyes, Jacob.

Those are real physician's eyes, just like your father's.' And another of their friends chimed in, 'He's going to be a wonderful physician.' And someone said to Jacob's mother, 'You must be very proud of him.' And his mother said she was.

So for a moment, only the woman Cousin Baruch was talking to heard Baruch say: 'He isn't going to be a physician.'

'What do you mean?' she said, so that several people turned to look. 'Of course he's going to be a physician.'

'Suit yourself,' said Baruch. 'I'm just telling you he doesn't want to be a physician.'

Jacob's mother heard that.

'What are you talking about, Baruch?' she demanded impatiently. She liked Baruch better than her husband did, because he was her family, but she didn't like him that much.

Baruch shrugged.

'I'm just saying he doesn't want to be a physician. He wants to work for me. Is that so terrible?'

'No he doesn't.'

'Ask him.' He pointed to Jacob. And everybody looked at Jacob. And Jacob looked back at them, and wished that the ground could open up and swallow him forever.

'I am very disappointed in you,' his father said later that night. 'I am sorry that you don't want to be a physician, because I think you would be a good one. But to go behind my back . . . You talk to Baruch, with whom we are not close, before you even talk to your own father. Then you make a mockery of us all. "Honour Thy Father and Mother": you break this commandment, on the very day of your bar mitzvah. Shame on you, Jacob. I hardly know whether to call you my son.'

That had been his first great crime. Even now, the memory of that day made him cringe with shame.

But in due course, he had started to work for Baruch, and for ten years he had continued with him, until Baruch dropped dead in the middle of an argument with somebody one day. By that time, Jacob had learned the business of moneylending very thoroughly, and he continued on his own. And thanks both to his skill, and to his father's many friends in the city, he was able to do very well.

He had married Sarah, and been happy, and started a family.

So what had possessed him to make the terrible error of judgement, to commit the unspeakable crime that had brought tragedy to his own life, misery to his family, and now the loss of his daughter?

If one were to seek deep causes, Jacob considered, one could say that it was the Crusades that were to blame.

Two centuries ago, when the first crusading knights had set out to win back the Holy Land from the Saracens, they'd been successful. They'd taken Antioch. Then Jerusalem itself.

But it had hardly been a year before the crusading cause had degenerated. A huge, motley army of adventurers and looters had swept across Europe in their wake. Finding the Jewish communities in the Rhineland and on the River Danube, they'd robbed and slaughtered them.

Christian kings, and even the Church, had been appalled.

But in the decades that followed, another process had slowly begun, and the mood of Christendom had changed. For the huge, unwieldy Moslem empire had not crumbled. It had fought back. And so the long series of Crusades had begun. Some were successful – in Spain, the Moslem Moors were being pushed back. But other Crusades had been disasters.

Churchmen were puzzled. Why hadn't God given them victory? Crusaders were frustrated. Everyone looked for scapegoats. And what better scapegoat than the Jewish community, which contained the moneylenders to whom kings, knights and merchants alike owed so much money? Soon, Jews were being accused of all kinds of crimes: even that they sacrificed Christian children.

In Paris, the Jewish community had occupied a quarter near the royal palace in the middle of the Seine, with a fine synagogue across the water on the Right Bank. In 1182, King Philip Augustus had turned their synagogue into the church of La Madeleine, and for several years the Jews had even had to leave his kingdom. With his city wall to build, and a crusading army to finance, he'd soon recalled them. The Jews of Paris had mostly lived near the northern city wall after that, grudgingly tolerated.

It hadn't been until the reign of Philip's grandson that the next attack had come. But when it did, it was cunning and insidious.

A Franciscan friar in Brittany named Nicolas Donin claimed that the Talmud not only denied the divinity of Jesus, but also the virginity of his mother, Mary. Soon the pope himself told every Christian king to burn the Talmud. Most of Europe's monarchs took no notice.

But pious King Louis IX of France did. The saintly monarch who brought the Crown of Thorns to Paris, built the Sainte-Chapelle and encouraged the dreaded Inquisition was not going to fail in his Christian duty. He burned every copy of the Talmud he could find, and made French Jews wear a red badge of shame.

Jacob's grandfather had worn the badge of shame. Yet even so, like most of the Jewish community in Paris, he hadn't wanted to leave. And Jacob could see why.

Paris was still one of the greatest cities in Europe, far larger than London. It was an intellectual centre. It had a huge trade.

By the time Jacob was starting to earn a living, things had seemed to be getting a little better. The grandson of saintly King Louis – tall, blond, Philip the Fair – had come to the throne. He claimed to be pious, but he always needed money.

'Finance my debts,' he told the Jews of France, 'and I'll protect you from the Inquisition.'

Jacob's house had been in the rue des Rosiers. It was a pleasant street under the north-eastern corner of the city wall. His business was prospering. He was about to get married. It had seemed that fate was smiling upon him.

Strangely enough, the first sign of trouble had come from the king of England. For the mighty Plantagenets had not been driven from all of France. They still held the rich lands of Gascony, in old Aquitaine. And in 1287, the English king had decided to kick all the Jews out of Gascony. By any standards, this was a distressing event. But at the time it had happened, Jacob had been busy making the arrangements for his wedding day. And besides, he need not concern himself too much with the follies of France's enemy, the Plantagenet king of England.

The next year had been one of family loss. Sarah had given birth to a baby boy, but it was clear at once that the baby was sickly, and it was not a shock that it did not last a month. A few months after that, Jacob's mother had died, very peacefully, and no one was surprised when his father, who was quite lost without her, had followed her before the year was out.

As a result of these changes, Jacob had suddenly found himself both head of the family, and still childless. He'd felt strangely lonely.

But then, a twelvemonth later, his little Naomi had been born. From the day of her birth, she'd been a strong baby. He'd been over-joyed. She'd continued to thrive. He was sorry that his parents had not been there to see it, but he faced the future with happiness, and hope.

Once, just once during those years, there had been a brief reminder that in the medieval world, the dangers of hysteria were never absent.

One Easter in Paris, a Jew he knew slightly, not an especially pleasant fellow, was suddenly arrested. The crime of which he was accused was serious, however, for he was accused of desecrating the Host.

A poor woman from a nearby parish claimed that she had brought a wafer to him from her church and that he had attacked it with a knife. Was it the truth? Who knew? But within days the story had grown. The wafer had run with blood. The blood had filled a bath. Then the wafer had flown about the house. Then the Saviour Himself had appeared to the Jew's terrified family. People often had visions, and they were often believed. In this case, a court had found the fellow guilty and, this being a religious crime, he'd been executed.

Jacob had shaken his head at the folly of it all, but he had not been astonished. One must be careful, very careful, that was all.

More serious might have been another development from across the sea.

It had been a July day. Jacob had been walking across to the Île de la Cité, and had caught sight of Henri Renard. He'd waved to him. And been surprised when Renard had hurried to his side and urgently seized his arm.

'You haven't heard?' Renard had demanded.

'Heard what?'

'Terrible news,' Renard continued. 'The Jews of England are all expelled. They're to leave at once.'

Jacob had hastened home. By that evening he'd discussed it with the rabbi and a dozen friends.

'The fact that the king of England strikes the Jews does not mean that Philip of France will want to copy him,' the rabbi pointed out. 'We have to wait and see. Besides,' he had added, 'what else can we do?'

By the next day, most of the Paris community had come to the same conclusion.

But it was then that Jacob's friend Renard had stepped in. He'd waited only days before he did so. Seeing Jacob in the market of Les Halles, he'd taken him to one side.

'We have known each other too long for you to take offence,' the merchant began quietly. 'So forgive me if I ask you something, Jacob, that I've been thinking about ever since the expulsion from Gascony.' He'd paused, embarrassed. 'Jacob, my friend, these are such dangerous times that I must ask you: Have you ever thought of converting?'

'Converting?' Jacob had stared at him in astonishment. 'You mean, to Christianity?'

'It's hardly unknown.'

Conversions had certainly happened in Spain. In France they were rarer. A generation ago in Brittany, five hundred Jews had converted all together – though that had been under the threat of death if they didn't.

'It would bring you safety,' Renard pointed out quickly. 'All the restrictions placed upon Jews would be raised. You could own land, and trade however you pleased. I'd gladly sponsor you for the merchants' guild,' he added.

Jacob knew his childhood friend meant to be kind. But he was shocked all the same. He'd shaken his head, and Renard had not raised the subject again.

And indeed, the Jews of Paris had been left in peace. England remained closed to Jews. As might be expected, the English king soon replaced them with Italian moneylenders, sanctioned by the pope. But Philip the Fair did not follow his example. The Jews of Paris breathed easier.

For Jacob however, the next years had brought problems of another kind.

The year after the expulsion from England, Sarah had given birth to another child, a son. But the tiny boy had been sickly and had not lived a week. Eighteen months later she had suffered a miscarriage. And after that, nothing. For some reason his wife had failed to conceive. It seemed that Jacob was not to be blessed with a son.

He accepted this blow, as he knew he must, but he could not help asking himself sometimes: Why had God singled him out for this misfortune? What had he done?

The old rabbi who had failed to impress Jacob's father had been succeeded by his son, a stocky fellow of about his own age. Naomi and the rabbi's son were part of a group of children who played together, another reason to keep friendly with him, and so Jacob had gone to consult him. The rabbi hadn't been much help, though. He found no fault with Jacob's conduct, and told him: 'We must accept what God decides. It may be for a reason you do not know.'

Was it from that time that the change within him had begun? Jacob himself could not say. There had been no sudden turning away. He'd attended the synagogue exactly as he had always done. But he got little pleasure or comfort from it. He was conscious of a sense that the Lord had somehow turned away from him, but whether this was a temporary trial, like the tribulations of Job, or whether it was something more permanent, he had no idea. Occasionally he failed to go to the synagogue and his absence was noted. Yet each night without fail he said his prayers and took comfort from them.

His greatest joy was Naomi. He doted on her. With her bright eyes and dark curls, she was an enchanting little girl. He taught her the Shema and said it with her every night, as his father had done with him. He would sit with her on his lap and talk to her on all manner of subjects. He taught her to read so that, by the age of eight, she could read and write better than most of the Jewish boys of her age.

He liked to take her about with him and he showed her the wonders of Paris, including the great churches.

So he was none too pleased, one evening shortly after Naomi's eighth birthday, to receive a visit from the rabbi, who'd asked to speak to him alone. Nor was his mood improved by the rabbi's opening remark: 'I've come, Jacob, not only for myself, but for some of your friends. For I must tell you there have been complaints. About your daughter.'

'What kind of complaints?' Jacob kept his voice quiet and even. 'Has she done something wrong?'

'Not at all,' the rabbi answered quickly. 'It is not what she has done . . .' He hesitated a moment. 'Jacob, have you ever considered that it may not be seemly for a girl to receive too much instruction?'

'You mean that she can read and write better than a boy?'

'Not everyone likes that. You are treating her as if she were your son. But one day she will grow up and marry, and it is for the husband to lead the family in these things, not the wife.'

'Anything else?'

'You take her everywhere. This is your choice, naturally. But when she is older, she will have to restrict where she goes. To family, to friends. We hope you make her understand that it is not seemly for Jewish women to wander about the town. Especially . . .'

'Especially what?'

'Jacob, you have been seen taking your daughter into Christian churches. Is that wise?'

'We live in Paris. She should know what the inside of Notre-Dame looks like.'

'Perhaps. But not all the community think so.'

'Is this all?'

'No, Jacob. It is not. She has been telling the other children stories. Of Saint Denis. Of Saint Geneviève. Of Roland.'

'But these are the heroes and heroines of France. Every Christian child in Paris knows the story of the killing of Saint Denis on Montmartre. They say now that he picked up his head and walked away with it. Absurd, but a children's tale. I told her how Geneviève – supposedly – saved Paris from Attila the Hun. I find these stories absurd, but shouldn't she at least know them?'

'When she is older, I would agree with you. But she tells these stories to your friends' children, and they don't like it.'

'They say nothing to me.'

'No. But to me they do.' The rabbi took a deep breath. 'Jacob, we are sorry that you have no son, but Naomi is a daughter. You cannot turn her into a boy.'

'Have you any other advice?'

'You do not always come to the synagogue.'

'Perhaps this is the real reason you are here.'

'No. But if you turn your face from God, then God will turn his face from you. This is certain.'

'I am grateful for your concern.'

'I have told you only what is for your own good.'

Jacob stared at him. He was angry. But he was also hurt. And the fact that some of the things the rabbi said might be true did not make it any better.

'I will consider your advice,' he said coldly.

'You should. It is good advice. I shall tell your friends that it has been given.'

This was the last straw. Was this rabbi really trying to impose himself between him and all his neighbours? Was this his object?

'You are a fool,' Jacob suddenly burst out. 'My father always told me your father was a fool. Your son will be a fool as well.'

'Do not speak to me like that, Jacob.'

'Get out.'

The next week, Jacob observed the Sabbath in his home. But he did not go to the synagogue. He did return the week after. But although he had many friends, an invisible bond between himself and the rest of the congregation had been broken. What else, he wondered, might his so-called friends say to the rabbi behind his back?

And then, as if to give the lie to the notion that God had turned His face from him, Sarah announced that she was going to have another child.

If Jacob was thrilled, he was also concerned. God might be smiling upon him again, but common sense told him to be careful. Two boys lost and a miscarriage: the record was not good. He resolved to take every precaution. He wished his father were still alive to give him guidance.

As the weeks went by, therefore, he protected Sarah night and day. He made her promise not to exert herself. If he was out in the city, he'd come back several times during the day to make sure that she was keeping her promise. He realised that he was giving less attention to Naomi than he usually did, and felt guilty about it. But though she was only eight years old, Naomi seemed perfectly to understand. Each evening he would read stories to them both in front of the fire.

They never discussed whether the baby would be a girl or a boy. The subject was too sensitive. But one day when Sarah was in her sixth month, a visiting neighbour remarked to him: 'I see your wife is going to have a boy.'

'Why do you think so?' he asked.

'By the way she carries the child, the way she walks,' the woman replied. 'I can always tell.'

And at this news, Jacob's heart leaped for joy. But he said nothing even to Sarah. And he was glad that he had not. For a few days later, passing the kitchen, he overheard Naomi say: 'I wonder if my father will still love me so much if the baby is a boy.' And he knew that his little daughter was right, and his heart went out to her. And he vowed on the spot that never, never would he love her any less, or show that he cared more to have a son than a daughter.

It was in the eighth month that things began to go wrong. The physician, a man whose judgement he trusted almost as well as he had his own father's, took him aside and told him: 'I believe this will be a difficult birth, Jacob.'

'You mean she may lose the child?'

'It may be difficult for both of them.'

'What can I do?'

'Trust in the Lord. I will do the rest.'

It was now approaching midwinter. Some mornings, the cobbles in the street were slippery with ice. He told Sarah that she must on no account go outside. He kept the fire burning night and day.

Two more weeks passed. Her time was drawing near.

Then one night came a knock on the door.

It was Renard. His friend came in quickly, embraced him, asked after Sarah and Naomi and then said in a low voice that they must speak alone.

They went into Jacob's little counting house and closed the door.

'No one must know that I came here tonight,' Renard began. 'What I have to tell you must remain a secret, for your own sake and for mine.'

'You can rely on me.'

'I know.' Renard took a deep breath. 'Jacob, I have a friend who is close to the counsels of the king. He has given me news that I share with you alone. I must ask you not to share it with others, however tempted you may be. Otherwise, I can tell you nothing. I beg you for your own sake and your family's to promise that you'll keep this secret.'

Jacob was not sure that he liked the sound of this. But he had no doubt that if Renard told him that it was for his family's sake, then it was so.

'Very well,' he said after a pause. 'Please go on.'

'The king has been persuaded to move against the Jews. I do not know when he will strike, but it will not be long.'

'What will he do?'

'I am not certain. But it's not just a fine. It is something more significant.'

'It must be expulsion, then.'

'That is what I think.'

Both men were silent for a moment. Where would the Jews go? The King of France controlled far larger territories than when Philip Augustus had briefly expelled the Jews a century ago. The nearest possible refuge might be Burgundy, if the Duke of Burgundy would have them.

Jacob thought of Sarah in her condition, and of the unborn child. Must he wander the world with his poor little family? Would they survive?

Then Renard spoke. His voice was quiet, though troubled.

'Years ago, dear friend, I made a suggestion to you. I never raised the subject again. I respected your wishes. But when I see the situation now, as your friend, I must beg you to reconsider. For your own sake. For the sake of your family.'

'You are speaking of conversion.'

'I am. I needn't remind you of the advantages. All the limitations placed upon Jews would be raised. You would be a free man. Your family would be safe. You could continue to reside here in Paris. I could do so much for you.'

'I must turn my back on my God to find safety?' Jacob said.

'Is it turning your back on God?' Renard responded earnestly. 'What is it, Jacob, that we Christians say? Only that Jesus of Nazareth was the very Messiah that the Jews were waiting for. Those Jews who realised it became the first Christians. We are waiting for the rest of the Jews to follow them. That is all that divides us in our religion, my friend. And to me it seems but a small step to take. The ancient Jewish prophecies have been fulfilled. That is all. It's a cause for rejoicing.'

Jacob smiled at his friend.

'You must talk to my rabbi,' he said wryly.

'One thing I must urge upon you,' Renard continued. 'If you are prepared to take this step, you'd better take it soon. The Inquisition desires that all men should be good Christians – of course. On the other hand, the Inquisitors are suspicious of converts, because they suspect their conversions may not be sincere. While the information I have given you remains secret, your conversion should be acceptable. But once it's known the king means to expel the Jews, then it might arouse suspicion.'

'This I understand,' said Jacob, but he gave no further answer before Renard departed.

Jacob did not sleep well that night. For a while, he lay in bed thinking. Then he got up and sat by the fire. Twice he took a candle and went softly to look at his wife, and at Naomi, as they slept. And all the time he pondered.

He did not care about the rabbi. He did not even care so much about the Jewish congregation. Not since some of them had shown themselves to be false friends.

But what of the Lord God of Abraham and his forefathers? If I have suffered when I have served the Lord my God, Jacob considered, will He not smite me with afflictions far worse, if I betray Him now? Besides, wasn't the Lord making His face to shine upon him, by granting him a son at last? To turn away from God after such a blessing would be madness indeed.

Yet was the baby a son? A neighbour's wife had said so. What of it? The truth was that he did not know. Besides, he'd lost two sons already. And now the physician was concerned about the birth itself. Even the safety of his wife was in doubt.

Hour after hour Jacob turned these things over in his mind. To trust in the Lord, or to betray his heritage. To save his little family, or to see them destroyed. Thus he passed the dark night of the soul. And it was only at dawn, when he heard his wife cry out in pain, and sent hurriedly for the physician, that, unable to bear it any more, he had made the terrible decision.

Jacob had been baptised into the Christian faith a week later. Renard had made the arrangements with a priest, and it had been discreetly done. For Jacob had been so afraid that the shock of his conversion might cause his wife to miscarry that neither she nor Naomi had any idea of it until two weeks after his son had been safely born. They called the little boy Jacob, since it was the family tradition. During this time, he did not go to the synagogue, but allowed it to be thought that this was because he would not leave his wife's side.

When at last he told Sarah, she had been greatly shocked. He ex-plained to her in secret what Renard had told him, and why he had done it. When he had finished, she said nothing for a few moments, and then remarked with some bitterness: 'So, I am to lose every one of my friends.'

Had she not been nursing her baby, and caring for Naomi, he supposed she might have said a lot more than she did.

As for Naomi, the little girl was mystified. The first night after she was told she was to be a Christian, he had come to say prayers with her as usual, and she had begun:

Shema Yisrael Adonai eloheinu adonai ehad . . .

But there he had gently stopped her, and explained that from now on she should begin her prayers with a new prayer.

'It is a very beautiful prayer,' he promised. 'It is addressed to the one Lord, the God of Israel, and of all the world. It begins "Our Father . . ."'

'Am I not to say the Shema any more?' she asked.

And with a sudden pang of grief he found himself telling her: 'Christians sometimes say the Shema, too, in Latin. But it's better that you use this other prayer instead.'

When Naomi asked her mother about it the next morning, Sarah told her firmly that she must obey her father and that he knew best. But that afternoon she came in crying because another little girl had told her that the prayer was used only by the enemies of her people. Soon, none of the other children in the quarter would speak to her.

She could not be told the secret about the coming expulsion. It was too dangerous, and she was too young. Jacob could only watch her suffering and comfort her as best he could.

It was clear they had to move.

If Henri Renard had been the cause of all this pain, he certainly kept his promise when it came to helping his friend once he had made the fateful decision. He had already prepared the ground, both with the priest who baptised Jacob, and with a wide circle of influential merchants and their families.

'You'll remember his father the physician, of course,' he'd say. 'One of the most trusted men in Paris. So Jacob grew up among Christians like myself from his childhood. He couldn't discuss it publicly, of course, but to my certain knowledge he's been considering converting for nearly a decade.' Technically, since he himself had broached the subject to Jacob years ago, this was true, if somewhat misleading.

As a Christian, Jacob was not supposed to practise moneylending. But in no time Renard had got him into the merchant guild. There were plenty of opportunities for a man of his skill and fortune to make money as a merchant, and he was soon an active dealer in the city's great cloth trade. Renard had also helped Jacob find the house in the rue Saint-Martin.

'It's only a short walk from Les Halles, and it's in my own parish of Saint-Merri, so we can hear Mass at the same church,' he explained. And he ensured that the newly converted family – for Sarah and Naomi, however unwillingly, had also been baptised – were welcomed by their fellow parishioners. So at least they now had neighbours who spoke to them, and Naomi had the chance to make new friends.

The greatest relief for Jacob, however, had been the health of his newborn son. The birth had not been as difficult as feared. The baby was in good health, and within weeks was giving every sign of being robust. So far, at least, it seemed that God had not turned His face away from Jacob. Indeed, Jacob even wondered if it was possible that the Lord might be pleased with his conversion.

Strangely, during the whole business, the reaction that troubled him the most, the words that haunted him, came from a man he didn't even care for.

The morning after his conversion had become known the rabbi came straight to his house.

'Is this true, Jacob ben Jacob? You have converted? Tell me this is not true.'

'It is true.'

He had expected the rabbi to be angry. But there was an even more striking reaction, a look so deeply carved in the lines of the rabbi's face that it gave him a new dignity. It was grief.

'Why? Why have you done such a thing?'

'I have decided that Jesus of Nazareth was the Messiah.'

It was not true. He could not tell the rabbi the truth. And as he stared at this man he did not like, he felt a sudden and terrible guilt. He longed to cry out: 'I did it because the Jews are going to be expelled. I did it to save my family.' But he could not. There lay his greatest crime. He was doing nothing to warn his own people. He was going to wait as their doom approached, watch while they lost everything, including their homes, and were cast out to wander the world.

'Will you betray us then, Jacob ben Jacob?' the rabbi asked bitterly. 'Will you be another Nicolas Donin?'

This was a searing accusation. For every Jew knew that Nicolas Donin, the Franciscan who'd persuaded Christendom to burn the Talmud, had been born a Jew himself. Nothing was more terrible, it was often said, than the vengeance of the traitor.

'Never!' he cried. He was deeply hurt. But it was the rabbi's parting words that would haunt him.

'You call me a fool,' the rabbi said. 'But it is you who are the fool, Jacob. You convert. You join the Christians. And you think: now I shall be safe. But you are wrong. This I know, and this I tell you.' He shook his head. 'You are a Jew, Jacob. And no matter what you do, no matter what the Christians say – believe me – you will never be safe.'

So Jacob attended church and learned what it was to be a Christian. In a general way, through his intimacy with friends like Renard, he had always known. But because it was his nature to be intellectually curious, he began to study the religion to which he had committed his family. The Old Testament he knew well. Now he studied the New. And he was interested to discover how directly, how intimately, the one grew from the other. To him, Jesus and his disciples did not seem like Christians at war with a Jewish culture they shunned. They were Jews. They were Jewish in culture, they obeyed Jewish laws, followed Jewish observances. They read from the Torah, and sacrificed at the temple in Jerusalem.

As for the Christian message of love, who would argue against that?

When Renard had urged him to remember that the Christian Church had begun as a group of Jews who recognised that their rabbi had been the promised Messiah, Jacob had assumed it was to help him convert and save his skin. And it probably was. But, in fact, Jacob now concluded, his friend had spoken the truth. As he read the Acts of the Apostles, it struck him forcibly to what an extent the first Christians were Jews, and how easily – but for Saint Paul's persuading the Saviour's reluctant family and friends to let the Gentiles join them – they might have remained a Jewish sect. Time, and the tragedies of history, accounted for all the rest.

But no man could ignore that long history. It could not be done. If the Church regarded him cautiously, if the rabbi no longer spoke to him, if his wife was unhappy and his daughter mystified, he could not blame them.

Meanwhile he waited, with a heavy heart and secret shame, for the terrible blow that was about to fall upon the Jews of France.

Weeks passed. Nothing happened. He wondered if Renard had made a mistake about the king's intentions. Had he put his family through untold misery for no good reason at all?

But Renard had not been mistaken. The king had indeed been planning to strike at the Jewish community – but not in the way that he and Jacob had expected.

For in the year of Our Lord 1299, Philip the Fair announced that he would no longer protect the Jews from the Inquisition. The blow was as cunning as it was vicious.

What had the king done? Nothing. What might the Inquisition do? Anything. Was the king losing any revenues he might collect from the Jews? No. Was he proving his piety? Yes.

And what did this mean for Jacob?

'That I converted, thinking that my own people would be thrown out of Paris. Whereas now they remain here, and hate me more than ever. That I converted to be safe. Whereas now, the Inquisition will be encouraged to watch me like a hawk, and if they decide that my conversion was not sincere, they will say that I am a Jew after all, and they will attack me for perjury, and who knows what else. For all I know, they will burn me alive. That is what the king's action means for me,' he said miserably to his wife.

'For us,' she corrected, grimly.

But the Inquisition had left him alone. In his favour was the fact that the Jews of Paris so clearly hated him, and that, thanks to Renard, the congregation of the Saint-Merri parish continued to embrace him as one of their own.

The family settled into a Christian life. It was strange to them not to celebrate the Sabbath on a Saturday any more. The observance of the Christian Sunday was a far more lax affair. He missed the passionate intimacy of the Jewish Passover. He missed the haunting, melancholy sound of the cantor in the synagogue. But the Christian services had their beauty too.

'Our life,' he told his family, 'is not so bad.'

Whatever she thought, Sarah saw no use in complaining. Little Jacob, growing up in an extended circle of the Renards and their friends, was too young to have known anything else. As for Naomi, she seemed to adapt. She made new friends. As far as Jacob knew, she never saw any Jewish children at all.

Jacob rented a storehouse nearby where he kept the great bales of cloth in which he now dealt. He took on an apprentice, who slept in a loft over the store to guard its contents. A year after converting, he had bought the orchard of apple and pear trees by the hamlet on the slopes to the north-east of the city, and on Sunday afternoons the family, often accompanied by the Renards, would usually walk out there and, after inspecting the orchards and gazing down upon Paris, return by another path that led them past the fortress of the Temple Knights and thence into the city. It was pleasant exercise.

Five years had passed in this manner, without incident.

Perhaps because it developed slowly, he never saw the crisis with his daughter coming.

He had taken the greatest care never to seem to neglect her for the baby. He continued to read and write with her and to teach her simple mathematics. He told her stories just as he had before. As little Jacob began to talk, he'd put the child on his knee and tell him a story, saying to Naomi, 'Do you remember how I used to tell this story to you?' And sometimes he would get halfway through and say, 'You finish it now, Naomi,' praising her when she did – so that soon she was proud of the fact that the little boy looked up to her as a second mother.

Naomi would help Sarah dress the child, and take him for walks.

'It's good for her,' Jacob would say contentedly to his wife. 'She'll make an excellent mother one day.'

He was also pleased to observe that his daughter was going to be a beautiful young woman. As a little girl, the most noticeable thing about her had been her wide-spaced blue eyes, set in a round face surrounded by a mass of dark curls. But by the time she was eleven, her face was already turning into a lovely oval. The curls were becoming rich tresses that fell thickly below her shoulders. Men were starting to turn to look at her in the street.

He had often wondered if she would make a good bride for Renard's eldest son, who was five years older. He didn't like to suggest it to his friend, who had already done so much for him. 'If he doesn't like the idea, I don't want to embarrass him,' he explained to Sarah. And Renard, so far, had never broached the subject himself. Jacob was also constrained by the fact that on the one occasion he had gently asked Naomi what she'd say if the offer were ever made, she'd said simply: 'I like him very well, Father. But I think of him as a friend, not a husband.'

'Friendship is the best basis for a marriage,' her father had responded. 'Your feelings might change.'

'I don't think so,' she said.

And though he naturally had the right to choose her husband, Jacob loved his daughter far too much to make her unhappy.

'I'll never give you to any man against your will,' he'd promised.

There was no shortage of offers from other families. He'd received three inquiries from worthy merchants in the city. He'd put them off for the time being, but there seemed little doubt that Naomi would have the chance to marry well.

Meanwhile, she displayed a wonderful understanding that delighted him. For having treated her more like a son than a daughter when she was young, he had found he couldn't suddenly change his intellectual relationship with her just because she had a brother. Often, therefore, he would discuss his business with her, or the events of the day. It was especially enjoyable for him because she not only grasped matters quickly, but her questions were probing. She asked not what had occurred, but why. He remembered one conversation in particular. It had been a little before her thirteenth birthday.

'Why is it,' she'd asked him, 'when the land of France is so rich, that the king is always short of money?'

'For two reasons,' he told her. 'First, because he likes to go to war. Second, because he likes to build. When he's finished enlarging the royal palace on the Île de la Cité, it will be the envy of all Christendom. And nothing in the world costs more than war, and building.'

'But why does he do this? Is this for the good of his country?'

'Not at all.' Jacob had smiled. 'You must understand, Naomi, that when a simple man, a merchant let us say, inherits from his father, that inheritance is his personal property. He seeks to enlarge his fortune and to become more powerful. Often, he also wants to impress his neighbours.'

'This may be foolish.'

'Undoubtedly, but it is human nature. And kings are the same, but with this one difference. Their inheritance is an entire country. But they still view it as their property, to do with as they please. So, King Philip desires to enlarge his kingdom, especially at the expense of his family's rivals, the Plantagenets of England. Down the generations, his family have pushed the Plantagenets out of Normandy, in the north, and both Anjou and Poitou, in the west. Now he hopes to press farther down the Atlantic coast of Aquitaine, and push them out of the great wine-growing lands around Bordeaux in Gascony. The king has also done very well in his marriage. His wife has brought him control of the rich plains of Champagne. This is a wonderful addition to his realm. But beyond Champagne he sees the lands of Flanders, with their rich towns, and he hopes to get some of Flanders as well.'

'This is all for his personal glory, then?'

'Certainly. He is just a man. In fact, rich kings often behave no better than spoiled children.'

'You think that wealth and power make men childish?'

Jacob laughed.

'I had never formulated the thought in quite that way, but you may be right.'

'So these things are not done for the good of his people?'

'Kings always say they are. But it's not true. Or if it is, then it's purely by chance.'

'But what of God?' she demanded. 'Shouldn't kings serve God? Aren't they afraid for their immortal souls?'

'Intermittently.'

'I think that rulers should be good men.'

'And it does you credit,' her father replied. 'But I will tell you something. A good man may not be a good king, Naomi. It all depends on the circumstances. There is something better than being good, in a ruler, and you will find it in the Bible.'

Naomi frowned, and thought for a moment.

'You mean King Solomon?'

'Exactly so. When Solomon became king, the Lord asked him what gift he would like to have. And Solomon asked for wisdom. I am happy if a ruler is a good man, but I would rather he were wise.'

'You do not think many kings are wise?'

'Not that I have observed.'

Jacob could see that the conversation had saddened his daughter, and he was sorry for it. But he wasn't going to lie to her.

Looking back, however, he sometimes wondered whether he'd been wrong to speak to her so frankly on that day. Had this been the start of that disillusion that was to lead to tragedy?

It might be so. But there had been no sign of it for more than a year after that.

During that time King Philip of France, as usual, had been trying to raise money. He'd tried all the usual expedients. He'd taxed the Jews. He'd even debased his own coinage. But nothing had been enough. So he'd tried another ruse, sudden and unexpected.

'We'll tax the clergy,' he declared.

There had been an uproar. The bishops had protested. The pope himself had told King Philip to remove the tax at once.

'Why did he do it?' Naomi had asked.

'The simple answer is because the Church has so much money,' her father replied. 'Perhaps a third of the entire wealth of France is owned by the Church.'

'But the Church doesn't pay taxes?'

'The Church may make a voluntary contribution to the king. But it is exempt from the usual taxes.'

'Because the Church serves God.'

'This is the idea.' He paused. 'But you must also understand that there is more at stake. It's a question of power.'

'Please explain to me.'

'It's been going on a long time. Essentially, because they say they represent the divine power, the Church claims that it is a heavenly kingdom, not subject to earthly kings. That's why there are Church courts, which often let people in Holy Orders off with a light penance for crimes that might lead to execution if they were ordinary folk. We see this in Paris every day, and many people resent it.'

'The students at the university are protected in this way.'

'Exactly. And at the highest level, popes have sometimes claimed that monarchs should answer to them for their kingdoms. A pope might even try to depose a king. As you can imagine, this idea is not popular with kings, even the most pious ones.'

'I did not realise it went so far.'

'It depends on the pope. Some popes have more lust for power than others.'

'But are they not acting for God?'

'That's the idea.' He considered. 'The great cathedral of Notre-Dame is a monument to God, is it not?'

'Yes, Father.'

'You know, there was a cathedral there before the present one. But the great Bishop Sully said that the old church was not big enough, and so he built it again, in the new style. It cost a fortune.'

'It is very fine.'

'Yes. But do you know that Bishop Sully also told a lie. The old church was almost the same size. But Sully wanted something more splendid, so that Paris would be proud, and men would say, "Look what the great Bishop Sully built." To the glory of God, of course.'

'And your point is?'

'Two things may be true at the same time. The Church is there to bring men to God. But bishops and popes are men, like kings. They experience the same passions. In the old days, the days of Saint Denis, for instance, when Christians were persecuted, as Jews are now, their faith was probably more pure. But now that the Church is rich and powerful, there will be some corruption. I think it's inevitable.'

Naomi looked down thoughtfully for a few moments. Then she turned her blue eyes on him.

'If the Church is corrupt, Father, why did you leave your faith to join it?'

He stared at her, taken aback. She had never asked him this question before. Of course, when he had first converted, he had given the expected reason – that Christ was indeed the Messiah that good Jews had been waiting for. And he had often pointed out to his children, at appropriate times during the year, how closely the Christian Church was following this or that aspect of the original Jewish faith. But beyond that, the subject was never discussed. He was sure that Sarah had seen to that.

So had Naomi been brooding about it all these years? It sounded as if she had. And was this the moment of reckoning, when he should tell her the truth? 'I converted to save your skin, and that of your brother, and your mother and, yes, my own as well.' Could he say that? He dare not. She was still a girl.

'Because I believe Jesus Christ was the Messiah,' he said. 'You know this, Naomi.'

She continued to stare at him, but said nothing more, neither then nor for many months. Whatever her feelings, she kept them to herself. He hoped it was because she loved him.

And perhaps she might have kept silent forever – who could tell? – had it not been for an extraordinary event that took place in 1305, when Naomi was fifteen.

The dispute between King Philip and the pope remained at a furious stalemate until, quite suddenly, the pope had obligingly died. Within months his elderly successor had followed him to the grave

– poisoned, probably. A new election was to take place in Rome, and Parisians waited to see whether the next pope would be any more friendly towards their master. The election was delayed. Word came that there was confusion in the Holy City.

It was mid-afternoon on a day in June when Renard arrived at Jacob's house. The little family were all there.

'I believe I am first with the news,' he declared. And seeing this to be the case, he quickly continued. 'We have a new pope. Can you guess who it is? The bishop of Bordeaux.'

'He's not even a cardinal!' Jacob cried.

'No. But he's French. He's King Philip's man. Our king must have been working behind the scenes.'

Kings often tried to influence papal elections, to get a pope who'd favour them, but this was an extreme case.

'He's just a puppet,' said Jacob.

'Then listen to the most extraordinary news of all. The new pope is not going to live in Rome.'

'Not at the Vatican?'

'He won't even be crowned in Rome. They'll do it in Burgundy. After that he's moving the papal court to Poitiers, right here in the domains of the King of France. There is talk of his moving down to Avignon in a year or two, but not to Rome. As of today, King Philip of France owns the papacy.'

He left them soon afterwards to spread the news. When he had gone, Jacob shook his head.

'In time of danger, popes have sometimes left Rome before,' he remarked, 'but this . . . I don't know what to say.'

Sarah's face was a mask.

Then Naomi spoke.

'I'm not surprised at all.' She looked steadily at her father. 'The Church is corrupt. You have told me so yourself. I don't think the Church has anything to do with God at all. In fact, it disgusts me.'

'Don't speak to your father like that,' said Sarah sharply.

But Jacob was not angry. He was grieved.

'You must be careful what you say, Naomi,' he said quietly. 'Such words are dangerous. And for a convert, they are more than dangerous.'

'I am not a convert,' Naomi cried bitterly. 'It was you who made me a Christian.'

'But you are a Christian now. No one, not even a servant in this house, must hear you say such a thing. It could place us all in great danger.'

Naomi was silent for a moment.

'I will say nothing,' she answered. 'But now you know what I think, Father, and that will never change.' Then she went out of the room.

What could he do? There was nothing he could do. He understood her feelings. In many ways he shared them. She was shocked at the corruption. So was he.

And she was young. By the time she reached his age, she might accept that the best to be hoped for were small adjustments to an imperfect world. But for the time being, her mind was made up, and he must respect it.

He was grateful also that she kept her promise not to reveal her feelings. She went about her daily business, helping her mother, in her usual quiet and cheerful way. She accompanied her family to church without complaint. She still joined him when he told stories to little Jacob, and she even started to teach the child to read and write herself. He would have preferred to reserve this task for himself, but he was pleased if it gave her an occupation, especially in the dark winter months.

For her greatest pleasure was to go out. She took little Jacob for a walk each day. Whenever her father went out to his orchard, she would always gladly accompany him. She would walk across to the Île de la Cité and light a candle in Notre-Dame. And since these visits appeared to the world as acts of religious devotion, her father did not discourage them.

'I think it helps her to get out of the house,' he remarked to Sarah.

And so their family life continued quietly, through the winter and into the spring. As the weather grew warmer, Naomi was able to walk a little longer. One day, she told him, she had crossed over to the Left Bank and visited the lovely Church of Saint-Séverin. With the warmer weather, her mood also seemed to lighten. Perhaps she had got over her shock of the previous year.

'The time is approaching,' Jacob said to his wife one day, 'when we may have to start thinking about a husband for her. As long,' he added uncertainly, 'as she isn't going to start airing her views on the pope to any prospective husband.'

The visit from the rabbi came in the middle of June. He arrived at Jacob's house a little before noon. Naomi was out with her little brother.

The rabbi had put on weight in the last few years. He sat down heavily on the bench in Jacob's counting house.

'What can I do for you?' Jacob asked warily.

'What can you do for me?' The rabbi stared at him. 'What can you not do for me?' He sighed, and shook his head. 'You do not know why I have come to your house?'

'I do not.'

'The wise man does not know.' He nodded. 'I am a fool!' he burst out suddenly. And then, very quietly: 'But I know.'

Jacob waited.

'Your daughter, Naomi, goes walking by herself quite often,' the rabbi continued.

'Yes. What of it?'

'Where does she walk?'

'It depends. Sometimes to Notre-Dame, or some other church.'

'And what does she do when she gets there?'

'Lights a candle. It is the custom. What is this to you?'

'Because your daughter does not walk to Notre-Dame. She walks to other places.'

'Where does she walk?'

'She can walk to Aquitaine for all I care! But she is walking with my son Aaron. That is why I am here.'

Aaron. Her childhood friend. A stocky boy, some years older than Naomi. Nothing special. Jacob hadn't given him a thought in years.

So Naomi's outburst had caused her to start seeing her Jewish childhood friends again. He could understand her doing so, but it was not wise, especially to be seen in the streets with the rabbi's son. It could give rise to misinterpretation. He wondered what other Jews she might have seen, and what she might have said to them.

'I did not know this. I will tell her she should not meet him any more.' He almost reached out his hand to touch the rabbi's arm, but decided not to, instead giving him what he hoped was a conciliatory smile. 'I am sure Aaron is a good young man. But in our situation . . .' He shrugged sadly. 'Their old friendship is no longer wise.'

'You have not understood,' said the rabbi. 'They want to get married.'

'Married?'

'Yes, Jacob ben Jacob. Married. Your daughter wants to return to the faith of her fathers. She wants to marry my son and be a Jew again.'

Jacob gazed at him. Then he bowed his head.

So. She had deceived him. Completely. For a moment it was like a blow to the pit of his stomach. He sagged forward.

She had turned away from him. She was no longer his. Did her mother know? Had his whole family secretly deserted him? He took a deep breath.

She was young. He must remember this. She might read and write, and think for herself, and show wisdom. But she was still young, and probably in love. He told himself this quickly, before the pain grew too great to bear.

'You are sure of this?' he asked, without looking up.

'Yes. My son has spoken to me.'

'Such a thing is impossible.'

'Of course it is impossible.'

'Does she not realise that this would put her whole family in danger? My own conversion would be questioned.'

'Your family?' The rabbi leaned forward, and began to speak, in a low voice that was intense with anger. 'Less than thirty years ago, Jacob ben Jacob, a Christian in Brittany converted to Judaism. Such a thing is very rare. We do not encourage it. But it happens. And when that convert died, he was buried as a Jew, in the Jewish cemetery. And do you know what the Inquisition did? They burned the rabbi at the stake. Because he let that man die a Jew, when he should have been buried in Christian, consecrated ground. Does this make sense? Not to me. But that is what they did.' He paused. 'So what will happen to me and my family if the Inquisition says that we are stealing a Christian convert back to Judaism? Who can tell? But for taking your daughter's soul into our evil clutches, they will probably burn me and my son as well. Our risk is not less than yours, Jacob. It is greater.'

'What have you told your son?'

'That I forbid him even to think of it.'

'And what does he say?'

'That he will marry no one else. I told him: "Then you will marry no one." ' The rabbi threw up his hands. 'He thinks that they can go to live in another city where they are not known. Arrive there as a married couple. This is foolishness. I have told him no. But . . . I don't know what they may do.'

'You don't think . . .?'

'That there is a child on the way? No. Thank God. He says they have not . . . But we had better be careful. You must lock your daughter up, Jacob, to stop this madness.'

'It is what I will do,' he said.

He tried to reason with her first.

'My child, do you think I do not understand?' he cried. 'When you are in love, the skies open, you think you see angels. Everything seems possible. But there are darker forces at work in the world, and I am trying to protect you from them.'

She listened to him. But when he asked her to promise never to see the young man again, she would not do it. And even if she had, he wasn't sure he would have believed her.

From that day, despite all her protests, Naomi was kept in the house. She could not even take her little brother for a walk. Jacob told her that she could come out with him, if she wished. But she refused, because she would not speak to him.

Though he was under close watch himself, Aaron tried to see her, and three times tried to sneak a letter in to her. But Jacob and the rabbi managed to prevent all these attempts from succeeding.

In the home, the atmosphere was tense. Jacob was not sure how long the family could continue to live like this.

'I have men with whom I do business in other cities,' he suggested to Sarah. 'Perhaps she could go and live with another family for a while.'

'And what might she do then? Will you have them keep her under lock and key?'

There seemed no solution to the problem. A month passed. In the Jewish calendar, they came to the fast day of Tisha B'Av.

King Philip the Fair was both ruthless and efficient. He'd shown it in getting a pope of his own. Now, on the twenty-second day of July, in the year of Our Lord 1306, which was the day following the Jewish fast of Tisha B'Av, he showed it again.

The preparations had been immaculate. No word of his intentions had leaked out. Renard the merchant had heard nothing. Every street, every house was known. The cordons were ready and moved into place during the night. And at dawn, his men struck.

The success was total. Every Jew in Paris was arrested. They, their wives, their children. Not a one was missed. By early morning they had been marched through the streets to the awaiting jails. There they were given the news.

They were to leave France at once. They might take with them the clothes on their backs and the paltry sum of twelve sous. Everything else was forfeit, to the king.

In the middle of the morning, Jacob met Renard in the street. They looked at each other.

'It came after all, then,' said Renard quietly.

'Yes.' There was no need to say more.

By mid-afternoon, much was known. The same thing had happened in every town in France where there was a Jewish community. They were to leave every territory that King Philip controlled. The usual reasons were given for the arrests – the Jews' religion, their practice of usury – but nobody was fooled for an instant. Jacob was in a group of merchants whom a royal councillor addressed in the market of Les Halles.

'None of the debt owed to the Jews is to be forgiven,' the man explained. 'Those debts are now the property of the king, and he will insist on their being honoured to the full.' This was not popular. But the next piece of news brought groans. 'Further, all debts must be repaid in the coinage in use at the time they were contracted. The king will insist upon it.'

This was devious. King Philip had just issued large quantities of clipped coinage. Clearly, he had no desire to be paid in his own debased currency.

The expulsion of the Jews from France was simple and straightforward. It was a confiscation of the entire assets of the financial community in order to pay the king's debts.

It took a couple of months to complete. The last Jews of Paris didn't leave until early October. During this time, Naomi was kept indoors, and Aaron was kept on a tight leash by the rabbi. At the start of September, Jacob heard that the rabbi and his family had gone.

For Jacob, the great expulsion brought horror. Horror at what was being done to his people.

True, he also felt vindicated. He could turn to Sarah and say: 'This is why I converted. This is what I feared.' The pain he had put his family through had not been in vain. He had indeed saved them.

But at what price in guilt? Every day, as more Jews left Paris, people would watch them go. But not Jacob. He kept away. He didn't want to see. Above all, he feared that they might look at him. For he couldn't have met their eyes.

And then, God forgive him, it also brought relief. Relief that the rabbi's son was leaving.

Where were the Jews of France going? Over the eastern border into Lorraine; or into Burgundy, or farther south. Or they might journey towards Italy, up into the Alpine territory of Savoy. But wherever they went, young Aaron and his family were gone. That danger, at least, was past. Life could begin anew.

Or could it? The first few days were difficult. Naomi wanted to follow Aaron. She said so plainly. And though he sympathised, Jacob could not help feeling a little aggrieved.

'She knows the danger for her family,' he protested to Sarah.

'She thinks it could be avoided. Aaron would be out of France. She thinks we could say she'd been sent to live with some merchant in another city.'

'These things get discovered. The risks are too great. She should know this.'

'She thinks it because she wants it to be true.'

'What would they live off anyway? Aaron has no money now,' Jacob pointed out sadly. 'The king's completely ruined them.'

'He'll be a rabbi. They always manage to live.'

'Well, she can't follow him, anyway,' said Jacob, 'because she doesn't know where he's gone.' And this was true.

But by winter, Jacob knew. He'd taken trouble to find out.

Aaron was far away, up in the mountains of Savoy.

If Naomi had been angry at first, after a time her temper subsided into moodiness. She was allowed once again to take little Jacob for walks, which she did listlessly. Often Jacob would come upon her sitting with her brother by the fire, but while the boy chattered, she would be staring off into space.

Jacob and Sarah both suspected that Naomi might be hoping to receive some word from Aaron, and they watched carefully to intercept any such message. But as far as they could tell, no message arrived.

December came and went. There was ice in the streets. Snow fell. And in those dark days of the year, their daughter seemed to be wrapped in a mantle of sadness.

They tried to behave as normal. They did their best to be quietly cheerful in her presence. Jacob told stories in the evening, as they all sat together, and she seemed to enjoy them. If he recounted some foolish joke he'd heard in the market, she would laugh quite easily. But as grey January began, he could see little joy in her face, but only resignation.

One day, returning home from some business, he saw her sitting on a bench by the fire. She was alone. She must have heard him come in, but she did not turn, as though silently letting him know that she wanted to be left alone. And he was about to go into his counting house, but then, thinking better of it, he quietly entered and sat on the bench beside her. He did not say anything, but observed the sad curve of her neck and the way she stared with stony eyes at the embers of the fire. And after a time he put his arm around her tense shoulders and said: 'I am so sorry, my child.'

She said nothing. But she did not draw away.

'I know you are unhappy,' he continued quietly. 'I am sorry that you wanted to leave us, but I understand.'

After a pause, she answered.

'The truth is, Father, that I no longer wish to live in a land where they do such things.'

'Ah.' He sighed. 'Aaron's father once told me, "You will never be safe." He may have been right. Whoever is born a Jew is never safe, no matter where he goes.'

'Why are we Christian, Father?' she asked.

And then, because it seemed to him at that moment to be the right thing to do, he quietly told her everything. He told her about Renard's warning, and his agony over what to do, and how he had feared for Sarah, the unborn baby, and herself; how he had converted, and the agony it had brought him. He told her everything.

'I may have been wrong, my child, but that is what I did and why. And now I have caused you great pain, which was never my intention, and I am sorry for it.'

When he had finished, she was very still, and he wondered if he had made her angry.

'I did not know,' she said at last.

'There was so much danger, I did not dare to tell you. I wondered sometimes if your mother had.'

'No.' She shook her head. 'Nothing.'

He had removed his arm from her shoulder while he spoke. Now he put his two hands together in his lap, and stared into the fire himself.

Then he felt her put her arm around his neck and as he turned towards her, she rested her head against his shoulder.

'I understand, Father, that you did what you thought you must.'

'I hope you do,' he replied.

'You know that I shall always love you, don't you?' she said.

He turned to look at her, and she smiled.

'Always,' she said. 'You are the best father in the world. Didn't you know?'

He could not answer, but he took her hand and squeezed it, and her words meant more to him, almost, than even the birth of his son.

From that day, she seemed to be less sad. Life began to return to its usual pattern. As spring began, Jacob asked Sarah if she thought they might begin to think about a husband for her again.

'Wait a little,' she advised.

'I leave it in your hands,' he wisely said.

At the end of May, Sarah told him, 'I think she is ready.' And a few days later, Naomi herself remarked to him quite casually: 'I am in no hurry to marry, Father, but when the time comes, I wonder if we should consider the Renard boy. I trust him and he has always been my friend.'

Jacob needed no further bidding. The very next day, seeing Renard walking along the street, he fell into step beside him. After a few pleasantries he remarked what a fine young fellow Renard's eldest son had become.

'I'm pleased with the way that Naomi's turning out as well,' he added.

They walked on a few more paces before Renard turned to look at him.

The two men showed their ages in very different ways. What little hair was left on Jacob's head was grey. Renard by contrast, like many redheads, had kept all his hair, and showed little sign of ageing at all. Only the deep, long lines that ran down his face like gullies betrayed his years.

'She's a beautiful girl,' he remarked. 'I should think you'll be looking for a husband for her soon.'

'Yes,' said Jacob.

'I remember so well,' Renard continued quietly, 'those days when you converted.'

'I owe it all to you.'

'Naomi would have been about nine at that time.'

'Indeed.'

'How did she take it, then – and later?'

'Well . . .' Jacob hadn't expected this question. 'She's an obedient girl, so she didn't question her father's judgement. And it's been so long now. All her friends are Christian. Her brother, of course, has been a Christian since birth.' It wasn't quite an honest answer, but it was the best that he could make.

Renard nodded thoughtfully.

'You know my affection for you and your family, Jacob. I'm glad of what I did to help you, and I would do it all again. But a marriage goes beyond that. My son loves your daughter as a friend. He will be her friend all his life. But he is also devout. Not all Christians are devout, God knows. But he is. Whoever marries my son will need to be devout. She cannot harbour any doubts.'

'Of course my daughter has no doubts,' Jacob said quickly. 'None at all.'

They both knew it was a lie, but that he had to say it.

'We must speak of this again some time,' the red-haired merchant suggested as he left him. But they both knew that they never would.

'I never thought he was so devout,' remarked Naomi, when her father told her about the conversation.

'Perhaps he isn't,' said Jacob quietly.

But he was not discouraged. By the end of the summer he had begun serious negotiations with the merchants who had expressed interest before, and two other new candidates also came forward. By the end of September, he was able to present his daughter with as good a set of choices as any girl could reasonably hope for. For her part, Naomi gradually entered into the spirit of the thing. Indeed, by the time he showed her the final list, she'd become quite cheerful, and appeared to find the process amusing.

'I'd like to have a little time now, Father. Two of the choices I hardly know yet. Could I have a month or two?'

'Of course,' he answered with a smile. 'Let us decide by Christmas.'

On Tuesday the eleventh of October, Jacob was down in the Grève market on the riverbank when he happened to see Renard. The two men chatted for a little while. And Renard was just departing when he casually remarked: 'Do you remember Aaron, the rabbi's son?'

'Certainly,' Jacob replied.

'Do you know, I could have sworn I saw him in the street yesterday. I don't suppose it was him. But if he's sneaked back into Paris, he'd better be careful. He could get arrested.'

Jacob stared at him in horror, but quickly recovered himself.

'I should think it's unlikely,' he said, with a shake of the head. 'He'd be a fool if he did come back.'

But the moment Renard was out of sight, he hurried out of the market at once.

'Where's Naomi?' he cried, as he burst into the house. Sarah told him she'd just returned from a walk with her little brother. 'She's here?' he demanded.

'She went out again. She's gone to that stall she likes in the rue Saint-Honoré, to buy some ribbon,' her mother replied. 'I'm sure she'll be back soon.

Then, in low tones, Jacob quickly told her about Aaron.

'Not a word to anyone,' he cautioned. 'Nobody must know. Go to the ribbon stall and see if you can find her. Then come back and meet me here.' Meanwhile he went to saddle his horse.

Sarah didn't find her. Within the hour, Jacob was on his way. He crossed the river to the Left Bank and took the rue Saint-Jacques, the pilgrims' path, that led towards the south. If they had started for Savoy, they would probably have gone that way.

And now, two days later, he knew he had lost her. Naomi's cunning letter made that quite clear. For a long time, he stared at the shining carpet of mist over Paris. The rising sun was starting to strike the towers of Notre-Dame, making them gleam.

He started to read the letter again.

It wasn't long. After some expressions of affection, she announced that she had news that she knew must cause them sorrow. She thanked her father for offering her such a fine collection of worthy suitors, and allowing her to choose a husband from among them. But now she must make a confession. She loved another.

> I love another. He is a good young man, but I know he would not be acceptable to you, for he has no fortune. He comes from Aquitaine, where his father is a miller. He came to Paris as a servant in a nobleman's household. But now he is returning to Aquitaine. And I go with him.
>
> I am his woman. We shall marry when we reach his home. He has promised it.
>
> Do not try to follow us. It is too late for that. But you shall hear from me again, once we are married. Until then, I beg your forgiveness, my dear parents.

He could not fault the letter's cleverness. There was not a word about Aaron, the Jewish boy. The miller's son was obviously Christian. Of course, he didn't believe in the existence of this boy from Aquitaine for a moment. But any outsider to whom the letter was shown would

147

see no reason to doubt it. All they'd see was that she'd run off with a poor boy. She was already living with him in sin. She'd disgraced herself and her family. Such things happened.

Nor was there any hint that she might have gone to Savoy. Just a false trail to Aquitaine.

Once or twice, he still asked himself if there mightn't be a chance of recovering her. What if he brought her back and married her to one of the eligible young men he'd chosen for her? But he knew it was useless. If Naomi was determined to run away with Aaron, then she was never going to settle down with a Christian boy, even if he led her to the altar in chains.

To make it believable, he'd probably tell a few friends what had happened, and set out for Aquitaine where, of course, he would not find her. Nor would any letter come from her. People would suppose that something had happened to her and her lover on the way, or that the young man had jilted her, and she was too ashamed to return to her parents.

He'd apologise to the families with whom he'd been negotiating her betrothal. He'd probably show them the letter. They'd hear about it anyway.

It would be highly embarrassing. But yes, he thought sadly, it would probably work.

For another hour, he paced about in his orchard, going over the thing this way and that, glancing from time to time at the city below, where the mist was gradually thinning and the houses beginning to emerge.

After that, he decided to return home. Out of force of habit, he followed the path that he and Naomi always took, which led down the slope and into the city past the great fortress of the Temple Knights. There were still some wreaths of mist where the ground fell away beside the lane, but he could see the fort's walls clearly enough from some distance.

He was about a hundred paces from the Temple's gateway when he saw the crowd. He wondered what it could mean. Then he noticed a gleam of swords and armour, and saw that a cart was emerging from the gate.

Was this a bullion shipment setting off? He drew closer. There was something odd about the cavalcade ahead of him, but he couldn't decide what it was. Another fifty paces, and he realised. The mounted men were not Templars. They were the king's men-at-arms. There was also a troop of men following the cart. They weren't armed, though. Some of them looked as if they were only half-dressed. As he stared, he saw that they were shackled together with chains. It seemed to him that he had seen some of their faces before. Then he realised.

They were Templars. Knights Templar. In chains.

'What is happening?' he asked a fellow in the crowd before the gateway.

'The Templars are being arrested.'

'Which Templars?'

'All of them. Every Templar in France. In all Christendom, I believe.'

'By whose orders?'

'King's orders. And the pope's.' The man grinned. 'Same thing these days, isn't it, now that our king owns the pope.' The fellow seemed rather proud that France now controlled the Holy Father.

'Upon what charge?'

'All kinds of crimes. They read the proclamation not an hour ago. Loose living, heresy, sacrificing to idols, magic arts, sodomy . . . You name it. They've done it all.'

'Heresy? Sodomy?' The Templars, sitting on their stupendous fortune, were often said to eat too well and drink too much nowadays. Jacob suspected people said this because they were jealous. And what if it were true? So did half the monks in Christendom. But sacrificing to idols? Magic arts? These other charges were clearly absurd. Jacob had no particular love of the Templars, but his sense of justice was outraged. 'Is there evidence?' he asked.

'There will be.' The fellow laughed. 'The Inquisition will see to that. After they've been tortured. You know the way of it.' They were going to torture the Templars, like common criminals. Like heretics. 'Once they've burned a few at the stake,' the man continued cheerfully, 'they'll talk.'

'But what about all their forts, and their money?' Jacob asked. 'What's to become of them?'

'Forfeit. The whole lot. They're bust, from dawn today.' This thought seemed to give the fellow particular satisfaction. 'These

Templars and their damned Crusades. They cost us a fortune and achieve nothing.' He shrugged. 'Look at Saint Louis.'

So impressed had the papacy been by the piety of King Louis IX of France that ten years ago the builder of the Sainte-Chapelle, and supporter of the Inquisition, had been canonised as a saint.

'He went on crusade,' the man went on. 'Got himself captured. And we, the people of France, had to pay his ransom. And all for what? He had nothing to show for his stupid war, and most of his troops died of disease. Damn the crusaders and damn the Templars who support them – that's what I say.'

Jacob knew that most Parisians nowadays would agree. But behind this attack on the Templars, he realised, was a simpler and more brutal truth. By disbanding the order, the king had just cancelled all his debts to them.

The heresy, the immorality and the arrests were all a screen. With the pope and the Inquisition in his pocket, King Philip the Fair was going to torture and burn God knows how many unfortunate men to get their bogus confessions. Every instrument of Holy Church was to be used. And all for what? To plunder the bullion of the Templars, and to renege upon his debts.

The expulsion of the Jews had been bad enough, but for the king to turn upon his own Christian soldiers, it seemed to Jacob, showed a cynicism that, in its way, filled him with an even deeper disgust.

There was no loyalty, no mercy, no interest in truth, nor thought of justice. There was no respect for God. There was nothing.

When he got home, Jacob told Sarah what he had seen. Then he went into his counting house and closed the door. He did not emerge all day.

In the evening his wife came in.

'Will you not eat something, Jacob?'

'I'm not hungry.' He stared at the table.

Sarah sat on the small wooden chair he used for visitors. She didn't say anything, but she rested her hand on his. After a while, Jacob spoke again.

'Naomi said she didn't want to live in a land with such a king. She blamed me for converting.'

'She is young.'

'She was right. I shouldn't have converted.' He was still staring at the table.

'You did what you thought was for the best.'

'You know' – he looked up at her now – 'I have no problem with the Christian doctrine of love. It's wonderful. I embrace it.' He shook his head. 'The trouble with the Christians is that they say one thing, and do something completely different.'

'The king is corrupt. The Church is corrupt. We know this.'

'Yes, I know this.' He was silent for a long moment. 'But if they are corrupt, then I am corrupt also.'

'What would you do? Stand before the king and curse him like one of the prophets of old?'

'Yes,' he cried, with sudden passion. 'Yes, that is what I should do, just as the prophets of my forefathers did in ancient times.' He threw up his hands. 'This, no doubt, is what I should do,' he added sadly.

'And what are you going to do?' Sarah gently asked her husband.

Jacob paused for a while.

'I have an idea,' he said at last.

Within a week all Paris knew. The lovely daughter of Jacob the merchant had run away with a poor miller's son. It was a humiliation. His family was dishonoured. But one had to respect his reaction.

For Jacob the merchant was leaving Paris. He, with his wife and son, were setting forth for Aquitaine, where it was believed the couple were, and would not rest until Jacob had seen his daughter properly married in church. Then it was their hope to return to Paris where, if the young man was up to it, Jacob would take him into his business.

Not many fathers would have done it. They'd have cast their daughter out. But it was generally agreed that he was showing a truly Christian spirit.

The luckiest person in all this, people also said, was the miller's son. He was going to get an heiress for his trouble.

'If only I'd known,' joked one of the eligible suitors for Naomi's hand, 'I'd have run away with her myself.'

It took Jacob ten days to close up his business and put his affairs in order. The merchant guild wished him a safe return. The royal authorities gave him a travel pass and wished him luck.

In the last week of October, in the year of Our Lord 1307, Jacob the merchant set out in a horse and cart, taking the rue Saint-Jacques, the old pilgrim's road that led up the hill past the university. Before passing through the gate, Jacob paused.

'Look back at the city,' he said to his son. 'I shall never see it again, but perhaps you will one day. In better times.'

A week later, they reached Orléans.

Two days after that, however, instead of continuing south-west towards Aquitaine, they took another road that led them eastward. Journeying south and east by stages they continued for another two weeks until they passed into Burgundy. And then they travelled for another ten days until finally, looking eastward early one morning, Jacob said to his son: 'What do you see in the distance?'

'I see mountains, whose peaks are covered with snow,' he answered.

'Those are the mountains of Savoy,' his father said.

By the time he reached them, he would be a Jew again.

And feeling a great weight of corruption and fear fall from his shoulders at last, he murmured the words he had missed for so long.

' "Hear O Israel: the Lord our God, the Lord is One." '

Chapter Seven

1887

They were all furious with him. Madame Michel was not speaking to his parents. As for Berthe, no one knew what she thought.

And how could he explain? He hadn't liked Berthe so much, nor her mother's business. He thought only of working on Monsieur Eiffel's tower. But even if his parents understood, he wasn't sure how much they'd care. His mother pursed her lips. His father looked glum. As well they might, having hoped he was going to feed them.

'I suppose,' his father once suggested, 'you could still be an ironworker and marry Berthe.'

'I don't think so,' said Thomas.

'The girl goes with the business,' said his mother simply. 'It's obvious.'

'You'll just have to find another rich girl,' said Luc with a grin, but everyone ignored him.

So it was partly to escape his family for a while that, within a week of starting work on the tower, Thomas made an announcement.

'I think I'd better get lodgings closer to my work.'

'It's only an hour's walk,' his father pointed out.

'More than that. And the hours are long. Monsieur Eiffel's got less than two years to build the tower.'

'You'll be paying rent to someone instead of bringing the money home,' his mother said quietly.

'Just while I'm working across the river.'

He was being selfish and he knew it. Nobody said anything.

He found the lodgings without much difficulty.

In almost every house and apartment building in Paris, up in the roof, there was a warren of servants' rooms, some of them garrets with windows, others hardly more than wooden-walled closets. Those not being used by servants could be let out by their owners to poor folk.

An advertisement led Thomas to the house of an elderly gentleman who lived alone, with only a single servant, across the river from the building site on an ancient street named the rue de la Pompe, which worked its way up towards the avenue Victor Hugo. Having given proof that he was respectably employed on Monsieur Eiffel's great project, Thomas was able to rent a tiny attic room with creaking floorboards, just enough space for a mattress on the floor, and a small round window through which he could look out at the surrounding rooftops. The old man asked a peppercorn rent, and it was only a short walk to the Pont d'Iéna, which gave straight on to the building site.

After that, Thomas went to see his parents every Sunday, and always gave his mother any spare money that he could.

Every morning, when he came on to the site, Thomas felt a sense of pride. As everyone knew from the newspapers, it was only three years since, in America, the 555-foot Washington Monument had surpassed the ancient pyramids and the medieval spires of Europe to become the tallest building in the world. But Monsieur Eiffel's tower wouldn't just beat the record. It was going to soar to almost twice that height – a triumph for France.

Yet the site was strangely quiet, almost deserted. In the huge open space, the tower's four mighty feet looked like the stumps of some vanished fortress in the desert. And as the four spread legs of the tower began to grow from those feet, with the workmen up in the iron girders, the ground below was often nearly empty.

'Why is there nobody here?' a visitor once asked Thomas.

'Because Monsieur Eiffel is a genius,' Thomas proudly replied. 'There are only a hundred and twenty of us workmen on the site at any one time. And we alone build the tower.'

Prefabrication. This was how it was done.

Out at the factory lay the network of girders, in their prefabricated sections fifteen feet long and weighing no more than three tons. Each day, the huge horse-drawn wagons would arrive at the site with just enough sections for that day's work. Big, steam-powered cranes would lift the sections up into position, and under the watchful eye of their foreman, Jean Compagnon, Thomas and his fellow workers – the flyers, as they were proudly called – would swing their hammers on to the hot rivets to fix them in place.

'The precision is astounding,' he told his family. 'Every piece fits exactly, every hole is drilled to perfection. I never have to pause in my work.' He grinned. 'The whole tower will go up like clockwork. It has to,' he added. 'The exhibition starts in eighteen months.'

Soon after he began work on the site, he took his brother, Luc, around it, and showed him how everything was organised. Luc was much impressed.

'And how's your head for heights?' Luc asked him.

'No problem,' Thomas told him. 'None at all.'

The foreman of the flyers, Jean Compagnon, was a sturdy workman who looked like a battle-hardened sergeant. His watchful eyes missed nothing. But Monsieur Eiffel himself was also on-site most days. Thomas took care never to interrupt the great man, but if Eiffel saw the young worker, he'd always give him a friendly nod.

As the huge lower legs began to grow, upward and inward, it appeared as if the tower's four feet were the corners of a vast iron pyramid. Day after day the sections went in. By the end of August, the legs were over forty feet high.

Early one evening, as he was looking at the progress before going home, Thomas heard a voice at his side.

'Well, young Gascon, are you enjoying being a flyer?'

'Oh yes, Monsieur Eiffel. It's so well organised, monsieur.'

'Thank you.' Eiffel smiled. 'I've done my best.'

'But I suppose this is the easy part,' Thomas ventured. 'When we get higher . . .'

'Not at all, young man. This is the hardest part, I assure you.' Eiffel pointed to the rising legs that sloped in towards the centre. 'Those legs are inclined at an angle of fifty-four degrees. Does anything strike you about them?'

'Well . . .' Thomas didn't like to say. But the great man nodded encouragingly. 'Won't they fall over?' he finally dared to ask.

'Exactly. They will fall over, I calculate, on the tenth day of October. To be precise, when they reach a height of ninety-two feet.' He smiled. 'But they will not fall over, my young friend, because we shall prop them up with big wooden pylons. You have seen the flying buttresses of Notre-Dame?'

'*Oui, monsieur.*'

'They will look a bit like that, only they will be inside the legs. Then we shall continue to build the legs up to the height of the first huge platform, which will hold them all together. That will be at a height of one hundred and eighty-two feet. And it will be necessary to put scaffolding under the middle of the platform while we build it, of course.' He paused. 'It's not easy to do all that, I assure you.'

'I understand, monsieur.'

'Then comes something rather special. I have to make sure that the platform is absolutely, and perfectly, level. How to do that, young Monsieur Gascon? Give it a shove?'

'I don't know, monsieur.'

'Then I will tell you.' He pointed to one of the tower's four great feet. 'Under each foot is a system of pistons, operated by compressed water, which allows me to make minute and subtle adjustments to the height and angle of each leg in three dimensions. Surveyors will take the most careful measurements.' He gave a broad grin. 'Then I'll go up and check with a spirit level.'

'*Oui*, Monsieur Eiffel.'

'Any other questions?'

'I have one, monsieur.' Thomas pointed to the great cranes that hoisted the girders up into position. 'Those cranes will go only so high. Nowhere near the height to which we're building. When we get to the height of the cranes, what happens after that?'

'Bravo, young man! Excellent question.'

Thomas politely waited.

'You'll see,' the great man said.

It was already growing dark as he crossed the Pont d'Iéna to the Right Bank. Ahead of him, on the slope overlooking the bridge, stood the strange, moorish-looking Trocadéro concert hall, built a decade ago for the last World's Fair.

Thomas smiled to himself as he passed this exotic palace. Ten minutes later he was at his lodgings. But he didn't go in. He was feeling hungry. If he walked for another five minutes up the rue de la Pompe to where it crossed Victor Hugo, there was a little bar where he could get a steak and some *haricots verts*. He'd earned it.

Still feeling rather cheerful, he trudged contentedly along. On his right he came to the railings of the Lycée Janson de Sailly, and this made him smile again.

All Paris knew the story of the grand new school that had recently opened on the rue de la Pompe. The rich lawyer whose name it bore had discovered his wife had a lover. His revenge had been sweet. He had disinherited her, and left his entire fortune, down to the last sou, to build a school – for boys only! Though the lycée had only just opened, it was already fashionable. Thomas wondered cheerfully what had become of the widow.

There was still a glow of gas lights coming through the windows. No doubt the cleaners were finishing their work. As he watched, he saw the lights starting to go out. He paused.

Why did he pause? There was no reason at all, really. Just idle curiosity, to see the cleaners come out.

A moment later they did. Two women, one old, one younger, though he couldn't see their faces. The older one crossed the street. The younger turned up it. He continued walking. He came level as she reached a lamp outside a doorway. He glanced at her. And stopped dead in his tracks.

It was the girl from the funeral. It had been so long since their brief encounter that he'd almost put her out of his mind. He'd wondered if he'd even recognise her. Yet now that he saw her, even in the lamp-light, he hadn't the slightest doubt. He'd looked all over Paris for her, and here she was, hardly a mile from where he'd first seen her.

She was a few paces in front of him now. He drew level again. She looked across sharply.

'Have you been following me?'

'No. I was walking up the street when you came out of the lycée.'

'Keep walking, then.'

'In that case, you will be following me,' he said cleverly.

'I don't think so.'

'I will do as you ask, but first I have to tell you something. We have met before.'

'No we haven't.'

'You were at the funeral of Victor Hugo.'

She shrugged.

'And?'

157

'You were in the front row, on the Champs-Élysées. A soldier made you move.' He paused. She gave no reaction. 'Do you remember a man hanging out from the railings of the building behind?'

'No.'

'That was me.'

'I have no idea what you're talking about.' But she was thinking. 'I remember a crazy man. He was saying vulgar things to a man below him.'

'That's right.' He smiled. 'That was me.'

'You're disgusting. Get away from me.'

'I went looking for you.'

'So now you've found me. Fuck off.'

'You don't understand. I went back to the same place in the Champs-Élysées for weeks. Did you ever go there again?'

'No.'

'Then I went from district to district, all over Paris, for over a year, in the hope of finding you. My little brother came with me sometimes. I promise you this is true.'

She stared at him.

'I work on Monsieur Eiffel's tower,' he continued proudly. 'He knows me.'

She continued to stare at him.

'Do you always piss on people's heads?' she asked.

'Never. I swear.'

She shook her head.

'I think you must be crazy.'

'There's a bar over there.' He pointed up the street. 'I was going to eat something. I'll give you supper. It's a respectable place. You'll be quite safe. When you want to leave, I won't follow you.'

She paused.

'You really looked for me all over Paris, for a year?'

'I swear to you.'

In the bar, he could see she was giving him a thorough inspection, but he pretended not to notice. They sat at a small wooden table.

He supposed she was two or three years younger than he was. There were even more freckles on her face than he remembered. Her eyes were hazel, but up close he could see different lights in them. A hint of blue or green, he couldn't decide which. Perhaps both. But it was her mouth that he especially noticed. He'd remembered that it was wide, but there was something potentially sensuous about her lips that excited him. And she had white, even teeth. He hadn't been able to see that before.

She was sitting across from him, leaning back slightly, as though to keep him at a distance. He could hardly blame her for that.

'My name is Thomas Gascon,' he said.

'I am Édith.'

'You come from this quarter?' he asked.

'We've always been here.' She shrugged. 'Since it was a village.'

'I'm from the Maquis. On Montmartre.'

'I've never been there.'

'It's all right. People come up there for the dancing, and the views. But our family name is Gascon, so Monsieur Eiffel says we come from Gascony.'

'Monsieur Eiffel seems to be important to you.'

'I worked for him on the Statue of Liberty. Then I got sick, but he let me work on the tower as a favour. He was talking to me this afternoon.'

'He must think well of you, then.'

'I'm skilled. That's why he hires me. It's important for a man to have a skill. If he can.'

'My mother and I clean. And I work for my aunt Adeline too. She has a very good situation.' She paused. 'Maybe I shall inherit her position one day.'

'Would you like to do that?'

'Certainly. She works for Monsieur Ney, the attorney.'

'Oh.' This meant nothing to him, but in her mind, evidently, he was as significant as Monsieur Eiffel.

She took a little wine, but she refused to eat, explaining that she was on her way to her aunt, who would be expecting to feed her.

She asked him some questions about his work and his family, then said that she must leave.

'I hope I shall see you again,' he said.

She shrugged.

'You know where I work in the evenings.'

'I don't get off work until late in the summer months,' he said.

'I don't get off work until late any time.'

'Can I see you safely to your aunt's?'

'No.' She seemed about to get up, then paused. 'Tell me one thing,' she said. 'Why did you waste your time looking for me all over Paris?'

He considered.

'I will tell you,' he answered. 'But another time.'

She laughed.

'Then perhaps I shall never know.'

But he did see her, a week later, and this time she consented to eat something, but only a *crêpe*. And towards the end of their little meal, she said: 'You still haven't answered my question.'

'About why I looked for you?' He considered for a moment. 'Because, when I first saw you, I said to myself: "That's the girl I'm going to marry." It was therefore necessary to find you.'

She stared at him in silence for a moment.

'You tie yourself to a railing and hang there offering to piss on people's heads, and then you catch sight of a person you've never seen before in your life, and you decide to marry her?'

'That's it, exactly.'

'You're insane. I'm eating with a lunatic.' She shook her head. 'No chance, monsieur.'

'You can't refuse.'

'I certainly can.'

'Impossible. I haven't asked you yet.'

'Ah. What an asshole.'

The next week, however, when she found him waiting for her one evening, she told him that, if he liked, they could meet on the following Sunday afternoon. 'Meet me in front of the Trocadéro at two,' she said.

Sunday was a warm September day. She was wearing a pale striped dress and sash.

On the slope below the Trocadéro's Moorish concert hall as it looked across the river to the site of Monsieur Eiffel's tower, there were some pleasure gardens, which contained two big statues, one of an elephant, the other of a rhinoceros.

'I remember my father bringing me here to look at these,' Édith told him, 'when I was a girl.' She smiled. 'So I like to come and see them sometimes.' She shrugged. 'It brings back good memories.'

'Is your father still around?'

She shook her head.

'There's an aquarium,' she said, pointing to a long, low building. 'Have you ever been in there?'

He hadn't. They spent a pleasant half hour looking at all manner of exotic fish. There was a small deep-water black squid that fascinated him. And exotic jellyfish with poisonous stings. Even more exciting was an electric eel that could kill a man. The power of these sea monsters attracted Thomas, and he pointed them out eagerly to Édith. 'They're even more impressive than the sharks,' he said. She looked, but preferred the brightly coloured tropical fish.

When they had finished, Édith led the way. He noticed that they were going towards the rue de la Pompe.

'When my mother was my age,' she remarked, 'this wasn't part of Paris at all. It was all the village of Passy.'

'Same with Montmartre.'

'Did you know,' she said proudly, 'that Ben Franklin, the great American, used to live up the street from here?'

'Oh.' He'd heard of Ben Franklin, though he couldn't remember much about him. 'I didn't know that.'

'On the west side of Passy, there was a small palace where Marie Antoinette used to stay.' She glanced at him. 'You can tell I'm very proud of Passy.'

'Yes.'

'So I'm going to show you something even more important.'

They kept walking until they came to the lowest section of the rue de la Pompe. Looking up the street, most of the houses were set in gardens. Some were hard-faced granite residences, newly built town houses for rich people. Others, somewhat older, were less formal suburban villas with shutters on the windows, set in leafy gardens where fruit trees suggested a more rural past. But the place where she stopped was the gateway to a courtyard containing some stables, and beyond which he saw a kitchen garden.

'Do you know who lived here before the Revolution?'

'No idea.'

'Charles Fermier himself.'

Thomas paused, unwilling to expose his ignorance. She was watching him.

'Well, who was Charles Fermier?' she prompted.

'I don't know,' he confessed.

'The ancestor of my father.' She smiled. 'He was a farmer. This area was mostly farmland then.'

'He owned the land?'

'Oh, no. Most of Passy was owned by a few big landowners. He rented his land. But he kept a lot of cows. We've been here ever since. Well, except my father. We don't know where he went.' She shrugged a little sadly.

'Your family didn't continue to farm?'

'My grandfather looked after the horses at a château on the far side of Passy. Then my father worked in a merchant's house until he left.'

They walked up the street. Just past a handsome horse chestnut tree they came to the house where Thomas lodged.

'I rent a place in there,' he said.

'It looks nice.'

He thought of his tiny room where he had just space to lie down.

'It's all right,' he said. 'I'm afraid the owner won't allow me to bring any women into the house.'

'I'm a respectable girl. I wouldn't go in if you asked me.'

They walked on.

I make good money working for Monsieur Eiffel, he thought. I could rent a nicer place if I didn't give my spare money to my mother. It was a moral conflict he hadn't thought of before.

'Where do you live?' he asked.

'My mother lives over by the Porte de la Muette,' she said a little vaguely, 'and my aunt Adeline in the other direction. I go between the two.'

Before they reached the Lycée Janson de Sailly, they turned right and soon came into a street of small stores, where they found a little place to sit down, and Édith ordered tea and a pastry.

'I've enjoyed my afternoon,' she said. 'But I have to go to my aunt now.'

'The one who works for the lawyer.'

'For Monsieur Ney.' Her tone was respectful.

'I should be curious to see such an important gentleman.'

'I must go,' she said suddenly.

'When shall we next meet?'

'Wednesday is a good evening,' she answered. Then she was gone.

And so their meetings continued for several weeks. On Wednesdays she would come out of work with her mother as usual, and then continue alone to her aunt Adeline's. Thomas would meet her. They would sit and talk for a while. She would let him accompany her some of the way towards her aunt's, but never the whole way. Some Sundays he would go to his family in Montmartre, on others she would agree to meet him, and they'd wander about together quite happily. It was clear that, for the time being at least, Édith was keeping him at a distance, and he was content to be patient. He supposed that it was only natural caution on her part.

But he also had a sense that there were aspects of her life that had not been fully revealed to him yet.

In the month of October Thomas made two discoveries on Monsieur Eiffel's tower. Both of them took him by surprise.

He had arrived as usual one morning when he saw a knot of people gathered by one of the tower's four feet. As he approached, he saw both Jean Compagnon and Monsieur Eiffel watching closely while a gang of workmen that he'd never seen before were assembling a large piece of machinery.

Thomas had been working on this leg the day before, but Compagnon directed him to join another crew. By the lunchtime break, however, the new piece of machinery was fully assembled, and Thomas eagerly went to inspect it.

Eiffel saw him and gave a nod as he addressed the men who had gathered around.

'Well, my friends, I was asked a little while ago how we should raise the girder sections into place when the tower grew higher than the cranes. Here is the answer. It is a creeper crane. It will run on rails inside each leg of the tower. And when the tower is completed, those same rails will carry the elevators that the public will use – unless they choose to take the stairs. Since the tower's legs are at an angle, the crane and later the elevators will also run at an angle. Just like a funicular railway.' He smiled. 'As we build up, they will accompany us. The arm of the crane will extend and allow each section to be raised, with the crane, so to speak, creeping along just behind. The cranes can also swivel, if desired, three hundred and sixty degrees.'

From that day, Thomas worked his way up the tower's huge iron leg with the creeper crane for company.

He made the second discovery in the last week of October.

One feature of the building site was the care that Eiffel had expended on the safety precautions. By its nature, work on iron structures like this was dangerous. It was a lucky builder who could complete a great iron bridge without at least one worker badly injured. And in the case of the tower, its height dictated that any fall would surely be fatal.

So Eiffel had designed an elaborate system of movable barriers and safety nets. His aim was to do the near-impossible, and complete the project without losing a single man. After all, his workers were all used to operating on high structures. With care and attention, he believed his ambitious safety record could be achieved.

Until then, Thomas had worked with the same crew. They got on well together, and evidently Jean Compagnon had been satisfied with their work. He'd have let them know soon enough if he wasn't.

One morning, there was a man short on a crew who worked near them, and Compagnon told him: 'I'm putting you on the crew that's short today.' So Thomas had gone up with them. He wasn't concerned. His own crew had worked on the outside edge of the building, while the crew he was joining worked on the inside edge, only yards away. Indeed, it crossed his mind that they might even have asked for him. The work, naturally, was identical. As they went to their workstation, he looked back at his old crew and waved.

When he got to his position on the inner edge of the tower, he glanced down.

And froze.

A second later, his left hand was gripping the edge of a girder just above his shoulder; his right had found a metal strut just behind him, and was clenched around it so tightly that he could feel the metal edge biting painfully into the flesh. But he could do nothing about it. He couldn't loosen his grip. A cold panic seized him, as though all his strength were suddenly draining away through his feet. He stood there, unable to go forward or back, his breath coming short.

Thomas Gascon had never experienced panic before. It had never occurred to him that the sensation of working on the inner edge of the tower's slope would be any different from working on the outer edge as he had been up till now. But yesterday, he'd had the network of girders under him. Today, there was nothing under his feet. Nothing except forty yards of empty space.

He'd supposed he had a good head for heights because he could stand on a hill and look down. And 120 feet wasn't so high, in any case. But this was like stepping on to a tightrope.

And then he realised that two men were looking up at him. Monsieur Eiffel was smiling. But the eye of Jean Compagnon missed nothing, and he wasn't smiling.

'What's the matter?' His voice was sharp. 'You want to come down?'

And at that moment Thomas Gascon knew that he was about to lose his job.

'*Mais non!*' he cried. And then, he hardly knew how he did it, except that he knew he must, he made himself lean out a little, and somehow let go of the girder with his left hand and saluted Monsieur Eiffel. '*Bonjour, monsieur,*' he called. 'I'm just waiting for your creeping crane to send me something.'

He could see Eiffel smile and nod, but Compagnon's gimlet eye was still fixed on him suspiciously. So Thomas, wondering if Compagnon could see the white knuckles of his right hand, which was still clenched tight on to the metal strut, carefully turned and looked at one of his crew. And when he took his eyes off the yawning chasm underneath him, he felt a little better. The man was looking at him curiously also, so he forced himself to smile.

'When I worked with Monsieur Eiffel on the Statue of Liberty, he told me it would be the most famous project he ever did. Now he builds this.' He managed to loosen his hand from the metal strut and shrugged. 'When we're finished I shall ask him: "So, monsieur, what will you do for an encore?"'

The men laughed. He felt calmer now. For the rest of that day, he would glance down every little while, and gradually he got used to it.

That weekend, when he was up at Montmartre and Luc asked him, 'How's your head for heights?' Thomas just smiled.

'No problem,' he said.

★　　★　　★

In the second week of November he decided to take the plunge.

'I have to go to see my family on Sunday,' he said to Édith. 'Would you like to come? I can show you Montmartre.'

She looked down thoughtfully.

'It's a long way,' she said.

'Not really. We can take a tram to Clichy and walk up the hill.' He could see her still hesitating. 'I think you should come if it's not raining. But if it's raining, there won't be any view to show you.'

'I could come if there's a view.'

'Exactly. I'll have to have lunch with my family, but then I can show you around. If it's a clear day, even in November, there are usually some artists painting outside.'

'All right,' she said.

They hailed a tram just north of the Arc de Triomphe. Since the trams had no official stops, but were hailed by people as they went along, the drivers used their discretion. For a respectable elderly lady, they'd pull up the horses, but not for young poor folk like Thomas and Édith. As she stepped on to the moving platform, Édith slipped, and if Thomas hadn't caught her with his arm, she might have fallen. He used the opportunity to pull her close, and she didn't seem to resist. But moments later she was sitting demurely beside him in the tram, and when he tried to put his hand on her leg, she gently removed it.

They got out of the tram at the Place de Clichy, and walked up the hill. As they neared the top, he guided her around the picturesque little streets and she remarked that even when she was a little girl, parts of Passy had still looked like this. The windmills on the hill delighted her. But as they started down the slope into the sprawling shanty town of the Maquis she said less, and it seemed to Thomas that she became a little thoughtful.

'It's not a palace, where we live,' he said.

'Who wants to live in a palace?' She gave him a smile.

When they came to the house and went up the steps, they found the two Gascon parents, Luc, and also Nicole. They were all rather surprised that Thomas had brought a young woman with him, but Thomas told them easily that Édith was a friend from Passy, who'd never been up to Montmartre. 'I said I would show her around, and that she could come and eat with us first,' he said to his mother. 'Is that all right?'

'But of course.' His mother was all smiles. God forbid that any French family should not have food on the table for a guest. Though it was as well, Thomas thought, that it was Sunday, or there might not have been enough. 'Did you go to Mass today?' she asked Édith.

'*Oui, madame.* With my mother,' Édith answered.

'You hear that?' said his mother to Nicole. 'Perhaps you will accompany me next Sunday, instead of lazing in bed.'

'I was tired, Maman,' said Nicole irritably.

'Passy, eh?' said Monsieur Gascon. 'Elegant quarter.'

'We used to have a farm there, monsieur,' said Édith, 'but not any more.'

'And what do you do, if I may ask?' inquired Thomas's mother.

'I help my mother, madame. She's the caretaker of the Lycée Janson de Sailly. But I also help my aunt Adeline. She has a very good position with Monsieur Ney the attorney, and it may be that I can take her place one day.'

'Janson de Sailly,' said his father. 'I hear that's very chic already.'

Thomas watched his mother making her own calculations with this information, while Nicole was eyeing Édith's skirt and blouse, and her shoes. The clothes looked all right to him. What Nicole thought of them he couldn't guess. Judging by his mother's expression, she hadn't made up her mind yet, but wasn't especially impressed.

'This year I started work as a housemaid in a doctor's house near the Place de Clichy,' Nicole announced.

'That sounds like a good position,' said Édith politely.

Nicole shrugged.

'It's all right.'

There was enough food. A big plate of *haricots verts* appeared. There was even meat, though Thomas saw his mother discreetly cut two of the portions to a smaller size, to provide for Édith. There was a fruit pie. He was glad that his family could eat respectably on a Sunday, and supposed that the money he gave his mother must be helping them to do so. They talked of this and that. His mother discovered that Édith was an only child.

Luc had been observing Édith, but unusually for him, he'd been rather silent so far. Édith asked him what he was planning to work at when he grew up.

'I shall work in Montmartre, like I do now,' he answered cheerfully. 'And then I'm going to be a great comedian, and make a fortune.'

'Oh,' said Édith.

'It's better than working,' said Luc.

'He's joking,' said Thomas, though he wasn't sure that his brother was joking at all.

To make conversation, Thomas told them how they had taken a tram, and how Édith had nearly fallen.

'Ah,' said his father. 'Thomas is working on his great tower, and people will come from all over the world to see it, but when they see how we move around the city, we shall be ashamed.'

'Why?' asked his wife.

'In London they have steam trains that take you all over the city. They go underground, many of them. We still have nothing like that.'

'And in New York,' Luc chimed in, 'they have elevated trains.'

'The English and the Americans can do what they like,' said Édith, 'but why should we spoil the beauty of Paris with soot and steam and hideous rail tracks everywhere? They may be more modern, but we are more civilised.'

'I agree,' said Thomas's mother, with approval. 'Life is more civilised here.'

After the meal, Thomas and Édith stepped out into the unpaved streets of the Maquis, and he walked her up the hill to the Moulin de la Galette. The day was clear but cold, and although it was a Sunday, there weren't many people up there. Then he took her through the little square where the artists liked to paint. There were just three men out there, wrapped in heavy overcoats and scarves, but doggedly applying paint to canvas. They looked at them for a few minutes, then proceeded to the great building site of Sacré Coeur. Though the huge stone walls of the church were steadily rising, all one could see at present was a great fortress of scaffolding in a sea of mud.

But from the edge of the hill beside it there was still a magnificent view.

'There are the towers of Notre-Dame.' Thomas pointed them out proudly: the golden domes of the Opéra, only a mile away, and Les Invalides farther off. 'And there' – he indicated the site some way to the right of Les Invalides on the panorama – 'that's where Monsieur

Eiffel's tower will soar above them all.' He smiled. 'I know the Maquis is a bit primitive, but I love Montmartre. There's nowhere else in Paris like it.'

'You're really proud of the tower, aren't you?'

'Of course.'

'That's nice.'

Before it grew dark, he took her back to Passy. On the avenue Victor Hugo, she thanked him, let him kiss her on the cheek, and parted from him. He thought she had enjoyed the visit, but he couldn't be sure.

The next Sunday, she wasn't free, and so he went to see his parents. His mother waited until the meal was nearly over before she brought up the subject.

'That girl you brought here: are you interested in her?'

'I don't know,' he said. 'Maybe.'

'You can do better,' said his mother firmly.

'You just say that because she isn't the daughter of the widow Michel,' he answered with a shrug. He glanced at his father, but his father refused to meet his gaze. He turned back to his mother. 'You seemed to get on.'

'You can do better.'

After the meal, he went for a walk with Luc. He hadn't been entirely surprised by his parents' reaction. Nothing less than the widow Michel's daughter was ever going to satisfy them now. But he hoped for something better from Luc.

So he was taken by surprise when Luc finally spoke.

'Was that the girl we went looking for?' Luc suddenly asked.

'Yes. How did you guess?'

'I don't know.'

'What do you think of her?'

Luc paused. Then he looked a little sad.

'She doesn't like me,' he said.

'Why do you say that? She didn't say so to me. Not a word. I think she likes you.'

But Luc shook his head.

'No. I promise you it's so. I can tell.'

'I'm sure you're wrong,' said Thomas. But he was puzzled.

*   *   *

169

Three days later Édith asked him if he would be free to visit her mother and her aunt that Sunday.

It was mid-afternoon when they met. She was waiting for him at the top of the avenue Victor Hugo. They walked around the great circle under the Arc de Triomphe until, directly across from the Champs-Élysées, the massive avenue de la Grande-Armée stretched down to the west. Turning down the avenue, they walked a few blocks, turned right and proceeded a little way. The houses in the street, though respectable enough, had a grey and dingy air that Thomas found depressing. One house on a corner, somewhat larger than the others with an impressive central door, also had a gateway beside it, leading to an internal courtyard, protected from intruders by a tall screen of iron railings. To the right of this iron screen was a door, and a bell chain, which Édith pulled. Somewhere within Thomas heard a small, harsh clang. Moments later, the door was opened.

'This is my mother,' said Édith.

One could see the likeness at once. The same freckles, the same wide mouth. But time had not been kind to Édith's mother. She'd been pretty once. He could see that. Then she'd become blowsy. But in recent years, she'd started to let herself go. She had dyed her hair with henna, some while ago, and the grey roots showed as cruelly as a wintry wind, winnowing the autumn leaves. The eyes that had once been bright were puffy. The skin on her neck was criss-crossed with deepening lines, and sagging.

'So you're the boy who works on the tower.' She managed a smile.

'*Oui, madame,*' he answered politely.

She led them down a narrow passage into a room. It contained a sofa with a curved back, two formal chairs, a sideboard on which a decanter, a bottle and some glasses stood, and a small table. The window, framed by heavy damask curtains, gave on to the yard, but the thick gauze in front of the glass only let in a modicum of light.

'My sister-in-law has a beautiful situation, *n'est-ce pas?*'

So Aunt Adeline was the sister of Édith's vanished father. Thomas hadn't realised that.

'Beautiful, madame,' he said.

'My aunt is the concierge,' Édith explained. 'She really looks after the whole place.'

'It's a big house,' said Édith's mother. 'A big responsibility. But she has the head for it. That's for sure.'

'And Monsieur Ney lives here?' said Thomas.

'Monsieur Ney owns the establishment,' said Édith's mother, with the pride of someone with a rich friend. 'His office is next door. And he has his own house nearby, where he lives with his daughter.'

'His daughter is called Hortense,' Édith explained.

'Ah, Mademoiselle Hortense,' said her mother. 'She'll make a fine marriage, one of these days. That's for sure.'

'Perhaps I should show Thomas the house,' suggested Édith.

Her mother glanced at the sideboard, and nodded.

'Tell your aunt that we're waiting for her.'

Thomas followed Édith up a small staircase, then along a passage that took them into the back of the main house. With a smile, she opened another door, and he found himself standing on a broad landing looking down a big staircase towards the front door.

'It's a handsome entrance,' he remarked. 'Do you ever come in that way?'

'Oh no. The front door is always locked,' she told him. 'Come.' She went to a door on the right, knocked softly, and entered.

The room was spacious. The panelling on the wall was a little cracked in places, but the general effect was grand. A picture of an eighteenth-century aristocrat with a face of perfect serenity hung over the fireplace. Coloured prints of ladies in court dress graced the walls. In front of the window stood a small, elegant rococo writing desk and chair. Against the wall to the right of the door was a fine walnut armoire. And on the side of the room across from the fire stood a magnificent eighteenth-century canopied bed where, propped up on pillows and cushions, sat a lady of distinction swathed in lace. She was reading a small, leather-bound book.

'Ah. *La petite Édith*,' said the lady whose face, were it not for the obtrusion of some poorly fitting ivory teeth, would have exactly resembled the serenity over the fireplace.

'May I present my friend Thomas Gascon, Madame Govrit?' asked Édith politely. 'He is working on Monsieur Eiffel's tower.'

Madame Govrit de la Tour gazed at Thomas over her book.

'I'm sorry to hear it, young man,' she said, quite calmly. 'I've seen the pictures in the newspapers of this tower of Monsieur Eiffel, whoever he may be.' She spoke the builder's name as though she considered it unpronounceable. 'You should find other employment.'

'You don't like the tower, madame?' Thomas offered.

'Certainly not.' She laid the book face down on the bedspread. 'When I think of what France has built in the past, young man – of the Louvre, or Versailles – and then I see pictures of this monstrous spike that will no doubt rust before it is even constructed, this barbaric seaside vulgarity that is to hang in the sky over Paris, I ask myself, what has France come to?' She picked up her book again. 'You seem to be respectable, but you dishonour France. You should stop this work at once.'

'Thank you, madame,' said Thomas, as he and Édith withdrew.

Once the door was closed, Édith giggled. 'I hope you don't mind.'

'Not really.' Thomas shrugged. 'It's what half Paris of thinks.' One could read articles saying the same thing in the newspapers every week.

'I know. But she has her own way of saying it. She's our aristocrat,' Édith said with a note of pride.

'So what is this place? Old people live here?'

'Yes, but it's very special. Monsieur Ney comes to a private arrangement with each person. Some of them give him a sum of money, others have a house, or land, or income of some kind, and then they come to live here, and he looks after everything for them. He's a lawyer, so he always knows what to do.'

'How many are there?'

'About thirty.'

'Don't they have families?'

'Some do. But they all know they can trust Monsieur Ney. They say,' she continued quietly, 'that one old lady was so happy that she left Monsieur Ney her entire fortune when she died.'

Thomas said nothing.

They looked into another room, not nearly as lavish as the first, where an old lady was sitting in the single armchair facing the window. She seemed half asleep.

'Madame Richard can be difficult. My aunt has to give her a little laudanum,' Édith explained.

As they went down the passage, a short, fat woman waddled out of one of the rooms. She was dressed in black, with a face so fleshy it was perfectly round. Could this be Aunt Adeline? he wondered.

'Have you seen my aunt, Margot?' asked Édith.

'*Non*. Haven't seen her,' the small round woman answered placidly. '*Bonjour, monsieur*,' she said to Thomas, as she passed.

'That's Margot, the nurse,' Édith explained. 'I wonder if my aunt could be upstairs.'

They reached the top floor of the house by a steep and narrow staircase. The passage was windowless, though some light came from a skylight at the end. Édith called out her aunt's name a couple of times, but there was no reply. She turned to go back down the narrow stairs. But just before he followed her, out of curiosity, Thomas opened the nearest door.

The room was almost bare. The window, which had surely not been cleaned that year, lacked any curtains. In several places, the walls were stained with damp. In the middle of the floor was an iron bedstead, painted black, covered with a red blanket under which, like a discarded garden rake, lay a bony old woman, whose grey hair hung in thin strands over the side of the horsehair mattress. She was very still. If she breathed, she made no sound. There was dust on the floor, but not a crumb to tempt a mouse. One thing, however, caught his eye. On the wall opposite the bed, in a thin metal frame, hung a cheap print of a Virgin and Child behind glass that had been polished till it gleamed.

'Thomas,' Édith called, 'what are you doing?'

'Nothing,' he said, and closed the door. 'Who's that in there?'

'Mademoiselle Bac. She's very poor. Come.'

By the time they got back to Aunt Adeline's quarters, the lady in question had arrived there. She gave Thomas a brief look and having, he suspected, seen everything she needed to know, asked him to sit down.

She went to the sideboard and picked up the bottle of cider.

'Will you take a little *cidre doux*?' she asked him.

'Perhaps the young man would prefer a cognac,' Édith's mother suggested hopefully.

'*Non*,' said Aunt Adeline firmly. '*Cidre doux*.'

'Yes, thank you,' said Thomas.

Aunt Adeline poured cider into small glasses for them all. She wore a starched white shirt and a long navy blue dress. Her dark hair was pulled back severely into a bun. Her eyebrows were thick, and her large dark eyes watchful.

'Where do you live, young man?' she asked.

'I lodge in the rue de la Pompe, madame. But my parents live in Montmartre.'

'Not in the Maquis, I hope.'

'In the Maquis, madame. But they're quite respectable,' he added. 'They sent me to school and made me take up a skilled trade.'

'I'm glad to hear it.'

'You've run this home for Monsieur Ney for many years, madame?'

'I have. It's a great responsibility.'

'That's for sure,' chimed in Édith's mother, though Aunt Adeline tried to ignore her. 'He started with a much smaller place, you know. He was a lawyer in the backstreets of Belleville then. Just two rooms in a tenement. One for Mademoiselle Bac, and the other for a widow whose husband left her quite a good little business. An ironmonger's. But she couldn't run it. No idea. He did everything for her. Ran the business, looked after her. And when she died, she left it all to him. That was the start of his fortune. Then he moved to a bigger place, near the Gare du Nord. And now this.' She nodded. 'But he's very loyal. He always took poor Mademoiselle Bac with him. She started in a tenement in Belleville, and now she lives in a big house near the Arc de Triomphe!'

'That's enough,' said her sister-in-law.

'He's got brains, Monsieur Ney,' continued Édith's mother, feeling rather pleased with herself. 'I asked him once, "What's the secret of the ironmongery business, Monsieur Ney?" And do you know what he replied? "It turns out," he said, "that it's nails." Think of that. Just nails.'

She seemed finally to have exhausted her store of information. Aunt Adeline looked relieved. Thomas didn't mind. He thought it was rather interesting.

'Shall I tell you something about Monsieur Ney?' said Édith. 'You've heard of the great Ney, who was one of Napoléon's marshals?'

'Of course.'

'Monsieur Ney and he are related. Isn't that right, Aunt Adeline?'

'I believe it may be so. Monsieur Ney is too discreet to say it.'

'And he runs a good business here,' said Thomas.

Aunt Adeline gave him a sharp look.

'Monsieur Ney is wonderfully kind,' she said with a hint of reproof. 'No one who has the good fortune to come here need ever worry again.'

'He's an angel,' cried Édith's mother, taking her cue at last. 'An angel.'

'And he has a daughter?'

'That's correct,' said Aunt Adeline. 'Mademoiselle Hortense is a charming young lady.'

'She'll inherit a fortune, and make a fine marriage,' said Édith's mother.

'No doubt,' said Aunt Adeline.

Thomas wondered if any food was to be forthcoming. It didn't look like it. And he was just wondering what he was supposed to do next, when there was a sound from the entrance. Aunt Adeline looked surprised. They heard a key turning in the outer door.

'It must be Monsieur Ney,' she said. 'He doesn't normally come at this hour.'

A moment later, there was a soft footfall in the passage, then a light tap at the door, which Aunt Adeline quickly opened, and the owner of the establishment entered the room. Édith and Thomas stood, and Édith's mother, unable to rise quickly enough, conveyed from her chair by an obsequious bow her cognisance of the profound respect that was due to him.

Monsieur Frédéric Ney was a small-time attorney of just under average height, but his presence gained its force from the fact that he was so remarkably thin, and that his pale face, which reminded Thomas of a fish, was too long for his body. His trousers fitted so tightly that they were almost like the stockings of the former age. His coat today was a dark chocolate colour.

He surveyed them all. Could some sixth sense have told him that an alien presence had entered his domain? His eyes fixed upon Thomas.

'*Bonjour, Monsieur Ney,*' said Édith with a winning smile – and a faint upward twitch of the corner of the lawyer's slightly fleshy mouth suggested that she was in his good graces. 'May I present my friend Thomas Gascon. He works on Monsieur Eiffel's tower.'

Monsieur Ney inclined his head.

'My felicitations, young man.' His voice was so quiet that Thomas had to lean forward slightly to be sure he heard. 'Opinions may vary about the tower, but I believe that we must not be afraid of progress, so long as we never forget tradition.'

'That's for sure,' said Édith's mother.

'I took him to see Madame Govrit,' said Édith to Ney. 'She doesn't like the tower at all,' she added with a laugh.

Again, the lawyer's lip twitched.

'Madame Govrit has a fine room, monsieur,' said Thomas, hoping to be agreeable. And he seemed to have succeeded, for the lawyer suddenly became quite animated.

'It is indeed, young man, as befits a person of her station. I'm proud to have such a room in this house. All our rooms, I hope, are satisfactory, but hers is, I may say, the best.'

Thomas knew that he shouldn't, but he could not resist.

'I also saw Mademoiselle Bac. Her room was not so nice.'

It was foolish of him to challenge Ney, but if he expected the lawyer to be embarrassed, he underestimated his man.

'Ah, poor Mademoiselle Bac,' said Ney with a shake of his head. 'She came to me many years ago, with little enough, but I took her in. And now . . .' He smiled. 'It is I who pay for her food and keep.' He made a little gesture with his hands as though to say, 'What can one do?'

'He's an angel,' murmured Édith's mother.

'And I'm sure that she's grateful, Monsieur Ney,' said Aunt Adeline, 'even if she can't express it.'

'I'm glad you say that,' Ney responded with feeling. 'I'm glad because there are two things in the world that I especially value.' He turned to Thomas. 'Take note, young man, for these will see you safely through life. The first is gratitude. And I hope that all the residents here may have cause to feel gratitude.'

'There is nothing that Monsieur Ney will not do for them!' cried Édith's mother. 'Nothing is too much.'

'I hope I provide everything they need, and more than that – if funds permit,' said Monsieur Ney. He turned to Thomas again. 'The second quality, young man, is loyalty – such as I am fortunate enough to receive from Madame Adeline here. Gratitude and loyalty. These are everything.'

Thomas had the feeling that if people were ungrateful or disloyal to Monsieur Ney, they might live to regret it.

'Are you grateful and loyal?' Ney suddenly asked Thomas.

'I am grateful to Monsieur Eiffel for giving me a job,' said Thomas. 'I should certainly be loyal to him.'

'*Voilà*. We are in perfect agreement,' said Monsieur Ney. He gave Thomas a glassy stare, then smiled at Édith. 'What an excellent young man.' He turned to Aunt Adeline. 'When I made my rounds yesterday, you may remember I was called away. And that is why I have come in today to see the three or four of our residents that I missed. Mademoiselle Bac was one of those.'

'Do you wish me to accompany you, Monsieur Ney?' asked Aunt Adeline.

'No. There is no need.'

'She always has her picture of the Virgin and Child,' said Édith. 'Margot polishes the glass whenever she goes in. You know how Mademoiselle Bac always seems completely still, but I can see her looking at the picture.'

'Religion is a great comfort,' said her mother with a wise nod of the head.

'Indeed,' said Ney, as he stepped towards the door, and Thomas secretly wondered if the comforting picture would remain.

'And Mademoiselle Hortense is well?' asked Édith's mother.

'She is.'

'Ah,' said Édith's mother, 'she has everything. She is beautiful, she is kind . . .'

Monsieur Ney left the room.

A few minutes passed in desultory conversation, then Aunt Adeline pulled out a little silver watch on a chain and looked at it.

'I have duties now, and Édith will be helping me,' she said.

Thomas took the hint and began to rise.

'Perhaps the young man would like to stay with me and have a cognac,' said Édith's mother.

Aunt Adeline looked at her as one might at a waterlogged old ship sinking inconveniently in a harbour.

'Sadly, I have to go, madame,' Thomas lied.

★   ★   ★

Outside in the street, he paused. He'd nothing special to do. Dusk would soon begin to fall. He went and stood opposite the handsome front door. Looking up, he was fairly sure he could identify the big window of Madame Govrit's room. As for Mademoiselle Bac's dingy attic, that would be up in the roof, towards the back, well out of sight.

Judging by what he'd seen of Édith's mother, he supposed the lodgings she and Édith shared were not a lot better.

He walked back past the archway and turned the corner. This side of the building consisted of a high house wall, punctuated by some small, narrow windows, which continued as the courtyard wall. As he moved along the house wall, he calculated that just before the courtyard began, he must be level with Aunt Adeline's quarters. Just above his head there was a small window that was slightly open. He guessed that it probably belonged to her kitchen. He paused there for a moment, wondering if perhaps he might hear Édith's voice.

But it was Aunt Adeline's voice that he heard.

'You heard him, *ma chérie*. That stupid comment about Mademoiselle Bac. He was just trying to be cheeky to Monsieur Ney.'

'Monsieur Ney called him an excellent young man,' Édith's voice replied.

'Yes. Out of kindness to you. But he wasn't pleased, I assure you. And you can't afford a young man who annoys Monsieur Ney.'

Édith said something else, but Thomas couldn't hear what it was.

'My child,' answered Aunt Adeline, 'I don't care if the young man went to the moon to look for you. We have one fool in the family already. Forgive me, but that's your mother. We can't afford two. Let us not see this Thomas Gascon again, if you please. You can do better.'

For the next three days, Thomas waited uneasily. He believed in fate. His parents might not like it, but he wanted Édith. Did she feel the same way?

On Wednesday, he waited near the lycée in the evening. Édith and her mother came out together as usual. But instead of separating, they went home together, and not wanting to encounter the mother, Thomas hung back. If Édith caught sight of him, she gave no indication. The next night the same thing happened.

Friday was a cold November day. An icy wind entered the city from the east. It hissed cruelly through the girders of the tower as he worked, biting his hands, and snaked down the boulevards, stripping the brown leaves from the trees.

Work ended at dusk and as soon as he got across the river he found a bar where he could get a large bowl of soup to warm himself up. Then he walked up the rue de la Pompe. The lights in the lycée were just being extinguished as he got there. He was determined to speak with her this evening, whether she separated from her mother or not. But a few moments later he saw her come out alone. He went straight up to her.

'Oh,' she said. 'It's you.'

'Of course it's me. Where's your mother?'

'She's sick today.'

'I'll walk with you,' he said. Then, as they passed a bar, he remarked that he needed to warm up, and guided her in.

'Only for a minute,' she said.

They sat at a table and he ordered them each a glass of wine.

'It's good to see you,' he said. 'I was glad to meet your family.'

'Yes.'

'What are you doing this Sunday?'

'Looking after my mother, probably.'

'We could meet for a short while, perhaps?'

She hesitated.

'I don't think so,' she answered. 'Everything is difficult at the moment.'

'You haven't time to see me?'

'Not at present. I'm sorry.'

'Do you want to see me?'

'Of course, but . . .'

He understood. He had thought that this was the woman whom fate had chosen for him. He had felt it to be so. Yet it seemed that his belief had been nothing but a foolish illusion.

That was bad enough. But why was she rejecting him? Because her aunt didn't approve of him. Because Aunt Adeline thought he was stupid. Because he had not shown enough respect to Monsieur Ney. And the fact that she was right, that he shouldn't have blurted out his foolish comment, only made his sense of resentment worse.

'Your family don't approve of me,' he said.

'I didn't say that.'

'You didn't say it, but it's the truth.'

She didn't answer.

'Tell me,' he asked, 'are you going to live your entire life under the thumb of Monsieur Ney?'

'He employs Aunt Adeline.'

'To help him steal money from a lot of helpless old women?'

'No.'

'Yes. That's what he's doing. And if you spend your life working for him, that's what you'll be doing.'

'You think you know everything, but you don't.'

'You think he's going to look after you? You think he's going to look after your aunt? I'll tell you how she'll finish up. Like Mademoiselle Bac.'

'You don't understand,' Édith suddenly cried out. 'At least Mademoiselle Bac has a roof over her head.'

He shrugged.

'I'd sooner be in the gutter.'

'You probably will be. My aunt's right. You're a fool.' She got up. 'I have to go now.'

'I'm sorry.'

'I have to go.'

So Thomas sat there feeling very angry, and it did not occur to him that when she was twenty yards down the street Édith had burst into tears.

That winter seemed long to Thomas Gascon. He was high above the Paris rooftops now, on the cold, iron tower. As he gazed down, grey day after grey day, the winter trees by the building site, and the long sweep of the Seine, looked bare and sad.

The work was hard. When the creeper cranes raised each section of the iron framework into place, the workmen swarmed over it. The sections came from the factory held together with temporary bolts, all of which had to be replaced with rivets.

It took a gang of four to rivet. First, the apprentice heated the rivet in a brazier until it was almost white hot, and swollen. The holder, wearing thick leather gloves, picked the rivet up with a pair of tongs and fitted it into the hole that was perfectly aligned between the metal girders or plates to be joined; then he'd block it in place with a heavy metal counterweight while the first of the two strikers would use a hammer to fashion a broad head on the other end of the rivet. Last, a second striker with a heavy sledgehammer would hammer the rivet down. As the hammered rivet cooled and shrank, it would grip the metal plates together tighter and tighter, finally exerting a force of three tons.

Each team had its own particular hammering sound, so that the men themselves could often tell without looking exactly who was working at any given moment.

The work was intense, and come rain, sleet or snow, it went on, eight hours a day.

Thomas was a striker. He usually liked to work with open-finger gloves, warming his hands from time to time with the heat from the fires used to heat the rivets. But he was obliged to abandon them for leather gloves, and often his fingers were numb. When the wind got up, it lashed his body as mercilessly as it would a sailor up a mast.

Early in the new year, however, the work of the flyers changed. For now they began to construct the tower's massive platform.

To Thomas, this felt quite strange. It was as if, building a table, he had suddenly moved from the vertical confines of the leg to the vast horizontal space of the tabletop.

'It's more like building a house,' he remarked. A house in the sky, to be sure – or rather, an enormous apartment block, constructed of iron.

The base of the platform was nearly two hundred feet in the air. In the central pit underneath, a huge square of scaffolding rose from the ground like a tree trunk, with branches spreading out to the underside of the platform's edge, so that away from the platform's centre, he was still looking down at an almost uninterrupted vertical drop. But he noticed that, since his eye was constantly led to look across the growing horizontal floor of the platform, he was hardly aware of the chasm below.

Structurally, Thomas well understood, it was this platform that bound the four great pillar stacks together and would provide the base for the soaring tower above. But even so, as the work progressed, he was astounded by the scale of the thing. The walk around the side galleries, from which there were fine views of Paris, was over three hundred yards long. There was space for numerous rooms, including a large restaurant.

This huge band of hollow space was carefully locked into place. It was, as Eiffel had foreseen, a mighty task, and it took time. It was not until March that, having finally checked that the basic structure of his four-legged table was solid and perfectly level, Eiffel gave the order: 'Proceed upward.'

Yet as the creeper cranes began their journey up the pylons again, Thomas noticed something else.

It seemed to him that the tower must be falling behind schedule. Eiffel's assistant engineers would sometimes be fretful. Thomas would see them shaking their heads. He knew from the drawings he'd seen that the massive span between the ground and the plat- form was to be finished with an elegant semicircular arch across the outside edge. Yet as April wore on and the pylons climbed into the sky above the platform, the whole underside of the tower looked a mess. But whatever was passing in his mind, Eiffel himself was always calm, polite, serene.

Only once did Thomas see Monsieur Eiffel angry. It was during the lunchtime break, one day in May. Eiffel was standing alone, near the north-western foot of his tower, reading a newspaper. Suddenly Thomas saw the engineer crumple his paper and slap it furiously against his side. Then, seeing Thomas watching him, he beckoned him over.

'Do you know why I am angry, young Gascon?' It was evident that he needed to get something off his mind.

'*Non, monsieur.*'

'They don't like my tower. Some of the greatest names in France hate it: Garnier, who built the Paris Opéra, Maupassant the writer, Dumas, whose father wrote *The Three Musketeers*. There have even been petitions against it. Do you know people who hate it?'

'*Oui, monsieur.* Madame Govrit de la Tour told me I should not work on it.'

'There you are. They even try to subvert my workmen. But this article in the newspaper today, young Gascon, surpasses everything. It says that my tower is indecent. That it will be nothing but a great phallus in the sky.'

Thomas didn't know what to say, so he shook his head.

'What is the greatest threat to a tall structure, young Gascon? Do you know?'

'Its weight, I suppose, monsieur.'

'No. Not really. It's the wind. The reason my tower has the shape it has, the reason it is constructed the way it is, all this is because of the wind, whose force would otherwise tear it down. That is the reason. Nothing else.'

'Is that why it's just iron girders, so the wind can blow through?'

'Excellent. It is an open-lattice construction, so that the wind can blow clean through it. And despite the fact that it is made of iron, which is strong, it is actually very light. If you put the tower in a cylindrical box, as a bottle of wine is sometimes sold, the air contained in the box would be almost as heavy as the metal tower itself. Amazing, but true.'

'I would never have imagined that,' Thomas confessed.

'But even this is not the point. The shape of the structure, its slender curve, is purely mathematical. The stress of the structure exactly equalises that of the wind, from any direction. That is the reason for its form.' He shook his head. 'The arts and literature are the glories of the human spirit. But all too often, those who practise them have little understanding of mathematics, and none of engineering. They see a phallus, with their superficial eye, and think that they have understood something. But they have understood nothing at all. They have no idea of how things work, of the true structure of the world. They are not capable of perceiving that, in truth, this tower is an expression of mathematical equations and structural simplicity far more beautiful than they could even imagine.' He looked down at the crumpled newspaper in disgust.

'*Oui, monsieur,*' said Thomas, feeling that, even if he did not understand the mathematics of the tower, at least he was building it.

'You'd better go,' said Eiffel. 'If you are late, tell Compagnon that it was my fault and that I send my apologies. It's not as if,' he murmured to himself, 'I want the building delayed any more than it already is.'

By the time Thomas got back to his station, he was a minute late. Passing Jean Compagnon, he began to explain, but the foreman waved him on.

'I saw you with Eiffel. He likes to talk to you.' He shook his head. 'God knows why.'

Since their parting the previous November, Thomas had hardly seen Édith. Once in December, and again at the turn of the year, he had deliberately encountered her outside the lycée, but each time she'd made it clear that she didn't want to see him any more. After that, he'd avoided the lycée, and although he would occasionally catch sight of her in Passy, they hadn't met.

Since he spent every Sunday with them now, it was clear to his parents that he wasn't seeing Édith. But nobody said anything. Once Luc asked him what had happened to her, and Thomas replied that it was over.

'Are you sad?' Luc asked.

'Oh,' Thomas replied with a shrug, 'it just didn't work out.'

Luc said nothing.

As spring began, he had thought about looking for another woman. But so far he hadn't met anyone he especially liked. Nor did he have much time or energy.

During May and June, the work on the tower picked up more speed. The men were now working twelve hours a day. The great arch under the first platform was accomplished, and the central scaffolding removed. Suddenly the tower began to put on a stately face. As the four great corner pylons swept up their narrowing curve into the sky, the next target was the second platform. At 380 feet above the ground, this would form a second four-legged table on top of the first. After that, the tower would soar in a single, narrowing fretwork shaft up to its dizzying height in the heavens. By the end of June, the second platform was already being built.

And this was admirable timing. For it was almost the fourteenth of July. *Le Quatorze Juillet*.

Bastille Day.

How fortunate it was for succeeding generations that when the ragged *sans-culottes* had inaugurated the French Revolution by storming the old fortress of the Bastille in 1789, they should have done it

184

on a summer's day. A perfect choice for a public holiday of celebrations, parades and fireworks.

'Monsieur Eiffel is having a party at the tower on the fourteenth,' Thomas announced to Luc. 'Do you want to come?'

It was a bright afternoon. As they crossed the Pont d'Iéna, Thomas glanced at his younger brother and felt rather proud of him.

Luc was now fourteen. His face had continued to fill out, and a dark lock of hair fell elegantly down over his brow, so that at the Moulin where he often worked, the customers often thought he must be a young Italian waiter. Indeed, despite his youth, his years spent up there had given him a mixture of smooth worldliness and boyish charm that his older brother could only watch in wonderment.

Today, he had put on a white shirt without a jacket, and a straw boater on his head.

By the time they arrived, there were large crowds walking around the site. The lower parts of the tower were festooned with bunting, displaying the red, white and blue of the Tricolour flag. There was a refreshment tent and a band smartly dressed in uniform.

Whatever the papers might have said about the ugliness of the tower, one could see already that its huge, two-tiered archway was going to provide a magnificent entrance to next year's exhibition. At 380 feet, the just-completed platform was almost three quarters as high again as the towers of Notre-Dame, and on a level with the highest cathedral spires in Europe.

All kinds of people were there, including the fashionable. Thomas and Luc stood near the refreshment tent. 'I'll introduce you to Monsieur Eiffel,' said Thomas proudly, 'if he comes by.'

They'd been there about five minutes when Luc suddenly said, 'Look who's over there.' But when Thomas looked, he couldn't see anyone particular in the crowd. 'Over there.' Luc indicated a knot of well-dressed people. And then Thomas saw.

It was Édith. She was wearing a white dress that must have been given to her, since she could never have bought such a thing herself, and a small bonnet. She looked very pretty. Beside her was Monsieur Ney, and a pale woman in her late twenties who must, Thomas guessed, be his daughter.

'I'll go and say *bonjour* to her,' said Luc.

'You can't do that. She's with Monsieur Ney,' Thomas cried. But Luc was already on his way.

Thomas watched, not knowing what to do, as Luc very politely took off his boater and bowed to Édith. He saw her say something to Ney, and then saw Luc bow to the lawyer and his daughter too. Then he saw Luc say something else, after which they all turned to look at him. Luc was smiling, indicating that he should advance.

When Thomas reached them, after a polite smile to Édith, he was careful to make a deeply respectful bow to Monsieur Ney.

'It is a great honour, monsieur, that you should visit the tower where I work.'

'I told Monsieur Ney that you had promised to introduce me to Monsieur Eiffel if he comes by,' said Luc. 'And Monsieur Ney said that he hoped you would introduce him too.'

Thomas stared at his little brother, dumbfounded. He, a humble worker, was to introduce the rich lawyer to Eiffel? But he saw to his further amazement that Ney was smiling with amusement. Obviously this charming fifteen-year-old boy in a straw boater could get away with things that Thomas himself could not.

'Of course, monsieur,' he said, wondering how on earth he was to do such a thing.

'Do you know my daughter, Mademoiselle Hortense?' the lawyer asked.

'Mademoiselle.' Thomas bowed again.

One could see the likeness at once. The same long, pale face, narrow body, slightly fleshy lips. To his surprise, he found the combination strangely sensual, and though of course he gave no outward sign, he wondered whether she had sensed it. She was dressed in pale grey. It occurred to him that the dress Édith was wearing might be an old one of hers. She did not smile, but observed him coolly.

Ney turned to Luc.

'And what do you do, young man?'

'I work mostly at the Moulin de la Galette on Montmartre, monsieur. But I run errands for people and perform services for them.'

'What sort of services?'

Luc smiled, and paused for just a split second.

'It depends what they ask, monsieur,' he answered quietly.

The lawyer looked at him thoughtfully for a moment, and Thomas had the sense that, in some way that lay outside his own experience, Monsieur Ney and his little brother understood each other perfectly.

He still hadn't said a word to Édith, and was just turning to do so, when Luc nudged his elbow.

'There is Monsieur Eiffel,' he said.

He was walking by, not ten yards away. Thomas took a deep breath, and went quickly over to him.

'Ah, young Gascon. I hope you're enjoying yourself.' The tone was friendly, but indicated that he was busy. There wasn't a moment to lose.

'Monsieur, I have my brother here, but also an important lawyer we happen to know, who wishes to be introduced to you.' He looked pleadingly at Eiffel. 'His name is Monsieur Ney. I'm only a work-man, monsieur, and I don't know how to do such a thing.' He indicated the Neys to him.

A glance at the lawyer told Eiffel that this was a man who might be useful. Besides, it was his day to work the crowd. Placing his hand on Thomas's shoulder in the most pleasant way, he went over with him.

'Monsieur Ney, I believe. Gustave Eiffel, at your service.'

'Monsieur Eiffel, may I present my daughter, Hortense.'

The great man bowed over the hand she offered him.

'Monsieur Gascon here has worked for me since the days when we built the Statue of Liberty,' said Eiffel with a smile. 'We are old friends.'

'And this is Mademoiselle Fermier,' said Ney in return, 'whose aunt is my most trusted assistant.'

Eiffel bowed to Édith.

'Are you by any chance connected to the great Marshal Ney, might I ask?' Eiffel inquired.

'Another branch, but the same family,' said the lawyer.

'You must be very proud of him,' suggested Eiffel.

'I am, monsieur. His execution was a stain upon the honour of France. I visit his grave and lay a wreath each year.'

After the fall of the great emperor Napoléon, the royalists had sentenced Marshal Ney to be executed. He had faced the firing squad bravely, pointing out that he failed to see that it was a crime to command French troops against the enemies of France. Most Frenchmen agreed, and he had since been interred with every honour in the cemetery of Père Lachaise.

They spoke briefly about the progress of the tower. Eiffel said that he hoped to welcome both the lawyer and his daughter to the top of it after the completion. And he was about to depart when he glanced at Luc.

'You're the brother of this hero, aren't you? I remember the day when you were lost, and your brother went to look for you.' He put his hand on Thomas's shoulder again. 'This is a loyal fellow. I hope you're grateful.'

'I am, monsieur.' Luc smiled charmingly.

After Eiffel had departed, Ney indicated that they also would be leaving. But it was clear that he was well satisfied with the service that Thomas had performed for him.

'Perhaps we shall see you again,' he remarked to Thomas. 'And you too, my young friend,' he added to Luc.

During all this time, Édith had not said a word.

'You're looking very well, Édith,' Thomas said to her. 'I hope your mother and your aunt are also well.' Receiving a nod from her, he added, 'Please give them my respects.' And it seemed to him that, perhaps, she gave him a smile.

He and Luc hung around the place for most of the afternoon. He introduced his brother to some of the men he worked with, and listened to the band. That night, Eiffel had promised a splendid fireworks display from the top of the tower's platform. But before that, Thomas and Luc crossed over the river and went into a bar to eat. As they finished eating, Luc remarked: 'I think that if you asked, Édith would go out with you again.'

Thomas looked at him thoughtfully.

'Why are you encouraging me to do that,' he asked Luc, 'when you think she doesn't like you?'

'Because I think you're unhappy without her.'

Thomas gazed at his brother fondly. Then he gently punched his arm.

'You're a good fellow, you know,' he said.

'Me?' Luc considered, then shook his head. 'Not really.'

'I think you are.'

'No, I'm not a good man, Thomas. In fact,' – he paused for a moment – 'I don't even want to be.'

Thomas held up his glass of wine and looked over it.

'I don't understand you, little brother.'

'I know,' said Luc. 'Will you see Édith?'

It was late July when people started to notice that something was wrong at the Eiffel Tower. All Paris knew that it must be completed in another eight months. And it still had to grow another six hundred feet. Yet day by day, as people looked out towards the huge stump from all over the city, it hardly seemed to be growing at all. Rumours began that the great engineer had hit a technical problem. After so much work – and so much publicity – would the great exhibition begin next spring with a huge unfinished stump at the entrance? Was France going to be the laughing stock of the world?

Certainly young Thomas Gascon was worried.

And yet, despite his reverence for the tower and its designer, there were moments when he scarcely cared. He had other things on his mind.

It was the first Sunday in August when he and Édith went out for the afternoon together. She was coming from her aunt's, so they'd agreed to meet on the corner of the avenue de la Grande-Armée. As the huge continuation of the Champs-Élysées swept down from the Arc de Triomphe towards the west, it reached the sprawling old village of Neuilly before ending at the huge wooded park of the Bois de Boulogne.

It was a hot summer's day. A perfect afternoon to enjoy the delights of the Bois.

For when Napoléon III and Haussmann had come to the old hunting forest at the western edge of the city, they had known exactly what to do.

'I want something like Hyde Park in London,' Napoléon III had said, 'but bigger and better.' Of course.

The Bois de Boulogne was considerably bigger than the English park. At its southern end they laid out the great racecourse of Longchamps, which was reached by a long and magnificent avenue.

Together with Chantilly to the north of Paris, and Deauville up on the Normandy coast, it was to offer some of the most fashionable race meetings in the world.

If Hyde Park had the Serpentine water, the Bois had two artificial lakes, joined by a waterfall. There were scores of delightful alleys of trees. In the north-eastern corner a children's zoo had developed into an anthropological theme park where one could admire some of the picturesque cultures of distant lands.

This was where they started.

There were plenty of people there as they went through the turnstile. Some were families from the professional classes, with children in sailor suits and muslin dresses; others were small clerks and shopkeepers, others manual working folk like himself and Édith.

Édith was dressed in a blue-and-white dress which she had enhanced with a small hat with a ribbon around the crown. She carried a parasol. Thomas guessed that the hat and parasol might be discards from Mademoiselle Hortense. The effect was to suggest that Édith might belong to the class above her own. But he had often noticed that women tended to dress up more finely than their men. His own short jacket was clean enough, but his boots had never been shiny even before they became caked with dust. It suddenly occurred to him to wonder how his little brother would have dressed for a day like this.

Édith liked the place. There was a little Oriental temple, and a number of curious animals. But it was also clear that a large area was being prepared for a new display, and they asked a uniformed warden what this was going to be.

'Ah,' he said, with a twirl of his moustache, 'that's for the exhibition, the World's Fair next year. Biggest show we've ever done. An entire village.'

'What sort of village?' Édith wanted to know.

'An African village. Native huts. The lot.'

'Any real natives?' Thomas inquired.

'But of course. They're importing four hundred Negroes. At the last big exhibition, back in '77,' he went on enthusiastically, 'we had Nubians and Inuit Indians on display.'

'Like a zoo?' asked Édith.

'But of course like a zoo. A human zoo. And do you know, it brought in a million visitors. Think of that. A million!' Thomas had heard about the human zoos, as these exhibitions were called, that were to be found in several countries. But the scale of this one was certainly impressive.

'It will rival Buffalo Bill and his Red Indians,' the warden proudly declared.

As they left the zoo and started walking through the Bois, Édith turned to Thomas.

'Will you take me to watch Buffalo Bill when he comes?'

'Of course,' said Thomas.

He took note of the signal. When he'd waited outside the lycée the week after Bastille Day, he hadn't been sure what to expect. She'd been cautious, and said she couldn't meet him until early August, but she hadn't said no. And now, after only an hour in his company, she'd just asked him to take her to a show the following summer.

A change of heart? Had Monsieur Ney indicated his approval? Or had Édith missed him? Well, he thought, he'd just have to wait and see. For the moment, he was glad.

He wondered if he dared put his arm around her. He glanced at her pretty hat and parasol and decided he'd better not. Not yet, anyway.

They came to a noble avenue. This, clearly, was where the fashionable ladies came to be seen in their fine carriages, while rich men and officers rode beside them. He wondered what it must be like to have no work to do, and realised that he had no idea.

But he knew how to treat a girl on a summer Sunday afternoon, and soon they reached the upper lake.

Fringed with trees, which gave it a rustic air, the lake was quite large. In the middle of its waters there was an island containing a café and restaurant in the form of a Swiss cottage. The overall effect was charming and romantic.

Thomas led Édith straight to the boatyard. Within minutes, they were out on the water with Édith sitting very prettily in the stern, under her parasol, and Thomas manfully plying the oars.

He'd been in a boat only once or twice in his life, but he took care and splashed Édith only a couple of times, which made her laugh. Since the day was hot, he took off his jacket and rolled up his shirt-sleeves, and felt more comfortable like that.

There were plenty of other boats out on the water. Most of the oarsmen were gentlemen, some of whom had taken off their jackets just as he had. But to his surprise, several boats were being rowed by well-dressed women, who seemed to think it a fine joke to compete with the men.

After rowing about the lake for nearly half an hour, he moored the boat at the island, and treated Édith to an ice in the Swiss cottage.

When they came back to the boat again, Édith said she wanted to row.

'Have you done it before?' he asked.

'I've been watching you,' she said.

So he helped her into the boat, and stepped in after her, but the boat moved in the water, and Édith lost her balance, and Thomas caught her as she fell, which was just as well because she might have cracked her head on the wooden seat otherwise. And he got a bruise on his leg, but he didn't mind. As they went down in the boat, he was underneath and she fell into his arms and he felt her body pressing into his, and his arms went around her, and for a moment or two they lay there like that. She was looking down into his face, and he was going to kiss her.

'Well, help me up, silly,' she said. But she was laughing with pleasure all the same.

Then she rowed him back to the shore. She splashed him several times. Once or twice he thought it was deliberate. And he was happier than he had ever been in his life.

They walked through the Bois after that. They were walking down a long empty alley when he put his arm around her. She didn't stop him. After a little while, they stopped. There was still no one in sight. And he kissed her, and she kissed him back. But when his hands started to rove too much she stopped him. Then they walked back, and he kept his arm around her until some other people came in sight.

The sun was behind them when they walked back up the avenue de la Grande-Armée, and ahead of them in the distance the Arc de Triomphe shimmered as if it were going to dissolve in the sunbeams.

The next weekend Thomas went to see his family at Montmartre.

'Did you take Édith out?' Luc asked, when they were alone.

'Yes, to the Bois de Boulogne. We went on the lake.'

Luc reached into his pocket.

'Take these,' he said. 'They're the best.'

Thomas looked down at the little packet in astonishment. They were condoms.

'My little brother is giving me *capotes anglaises*?' It was a cultural curiosity that the French and English nations had decided to attribute these artifacts to each other. The French called them English hoods; the English, for reasons obscure, called them French letters. They were mostly made of rubber, could be reused, but were not too reliable.

'Why not? One of my rich customers gave them to me. These aren't the usual ones. They're finer. He told me they're the best.'

Thomas shook his head. At the age of fifteen, his little brother was mixing with some strange company. But what could one do? There probably wasn't a child of ten in all the Maquis who was innocent.

'She's not that kind of girl,' he said.

'Keep them all the same,' said Luc.

So Thomas laughed and put them in his pocket. And as he did so, he wondered: Might he need them after all?

In September 1888, after several weeks of agonisingly slow progress, the tower suddenly began to increase in height at great speed.

It should have begun after Bastille Day. For above the second platform, the curve of the tower was such that it became much thinner. Instead of building horizontally, as they had in the lower sections, the flyers were now building almost vertically. The same number of men, installing the same number of sections, could add two, three or more times the height each day than they had done before. While some of the gangs, including Thomas's, continued going up the tower, others were redeployed to the filling-in work on the great platform and the arches below.

Yet one problem had almost brought progress to a grinding halt.

It was the cranes. The ingenious creeper cranes were splendid, but they were slow. And now, as the cranes had to crawl up hundreds of feet, the flyers would quickly install the sections they brought, and then wait, uselessly, for the next sections to make their slow journey back again. The work was falling behind. Tempers frayed.

One day Jean Compagnon stopped Thomas.

'At least you look cheerful, young Gascon. You've got a girl? Is that it?'

'*Oui, monsieur.*' Thomas grinned.

'Well, good for you.' He nodded thoughtfully. 'I don't like the look of the men, young Gascon. Do you know when there's trouble at work?'

'*Non, monsieur.*'

'Well, I'll tell you. It's not when the men are working too hard. It's when they haven't got enough to do. I've seen it time and again. So think of your girl and stay out of trouble, you hear me?'

'*Oui, monsieur.*'

The solution that Eiffel found took time to put in place. But at last it was ready. And as soon as it was set in motion, the entire mechanics of the operation changed.

Machine-driven winches would hoist the sections vertically from the ground to the first platform. As soon as the sections arrived, they'd be reattached to a second lifting system which hoisted them vertically another two hundred feet up to the second platform. 'And as we get higher, we'll have another winch at about six hundred and fifty feet,' Eiffel informed them. The winching process would be accomplished in minutes. From there, creeper cranes could go up the tracks to where the sections were needed. The entire process could be completed in a little over a quarter of an hour.

Eiffel also announced a pay increase up to ten and sixteen centimes an hour. The tower was ready to soar.

But if the mechanics of the operation had changed, another problem returned.

It was one of the first mornings of this new regime, in the middle of September, when Thomas came down to the Seine and found that he could not see the top of the tower. Above the second platform, the girders had vanished into an autumn mist. He was rather excited as he went up the tower. It would be like working in the clouds, he thought. As work began, the fires for heating the rivets glowed eerily in the surrounding mist. There was only one thing he'd forgotten.

The cold. Up there, at over four hundred feet, the temperature was lower. Though Thomas was working hard, it wasn't enough to stop the damp cold seeping into his bones. He looked around him. The other men on the tower were feeling the same thing. When they went down for the lunchtime break, he could hear men cursing all around him. Was the terrible cold of the previous winter going to return – and so early?

There was a new fellow on his gang that week. Their holder had fallen sick, and been replaced by a cheerful Italian fellow, younger than himself, whom everyone called Pepe. 'You must be used to better weather than this,' Thomas remarked as they went down.

'It's true. But I'm happy to work on the tower,' Pepe replied, and grinned at him. 'My father build roads. He work in a hole. I no want to work in a hole. So I work in the sky.'

Thomas smiled and tried to be cheerful too.

That afternoon, the mist cleared, but a cold wind got up, moaned around the girders, and lashed the men as they worked. Everyone was blue with cold by the end of the day. Even Pepe stopped smiling.

The next workday – it was the nineteenth of September – when he arrived at the site, Thomas found a crowd of men standing at the foot of the tower. Jean Compagnon was standing apart, looking grim. The wagons bearing the sections for the day had all arrived, their teams of horses standing silently. But none of the sections had been picked up by the crane, and nobody was going up the tower.

He saw Pepe.

'What's up?'

'The men strike. They want more pay.'

In a few minutes, when the workers had all arrived, one of the older flyers, a tall, bony-faced man named Éric, addressed them.

'Brothers, the conditions under which we're working are a disgrace. So last night a group of us got together and now we're asking you to join us and call a strike. We have agreed on our main grievances. If you want to add to them, then now's the time to raise your complaint. Do you all agree that I should read our grievances out?'

There was a chorus of approval.

'First: we are being asked to work under dangerous conditions. No one has ever had to work at heights like this. Yet the workers on this tower are being paid the same as if we were working on an ordinary building. Further, as soon as the winter ended, Monsieur Eiffel demanded that we work a twelve-hour day. And long hours cause fatigue – which in itself is dangerous on a high building. Eiffel is trying to squeeze every last drop of blood out of the workers on this tower, brothers. The workers are being exploited.'

There was a broad murmur of agreement. 'And what about the wages?' someone called.

'Exactly. Second: Monsieur Eiffel has announced a small increase in wages. The top men will be getting sixteen centimes an hour. Note this. Per hour. But we are just about to go back to winter hours. Will you get any extra money for your trouble? Not a centime. We're going to be exploited even further, under arctic conditions. And Eiffel doesn't care. The only way to get his attention is a work stoppage.'

'You mean a strike?' someone called out.

'We stop work now. That's a stoppage. If we're not satisfied by the end of the day, you can call it a strike.' He looked around at them all. 'Brothers, I open the meeting. Who wants to speak?'

Several men stepped up. One spoke of the need for hot drinks in the cold, another about the need for special clothing. Two more complained about the wages and the hours. Yet as Thomas listened, he didn't feel comfortable with what was being said. Rather to his own surprise, he found himself coming forward.

'I agree about the cold and the need for hot drinks,' he said. 'My hands were freezing last winter, and the higher we go, the colder it seems to get.' This was met with nods. 'But I'm not sure about the extra danger.' He shrugged. 'The safety barriers and netting are pretty good. Nobody's fallen so far. But I mean, if you did fall,' he shrugged, 'two hundred feet, or four hundred feet, doesn't make a difference. You're going home in a box anyway.' A few of the men laughed at this, but Éric was not pleased.

'Don't you want to be paid for the extra height?'

'I'll take more money as soon as the next man,' Thomas answered, 'but we signed on knowing what the wage was, and we're getting more than the usual rate anyway.'

It was true, but it wasn't what the men wanted to hear. There were some growls. Suddenly, Thomas found Éric standing beside him. The tall man put a large, hard hand on his shoulder.

'Now we all know that this young man is a friend of Monsieur Eiffel. So maybe he's not exactly on the same side as us.' This caused a murmur of agreement that was none too friendly. Thomas was taken by surprise. He hadn't realised that the fact he'd worked for Eiffel before, or that Eiffel sometimes chatted with him, might be turned against him like this. Éric was well into his stride now, though. 'No, brothers, no, I don't believe the young man means any harm by it. He's a good young fellow. But, brothers, there are two things we need to remember. The first is that our demands are reasonable, and we all agree about that – well, perhaps my young friend here doesn't. And second,' – he gave the men a knowing smile – 'this is a negotiation.' He paused to let the thought sink in. 'My friends, Eiffel has to finish this tower. His entire reputation and his personal fortune are at stake. If he fails, he's bust. And he's running late.' He grinned. 'We've got the bastard over a barrel.' He paused once more. 'Anyone else want to argue?'

They didn't. There were shouts of approval. Éric kept his hand clamped on Thomas's shoulder.

'If the tower's not finished,' Thomas said, too quietly for anyone to hear, 'we shall have dishonoured France in the eyes of the whole world.'

'It'll get finished,' Éric replied, just as quietly. 'But I'd keep my mouth shut, if I were you. Wouldn't want you falling off the tower, would we?'

The work stopped that day. Eiffel turned up at the site an hour later and had an urgent conversation with Jean Compagnon. Then the two of them went to talk to Éric. The engineer looked furious, but it seemed he didn't give way. The men stood around all day, but nothing happened. Late in the afternoon, the foreman told them they might as well go home for the day.

As Thomas was walking off the site, Pepe fell into step beside him. 'Want a drink?' he said. As he had nothing else to do, he agreed gladly enough. Pepe lived in the sprawling quarter on the Left Bank to the south of the tower, and he took Thomas to a bar there.

'I didn't dare say what you did,' Pepe told him, 'but I think you were right.' Then they talked about his family, and the Italian girl he was hoping to marry, and Thomas told him a little about Édith, but not too much, and they agreed that they'd all meet one Sunday, and Pepe would take them to a place where they could get an Italian meal for not too much money. After parting the best of friends, Thomas walked back, crossed the river in the usual way and made his way home.

He came to the rue de la Pompe. His lodgings were not far ahead. He passed the darkened gateway to the yard that had once been the farm of Édith's family.

The strong hand that clamped on his shoulder took him completely by surprise. He lunged forward to run, but felt his other arm held in a grip he couldn't break out of. Someone powerful, very powerful, had moved out of the shadows. He twisted, punched hard over his shoulder at where his assailant's face might be. But the unseen figure anticipated him. He kicked back hard with his right boot, and felt the body behind him shift skilfully. Whoever it was knew how to fight. And he was just opening his mouth to shout for help, when a familiar voice spoke into his ear.

'Keep still, you fool. I need to talk to you.' Then the grip relaxed, and he turned to face the burly figure of Jean Compagnon. 'Stay in the shadow,' the foreman said, so Thomas stepped into the gateway.

'Couldn't you have met me in a bar?' Thomas asked, having recovered himself.

'Bad idea. Never know who might see you. The men already think you may be a stool pigeon.'

'But I'm not.'

'That's not the point. It was brave, what you did today. Took me by surprise. But now you've got to be careful.'

'You mean Éric might push me off the tower?'

'No. Not unless you annoy him. You were quite useful to him today, you know. You provided a focus. Anyone who thought of disagreeing with him would be pointed at as one of your friends. A stool pigeon of Eiffel's. That suits Éric very well.'

'The son of a bitch.'

'That's politics. Éric won't hurt you, but one of the men might. You never know.'

'What do I do?'

'Nothing. Keep your mouth shut and your eyes open. I've enough troubles without having to look out for you all the time. I did that once already.'

Thomas was silent for a moment. Was Compagnon letting him know that he'd noticed him that day he'd panicked when he'd looked down in the early days of the tower's building? Probably.

'What's going to happen about the strike?' he asked.

'Eiffel's furious. But Éric's right. He'll have to settle. It'll take a day or two.'

'Won't Éric just do it again?'

'I don't think so.'

'How can you be sure?'

'I'll make sure. Now, lad, I've got a home to go to. Are you going to keep your mouth shut?'

'Yes.'

'Don't talk to me. Don't talk to Eiffel. Keep your head down. Now beat it.'

So Thomas walked up the rue de la Pompe. He supposed Jean Compagnon stayed in the shadows for a while. He didn't look back.

The bargaining lasted three days. In the end, the men were given a bonus that would reach an extra four centimes a day. They were given waterproofs, and sheepskin clothes, and mulled wine to warm them up. Eiffel also set up a canteen on the first platform.

The men went back to work. Although Thomas was aware that he was regarded with suspicion, nobody gave him any trouble. During the month of October, the tower rose rapidly.

Thomas saw Édith regularly now. One Saturday night they went out with Pepe and his friend Anna, a pleasant, round-faced Italian girl, who took them to a little place that served Italian food, which neither Thomas nor Édith had ever eaten before. It was a good evening. He discovered that Pepe had a good voice and liked to sing Neapolitan songs.

Thomas would often kiss Édith. But so far at least, he had never had the chance to use the *capotes anglaises* that he sometimes secreted in his pocket. For Édith would never let him go all the way.

They went to see her aunt again. This time Édith's mother was not there. Aunt Adeline probably wasn't overjoyed to see him, but she didn't show it. Monsieur Ney, however, chancing to look in again, welcomed Thomas politely and urged him, 'Next time you visit, young man, don't forget to bring your little brother.'

So when, halfway through November, he and Édith agreed to meet the following Sunday at her aunt's, he told her: 'Say to Monsieur Ney that I will bring Luc with me.'

★　　★　　★

On Sunday, he met Luc near the Arc de Triomphe. As they walked down the avenue de la Grande-Armée, Luc was in a cheerful mood.

'I don't know why Ney wants to see you,' Thomas admitted. 'But I thought I'd better not disappoint him.'

'He has no particular reason,' Luc assured him. 'Do you remember the giant squid that attacked the submarine in *Twenty Thousand Leagues Under the Sea*?' One didn't need to have read Jules Verne's classic tale to remember the giant squid. Popular illustrations had made highlights of the story familiar to almost every child in France. 'People like this *notaire* spread their tentacles out to catch anything they can. If he thinks it's possible I might be of use to him one day, he'll want to get one of his tentacles around me, that's all.'

'How would you be of use to him?' Thomas asked.

'Who knows? I'm just a young fellow who does things for people, and I don't ask questions. That's all he needs to know.' Luc smiled. 'He's right. I might do something for him one day. As long as he pays me.'

'If you say so, little brother,' said Thomas.

Édith met them at the door. She greeted them both, offered her cheek to Luc to kiss, as he was Thomas's brother, and took them inside.

'Monsieur Ney is out, but he's coming here shortly,' she told them. 'But Mademoiselle Hortense is here. She's calling on Madame Govrit, and my aunt says you should go up there to relieve her. Madame Govrit likes to see new people.'

The old lady was propped up in her handsome bed as usual. She had a lace cap on her head. On the bed lay some magazines that Mademoiselle Hortense had brought her, and as they entered, the lawyer's daughter was sitting very upright, with perfect posture, on a chair beside the bed. Thomas and Luc bowed to them both politely. Madame Govrit stared at them.

'I remember you,' she said to Thomas. 'Are you still building that monstrous tower?'

'Yes, madame. It's my job. I'm sorry.'

The old lady gave a sniff.

'Well, you'd better come closer so I can hear you better. And who's this?' She indicated Luc.

'My little brother, Luc, madame.'

'Is he building the tower too?'

'*Non, madame.*'

'I'm glad to hear it. He has more sense than you.' She looked appraisingly at Luc. 'He'll be very handsome, this one, don't you think?' she remarked to Hortense. Hortense bowed her head slightly to indicate that it might be so. 'He looks sly. I like him. Are you sly, young man?'

'I am whatever a lady likes me to be,' said Luc in his smoothest manner.

'Oh, what cheek!' exclaimed the old lady with delight. 'What a young villain.' She addressed Hortense again. 'Do not marry the young one, my dear. He'll lead you a dance. The older one looks more stable, I think. Not so amusing, but . . .' She shifted her gaze back to Luc. 'Ah, but he has mischievous eyes.'

Mademoiselle Hortense slowly turned and looked at the two Gascon boys. Her eyes rested on Luc, but only briefly. Then she transferred them to Thomas.

Her eyes were a very deep brown. He hadn't noticed before how dark they were. Almost chocolate. The colour was deep, but the eyes gave nothing away. He could find no emotion in them, nor any expression on her long, pale face. She was wearing a fashionable riding habit, whose narrow waist and swelling line accentuated her small breasts. Even more than before, the pale lawyer's daughter seemed to suggest erotic possibilities to him. She rose.

'I must leave you with these two young men, madame,' she said in a low voice. Yet as she passed him, Thomas thought that she paused, just for a moment, before moving to the door. And however absurdly, the thought came into his mind: perhaps, if she liked him . . . after all, she must be nearly thirty, and wasn't married yet . . . what a surprise for his family if, having turned down the daughter of La Veuve Michel, he were instead to waltz off with the heiress of rich Monsieur Ney, the *notaire*.

Luc meanwhile was wasting no time in amusing old Madame Govrit.

'Do you play cards, madame?'

'I used to, young man, but I haven't any cards now.'

Luc reached into his pocket and produced two packs of cards.

'*Tiens*!' she cried. 'This young man has everything. You have two packs?'

'*Oui, madame*. Shall we play bezique?'

She clapped her hands with pleasure.

'Excellent.'

As bezique was played by two, Thomas contented himself with supplying a tray, which was placed on the bed, and with watching while the old lady and his brother played. He couldn't tell whether Luc was letting her, but the old lady was taking more of the tricks and becoming quite animated. This continued very agreeably for almost half an hour. At the end of the game, the victorious lady gave them both a smile.

'That's enough, young man,' she said to Luc. 'But you have given me great pleasure.' She nodded at Thomas. 'I hope you have not been too bored, monsieur.'

'Not at all, madame. My little brother has too good an opinion of himself, so I like to see him defeated.'

'And what do you think of this tower your brother is building?' she asked Luc. 'They say it is seen from all over Paris, but I can't see it from my window.'

'It's already taller than the highest cathedral spire in Europe,' Luc told her. 'You can certainly see it from the avenue de la Grande-Armée.'

'I want to see it,' Madame Govrit declared. 'I want to see it now. We still have a couple of hours of light. Will you young men take me to the avenue?'

'Certainly, madame,' said Luc. 'It's not far away.'

Madame Govrit turned to Thomas.

'Do me the kindness, young man,' she commanded, 'to tell them that I wish to go out.'

For a moment, Édith was speechless.

'Go out? Nobody ever goes out. I don't think they're allowed to.'

They went to find Aunt Adeline.

'Everything that the residents need is here,' she told them firmly. 'And if not, it is bought for them. I'm sure Monsieur Ney would not hear of it.'

'You'll have to tell her, Aunt Adeline,' said Édith. 'We can't.'

Even Aunt Adeline hesitated at the thought of this ordeal. But the situation was quickly put in other hands by the arrival of Monsieur Ney himself.

'Ah, you are right, this is difficult,' he agreed, as soon as Aunt Adeline had told him the situation. 'Normally we do not let the residents out,' he explained to Édith and Thomas, 'because most are infirm, some confused. Funds do not permit that we should employ staff to take them out on the streets, and they cannot go alone. Imagine if we had them wandering all over Paris. But Madame Govrit . . .' – he nodded thoughtfully – 'she is perhaps a special case.' He looked at Thomas. 'She really wants to go out?'

'I'm afraid she was most insistent, monsieur.' Thomas realised that, inadvertently, he was falling into their way of talking, but he couldn't do anything about it. 'She had been playing cards with my brother. And now she wants to go as far as the avenue to get a glimpse of Monsieur Eiffel's tower – though I don't think the sight will please her.'

'Couldn't we tell her it's cold, and that she should wait until another day?' Édith suggested.

'With another resident, yes,' said Monsieur Ney with a faint smile. 'But Madame Govrit won't forget, I assure you.' He turned to Thomas again. 'I cannot spare Édith or her aunt, but might I ask if you and your brother would convey her to the avenue?'

'Of course, monsieur.' His chance to get in favour. 'With pleasure. We should take the greatest care.'

'Thank you,' said Ney. 'I will go and speak to her myself.'

They escorted her carefully down the main stairs. She insisted that she would walk with her sticks, but it was as well that the two Gascon brothers went one on each side of her. For the occasion, the handsome front door had been opened. 'My aunt says the last time it was unlocked was when Madame Govrit first arrived,' Édith had whispered. Down the front steps they went into the street, where they helped her into the large wheelchair that Monsieur Ney had provided.

It was certainly a magnificent conveyance. With two large side wheels and a single front wheel, the body of the chair was of handsome wicker basket construction. It took a minute or two before

Madame Govrit was ensconced, wrapped with a shawl around her neck and a blanket to cover her body. But when all was ready, with Thomas pushing, the chair moved slowly away from the spectators at the front door with the solemn dignity of an ocean liner leaving port.

The wicker wheelchair was heavy. Thomas and Luc took turns pushing it. Madame Govrit meanwhile, rather flushed from the cold air, was observing the proceedings carefully. They negotiated one street, turned into another, crossed by a small church. Madame Govrit remarked that it was cold. Thomas politely asked if she wanted to turn back.

'Never,' she cried, though Thomas noticed a minute later that she had closed her eyes. For a minute or so she nodded off, but was wide awake again by the time they reached the broad avenue de la Grande-Armée.

It was a quiet Sunday afternoon. The trees in the avenue were bare. To the left, up the avenue's gentle slope, the Arc de Triomphe filled a portion of the grey November sky. Across the avenue, the long, low line of buildings stared dully at their counterparts. Here and there, carriages haunted the empty thoroughfare like boats on a deserted waterway. There were few pedestrians about.

Thomas pointed across the avenue and to the left.

'There it is, madame,' said Thomas. 'There's the tower.'

Had there been a sun in the west, its low rays might have bathed the girders in its softening light, so that they appeared like a mighty Gothic spire, full of romantic promise. But there was no sun. All that was to be seen, a mile away over the rooftops, was a grim, industrial tower attacking the heavens with its jagged iron spikes.

'*Mon Dieu!*' cried the old lady in horror. 'But it's frightful! It's terrible! It's worse than I could have imagined!' She slapped her hand on the arm of the wicker chair. '*Ah non!*'

'When it's finished . . .' Thomas began, but the old lady wasn't listening.

'What a horror!' she screamed in rage. She started to struggle forward, fighting with the shawl and blanket, as if she meant to rise and tear down the offending tower with her own hands. 'They must be stopped!' she cried. 'Stopped! Ah!'

She got tangled in the shawl and fell back into the chair. Thomas looked at Luc in consternation. Luc shrugged.

'She chose a bad afternoon,' said Luc.

Madame Govrit seemed to be almost panting after her exertions, but then apparently gave up in despair at what she had seen. She shuddered under the blanket. Thomas tried to straighten her blanket and shawl for her.

'I'm sorry, madame,' he said. 'Do you want to return?'

But Madame Govrit refused to answer him. He looked at Luc for help, and Luc leaned down.

'You know, madame,' Luc began, but then stopped and gazed at the old lady thoughtfully.

'What?' asked Thomas.

'She's dead,' said Luc.

December passed without incident at the tower until the twentieth of the month. On that day, one of the flyers claimed that he had been shortchanged an hour on his timesheet. Within the hour, it seemed that the men might go on strike again. This time, Eiffel promised a princely bonus of one hundred francs to each worker who continued until the building was finished. But anyone who didn't go back to work at once would be fired. Whatever arrangements Jean Compagnon had made seemed to give him confidence, and Éric did not press his case so hard this time. The few workers who held out were duly fired, and replacement workers appeared at once. As Christmas came, the tower continued to rise.

But Eiffel did one other thing that impressed Thomas very much.

'I shall paint the name of every man who worked on the tower from start to finish on a plaque, for all the world to see.'

'Just think of that,' Thomas told his family. 'I shall be immortal.' His mother said she was pleased for him, but his father was profoundly moved. 'Ah, now that's something. The first time our name has ever been written up.' It seemed to Thomas that his father was even more pleased by this addition to the family honour than he would have been if he'd married Berthe Michel.

If the start of the New Year was normally the day of greeting in France, the Christian festivals were well observed. Early in December came the Feast of Saint Nicolas; early January saw the season of Epiphany. As for Christmas, it was quieter than in some other lands, and was perhaps the better for it.

Monsieur Ney did not stint when it came to Christmas. On Christmas Eve, before celebrating the Midnight Mass at his church, the local priest came earlier in the evening to say a Mass for the old people in the house, which he did in the hall by the front door. As for the Réveillon feast that celebrated Christ's birth after the Midnight Mass, this was deferred for the old folk until lunchtime on Christmas Day.

Up in Montmartre, the Gascon family would be celebrating the feast with their neighbours up at the Moulin de la Galette into the early hours. So when Édith told Thomas that he was invited to join Monsieur Ney's lunchtime feast on Christmas Day, he didn't hesitate to accept.

For a week after the death of Madame Govrit, he had been afraid that the lawyer might blame him in some way. But since he and Luc had taken her out at Ney's own request, this would hardly have been reasonable. And while Ney was certainly upset to lose his prize resident, whose aristocratic name and presence lured others to place themselves in his hands, there had been compensations.

For soon after her death, it was discovered that, in addition to the moneys she had paid Monsieur Ney upon her arrival, she had also left a most generous bequest to Hortense.

'She was always very fond of Mademoiselle Hortense,' Aunt Adeline explained. The residue of her estate was to pass to the daughter of a poor cousin who had no idea she was to receive anything.

'Madame Govrit was kindness itself,' Monsieur Ney declared. 'She thought of everyone.' As executor of the will, he had told Aunt Adeline, it would give him particular joy to convey her bequest to this poor relation, as far as funds permitted.

Meanwhile the other residents were reminded, by the cautionary tale of what had befallen Madame Govrit, how wise it was of Monsieur Ney to insist that they should not go out.

When Thomas arrived, he found Édith and her aunt already helping those who were not bedridden into a long, narrow room off the hall, where a dining table had been set up. By the time this process was complete, there were nearly twenty old folk seated. Monsieur Ney took the head of the table, and Aunt Adeline the other end. Mademoiselle Hortense was not present. Secretly Thomas had rather hoped that she might be, as he wanted to observe her some more.

'Sadly, my daughter is unwell,' Ney explained. 'I think it was brought on by her distress over the loss of her friend Madame Govrit, but she suffered a bad cold, and I was obliged for her health to send her to the south. I hope the warmer weather in Monte Carlo may restore her.'

The lawyer had brought in two women from his own house to help serve at table. Édith and Margot, the old nurse, took food up to the bedridden in their rooms. Thomas offered to help them, but Ney wouldn't hear of it.

'You're our guest,' he directed, and Thomas was seated between Édith's mother and an old lady who seemed quite content to masticate her food while he talked to her, without making any reply.

The food was good. They began with oysters, accompanied by a glass of champagne. Then turkey with chestnut stuffing, and *boudin* pudding, with which a red bordeaux was served. The old folk were given just a glass, but Ney indicated to Thomas that he should fill his own glass as much as he pleased. As for Édith's mother, she needed no bidding, and it was clear that on this occasion at least, Aunt Adeline and Monsieur Ney were content to let her drink as much as she liked, on the premise that she would soon enough fall asleep.

Once, it seemed that Édith's mother wanted to rise to propose a toast, but Aunt Adeline gave her such a look that, flushed though she was, she kept quiet.

'An excellent meal, madame,' Thomas offered quickly.

'That's for sure,' she said.

Then came the highlight of the feast, the Christmas cake. Not the heavy fruitcake that the English favoured, but the light sponge covered in thick, chocolate butter cream, and rolled into a cylinder. Here Monsieur Ney had outdone himself. He had gone to one of the best patisseries in Paris, and bought a cake that stretched halfway down the long table. The Genoise sponge was golden, and the thick spiral of filling in each slice was of chocolate flavoured with chestnut. The outside was dusted with powdered sugar.

'The *patissier* has invented a charming name for the cake,' Monsieur Ney told them. 'He calls it a Yule log – *bûche de Noël*.'

By the end of the meal, everyone was satisfied. Ney, like a monarch who knows that his people will be obedient if they are entertained from time to time, was surveying the room with a look of calm benevolence on his narrow face. The old folk, sleepy and contented, were taken back to their rooms, with Thomas helping, while the table was cleared.

Édith and Margot the nurse appeared, having completed the feeding of the other residents in their rooms. Two places had been set for them at the empty table, and their food, kept warm in the kitchen, was set out under covers. Monsieur Ney thanked them both for their efforts, and left them with a bottle of wine before departing to his own house. Aunt Adeline retired to her quarters with Édith's mother, who was already half asleep. And Thomas joined Édith and old Margot at the table.

Margot ate stolidly and in silence. Édith poured wine for herself, and for Thomas.

'I've drunk too much already,' he said.

'Keep me company.' She smiled.

He watched her. She had grown her hair out in the last few weeks. Instead of being frizzed, it was fuller now, with soft curls just above her shoulders and a parting near the middle. Her face was perhaps a little fuller too.

More than ever, he found her desirable. It hadn't been appropriate to bring his *capotes anglaises* to Monsieur Ney's Christmas feast, but he hoped that before too long he might get the chance to use them.

Did she have the same feelings for him? He thought she did. After all, she went out with him, and let him kiss her, and asked him to the Christmas feast. But she was still cautious about letting her feelings show. She held back.

When Margot had finished eating, she waddled off to the kitchen, leaving them to sit and talk. They finished the bottle of wine. Édith added a little water to her wine, so he was actually drinking more, and on top of what he'd already had, he felt pleasantly flushed. She put her hand on his arm.

'You'll have to go soon,' she said. 'I'll have work to do at the end of the afternoon, and I need a little rest.'

'That's all right.'

'Thank you for coming. I'm glad you came.' She got up to take the remaining things to the kitchen. He stood to help her. 'Stay here,' she said.

A couple of minutes later she returned.

'My mother's asleep, of course, but even Aunt Adeline's nodded off.' She sat down beside him and he kissed her, but it wasn't very satisfactory in the upright chairs.

'I'd better rest,' she said.

'All right.' He stood. 'By the way,' he said, 'have they found a replacement for Madame Govrit yet?'

'No.' Édith shook her head. 'That may take time. Monsieur Ney will want a very special person for that room. You know, Mademoiselle Hortense has already redecorated it.' She smiled. 'Do you want to see it before you go?'

'Certainly.'

She led him out into the hall and up the main stairs. One of the steps gave a noble creak as they passed.

'Here we are,' she said, as she opened the door.

He recognised the bed, the armoire and the pictures, which were the same as before. But the panelling had all been repaired and painted. The bed had a new cover, very handsome, in heavy damask, and in front of the fire a small Second Empire sofa with a curved back, upholstered in the same material, had appeared. On the mantel over the fire there was now an ormolu boudoir clock whose dial was held by two gold cherubs; and to the left and right of it, a pair of pretty porcelain figures from the court of Louis XVI. There was a new rug on the floor. Together with the little rococo desk by the window, it all made a charming if slightly predictable ensemble.

It had all been accomplished so quickly, that Thomas wondered if some of these items might have come from the lawyer's house, perhaps from the room of Mademoiselle Hortense herself.

'As you see,' Édith remarked cheerfully, 'it's all ready to be shown off. We have a vase for flowers, when somebody comes to see it.'

He nodded. The room was clearly ready for another Mademoiselle Govrit de la Tour. Feminine. Perhaps even sensuous.

As Édith closed the door, she gave him a funny look.

'You could kiss me if you like,' she said. And he was just moving to do so when she went to the bed, pulled back the damask cover and lay on top of the blankets. 'Only a kiss,' she reminded him.

But half an hour later they were still there, with fewer clothes on. Thomas was wishing he had brought those *capotes anglaises*, only he'd never thought things would turn out like this. Then Édith got up, because she didn't dare use the sheets, and fetched a towel from the armoire and spread it on the bed and said, 'You must be careful.'

And Thomas kissed her and held her and said, 'I'll be gentle. Just tell me if it hurts.'

But Édith smiled and said that he didn't have to worry about that, and when he looked surprised, she said it was nothing important and a long time ago. And Thomas realised it was too late for him to think much about that now.

A little time passed. And then she cried, 'Oh, you mustn't,' but it was too late.

During the first two months of 1889, the Eiffel Tower raced towards completion. The progress was astounding. By March, it soared to over nine hundred feet, where the third and final platform was being constructed. Enclosed by glass, this observation platform would offer the astonished visitors a panoramic view with a radius, on a clear day, of thirty-five miles – northwards to the lovely park of Chantilly, southwards to the great Forest of Fontainebleau, and on its western side, far over Versailles and almost to the twin spires of Chartres Cathedral. The whole tower was being painted a bronze colour, gradually getting paler as the tower grew higher to increase its appearance of soaring elegance.

The greatest difficulty in these later stages was the installation of the elevators. For though there were stairs that went all the way up to the top, few people would care to mount 1,665 steps – and descend them again.

This work had to be subcontracted, and several companies were tried. But the task was almost beyond them, and they could hardly be blamed. Never before had they been asked to take such huge numbers of passengers up to such unheard-of heights. The elevators taking passengers the 550 feet from the second platform to the top posed less of a problem. But how to raise an elevator that was to travel from the ground, nearly 400 feet to the second platform, on tracks with a variable curve?

In the end, two systems were used for the four feet of the tower. French engineers supplied two inventively designed chain elevators that at least got people from the ground to the first platform. But the American Otis Elevator Company had invented a brilliantly contrived system, part hydraulic elevator, part railroad, that took passengers up the other two legs of the tower, and continued all the way up to the second platform.

Thomas would tell her enthusiastically about all that was happening.

'Monsieur Eiffel says the Otis elevator designs will be years ahead of the French. But we mustn't say so,' he confided. 'When the gallery is completed up at the top, they're building a private office for Monsieur Eiffel above it. He says that's going to be his office for the rest of his life. Imagine it: working each day up in the clouds like that, like a god.'

If Thomas loved his work, Édith thought, so much the better. And if he worshipped Monsieur Eiffel, there was no harm in that. 'Just think,' he'd often remind her, 'very soon, my name will be painted up there on the tower, because I helped to build it.'

Sometimes, during these weeks, Édith would walk over to the Trocadéro before she went to work in the lycée and gaze into the sky where Thomas was working. If the day was misty, she might not be able to see the upper part of the tower at all. More often, under a blanket of cloud, and through the smoke from a thousand chimneys, she would see a faint hint of firelight in the sky as the rivets were heated on their little braziers high in the girders. But sometimes, if the sky was clear, she would see those same braziers twinkle like stars, and smile, wondering if Thomas was standing with his hammer beside one of them.

They had not made love again after Christmas Day. He had wanted to. 'I have protection,' he had told her. But she had been reluctant. 'Not just yet,' she had told him, several times. He'd been rather hurt and frustrated, and she knew that her refusal made no sense. But for reasons she could not explain, she did not want to give herself to him again. Not yet. Not until she had decided what to do.

It was in mid-January that she had started to get alarmed. But she hoped she might be wrong, and she told nobody. By mid-February, there could be no doubt. It was useless to talk to her mother, but she went to see Aunt Adeline.

'Idiot!' her aunt cried. 'When?' – and when Édith told her the when and where, 'You're insane. And he took no precautions?'

'We weren't planning to. It just happened.'

'Have you told him?'

'No.'

'Why?'

'Because he'd want to have the child and get married. I know him.'

'Ah.' Aunt Adeline considered. 'Faced with the reality, he might not be so keen.'

'No. It's his character.'

'Do you love him?'

'He looked for me all over Paris, for a year. I couldn't believe it, but it's true. And since he found me, he's never given up.'

'I didn't ask if he loved you. I asked if you loved him.'

'He's nice with me. He's considerate. He tries to please me. And he's honest. I like that. And I find him seductive. I want him when he's there.'

'He has no money.'

'I can't complain. Nor have I.'

'We'll try to get you a little. You know that I think you can do better.'

'People with a little money like to find other people with a little money too. Maybe rich people marry who they like.'

'No, they don't. Their families see to that.'

'He's loyal. At least I don't think he'd walk out on me like my father.'

Aunt Adeline was silent for a moment. Then she said: 'I don't want to tell Monsieur Ney. He wouldn't be pleased at all.' She considered. 'Perhaps I could arrange for you to go away for a while. You could have the child. But we'd have to give the child up for adoption. Nobody need be any the wiser. That's one alternative.' She looked sadly at Édith. 'Or, I know a doctor who could take care of it . . .'

'I'm afraid of that.' Édith shook her head. 'It can be dangerous.'

'You know, my child, that if you have the child and keep it, you have no chance of making a respectable marriage, don't you? Unless you marry this boy. But I foresee a life of poverty.'

'I know. I need to think.'

'Well, don't think for too long. It'll show in a while.'

'I feel as if it does already.'

'That's just your imagination. But during the spring . . .'

And now March had begun, and still Édith hadn't decided what to do. Nor had she told Thomas.

Édith didn't often think about her father. The truth was, she hardly remembered him. But she knew what he looked like. Her mother had no picture of him, but Aunt Adeline did. The picture showed quite a handsome-looking man. His hair appeared to be the same dark colour as Aunt Adeline's, but where hers was neatly pulled back, his was shaggy. There was something boyish about him. He was wearing a jacket, but his shirt was open at the collar. He looked like what he was, an intelligent working man, a builder, Aunt Adeline said.

Had he left because his wife was a foolish drinker, or had she got that way because he left? Édith suspected it was the latter, but she wasn't sure, and Aunt Adeline would never discuss it. Where had he gone? 'Who knows?' her aunt would say with a shrug.

Sometimes Édith would imagine that Aunt Adeline did know where her father was and that she was keeping it a secret. Perhaps he did not want to live with her mother. Perhaps there was some other trouble that he had to hide. Perhaps he was in prison. But she liked to think that, wherever he was, he cared about her. She pictured him asking Aunt Adeline for reports of her, and listening to them eagerly. He might know all about her. He could even be secretly watching her sometimes as she walked down the street – watching her with love and pride. It was possible. You never knew. She realised that these were childish fantasies, but she could not help it if, when she was in her bed all alone at night, she sometimes allowed herself to dream of such things before she went to sleep.

Lately, she had been thinking of her father more often. And she compared in her mind the feelings of warmth that these foolish dreams brought her with the feeling of warmth and comfort she experienced when she was with Thomas, and he put his strong arms around her, and held her. And sometimes when she thought of him like that, she thought she would tell him about the baby growing within her, and sometimes she wasn't so sure. But she was beginning to think that perhaps she would.

So when he suggested that they meet Pepe and Anna on Sunday, because Pepe had discovered an Irish bar where you could eat cheaply

– he was always inventive like that – she'd agreed, thinking that maybe at the end of the day, when she and Thomas were walking back together, she might tell him her secret.

They met at the Irish bar in the middle of the day. It was on the edge of the Saint-Germain quarter near the old Irish College. The two young men were especially pleased with themselves because their crew had been among the last twenty men working at the top of the tower. This was a special badge of honour.

Pepe insisted they all drink the dark Irish Guinness with their meal, which they were not used to. Then they drank some red wine. Thomas amused them all by confessing how he'd sworn to Monsieur Eiffel that he had an excellent head for heights, and then frozen with panic before the building even got to the first platform. Anna told them stories about her huge family in Italy. By the time they were finally ready to leave, they were all very happy, but a little tipsy.

They strolled back together, along the left bank of the Seine. The tower, virtually completed, rose into the blue sky ahead of them. They reached the great site, where numerous halls were already being prepared for the huge exhibition. Some way off, there were people on the bridge staring up, but the fenced-off site was empty.

And they were just about to go their separate ways when Pepe said: 'And now, Thomas and I will give you a demonstration of the fearless flyers of the Eiffel Tower.'

He led them to a small gap in the fence and in another minute they were in the quiet space under the huge southern archway of the tower.

'Want to come up?' he asked the girls.

'No,' said Édith. 'Anyway, it's all locked.'

But Pepe only laughed.

'Come on, Thomas,' he cried. 'Let's go.'

Édith stared in horror. It suddenly occurred to her: if anything were to happen to Thomas, now of all times . . .

'Stay here, Thomas,' she begged him. 'Don't go up. You've been drinking.'

'We're not drunk,' Pepe cried. 'They give us wine up the tower every day.'

'Please, Thomas,' she implored.

But the two men were already swarming up the huge framework. After a while they got into the stairs. She and Anna could see them running happily up them, laughing as they went. Then, for a short while, they couldn't be seen.

'Where do you think they are?' she asked Anna.

'Perhaps they're going to the top,' Anna suggested.

'Oh my God, don't let them do that,' Édith prayed. She looked up the huge iron network reaching into the sky. The safety barriers were all gone now. There was nothing to protect anyone out there on the girders. She still couldn't see them. She and Anna moved in closer, almost under the arch.

Then, somewhere up there, she heard Thomas's voice calling down.

'Édith! Can you see me?' And then, just behind the huge arch under the first landing, she saw him balanced on a girder.

'Yes. But take care!' she cried.

'It was here exactly. This is where I panicked.'

'Are you all right?'

'But of course.' He waved.

'Where's Pepe?' called Anna.

There was a brief silence. Then Pepe's voice floated down to them.

'Anna. Look to the left of Thomas.'

He was on a beam, a little higher, standing very comfortably with his hands on his hips, and staring down at them as if he owned the place.

Édith called out to them both that they should come down now or someone would see, and they'd all get into trouble. Reluctantly, Thomas moved to one side, and she could see him getting near the stairs. But Pepe hadn't come in yet. And then, suddenly, he began to sing.

O dolce Napoli
O suol beato . . .

The strains of the Neapolitan song wafted down. He had a pleasing tenor voice. Édith could hear every word. Anna clapped her hands with pleasure. Could the people out on the bridge hear this concert performance emanating from the depths of the huge iron structure? It was possible. His voice was very clear. He came to the chorus.

Santa Lucia, Santa Lucia . . .

Anxious that he shouldn't sing another verse, Édith applauded vigorously. And then, hoping to get him off the tower quickly, she shouted out: 'Take a bow, Pepe, and come down.'

Pepe obliged. He made a magnificent, theatrical bow. Then another to the left, and also to the right, and a final, still deeper bow to the centre again. And lost his balance.

It happened so quickly that, apart from a tiny motion with his hand as he reached out for something to hold on to, it was almost as if he had purposely dived. His body fell. How tiny it seemed under the massive iron arch. They heard his voice, a single, fearful 'Oh . . .' And strangely, neither she nor Anna screamed out, but watched, stunned, as the little body plummeted, one, two, three seconds and then, not sixty feet from her, hit the hard ground with a thud so terrible, so final, that she knew instantly that there could not be anything left of the person that, a moment ago, had been Pepe.

Thomas Gascon never knew he could think so fast. A year ago, on these same girders, he had stood paralysed in panic. Today, as he clattered down the metal stairs, more than three hundred of them, flight after flight after flight, taking them almost at a run, he found that he saw everything with a cold clarity that amazed him. By the time he clambered out on to the girders, slid down over the concrete base, and raced across to Édith and Anna, he knew exactly what must be done.

Anna was crouched on the ground beside Pepe's body. She was shaking with shock. At least, thank God, she wasn't screaming. Édith had her arms around her.

Thomas quickly inspected poor Pepe. His small body was a crumpled mess. His neck was twisted at a strange angle, a pool of blood already forming in front of his open mouth. He reminded Thomas of a baby bird that has fallen out of a high nest. Wherever the spirit of his cheerful friend had gone, it was already somewhere far, far away.

'Édith,' he asked, 'does Monsieur Ney have a telephone?' He knew there were only a few thousand people in all Paris who had one, but he thought the lawyer might be one of them.

'I think so.'

'Go to him as fast as you can. Tell him what happened, and that Monsieur Eiffel must be informed at once. Also the police. He will know what to do. Then you stay with your aunt. I shall wait here with Anna.' He reached into his pocket and gave her money. 'If you walk fast you can reach him in less than half an hour. But if you see a cab, take it. And don't say anything to anyone, even the police, until you get to Ney.'

'If he's out?'

'Your aunt will help you. Try to find him. We have to tell the police, but it's essential Monsieur Eiffel knows at once.'

Édith didn't like to leave Anna, but she agreed to go. As she left, Thomas kissed her and repeated quietly, 'Don't come back.'

As she left, he wondered if anyone on the bridge had seen Pepe fall. They might have. But they might not. If they had, the police would probably arrive quite soon. That couldn't be helped. But at least he'd done his best to protect the two people who mattered: Édith and Monsieur Eiffel.

Then he sat down, put his arm around Anna, and waited.

He waited an hour and a half. It seemed an eternity. Then a group of people all arrived together. Monsieur Eiffel and Ney and a small man with a neatly trimmed moustache were closely followed by a uniformed policeman, a young man with a camera apparatus and two men with a stretcher.

While Eiffel moved slightly apart, Ney spoke.

'As you see, Inspector,' he addressed the man with the moustache, 'my client awaits you exactly as I said he would. And this young lady I am sure is the friend of the unfortunate young man.'

The inspector glanced at Thomas briefly, moved to Pepe's body, gave it the briefest inspection, glanced up at the tower and nodded to the young man with the camera, who was already setting up a tripod to take photographs.

Meanwhile Ney had gone to Thomas's side.

'You have shown intelligence by your actions, young man,' he said in a low voice. 'Now listen carefully. Answer the questions that the

217

inspector puts to you, and answer them very briefly. That is the only information he wishes to know. Add nothing. You understand? Nothing.'

Thomas saw the inspector look at Ney inquiringly. The lawyer gave him a slight nod.

'My client is ready to help you, Inspector.'

The inspector came across. Apart from his moustache, his face was clean-shaven. His hair was thin over a broad brow. His eyes reminded Thomas of oysters. They were watchful and somewhat sad. He took out a notebook.

The preliminaries were brief: his name, the address where he lived – Thomas gave his lodgings in the rue de la Pompe. The time of the incident. The name and occupation of the deceased. He had been with the deceased before the incident? Where? The Irish bar.

'Had the deceased drunk anything at the Irish bar?'

'Yes, monsieur. Both Guinness and wine.'

'Was he inebriated?'

'Not drunk. He had control of himself . . .'

'But he had consumed both beer and wine.'

'Certainly.'

'Then he climbed up the tower.'

'Yes, Inspector.'

'How?'

'Up the girders at first, since the staircase is closed. Then into the staircase and up to the first platform, then out on to the girders.'

'You saw him do this?'

'Yes.' He was about to explain that he had gone up with him, but remembering what Ney had said, and since the inspector had not yet asked where he was himself, he did not offer this information.

'What did he do up there?'

'He sang an Italian song.'

'Then what?'

'He fell.'

'How?'

'He took a bow, quite a big one. Three times. Centre, then left, then right. Then he took a final bow, deeper than the others, and lost his balance. Then . . . it was very sudden.'

'This girl is his friend?'

'Yes. She is very shocked.'

'Naturally.' The inspector turned to Anna. 'I understand you are distressed, mademoiselle, but I must ask you a few questions.'

Her name and address. Pepe's name and address. Was he of Italian family? Was she? How long had she known him? Had she drunk Guinness and wine with him at the Irish bar? Did he climb the tower and sing an Italian song? Was she standing below? Did he take a bow three times, then a final bow, and lose his balance? Did she see this, and was this what happened?'

'Yes. Yes it was.' She burst into tears.

The inspector closed his notebook, and turned to Ney and Eiffel.

'It is very clear. I am satisfied. There will be some formalities later, of course, but unless Monsieur Eiffel wishes it, I personally see no need to take matters further.'

Eiffel indicated that he also was satisfied. At a nod from the inspector, the two assistants put Pepe on the stretcher and started to carry him away.

'I think I should take Anna to her home,' said Thomas.

Ney glanced at Eiffel, who said he was going to remain at the site for a while. Then Ney told Thomas that he and Anna should come with him, and he would convey them home. Thomas wondered if he should say something to Monsieur Eiffel, but the engineer had already turned his back.

By the bridge, the lawyer had a small *fiacre* waiting. The two men put Anna between them, the cab driver whipped up his single horse, and they set off.

Anna lived with her parents in a small tenement near the southern Porte d'Italie. It took them nearly half an hour to reach it. When they got there, Ney went in with Anna to speak to the girl's parents. When he emerged he told Thomas that he would return him to his lodgings.

'You must not try to see Édith today,' he told him. 'She is resting.'

They had gone a short distance when Thomas ventured to speak something that had been on his mind.

'You were good enough to say to the police that I was your client, monsieur, but you know I haven't much money.'

'You need not concern yourself with that,' the lawyer replied. 'Monsieur Eiffel wishes it.'

'I am amazed he would do such a thing for me. Does he know that this is partly my fault?'

'Do not deceive yourself, young man. Monsieur Eiffel is not pleased with you at all. But there is more at stake here. The tower is the centre of the Universal Exposition, the World's Fair that is about to open. The honour of France as well as that of Monsieur Eiffel are at stake. Having heard the details from Édith, I was able to point out to him, and also to the inspector, that tragic though the business is, it is somewhat fortunate, to put it bluntly, that the deceased young man was Italian. No one wants a Frenchman to be involved with such an embarrassment. It is in nobody's interest that your part in this should receive publicity. I was therefore able to protect both Édith and yourself.'

'That is why the inspector never asked me where I was when Pepe fell.'

'Precisely. He had no wish to know. If there were any doubt that this was a stupid and terrible accident, it would be another matter. But that is not the case.'

'His fall was exactly as I described it, I assure you.'

'If the authorities require you to testify again, they will come to me, and I shall tell you what to do. But in the meantime, I must stress to you that nobody must know of your part in this. I have made the parents of Anna quite terrified. She will not speak of it at all. Édith you may be sure has no reason to do so. But you must keep silent, or Monsieur Eiffel will be very angry. Technically, you know, he could prosecute you for entering the tower the way you did.'

'I shall not speak a word.'

'Good. I was able to tell Monsieur Eiffel that, as a lawyer, I thought you had acted very wisely after the accident.'

Clearly Ney had lost no time in making himself useful to Eiffel, thought Thomas. One could only admire him for it.

But after the lawyer dropped him off in the rue de la Pompe, he suddenly found he was very tired.

By the time he went to work the next day, Thomas was ready with his story. In the first place, he'd say nothing. If by chance anyone knew he'd met Pepe for a meal on Sunday, he'd simply say that he'd parted from him immediately afterwards, and known nothing about the accident.

If there had been any doubt in his mind about the consequences of saying anything else, they ended as he walked down the rue de la Pompe.

He was just passing the place where Édith's family had once had their little farm when Jean Compagnon fell into step beside him.

'Nice day,' said the foreman.

'It is,' said Thomas.

'Keep your mouth shut,' said Compagnon.

'Don't know what you mean,' said Thomas. 'But I always do.'

'If anyone finds out, Eiffel will fire you. He'll have to.'

Thomas didn't answer.

'But that,' continued Jean Compagnon pleasantly, 'will be the least of your troubles. Because I'll be waiting for you, and you'll join your friend Pepe, wherever he may be.'

'I don't know what you mean,' said Thomas, 'but I'm sorry if you don't trust me.'

'I trust you,' said Jean Compagnon. Then a moment later he turned abruptly into another street, leaving Thomas to go on alone.

Thomas was strong, and he knew how to fight. But he wasn't under any illusions. If the burly foreman wanted to kill him, he could do it.

At the tower, Pepe was replaced without any explanation. They were doing the finishing touches now. Not all the men were needed any more. No doubt the news of the accident would be out soon, but obviously it had not been released to the newspapers yet. The day passed quietly.

It did not pass so quietly for Édith. She had slept through the night in her aunt's quarters, because Aunt Adeline had given her a sleeping draught. She awoke and took a little tea and a croissant.

But even while she was eating this *petit déjeuner*, the terrible feeling that had been gnawing at her the day before came back, with just the same awful, insistent coldness, so that she cried out to Aunt Adeline in agony: 'It was me that killed him! It was my fault.'

Her aunt sighed.

'You're quite wrong.'

'I told him to take a bow. If he hadn't done that . . .'

'He would have done it anyway.'

'Maybe not.'

'He had the choice. People have to take responsibility for their actions. It was he who decided to go up the tower, anyway, in the first place.'

There was truth in this. But not enough, Édith felt, to absolve her. She sat with her head bowed over her cup of tea, shaking her head slowly.

And then something happened.

At first, when she felt the little gush, she didn't understand. She went into the bedroom where she slept and used the bed pan. A few minutes later, she called her aunt.

Aunt Adeline was very calm. She told Édith to stay where she was and that she'd be back in a few minutes. Then she went out to fetch the doctor.

Later in the morning, the doctor gave her the news. She had lost the child.

'Thank God,' said Aunt Adeline.

It was a week later that Thomas was told Monsieur Eiffel wanted to see him in his office.

The great man had wasted no time installing himself in his office at the top of the tower. Since the elevators were not operating yet, it meant a huge climb; but Eiffel didn't seem to mind. From the third platform, a small spiral staircase led directly up to his quarters.

As he knocked on the door and went in, Thomas was struck by how comfortable the office was. The wall had already been papered in a dark, striped wallpaper. There was a patterned carpet on the floor. Eiffel had a table, a desk and a couple of chairs, and a few small ornaments. And one could look out on a breathtaking panorama. Monarchs and presidents might have palaces, but Monsieur Eiffel, without any doubt, now had the finest office in the world.

There was quite a strong wind blowing that day. As he stood close to the pinnacle of the great tower, Thomas could just feel the faintest motion.

Eiffel was sitting at his desk. He was looking at some papers. Without looking up, he read Thomas's thoughts.

'The maximum sway caused by the wind is about twelve centimetres,' he remarked drily. He finished checking a list, then looked up. 'You know why I sent for you?'

'I think so, monsieur. I apologise.'

'When the Russian tsar built his city of St Petersburg, he drove his workers relentlessly. Do you know how many men died working on that great enterprise?'

'*Non, monsieur.*'

'A hundred thousand. St Petersburg rests on their bones. When we began work on this tower,' Eiffel continued, 'it was assumed there would be accidents. There always are on big projects, alas. But I took exemplary care. I put in movable barriers and screens – safety precautions more sophisticated than anything used on a building site before. And we built the tower without the loss of a single life.' He paused. 'Until the other day.'

'It was not your fault, Monsieur Eiffel. It was mine. It was an accident.'

'Do you think that anyone will remember that? All that will be remembered will be that one of the workers on my tower fell to his death.'

'I am truly sorry, monsieur.'

'I made space for you, when you asked me if you could work on the tower. This is how you repay my kindness. You have dishonoured me.'

Thomas bowed his head. The children of the Maquis, like the knights of old, understood honour. Every Frenchman understood it. And he had dishonoured his hero.

'I have in front of me the list of names of the workers on the tower,' continued Eiffel. 'As I promised, they will be painted on a plaque where they may be seen. But I cannot bring myself to add your name to the list. Do you understand? You will receive your bonus of a hundred francs, but no public recognition.'

Thomas nodded. He did not look up. He could not speak.

'That is all,' said the builder of the tower.

Thomas had seen Édith only once since the accident. He had met her as usual outside the lycée. She had been off work for a couple of days, she told him, and she wouldn't be free that Sunday. He wanted to talk a little about what had happened, but she seemed preoccupied, and he left feeling uncertain about where he stood with her.

So it was not surprising if, up on Montmartre that Sunday, his family found him rather subdued. Was everything all right at work, his father asked?

'Not bad,' he replied. 'Monsieur Eiffel himself told me I'd be getting my bonus at the end.'

'And your name written up,' his father said proudly.

Thomas changed the subject.

'I'll be looking for work again, as soon as I'm finished on the tower,' he reminded them.

In the afternoon, he went for a walk with his brother.

'How's Édith?' asked Luc.

'All right.'

'That's good.' It seemed to Thomas that his brother had something he'd been waiting to tell him. But they walked on in silence for a little way before Luc asked him casually: 'Have you seen the posters for the Wild West show?'

One could hardly miss them. They seemed to be sprouting on every billboard in Paris. A huge buffalo, racing across the prairie, took up most of the picture. Inset on his powerful body, however, was an oval portrait of the handsome and unmistakable features of Colonel W. F. Cody, Buffalo Bill himself, with beard, moustache and cowboy hat, and underneath him just two words in French.

Je Viens: I am coming.

Everyone had heard of Buffalo Bill's circus. It had already had a triumphant tour in England. People might not be sure exactly what the spectacle entailed, but it was known to be exotic, and exciting. It would be one of the biggest side attractions of the Universal Exposition.

'I was given a couple of tickets,' said Luc. 'Thought you might like them. You could take Édith.' He pulled a little packet out of his pocket, carefully extracted two tickets, and handed them to Thomas to see. Thomas stared at them.

'But this is for the grand opening! How in the world did you get them?'

'A gentleman gave them to me.' Luc grinned. 'I'd helped him with something.'

'But you should go,' protested Thomas.

'No. I want you to have them.'

'But they're for the grand opening,' Thomas repeated.

'That's right,' said Luc.

It was Wednesday before he saw Édith, but this time she agreed to accompany him to the bar they'd gone to the first time they met. She even agreed to eat a little.

All the same, Thomas sensed that she was uncertain about something, and he was anxious to find out exactly what it was.

'I've been worried about you,' he said.

'I'm all right.'

'I feel terrible about what happened. I never meant to put you through that.'

'You shouldn't. After all, it was my fault.'

'Your fault?' He stared at her in astonishment.

'Yes. If I hadn't told him to take a bow . . .'

'Édith.' He put his arm around her shoulder. 'I never even thought of such a thing. Pepe was going to do that anyway, I promise you. That's just the way he was.'

She didn't say anything for a moment, but she was weighing his words.

'You really think so?' she said at last.

'Of course. I know it.' He reached over and kissed her head. 'You can put that idea out of your mind. It isn't so.'

She stared down at the table. After a pause, she picked up her glass of red wine, took a slow sip, and put it down on the table again, still holding the stem for a little while, before finally releasing it.

'There's something else you should know,' she said, and looked up into his face.

Then she told him about the miscarriage.

When she had finished, he was left staring at her open-mouthed.

'I had no idea you were pregnant,' he said.

'I know.'

'Why didn't you tell me?'

'I don't know. I didn't want to.'

'I thought . . . after what happened at Christmas, and then you were suddenly cold . . .'

'I was anxious. And upset. Perhaps I felt angry with you. I suppose . . . it makes no sense, but I was afraid to be with you.'

'I thought maybe you didn't like me.'

'I know.'

'Oh.' He considered. 'Are you still angry with me now?'

'No.'

'How do you feel about everything?'

'When you lose a baby, even so early when, you know, there's hardly anything, you feel a sort of grief.' She shrugged. 'But now, I feel relief. I can't deny that. I don't want a baby, Thomas. I mean, not now.'

'Of course.' He pulled her to him and held her closer. 'You could have told me. You can trust me.'

She nodded silently. She knew that.

They talked quietly for a little while. It seemed to Thomas that her mood was lightening. She felt warm beside him.

'Would you like to do something dangerous?' he suddenly asked. He felt her stiffen, and he laughed. 'Would you like to go to the Wild West show?'

On the first day of April 1889, at the start of the afternoon, Monsieur Eiffel gave a party at the tower for the workers, almost two hundred of them, in the presence of a large company of the great men of the city. The prime minister was there, the entire municipal council, numerous dignitaries, all formally dressed in top hats, together with their wives and children. Among these, Thomas noted with amazement, were Monsieur Ney and his daughter, Hortense, elegant in a blue silk dress in the latest fashion. Somehow, deploying his two hounds, Loyalty and Gratitude, the huntsman from his small attorney's office had managed to bring down this impressive quarry. Hortense, as usual, looked pale and strangely sensual as her father quietly insinuated himself into one group after another. Surely, Thomas thought, amid such a distinguished gathering, the small-time attorney should be able to find a worthy suitor for his daughter's hand.

It was a windy day. The sun showed through the clouds as they chased across the sky.

Recently Thomas had gone to a tailor in Montmartre who made men's clothes for a price that the artists and artisans could afford.

From the tailor he had acquired a suit with a short coat in which he looked very smart, and he was wearing it today.

At one-thirty precisely, Eiffel and a party of more than a hundred dignitaries prepared to ascend the tower. It was a pity that the elevators were still not working, but that did not deter them from ascending the stairs to the first platform. One of the deputies, afraid of heights, insisted that he would go up all the same, which he did with a silk scarf wrapped around his eyes.

Eiffel took his time. Every little while he would pause to explain this or that detail of the construction, and let the visitors catch their breath. On the first platform, the bar, brasserie and two restaurants, one French and one Russian, were still being fitted out for the public opening the following month.

The more determined members then accompanied Eiffel on the long climb up to the second platform. And a still smaller group ascended to the very top, where Eiffel ran the national Tricolour flag up the flagpole where it flapped in the wind, a thousand feet high in the sky. And at this patriotic signal, a burst of fireworks sent out the equivalent of a twenty-one-gun salute from the second platform.

It took a long time for them to come down. The wind was growing stronger, and Thomas wondered if it was going to rain. But they all sat down to their feast of ham, German sausage and cheese.

And if there was a hint of Eiffel's Germanic origins in this choice of food, it was quickly dispelled both by the champagne which was served, and the patriotic speeches which followed.

Eiffel thanked them all, and announced that the names of France's greatest scientists would be painted in gold on the frieze of the first platform. The prime minister thanked Eiffel, and invested him as an officer of the Légion d'honneur. They all toasted the builder, and each other, and France.

Then, as the wind got up and the rain threatened, they all dispersed to their homes. But not before one tiny incident occurred.

Thomas was just heading towards the Pont d'Iéna, with the first drops of rain patting his face, when he felt a hand on his arm. It was Jean Compagnon.

The burly man shook his hand and gave him a small card. On it was written the name of a bar.

'They always know where to find me there,' he said. 'Let me know if you need a reference.' Then, before Thomas could thank him, he was gone.

The Universal Exposition of 1889 officially opened on the sixth day of May. Visitors looked in awe at the vast iron tower under which they passed. They had to wait until the fair's second week before they could go up it, but even if they didn't ascend, they found plenty in the huge fair to interest them. There were exhibits from all corners of the world. There was a replica of a Cairo street and Egyptian market, with cafés serving Turkish coffee and entertaining the customers with belly dancers. The site was so huge that a delightful miniature train took passengers from the Champ de Mars to the esplanade by Les Invalides, where they found Oriental rickshaws.

The fair might be celebrating the centenary of the French Revolution and its ideals of Liberty, Equality and Fraternity, but the honour of France demanded that visitors should also be reminded of her far-flung colonies; and so there were large and exotic exhibits from the colonies of Algeria, Tunisia, Senegal, Polynesia, Cambodia and others. If the British had an empire, so did France.

But while the Eiffel Tower was the staggering glory of the fair, it had to be admitted that the pavilion which astounded everyone was the one supplied, at his own expense, by Thomas Edison, who was sailing from America to Paris himself in August. The range of inventions on view was staggering, and in keeping with the shared republican values of America and France, it showed how, very soon, the advances of modern science would bring electricity, telephones and other wonderful new conveniences not only to the wealthy, but to the masses. Most fascinating of all was the new phonograph with its cylinders, which no one had ever seen before.

The huge numbers of Americans who were filling Paris to see the exhibition might feel delight and gratification that the man who'd built the Statue of Liberty and their own Thomas Edison were the stars.

And then of course, just twelve days after the opening of the fair, Buffalo Bill's Wild West show was due to open on a Saturday afternoon.

★   ★   ★

On the evening before, Thomas went up to Montmartre to see his family. He ate with his parents and sister. Luc was working, and Thomas decided to stay the night up at the house so that he could see his brother. It was after midnight when Luc arrived, and as it was warm, the two brothers sat out on the wall nearby under the stars to chat awhile.

'I went to the tower this afternoon,' Luc informed him. 'It's only been open two days, and you still can't use the elevators, but I wanted to go and see.' He smiled. 'Most people only walk up to the first platform, but I went on to the second. It's still not open above that. And guess who I met there?'

'Tell me.'

'The man himself. Monsieur Eiffel. He was walking up to his office at the top. He's certainly fit. He told me he does it every day.'

'You spoke to him?' After his disgrace, Thomas was a little nervous of what the great man might have had to say.

'Certainly. He recognised me. He said I could walk up to the top with him if I liked. So of course I did.'

'I see.'

'And I saw the plaque with all the workers' names on it.'

'Ah.' Thomas sighed. 'I didn't tell you yet. But unfortunately . . .' he began.

'I saw your name.'

Thomas started. His name? Could there have been another Gascon working on the tower he didn't know about?

'My name? You're sure?'

'It was Monsieur Eiffel who pointed it out to me. "There's your brother's name," he said. "Don't forget to tell him you saw it."'

'Oh,' said Thomas.

'So I went up to the top and he went up into his office and I walked around the viewing platform. Quite a view. It must be like that when you're up in a balloon.'

'What did you do then?'

'I came down, of course. What else?'

'Nothing.'

'*Il est gentil*, your Monsieur Eiffel. He's nice.'

'Yes,' said Thomas. 'He is.'

★　　★　　★

Édith wasn't sure. Aunt Adeline was.

'This is the time to end it. You made a mistake, but now that's over. You're not pregnant any more. You're free. He's a nice boy, but he seems to have a talent for getting in trouble, and he hasn't a sou.'

Even Édith's mother did her best to give her good advice.

'You know that butcher up at the top of the rue de la Pompe? Well, his son has his eye on you. And that junior master at the lycée, the one with the little beard, I see him looking at you when he leaves the building. You should encourage him, you know.'

'A schoolmaster's never going to marry me.'

'You never know. I could talk to him.'

'That may not help.'

She was determined to decide for herself, but she couldn't deny that her aunt was right. Thomas might be as much as she could hope for, but he was no safe haven.

And then there was his family. Better than many in the Maquis, she supposed, but she hadn't felt any particular kinship with them. She'd probably finish up working to support them.

As for his little brother Luc . . . There was something about young Luc that she didn't like. She wasn't sure what it was, but she didn't trust him.

So what did that leave? Only the fact that when she felt Thomas's strong arm around her, she was at peace. That he was attentive to her, and that she was happy in his company. That he loved her, and that she liked the way his body was made, and the scent of it. And that she knew he was a good man. And that therefore, taking all these things together, she supposed that in a modest way she loved him. And that sometimes she yearned for him. But that at other times she could almost forget him.

So she still didn't know what to do, and she wished that she did, because she didn't like to be dishonest with him. And perhaps that was why, recently, she had somehow avoided him.

During April, she'd seen him several times, but only in the evenings after her work. She hadn't been out with him at a weekend. There had been things to do helping Aunt Adeline, of course, but she knew she could have made time for him if she'd really wanted to.

He'd asked her to the World's Fair. But she had an easy excuse for putting that off. She wanted to go up the tower. 'And I'm not walking,' she said. 'I want to take the elevator.' The tower had finally opened to the public three days ago, but the elevators still weren't fully operational, and probably wouldn't be for another three weeks. And by that time . . .

For by the start of May it seemed to her that, if it hadn't been for the tickets to the opening of the Wild West show, which she really wanted to see, she might have broken with Thomas already.

Thomas came to pick her up at noon. Soon, they were walking down the avenue de la Grande-Armée westward towards Neuilly. Thomas was wearing his new suit that he was proud of. She was wearing a summer dress with a silk shawl that Aunt Adeline had found for her. Thomas offered her his arm, and she put her hand through it. She liked walking with him like that.

At the bottom of the avenue where it reached the Bois de Boulogne they turned right, and soon came to the part of Neuilly that was still open ground. In the middle of this open space stood the remains of an old fort, and here Buffalo Bill had built his camp.

There were two hundred tents, and big corrals for the horses and the shaggy buffalo – which had caused a sensation when they were led down the road from the railway station to the camp. And in the centre of it all were the splendid arena and a newly constructed grandstand that would hold fifteen thousand spectators.

'Look at the crowd,' said Thomas. They were early, but already a sea of people was flowing through the entrance. And it wasn't just any crowd.

The president of France, Monsieur Carnot, and his wife were to be present. Royalty and ambassadors, generals and aristocrats, distinguished visitors from all over the world, including a large party of visiting Americans – the stands were packed. Everyone who was anyone was there. And so was Thomas Gascon.

It amused him that he and Édith were there and that Monsieur Ney and Hortense were not.

And all that packed crowd – except of course the Americans – were united by two things. They were all excited to be there. And they were not quite sure what the show was about.

The opening of the show was clear enough. It was a huge parade around the ring of all the colourful cast. Cowboys and cowgirls with whirling lassoes, magnificent Indians in feathers and warpaint,

Mexicans, Canadian trappers – French Canadians, of course – with their huskies, all that was brave and dashing and exotic in the huge, wild North American spaces. The crowd was delighted. Then came a single young lady, Annie Oakley, with her guns. The crowd clapped politely, not knowing much about her. And finally, the hero of the West, the greatest showman of them all, Buffalo Bill himself in his buckskins and big cowboy hat, his hair flowing behind him, entered at a gallop, whirled around the ring and made a magnificent, sweeping salute to the president of France.

The crowd roared. So far so good.

Thomas offered Édith the bag of popcorn he had purchased at the entrance.

'What is it?' she asked uncertainly.

'God knows. It's American. Try it.'

She did, and made a face. But a few moments later, she dipped her hand in again.

The first re-enactment of Wild West history was the attack of the Redskins on the Pioneers. The show's regular man, to whom God had given a magnificent, carrying voice, declaimed the narrative so all could hear, the trappers formed their wagons into a circle, the Indians whooped – the riding and the action were altogether splendid.

There was only one problem.

'What's going on? What's it about?' asked Édith.

'I don't know,' said Thomas.

Nor, apart from the Americans in the stand, did anyone else. For although the announcer had a mighty voice, and although he'd been practising his lines in French for weeks, his idea of French pronunciation was even stranger to his audience than the Wild West itself. As the trumpet sounded, and the US Cavalry came riding in to the rescue, the French were not quite certain who the men in uniform were, or why they were there.

As the thrilling scene ended, they waited in silence.

'Is that it?' whispered Édith. 'Should we applaud?'

'Let's wait till someone else does,' said Thomas. Most of the audience was in the same dilemma. Fortunately the Americans started to applaud, and so everyone thankfully followed suit. But it was not the start that Buffalo Bill was used to.

So as the audience waited for the next tableau, and prepared to strain their ears to try to decipher the announcement – for they all wanted to be pleased – they were a little surprised to see instead the slim young lady walk into the ring, accompanied by some assistants and a table of guns.

Thomas frowned. This surely was an *entr'acte*, supposed to come later in the show. The first piece of action had at least been exotic. The young lady seemed pleasant enough, but not very exciting. He hoped Édith wasn't going to be disappointed by the whole thing.

The young performer was looking around at her audience, sensing them. But she remained composed.

From somewhere, a glass ball rose high into the air. Easily, hardly glancing at it, she raised her rifle and shot it so that it burst into a thousand fragments. A cool shot certainly. Another ball, and a second. Two shots, so close together it seemed hardly possible. Both glass balls burst. Very good, it had to be said. She went to the table and picked up another gun. As she did so, three balls went up, in different directions. Three bangs, three hits.

And now it began. Glass balls, clay pigeons, a playing card, a cigar, objects on stands, things tossed in the air, in front of her, behind her, faster and faster, high and low. She was grabbing guns from the table and throwing them down with bewildering speed. Generals boggled, sporting aristocrats leaned forward in their seats, ladies dropped their fans. Annie Oakley did not miss. They had never seen anything like it. The cries of astonishment rose; people were standing in their seats. And when she had exhausted every gun and the haze of smoke was hanging over the centre of the arena, and she took her bow, the audience roared, and threw handkerchiefs at her feet.

She ran off gaily, and the audience sank into their seats.

And then she was back again, but riding a horse. Around the arena she rode, and the balls started rising into the air, and she shot them as she went. And then silver French coins went up, sparkling in the sun, and she shot them too. But now the audience was beyond ecstasy. As well they might be. For what they were seeing was close to a miracle, and Annie Oakley was, quite likely, the finest shot the world has ever known.

After that, the audience was won. They cheered the Mexicans, and the buffalo, and the Indian battles and the taming of the West.

They might not be sure exactly what it all signified, but they didn't care.

Buffalo Bill was a big success.

And it was understandable. The Americans might speak abominable French, but weren't the two countries historic soulmates? France, for whatever reasons, had helped the American colonies break free of England in the American Revolution, which in turn inspired the French to follow with an even greater revolution of their own. And if the French Revolution had been for Liberty, Equality and Fraternity, were these not, in a different manifestation, the watchwords of the American Wild West as well?

Indeed, many in that audience may have reflected, after France's humiliation by Germany not twenty years ago, perhaps she needed heroes with the brave spirit of Buffalo Bill to restore her honour still.

He was the toast of the town all summer.

So it was a flushed and excited Thomas who conducted Édith away from the Wild West show late that afternoon. Then, when they got to the bottom of the avenue de la Grande-Armée, instead of walking up it, they turned into the leafy Bois de Boulogne, and walked along a pleasant alley a little way.

Then Thomas kissed Édith, and she kissed him back. And he hadn't planned it at all, but there was no one else in the alley just then, and so he suddenly went down on one knee and said: 'Will you marry me?'

Chapter Eight

1462

In the tavern they called the Rising Sun, Jean Le Sourd was holding court. Le Sourd. It meant 'the Deaf One'.

Not that Jean Le Sourd was deaf. Not at all. He could have heard a pin drop in the street outside. It was said he could hear men's thoughts. Certainly, if a man even thought of reaching for a knife, Le Sourd's own knife would be at that man's throat before he had a chance and, like as not, have slit that throat from ear to ear, not out of malice, but just as a precaution.

Rouge Gorge, they also called him. Red Throat.

But mostly they called him Le Sourd because, if a man crossed him, he was deaf to all entreaty. There was no second chance. There was no use pleading. There was no mercy. And within the territory comprising a network of a dozen streets on one side of the old market of Les Halles, Jean Le Sourd was king. The Rising Sun tavern was where he liked to hold his court.

Despite its name, there was nothing sunny about the place. The small street in which it was to be found was dark and narrow. The alley that ran down beside it, and where Le Sourd lived, was scarcely wide enough for two cats to walk side by side, and the overhanging storeys above drew so close together that a mouse could leap across, and the stench of urine clung to the walls.

And the streets had names befitting their condition: *Pute-y-Muse*, Lazy Whore; *Merdeuse*, Shit Street; *Tire-Boudin*, Cock Puller; and other names worse, far worse. And the people who lived there were whores, and thieves, and pickpockets, and did other things worse, far worse.

Jean Le Sourd was a large, strong man with a great mane of shaggy black hair. He sat at a wooden table in the middle of the tavern. At his table were several men, some who looked like murderers, but one of them, who had an aquiline face and a sallow complexion, looked as if he might be a defrocked priest or scholar. Standing behind Le Sourd was his son Richard, a ten-year-old boy, his face not yet hardened, but with a mop of black hair like his own.

A stooped man came through the door. He was tonsured, suggesting that he might be a cleric of some kind, and he moved with a curious motion, like a bobbing bird. He went straight to the central table and, taking something out from under his shirt, laid it in front of Le Sourd.

Le Sourd picked it up and examined it carefully. It was a pendant on a golden chain.

'Unusual,' said Le Sourd. He passed it across to the man who looked like a scholar. The scholar inspected it, remarked that it wasn't from Paris, and gave it back. Le Sourd turned to the stooping man: 'We'll have to find out what it's worth. You'll get your share.'

Those were the rules of Le Sourd's kingdom. Whatever was stolen was brought to him. He found the market and gave the thief a share. Once or twice men had tried to bypass the system. One was found with his throat slit. Another disappeared.

The stooping man moved to the back of the room to join some of his fellows. Jean Le Sourd resumed his conversation with the scholar. And several minutes passed before the door of the tavern opened again.

This time however, as the newcomer entered, the buzz of conversation died down to a hush.

He was a young man. Twenty years old, perhaps. He had fair hair and blue eyes. He was wearing a short cloak and a sword that immediately proclaimed he was a noble. And the fact that he had entered such a place alone told everyone that he did not know Paris.

It might be dangerous to kill a noble, but the inhabitants of that quarter were no respecters of persons. One of the men nearest the door quietly rose, with a knife in his hand, and stood behind the visitor, awaiting a signal from Le Sourd.

At the same time, the stooping man at the back of the room shifted position slightly, so that he was in the shadows. But he spoke a word to his neighbour, who walked over to Le Sourd and whispered something in his ear.

Le Sourd looked at the intruder thoughtfully, while everyone waited. They all knew what the young man did not: that his chances of leaving the Rising Sun alive were not good. Not good at all.

Guy de Cygne was in Paris for only a week, and this was his second day. His parents had made him come and, from the moment he came through the Porte Saint-Jacques, he couldn't wait to leave.

For Paris was rotten. It had been rotten a century ago when the Black Death came and killed nearly half its people. It was even more rotten now.

Worse, despite plague, famine and war, like a pestiferous plant, Paris had grown. On the Right Bank, they had built a new fortification line, hundreds of yards beyond the old wall of Philip Augustus, so that the Louvre was now well inside the city gates, and the former Temple too. Country lanes had turned into narrow streets, orchards into tenements, streams into open sewers. And two hundred thousand souls now dwelt in this dark, godforsaken city.

Had God truly forsaken Paris? Certainly. For over a century, God had forsaken France itself. And why? Few Frenchmen had any doubt.

Because of the Templar's curse.

Young Guy de Cygne's father had explained it to him when Guy was still a boy.

'After King Philip the Fair arrested the Templars, he tortured some of them for years. He got his puppet pope to disband the order all over Christendom. Finally, he took Jacques de Molay, the Grand Master – a man of unimpeachable character – and burned him at the stake. And as he burned, de Molay cursed the king and all who had destroyed the Templars.'

'And did it work?' Guy had asked.

'Certainly.'

Within the year, both the king and his pope were dead. But that was only the beginning. Within a few years, all King Philip's sons were dead as well, and another branch of the family, the Valois, took over.

Even that was not enough. King Philip's daughter had married the Plantagenet king of England, and soon the pushy Plantagenets were after the throne of France as well.

For more than a hundred years, an on-and-off war had continued. Before and after the Black Death, England's longbowmen had smashed the chivalry of France at the battles of Crécy and Poitiers. The Plantagenets had taken Aquitaine and half of Brittany. Scotland, France's ancient ally, had deflected the English for a while. But at the end of the dismal fourteenth century, the king of France had gone mad; and in the chaos that ensued, the greedy Plantagenets came back once more, to see what else they could grab.

By the time Guy's father was a boy, Henry V of England had smashed the French at Agincourt, and married the French king's daughter. It seemed the Plantagenets would be kings of France as well.

And then, at last, God showed his mercy. Just as He had a thousand years before, when He inspired Saint Geneviève to save Paris from Attila the Hun, He sent the peasant girl, Joan of Arc, to inspire the men of France. Her career had been brief. But her legacy had lived on. Gradually the English had been pushed back. By now they were almost out.

So had the Templar's curse been lifted from forsaken France? Had Christendom returned to its normal state?

Perhaps. At least there was now a single pope, in Rome. After seventy years of French popes at Avignon, then another half century of rival popes and antipopes, the Catholic schism was over.

But what was Paris? A sink of iniquity. A place of darkness. And judging by what he saw before him now, in the tavern of the Rising Sun, it did not seem to Guy de Cygne that there was any good day dawning.

Le Sourd gave a single rap upon the table, and the tavern fell silent. He gazed at the young noble.

'You are a stranger here, monsieur. Can we help you?' The tone was quiet, but it was clear that he was in charge.

'I am searching for something,' Guy replied calmly. He was not sure how much danger he was in, but ever since he was a little boy, his father had told him: 'In front of animals, or a mob, never show fear.'

'What is it you seek?'

'A gold pendant. It was on a chain. It is not of great value, but it was given to me by my grandmother just before she died, and for that reason I would not lose it for all the world.'

'But why do you come here, monsieur, to the tavern of the Rising Sun, where there are only honest men and poets?'

If there was some ironic humour in this, the young man ignored it.

'I saw the man who robbed me. I followed him. And I am sure he came in here.'

'No one has come through the door in the last hour, except yourself,' Le Sourd answered blandly. 'Isn't that right?' he asked the room, and forty throats echoed his sentiments, until Le Sourd raised his hand and they instantly fell silent.

Young Guy de Cygne let his gaze travel around the tavern. It was hard to see into the shadows.

'You will not mind, then, if I satisfy myself that the man I seek has not slipped in by some other entrance,' he replied coolly.

Le Sourd gazed at him. This young aristocrat might be a stranger, but he could not fail to realise that he was at their mercy. The cool effrontery, the reckless courage of the fellow appealed to the ruler of thieves.

'Please do so,' he said.

Guy de Cygne moved swiftly around the big room. He knew he might be about to die, but he could not go back now. In the shadows, he found the stooping man.

'This is him,' he said. 'He's tonsured like a priest, but this is him.' He'd heard there were cutpurses and other rogues in Paris who tonsured themselves in the hope of being tried by the protective Church courts instead of the harsher provost. He assumed this fellow must be one of them.

'*Connard!*' Le Sourd called out to the stooping man. 'Let this gentleman search you.'

The stooping man submitted. Guy de Cygne found nothing.

'This man of God has been here all day,' declared Le Sourd. 'But I can think of others in the quarter who resemble him. It must have been one of them.' He paused. And now his voice became soft and dangerous. 'I hope you will not call me a liar, monsieur.'

Guy de Cygne had been made a fool of. He knew it and they knew it. But there could be no mistaking Le Sourd's meaning: call him a liar in this den of iniquity, and he'd be dead.

Yet he must retain some honour.

'I have no reason to call you a liar,' he answered calmly. He moved carefully to a place where he could draw his sword and use it. If they attacked him, he could probably kill two or three before they brought him down. The men in the room noticed, but nobody moved.

And now Le Sourd had an idea. He glanced at his son, who was watching carefully. Richard knew that his father's word was law. He knew that his father could kill this young noble if he chose. This was his father's power.

Should he show the boy something even better? Should he humiliate this noble, make him apologise to the stooped man before he left? The young noble might refuse, in which case he'd have to kill him. Or he might accept and leave with his tail between his legs. But either way, it was a petty gesture, unworthy of a father who, in his own way, still wanted to be a hero to his son.

No. He would show the boy his father's magnificence. For wasn't he a monarch in his own small kingdom? And weren't the great nobles men like himself, but on a larger scale?

'Perhaps I may be able to help you, monsieur. I invite you to sit at my table.'

Guy de Cygne stared at him. This was obviously a trap. He'd be unable to see behind him, or to draw his sword. The quickest way to get his throat cut. Le Sourd read his thoughts.

'You are my guest, monsieur, and under my protection. It would be an insult to refuse me.'

Still de Cygne hesitated. But then the scholarly-looking man sitting on Le Sourd's right came to his aid.

'You may safely sit, sir,' he said in a voice that was clearly educated. 'And I advise you to do so.'

Thinking that this might be the last thing he did, Guy de Cygne sat down in the place offered, opposite Le Sourd, with half the tavern behind him.

Le Sourd ordered his son, like a young squire, to pour their guest a goblet of wine.

'I am Jean, called Le Sourd,' he introduced himself. 'This gentleman' – he indicated the scholar – 'is my friend Master François Villon. He is a notable poet, his uncle is a professor at the university' – he grinned – 'and he has twice been banished for murder.'

'Which I did not commit,' said the poet.

'Which he did not commit,' Le Sourd continued. 'So you see, monsieur, that you are in the company of distinguished and honest men.' He glanced at young Richard. 'And this young fellow who poured your wine is my son.'

The name of Villon meant nothing to Guy de Cygne. He noticed that the poet had just peeled an apple with a long, sharp dagger which rested on the table. He suspected that the dagger had been used for less domestic purposes. He gave a faint nod to them all.

'I am Guy de Cygne, from the valley of the Loire.'

Le Sourd glanced at Villon.

'I've heard the name,' the poet remarked. 'Noble family.'

Le Sourd was satisfied. It was the first time a noble had sat at his table. Now he'd let Richard see that his father knew how to conduct himself with an aristocrat.

'There are many fine estates in the valley of the Loire,' Le Sourd remarked as he handed the young man a dish of sweetmeats.

'And many, like ours, that have been ruined,' de Cygne replied frankly.

'That is unfortunate. May we ask how that came about?'

It was none of this evil man's business, Guy de Cygne thought. But situated as he was, he may as well play along, so he answered honestly.

'It has taken time. The plague did not help.'

This was an understatement. In 1348, when the Black Death reached France, it had struck their small village especially hard. Only one of the de Cygne family, a boy of ten, had lived, with only the family motto – 'According to God's will' – to guide him. Clearly God wished the family to survive. And this was enough to keep him going. But life had been hard.

'My own family had an important position at that time,' Le Sourd remarked with a wicked smile. 'My great-grandfather was the finest cat-killer in Paris.'

It was true that the Paris authorities, convinced that it was cats rather than rats which carried the plague, had caused huge numbers of them to be killed. Though whether his host was serious or joking, de Cygne wasn't sure.

'But it was the English who ruined us,' he continued. 'My ancestor fell at the battle of Crécy. Ten years later, his son was taken at Poitiers and we had to ransom him. That cost us half our land.'

'He was in good company,' Le Sourd remarked. 'The king of France himself was taken at Poitiers, by the Black Prince of England. They put him in the Tower of London.'

'And all France had to pay his ransom,' Villon added sourly. It seemed to Guy de Cygne that the poet didn't think the king was worth the price.

'Then the English mercenaries came and looted us,' he said.

'They looted half France,' Le Sourd agreed. 'A plague of locusts.'

'And we had only a generation to recover from these misfortunes,' Guy went on, 'before the English returned again. My grandfather died at Agincourt.' He paused and looked at them with the pride of a noble whose fortunes might be low, but whose ancestors fought with honour.

Le Sourd nodded slowly. He, who lived by the knife, could respect those who died by the sword. If he wanted an aristocrat at his table, young de Cygne was the real thing. Just as well he hadn't killed him.

'The ruin of my family was completed,' the young nobleman calmly continued, 'by my own father in the time of Joan of Arc.' He paused. 'But that may be a story it would bore you to hear.'

'Not at all.' Despite himself, Le Sourd was coming to like this aristocratic boy. 'Please continue.'

Young Guy de Cygne was just about to begin when he realised that he could be about to make a terrible mistake. He had forgotten to ascertain Le Sourd's politics. He thought quickly, but it was too late. He'd have to tell the story as it was, and take a chance.

'Paris was under the rule of Burgundy and England,' he began. 'But Joan of Arc had just appeared.'

It had been a miserable period. After the poor king had gone mad, his family had formed a regency council. But regencies usually mean trouble, and soon two factions within the extended royal family were vying for control. One was the Duke of Orléans. The other, also royal, was the Duke of Burgundy. For after the old dukes of Burgundy had died out, and their huge territories, which included many Flemish cloth towns, reverted to the crown, Burgundy had been given to a royal younger son. The Burgundian faction favoured the great cloth trade with England, which supplied the wool for their rich Flemish towns. The Orléans faction, known as the Armagnacs, favoured rural France.

Soon the factions were fighting in open war. The Duke of Burgundy courted the merchants of Paris, and soon the capital was under Burgundian control, while the mad king's son, the dauphin, and the dispirited Armagnacs were pushed out to the Loire Valley and old Orléans.

So perhaps it was inevitable that when yet another generation of greedy Plantagenets came, like hyenas, to see what they could tear from the bleeding body of France, the Burgundy faction did a deal with them. After all, England's wool merchants were their business partners.

They supported the Plantagenets' bid for the throne of France.

When the strange peasant girl Joan of Arc appeared with her sensational message – 'The saints have told me that the dauphin is the true king of France' – and gave the Armagnacs new spirit, the Burgundians were alarmed. When Joan and the Armagnacs drove the English back and crowned the dauphin in holy Reims, they were horrified.

But then the Burgundians captured Joan of Arc, and sold her to the English – who had her judged a heretic and burned her at the stake.

It had been in the first, magic moment, Guy de Cygne now explained, when Joan had arrived in the Loire Valley with her message from God, that his father had made a dangerous journey. Determined to play his part, he was ready to sell some more of his remaining land to equip himself for the fight. He tried to transact the business in Orléans, but the city was so depressed that he could get no takers. He knew a merchant in Paris, however, whom he could trust; also an old aunt he had not seen in years. Using the plausible story that he had come to see the old lady, he managed to get into the city, and sell his land. The merchant, who was a secret Armagnac himself, even promised that if de Cygne found the money within five years, he could have his land back.

'Well pleased with this, and with a small chest of coins, my father passed a night in a tavern before leaving the city. There were Englishmen there, but to them, he was just another Frenchman. A party of Burgundian soldiers became suspicious of him, however. One of them knocked him on the head, and when he woke up, both his money and his horse were gone.'

Guy de Cygne stopped and looked at Le Sourd. Had the story been a mistake? Many of the Parisians had preferred the Burgundian party and their merchants. Was he about to lose the sympathy of his host? Was he going to get his throat cut?

He saw Le Sourd raise his hand. He reached for his sword. But the hand came down on his shoulder.

'Damned Burgundians!' the big man roared. 'If there's one thing I hate more than an Englishman, it's a Burgundian. So your father could not fight?' he asked.

'Not armed and mounted as he wished. So he went on foot as a humble man-at-arms. He said it was his pilgrimage.'

'Ah. Bravo, young man!' cried Le Sourd. 'Magnificent!' He seized his goblet and raised it. 'Let us drink to the Maid of Orléans,' he called, 'to Joan of Arc and all who fought for her.'

Guy de Cygne allowed himself to smile. It was all right. He'd taken a chance, and it had paid off.

For as it happened, though the stories about his ancestors had all been true, the one about his father was not. He'd made it up on the spur of the moment. The truth – that his father, as a young man, had stupidly gambled away some of his small inheritance – was hardly heroic. But the tale he had told was much better, and it amused him that this villainous rogue had believed it.

When the toast had been drunk, his host turned to him in a manner that was almost solicitous.

'So tell me, monsieur, have you come to Paris to serve our new king?' he inquired.

It was only a year since King Louis XI of France had come to the throne. But it was already clear that the new king meant to make changes. Louis's father had been content enough, thanks to Joan of Arc, to keep his battered kingdom. King Louis had made no secret of the fact that he wanted far more. Ambitious, cunning and ruthless, he intended to destroy all opposition, and raise France to glory, and he'd do whatever it took.

And if Guy de Cygne's family could have afforded armour and a fine warhorse, then this might have been an option. But they couldn't, and their reason for sending him to Paris was more prosaic.

'I have come here to meet my bride,' he answered, without enthusiasm.

It was a friend of his father's who'd arranged the business. The girl was from a rich merchant family, and Guy's parents had been well satisfied with the dowry offered. But his father had left Guy a choice. 'Go to Paris and meet the girl,' he'd instructed. 'If you truly dislike each other, we'll call it off. Although,' he added, 'I've known couples who got on perfectly well for years without liking each other in the least.' He shrugged. 'However, I suppose you may as well like each other at first.' Guy was due to meet the girl the following day.

'Your bride is noble?' asked Le Sourd.

'She is of a merchant family,' de Cygne said quietly. His lack of enthusiasm was evident.

Villon, who'd been listening carefully, shook his head.

'Take care, young man,' the poet cautioned. 'This is Paris, not the countryside. Do not despise the Third Estate.' Of the Three Estates that the kings of France occasionally summoned to advise them and vote them taxes, the first two, the nobles and the Church, had traditionally been more important. But times had changed. 'Even back in the days of Crécy and Poitiers,' Villon continued, 'don't forget that Étienne Marcel, the city provost and leader of the merchants and artisans, practically ruled Paris. It was he who made the great ditch and ramparts that became the new wall. Even the king had cause to fear him. Today, the richest merchants live like nobles, and you despise them at your peril.'

'It is true,' Le Sourd said quietly, 'but I have a feeling that Monsieur de Cygne would rather marry a woman of noble birth.'

And Guy de Cygne blushed.

Le Sourd glanced up at his son. Young Richard was taking everything in, that was clear. He was learning about the world. He had seen a noble blush from embarrassment, and now he should see his father save the noble further embarrassment by changing the subject. And amazed at his own fineness, Le Sourd now turned to the poet, like a king in his court, and said: 'Give us one of your verses, Master Villon.'

'As you like,' said the poet. He reached down into a leather satchel at his feet and drew out some sheets of paper on which long columns of verse could be seen in his spiky, scholarly hand. 'Last year,' he explained, 'I finished a long poem called "The Testament".' It has several parts. Here is a pair of ballads from it.'

The first was a short, clever ballad asking what had become of the classical gods, of Abelard and Héloïse, and even Joan of Arc. It was simple, but elegant, and a little melancholy as it echoed the passing of time. At the end of each verse came the haunting refrain: 'Where are the snows of yesteryear?'

Mais où sont les neiges d'antan?

The second was similar in form, and spoke of the vanished rulers of the earth, not without humour. Where was the famous Pope Callixtus, the king of Scots, the Bourbon duke; where was the worthy king of Spain, of whom he did not know the name? And again, with each verse, a refrain: 'And where is mighty Charlemagne?'

'Excellent,' said his host. 'And is there anything new?'

'I have started something. Some fragments so far.' He shrugged. 'I hope to finish it before my ruin.'

Frères humains qui après nous vivez
N'ayez les cœurs contre nous endurcis
Car, si pitié de nous pauvres avez
Dieu en aura plus tôt de vous mercis.

Brothers who are alive today, when we
are gone, do not be hard, but pity us
Beg God's forgiveness for us now, that He
may sooner pity you, when you are dust.

It was a poem about a group of men in jail, awaiting execution. He had written only a couple of verses so far. But as he read them, a strange quiet fell over all the men listening. For it was a fate, like as not, that awaited themselves one day, and his words were sad, and dark, yet full of pity.

And as Guy de Cygne heard Villon recite his verses, he could not help being struck by the haunting melody in them. Whoever he might be, this fellow was clearly a scholar, yet one who lived with murderers. He might be a thief himself, yet he could write poetry that moved the other thieves.

When Villon was done, there was a brief silence.

'Master Villon,' said Le Sourd, 'your poems should be printed.'

'I agree,' said the poet with an ironic smile, 'but I can't afford it.'

'Could your uncle the professor help?'

'He can tolerate me, occasionally. That is all.' Villon shrugged. 'It is my fault.'

Le Sourd nodded, took a long sip of his wine, then turned to de Cygne.

'Master Villon is fine, is he not?'

'I agree.'

Le Sourd gazed around the room, and nodded to himself thoughtfully, then shrugged.

'This is our life,' he said quietly, almost to himself. Then, after another sip of wine, he turned to his guest and the matter still in hand. 'So, Monsieur de Cygne, let us return to the question of your missing pendant. Can you describe it to me?'

'It is gold. There's a design upon it, from Byzantium, I believe. My grandmother always told me her father got it in the Holy Land.'

'I cannot tell you where this pendant is, monsieur,' said Le Sourd, 'but if I make inquiries in this quarter, I may find the man who has it. But theft is like war. Whoever has your pendant will want a ransom before he yields it up.'

'I can offer a hundred francs,' said de Cygne. When one of the king's new francs was officially the same as an old-fashioned livre, a pound of silver, it had once been a lot of money. But time and devaluation had done their work. A hundred francs was now a modest sum.

'I should think it's worth more than that,' said Le Sourd.

'It may be, but that's all I can afford.'

'Well then,' said his host, 'I promise nothing, but let me see if I can recover it for you. I have influence in this quarter. Would this be agreeable to you?'

Guy de Cygne gazed at him. He wasn't deceived. This rogue probably knew where the pendant was at this very moment. But if courtesy was the way to get it back, then so be it.

'You are very kind,' he said. 'I should be in your debt.'

'Then let us drink to that,' cried Le Sourd, suddenly cheerful. 'Will you raise your goblet with me, as a man of honour? I know that this place is not where you would normally come, monsieur, but'

– he looked around the room and spoke the words clearly so that every man in the place should hear – 'you are welcome at my table any time, and from this day, all men here are your friends.' He paused and looked at de Cygne in a way that indicated that he too, in his own way, was a man of honour. 'Should you ever be in trouble in the streets of Paris, monsieur, tell them that Jean Le Sourd is your friend, and you will never be harmed.'

This grandiloquent statement was probably true. Even the thieves in the other quarters of the city would respect the protection of a powerful chief like Le Sourd. And had Guy de Cygne been a native of Paris, he would have understood that he had just been given a gift worth far more than his golden trinket from the Holy Land.

But he raised his goblet of wine all the same, and thanked his host for his hospitality and friendship. And Le Sourd glanced at his son, and then looked around the tavern like a satisfied monarch, and told himself again that the kings of the feudal world were, after all, nothing more than himself writ large – in which belief, it must be said, he was entirely correct.

'My son, Richard, will accompany you to where you are staying so that we may know how to find you,' he said. And although Guy wasn't delighted by the idea of taking Le Sourd's son to the house of his father's friend, it seemed the only way to get his pendant back. So after renewed expressions of mutual esteem, he and Richard set off.

He met the girl the next day. The Renard family lived in a fine house on the Right Bank near the river. She wasn't so bad. Her name was Cécile. She had red hair and a pale oval face. Some people would have thought her beautiful. His father's friend, who knew the Renard family well, came with him, and on their way back he told Guy: 'She likes you. So did her parents. It's up to you now, young man.' And his tone of voice said: 'If you turn down this dowry, you're a fool.'

'Does she want to live in the country?' Guy had asked.

'Of course she does.'

'She didn't say much, but her family talked about Paris a lot.'

'Naturally. That's all she knows. She'll love the country when she gets there.' His father's friend smiled. 'You might as well say an unmarried girl's a virgin, therefore she won't enjoy being married.'

He was quite surprised when they returned to find Le Sourd's son, Richard, awaiting them. He came forward and made a polite bow with his shaggy black locks. As he looked up at de Cygne, he smiled.

'I have good news, monsieur,' he said. And he held out his hand. 'Is this the one?'

It was. So the rogue had had it all the time, as Guy had thought. But he kept up the little comedy.

'And what is the ransom demanded?' he inquired.

'Nothing, monsieur. My father was able to persuade the man who had it to part with it for nothing. My father told him that, perhaps, this good deed might save his soul.'

'Let us hope so,' said Guy. It was hard not to smile at the rogue's cheek.

'My father sends you his respects, monsieur. Is there any message I should take back to him?'

Guy de Cygne considered. He knew what he thought: that Le Sourd was a thief and prince of thieves. On the other hand, the thief had given him back his pendant.

'Please tell your father that Guy de Cygne thanks him for his hospitality, and thanks him for his help.'

'Thank you, monsieur.' The boy smiled. 'May God keep you.'

'And you too.'

That night Guy de Cygne thought long and hard. There were terms the nobles used for marrying a rich bourgeoise: 'Putting gold on the coat of arms.' Or, less lovely: 'Putting dung on your land.'

Cécile Renard was all right. He imagined he could love her, but he doubted that she'd be happy in the country, and this troubled him a little. But then he thought of what her dowry could bring. He would be able to enlarge the estate. He could make improvements to the manor house.

He knew his duty. Before he went to bed, he said his prayers. He knew, he told God, that he should honour his father and mother, and if he married the girl, he'd certainly be doing that. But the family motto also came into his mind. 'According to God's will.' He would be guided by it. If God sent him a sign – if, for instance, his bride should die before their wedding day – that would be a clear signal that God did not want the marriage. But if there was no sign, he'd take it as consent. And he gave the Almighty the assurance that he would try to make the girl's life pleasant, if it could be done.

The marriage took place three months later. The ceremony was in Paris, at the house of the Renard family.

It had to be said that they did the thing handsomely – far more so than the de Cygne family could have done at their crumbling manor. But there was something that his parents were able to do that clearly satisfied the bourgeois Renards.

They were able to summon noble kinsmen that Guy had hardly known he had. He might not be making a noble marriage, but it seemed the news that he was marrying an heiress was enough for all kinds of family friendships to be renewed. A score of noble names appeared, with their sons and daughters. If the Renards had been counting on this, then they had received their part of the bargain.

Even before the marriage took place, Guy suddenly found himself with kinsmen who declared that his bride was charming, and sweet, and all the other things that are said of a rich young girl – as long as she doesn't make herself unpleasant – when she arrives on the social scene. Cécile seemed delighted by their friendly attentions, and was promised all kinds of amusement when she came to the country. As for Guy, his kinsmen soon introduced him to their own friends so that, by the time he married, he was on friendly terms with young men who belonged to some of the greatest families in the land.

The wedding was a success in every way. By the third day, he and Cécile had decided that they liked each other very much indeed. Meanwhile, a week of gaiety in Paris was called for, before he took her down to the valley of the Loire, to see the modest estate which so urgently needed her love.

He was in a company of a dozen nobles, three days after the marriage, when they had dismounted to wander through the great market of Les Halles. And he was just standing beside a brightly coloured stall that offered herbs and spices when he heard a cry from nearby.

It was Charles, son of the Comte de Grenache, with whom he'd been riding only minutes before. He ran over to him.

'What's the matter?' Guy asked.

'Someone just stole my purse. It was hanging on my belt, on a strap, and the cursed fellow must have cut it off with a knife. My God he was fast.' Charles de Grenache shook his head. 'I had thirty francs in there.'

'Did you see him?'

'I'm not certain, but I think so. A fellow with a stoop. Tonsured like a priest. His head bobbed like a pigeon.' The young aristocrat looked around. 'He just vanished in the crowd. I'll never see him again. Or my money.'

Guy smiled.

'As it happens,' he said, 'I may be able to help you there.'

It took only a few moments for Guy to explain what he required. One of the party, a young squire, volunteered to go with him. Then, leaving the others in the market, Guy and the young squire set out.

They moved swiftly and by the most direct way, to a street where they could see the door of the Rising Sun. They hadn't long to wait. Having taken a more circuitous route, the stooped man appeared from an alley, and having glanced behind him furtively, went in through the tavern door.

Guy gave him time to get well inside, and then, keeping the squire with him, he strolled casually to the tavern and opened the door.

Jean Le Sourd was in a good mood. He sat with his son beside him at his table, on which the leather purse had just been placed. He poured out the gold and silver coins and quickly reckoned. Thirty francs' worth. He scooped the money back into the purse, and nodded to the stooping man.

'You'll get your share,' he said.

'How much?'

'Whatever I give you,' said Le Sourd sharply. 'Sit down.'

As the stooped man was about to turn away, there was a movement at the door, and Le Sourd looked up in surprise to see the fair-haired young noble who'd come there three months ago enter with a youth.

Was it possible the stooped man had stolen from him again? He looked inquiringly at the cutpurse, who gave a shrug which said, 'I've no idea.'

De Cygne was looking at him and smiling.

'I hoped I'd find you here,' he said. 'I am in Paris only another day.' He paused. 'You said I was welcome at your table. Is the offer still good?'

Le Sourd kept his eyes on him thoughtfully, at the same time taking the purse off the table and placing it at his feet.

'Of course.' He glanced at the door, and one of his men slipped out.

De Cygne turned to the youth.

'Go to my father and say I shall return in an hour or two. Tell him I am dining with friends.'

He advanced towards the table, gave a friendly nod to young Richard, and addressed his host again.

'I have not forgotten your kindness to me, you see. And I came to tell you my good fortune. I was married, two days ago, here in Paris.'

'Ah.' Le Sourd nodded. 'To the heiress.'

'It turns out she is an angel. I am taking her down to our poor manor this week.'

'An angel of mercy. The fields will rejoice.'

'No doubt. May I sit down?'

The man at the door came back in and signalled that the coast was clear, and the visitor had come alone.

'Of course.' Le Sourd smiled expansively. 'Wine for our friend,' he called.

It seemed he could relax a little. This show of courtesy was more than he'd expected, but one never knew with these nobles. He gave his son a look that told him to take note of this courtesy to his father.

'Master Villon is not here?' de Cygne asked.

'No, monsieur. He is away.'

So they talked of this and that. De Cygne could not ask Le Sourd much of what he'd been doing, since he'd only been robbing people. But young Richard wanted to know about the wedding, and so, without making too much of the disparity between the richness of the scene and the poverty of the tavern, he was able to describe the bright clothes of the men and women, and the food. 'A great haunch of venison. A boar's head stuffed with sweetmeats, a huge pie made from – I don't know – a hundred pigeons. Ah,' he told the boy cheerfully, 'the smell of it . . .'

'And wine, monsieur?'

'All you could drink.'

'And many guests?' asked his host.

'I never realised,' Guy smiled, 'I had so many friends.'

'Keep your money, monsieur, that your friendships may last.'

'I know,' Guy answered quietly. 'Remember, I have been poor.' And reading the other's thoughts: 'The estate has value, of course, but not until money is spent on it.'

They continued awhile. They discussed the doings of the king. Guy even suggested that perhaps, one of these days, he might be in a position to have the verses of Master Villon printed. And this, he noted, seemed to evoke a response of genuine enthusiasm in his host.

And then the tavern door burst open.

Le Sourd looked up. Through the door came a young man with a drawn sword. Moving swiftly forward he gave a loud cry: 'In the name of the king, nobody move!'

The man by the door leaped towards his back with his knife, but let out a scream as a second swordsman, coming through the door, put a blade through his ribs from behind. More men were pouring through the entrance now: five, ten, fifteen, fanning out through the room with swords drawn. Even the thieves and murderers who filled the place knew at once that they hadn't a chance. These invaders were young knights, trained in the use of arms. By coming in the king's name, they had all the legal excuse they needed. And they had one other advantage also. They were noblemen, and as such they were ruthless.

When a huntsman killed a deer, he might see the beauty and the nobility of the creature, as he did in much of God's creation. But when a knight was confronted by such men as kept company in the Rising Sun, he'd kill them with no more compunction than he'd use towards a sewer rat. And Le Sourd's men knew it.

While Le Sourd's attention was distracted by the men who were pouring in through the door, something else was happening at his own table.

Guy de Cygne had suddenly leaped up from the bench, drawn his sword, and by the time Le Sourd turned back to him, he found that he was looking along a blade whose point was tilted tight under his chin.

And as young Richard reached for his knife to protect his father, Le Sourd's voice called out with an urgency and command that could not be ignored: 'Leave your knife, my son. Keep still.'

Then, in the heavy-breathing silence that followed, Guy de Cygne's voice came crisply: 'This is your man, Grenache. The purse is by his feet.'

Le Sourd watched as the young man who'd been first through the door advanced to his table. Carefully, with the point of his sword, Charles de Grenache felt for the purse, and drew it across the floor until he could see it clearly. Still using the sword point, he lifted the purse and let it fall upon the table.

'That is my purse,' he confirmed. He turned and surveyed the room until his eyes rested upon the stooped man. 'And that's the fellow who took it,' he added.

'He works for this villain,' said de Cygne. 'They all do. That's why he's got the purse now. He's called Le Sourd.'

Le Sourd was a hard man. He'd killed many times. He'd been cautious when de Cygne had first arrived, and he cursed himself now, for allowing the young man to ambush him.

Yet even so, he was taken aback by the completeness of the transformation. The courtesy de Cygne had shown, the confidences he'd shared, had vanished so suddenly, it was as if they had never been there at all. Vicious though he was himself, Le Sourd was astonished. He stared at the young noble with hurt and almost disbelief.

But then he saw, in a flash, into Guy de Cygne's soul. The young man had been poor. Now he was rich. But it hardly made a difference. For Guy de Cygne was noble. And Jean Le Sourd was not. And it was that social chasm, more even than the fact he was a thief, that made the difference between them.

Before, the young man had to wear a mask. Now, backed by his noble friends, the mask was dropped.

To Guy de Cygne the hospitality of a Le Sourd was nothing. The friendship, the gift: nothing. His honour – for even thieves have honour – nothing. His son, nothing. His very soul – for even thieves have souls to be saved – also, nothing. He was less than a horse, less than a dog. He scarcely had the merit of a rat. Because he was not noble. Jean Le Sourd understood, and he looked at his son, and he knew bitterness.

'Well, Le Sourd,' said Charles de Grenache, 'you and your stooping friend are going to hang.'

It was a month later that they brought Jean Le Sourd to execution. He and the stooping man had been kept in the Châtelet's stout jail. Naturally, the provost had ordered them tortured. It was assumed that Le Sourd in particular had murders to his name, and the provost wanted confessions. It took a little while, but he got them. After a certain amount of pain, most men would confess to anything if they knew they were going to die anyway. It was only reasonable.

The stooping man's claims to be a churchman had been easily disposed of. He had no proof, and he couldn't read. They'd hanged him the day before on one of the city gallows. But Le Sourd was special. They needed to make an example of him. And the crowds always liked to see a powerful villain die.

Early in the morning, they'd erected a gallows with a high platform in the open spaces of Les Halles, his centre of operations. The whole market would be there to watch. And it was a sunny day as well.

But they had let him see his son.

'Are you going to watch?' he asked the boy.

'I don't know. Do you want me to?'

'They'll take me from the Châtelet to Les Halles in a cart, so that everyone can see me. You can watch that. Then go away. You know what they're going to do to me? Hang me for a while, then cut my head off.'

'I know.'

'I don't want you to see that.'

'All right.'

'Go away just before we enter Les Halles. Otherwise you'll be tempted to stay.'

'Will you look for me in the crowd? I don't know where I shall be.'

'No. I shan't look for you. Don't try to wave at me or anything. I shall stand proud. Promise?'

'I promise.'

'Did you see Master Villon?'

'No. I don't think he's in Paris.'

'He'll go the same way as me, you know.'

'You'd have been all right if it wasn't for that cursed de Cygne.'

His father shook his head.

'I'd have swung for something sooner or later. I could have swung so many times before.'

'If he comes back, I'll kill him.'

'No you won't. That's an order. I don't want you to swing as well.'

'What am I to do, Papa?' The boy's voice suddenly started to break down.

'Get yourself apprenticed to a trade. You know where the money's hidden. Enough there to pay a master to take you on. I was going to get you apprenticed to someone next year.'

'Why?'

'Not much money in thieving really. And you never have any peace. And then . . . there's this.' He shrugged. 'It's my fault. I've taught you all I know about thieving, which is a lot, and it's still a waste of time.'

'I dunno, Papa.'

'Yes, you do.'

'I wish I had a mother.'

'Well you don't, so do as I say.'

'I suppose so.'

'As for de Cygne. Leave him alone. You'll probably never see him again, but leave him alone. But there's one thing you've got to know. About the nobles – not just de Cygne, all of them. They don't care. Just remember that. Do what you have to do with them, because they have the power. I don't know if they'll always have it, but they do now, and they'll have it as long as you live, my son. So don't ever go against them. But just remember, no matter what they say, don't ever trust them. Because they don't care about you, and they never will, because you're not one of them.'

He looked up. The jailor had come in.

'Say good-bye to your father now,' he said to his son. They kissed. 'Now go.'

An hour later Richard heard the crowd roar, and knew that he didn't have a father any more.

Chapter Nine

1897

As the month of October began and Jules Blanchard considered his family, he decided that he wasn't worried about his daughter, Marie. She was everything a young woman of her age should be.

Her hair had changed. The golden curls of her childhood had given way to light brown hair, parted in the middle and fluffed into soft waves. But her eyes were still china blue. She had a perfect peaches-and-cream complexion, and her father adored her. No doubt she'd be married before long, but he could only pray that whomever she married wouldn't take her far away.

The boys were different. They'd both gone to the Lycée Condorcet, near their home, and done well. But after that, their paths had diverged entirely.

Gérard had been everything his father could reasonably have asked. He'd been eager to go into the family business and he'd worked hard at it. Jules could already rely on him to keep everything running smoothly. Only months ago, he'd married an entirely suitable girl from a good family with plenty of money. He gave his father no worries.

But his younger son was another matter. He worried about Marc.

He hadn't minded when Marc had been accepted by the École des Beaux-Arts. He liked the art school's classical facade, which stared so handsomely across at the Louvre from the Seine's Left Bank. The place had prestige. It sounded quite well to say that his younger son had been there. But somehow he'd supposed that after this, Marc would want to engage himself in the business or administration of art, rather than put paint on canvas himself. True, Marc had done a fine portrait of his mother, which now had pride of place in the salon of the family's big apartment. But Jules would rather see his son as a gifted amateur than a professional painter.

His wife was of the same opinion. Only his sister Éloïse had stood up for the boy.

'If he wants a career in the art business,' he'd remarked to her, 'I know the Durand-Ruel family. They've three galleries in Paris now, and another in New York. They're starting to make money selling the Impressionists. Or I can easily get an introduction to the Duveens. They handle the Old Masters. They could give him advice.'

'But Le Bon Dieu may have given Marc a special gift,' Éloïse had pointed out. 'If so, it's his duty to use it. He's creative, a free spirit.'

'That,' confessed his father, 'is what worries me.'

'You created the Joséphine store.'

'Not the same.'

'Besides,' his sister pointed out, 'a painter can become a great man. Think of Delacroix. He was magnificent. You'd be proud to have a son like that.'

'Hmm.' Jules pulled a face. 'Delacroix had Talleyrand to ensure him a great career.'

It was true that France's epic romantic painter had obtained important state commissions from the powerful minister Talleyrand – and many believed that Talleyrand, a close friend of the Delacroix family, was actually the artist's father.

'Well, you have the resources to help him,' Éloïse pointed out. 'And you're his real father, too.'

Jules Blanchard considered.

'I just think it's all too easy for him,' he complained. 'He hasn't suffered. Think of all those years I had to suffer working for our father.'

'You didn't suffer so much,' his sister said tolerantly.

'I suffered,' he insisted.

'He will suffer for his art,' said Éloïse.

'I doubt it.' Jules Blanchard gave his sister a searching look. 'Do you really believe the boy has the passion to be an artist? Do you think he'll stick at it?'

'I don't know, Jules. But if you want my opinion, you should trust him. You should give him the chance to succeed – or to fail.' Éloïse paused. 'If he is not good enough, he will realise it himself. But if he never tries, he'll always regret that he didn't.'

That had been two years ago, and soon after the conversation, Jules Blanchard had made Marc an offer.

'I will support you for five years,' he told him. 'But if you have not met with any success by that time, then you will have to reconsider, and find some other employment. During those years, from time to time, I may ask you to do certain small projects for me. I shall not ask for more than one a year. Do you agree?'

'Yes, Father. That seems reasonable.'

'Good. Now, you will need a studio. There are a number to be had between the boulevard Haussmann and the Gare Saint-Lazare. Manet had a studio there, and Morisot and a number of our modern painters, and it will be close to our home as well.'

Marc smiled to himself. The area would be close to home and also to his father's office. He had no wish to live under the parental eyes.

'In fact,' he said with perfect truth, 'you're more than a decade out of date. Some of the artists you're thinking of have moved out of town altogether. A few went across the river. But the place for any artist to be nowadays is just below Montmartre, in the Place de Clichy area.'

'A bit unsavoury.'

'Not really. And if I'm going to do it, I should be in the community, don't you think? What's the first project you'd like me to do?' he asked obligingly, to change the subject.

'Your mother wants a new set of dining room chairs. I want you to design them. Something striking, out of the ordinary. I've got an excellent man who can make them.'

A month later, Jules and his wife had been astonished when Marc had come in one evening and laid his designs out on the dining room table. The work was unlike anything they had seen before. Over the rich, full-bodied shapes of the chairs were carved elegant, sinuous, tendril-like lines that suggested delicate plants.

'It reminds me of Gothic decoration, yet strangely modern,' remarked his father.

'It makes me think of orchids,' said his mother. 'Where does it come from?'

'I have a friend at the School of Decorative Arts,' Marc told them. 'He's been showing me all the latest designs from Germany and England. It's the coming thing.'

'Does this style have a name?' asked Jules.

'My friend calls it Art Nouveau. You'll be setting the fashion. If you don't mind being a little courageous.'

'Well' – Jules looked at his wife – 'I asked for something striking. Do you like them?'

Madame Blanchard thought of the effect they would have on her dinner guests. She imagined herself saying, 'My son Marc designed these, after he finished at the École des Beaux-Arts.'

'One would need a table to go with them, or they won't look right,' she said.

'Ah. I thought you might say that.' Marc unfurled more plans: for the table, a sideboard, new window treatments, and new wallpaper. 'The wallpaper you'll have to get from England,' he explained. 'I checked out the designs already before I designed the chairs.' And he handed them a catalogue. 'I'm afraid it's expensive having an artist in the family,' he said with a grin to his father.

His father considered. The entrepreneur in him understood what his son had done at once.

'It's bold,' he said. 'Completely bold.' He nodded. 'We'll do it.'

The next day he showed the designs to his sister.

'But it's magnificent!' cried Éloïse. 'He really has talent, Jules. I'm delighted.' She thought for a moment. 'You know,' she said quietly, 'Gérard is a good organiser, but he'd never have thought of this in a thousand years.'

Jules said nothing. But she knew that he knew it.

Soon after this, Jules had taken Marc to the rue du Faubourg-Saint-Antoine to see Monsieur Petit, the cabinetmaker.

Petit was a small round man who moved with a certain gravity. He lived over his workshop in the Faubourg Saint-Antoine, as his family had done since before the French Revolution. He took several minutes inspecting the drawings, while his daughter, a pretty young thing of about sixteen, entered the workshop to offer them refreshments. When Petit had completed his inspection, he addressed Marc with the respect of a craftsman for a proven artist.

'This is the first time I have ever been asked to make furniture to designs like these, monsieur,' he explained, and for the next twenty minutes, he and Marc went over them in detail together, the crafts-man asking numerous questions as to measurements, and requesting a few minor design alterations to aid in the making. It gave Jules pleasure to see his son and the craftsman so deep in their discussion that when the pretty girl came in again with their tea, neither Petit nor Marc noticed her at all.

It had taken many months to make the furniture. Petit asked Marc to come to his workshop several times to ensure that everything was done as he wished. But when the project was completed, Madame Blanchard's Art Nouveau dining room created a small sensation.

Meanwhile, Jules was able to get Marc two or three portrait commissions, which Marc completed to everyone's satisfaction.

It was the success of the first project that had encouraged Jules to suggest the second.

For some time, he had been considering a remodelling of his department store. But he hadn't been sure exactly what he wanted to do. The moment he'd seen Marc's designs, a plan had begun to take shape in his mind.

'I want something like what you have done for the dining room, but lighter, more airy. I want to use glass and steel, something absolutely modern, but at the same time sensuous. A big part of our business is selling clothes to women, after all. The Art Nouveau style is perfect for that. I want to design one big room. Then, if we like it, I shall convert the entire store.'

'That's a huge project,' Marc pointed out. 'I'll make designs, but I can't oversee their development and execution. We'll have to work with architects.'

This was clearly sensible. Marc had found a firm of architects, and they in turn had found contractors who specialised in the finest steelwork.

Although Marc had said that he couldn't supervise the work, his father was aware how often he looked in at the workshop where the decorative steel was being made. And when the actual building was being done, he was on-site in the store almost every day.

Jules also noticed something else. Marc seemed to have a natural talent for getting on with the workers, who clearly liked him.

'Did you know,' Marc asked him one day, 'that the steelworkers' foreman worked for Eiffel, both on the Statue of Liberty and the Eiffel Tower?'

'I must confess I didn't.'

'He's very proud of the fact. He was a riveter by trade, but he understands what we're doing. You should talk to him sometime.'

'What's his name?' Jules inquired.

'Thomas Gascon.'

And if Jules hadn't had time to do so, he'd been pleased that Marc discovered these things.

So why, as the third of the five years he had promised Marc began, should Jules Blanchard be worried about his son?

It was instinct, perhaps. Instinct, combined with some observation. It seemed to him that Marc was drinking too much. Not that he was getting drunk, but once or twice when he'd dropped by in the evening, his speech had been a little slurred. Jules had told him to take more exercise, but he doubted that Marc had done so. Occasionally he'd go by the studio, a big attic space at the top of a house next door to a small emporium selling *charcuterie* near the Place de Clichy. There was no doubt that Marc was working. The place was full of canvases. But it seemed to Jules that too many of them were studies of naked women. Of course, that was to be expected in an artist's studio, but he couldn't help asking once: 'Do you ever paint women with any clothes on?'

'Certainly, Father. When you got me that commission to paint Madame Du Bois, I not only painted her fully dressed, but wearing a hat as well.'

That a sketch also existed of the lady wearing the hat, and nothing else, was something there was no need for his father – or the lady's husband – to know.

When he expressed his reservations to his sister, however, Éloïse was dismissive.

'My dear Jules,' she told him, 'you are worrying about the wrong member of the family entirely.'

'What do you mean?'

'The person in the family who needs your care and attention isn't Marc at all. It's Marie.'

'She seems happy enough.'

'That's because you like having her at home. But she's almost twenty-three. She needs to find a husband. I'm sorry to say it, but for once you are neglecting your family duty. It's high time that you did something about it.'

★　　★　　★

262

There were twenty of them, gallant young officers, sitting all together. They were in high spirits. As well they should be. For they were at the Moulin Rouge.

Not only that. Tomorrow evening, one of them was going to sleep with the most beautiful woman in Paris. But who?

The Moulin Rouge was a work of genius. It had been going for only a few years, but it was already a legend.

It was to be found at the foot of the hill of Montmartre, on the broad and leafy boulevard de Clichy that effectively marked the frontier where the serried order of Baron Haussmann's Paris met the steep chaos of Montmartre. It occupied a former garden plot sandwiched between two respectable, six-storey blocks, its large street-level front forming one edge of a platform. And upon this platform rose an almost full-scale model windmill, painted bright red.

Even by the exuberant standards of the Belle Époque, as this age would come to be known, the Moulin Rouge was preposterous. The louche old windmills on the hill above had always been there, but this bright red dummy down below was a loud affront to the baron's bourgeois boulevard, and meant to be so.

As such, it was wonderfully French.

For if, since the time of Louis XIV, governments had tried to impose a stern classical order on the ancient, often tribal lands of France – each with their own dialects, each with probably a score of local cheeses – they hadn't found it easy. And even here in the nation's capital, the spirits of old medieval Paris, of markets and alleys, and jostling crowds, kept bursting up, like brightly coloured plants and irreverent weeds, breaking through the tightly cemented surfaces and angry order of monarchs, bureaucrats and policemen.

The Moulin was just such a plant. It was coloured bright red. It had the finest cabaret in Paris.

And everybody went there. Working men went there. Ladies of the night, of course. Middle-class Paris went there, and the aristocracy. Even Britain's Prince of Wales had gone there.

The young officers were aristocratic. They were all brother officers in the same regiment. Most of the time, they might expect to be stationed in other places, usually on France's eastern borders; but for the present they were stationed in Paris, and they were determined to make the most of it.

Like most of the aristocratic regiments of the day, they patronised a particular brothel. If the brothels of Paris were legally regulated, with twice-weekly medical inspections, the grandest of them were like private mansions, whose rooms might have exotic themes – Moorish, Babylonian, Oriental. Whenever the Prince of Wales visited Paris, he frequented a very chic brothel where he installed his own bathtub, which he liked to fill with champagne. The house where the officers of the regiment went lay in the quarter between the Opéra and the Louvre. It was discreet, delightful, and was patronised by several great nobles.

But above all these lay the world of the private courtesan, the *grandes horizontales*. Though many were kept by a single rich man, others took lovers, sometimes for just a night at a time. The luckiest courtesans might marry a rich and elderly client, even one with a title; and if widowed young enough could live in a mansion of their own, and hold a salon – and take fresh lovers too, of course, as long as they understood that she expected to receive gifts, in cash or kind, for the interest she took in them.

The courtesan known as La Belle Hélène was as renowned for her charm as for her many other accomplishments. To spend a night in her company was considered a great privilege. It was also very expensive indeed. Even the richest of the aristocratic young officers baulked at the price. So they had come up with an agreeable solution.

Each of the twenty men had contributed the same amount – more than they would have had to pay for a visit to the discreet mansion near the Opéra – into a fund. And tonight they were going to draw lots to discover which of them was to take the money and visit La Belle Hélène.

But before the lottery took place, they would drink champagne and enjoy the show at the Moulin Rouge.

Roland de Cygne had never been to the Moulin Rouge before. He'd often meant to go. But as a regular patron of the rival Folies-Bergère, which was nearer the centre of town and whose first-rate comedy and modern dance had always satisfied him, he'd somehow never got around to the Moulin Rouge with its saucier fare. Needless to say, as soon as his companions had discovered this fact, he'd had to endure some teasing, which he did with good humour.

His brother officers liked Roland. He'd shown a fine aptitude for a military career right from the start. When he'd attended the military academy of Saint-Cyr, he'd come out nearly top of his class. Perhaps even more important to his aristocratic companions, he'd shown such prowess at the Cavalry Academy at Saumur that he'd almost made the elite Cadre Noir equestrian team. He was a good regimental soldier, respected by his men, a loyal friend with a kindly sense of humour. He could also be trusted to tell the truth. And he certainly looked the part of the cavalryman. He was a good height, a little taller than his father. His fair hair was parted in the middle, from which it marched out in close-trimmed waves. He wore a short moustache, brushed outward but not curled. The effect was handsome and manly.

Yet sometimes one might notice a quiet thoughtfulness in his blue eyes, even a hint of proud melancholy, and his brother officers thought it was their job to tease him about this too.

'There is an air of mystery about you, de Cygne,' one of them now remarked. 'Like Athos in *The Three Musketeers*, I think you have a hidden past. A secret sorrow. Is it a woman?'

'Of course it is,' the youngest cried. 'Tell us, de Cygne. Your secret is safe with us. For at least ten minutes!'

'No,' the oldest of them, a captain, corrected. 'Hidden in that handsome cavalryman's head, I detect an idealist. One day, de Cygne, you will be a hero, as famous as the great knight Bayard, *sans peur et sans reproche*. Fearless and beyond reproach. Or you'll surprise us all and enter a monastery.'

'A monastery?' cried the youngest. 'What are you talking about? We're at the Moulin Rouge, for God's sake!'

'I agree,' Roland responded with a smile. 'Anyone wishing to become a monk will be reported to the management.' It was time to end this probing into his character. He glanced around the table. 'I think we need more champagne.'

The captain signalled to the waiter, who was at his side in an instant.

'More champagne, Luc.'

'At once, *mon capitaine*.'

A few minutes later, the floor show began.

It had to be said, Roland thought, the Moulin Rouge did what it did supremely well. The cavernous space had room for dozens of tables, but the view of the stage was excellent. Part of the atmosphere of the place was created by its particular light. There were numerous gas lights, which provided a warm glow, but the owners had supplemented these with the latest electric lights, which provided a sparkling overlay, magnified in the huge mirrored glass by the stage that reflected the whole scene. The effect was both risqué and magical at the same time.

The orchestra was excellent. And then there were the dancers.

They danced a medley of arrangements that night. There were exotic dances, gymnastic dances with one dancer after another dropping down dramatically to do splits, and then, of course, the dance that had become the Moulin's signature: the cancan.

'I'm sorry you never got to see La Goulue perform this,' the captain said to Roland, who nodded. In the space of five years, La Goulue had made herself a legend. Now she'd gone off with a circus on her own. But her replacement, Jane Avril, already made famous thanks to a poster by Toulouse-Lautrec, was quite as good. And where La Goulue was loud and outrageous, Avril was a little more elegant.

The troupe came on, in silk dresses, black stockings and extravagant, frilly petticoats. They began in a line, swishing their skirts, and performing half kicks. Then they broke up into a complex choreography. The kicks grew higher. One did a cartwheel. Two others dropped into the splits. They formed back into two lines. And then Jane Avril made her entrance.

If the troupe was athletic, Avril was something more. If the girls had formed a line to support each other as they performed the high kicks, Avril could balance on one leg, like a ballerina, performing half kicks and high kicks one after the other as she made a pirouette. Minute after minute, while the troupe performed all the cancan moves and the tempo increased, Avril was out in front of them, dancing a sort of descant to their tune, before sinking at last, in a single, fluid fall, into a split that made it look like the most natural thing in the world.

It was the cancan, yet beyond the cancan. It was a work of art.

When it ended, no one rose to their feet faster than Roland.

'Magnificent!' he cried as he applauded.

When the audience had finished applauding, the master of ceremonies announced that there would now be a pause for the orchestra to take refreshments before the general dancing began.

For the officers at the table, the moment had come. The captain took command.

'On this sheet of paper,' he announced, drawing it from his pocket, 'are written the twenty names of the officers in the draw. Against each name is a number. On each of these small cards' – he produced them with a flourish – 'is written a single number from one to twenty. Please inspect them.' He laid them ceremoniously on the table. 'Very well. To ensure absolute fairness, I have here a blindfold.' He produced a black silk bandana. 'Luc!' he called to the waiter. 'Come here and bring me a large soup bowl.'

Luc obliged at once.

Roland noticed that the waiter was quite a handsome young man, with a broad, intelligent face and dark hair, a lock of which fell down over his broad brow. He might be French or possibly Italian, Roland thought. But his age was hard to guess. He had a lithe way of moving that suggested he might be only twenty, but there was a smoothness and worldliness in his manner that belonged to an older man.

'Luc,' announced the captain, 'I am going to blindfold you.' And he began to tie the black bandana around the waiter's head.

As Jacques Le Sourd entered the Moulin Rouge, he did not see the officers at first. He certainly wasn't looking for them. He'd come there to dance.

Jacques was a busy man. After a brief spell as a teacher, he had turned to his father's trade as a typesetter. The work was hard, but he still found time to write articles for the various socialist journals that had sprung up. Today had been a free day, and he'd spent it working on an article he was writing for *Le Parti Ouvrier* about the anarchist movement.

It had been a long afternoon. He'd been up on Montmartre, in the Lapin Agile bar, a picturesque establishment on the back slope of the hill, where artists and people with anarchist views liked to congregate. He had interviewed three anarchists. By the time he was finished, it was well into the evening.

He had wanted to write on the anarchists for a while. During the last few years there had been a number of incidents in France that were supposed to be their work. Bombs had exploded, quite a few people had been killed. There had been a government crackdown, and a number of anarchists had fled to England.

But what was anarchism for? What did it achieve?

There were so many groupings on the Left. If radicalism was a tree that had grown from the ideals of the French Revolution, the midcentury graftings of Marx and Engels had now produced a plant of many branches. There were kindly utopians, trade union men, socialists, communists, anarchists and many variations in between. They all opposed the monarchy. They were all suspicious of the Church. And they all longed for a perfect society of free men. But what that society would be, and how to achieve it, was the subject of endless discussion. And no subject was more disputed than the role of the anarchists.

Le Sourd knew that the true anarchist movement, the anarchism of men like Proudhon in France, followed by Bakunin and Kropotkin, called for the overthrow of the state, which would be followed by a utopian world of friendly collectives. For these men, the violent outrages, the bombings and terrorist acts were only a catalyst – the shock needed to trigger a huge reaction – in which the state, which lacked all moral validity, would collapse. After that, miraculously, poverty, exploitation and human suffering would end.

Jacques was not an anarchist. He thought that even the original anarchist philosophers were utopian dreamers, and that most of their followers were dangerous fanatics. And the three men he'd talked with that day had confirmed all his worst opinions.

Hadn't they learned anything from the Paris Commune? The Commune for which his father had fought and died? During its brief reign, it had run Paris successfully. But it lacked a proper army. The Communards hadn't got an organisation outside the capital, and the forces of reaction had been able to march into Paris and break them. The present regime, republican but corrupt, had been in power ever since.

The more he'd listened to the men this afternoon, the more he had appreciated why his father's Commune should be his guide. The anarchists he'd spoken to wanted to throw a bomb and run away. There, they seemed to think, their responsibility ended. But his father and his friends had stood up for their beliefs, fought for them, tried to construct something concrete, and been killed for it.

Compare these anarchists with that other heroine of the Commune, still living, Louise Michel. She'd fought for the Commune up in Montmartre. Afterwards, at her trial, she'd challenged the government to execute her. 'Put a bullet in me,' she had cried, 'for if you don't, I'll go straight back to opposing you.' And if she hadn't been a woman, no doubt they would have shot her. But she'd been as good as her word. Deported, in and out of jail ever since, she'd taught, preached revolution, even taken up arms again. People called her an anarchist, but properly speaking, in Jacques Le Sourd's opinion, she was a revolutionary.

Perhaps, he thought, this comparison might provide the structure for his article.

For Jacques had long ago concluded that the Marxists were right. There must be central organisation. There must be a proper power base. Just days ago, the Jewish Workers in Russia and Poland had formed a party to promote socialism and equal rights for women. They were calling it the Bund. This was the sort of well-established development that would be needed, years of it, before the revolution would be ready.

And who knew, when the revolution did come, it might be worldwide. He hoped so. Until then, the anarchist bombs were as useless as they were cruel.

After four hours of listening to these men in the Lapin Agile, who thought that outrage was an end in itself, he'd come to the conclusion that they were vain, self-centred lunatics and artists, and he'd left in disgust.

So having walked down the hill to the boulevard de Clichy, and seeing the bright lights of the Moulin Rouge, he had decided to go in there to relax a little. He might be a revolutionary, but he still loved to dance.

The big hall was packed as usual. Here and there he saw tables where groups of women sat. Some were there to look for clients. Others were just there to have a good time. Either way, since he was tall, and dark, and danced well, he always found women happy to dance with him. And if he wanted more, he could often find that too, without having to pay for it.

Of course, when the revolution finally came, scenes of bourgeois decadence like this would surely have to go. Most of his friends said that even the small café owners would be swept away, and be replaced with cooperatives. There were already quite a few food cooperatives operating in Paris. Whether a family was operating an emporium or a tiny café, they were still profiteering, and exploiting the workers.

He shrugged. That was for another day. His eyes began to travel around the tables where the women sat.

And then, from over on his right, there was a roar. A waiter wearing a blindfold was standing by a long table of young men, who were starting to applaud. People were turning to look. The young men were laughing.

'Bravo, de Cygne,' one of them cried out.

'Bring champagne.'

'No. Oysters. Bring oysters.'

'The honour of the regiment is in your hands.'

'The honour of the regiment is between your legs!'

'Oysters for de Cygne!'

One of the officers had got up to take the blindfold off the waiter, who was smiling broadly. Now the waiter made a congratulatory bow to one of the seated men.

A few moments later the waiter came past him, still smiling to himself.

'What was that about?' Jacques asked.

'Oh, something very amusing, monsieur. A party of young cavalry officers clubbed together so that one of them could pay a visit to, one might say, the most desirable woman in Paris. I had the honour of making the draw.' He nodded. 'It must be said, the cavalry has style.'

'I thought I heard the name de Cygne. Would that be the son of the Vicomte de Cygne?'

'I couldn't say,' Luc replied discreetly.

'It's an ancient name,' Jacques remarked casually.

'No doubt, monsieur.'

Jacques would have liked to ask the name of the lady in question, but there was no need. For at that moment, a young officer rose unsteadily to his feet, and raising his glass cried out: 'To our noble friend de Cygne, and La Belle Hélène.'

Jacques Le Sourd smiled.

'Lucky man,' he said to the waiter. All Paris had heard of La Belle Hélène.

'Tomorrow night, monsieur, the gentleman will be in paradise.'

'Indeed,' said Jacques thoughtfully. Then he looked around the Moulin Rouge at the women again. He saw one or two he'd danced with before. Perhaps he'd get to paradise himself tonight.

A few minutes later, Luc was back at the table. This time, he spoke softly to Roland.

'If you will permit me, monsieur, I have heard that the lady is particularly well-disposed towards those who send flowers to her before their arrival. And she has a particular taste in flowers. If you would allow me, I could make all the arrangements for you. I think you would be well satisfied.'

Roland was surprised, and not altogether pleased. Why was this waiter insinuating himself in his business? But before he could reply, the captain interposed.

'My dear friend, you can put your trust in Luc, I assure you. He knows everything in Paris.' He gave the waiter a wry look. 'How he knows all these things, we do not ask. But let him get the flowers, and it will be to your advantage. Give him some money and he'll take care of it.'

'How much?' Roland asked with a frown. Luc leaned down and murmured something in his ear.

'For flowers?' Roland was incredulous. He stared at Luc suspiciously.

The captain glanced at the waiter. 'Special flowers, eh?'

'Very special, *mon capitaine*,' Luc replied quietly, and the captain nodded.

'My dear de Cygne,' he said to Roland, 'take my advice, there's a good fellow. I want you to leave this in the hands of my friend here. Trust me, you won't be sorry.'

At about the same time the following evening, a covered horse-drawn cab containing Roland de Cygne rolled from the Arc de Triomphe down the avenue Victor Hugo. It was cool but not cold. A half-moon hung in the sky. By the soft lamplight, Roland could see the yellowed leaves still on the trees that lined the street.

Not surprisingly, he felt excited.

When his companions had teased him the previous night, they had been quite perceptive. He'd never regretted his choice of career.

271

At the age of twenty-five, he was happy in the army. He enjoyed the brotherhood and companionship it offered and he was as proud of his regiment as he was of his name. But though he kept such thoughts to himself, he could not help the fact that he was a de Cygne, whose life – the family motto demanded – must be 'According to God's Will'.

Did that make him a romantic? Certainly some would say that his view of the family's relationship to the monarchy, to God and to an almost mystical notion of France was romantic. But it was a sense of identity that fortified him for whatever noble task might lie ahead. And if the seeds of those ideas had been implanted by Father Xavier during a walk in the Tuileries Gardens which Roland had long since forgotten, everything in his life so far had served to nurture them.

Was his religion nothing more than a sense of family pride? Only if it was pride that made him cherish in his heart the memory of his mother and her gentle prayers like secret icons, as holy to him as the pure red flame that glimmered over the Host in every Catholic church. Moreover, he was ready to sacrifice his life for that tiny flame, in the hope of a greater light beyond. So that, when he looked dispassionately at the teeming life around him, the desire of the socialists to change the impurity of the world by mere material manipulation seemed as deluded to him as his hopes of redemption seemed illusory to them.

None of these reflections, however, prevented him from being a good companion to his brother officers, and he certainly wasn't a prude. Fastidious, yes – as the madam at the regiment's private house had discerned at once the first time he had gone there, when she selected a very sweet girl for him. But he liked women, and felt that some modest career with them, at least, was as much a rite of passage in his life as passing out of Saint-Cyr or the school of equitation. As for the fact that such adventures counted as sins of the flesh, he would go to confession in due course and receive a penance. Meanwhile, though he might not have put the thought into words, he had to assume that the deity, having destined him to be an aristocrat, would understand that it would be necessary to behave in the appropriate manner.

Indeed, the adventure tonight was something of which he could be justly proud. It was almost as good as if he'd got into the Cadre

Noir. For a de Cygne to have spent the night with the most celebrated courtesan in Paris was done partly for the honour of the family. It was something to tell his sons and grandsons about – when they reached a certain age, of course.

The cab had reached the intersection where the avenue Victor Hugo was met by the rue de la Pompe and several others. Here it turned right, into a quiet but elegant street known, on account of the leafy trees that had formerly graced the place, as the rue des Belles-Feuilles – the street of beautiful leaves. The short downward slope of the street led out on to the broadest and grandest of the lateral avenues that emanated from the Arc de Triomphe, and the little quarter contained a number of diplomatic residences and some of the lesser embassies. Halfway down it, in a small, ornate mansion, whose entrance was reached up a half dozen marble steps, lived La Belle Hélène.

Jacques Le Sourd had first arrived there two hours ago, just after dusk.

It hadn't been difficult to discover where La Belle Hélène lived. He'd remembered her real name, and a quick perusal of some directories in the morning had given him the address he needed.

First, he'd stood around by the top of the street, looking down it, and quickly ascertained that it was very quiet. During ten minutes, he saw only one person enter it at all. Then he walked casually down the street, taking note of her house and those on each side. After that, he'd gone out into the big avenue below, and let a little time pass. The houses on this avenue were set back even farther than those on the Champs-Élysées, and the view up the long slope towards the Arc de Triomphe was so broad and so grand and so blank that it was almost frightening. And that circumstance, it occurred to him, was curiously appropriate for his mission.

For tonight, Roland de Cygne was going to die.

Next, he went up the street again, on the other side. This time he was looking for places where he might conceal himself. This was not so easy, but there was a tradesman's entrance to the house just down-hill from La Belle Hélène's. The fact that there was no light above this doorway was not only helpful, but it suggested that it was not much used after dark, and it was a few feet back from the street, which made it less visible. He was just eyeing this from a few yards away when a cab drew up outside the lady's little mansion.

Surely de Cygne couldn't be arriving so early? He wasn't ready. But all was well, for out of the cab, carrying a huge bunch of flowers, came a man that Jacques Le Sourd thought he vaguely recognised. The fellow went straight to the side door, which was opened by a maid. Jacques saw the fellow have a brief conversation with her, then turn. And at that moment he remembered. It was either the waiter that he'd spoken to in the Moulin Rouge last night, or someone very like him. The man glanced towards Jacques, but gave no sign of recognition at all, and got back into the cab, which immediately rattled away. Jacques shrugged. A coincidental resemblance perhaps. Or if it was the waiter, the fellow clearly hadn't recognised him. He put the incident out of his mind.

When he thought that he had done all that he usefully could, he left the rue des Belles-Feuilles. For there was still another equally important task to complete. He had to plan his escape.

He wasn't worried about the moment of the killing itself. If there were people in the street who could identify him or give chase, then he wouldn't shoot. De Cygne could always die another day. But the odds were good that the street would be empty. If destiny had thrown this opportunity in his way, it must be for a reason.

Then, assuming that de Cygne didn't come on foot, there might be a coachman to deal with. The chances were that the coachman would be too shocked to react in time. But if he tried anything, then Jacques decided he'd shoot him too. It was simpler.

For half an hour he wandered about the area. The first thing to consider was the pistol. He felt inside his overcoat. It was safely concealed there, tied with string around his waist. After firing it, he wanted to dispose of it as soon as possible. He could throw it almost anywhere, but thirty yards down the street on the right was a high wall enclosing the garden of a large mansion. He could easily toss the gun over the wall as he ran past.

At that point he'd already be running down the hill, so it would be sensible to continue in the same direction. The huge avenue would be quiet at night. He could turn down it, run to the end, which wasn't far, and then into the Bois de Boulogne. But should anyone see him, it would immediately invite suspi-

cion. The police were quite good at sweeping the Bois for criminals at night.

At the bottom of the rue des Belles-Feuilles, however, before one
reached the avenue, there was an intersection of small streets which
led into a network of lanes. It didn't take him long to find a route that
took him through a succession of these lanes and led him back into
the avenue Victor Hugo, where there were always people, bars, a
brasserie or two. He could hail a cab if he saw one, or even stop for
a drink.

Satisfied with this plan, he made his way slowly back towards the
rue des Belles-Feuilles.

The street was empty as he went down it. He came to the darkened doorway he had selected and stepped into it. Carefully he drew
out his pistol from its hiding place. All he had to do now was to wait.
He felt very calm.

He'd always known he would kill Roland de Cygne. He'd made a
vow to do it, and that was enough. But it had also become clear to
him that he could take his time. When he could do so without risk,
he'd do it. Until then he would wait. For there were other things,
more important things, that needed to be done. When he was a boy
he hadn't really understood that, but now he did.

Like Roland de Cygne, he believed in a higher cause, a pure ideal,
the freedom of the human spirit. Like Roland, he was proud of
France. For wasn't France the home of revolution? True, the
American Revolution had been a noble precursor. A bourgeois revolution for a capitalist country, a step along the way, but no more. The
true ideals – sullied since by dictatorship and compromise and
corruption – had been born in France. And when the new international order came into being, France would have her place of honour
in the history of the world.

Above all, Jacques now believed, the final resolution of the long
historical struggle was inevitable. It might take time, but the earthly
apocalypse, when all men should be free – free of oppression, free of
bogus bourgeois comfort, free of superstition – would come. It was
destiny. And that certitude gave him strength and comfort.

The death of Roland de Cygne was just a tiny part of that process,
of no great importance. But it was a debt of honour he owed his

father, and the memory of the Commune, and when the time was right, he would accomplish it.

He'd continued to keep an eye on Roland. He'd known when Roland went to Saint-Cyr, and the school of equitation, and when he was away with his regiment. But he hadn't realised that the regiment had been posted to Paris recently. That had been careless of him.

So when he had suddenly caught up with him in the Moulin Rouge last night, it had seemed to Jacques that this must be destiny. The opportunity was too good to miss. There was nothing to connect him to Roland or La Belle Hélène. If someone shot the young man as he entered her door, the police would probably assume that it was a jealous lover. Paris took some pride in its crimes of passion. All he had to do was to vanish back into the streets, and the thing was done.

How appropriate that the aristocrat, the new representative of the old monarchist order, should die while visiting a whore.

He waited patiently for Roland to appear.

During the first hour, only half a dozen people entered the street. A manservant went into one of the houses, the rest passed through.

It was past eight o'clock when the cat appeared. It was a small black-and-white creature, hardly more than a kitten. Where it had come from he wasn't sure, but the little creature sidled up to him and started rubbing itself against his feet. It was so light and dainty that he could scarcely feel it. But he didn't want it there, and gave it a gentle shove with his foot. This seemed to make the tiny cat even more interested. Perhaps it thought this was some kind of game. This time it got a good grip on his right foot with its sharp little claws, and started attacking the laces with its teeth. Starting to get irritated, he made a kicking motion with his foot that was strong enough to send the kitten flying out into the roadway. Disgusted, it turned towards him and gave a hiss that was unmistakably an insult.

And at that moment, a cab came down the street and pulled up outside the house of La Belle Hélène.

He glanced up and down the street. Not a soul. The door of the cab opened. There was only a single lamp by the door of La Belle Hélène's house, but it gave enough light to see the face of Roland de Cygne.

The moment had come. Holding the pistol firmly under his coat, he stepped out of his hiding place just as Roland took the first step up to the mansion door. It took only two paces to reach the street. At his normal stride, he should be directly behind de Cygne just as he had reached the door. He took the first step.

'Here, kitty kitty kitty. Where are you, little cat?'

Jacques stared in stupefaction. The servant he'd seen earlier had suddenly appeared from the house below, directly in his path. He couldn't see the fellow's face, but judging from the way he was bent, it was an old man.

'Kitty kitty kitty.' The old fellow was moving straight towards him. Jacques was so surprised that he missed taking a step. At this rate he and the old man would meet exactly at the foot of the steps where he had intended to fire. Worse, de Cygne was turning to look. He had counted on him presenting an easy target, outlined in the doorway with his back to him.

'Kind sir, you have not seen a little cat?' The old servant hadn't looked up, but the question was addressed to him. De Cygne was turning towards him now. At least he couldn't see his face in the darkness. The coachman was turning to look at him too.

It was no good. The business was getting out of hand. With a muttered curse he turned around, crossed the street and strode rapidly away.

A female servant let Roland in. For apart from her visitors, La Belle Hélène had no men in the house. The coachman, whose son acted as groom, lived in the coach house at the end of the garden.

If his father's masculine mansion evoked the grand, baroque spirit of Louis XIV, the house of La Belle Hélène was full of the lighter spirit of Louis XV, the Sun King's successor. On the left side of the hall, an elegant marble staircase curled up to a gallery above. Against the opposite wall, under a gilded rococo looking glass, a turquoise marble side table, on sinuous gilded legs, supported a vase of creamy Paris porcelain, decorated with blue and pink flowers and a charming shepherd playing a pipe. The vase was full of flowers. Beside it he noticed a small silver salver.

As the maid took his top hat and coat, she softly suggested that if he wished to leave an envelope, he might place it on the salver.

This done, she ushered him into the salon, saying that her mistress would be with him shortly. Then she disappeared with the salver.

The salon was furnished with rococo gilt furniture. He noticed a beautiful little writing table with a marquetry top and polished curves. Sèvres porcelain graced the chimney mantel. On the walls were charming paintings by artists like Boucher and Watteau of gods and goddesses, or frivolous ladies and gentlemen of the court, in pastoral landscapes, enjoying themselves in various states of dress or undress. On one wall, however, was a large painting belonging to the present century, of a handsome lady, as clearly drawn as a portrait by Ingres, wearing a wonderful pink silk dress, and walking in a garden that contained a sumptuous peacock.

Everywhere he saw pinks and soft blues, delicacy and charm: it was the most feminine house he'd ever been in. He'd been waiting there only a minute or two when the lady appeared.

La Belle Hélène was wearing a long, light silk gown, cut low over her lovely breasts – a little simpler than she would have worn if she were dining out – which darted to a fashionably narrow waist and laced, or unlaced, at the back.

She looked radiant.

She was in her early thirties, he supposed. Like his, her hair was fair and wavy, and her eyes were blue. But beyond these superficialities, they might have come from different planets. For though the aristocrat was perfectly tailored, shaved and barbered, it was the lady who was sophisticated, in ways of which he was only dimly aware.

Her hair, her skin, her teeth were flawless, and kept that way at great expense. She was waxed and powdered, manicured and scented, until she was a work of art. Her eyes were wide apart and took in everything without seeming to do so. Her face was turned slightly upward, her mouth smiling pleasantly. She was available to him – that was already established – yet she remained perfectly poised.

'Thank you for the beautiful flowers, monsieur,' she said, 'which I hope you noticed in the hall. It seems you know exactly what I like.' She smiled. 'I see that you understand that flowers are to be smelled as well as looked at.' She paused just an instant. 'I collect pollen like a bee. But just a little. Never too much.'

He bowed and smiled, though he had still not comprehended that when Luc had delivered the flowers, neatly tied to the stem of one of the roses was a little packet of cocaine. Not that he need have been shocked if he had known; for cordials containing cocaine were even then being enjoyed, and publicly recommended, by such worthy persons as Thomas Edison in America and Queen Victoria in Britain.

The maid appeared with two glasses of champagne. The glasses were the broad *coupes* then in fashion. La Belle Hélène used a golden swizzle stick, with a tiny flail at the end to reduce the bubbles in her glass.

'I prefer less bubbles,' she remarked, 'though my friends tell me I should not.' Then, as they sipped their champagne, they began to talk.

La Belle Hélène was a beautiful woman. But the reasons she was a great courtesan began with her conversation.

It took her only moments to put him at his ease. Within five minutes, he was having the most delightful conversation he had ever had in his life. She told him a little about herself or, like as not, made reference to something some friend of hers had experienced or told her about, but she seemed chiefly interested in learning about him. And soon she knew far more about him than he guessed.

For her success, her mansion, the works of art on the wall and her friendships, which were genuine, all derived from this one fact: that she studied men. She discovered their strengths and weaknesses, what they felt and what they wanted, and then she set her entire intelligence and imagination to making them happier than they had ever been in their lives. She fulfilled their every desire, and even desires they did not know they had. And they showed their gratitude as only very rich men can. The house and much of the art came from an elderly industrialist, who would have married her if he could have.

In the course of this career, she had amassed not only a little fortune, but a large stock of knowledge about many subjects, from finance and art to wines and the racetrack.

By the time they moved into the little room which she used for intimate dining, she already knew about his regiment, his family and the fact that he liked the Folies-Bergère.

They started with caviar, then a delicious oyster bisque, some hors d'oeuvres and a light, poached turbot, served with an asparagus gelatin. The main course was sliced pheasant breasts cooked with Normandy apple, a speciality of her cook.

Though she served excellent wines, including a wonderful Hermitage with the pheasant, Roland noticed that La Belle Hélène drank almost nothing, and he took care to drink only moderately himself. The food was carefully calculated to be delicious but not too filling, with sorbets to keep the palate clean. They finished with some cheeses and a little fruit.

And all the while, they talked. She wanted to know about his childhood, his likes and dislikes, his views on politics, his travels — which were few. He had never had any woman take such an interest in him, let alone such a woman as this. Though there were some rich aristocrats who could, neither he nor even his father could afford to keep such a lady, and for the first time in his life, Roland experienced a moment of envy for the rich bankers and industrialists who were able to.

At one moment, after they had been discussing his favourite light opera, she gazed at him thoughtfully and asked, 'Tell me, my friend, have you ever heard any of the music of Debussy?'

'I'm afraid I haven't.'

'The other day I went with friends to a concert in which a recent piece of his was played. 'Prélude à l'après-midi d'un faune'. It's one of the most sensuous things I ever heard. Quite short. Ten minutes or so.' She paused. 'You need to close your eyes and just let it waft over you. Don't think at all. Like listening to some of Baudelaire's poems. 'L'Invitation au Voyage', for instance.'

'My father likes that poem. He told me so years ago.'

'One should always listen to one's father.' She smiled. 'I have the impression that you should learn to surrender yourself sometimes.'

Roland frowned. 'Surrender' wasn't a word he used if he could help it.

'Well,' La Belle Hélène continued gently, 'perhaps you may surrender to me. If you like.'

By the end of the meal he noticed that her gown had discreetly shifted down to reveal more of her breasts, in a most enticing way. She rose.

'If you would like to come upstairs in a few minutes,' she said, 'you will find a dressing room on the right. You will see where to go after that.'

The dressing room was panelled, with a washbasin, water jug and all the things that a man might require for his *toilette*, including a pair of ivory-backed hairbrushes so miraculously clean that one might have supposed they had never been used before. A nightshirt and an embroidered silk dressing gown of just his size were hanging ready for his use. When he had changed, he went through the small door he saw in front of him, and found himself in the bedroom of La Belle Hélène.

If her salon had been charmingly in the style of Louis XV, La Belle Hélène's bedroom evoked a more recent style, and was designed entirely for comfort. By the window was a nice little Second Empire sofa, well upholstered and just big enough for two. By the fire was a broad bench, similarly upholstered, where two people might sit very companionably and gaze at the flames. The walls of the room were covered in pink silk. There was a hidden closet in one corner, containing various items that the lady did not think would be needed tonight. Also, strategically placed, but hidden behind curtains for now, two large looking glasses. And then there was the bed itself. It was quite a large four-poster, elegantly draped, but very solidly constructed. And in the middle of it, her hair now loose, and wearing only a satin nightdress, was La Belle Hélène.

Roland de Cygne had made love to some beautiful women, but what he experienced in the next hour and a half was beyond anything he had imagined. La Belle Hélène was not only skilful, she was full of surprises. At one moment he could not believe she could seem so light. At another, he would be amazed by her suppleness and strength. She coaxed him, challenged him; but above all, she was so delicious that he could not stop exploring, could not get enough of her. It was a play without an intermission.

Finally, they rested awhile.

'I feel,' he confessed, 'like one of those lucky fellows centuries ago in a Persian garden.'

'Do you remember the start of Omar Khayyám?' she asked.

'Remind me.'

> Awake! For Morning in the Bowl of Night
> Has flung the Stone that puts the Stars to Flight:
> And Lo! the Hunter of the East has caught
> The Sultan's Turret in a Noose of Light.

He nodded. An Englishman had translated the old Persian poem of love, and fate, and nothingness decades ago, and now it was a bestseller all over Europe.

'But it isn't morning yet,' he objected.

'No,' she said. 'It certainly isn't.'

And then they made love again. And this time, when he was ready to come to a climax, he discovered another of her talents, as she held him in the delicious squeeze for which she was known by her fortunate lovers.

Afterwards, he lay quite still and closed his eyes, and it seemed to him as if he were in some faraway place, a Persian garden perhaps, or an endless, timeless desert, under the stars, and he heard her say that he should sleep awhile.

Luc Gascon was puzzled, but he didn't mind. He loved intrigue.

If Jacques Le Sourd had imagined that he hadn't been noticed when Luc was delivering the flowers to La Belle Hélène that evening, he didn't know his man. Luc noticed everything. He'd trained himself to do that ever since he'd worked up at the Moulin de la Galette as a boy, and now, at the Moulin Rouge, a customer only had to blink his eyes for Luc to be at his side in an instant. As for the discreet errands in which he specialised, errands that often required that he not be observed, he'd become a master of that game. If a man needed a message to reach another man's wife, Luc would find a way to deliver it. If a man wanted to know if his own wife was unfaithful, Luc could probably find that out too.

Above all, in these and many other encounters, Luc had learned never to show that he had noticed anything.

When Jacques Le Sourd had asked about de Cygne at the Moulin Rouge the night before, Luc had taken note of his face. So when he caught sight of him loitering in the rue des Belles-Feuilles this evening, he had remembered him at once. And the fact Le Sourd was in such a quiet street, where de Cygne was shortly to arrive, could not possibly be a coincidence.

He didn't yet know Jacques's name. But it was evident that he was not a rich man or an aristocrat. Almost certainly he meant harm of some kind to de Cygne. And de Cygne was now a client, a friend of the captain, moreover. This was really all that Luc needed to know.

His clients were his livelihood. Every client for whom he could do a favour was an investment. His clients were to be protected.

Besides, it was his nature to be curious.

His cab had gone only halfway up the avenue towards the Arc de Triomphe, therefore, when he paid the coachman and stepped out. Then he'd made his way back to the rue des Belles-Feuilles and kept watch.

It had been easy to spot Le Sourd returning to take up his hiding place. The way that he briefly touched his stomach with one hand suggested to Luc that he was carrying a weapon of some kind.

More skill had been needed to enter the street and take up a position out of sight nearby, but Luc had accomplished that without too much difficulty. Now he could observe everything that passed.

And if this fellow tried to attack de Cygne, what was Luc going to do? Luc hadn't the slightest doubt. He was going to save the aristocrat. That was where his interests lay. The only question was, how?

Luc wasn't afraid for himself. Once he got close, the stranger would have to be very fast indeed to escape the stiletto Luc always carried, and which would have done its work before the stranger even saw it coming. But it would be best if he could intervene without causing any stir at all. No noise. Luc's world was a private world, and he meant to keep it that way.

A simple ruse would be to pretend to be a servant whose master next door had long been expecting a guest, and who believed that de Cygne was entering the wrong house. He'd done something like that once before, and it was enough to create confusion and interpose himself between de Cygne and his attacker. But then the little cat had entered the picture, and this was better still. The fact that the little performance was absurd mattered not in the least. He could be bent, apparently looking for the cat, so that his own face was hard to see. In case of need, the stiletto would be already in his hand, held against his stomach.

And the business had gone off perfectly. He'd seen the stranger's pistol, but the stranger had never had the chance to use it, nor had he seen Luc's face. It had also been clear from the stranger's actions that he did not want his own face to be seen either. That was useful information.

In less than half a minute, de Cygne was safely inside, the stranger was gone and the cab was rolling away.

One possibility remained, that the stranger might come back later, in the hope of accosting de Cygne when he came out. But Luc knew he needn't worry about that. He knew very well that those fortunate to spend the night with La Belle Hélène remained with her until long after the sun was up; and it was clear that the stranger had no wish to make his attack in broad daylight.

All that remained now was to find out more. It might well be that he would warn de Cygne of his danger. But he'd rather investigate first.

An ordinary person might have gone to the police. That never crossed Luc's mind. What profit to him if he did that? What if de Cygne were involved in something he wanted hidden, and a police intervention brought it to light? None of his clients would think much of that. In general, as far as Luc was concerned, the police were to be avoided. A blunt and destructive weapon, of little purpose to a man who liked creativity and finesse.

No, his first task was to find out who this would-be assassin was. Then he'd decide what to do.

The sun was well up when Roland de Cygne awoke. The curtains had been scooped and tied. One window had been opened a fraction to let in a little cool fresh air.

La Belle Hélène was already up, wearing a loose silk robe. A faint fragrance suggested she had already performed some part of her *toilette*. Her hair was lightly brushed, but that was all. She looked wonderfully fresh.

'Will you join me for a little breakfast?'

'Certainly,' he said. He put on his dressing gown and went to the dressing room. By the time he returned, some fresh coffee, hot milk and fresh bread had appeared on a low table by the sofa. She motioned him to the settee. She poured coffee for him. She had pulled up a little chair for herself, from which she now observed him, it seemed with pleasure.

'I could live here forever,' he said, and meant it.

She bowed her head at the compliment. He expected she had heard it many times before, but he didn't suppose she minded hearing it again.

'You will find yourself a charming wife one day, monsieur, and' – she returned the compliment – 'in my opinion she will be a very lucky woman.'

He sipped his coffee. He felt very happy. She continued to observe him.

'Tell me one thing,' she said. 'I was a little curious. The appointment was made by a certain captain of your regiment, who informed me that the gentleman would be coming incognito. Normally I might have refused, but the captain's reputation is of the highest, and I thought perhaps my visitor might be a person whose identity was too significant to be mentioned by name.'

It was true that great men, especially royal personages like England's Prince of Wales, frequently went about the town under other names. Roland laughed.

'And all you got, madame, was a humble young officer named Roland de Cygne.'

'I assure you that I was entirely delighted with what I received, monsieur. But I did not know your identity until your card arrived with your flowers. I was just curious as to why.'

So then Roland told her the truth.

'You won me in a lottery?'

'Madame, not all the officers in the regiment are so rich. But we are loyal. All for one, and one for all.'

She put back her head and laughed. It was a charming laugh.

'That is the funniest thing I ever heard. And you say there were twenty of you?'

'*Oui, madame.*'

She got up and went to the window, and looked out. The sun caught the silhouette of her body through her silk robe. He discovered that he suddenly wanted her again. He rose and went towards her. 'I suppose . . .' he asked, 'you would not consider . . .'

She turned and smiled, and put her arms around his neck.

'*Avec plaisir, monsieur,*' she said.

It was about three quarters of an hour before he finally left the house. She came down into the hall with him herself. Just before they reached the door, she put her hand on his arm.

'One moment,' she said. 'I have a present for you.' Disappearing for a moment she returned with an envelope. 'Now, my dear de

Cygne, I want you to do something for me. You are to take this. It contains one twentieth of what you brought with you last evening. And you are to tell your brother officers that you, and you alone, are the man who received the favours of La Belle Hélène as a gift, for free.'

He gazed at her in amazement. Then, before putting on his hat, he bowed.

'If I live to be a hundred, I shall never feel more honoured.'

'Don't say that. You might even get the Légion d'honneur.'

He grinned.

'Not even the Légion d'honneur, madame,' he said gallantly, and left.

As he put on his top hat and strode up the street, Roland de Cygne felt happier and more proud of himself than ever before in his life. For just a moment, he considered the possibility that some other man might be in La Belle Hélène's house that very night, but he put the thought from him. Across the street he noticed a small black-and-white cat. Probably the one that fellow was looking for last night.

After he had gone, she smiled. He was a nice boy. Too preoccupied to be entirely sensuous, but nice. As for the gift, she was amused. And for five per cent of one night's work, she had purchased a story that would travel all around Paris to her credit. It was always a good thing to be liked.

It took Luc only a day to find out about Le Sourd. A couple of the regular women at the Moulin Rouge had danced with him. One had slept with him.

'You want to know what he's like, dear?' she asked.

'No. Just his name.'

She knew that. And that he was a printer who wrote articles for the radical press. That was all Luc needed. But he thought carefully before he made his next move.

The captain was most surprised at the barracks to receive word that a Monsieur Gascon from the Moulin Rouge wished to speak to him in private. He came out of his office to make sure it was Luc, then called him in.

Luc told him quickly and concisely what he knew.

'I don't know what it means, *mon capitaine*, but I thought I should be discreet. I haven't told Monsieur de Cygne. I thought it better to tell you.'

'My God.' The captain stared at him. 'And you've already saved his life, by the sound of it. You think this is some affair of the heart? A jealous husband?'

'He's not married. He likes to dance with girls and sometimes . . .'

'Why on earth would he want to shoot de Cygne then?'

'I don't know. But he's political. Radical.' Luc made a face.

'You don't like the socialists?'

'There are not many people in the restaurant and entertainment trades who do, *mon capitaine*. They think we're decadent and want to close us down.'

'A little decadence does you good, eh? Well, I entirely agree.' He leaned back in his chair thoughtfully. 'The de Cygne family is old, monarchist, Catholic, of course. But so are half the officers in the French army. There's got to be more to it than that. I'm interested that you didn't just tell de Cygne himself all the same. He could show his gratitude to you for saving his life, at least.'

'I don't know him, *mon capitaine*, nor what this means, nor what he might do. So I came to you.'

'You're a clever fellow, Luc, and we're in your debt. I shan't forget that,' said the officer. 'I want to think about this. But in the meantime, I need to protect de Cygne.'

'I do have one suggestion,' said Luc. 'With your permission.'

It was two days later when the errand boy at the printers came back to where Jacques Le Sourd was working and told him that there was a policeman at the door who wanted to see him.

The boy noticed Le Sourd go very pale, but he followed the boy to the front door, where the policeman was waiting for him. The policeman was a tall, severe-looking man who looked at him coldly.

'You are Jacques Le Sourd?'

'Yes.'

'This is for you.' The policeman handed him an envelope. Then, to Jacques's astonishment, he walked swiftly away.

Jacques opened the envelope, frowning. Was this some kind of legal summons? To what did it refer?

The envelope contained a single sheet of paper. On it were written just two short lines in capital letters:

> *RUE DES BELLES-FEUILLES*
> *YOU ARE BEING WATCHED*

For the rest of that day, Jacques wondered what to do. The message was clear enough. Someone had seen him waiting for Roland de Cygne. That person, or whoever had informed him, appeared to be a policeman. But how much did he know, and what did he want?

Was it a policeman who had given him the envelope? Here his own fear had let him down, and he cursed himself for it. He'd been so afraid at the moment when the tall man arrived that he had just assumed it was a real policeman. But a real policeman arrests you. He doesn't give you a cryptic message and walk away. Does he?

What was the meaning of the cryptic message, anyway? Was it a warning, telling him to be careful? Or was it a threat to expose him?

And how much did this person – or persons – know? If someone recognised him loitering in the rue des Belles-Feuilles, they might suppose that he was planning to burgle one of the houses. If so, they certainly didn't know him. If somehow they had an inkling of his true intent, that would be another matter.

His work ended without his being any the wiser. He started to walk home. It was already after dusk. Once or twice he had the feeling that he was being followed. But though he glanced behind him, he saw nothing suspicious, and told himself that he was imagining things.

He was nearing his home when a young street urchin approached with his hand held out for money. Jacques shook his head. And before he knew it, the boy had thrust something into his hand and run away.

It was another envelope. This time, the message told him more. It began with just two words in capitals, like the message before:

> *DE CYGNE*

And below it, in smaller letters, a message that told him, without fail, to leave the sum of 250 francs in an envelope in the Bois de Boulogne's long allée de Longchamp, at the foot of the twentieth tree on the left, at six o'clock the following evening.

So they knew. And it was blackmail.

But who knew? The only link he could think of was the waiter at the Moulin Rouge. Even assuming it was him, however, it seemed likely that he had accomplices, which included the tall fellow dressed as a policeman. The threat was clear. Pay up or the police would be informed. Indeed, it might be that the tall messenger really was a policeman – a corrupt one, but no less dangerous for that.

Should he bluff it out? Perhaps. No crime had been committed. Nothing could be proved. Whereas if he paid, he was virtually admitting that he'd intended harm to an officer of the French army. On the other hand, if the sender of the messages chose to accuse him, he'd have to explain to the police why he was hiding in a doorway watching for de Cygne. Investigations would be made. He'd probably be under police suspicion for the rest of his life. He was still thinking about this conundrum when he reached his lodgings.

The building where he lived was one of a pair of tenements in Belleville, between the cemetery of Père Lachaise and the park of Buttes-Chaumont. It was six storeys high, and he occupied a single, good-sized room on the fifth floor, with a small washroom and kitchen attached. His mother lived in a similar apartment on the raised ground floor of the building next door. It wasn't a bad arrangement. The rents were low. He could lead his own life but keep an eye on his mother as well.

He made himself a little food, and drank a glass of wine. He went to the bookshelf and pulled out a book. Between its pages were concealed a number of banknotes. Not a huge sum, but enough to hide from any casual intruder. He had 150 francs.

And that was all he had. He'd never saved. He supposed he might one day, but so far he had preferred to work just enough to live, and to devote his spare time to study and political work. With a shrug he went down the stairs and into the building next door. He usually looked in on his mother each day.

The widow Le Sourd was sitting by her window, as she usually did when she wasn't working, watching the street. Her hair was no longer grey, but white these days, and she had grown a little thinner in the last few years, but she was still the same stern, gaunt figure that he remembered from his boyhood. He leaned over and kissed her.

'I saw you come in. Have you eaten?'

'Yes, Maman. And you?'

'Of course. But there is some cake in the kitchen if you want it.'

'No. Maman, have you any cash?'

'Perhaps. How much?'

'A hundred francs.'

'A hundred? That's quite a lot.'

'Can I borrow it?'

She stared at him silently.

'What would your father say? That his son should have to borrow from his mother?'

'I have given you money before.'

'That is true.' She sighed. 'I work, Jacques, but I save. A little.'

'I know.'

'You work, but you do not save.'

'I know that too.'

'What is it for? Some woman? You should marry. It is time you married.'

'It's not for a woman.'

'What then?'

'I cannot tell you. I may not need it, but if I do, I will pay it back.' He paused. 'It is for a good cause.'

She looked at him sharply.

'Tell me.'

'No. It is better you do not know.'

She shook her head sadly.

'You are speaking of politics?' Seeing him indicate that he was, she pursed her lips. 'Whatever you do, be careful. I have always told you to be careful.'

'I am careful.'

'There is a leather wallet in the top drawer of the desk. Bring it to me.'

'You should hide your money better, Maman,' he remarked as he did so.

She shrugged, took the wallet and counted out the notes.

'There are not many more,' she said.

Soon after this, Jacques Le Sourd went back to his own apartment. He worked on the anarchist article for a little while, then turned in to sleep. He still hadn't decided what to do.

The following evening, he went to the Bois de Boulogne. It was certainly a good place to make a drop of this kind. Anyone could be hiding in the trees, slip forward to pick up the envelope and vanish into the trees again.

He left the money by the tree. Inside the envelope with the money was a note. It was written in capital letters and unsigned. It said: 'THERE IS NO MORE'.

As he left the park, he reflected that to escape further trouble, he'd better stay away from Roland de Cygne for a time, perhaps a long time.

It had not occurred to him that this was exactly what Luc Gascon and the captain had intended.

'In the name of the Father, and of the Son . . .' The voice of Roland de Cygne came through the screen of the confessional. Old Father Xavier listened attentively.

'Bless me, Father, for I have sinned,' Roland's voice continued. 'It has been a month since I last confessed.'

Father Xavier knew that. The last confession had been quite boring. Indeed, as a friend rather than a confessor, he sometimes felt his young protégé needed to get out and sin a little more.

So he was rather pleased when, a couple of minutes later, Roland confessed to the sin of fornication.

'With one woman or several?' he quietly inquired.

'One.'

'How many times?'

'I slept with her one night. And again in the morning.'

'With what sort of person was this?'

'A courtesan.'

'When you say a courtesan, my son, you mean a prostitute?'

There was a momentary pause.

'She was not what you'd call a prostitute. She is known as La Belle Hélène.'

'La Belle Hélène?' Father Xavier shifted on his seat. This was getting interesting. Could the Vicomte de Cygne really be giving Roland such a huge allowance? 'Very well. You paid for her services, in any case.'

Another hesitation.

'Well, yes and no.'

'My son, either you paid her or you didn't. The sins of fornication and prostitution are slightly different.'

So then Roland explained.

For a few moments after he had finished, no clear sound came from the priest on the other side of the screen. Then, in a slightly strangulated voice, Father Xavier spoke: 'The sin of prostitution is greater than that of ordinary fornication, because each person treats the other heartlessly, as an object rather than a child of God. In this case, given the circumstances, I think we may say that the sin does not quite – I say quite – constitute prostitution, and your penance may therefore be somewhat less. Have you other sins to confess?'

Roland listed a few minor transgressions.

'And do you repent of your sins?' asked the priest.

Again a hesitation. The young man was really too honest for his own good.

'I am trying to, Father,' he said.

'That will do, as a start.' Father Xavier pronounced a penance that would take Roland a couple of hours and gave him absolution, before dismissing him.

After Roland had departed, and no other penitent had come, Father Xavier sat quietly contemplating the tale he'd heard, and practically hugging himself with amusement and with pleasure.

Of course he knew, theologically, that it could not be so; yet it was hard for Father Xavier not to believe, loving the aristocracy as he did, that La Belle Hélène's rebate was a divine dispensation for the family of de Cygne, which had served Him so faithfully and for so long.

It was a month later that the three men met for lunch at the Café de la Paix. They met for a purpose, and the purpose was a worthy one. But each of them, also, had a secret agenda of his own.

Jules Blanchard had chosen the Café de la Paix for two reasons. It was large and fashionable. Being almost opposite the Opéra, it was convenient for him, in that he could walk over from his office in the department store on boulevard Haussmann. Convenient also for the Vicomte de Cygne, whose coachman only had to cross the river to reach it, and then take the vicomte to certain shops he liked to visit afterwards. As for the lawyer they were going to meet, no doubt he'd be pleased to be there anyway, convenient or not.

He wondered what this legal fellow was going to be like. Neither he nor the vicomte had ever heard of him.

Whatever the man was like, it was a noble object that brought them together. It concerned the honour of Paris, and indeed of France.

The magnificent statue of the mounted emperor Charlemagne on the parvis of Notre-Dame was a national treasure. It might not be ancient, but it was heroic, a latter-day Gothic masterpiece. It was also falling apart – or, to be precise, it needed a new and suitably handsome plinth to stand upon. The old one had been small and temporary and unless something was done soon, the emperor of the Franks would have to be carted away.

Yet was the city of Paris prepared to spend a sou on it? No it wasn't. An informal committee of citizens had got together to raise money. He'd joined it because he admired the statue, and as the owner of the Joséphine department store, it was the sort of thing he ought to be seen supporting. The Vicomte de Cygne had joined because he descended from the emperor's legendary companion Roland.

But although Jules and the aristocrat came from rather different social worlds, they had soon discovered that they liked the same operas, smoked the same cigars and even occasionally frequented the same salons. In short, they had found each other rather congenial.

The members of the group could have found the money for the plinth between themselves. But everyone agreed that Parisians ought to express their appreciation for such an ornament to the city with a public subscription of some kind. So when the committee received a note from a city lawyer who thought he could help them do so, it was agreed that Blanchard and de Cygne should meet him and find out what he had to offer.

Jules got there a few minutes early. Almost immediately afterwards, the Vicomte de Cygne arrived. That summer he had grown a fashionable pointed beard and moustache – grey and close-cropped – which suited him rather well. He greeted Jules and they sat down to wait.

Exactly at the appointed hour, they saw a waiter leading a man across the grand spaces of the Café de la Paix to their table. A somewhat small, thin man, very neatly dressed, with a long, pale face.

Monsieur Ney bowed to them both and took the proffered chair. Drinks were ordered. Ney was polite. He apologised that he might be called to the front desk to sign a document – only for a moment – towards the end of the meal: a piece of information which did not endear him to the vicomte. But he had certainly taken the trouble to inform himself thoroughly about the business at hand. He knew that the artist had sadly died before the plinth could be installed, and that the artist's brother had almost bankrupted himself providing a stone plinth that he couldn't pay for.

'I am appalled that the city has not played its part,' he announced. 'The site in front of Notre-Dame seems well chosen, and the statue is a marvel.'

'And what brought our project to your attention?' asked Blanchard.

'To tell you the truth, monsieur, it was my daughter, Hortense, who learned of it, and told me I should be doing something. She interests herself in everything in the city. And as she is not yet married and has no children to worry about, she finds good causes every day. Her generosity will probably ruin me,' he added with a smile, which gently indicated that he was far from being ruined.

So, thought Jules, the true object of the lawyer was revealed. It was to promote his daughter. He thought of how his sister had taken him to task on the subject of Marie, and felt a pang of guilt. He couldn't blame the lawyer for doing what he ought to be doing himself. It remained to be seen what the fellow had to offer in return.

'What we really want,' he explained to the lawyer, 'is not only to raise money – which of course we wish to do – but to enlarge the network of people involved in the project. I wonder if you have any suggestions.'

'As far as funds are concerned, naturally Hortense and I would wish to contribute. I also know an old lady of large fortune who is good enough to take my advice on matters like this. But to enlist public interest, I wondered if it would be a good idea to ask Monsieur

Eiffel to give the project his blessing. We happen to know him.' He paused. 'And if only to please Hortense, I think he might take an interest.'

'Indeed.' The lawyer might not be quite the company he'd choose, but Jules was impressed. 'That might be very helpful,' he said.

The meal passed pleasantly enough. De Cygne let Blanchard do most of the talking, but inevitably the aristocrat asked Ney if he was related to the great marshal of the same name.

'I am, Monsieur de Cygne, and I am very proud of it. I know the marshal's loyalties might not be your own, but I honour him as a brave soldier.'

De Cygne greeted this with a nod.

The lawyer then gently turned the conversation to his daughter, Hortense. Ney did not say more than a fond father should, but it was clear that the young lady was as good as she was beautiful.

Now it was time for Jules to pursue his agenda too.

'You've had her portrait painted, no doubt,' he remarked easily.

'In fact, I have not,' the lawyer confessed.

'Oh,' said Blanchard, as if this was rather strange. 'I always think these things add to the reputation of a young woman. People see them, you know.'

'Have you an artist you'd recommend?' Ney innocently inquired.

'It would depend what sort of portrait you wanted, I suppose,' Jules answered. 'My son Marc is a painter. Rather in the style of Manet, you might say. He did Madame Du Bois the banker's wife, the other day. They seemed pleased.' He smiled. 'You'd better move fast if you want him, though, before his prices shoot up.'

'I should be most interested,' Ney responded, 'if you'd care to put us in touch.'

He'd understood, of course. A commission for Marc. A place on the committee perhaps, for himself and visibility for his daughter. So far so good.

Just as the meal was about to end, a waiter came and whispered in Ney's ear, and with profuse apologies, he left them for a moment to go to meet his clerk at the entrance. While he was gone, de Cygne turned to Blanchard.

'His game is the daughter, then. He wants to infiltrate her into society.'

'Undoubtedly,' Jules agreed. 'But one can't blame the fellow. He's only doing what a father should.' He shrugged. 'Who knows, she may be pretty. And I'm sure there will be a fine dowry.'

De Cygne grunted in a manner that indicated he couldn't care less.

'I enjoyed listening to you get your son a commission, though,' the vicomte added with a wry smile.

'When lawyers take so much in fees, one must claw back what one can,' Blanchard replied cheerfully. 'But if the fellow can deliver Eiffel, as he claims,' he continued more seriously, 'that would be a great draw to the public. And I think we ought to encourage him.'

'You're right, of course,' said the vicomte. He glanced towards the distant figure of Ney with distaste. 'But Eiffel is a great man. I am not going to be introduced to him by a back-streets attorney.' He gave an apologetic shrug. 'I'm a snob.' He reached across and touched Blanchard's arm. 'You could introduce me to Eiffel. That would give me great pleasure.'

Jules laughed.

'Perhaps the solution will be for Ney to introduce me to Eiffel. And then I can introduce Eiffel to you!'

'In that case, *mon ami*,' de Cygne said, 'I shall be in your debt forever.'

Ney rejoined them. They finished the meal.

And it was then that the Vicomte de Cygne, feeling that he ought to make an effort with this potential contributor, asked him pleasantly: 'Tell us, Monsieur Ney, as we know you are related to a military hero, have you other interesting figures in your ancestry?'

Ney hesitated.

'As it happens, Monsieur de Cygne, I have never been able to discover the connection, if it even exists, but my mother's maiden name was Arouet.'

'Arouet?' cried Jules Blanchard. 'But that's the family name of Voltaire.'

'As you say, monsieur,' answered Ney, 'before the great philosopher decided to call himself Voltaire, he was plain Monsieur Arouet.' He smiled. 'And his father was a notary, too.'

Blanchard gazed at Ney. Though the notary didn't exactly look like the great hero of the eighteenth-century Enlightenment, there was some resemblance, at least in their small, thin physiques.

'I'm surprised you don't claim it,' remarked de Cygne drily.

'I am a lawyer, Monsieur de Cygne. Others might demand proof, and I do not possess it.'

But the aristocrat wasn't going to let the matter drop just yet. He was going to punish the lawyer, just a little, for intruding upon him. He considered.

'What was that story about Voltaire? When he was quite young, he ran a national lottery, collected all the money and then awarded the prize to himself. Wasn't that how he made his first fortune? Something like that.'

If this was intended to embarrass Ney, it failed. He smiled.

'In fact, monsieur, he and several others realised that in a certain national lottery, the government had made a mathematical mistake in calculating the odds. They put together a syndicate, bought blocks of tickets, and made a great fortune. But it was perfectly legal.'

'Oh,' said de Cygne, and shrugged. 'Well, I prefer my story.'

'So do I,' said the lawyer with a laugh. 'So do I.' And then, just for once, Monsieur Ney inadvertently let down his guard. 'Think of it,' he cried: 'Oh what a fraud! How delicious! If a man could get away with that, and not get caught . . .'

And, quite forgetting himself, he let out a loud, gleeful cackle that was almost fiendish, while the businessman and the aristocrat stared at him in fascinated horror.

There was a silence. The lawyer dabbed at his face with a silk handkerchief.

'Well, Monsieur Ney,' said Jules Blanchard, 'it has been most interesting to meet you.' And he politely escorted him to the entrance. 'I shall be in contact very soon. Did you really want me to put you in touch with my son Marc?'

'Assuredly, monsieur,' said Monsieur Ney. 'As soon as possible.'

'Then in that case,' he wrote on the back of his card, 'all you need do is write to him at this address. It's his studio.'

When Jules got back to the vicomte, that gentleman declared that they both needed a brandy.

But he didn't want to discuss Ney any more. It seemed that the lawyer had already been expunged from his mind. It had not occurred to Jules that the aristocrat might also have a hidden agenda, but as the vicomte looked at him reflectively, it seemed that he might.

'I see that you are a good father,' said de Cygne.

'You mean the commission for Marc? I'm sure you do things for your son too, Vicomte.'

'I lost my wife when my son was a young boy. It makes it more difficult. I worry about him, still. Do you worry about your children?'

'Of course.' He told de Cygne briefly about Gérard and Marie. 'They're all right, I think. But I worry about Marc.'

'You see your children often?'

'At least once a month, the whole family meets for Sunday lunch, either in Paris or at Fontainebleau. They bring their friends. For better or worse, it's family.'

De Cygne thought of his own quiet house and nodded.

'That is how it should be. Do you ever have older guests?'

'Certainly.' Blanchard looked at him curiously.

'Might I be a guest at one of your lunches?'

'By all means.' Blanchard hesitated. 'They are quite informal, you understand. The Blanchard family is entirely bourgeois. It might not be to your taste, you know.'

De Cygne reflected that if Blanchard wanted to, he could probably buy the de Cygne house, château and estate, and have change to spare. But that was not the point. It was another little plan that was framing in his mind, and the Blanchard family was exactly to his purpose.

'If you would invite me,' he said, 'I should be delighted to come.'

'Well,' answered Jules, 'Christmas and the New Year are almost upon us, but what about the third Sunday in January? The sixteenth. In Paris.'

'Excellent,' said de Cygne. 'I shall be there.' Even though, in truth, he hadn't the least intention of going.

It had never occurred to Roland de Cygne that his father's life might be drawing to a close. The vicomte appeared to be in excellent health. So he was always glad, afterwards, that when his father had suggested he come down to the château and stay with him awhile, he had accepted.

The last couple of months in Paris had passed quietly enough for Roland. His regimental duties kept him busy. Indeed, he sometimes felt that he was being given extra duties. 'That's to compensate for your winning the lottery for La Belle Hélène,' the captain told him cheerfully. He didn't have time to go out on the town very much. But whenever he did go to the Folies-Bergère, or to see a play, or just to dine out, his brother officers were always eager to accompany him. The captain in particular seemed to want his company. He had no objection, but sometimes he might have been just as happy to go out for an evening alone.

In the middle of December, however, he was due some leave, and he'd been wondering what to do.

Many people, having spent the summer months in the country, would have remained in Paris for the winter season unless, like the fashionable English, they liked to travel down to places like Nice and Monte Carlo on the Mediterranean, or venture into the snowy magnificence of the Swiss Alps, where a few hardy souls would even hike across the mountain trails on skis.

But his father had recently decided it was time he paid more attention to the family estate. 'The house needs attention, so do the farms,' he told Roland. 'I want to leave things in good order for you. And before I die, I'm going to sort all the family papers that nobody's touched in a hundred years.'

'In that case, Father,' Roland answered with a smile, 'you may have to live a long time.'

So now, knowing that the regiment would certainly be posted, possibly far away, at some point, and having received his father's invitation, he'd decided to keep his father company in the country.

The Château de Cygne was not large, but it was full of character. At various times in its history, when the family could afford it, the old building had been altered or added to, so that the final result was a charming mixture of styles. Hidden inside were thick walls belonging to the original little fort, which went back eight hundred years.

But the oldest part visible from the outside dated from the late fifteenth century, when the son of Guy de Cygne, using the moneys from his mother, Cécile Renard, and the noble heiress he'd married himself, had created a small, romantic château, with a steep roof, round towers and pointed turrets at the corners.

This charming little French castle also contained the family's favourite room – a large hall, with quite a low ceiling that was crossed by dark, friendly old beams, and a huge fireplace that could have held a dozen men. On one wall of the hall, looking as if it had always been there, hung the lovely unicorn tapestry supplied by Monsieur Jacob.

Another wing, equally delightful in decorative brick, had been added a century later, in the rich and cheerful style of the French Renaissance. Finally, in the eighteenth century, yet another wing and court had been added in the classical style. This perhaps was less satisfactory, but a wide ornamental terrace, with a formal garden and elegantly clipped trees, had brought the whole ensemble together in a way that felt pleasing. It was not uncommon to find such places in the lovely Loire Valley region.

During that Christmas season, Roland and his father had time to discuss many things together. Roland told his father about his adventure with La Belle Hélène, which amused and pleased the vicomte greatly. They also discussed ways to improve the estate. The woods could be used for boar hunting. 'We could also raise pheasants for shooting, like the English do,' the vicomte believed. 'The château itself is in fair shape,' he informed Roland, 'but the upper floors need restoring, and in another dozen years we'll have to reroof the whole place. One day you may need to sell the house in Paris, unless you can marry a rich woman,' he added.

Yet sometimes, it seemed to Roland, his father was troubled by darker thoughts.

'The situation in Europe worries me,' he confessed one evening. 'I just hope you won't have to fight a war, like I did.'

'The great empires have treaties to maintain the balance of power,' Roland pointed out.

'Yes. But Germany is still jealous of Britain's empire. When old Bismarck was running Germany's policy, for all his ambition, he knew the limits of power. But the people around the young kaiser now are hotheads. I fear for the future.'

On the state of France itself, however, it was he rather than his father who was the pessimist.

'The corruption of the government is so complete, Father, I can't understand why most of the deputies don't shoot themselves in shame. When I think of the Panama Canal . . . I despair of my country.'

It was true that the catastrophe of the Panama Canal had shocked all France. At first, it had been advertised as a great French enterprise. Its builder, de Lesseps, had triumphantly engineered the Suez Canal some years earlier. Now French expertise would astonish the New World as well. But not only had the plans been misconceived, not only had the entire business gone bankrupt, taking with it the savings of ordinary people all over France, but de Lesseps and his friends had mounted one of the biggest cover-ups the world had ever seen, bribing innumerable politicians high and low to conceal the disaster. Even Eiffel, who'd been called in to try to correct the engineering when it was far too late, had almost been tarnished with the scandal.

Respect for the political class had been destroyed for a generation.

'My son,' the vicomte had replied with a shake of his head, 'I share your outrage, but scandals like these have been found in every country, and I suspect they always will be.'

'I do not accept that nothing can be done,' Roland replied. 'But I think it's proof that we cannot trust our elected officials.'

'And you would replace it with a monarchy? A sacred king?'

'I consider the monarch to be sacred. Yes. He is anointed by God. But if not a monarch, perhaps a man who is above mere politics. A man of destiny.'

'That is how Napoléon first portrayed himself, yet you do not approve of him.'

'I mean a religious man.'

'A few years ago, General Boulanger seemed like such a man, yet when perhaps he could have made a bid for power, he shied away from taking up such a burden. I cannot think of any plausible figure in France today. Nor am I so sure that I trust any single man, even an anointed monarch, so much better than I do one who is an ordinary politician.' The vicomte sighed. 'All governments are corrupt. It's just a question of degree.' He smiled wryly. 'And whether they're any good at it.'

And just as he had when he was a boy, while he loved and respected his father, Roland felt a sense of sorrow that the vicomte could not, or would not, take a moral stance when he should.

★   ★   ★

Sometimes the Vicomte de Cygne wondered if he should have married again. Not so much for his own sake as for his son. The trouble was that at the time when little Roland had probably needed a mother most, he himself had been grieving far too deeply for his lost wife even to think of marrying another.

Since then he'd been fortunate in having a number of romantic friendships. One woman he might have married if she had been available. Another was available, but she would not have been accepted socially by his friends. Others had usually followed a similar pattern – discreet, safe, amusing. He had not been unhappy.

As for his domestic situation, his Paris house was very effectively run by Nanny, even in her old age. And at the family château, where certainly, a woman's hand was called for, he wasn't sure he'd really be able to tolerate anyone else's interference nowadays. He'd long ago decided to keep it the way it was, in somewhat masculine order, until such time as Roland should marry and his wife and children could do as they pleased with the place while he watched, no doubt with horror as well as amusement. He'd supposed that was the natural order.

But as he looked at his son today, the vicomte couldn't help feeling that he had let him down. Plenty of other boys had grown up without a mother, of course. But Roland's upbringing had been too masculine. He lacked balance.

I shouldn't have let Father Xavier influence him so much, either, the vicomte thought.

He'd never objected to the priest, who was so obviously in love with his wife. He'd rather sympathised with him. He had known Father Xavier's love would remain entirely platonic. The priest was correct, and pure. But perhaps that was why he harboured doubts about him. For during the course of his life, rightly or wrongly, the vicomte had developed a certain suspicion of men who were too pure.

God knows what stuff that priest had put in his son's head down the years.

Not that the Vicomte de Cygne objected to his son's being a monarchist, nor a devout Catholic, nor a young aristocrat, proud of his ancestry and with the prejudices of his class. The vicomte shared most of those prejudices himself. In fact, he rather enjoyed these aristocratic snobberies. But he enjoyed them without believing in them too much. Indeed, the very fact that, as an aristocrat, he looked down upon most of humanity – and that he also knew the shortcomings of his fellow aristocrats – made it easy for him not to expect too much from imperfect human nature, nor to judge people too harshly.

But his son believed too much. And a lifetime of observation, including the horrors of the Commune, had led the vicomte to think that when men believed too strongly, it made them cruel.

He was especially concerned by a conversation they had just after Christmas.

It concerned an army officer. His name was Dreyfus and, unusually for an officer, he was Jewish. When a minor spying scandal had emerged, he had been accused of passing secrets to the Germans, court-martialed and sent to prison on Devil's Island.

Some people had said that the prosecution was badly flawed, and even that Dreyfus was innocent. As one might expect, the military authorities refused to contemplate the idea that there had been any mistake. And there the matter had rested.

The subject had come up quite casually when they were talking about the difference between civilian and military courts, and the vicomte was remarking that no system of justice could ever be perfect.

'That Dreyfus fellow, for instance: I dare say he's guilty, but it may turn out one day that he wasn't. That's just the way it goes.'

'Oh, I think we can be sure he's guilty, Father,' Roland replied. 'After all, the man's a Jew.'

'My dear boy, you can't say he's a traitor just because he's a Jew.'

'Perhaps not. But it makes him suspect, doesn't it?'

'I don't think so. What is it you object to about the Jews?'

'Apart from the obvious fact that they are not Catholics, one can never be sure of their loyalty. One never knows what they're up to.'

'You mean there's a general conspiracy?'

'The Jews all stick together, don't they?'

'But you surely don't think that our friend Jacob, for instance, who sold me that wonderful tapestry, is part of a conspiracy?'

'I don't know, Father. He may be.'

'And do most of your fellow officers believe such things?'

'Of course. And as far as this Dreyfus is concerned, most of them think that Jews shouldn't be officers at all.'

'There is no evidence for a conspiracy, you know.'

'Naturally. It's a conspiracy.'

His father sighed.

'My dear son, that has been the doctrine of every maniac in the secret police since the days of Babylon. If we can see a conspiracy, then it's proved. If we can't see it, then the conspirators must be hiding it. This is a logic from which there is no escape.'

'Exactly.'

'But there may not be a conspiracy, my dear boy. Has this not occurred to you?'

Roland was silent.

The vicomte was proud of his son. He could see that through these prejudices, which unfortunately were commonplace, Roland was expressing the idealist's desire to serve a cause. The fault in his son lay not in his nature, which was honourable, but in his perceptions, which were limited. All the more reason, he considered, that he should try to render his son one important service.

He must broaden the young man's mind, teach him that there were many ways to live, and that there was virtue in tolerance, too, in an imperfect world.

So he was all the more glad of that idea he'd had when he met Blanchard and that appalling lawyer the other day. Not that he'd have any objection to having Sunday lunch with the Blanchard family, but his intention had been to send his son instead. Roland should mix with some other kinds of people. The Blanchard family would be a good start.

The fact that Blanchard had an unmarried daughter who would undoubtedly bring with her an excellent dowry had also crossed his mind. True, she wasn't an aristocrat, but one must move with the times. A girl like that might be what Roland needed.

The important thing was not to give his son any idea of his plan. The boy would be sure to rebel if he thought he was being manipulated.

And here events played nicely into his hands. Early in January, there was a heavy fall of snow. It made the château look magical. But unfortunately, in the ensuing frost, some pipes froze, and by the second week in January when a thaw began, it was discovered that the cellars were flooding quite seriously.

Roland's leave was ending in any case, and he had to return to Paris. So the day before he was due to depart, the vicomte called him into his estate office.

'My dear son, I have two small favours to ask of you. The first is that I have just found this letter in my desk, which I received six weeks ago and entirely forgot. It's from a man in Canada who thinks he is related to us. I don't believe he is. As far as I know, no member of the family has ever gone to Canada. But I don't think that he is trying to insinuate himself. He writes very charmingly. Anyway, as I have so much to do here, and I'm embarrassed to have taken so long to reply, would you do me the kindness to reply to him. Write something nice. One never knows when one might need a friend in Canada.'

Somewhat unwillingly, Roland agreed to do so.

'And what is the second thing?' he asked.

'Ah. I had planned to go to Paris with you, but with all this water trouble, I think I should stay at the château. Would you go in my place to a luncheon I had promised to go to? In fact, to tell you the truth, I practically invited myself.'

'When, Father?'

'On the third Sunday of this month. That's the sixteenth, I think.'

'I suppose so. Who's giving the lunch?'

'A friend of mine named Jules Blanchard. He owns the Joséphine department store, you know. I met him through the business over the Charlemagne statue.'

'But Father, I don't know any people like that. I wouldn't know what to say.'

'My dear son, you don't have to say anything. Just go there as my representative. I don't want to offend him by not turning up. In any case, you'll find him excellent company. He knows how to behave. Quite a man about town, in fact. And it certainly won't do you any harm to meet some people like that. They're important, you know.'

'I shall be a fish out of water.'

'Just turn up as a kindness to me.'

'As you wish.'

The following morning Roland left for Paris. It never crossed the mind of either father or son that they would never meet again.

Jules Blanchard lived in an apartment. Ten years ago, he and his wife had considered buying a handsome house near the Parc Monceau. But in the end they'd both decided against it. 'The house at Fontainebleau is enough work to keep up,' Jules had remarked. And the apartment they had, which was already large, was so close to his beloved department store, and so convenient for the Opéra and the other amusements they both liked, that they decided to stay where they were. They had never regretted the decision.

On the morning of the third Sunday in January in the year 1898, while his wife and Marie were still at Mass, Jules Blanchard rose from the breakfast room, and made his way to his small library, where he meant to read the newspaper in peace for a couple of hours. God knows there was a lot to read about that week. After that, he'd prepare for the family gathering at lunchtime.

He was feeling quite pleased with himself.

In the last few weeks, he had taken his sister's words to heart. Though Jules had always had a large circle of friends, in recent years he'd been so involved with the department store, which truly fascinated him, that he had often been content to stay at home in the evenings with his wife when they might have gone out. They entertained a little, especially now that they had the new dining room to show off. Both Jules and his wife liked small dinner parties for just six or ten, and sometimes these included guests who might be of interest to Marie. But too often they had been middle-aged people that were of interest to Jules – businessmen, professional people, sometimes a politician.

Not that Marie had been without friends. Far from it. She and her mother went out to galleries and to visit family friends. Her aunt Éloïse went out with her to something interesting at least once a week, and had introduced Marie to quite a few people in the circles that she herself enjoyed. But these tended to be intellectual people – charming to add to the right sort of dinner party, but not quite as financially solid as he'd want for his daughter's husband.

Marie's brothers might have done more for her, but there was a problem. Gérard and his new wife had friends. But though Marie was on perfectly friendly terms with Gérard, she wasn't close to him. Never had been since she was a child. They met whenever the family gathered, but that was all.

Marc, on the other hand, she loved. But though Jules Blanchard admired his younger son's talent and imagination, he wasn't too sure who his friends might be, and what sort of lives they led. And if one thing was certain in his mind, it was that his daughter should have a blameless reputation. It was one thing for an unmarried man of his class to have a mistress. But the rules for women were entirely different. Marie was intelligent, charming, everything that a man of her class might want in a wife – which included the facts that she was respectable, of unblemished reputation and sexually innocent. Mostly, even at the age of twenty-two, Marie went hardly anywhere without a chaperone. And Marc knew the rules. Marie might meet his respectable friends, but could never be left alone with any man. This by no means prevented Marc from entertaining his sister, but it also meant that there was a good deal of his daily life that she could not see.

In the last few weeks however, Marie's parents had made a huge effort. There had been some delightful little parties. They had gone out a lot. She had met perhaps a dozen suitable men, and it seemed reasonable to assume that soon a good candidate would appear.

Even today's lunch had been a possible occasion to invite a suitable man to join them. Given that it was a family affair, Jules had tried to think of neighbours or friends they knew.

Éloïse had always liked Pierre Jourdain, that boy Marie had taken such a fancy to when she was a little girl, but he'd recently got engaged. Then there were the sons of their close neighbour Dr Proust, a most distinguished man. True, his wife was Jewish, but his sons were brought up Catholic, which Jules supposed was all right, and the family was well-off. The trouble was that the elder son was a dilettante with no proper career, while his younger brother, Robert, who looked far more promising, was still a bit too young.

Then, out of the blue, had come a note from the Vicomte de Cygne regretting that he was unable to get into Paris, but hoping that his friend would forgive him if his son, Roland, came in his place.

Could it be that the aristocrat had decided that his son should meet Marie? If so, it was cleverly done. This apparently chance arrangement gave no embarrassment to anyone. And God knows, Jules thought, the vicomte knows exactly who and what sort of fellow I am. He shook his head in amusement. Anything would depend of course on the character of Roland de Cygne and whether Marie liked him, but he couldn't deny that a marriage with such an aristocratic family would be as gratifying as it was unexpected.

Who else was coming? His sister, Éloïse, Gérard and his wife. Marc was bringing a young American – respectable, Marc said, but whose French wasn't too strong. And bearing that in mind, Jules had done something rather clever. He occasionally needed to transact business with English companies, where legal work was required, and had found an excellent English legal firm in Paris, a Mr Fox and his son, the latter being about Marc's age. Not a prospect for Marie of course, since he was undoubtedly Protestant. But since he spoke both French and English fluently, Fox would help with the American.

All in all, the day was looking very satisfactory.

Monsieur Petit stood and stared at his daughter Corinne. His fists were clenched. He was shaking with rage.

'I am going to see Monsieur Blanchard now,' he said.

'What for?' she cried. 'What good will that do?'

'He is a man of honour. Perhaps he will make his son marry you.'

'He will not do it. He cannot do it.'

'That may be so.' He spoke quietly now, and that was even more frightening. 'But if there is no marriage, then you will leave this house, and I shall never see you again.'

Paul Petit did not know when his family had first come to the Faubourg Saint-Antoine, but they were certainly there by the time of the French Revolution. And on the great day when the Faubourg Saint-Antoine arose, and marched up the long eastern thoroughfare to storm the Bastille, the Petits marched with them. They had supported every republican uprising since.

Though his wife went to Mass, which he considered a harmless women's foible, Paul Petit despised all priests. 'They are monarchists and bloodsuckers,' he would declare. But that did not mean that his children could ignore the last six of the Ten Commandments, and woe betide them if they did. Paul Petit came from a family of twelve children. He had eight of his own. Like his father before him, he was a hardworking craftsman. There was enough money to put food on the table, and clothe all the children decently. But not more. One slip, and the family would descend into chaos. That was all it would take. 'The gutter,' he would warn his children, 'lies just outside the door.' If he was stern, therefore, it was to ensure the family's survival.

And when he had to be, Paul Petit was hard. Very hard. He was about to cast his daughter out of his house. He had to, if only as an example to her sisters.

As he set off to walk to see Jules Blanchard, he was still shaking. It wasn't only Corinne's crime that was tearing him apart. It was the fact that she had lied to him. And not just once, but coolly and calmly over many weeks. It enraged him, and it hurt him.

He remembered the start of it so well. She'd taken a message from him to a customer near the Parc Monceau and taken a long time to return. But when she'd explained her long absence, he'd been rather pleased.

'Father, I met Monsieur Blanchard in the street, and he made me return with him to see his wife. She needs extra help in the house two afternoons a week, and wondered if you could spare me.'

The Blanchards were highly respectable, as well as valued customers. If Corinne could earn a little extra money in this way, her parents had no objection at all.

The arrangement had lasted three weeks when Corinne told them that Gérard, their recently married son, and his wife could use her for a third afternoon. Weeks had passed, Corinne had brought home some modest wages from this work, and it had never occurred to her parents to question the business.

Once, just once, he might have detected something, when he remarked that he wondered if there were any store fittings that Monsieur Blanchard might need at Joséphine, and whether he might call upon him. He'd noticed Corinne suddenly go a little pale. But his wife had promptly remarked: 'I'm sure he has you in mind, Paul, with his kindness to Corinne, and her being in his house every week. I don't think you should go calling on him for other favours. He might feel it was too much.'

'You're right, my dear,' he'd agreed at once, and put the idea out of his mind. 'Keep your ears open, though,' he'd said to Corinne.

So when, this morning, his wife had told him that Corinne was pregnant by Marc Blanchard, that she'd been modelling for him in his studio, and that she'd never been near the house of Monsieur Blanchard or his son Gérard, Paul Petit had found it quite difficult to believe that it was true.

'And when did this start?' he had demanded. 'How could such an idea enter your head?'

'I used to speak to him a little when he came here. I knew he painted people in his studio,' Corinne had confessed. 'But then I met him in the street that day I went to the Parc Monceau. He was going to see his parents. He suggested that I come and model for him. It sounded . . .' She wanted to say interesting, or exciting, but didn't dare. 'I didn't think you would allow it . . .'

'Of course I should not allow it!' her father had shouted.

'So I made up the story. I thought it would be just for a few afternoons, and then it would be over.'

'So you went and sat in a chair and he made drawings of you . . . How did this lead to what has happened now? Did he force himself on you?'

'No, Papa. It wasn't quite like that. Artists' models . . . they are not dressed, you know.'

'You were undressed?'

'And then, the third week . . . one thing led to another . . .' She trailed off.

'You became his mistress.'

'I suppose.'

'You suppose?' And only his wife throwing herself between them had prevented him from striking her. 'You bring shame upon your family,' he cried. 'Shame upon your parents, upon your poor brothers and sisters. And ruin upon yourself. But do not think that I will allow you to ruin this family,' he told her furiously. 'For when a branch is rotten, it must be cut off.'

The rue du Faubourg Saint-Antoine was a very long street. It began out in what had formerly been a faubourg, a suburb, on the eastern side of the old city. Long before the Revolution, it had been an artisans' quarter, where most of the carpenters, furniture makers and cabinetmakers were to be found. Most were republicans, some radicals, but like Petit, many of these skilled workers, craftsmen and small shopkeepers were sound family men of conservative instincts. But as monarchs had found in the past, once stirred, they were implacable.

Petit began his walk at a furious pace. The recent snows had melted away, and the streets were dry. After a short while, he came to where the old Bastille fortress had stood. There was nothing to be seen of it now, just a big open space above which the dull grey sky gave no hint of comfort upon his quest.

This marked the beginning of the old city, so that from now on the street lost the name of Faubourg, and became simply the rue Saint-Antoine. After a few hundred yards, however, it changed its name again; for now it became the rue de Rivoli. And it was under that fashionable name that it led past the old Grève marketplace on the riverside, where the city hall, the Hôtel de Ville, had been rebuilt to look like a huge, ornate château; and then the old Châtelet, where the medieval provost had held his court. By now Petit had slowed his pace to a fast walk, and despite the cold air, he was sweating a little.

Finally, he unconsciously brushed the sleeves of his coat as he entered the rue de Rivoli's grandest section – the long, arcaded thoroughfare that ran the entire length of the solemn Louvre Palace and the Tuileries Gardens beyond, until at last he came out into the vast open space of the Place de la Concorde.

He'd been walking almost an hour by now. His anger was no less, but it had slowly changed into a sullen rage bitterly flavoured with despair.

He turned up towards the lovely classical temple of La Madeleine.

Just to the west of La Madeleine, another of Baron Haussmann's huge residential boulevards began. The boulevard Malesherbes strode up from La Madeleine on a grand diagonal that took it past the edge of the Parc Monceau and on to one of the city's north-western gates. If the boulevard was solidly respectable, the sections nearest La Madeleine were distinctly fashionable. And it was here, in a large Belle Époque building, that he came to Jules Blanchard's apartment.

Jules was most surprised, at half past ten that morning, when a servant announced that Monsieur Petit the furniture maker was there to see him, but he told the servant to bring Petit to the library at once.

As Petit told his tale, his hands clenching his hat in a mixture of embarrassment and determination, Blanchard understood him completely. He kept his own face grave and immobile throughout, giving nothing away, but inwardly he did not doubt a word that the craftsman was saying, and his heart went out to him. He understood his embarrassment, his shame and his rage.

When Petit was done, however, Jules remained calm and noncommittal.

'You must understand, Monsieur Petit, that I know nothing of what you have just told me.'

'I understand this, monsieur.'

'First of all, therefore, I must speak to my son. But since you and I are together, let us for a moment consider the matter as far as we ourselves know it. You are sure that your daughter is pregnant?'

'My wife says so.'

'I would advise you to seek a doctor first. It might turn out that she is not. And there is always the chance, even if she is, that nature will bring the matter to an end. This can often happen, after all.'

'Perhaps, monsieur.' Petit looked doubtful.

'Even if – I say "if" for the time being – it should be that my son is the cause of your daughter's condition, I think we must put out of our minds the idea that my son would wish to marry your daughter. I say this simply because we must not deceive ourselves. I should be surprised if Marc wishes such a thing, and I should not be in favour of it myself.'

Petit said nothing. What could he say? He already knew it was true.

'If that were the case,' Jules continued, 'what would you do?'

'She will leave my house. I will never see her again.'

'You would not forgive her?'

'I cannot, monsieur. I have my family to think of. But your family has a responsibility, monsieur.'

He was probably losing a customer by saying it, but then he was sure he'd lost Blanchard as a customer anyway.

Jules wondered if the girl would consider an abortion. Such things could be arranged. This was not the moment to raise the matter, however.

'I make no comment until I have spoken to my son. But you may be sure that you will hear from me afterwards.'

The interview was at an end. As soon as Petit had left, Jules sent a servant to Marc's lodgings with a message that he should come to see him at once.

'Not later this morning,' he reiterated. 'At once.'

Marc arrived at twenty minutes before noon. He was smiling broadly. He had his American friend already with him, and cheerfully introduced the fellow, who seemed harmless enough, to his parents before his father asked him to step into his library for a private word.

Jules closed the door.

'Corinne Petit is pregnant.'

'She is?' The surprise on Marc's face was genuine.

'Her father was here this morning. He wants to know what you mean to do about it. Is there a chance you are not the father?'

Marc considered.

'I imagine I am.' He shrugged. 'She was innocent.'

'A virgin?'

'Yes. And ... I doubt she would even have had the opportunity ...'

'He thinks you should marry her.'

'*Ah, non.*'

'You know what will happen to her, don't you? Her father is going to throw her out into the street. She is dead to him. Ruined.'

'*Mon Dieu!*'

'What do you expect? Have you no sense of responsibility?' His father's voice was rising. 'You seduce the young daughter of a man who does work for our family, who trusts us and holds us in respect. You ruin her and think there will be no consequences? How do you think I felt, watching the poor fellow's rage and agony? How do you imagine I should feel if some scoundrel, yes, some scoundrel like you had ruined your sister? Villain!' he shouted. 'Cretin!' He was almost panting with rage.

Marc was completely silent. Then, after a pause, he answered with a single word.

'Joséphine.'

'What do you mean, Joséphine?'

'You insult me and call me names, Father, but it was you who called your department store, for which you and our family are known all over Paris, by the name of your former mistress.'

'Nonsense. It's named after the empress Joséphine. Everyone knows that.'

'Don't worry. Maman has no idea.'

'She has no idea because it is not the case,' his father answered sharply.

Marc shrugged.

'As you like.'

'If,' said his father quietly, 'you had a charming mistress, a woman of the world who could take care of herself, I'd have no objection whatsoever.'

'I should need a larger allowance.'

'But this case,' his father continued, ignoring the impertinent interruption, 'is entirely different.' He paused. 'We could take no notice of the girl, of course, we could say that she is just a little whore and that you may not even be the father. I know many families who would do exactly that. Do you wish me to do so?'

'No.'

'I am glad to hear that, at least, since I am not disposed to do any such thing. We shall have to see what arrangements can be made. She can have the child out of sight in the country. That's not a problem. It could be adopted. If need be, I can pay for its upbringing. But I'm afraid that Petit still won't have his daughter back in his house. I understand it, but it's tragic.' He looked at his son bleakly. 'Meanwhile, in order to help you reflect on this, I am stopping your allowance.'

'For how long?'

'Until further notice.' He signalled that there was nothing more to say. 'You had better rejoin your American friend. Our other guests are about to arrive. Oh, and one more thing,' he added. 'Your sister is to know nothing about this business. You understand? Absolutely nothing.'

Frank Hadley was a very decent fellow. He'd come to Paris to study art, and he'd been there only a couple of weeks when he bumped into Marc Blanchard, who'd befriended him, taken him around and now invited him to meet his family.

He was twenty-five years old, tall, well built, with a mane of brown hair, honest brown eyes set wide apart, and whose strong, athletic frame suggested that he might be a good oarsman, and probably swing the lumberjack's axe as well – both of which guesses would have been correct. During his education, he'd picked up enough French to make a start when he got to France, and he was studying the language hard for two hours every morning.

He looked around the apartment with interest. It was obvious that Marc's family had plenty of money, but it was bourgeois money. There was none of the stately Louis XIV furniture favoured by the aristocracy, nor the lighter, rococo furniture of the gilded age. The furniture of the Blanchards' large apartment was mostly nineteenth-century – sofas and chairs with curling legs and backs, lacquered cabinets, here and there a desk in the simpler, more severe Directoire style of the Napoleonic period. And above all, a profusion of potted plants – palm trees in tubs standing in corners, flowering plants on tables. The haute bourgeoisie of France, almost as much as the entire middle and upper classes of Victorian England, had taken to indoor plants.

He'd done his best to make small talk with Marc's mother. But although she couldn't have been a more kindly hostess, her English was limited, and their conversation had not been sparkling during the first couple of minutes. So he'd been relieved when an elegant lady, who explained that she was Marc's aunt, and a pleasant, fair-haired girl, who turned out to be Marc's sister, had entered the room. The girl spoke only a little more English than her mother, but Aunt Éloïse spoke English quite fluently, and it was quickly apparent that she was a cultivated and well-read lady. This was just the sort of person, he thought, that he should get to know.

They'd been talking only a couple of minutes, however, when, quite unmistakably, they heard the sound of Monsieur Blanchard's voice raised in anger. They couldn't hear what he was saying, but Frank was almost sure he heard the word 'Villain!' being shouted. And then: 'Cretin!'

He glanced inquiringly at Marie, who blushed with embarrassment. He had a sense that Marc's mother might know what this was all about. He wondered for a moment if perhaps he ought to go.

It was Aunt Éloïse who calmly took command of the situation.

'Well, Monsieur Hadley, it seems that Marc must have displeased his father. We do not know what he has done, but I think we can say it is quite certain that he has done something.' She smiled. 'Perhaps your father was sometimes angry with you.'

'I seem to remember being taken to the woodshed, as we say, when I was a boy.'

'*Voilà*.' She made an elegant motion with her hand. 'Then it seems that all families in the world are the same. So. As we have guests coming at any moment, my dear Hadley, you will now immediately have to become one of the family. We shall carry on exactly as if nothing had happened at all, *n'est-ce pas?*'

Frank grinned.

'I can do that.'

'Excellent.' Aunt Éloïse looked around. It did not seem that Marie or her mother were ready with any observations at this moment, so she continued in the same vein. 'Very soon, Hadley, we shall ask you all about yourself, but I shan't ask you yet, or when the others come you will have to say it all again.' She paused, but only for a moment. 'In France, you will soon discover,' she continued, as if, indeed, nothing had happened at all, 'we often raise our voices when we are discussing matters which are of absolutely no importance whatsoever. Philosophy, for instance. Everybody shouts and interrupts each other. It's most agreeable. If, however, the world is coming to an end' – she raised her finger – 'it is de rigueur to remain very calm, and, if possible, to look bored.' She gave him a wry look. 'At least, this was the ideal in the best circles, before the Revolution. And we still remember it.'

'We have the stiff upper lip in America,' Frank said, 'but we haven't yet mastered the art of being bored.'

'If you stay with us long enough, my dear Hadley,' said Aunt Éloïse with a smile, 'I'm sure that we can bore you. Ah.' She turned. 'People are coming.'

Everyone was arriving now. Gérard and his wife, Marc, who was looking a little pale, and moments later a pleasant Englishman named James Fox. Just after that, Monsieur Blanchard also returned to the room. He welcomed Fox, embraced Gérard and his wife, and if he did not look at Marc, gave no other sign that anything might be amiss between them.

His sister, Éloïse, turned to him.

'My dear Jules, while you had your passionate discussions with Marc, I have been having a charming conversation with Hadley

316

here, who is now quite one of the family.' She gave her brother a stare.

She spoke in French, but Frank got the gist of it, and he smiled to himself. The French manners might seem a little artificial, but Aunt Éloïse had just gently let her brother know that their American guest had heard him shouting.

'Ah.' Jules Blanchard glanced at him. 'Well,' he announced to the gathering, 'everyone is here except Monsieur de Cygne.' And seeing some surprise on their faces: 'I had better explain who he is.'

As Roland walked into the boulevard Malesherbes from La Madeleine, he wasn't very happy. He didn't want to go to this lunch. He'd do his best, because his father had asked him to; but he wasn't looking forward to it.

He'd had an irritating morning as well. He'd put off answering the letter from the Canadian that his father had given him, and decided that he really must deal with it today. So he'd read it.

The letter was perfectly polite. It informed him that although the writer's family name was spelled 'Dessigne' these days, they had always understood that they were a branch of the noble de Cygne and that since the writer was making a visit to France that summer, and had the idea of visiting some of the châteaus of the Loire, he wondered if he might be allowed to see the old family château one afternoon.

Whatever the man's intentions, it was quite clear that he was mistaken, and Roland had no intention of letting him through the door. But how to get rid of him politely? He had tried to compose a suitable letter for two hours, and each time he tried, he had felt more and more irritated, so that in the end he had been forced to leave for lunch with the letter unfinished.

Part of the trouble was that he had been in a bad temper from the moment he woke up. In fact, he'd been in a foul mood since Thursday. And for this he could not be blamed.

The cataclysm that had taken place in France on the Thursday of that week, and was to echo down French history for generations to come, consisted of a single letter. It wasn't even written by anyone important – just by a popular novelist named Émile Zola. And it concerned that obscure Jewish officer, Dreyfus.

'*J'accuse . . .*' the letter said. 'I accuse . . .' Who did Zola accuse? The French establishment, the justice system and, worst of all, the army itself.

They knew that Dreyfus was innocent, he said. The army and the government were involved in a disgraceful conspiracy to keep an innocent man in the tropical penal colony of Devil's Island, rather than admit the evidence that another officer, who had been identified, was the real traitor. And why were they all prepared to pervert the course of justice? Because Dreyfus was a Jew.

Before the spring was out, all France would have taken sides. For the moment, the government was furious, and as for the army, there was not the faintest question among Roland's fellow officers.

'Zola ought to be shot.'

Frank sat at the dining room table. Marc's family were certainly making things very easy for him.

He'd heard that in France, as in Spain, it wasn't always easy to get into people's houses, and that one would never really understand the country until one did. He'd also heard that the French could be difficult. Here Marc had already given him excellent advice.

'All you have to do, Frank, is to show respect. You must remember that the English defeated Napoléon in the end, and that they have the biggest empire in the world, so they are inclined to be arrogant. French is the language of diplomacy, of course, so we have no problem with the English diplomats. The rest of their countrymen, however, come over here and try to order us about in English. Naturally, we don't always like it. However, if you show respect, and make an effort to speak French, everyone will help you.' He'd paused. 'I have to tell you, all the same, that there is one small problem.'

'What's that?'

'The Americans have terrible difficulty with the French accent. I don't know why, but I have noticed that it is so. Sometimes an American will learn French, and we listen hard, because we realise they are speaking our language, but we can't understand what they're saying.' He shrugged. 'It's a pity.' Then he'd grinned. 'But don't worry, *mon vieux*. If you do your homework with the language, I personally will take care of your pronunciation.'

Manners dictated that Madame Blanchard, who spoke little English, should put de Cygne on her right and Frank on her left. But Fox the Englishman was on the other side of him. De Cygne spoke a little English. On the other side of de Cygne was Marie. Jules Blanchard took the other end of the table, with his sister, Éloïse, on his right and his daughter-in-law on his left.

The conversation was general, with Fox quietly supplying translations when they were needed. And since Hadley was the guest from abroad, the whole table demanded, in the most friendly way, to know all about him.

Where was he from? his hostess asked. He explained that he'd been brought up in several places because his father was a professor and had moved around several universities before retiring recently to Connecticut.

'A professor of what?' asked Aunt Éloïse.

'Of Latin.'

'Your family were always academic?' she asked hopefully.

'No, ma'am,' he replied. 'My grandfather made a pretty good fortune in the dry goods business, but my father liked to study, so he followed an academic career.'

'Dry goods, you say?' Gérard Blanchard asked from down the table. 'Wholesale or retail?'

'Both.'

'So, your family is like ours,' Gérard said with approval. 'Solid.'

Aunt Éloïse looked faintly irritated, but Frank smiled.

'We like to think so,' he answered cheerfully.

Aunt Éloïse wanted to know what had caused him to study art, and he explained that his mother was a talented musician and artist.

'I went to a small university called Union College, pretty much in the area where the Hudson River School of painters found their inspiration,' he explained. 'Scenery of amazing grandeur. That as much as anything got me started.' He suddenly turned to look up the table to Marc. 'You told me Americans have difficulty pronouncing French, Marc. So let's see how you get on in American. My university is in a little city on the Mohawk River called Schenectady. Who here can pronounce that?'

After everyone at the table had tried, he shook his head.

'Fox got pretty close, but he's English. The rest of you: nowhere near!'

His French hosts seemed to enjoy this very much. There were cries of genial protest: 'It's impossible. It cannot be done.'

'But why did you come to France, Monsieur Hadley?' Marie ventured, a little shyly.

'Impressionists, mademoiselle. The French Impressionists became all the rage in America, and so every ambitious young painter in the United States wants to come to France now. I guess I'm just one of a tribe.'

'It's true,' Marc informed them. 'Soon I believe there will be more American Impressionists in France than French ones. But I've seen Hadley's work, and he has a lot of talent.'

'You study and paint, Monsieur Hadley,' de Cygne remarked, 'yet you look to me like a man who enjoys outdoor pursuits as well.'

Frank smiled.

'To tell you the truth, I wasn't sure what I wanted to do after I left Union College, so I went west for a year and worked on a ranch. Loved it. Big open spaces, and I like physical work. By the end of it, though, I was sure I wanted to study painting.'

'So you ride?'

'I do.'

'Western?'

'I use an English saddle in New England, but I like to ride western. You ride?'

'I am in a cavalry regiment, monsieur. So, yes. As for the western saddle, ever since Buffalo Bill was here, everyone wants to try it.'

From the far end of the table, Jules Blanchard gently intervened.

'Monsieur de Cygne is too modest to say it,' he said, 'but I happen to know from his father that he almost made the elite Cadre Noir team. That means, Hadley, that he's one of the best horsemen in France.'

'I wouldn't say that,' said the aristocrat, but Hadley could see that he didn't mind the compliment. He noticed that Marie was impressed, as well.

It seemed to Hadley that he'd provided quite a useful diversion from whatever Marc and his father had been quarrelling about. Everyone seemed to be in a pretty good mood.

But now Gérard had a question.

'Tell me, Monsieur Hadley, if you fail to make a career as a painter, what will you do then? Will you work?'

'*Ah non!*' cried Aunt Éloïse. '*Assez*, Gérard. Enough.'

Hadley laughed.

'I see you like to get to the point,' he said good-humouredly. 'And it's a fair question. My father's been generous, and I'm going to give it all I've got for a few years. But if I can't really achieve anything, then I think I'll go into business. And I believe I know what business I'd like to get into.'

'Dry goods?'

'No. Motor cars. I think they have a huge future. Just in the last year or two, Ford in America, Benz in Germany, Peugeot in France, have all started turning from steam cars to the internal combustion engine. I believe that's going to be a very exciting business.'

Gérard seemed impressed. De Cygne looked thoughtful.

'I know one or two rich men who want motor cars,' the aristocrat remarked, 'as a rich man's toy, of course. But you think in America it will go further than that?'

'Not yet awhile. But within a generation, I suspect so. And not just in America. All over the world.'

This thought silenced the whole table for a moment. But Jules Blanchard was looking at Hadley with particular approval, and thinking that this was just the friend that Marc needed to give him some balance and steadiness.

Fox had contented himself with offering instant translations so far, but now he entered the conversation. He was an interesting-looking fellow, Frank thought. Nearly as tall as himself, but more sparely built and with the quiet face of a professional man.

'The great change in transport that we're about to see in Paris,' he informed Hadley, 'is the Métro. They won't start tunnelling until late this year – the French are years behind the Americans and the English, I'm afraid, but the plans are very extensive. Now it's happening, the whole network may come very fast.'

'And don't forget the designs for the entrances and exits,' Marc added. 'The plans are for the most lovely Art Nouveau metalwork. It's going to be elegant.'

The main course had arrived. And it was a triumph. *Bœuf en croûte*, made to perfection. A tenderloin of beef, a thick layer of rich *foie gras* around it and the whole encased in a puff pastry. The aroma alone was sumptuous. Even de Cygne was impressed.

'Madame,' he said to his hostess, with feeling, 'you have a wonderful cook.'

As Roland looked around the table, he had to confess that this meal with the Blanchard family hadn't been as bad as he'd expected. True, they weren't his sort of people. The apartment was not to his taste, and as for the Art Nouveau dining room they were so proud of, it seemed vulgar to him, simply because it was new.

But his father had been right. He should meet different sorts of people. The Blanchard sons might not be his style, and their aunt seemed too intellectual, but Jules Blanchard was a sensible man. As for the other guests, he liked Hadley. These Americans had a naturalness that was pleasing. Fox was that most British invention, the English gentleman, who had a code of manners that nobody could complain about – and he was certainly behaving very nicely by acting as interpreter.

That left Marie and her mother.

He'd been watching Madame Blanchard since the start of the meal. She was a pleasant-looking woman, a little thicker in the waist now than when she'd been a young woman, no doubt, but with her regular features and blue eyes, she looked somewhat younger than her years. Any middle-aged man with a wife like that might count himself lucky.

She had, of course, a cook and servants to prepare and serve the meal, but he could see from the way that she glanced at each dish, and observed the servants at their work that she was completely the mistress of her household. She knew exactly how everything had been prepared. If there'd been a single fork out of place, she'd have indicated the fact to one of the servants with the faintest nod, and the error would have been instantly corrected.

He discovered that she and her husband were second cousins – just as half the aristocrats he knew had married their relations – and it was evident from things she let fall that her own parents had been no poorer than her husband's. In short, without needing to assert herself in the least, Madame Blanchard was a woman who was completely sure of herself and comfortable with who she was. He respected that.

And as he observed Marie, it occurred to him that one day she would be just like her mother. She was a little quiet, but then she had been strictly brought up. So much the better. He learned from her mother that she and Marie had both been to Mass that morning, and that they went every Sunday. The girl was a good Catholic. He approved of that too.

She was pretty. He wondered what it might be like to awaken passion in her. Very pleasant indeed, he would guess.

And it suddenly occurred to Roland, who had hardly known what it was to have a mother and a normal family life himself, that this delightful comfort could be his if he were to marry this girl.

Was it breaking the code? Would it be letting the family down if he married into the bourgeoisie? Certainly he'd never imagined himself doing such a thing. What would his friends say? Perhaps not so much, if she were rich. What would his father say? He suspected that his father might have maneuvered him into attending this lunch for precisely this purpose. I must ask him, he thought.

Just then, Marie asked whether Hadley intended to travel in France, and what places he meant to visit.

Everyone had a piece of advice to offer. Hadley explained that he was hoping that by the early summer his French might have improved a good deal, but that the weather hardly invited going anywhere outside Paris just yet.

'You could go to Versailles,' de Cygne suggested. 'Much of what one sees is indoors. And it's only a short journey by train.'

'Is it open this time of year?' asked Jules.

'I could arrange a private visit,' de Cygne offered, which impressed everybody.

'You should accept at once, Hadley,' Jules told him.

'If you and Marc would like it, I could conduct you myself,' de Cygne continued. 'My family has some connection with the place. Perhaps Mademoiselle Marie would like to accompany us.'

Marie glanced at her mother, who nodded and looked at her husband.

'Certainly,' said Jules. With her brother there, the outing was entirely respectable. Indeed, it was a charming way for de Cygne to reciprocate for the lunch. And if the aristocrat liked to see more of his daughter . . . well and good.

'Have you room for a translator?' Fox inquired.

'Certainly,' answered de Cygne. He didn't want to take too obvious an interest in the girl just yet. The polite Englishman would be excellent additional cover.

So it was all agreed, and a date set for the following Saturday.

It was a pity therefore that a minute or two later, in all innocence, Frank Hadley should have chosen to ask de Cygne: 'What exactly is the business with this army officer that the newspapers seem to be so excited about?'

Roland de Cygne began very carefully. He assumed that this solid Catholic family would feel as he did, but it was wise to be cautious.

He explained briefly how Dreyfus had been tried for treason and found guilty. How another officer, Esterhazy, had subsequently been investigated, but had been cleared. Not everyone, he explained, was convinced, but there the matter had rested until, this week, a well-known novelist named Zola had written an open letter to the president of France that made serious allegations of a conspiracy to cover up the truth.

'As far as I know,' he concluded, 'Zola has no special knowledge or standing in the matter, whatever he may say. And it may be that the government will prosecute him. But we shall see.'

'And you may be sure, Hadley,' Marc added, 'that the army is not happy either. Would that be fair?' he asked de Cygne.

'Certainly,' de Cygne answered straightforwardly. 'Most, I think all, of my fellow officers feel that the army has been insulted by Zola. I do not suppose,' he continued, turning to Hadley, 'that the army of the United States would be happy if they were publicly accused of injustice and dishonesty.'

From down the table, Jules Blanchard moved quickly to avert any trouble.

'You understand, Hadley, that cases like this arise from time to time in every country. What is unfortunate is that Zola chose such an inflammatory way to approach the subject. But I have no doubt' – he looked around the table firmly to make his message quite clear – 'that calmness and wisdom will soon prevail.'

And now his wife showed that she, too, could command the situation when she chose.

'I am very disappointed that no one has tried the fruit flan.' She nodded to the servant who was holding it to move forward. 'Monsieur de Cygne, you will not insult my flan I hope.'

'It looks delicious, madame.' Roland took his cue at once, and accepted a slice.

'I know you have been at your château on the Loire,' she continued firmly. 'Do tell us about it. Is it of great age?'

Fox, also ready to help, immediately asked Gérard a question about his business.

But it wasn't enough.

'All that you say is true, Monsieur de Cygne.' Aunt Éloïse was speaking. 'But you have not mentioned the matter that is central to Zola's accusation. Namely, that Dreyfus is a Jew.' Hadley saw Jules Blanchard put his hand on his sister's wrist. But it did no good. 'It's true, Jules,' she cried. 'Everybody knows it.'

No one spoke. Roland had no wish to respond, but it seemed he couldn't avoid it.

'Dreyfus was not on trial for his religion, madame, but for passing secret information to a foreign power. He is suffering on Devil's Island. If he is innocent, then I am sorry for it. But no one has proved that it is so. That is the truth, pure and simple. What I resent in this business hardly concerns Dreyfus himself, guilty or not. It is Zola that I resent. Because he seeks to undermine the reputation and the honour of the army. And the army together with the Church are the two institutions in France which are above reproach. I say this not as an aristocrat, nor even as an officer and a Catholic, but as a soldier, a Christian and a patriot.'

Gérard Blanchard gave a murmur of approval. So did his wife. Jules too nodded, out of respect and good manners, at the least.

'Do you make any distinction between a Jew and a Christian?' Aunt Éloïse asked quietly.

'Certainly, madame. They follow different faiths.'

'And you think that Zola should be in jail as well?'

'It would not worry me if he were.'

'In America,' said Aunt Éloïse to Hadley, 'you have free speech. Your constitution guarantees it. Despite the Revolution, it seems that we in France do not, and I am ashamed of my country.'

Hadley said nothing. But Roland did.

'I am sorry that you are ashamed of France, madame,' he said icily. 'Perhaps you and Captain Dreyfus and Zola could find some other country, more to your liking.'

'I don't think it's necessary to elevate all this to a question of principle,' remarked Gérard. 'I don't know if Zola had broken the law or not by writing his letter. If he has, then that's for the courts to decide. And if there's no crime, then they won't. That's all. It's not so serious.'

For once, Gérard was actually trying to be helpful. It didn't do him any good.

'My dear Gérard, you run a business very well, I'm sure,' said Aunt Éloïse irritably, 'but I have known you all your life, and you wouldn't know a moral principle if it came up and smacked you in the face.'

'And you, Tante Éloïse, live in a little world of your own,' Gérard retorted furiously. 'May I remind you that it was our family's wholesale business that made the money that allows you to sit around all day reading books and thinking yourself superior to the rest of us.'

'This has nothing to do with Dreyfus,' said Aunt Éloïse coldly.

'Well, I'm with Monsieur de Cygne anyway,' said Gérard. 'I don't say all Jews are traitors, but this is a Christian country, so they can't feel the same as we do. That's all.'

And now, to avoid any more bloodshed before the situation got completely out of hand, Jules Blanchard put his foot down. To be precise, he rapped on the table and stood up, because it was the only way of getting their undivided attention, and then he made a little speech.

It was a good speech. And it proved in the months and years ahead to be more prescient than he could have guessed.

'Monsieur de Cygne, Hadley, Fox and my dear family. This is my house, and for myself and my wife, I demand that this discussion end. Completely. But there is something more to say.

'Today, we have very nearly quarrelled. We have not quarrelled' – he looked at Gérard and Éloïse sternly – 'but we have nearly done so. And let us be grateful that from this we have learned an important lesson. For if the people here – who are all kind, and well mannered – can come so close to blows, then I wonder what will happen when other, less well-disposed people discuss this difficult subject.

'Three days ago, when I read Zola's letter, I confess that I was surprised and shocked. But I did not understand the effect it would have upon people. Now I believe that this letter is going to create a great chasm in our French society. It may tear us apart. And whatever the rights or wrongs of the matter, I regret the destruction of good relations between honest people.

'So at the least let us all learn' – he looked around the whole table and smiled – 'that this is a subject for carefully controlled debate, but that none of us will ever allow ourselves to discuss it at any lunch or dinner party again. Because if we do, we shall inevitably lose all our friends!'

Even de Cygne, furious though he was, could only admire his host. His father had been right. This was a superior man. A states- man. From his end of the table, he gave a polite nod of respect as Blanchard sat down.

Aunt Éloïse was not mollified, but she said nothing. Fox murmured, 'Very wise.' And Frank Hadley could not help reflecting that if Aunt Éloïse had been right in assuring him that the French only argued passionately about matters of no importance, then this Dreyfus affair must be the exception that proved the rule.

The rest of the meal passed off without incident. But it was subdued.

As they were leaving, Frank went up to de Cygne and quietly asked, 'Is the visit to Versailles still on?'

'Certainly,' said the aristocrat, and quickly confirmed the arrange- ment to Jules Blanchard.

Frank would have liked to talk to Marc about the whole business after they'd gone out together. But their discussion had hardly begun when Marc clapped his hand to his head.

'My dear fellow, with all this drama, I almost forgot, I have some- one coming to sit for a portrait at four o'clock. Let's have a drink tomorrow evening and discuss everything.'

So Frank decided to turn into the Champs-Élysées and walk up to the Arc de Triomphe for a little exercise. Perhaps, if he felt in need of more, he might walk on as far as the Bois de Boulogne.

When Roland got back to his barracks, he was still furious. His anger was not directed against the Blanchard family particularly, with the exception of Aunt Éloïse, who besides being an intellectual, which automatically made her suspect, was clearly a republican. The very fact of her existence might have put him off the rest of the Blanchard family too, but he'd seen that Marie's brother Gérard and his aunt were hardly on speaking terms, and this suggested that it might be possible to be one of the family and still keep the wretched woman at arm's length.

But he still needed someone or something to vent his anger upon. So he was almost glad to see the unfinished reply to the Canadian still lying on his writing table. He sat down to compose.

> *Dear Sir,*
>
> *Your letter has been handed me by my father, the Vicomte de Cygne, for reply, as he has not time to reply to you himself.*
>
> *Quite apart from the fact that the spelling of your name in no way suggests that it has any connection with that of the vicomtes de Cygne, I can assure you that no member of our family has ever migrated from France to Canada, nor even visited that country. We should certainly know it if they had. The idea of a Canadian branch of our family is therefore entirely fanciful.*
>
> *I do not think that a visit to the Château de Cygne could be of interest to you therefore, and the house itself will in any case be closed for major repairs this summer.*
>
> *No doubt, monsieur, you have French ancestry. But if you wish to find connections in France, you will have to look elsewhere.*

He put down his pen with grim satisfaction. That should dispose of Monsieur Dessignes, whoever he might be. He signed and sealed the letter and laid it on the desk. A task completed. It was just four o'clock.

At the very moment that he sealed the letter, a pale, well-dressed lady reached the door of the house near the boulevard de Clichy where Marc Blanchard had his studio. She looked about her uncertainly, not having been there before. But the address was correct.

Wondering what it would be like to have her portrait painted, Hortense Ney started up the stairs.

Chapter Ten

1572

He was just a very ordinary little boy. No one would have imagined that he'd change the history of his family by opening a window when he had been told that he must not.

On this Monday morning, the eighteenth day of August in the year of Our Lord 1572, young Simon Renard was excited. His father's cousin Guy was about to arrive. And then Uncle Guy, as he called him, and his father were going to take him to see the royal wedding. He'd never seen such a thing before.

And he was doubly curious after his father had told him: 'This is the strangest royal wedding that's ever been seen in Paris.'

Simon was eight years old, and he lived with his parents, Pierre and Suzanne Renard, in a small house that lay down an alley of store-houses, near the fortress of the Bastille.

Simon liked the old Bastille. He knew that long ago it was put there to protect the Saint-Antoine city gate from the English. But there was no fear of English attacks nowadays.

In the previous century, cunning King Louis XI had seen to that. He'd wanted to make his kingdom into a mighty country, and he'd succeeded. While in England, the Plantagenets had torn each other to pieces in the Wars of the Roses, King Louis, by fighting, and by devious diplomacy, had spun his spider's web until he'd gathered all the great independent regions – Normandy and Brittany in the north, Aquitaine and warm Provence in the south, mighty Burgundy in the east – into the huge, hexagonal entity that would be known henceforth by the single name of France. For a while the English had kept one town, the northern port of Calais. But now they'd lost that too. The English threat was over. Paris was safe. And the Bastille just seemed a friendly old place to the little boy.

He'd also grown up with a deeper security.

Pierre and Suzanne Renard were good Catholics, and they loved their only son. Two little girls had been born after him. Both had died in infancy. But Pierre was in his early thirties and his wife a little younger. So they still had every hope of having more children, if it was God's will. In the meantime, Simon knew, the two baby girls were safely with their Father in heaven.

Apart from his parents, there was only one serving girl to help his mother, and an apprentice. The serving girl slept in the attic; the apprentice in the loft over his father's storehouse behind the house.

The little family was particularly intimate, therefore. Each day Simon helped his parents. Each night they said prayers together before he went to bed. And thanks to this gentle rhythm of life, Simon knew in his heart that his parents loved him and that his soul was protected by his Saviour.

He did wonder sometimes about his wider family. His mother had come from a village the other side of the city of Poitiers, and though they had travelled down there once when he was a very little boy, he hardly remembered them. He knew that his father had relations in Paris, but for some reason, apart from Cousin Guy, he never seemed to meet the other members of the Renard family.

He liked Guy, though, very much. Guy was in his late twenties, not married yet, and lived in another part of the city. He was a handsome young merchant with a short, neat beard and moustache and thick, dark red hair which he wore swept back. Every month or so he would look in, and whenever he did, he would talk to little Simon and make him laugh. Simon was very glad that Guy was taking him to see the strange royal wedding today.

As Guy Renard drew near the house, he silently cursed. He did so for two reasons. The first was that he always felt irritated when he went to see his cousin Pierre.

Why did Pierre have to be such a fool? He shrugged. Because Pierre's father, Charles, had been a fool too, he supposed.

A century ago, when Cécile Renard had married young de Cygne, the family had been at the height of its wealth. The next generation produced several Renard sons, who'd shared that wealth.

But it was in the time of their children, in the glorious reign of King François I, that the parting of the family ways began.

What a time that had been. The age – as history would call it – when the Renaissance came to France. Italian architecture had been transformed by the warm and delightful sensuality of the French into the glorious royal châteaus of the Loire. Humanist writers had been nurtured in that soil, like Ronsard the poet, and earthy Rabelais.

And François was everything a Renaissance prince should be: tall, handsome, a patron of the arts. The scandalous but brilliant gold-smith and sculptor Benvenuto Cellini had worked in Paris. New improvements were undertaken on the growing royal palace of the Louvre. And Leonardo da Vinci himself, bringing the *Mona Lisa* with him, had come to spend his last days in the valley of the Loire, and died in the French king's arms.

The king was a man of vision too: Verrazano's voyage to America was financed thanks to him; colonies in Canada were founded; explorers sent to India and beyond. He'd opened trade across the Mediterranean with Morocco. To balance the power of the Hapsburg Holy Roman emperor, he'd even formed an alliance with the Moslem Suleiman the Magnificent, of the Turkish Ottoman Empire. Though he'd also married his son to Catherine de Médicis, of Florence, with a rich dowry promised by her kinsman, the pope.

But Guy's favourite tale was what happened when King François had met that great bully, Henry VIII of England.

'Imagine it,' he gleefully told his little cousin Simon, 'they met at a magnificent congress called the Field of the Cloth of Gold. And Henry of England, who was big and powerful and very pleased with himself, challenged King François to a wrestling match. The two men wrestle. The crowds are watching. They are both strong. But maybe François is stronger, or more skilful, and no doubt more intel-ligent . . . and suddenly – oopla – Henry's in the mud. He's flattened. King François beats him.'

'Was King Henry angry?'

'He was furious. But there was nothing he could do. He was beaten.'

'Was it King Henry who had six wives?'

'Yes. But it didn't do him much good. He was a terrible man. Whereas King François was a great man. And of course,' Guy added proudly, 'he had many beautiful mistresses.' Like most Frenchmen, and certainly Frenchwomen, Guy liked his rulers to have mistresses. It showed they were virile, and powerful. Either that, or they could be saints.

'Why do kings have mistresses, Uncle Guy?' Simon asked.

'For the honour of France.'

But what Guy was really thinking – though he did not say it to the boy – was that the reign of François I had been the time when his own father and his uncle Robert had both made large fortunes. The king might have spent too much, but the Renard brothers had done very well out of supplying his court.

Whereas Simon's grandfather had not. Uncle Robert had even offered to bring him into his own business, but Charles had refused. In that glorious age of adventure, he'd managed to lose most of his money.

And to make matters worse, his son Pierre had no interest in getting the money back. He worked just hard enough to get by, and hardly that. He seemed to have no ambition of any kind. He didn't want any help. He was completely placid. As the years passed, this younger branch of the Renards had been written off by the rest of the family as poor relations. But Pierre didn't seem to mind. He was always cheerful.

And this situation irked Guy. He couldn't help it. He was proud of his family's success. He was ashamed if any of them went down in the world. And so he'd gone on a personal mission to see if he couldn't do something about it.

'It's good of you to try,' his father had told him, 'but I'm afraid you're wasting your time.'

'Pierre's hopeless,' Guy agreed, 'but the boy's a dear little fellow, and he seems quite intelligent.'

Once when he was visiting the family, Guy had casually mentioned the marriage of Cécile Renard to de Cygne. Young Simon had turned to his father in astonishment. 'Our family married nobility?' he'd cried.

'Oh, that was just one rich lady, centuries ago,' Pierre told him. 'Nothing to do with us.' And afterwards he'd taken Guy aside and gently requested: 'Don't put ideas into the boy's head. We live in quite a different world these days.'

'What are your plans for Simon?' Guy had asked him once.

'One of our friends is a baker, and he's suggested he might take Simon as an apprentice in a few years. Simon quite likes the idea.'

Guy was careful after that. If he was going to have any hope of doing something for Simon, he knew he had to keep on good terms with the parents. He never let his irritation with Pierre show. But he was constantly on the lookout for ways to engender some spark of ambition and adventure in the boy. If young Simon showed that, then the rest of the family might be prepared to do something for him when he was older.

He'd tell Simon stories of the great merchant heroes of the city, like Étienne Marcel, who'd built the city fortifications; he'd talk about the adventurers sailing to the New World; he'd tell the boy about how this small merchant or that had made his fortune through hard work or ingenuity. So far, he had no idea whether he was succeeding or not, but he wasn't going to stop trying. He was a Renard, after all.

It wasn't surprising, then, that each time he saw his cousin's house, he secretly cursed Pierre for putting him to all this trouble.

The second reason he'd cursed, however, belonged to the day. In fact, he wasn't sure they should be taking little Simon out into the streets at all. Because Guy Renard trusted his instincts – and he scented danger.

There was something very suspicious about this royal wedding.

Guy was watchful as they came down past the Convent of the Celestines to the riverside. A defensive wall ran along the bank of the Seine for a little way. After that, they could look across the water to the Île Saint-Louis, the small, bare island covered with woods and rough grazing that lay just upstream from the Île de la Cité, where the grey mass of Notre-Dame loomed ahead. They passed the old Grève embankment, where a couple of watermills on a quay jutted out into the water. The roadway was full of brightly dressed people, moving in the same direction. Along the waterside, the tall, steep-gabled wooden houses with their open galleries and balconies hung with festive garlands and ribbons stared over the river, which was full of boats and barges.

Young Simon was walking happily beside him, his father on the other side. So far, no sign of danger.

The ceremony was being held under a magnificent awning on the parvis of Notre-Dame, just in front of the cathedral's great west doors. There the king's little sister was going to marry her kinsman, Henry of Bourbon, King of Navarre.

In a way, it was a dynastic marriage – perhaps a necessary one – for her family and for France. For although her two brothers were living, they had no male children as yet. In another generation, the Valois line of the ancient Capet royal family would die out. And who was next in line? Quite a distant cousin, as it happened. The Bourbon line descended directly from a younger son of that saintly King Louis who'd built the Sainte-Chapelle two centuries ago. The bridegroom's father had married the queen of the little mountain kingdom of Navarre that lay between France and Spain in the Pyrenees, of which his son Henry was now king. So if Henry of Navarre did inherit the throne of France, the Bourbon and Valois lines would be conveniently joined again.

But despite the dynastic convenience, this marriage provoked one, very big question.

'Cousin Guy,' Simon now demanded, 'why is the Princess of France marrying a Protestant?'

It was amazing really, Guy considered. Fifty years ago an obscure monk named Luther had challenged the Catholic Church, and because of it the whole of Western Christendom was now divided into two armed camps. To the north and east, the Netherlands, many of the German principalities and much of Scandinavia was in the Protestant camp. England was too. The pope had just excommunicated the heretic Queen Elizabeth, and invited good Catholic rulers to depose her. Spain, meanwhile, and the Holy Roman Empire of central Europe were in the hands of the most Catholic Hapsburg dynasty.

And France? The humanist King François had tolerated Protestants in his realm for a while. By the time he'd decided they were dangerous, it was too late. The north of France was solidly Catholic. So mostly was Paris. The modest numbers of Protestants in the city worshipped quietly, in their own houses mostly, and took care not to draw attention to themselves. But in the southern mountains and Atlantic ports like La Rochelle, huge numbers of people had taken the new faith. They went by many names – Protestants, Reformers, Calvinists,

Huguenots. Many were humble craftsmen, but others were merchants and knights. Admiral Coligny, the finest military commander in France, had gone over to the new faith. And the mother of Henry of Navarre had also converted, and taken her family with her.

The Protestants had demanded freedom of worship. The royal government had clamped down. There had been a succession of regional conflicts and truces.

'You know,' Guy said to young Simon, 'that there has been fighting with the Protestants in recent years? Not here in Paris, thank God, but in other places.'

'Yes. But we are in the right, aren't we? The Protestants are heretics.'

'Yes, you are a good Catholic and so am I, little Simon. But it is sad that Frenchmen should kill each other, don't you think?'

'Yes.'

'Well, it is hoped that this marriage will help to stop any more fighting.'

'And after this marriage,' Simon asked, 'will the Catholics and Protestants be able to agree?'

'That may be difficult. We just hope they won't fight any more.'

That was the official explanation. It satisfied many people. The boy seemed to believe it, anyway.

They were approaching the great bridge that led across to the Île de la Cité. This had been magnificently rebuilt in stone around the start of the reign of the great King François. As well as the roadway, its high arches also supported a line of tall, gabled houses that acted like a curtain, blocking off the view downstream. This was the way to Notre-Dame.

But when they reached it, they found that the press of people was so great that it was impossible to cross. Simon was disappointed. He wanted to see the wedding. Guy was secretly glad. If there was going to be trouble, he'd sooner be here on the open Right Bank than trapped in the narrow confines of the city's central island.

'We'll try the next bridge,' he suggested.

But the Pont au Change, also covered with houses, was blocked too. And further downstream, the untidy old bridge of watermills – most of which had been converted into private houses now – had been sealed off to all traffic.

'I'm afraid we can't get across,' Guy said. 'And if we want to watch the nobles riding back afterwards, we'd do better to find some open space. Let's walk a bit farther.'

Downstream from the bridges the view opened out a bit. Ahead, the towers of the old Louvre fort rose over an unfinished collection of royal buildings that seemed still to be struggling against each other to form a cohesive royal palace.

Simon wanted to run ahead a little way. The two men did not stop him.

They were coming level with the downstream tip of the island when Pierre turned to Guy and asked him quietly: 'You seem uneasy. Why is that?'

'This wedding frightens me.'

'You don't think it may bring peace to France?'

'No.' Guy glanced bleakly at Pierre. 'I don't think it's intended to.'

'Explain to me. You know I am not worldly.'

'Who arranged this wedding?'

'The king and his mother, I suppose.'

'Forget the king. His mother. Catherine de Médicis. She was the one who was so determined on this marriage. When her daughter tried to refuse to marry a Protestant, she whipped her soundly. That's the word I hear. Even tore out the poor girl's hair.'

'That is terrible.'

'Now consider something else. For the last year or so, Catherine and her inner council have been courting Admiral Coligny, the Protestants' great commander. Inviting him to visit them. Flattering him. And what does Coligny want?'

'He wants freedom for Protestants to worship.'

'Yes, certainly. He also wants to help the Protestants in the Netherlands against their Catholic oppressors, the mighty Hapsburgs. Quite apart from the fact that I am a Catholic, I happen to think it's madness. The last thing we need is to put ourselves at war with the Hapsburg king of Spain.'

'God forbid.'

'Indeed. Yet now, to please Coligny, Catherine has even sent some troops to the Netherlands to support the Protestants. What do you make of that?'

'To me, it is very strange.'

'Well, I think it's more than strange. I think it's unbelievable. Are we really suggesting that an Italian Médicis, the kinswoman of popes, is going to tolerate Protestants in her realm?' He paused. 'There is one more person to consider. Who is Catherine's greatest supporter?'

'I should say the Duke of Guise.'

'Indeed. The mighty house of Guise. Her closest counsellors. The duke's uncle is a cardinal in Rome. And let us not forget Mary, Queen of Scots. Devout Catholic. Rightful Queen of Scotland. Claimant to the throne of England. Elizabeth of England holds her in captivity now, and fears her. And who was the mother of Mary, Queen of Scots? The cardinal's sister, Mary of Guise.'

'Unlikely sponsors of Protestants.'

'Exactly. Now I have one last question. Knowing what we do of Catherine de Médicis, by what principles will she be guided in all her actions?'

'By her faith, surely.'

'I said in her actions.'

'I do not understand.'

'You have heard of the great Machiavelli, I am sure.'

'Who has not? An evil man.'

'He merely described the ruthless cunning, the cold calculation, the poisonings and murders that he saw all around him among the rulers of Italy – the Florence of the Médicis in particular. Our queen mother will act exactly like that.'

'And so this wedding . . .'

'Is a diabolical trap. Think of it. Coligny is here. Almost every leading Protestant in France has come into Paris for this wedding, along with their followers. What a chance.'

'I don't understand.'

'She's going to kill them all. She and the Guises.'

'But there are hundreds of them.'

'Thousands. It's most convenient.'

'But that is evil. Unspeakably evil.'

'You have missed the point. It is logical.'

'But we are Christians.'

'You think the pope is going to object?'

'But what of Henry of Navarre? The bridegroom?'

'Ah. That is interesting. Catherine has already isolated him. Very cleverly.'

'In what way?'

'Who made Henry a Protestant in the first place?'

'His mother, the Queen of Navarre.'

'And what happened to her?'

'She died.'

'Exactly. Not long ago. When she was visiting the queen mother, who had begged her to come – so that they might learn to be friends.'

'What are you saying?'

'Catherine poisoned her.'

'There is no proof.'

'There never will be. But once Henry is left married to Catherine de Médicis's daughter, with his mother gone, and Coligny and all his supporters murdered, he will be entirely isolated. He will either convert to Catholicism, or . . .'

'This is terrible.'

'I agree.'

'I shall pray that you are wrong.'

'Will you?' Guy gazed at him coolly. 'Neither you nor I would do this deed. But will we regret it when it's done?' He paused to let the cold truth sink in. 'Do you want civil strife, Pierre? Do you want a Protestant king?'

But Pierre had done with questions.

'I thank God,' he said quietly, 'that my home is a haven of peace.'

'May it always be so,' answered his cousin. 'Ah, here comes young Simon, back again.'

They stayed out in the street several hours, and learned that the wedding had been safely accomplished, and saw many fine noblemen ride by that day.

And by evening, when nothing untoward had occurred, Guy almost dared to hope that he'd been wrong.

For Simon, the next three days were quite annoying. News came of the great feasts and tournaments taking place between the Louvre, the Île de la Cité and the Latin Quarter, and he would have liked to go and watch.

'Can we not see the knights jousting?' he cried.

But his father was always pleading that he was too busy, or giving some excuse why he couldn't take his son out. He wouldn't let the apprentice go either. And both his parents adamantly refused to let him wander off alone, even to one of the great aristocratic houses in the nearer part of the city, where he could at least have hung around by the gates and watched the parties of noblemen and their liveried retinues as they came and went between the celebrations.

If the royal marriage was intended to improve relationships between the Catholic followers of the Duke of Guise and the Protestant followers of Coligny and Henry of Navarre, then things appeared to be getting off to a good start.

On Friday morning, Pierre had to go out to the market, but he made Simon stay at home.

At noon, his father came back ashen.

'Coligny has been attacked. Stabbed.'

'Is he killed?' asked Suzanne.

'No. Wounded, but not badly. The assassin got away. Nobody knows who it was or where he is. But Coligny's people are furious. Most of them think this was the work of the Guises, or even the king's mother. One way or the other, everyone's afraid there's going to be a fight.'

Simon wasn't allowed even to go into the street after that. At the end of the afternoon his father went out again to gather news, but returned without anything definite.

Saturday morning came. Coligny was safely in his lodgings. The old hero had lost two fingers, but that was all. He was receiving people. The royal family had been to see him. They were determined to find his attacker. The only fear was of a Protestant backlash. And with large numbers of Protestant knights and men-at-arms being lodged in the buildings of the Louvre, this was frightening indeed. But as the hours passed, nothing happened. Whatever their suspicions might be, the Protestants were holding back.

It was a long, hot August day. As evening fell, a dusty warmth pervaded the streets. Tomorrow, in the calendar of the Catholic Church, it would be the Feast of Saint Bartholomew. Both the serving girl and the apprentice had been allowed to go to their families for the day, so Simon and his parents were quite alone in the house.

Dusk was just falling when there were the sounds of a horseman coming to the door of Pierre Renard's little house. The horseman entered quickly. It was Guy.

He came into the room where the family was sitting. His face was pale.

'Pierre. You must take these.' He held out a handful of white objects to his cousin. Simon watched curiously as his father inspected them. They were white armbands. 'Put them on. All of you. Keep them on. Don't take them off even when you are sleeping. At dawn, you will hear bells. Stay indoors. Do not go outside. Whatever else you may hear, besides the bells, do not open the door. But if for some reason, Pierre, you should have to step outside, then be sure to wear a white armband. On no account be in the street without it.'

'What is this about?' demanded Pierre.

'Do not ask. And do not speak of this to anyone else. I should not be here, but you are my family.'

'Should we be afraid?'

'No. Just thank the Lord that, in His grace, He has made you a member of the true Church. But stay indoors all the same. And speak to nobody.'

Simon watched his father's face. Pierre was looking very grave, and thoughtful.

'This is terrible,' he said to Guy.

'I know.'

'Will people come to the door and ask to see the armbands?'

'They might. But it's unlikely.' He gave his cousin a grim look. 'We already know where all the Protestants live.'

'We? You are part of this?'

'I didn't say I liked it.' He turned. 'Do as I've told you, Cousin,' he said, and was gone.

The night was silent. The family slept in two rooms. Simon's room was tiny, but it had a small, square window that looked out into the alley.

He slept soundly for several hours, even as a single bell began to toll, somewhere near the Louvre. Soon other bells were following, but still he slept.

Suddenly, he sat up in bed. He did not know it was a terrible scream that had awoken him. He listened. Then he got up and went to the window. It must be early morning, but without opening the shutter, it was hard to tell what time it might be. He hesitated. He heard a party of horses going by in the street at the end of the alley, but they didn't turn into the alley itself. He went to the door of his room. A sound from the back of the house told him that his mother was in the kitchen downstairs. He went back to the shutters and pushed them open, just a little.

The alley was deserted. Usually, first thing in the morning, the yard gate to the wooden storehouse just up the alley was opened by an apprentice. But today was Sunday, and it was still closed. There was something, though. A sack, by the look of it, lying in the road. He couldn't see it clearly enough to be sure what it was.

Then he heard another sound, nearby. A scuffling sound. It was almost under his window. A dog or a cat, perhaps. He pulled himself up, got his stomach on the window ledge and leaned out.

It was a dark-haired little girl. About five years old, by the look of her. She was wearing just a nightdress. Her small round face was looking straight up at him. Her eyes were wide with terror. She was trembling, white as a ghost. He gazed at her.

'What are you doing?'

She didn't answer. She was staring at him with fear.

'I'm not going to hurt you,' he said.

She continued to stare at him.

'Why are you all by yourself?' he asked.

She still didn't answer.

'I'm Simon,' he said.

'That's my mother,' she whispered. She pointed up the alley. And Simon realised that she was pointing at the shape he'd thought was a sack.

'Where's your father?' he said.

She didn't reply, but she shook her head in a way that was so final that he supposed it could mean only one thing.

'Wait,' he said.

He crept down the wooden stairs. At the bottom, he paused. He heard his mother shovelling ash out of the grate in the kitchen. She'd be taking the ash out into the little yard at the back. His father usually went into his small store, off the yard, first thing in the morning.

He knew he should go and ask his parents what to do. He knew that, on no account, should he open the door or go outside. So he did exactly what most children in his place would do.

Very carefully, he slid back the bolts of the street door. He looked outside. The little girl hadn't moved. The alley was empty. He stepped out and took her hand.

'Shh,' he whispered, 'Don't say a word.'

They stepped inside. He closed the door carefully and bolted it again. He could still hear his mother in the kitchen. Softly he led the little girl to the stairs and they crept up together. He put her in his bed. She was shivering, so he covered her with a blanket. Then he sat down beside her.

'What's your name?' he whispered.

'Constance.'

'You'll be all right here. But don't make a noise. I wasn't supposed to open the door.'

She lay still. She was still shivering a bit. She was watching him, still uncertain, he supposed, whether she was really safe there.

'Do you have any brothers or sisters?' he asked.

She shook her head.

'Nor do I,' he said.

For about a quarter of an hour they stayed like that. He said nothing. She watched him. Then he heard his mother's voice, calling softly up the stairs to see if he was awake. He thought quickly. He didn't want his parents coming up to his room.

'I'd better go down to my mother,' he said to the little girl. 'You stay here. All right?'

She nodded.

His parents were sitting in the kitchen. They were looking solemn.

'I heard the bells,' he said.

'We must stay inside today,' said his mother.

'Are they killing people?' he asked.

'Why do you say that?' said his father.

'I don't know.' He waited for a reply, but none came. 'Can I have some bread and milk?' he said. His mother gave it to him. 'I think I'll take it to my room,' Simon said. 'I feel sleepy.' And his parents seemed quite glad that he should go back up there.

When he got back to his room, he gave the bread and milk to the little girl. After she'd finished it, he put his arm around her. Then she fell asleep.

It was about an hour later that he heard a horse's hooves outside his window. Then a rap at the door. He stole out of his room to the top of the stairs. He saw the top of his father's head as he went to the door and called out, 'Who is it?' Then he heard the door open.

'I can't stop, Cousin.' Guy's voice. 'Don't go out there. They've killed Coligny, and all the Protestants staying at the Louvre. Every one of them. They've been going around every lodging where Protestants are staying. The Protestants have realised what is happening and they're trying to leave the city. But they can't. All the gates have been locked to keep them in. You don't hear it here, but they're hunting them down in the streets. I saw twenty bodies floating in the river as I came this way. There's a dead woman in the street at the end of your alley.'

'A woman?'

'They're killing all the Protestants, Pierre. Men, women, children, all of them. It's even worse than I imagined. I don't know if it's part of the plan, but there are mobs out in the street now. If they think someone might be a Protestant, they butcher them. One Catholic family were sheltering a Protestant, and so they killed them as well.'

'This is terrible. It must be stopped.'

'By whom, Pierre? Who's going to stop it? This is all done by royal order. It's the churchmen who are ringing the bells.'

'But it is evil.'

'Don't say that, Cousin. They'll say you're a heretic and butcher you too. Keep your mouth shut, I beg you. And keep your door shut too. And wear those armbands. I have to go.'

Simon heard his father close the door and slip the bolts.

Then he went back into his room, and sat on the bed beside the little girl, who remained asleep, and wondered what he should do.

It was an hour later that he went downstairs into the kitchen, found his parents alone and told them what he had done.

'You did what?' His mother was past him in a flash and up the stairs. Moments later she came down again. She looked at her husband, then at Simon. It was a look of reproach, almost of hatred, that he would never forget. 'She must go, Pierre,' said Suzanne. 'We must put her out.' She made a gesture of desperation. 'We have to.'

Simon shook his head.

'Maman, Papa hasn't told you what Uncle Guy said when he came to the door. But I heard him from the top of the stairs. They are killing the Protestant children in the street. They will kill the little girl.' He looked from one parent to the other. 'How can we put her out?'

Neither of his parents spoke.

Just then, they heard a small bump on the staircase. Then another. The child was coming down. She reached the foot of the stairs and walked back to the kitchen doorway. She looked a little sleepy. But when she saw Simon she went to his side and took his hand.

'I am Constance,' she said.

They kept her for two weeks. The difficulty was where they were to hide her.

'Nobody must know she is here,' Pierre insisted. Neither the apprentice nor the serving girl must know. Nor even his cousin Guy. 'One careless word, one slip and the secret's out.' He did not want to say what that could lead to. And there was only one way to achieve that.

'She will have to stay in your room with you, Simon. All the time. And no one must ever go in there. You will have to pretend to be sick.' He did not say so, but the message to his son was clear: 'You have brought the girl in, and now you will have to suffer the consequences.'

As for the little girl herself, Pierre was kindly, but blunt. The first thing he did was to put a white band around her arm.

'If anyone ever asks,' he told her, 'you must say that you are Catholic. If you say you are Protestant, they will kill you, like your mother and father. Do you understand?' It was a terrible thing to say, but he knew it was necessary. 'They will probably kill all of us too,' he added.

Little Constance nodded solemnly. She understood.

'If anyone ever sees her,' Pierre continued, 'we shall have to say she is a cousin who is visiting us. But people will be suspicious. So let us keep her out of sight until we can find out what to do.'

By gentle questioning during that very day, her story became clear enough.

Her parents had come from the great western port of La Rochelle, with a party of other merchants and craftsmen who had thought this a safe opportunity to see the capital. Dragged from the tavern where they were staying, her father had been killed at once, but her mother had managed to escape. As she ran down the street, hearing a horse's hooves coming around the corner behind her, she'd whispered to the child to hide, and shoved her into the shadows of the alley as she passed. A moment later, she'd been cut down.

'Did other family come with you to Paris?' Suzanne asked her. The child shook her head.

'Have you family in La Rochelle?'

'My aunt and uncle.'

'God willing,' Pierre said to his wife afterwards, 'we can return her to La Rochelle when it's safe to do so.'

They were both silent for a moment. Neither of them spoke the thought that was in their minds: unless the Protestants of La Rochelle had all been killed as well.

During the first days, the Renard family were very frightened. For the terrible massacre on the Feast of Saint Bartholomew lasted well past the day itself. Estimates varied, but thousands were slaughtered in Paris alone. Soon news came that the massacres were taking place in other towns and cities as well. What the royal family and the Guises had started in Paris, the mob continued all over France. Orléans, Lyon, Rouen, Bordeaux, in one after another, Catholic mobs massacred Protestants in the thousands. As yet, it seemed, the great stronghold of La Rochelle had not been touched. But who knew what might come next?

Outside France the news of the massacre travelled like wildfire. The pope sent the King of France a formal congratulation, had Vasari commemorate the event in a fine painting and ordered a Te Deum to be sung in celebration upon that day for years to come. It was said that when the King of Spain heard of the massacre, it was the only time he was ever heard to laugh. Only one great Catholic ruler seemed to have doubts about the merits of the murders. The Holy Roman Emperor, though he was the King of Spain's cousin, thought that it was not a Christian thing to do.

In France itself, however, the massacre had one immediate effect. Guy Renard brought the news to his cousin's house on the morning after the massacre.

'King Henry of Navarre has converted to Catholicism. So now our Médicis queen has a Catholic son-in-law.'

'Do you think it was a sincere conversion?' asked Pierre.

'Oh, very. He was told to do it on the spot or they'd cut his head off.'

It was a strange existence for Simon and little Constance. The door of his room was kept shut all the time. Now and again his mother would come in with a little broth or some other food that might nourish an invalid, and then she'd put some of it in a second bowl she'd concealed and feed them both. At these times she'd stay and talk in low tones to them both, though only Simon was permitted to reply. After she had gone, the two children would remain as quiet as a pair of mice.

The serving girl came past the door each day, but she never dared open it. Suzanne had told her firmly that she'd be whipped if she did.

'I don't want you getting sick as well. You've work to do,' she said.

The apprentice once asked Pierre if he thought that the shock of the massacre had caused Simon to fall sick, but Pierre was dismissive of the idea.

'He started looking feverish the afternoon before,' he remarked. 'And he certainly never saw anything.'

Each afternoon, however, he and his wife contrived that the house would be safe for the children to come out of the room. Either Pierre would take the apprentice out and Suzanne send the serving girl on an errand that would take her some time, or vice versa. Then, most days, with one or the other parent guarding the door, the two children would come down, and go into the yard at the back, where no one could see them, and walk about and get some fresh air. They could even play ball, so long as they spoke only in whispers. In this manner, they usually got out of Simon's little room for an hour or two each day.

For the rest of the time, however, they had to devise ways of keeping the children amused. Fortunately, the little girl liked to draw. And Simon could read. But within a day or two, her curiosity about what he was doing led to a new game. He taught her the letters of the alphabet.

346

Constance would make a drawing of a simple object – a cat, a dog, a house – and Simon would write the word in question and, in the lowest whisper, explain to her what sound the letters made, and show her how they were formed. Since they had nothing much else to do, it was not many days before the little girl knew the whole alphabet. Simon was impressed with how quickly she understood things.

After a few days, his mother brought them a checkerboard, and he showed Constance how to play checkers. It took only a couple of days before she could hold her own. Sometimes she beat him.

And so the two children lived their strange and secret life. And each night little Constance would curl up in Simon's arms and fall asleep, and he would sleep contentedly too, knowing that he was her protector.

Once or twice Uncle Guy came to see Simon's parents. He was sorry to learn that Simon was unwell, and wanted to come up and see him, but Pierre and Suzanne would tell him that it was better he not. 'He'll be up and about soon enough,' Pierre promised. And although Guy was slightly annoyed at not being allowed to see the boy, there wasn't much he could do about it.

Even though Simon always heard Guy arrive, he could not hear what was said in the parlour. But once, after Constance had been there for ten days, he did overhear one scrap of conversation as Guy was leaving. He had mounted his horse just under Simon's window, so his head was only a few feet away. He had turned down to his cousin, who was standing in the doorway.

'You know, Cousin,' he remarked, 'this killing of Protestants is a nasty business, no question. Yet when it's all over, we may be glad of it. If destroying one community of heretics is the price of uniting France, maybe we should pay it.' Then he had ridden away.

The words had come through the window quite clearly. Simon looked down at little Constance. Had she heard? Had she understood? Yes. Her face was quite still, but her mouth was open in shock. He put his arm around her. After a few moments he felt her shaking, and saw the tears roll down her cheeks, but she cried silently, because she knew she must not make a sound.

And somehow, after that, he could never love his uncle Guy the way he had before.

Constance had been there for two weeks when Pierre told his son that it would be safe for him to take her to her family in La Rochelle. 'There has been no assault on the town so far,' he explained, and the roads seemed to be clear. 'I shall say that I am returning a niece to your mother's family in Poitiers. That's well on the way. I should be able to get Constance safely across from Poitiers to La Rochelle.'

He was going to leave the city the following afternoon. Simon's mother would take both the apprentice and the serving girl out with her while they left.

'Just think,' Simon whispered to her before they went to sleep, 'you'll see your family soon.'

'I shall miss you,' she whispered back. 'Will you come to see me?'

'Of course,' he said, though he had no idea whether such a thing would ever be possible.

They were standing together in the parlour the next afternoon, while Pierre was saddling his horse. The house was empty. Simon looked at the dark-haired little girl he had been living with for the last two weeks and felt the need to say something.

'When I'm grown up, I shall marry you,' he declared.

'You will?'

'If you like.'

Just then, Pierre came into the room.

'Time to go,' he announced, and took Constance by the hand.

But when they got to the door, she turned and ran back to where Simon was standing, and kissed him before his father led her out.

Chapter Eleven

1604

Sometimes brothers quarrel. Robert and Alain de Cygne didn't. Maybe it was because they were close in age, yet with quite different characters. One would hardly have even guessed they were brothers, to look at them: Robert had thin, dark hair which was already showing the first hint of a receding hairline. He had an almost scholarly bent. Alain was more robustly built, his hair a lighter brown, and thick as thatch. He loved the great outdoors. He'd rather hunt than read a book on any day. But each was the other's greatest friend.

Robert was the older by just two years. He was the quieter one; Alain could be a little wild. All through their childhood, neighbouring families spoke of them as 'the de Cygne boys', or even sometimes as 'Robalain'. They went about as a pair. They were invited as a pair.

Robert, as the elder son, was to inherit the family estate and fortune.

'If anything happens to me,' he would tell Alain, 'I shall have the pleasure of knowing that the estate will go to you.' Alain might be a bit wilder, but Robert knew that he'd be an excellent steward of the family fortunes if they came his way.

'No,' Alain would reply, 'you get married and have children. I'd rather make my own way in the world.' And Robert knew that his brother was telling the truth. It was the challenge and the adventure that Alain loved. Robert sometimes thought they were even more important to him than the end result.

Assuming that he lived and produced a family, then Robert's dream was that he and Alain should have fine houses and estates near each other. And to this end, he was doing everything he could to secure his brother's advancement in the world.

That was why, six months ago, he had left Alain in the country to run the estate for him, and come up to Paris to see what he could do for his brother. Taking a house in the fashionable Marais quarter, he'd set to work.

It had been agreed that Alain would come to Paris in September. Robert knew his brother was excited about the prospect. And now September had come. Alain had arrived. And Robert was faced with one awful dilemma.

Should he tell his brother how completely he had failed?

Or that the meeting they were going to this autumn day was his last big chance?

They were walking through the quarter known as the Marais, the marsh, that lay just north of the axis that ran from the Louvre to the Bastille. Whatever marsh remained was mostly drained now – although hints of the old mire could be smelled in the streets on many days – and during the last decades, some of the greatest men in France had built their mansions there.

Alain was plainly excited by the magnificence of some of these aristocratic 'hôtels'. Mostly they consisted of a big courtyard behind a gateway – this was known as the *cour d'honneur* – a splendid mansion with wings, and a garden behind. As they stopped in front of the Hôtel Carnavalet, he cried out: 'Just imagine, Robert, if our family could have a place like this!'

'Either you or I,' said Robert with a smile, 'would have to be one of the richest men at court. So don't get your hopes up just yet.'

Robert looked at his brother affectionately. He knew that Alain was already planning to live there, with the fortune that he did not have. He hoped so much that he might be able to help his adventurous younger brother towards his dreams.

In one respect at least, young Alain had a great advantage over the generality of men. He was an aristocrat.

Those advantages were large. Aristocrats were exempt from many of the taxes that ordinary folk had to pay. Their social prestige gave them a better chance of finding a rich wife. And above all, the best positions in the king's administration almost always went to nobles. A man of outstanding ability might rise in the king's service. But at a certain point he would nearly always find that the position he sought, and had earned, and the rewards that went with it, would be given to a nobleman to whom he must submit.

So far, however, these advantages hadn't produced any results.

Robert's first prospect had been a tax farmer. The system of farming might not be popular, but it worked quite well. Instead of maintaining a huge network of officials, who might be corrupt anyway, the royal administration subcontracted the whole business to independent operators. The tax farmers guaranteed a given income to the crown, and anything more they could extract from the people, they kept. The king knew what he would receive, the tax farmers got rich, and of course, if the people were discontented, they blamed the tax farmers first, before they blamed the king.

So when Robert had found a tax farmer with a marriageable daughter, he'd gone to work. The deal was simple enough. The girl would get the benefit of social status, and with her father's financial backing, her noble husband might make a great career. Everybody benefited. Robert had a charming miniature of Alain, which was quite true to life. The girl and her parents had seen the picture and liked it. He was on the point of summoning Alain to Paris when the tax farmer had regretfully informed him that he had a better offer. These things happened, but it was a blow.

Then he'd got an introduction to the great Sully himself.

Maximilien de Béthune belonged to one of the oldest families in Europe. With branches in France, England and especially Scotland, where their name was often spelled as Beaton, every generation seemed to produce men of talent. Created Duke of Sully for his services, the soldier administrator was the king's right-hand man, and already he had transformed the country's finances from loss to profit.

When Robert was ushered into his presence, he found a man well into middle age, with thinning grey hair and a somewhat domelike head, from which a pair of shrewd grey eyes looked out at him with a hint of amusement.

'So Monsieur de Cygne,' he remarked with a smile, 'you have not come to ask for something for yourself, but you want me to help your brother. Very commendable. Has he a particular skill?'

'His talents are general, monsieur.'

'I'm sure they are. Does he by any chance have knowledge of the linen business, or perhaps glassmaking, or silk weaving?'

'No, monsieur.'

'I didn't expect it, but one never knows. More important by far however, has he knowledge and experience in building bridges or roads?'

'Not as yet. But I'm sure he could learn.'

'I dare say. But I need men with experience.'

There was a brief silence.

'I was hoping,' Robert ventured, 'that something might be found for him. Our family has always . . .'

'My dear Monsieur de Cygne,' the great man gently interrupted him. 'Your family is known to me. If I had something to offer, I assure you, I should oblige you at once.' He paused and gazed at Robert kindly. 'Do you know how to govern France?'

'Well . . .' Robert was stumped. It was not a question he had been expecting.

'Very few people do. The answer, however, is wonderfully simple. It is to do as little as possible.' Seeing Robert's look of stupefaction, he raised his hand. 'You are thinking that the king and I are busy, and we are. Allow me to explain. You see, the rulers of France usually spend their time destroying the country. They engage in wars. The trouble of recent decades has made a terrible mess of the countryside, and that is why I need men to build roads and bridges. Kings also have a deplorable habit of extravagant building, and of giving away money to all their friends. The present king is no better than the rest.' He smiled again. 'Don't worry, I tell him so to his face every day. But here is the point, Monsieur de Cygne: despite the attempts of every generation to ruin France, they cannot do it. The land is so large and so rich. The endless wheat fields that stretch from Chartres to Germany, the orchards and cattle farms of Normandy, the wines of Burgundy . . . the list goes on forever. Leave it alone for a year or two and the land recovers itself.

'All I have done, therefore, is to stick to the essentials, employ only people who are useful, build what is needed, and if possible, stay out of unnecessary wars – for as a soldier I know that war is ruinous – and if I do that, then the wealth of France will flow like a great river. That is why we now have a surplus in the treasury. And it is why I cannot create an unnecessary position for your younger brother.'

As Robert was sadly leaving, the great man did say one other thing.

'Perhaps you should try to get to know the king. I don't control him.'

It had taken time. Robert had got to work on people that he knew. And finally he had been presented to the monarch. Here his name and his family's centuries of loyal service had earned him a cordial enough reception. And the king was a very genial monarch. When he had finally plucked up the courage to ask if he might present his younger brother when he came to Paris, the king had told him that he expected it.

This was their mission today. Would the king do anything for Alain if he liked him? Who knew?

He'd discussed the meeting carefully with Alain. For once, his younger brother was nervous. 'What shall I do? What shall I say?' he'd asked.

'Just be yourself, my dear brother. People always like you exactly as you are. And even if you tried to pretend to be something else, the king would see through you at once. Remember, there isn't much in life he hasn't seen. There are just four things you need to know.'

'What are those?'

'First, wherever he goes, there will be women. Be polite to them all. Any one of them may be a mistress; perhaps several of them. One of them may even be his wife.

'Second, you love his new bridge. The one that's nearly finished. I showed it to you the other day. Do you remember what I told you?'

'The Pont Neuf. Built in stone. Goes right across the whole river, just touches the tip of the central island on the way.'

'And? You've forgotten something.'

'Ah. It will have no houses on it. Just a bridge. Pure and simple. First one in Paris without houses. Why does it matter?'

'Because one will have an unobstructed view along the river to the Louvre, which will look more gracious. The king is obsessed with this idea. On no account forget it.'

'I won't.'

'Third, if he asks you to gamble, accept at once, even if you haven't any money.'

'But if I lose?'

'Very unlikely. The king nearly always loses. He loves to lose. He loves giving money to people. Sully has to find the money to settle all his gambling debts. It drives the old man mad. I suspect the king finds that amusing.'

'You said there were four things. What's the fourth?'

'Ah. Yes. That's a bit special.' Robert grimaced. And then he told his brother what it was.

'Oh my God,' said Alain.

King Henry IV of France. King of Navarre. Born Catholic. Made a Protestant by his mother. Remained so until, on that fateful Saint Bartholomew's Day, Catherine de Médicis threatened him with death if he didn't become a Catholic.

And who knew, he might have remained a Catholic if Catherine and the Guises hadn't made one miscalculation. They'd supposed the massacre of 1572 would terrify the remaining Protestants into silence. It didn't. Though royal armies attacked in force, the great Protestant strongholds like La Rochelle held out. Soon they were pressing the government for freedom of worship just as strongly as before.

Once again, Henry of Navarre became a Protestant. It took him years to get his following back, but finally, he had a Protestant army behind him.

Would the throne of France be his? Nostradamus had said it would. When Catherine de Médicis had paid him a visit, he'd told her things would fall out this way. None of her sons left a legitimate male heir. Her last son, a talented transvestite, had no interest in producing one. Upon his death, therefore, the throne was Henry's to inherit.

But the Catholic Guises were not done yet. They formed the Catholic League. Spain came to their aid. When Henry and his army came to Paris, they found a Catholic city, reinforced with Spanish troops.

There was a siege. There were endless talks. But in the end Henry had no choice. Paris, as people said, was worth a Mass. He became Catholic again, and got the throne of France. But he did not turn his back on his Protestant followers. In 1598, he issued the great Edict of Nantes, which allowed Protestants to worship as they pleased.

And he reigned, for all his faults, the most genial king the French had ever known.

They found him in the huge courtyard of the Louvre. There was a party of people with him, more women than men.

'Is the queen there?' Alain whispered as they approached.

If the king's love life was busy, his marriages were somewhat eccentric. The marriage to Catherine de Médicis' daughter, back in 1572, had not been a success. Henry and his wife had been cheerfully unfaithful to each other and in the end the pope had obligingly annulled their marriage. They remained friends, however, and Henry had recently built her a splendid palace near the Louvre. For years he had lived only with his mistresses. But finally he had married yet another of the Médicis family.

Marie de Médicis was not among his women today, however.

'They say her conversation's pretty limited,' Robert informed his brother. 'But she is wonderful at breeding children.' The Bourbons didn't want to run out of heirs like their Valois cousins.

A courtier came to intercept them, remembered Robert, greeted Alain most amiably and led them towards the king. As he approached, Alain had a chance to observe the monarch. His curly hair and pointed beard were greying and clipped short. His face was full of intelligence and cunning, and amusement. He wasn't especially tall, but he held himself very erect. He reminded Alain of a ram entering a field of sheep.

'Remember the fourth thing I told you,' whispered Robert. The king was only ten paces away now.

And then it hit them. Robert smiled. Alain also tried to smile, but it wasn't easy.

For he had just smelled the king.

King Henry IV stank. He did not like to wash. The acrid smell of stale sweat that emanated from his body was striking even in an age when baths were rare. As for his breath . . . the combination of garlic, fish, meat and wine consumed over days, and never washed out of his mouth, produced a halitosis so thick, so putrid, that as Alain drew close, he almost retched.

How in the world, he wondered, can he stink so badly and still keep all these women?

But he made his deepest bows and found the king's swarthy, intelligent face looking at him with every sign of approval.

'Welcome to Paris,' the monarch said genially. 'Do you like it?'

'Most certainly, Your Majesty.'

'Have you seen my bridge?'

'I understand, Your Majesty, that they started building it wide, to support the usual houses, but that you forbade them to build any houses. I think it will look magnificent.'

'Excellent. Whoever told you to say that was quite right.' The king laughed. Alain almost winced as the breath reached him, but managed to smile instead. 'Rather than putting houses on the bridge and spoiling the view, I intend to build some splendid town houses on the triangle of land where the bridge crosses the tip of the island.' The king nodded with satisfaction. 'And as you see,' he continued, making a sweeping gesture towards the long building behind him, 'we are building in the Louvre as well.'

It had to be confessed, the huge palace was still a mess. During the course of the last century, the kings of France had discovered that it was one thing to abandon the old royal palace on the Île de la Cité for the huge site around the Louvre, but it was another to decide what they wanted once they got there.

Not that anyone wanted to move back to the island. Apart from the Gothic glories of the Sainte-Chapelle, the old palace on the Île de la Cité had turned into a huge warren of law courts, dungeons and royal offices. But over at the Louvre, each generation seemed determined to make their mark, and the result was a failure of unity.

The central, Renaissance palace was promising, but Catherine de Médicis had built a palace of her own at the far end of the Tuileries, cutting off what might have been a noble view towards the west. A much better enterprise, which King Henry had now taken in hand personally, was the splendid series of galleries running westward from the Renaissance palace along the bank of the Seine. It ran for a quarter of a mile.

'Some people say,' Robert had told his brother, 'that if there's ever serious trouble, King Henry reckons he can run along the galleries and escape from a discreet side door at the western end. Like some of the palaces in Florence.'

More likely, the galleries were to be a noble setting for impressing visiting foreigners with the splendours of the royal art collections.

So when the king turned to Alain now and asked him, 'Do you know what is so important about the long gallery?' Alain went for the art collection.

'Not at all. It's the lower floor that's the best thing about this new wing. Do you know what I'm going to use it for? Workshops. Artists' studios. Scores of them. We'll give the craftsmen space there. It'll be like a huge academy. A hive of activity.' His enthusiasm was palpable. 'A country is nothing, de Cygne, until it has peace. And a king is nothing if he does not promote the arts and crafts of his country. And a palace is nothing but an empty shell, unless it is the centre of useful activity. So I am going to fill this palace with workshops.'

He turned to Robert.

'You are staying in the Marais, aren't you?'

'I am, sire.'

'You must show your brother the site of my new square. They've started clearing the ground. It's on the rue des Francs-Bourgeois, before you get to the Bastille. There'll be colonnades at street level where people can walk. And above that, houses and apartments for honest working people. All built in brick and stone. A haven for modest townsmen, in the aristocratic quarter. I'm going to call it the Place Royale.' He suddenly looked at Alain. 'Do you approve of my efforts for ordinary people, monsieur?'

'Yes, sire.'

'Why?'

Alain paused to think. He really hadn't considered such a proposition before.

'I suppose,' he said, 'it's similar to the religious question. France is at peace now after being torn apart by religious divisions. But men can be divided by other things as well. If there is hatred between the classes, that is dangerous too. After all, there have been peasants' revolts in history, and they were terrible. It seems to me that Your Majesty is seeking to make France at peace with itself.' He stopped, afraid that he might have spoken too much.

'Good,' said the king. He nodded approval. 'Now then, to business, messieurs,' he continued. 'As you have only the one estate,' –he addressed himself to Robert – 'your brother will have to make his way in the world. Have you been to see Sully?'

'Yes, sire.'

Alain did not know what this meant, but Robert did. The king's question was not really a question at all. It was a broad hint that Sully had already told him about his efforts on behalf of his brother.

'I doubt you got anything from him,' the king remarked. 'He never wastes money. Did he tell you I was extravagant?'

Alain's mouth opened wide. What a question. How on earth did one respond to that? But Robert knew better than to tell his king a foolish lie.

'He did, sire,' he replied with a smile. 'But I did not believe it.'

'What a good answer!' The king grinned. 'You can never believe a word that comes out of Sully's mouth. If you see him again, tell him I said so.'

And this promising conversation seemed about to take a useful turn, when a group of ladies came up to the king.

'Your Majesty is neglecting us,' one of them said reproachfully. 'You were going to tell us what happened at Fontainebleau.'

Robert looked dismayed at this sudden interruption. Just as they had the king's attention, were they about to lose it?

King Henry turned to the ladies.

'So I was.' He nodded. 'You shall all hear it,' he called out. And at this signal the entire company hastened to gather in a circle around the monarch. 'It happened last week, at the Château de Fontainebleau,' the king explained. 'I was there, my wife was there, my little son, and the usual company. And we had an unusual entertainment, arranged by the English ambassador. A company of players. They gave us a play by a man named Shakespeare. Has anyone heard of this writer of plays? No? Well, nor had I, but they think highly of him in England. And you can imagine my excitement when, as I supposed, they told me their play was about myself.'

'A wonderful subject,' cried one of the courtiers.

'I quite agree,' said King Henry amiably. 'But it turned out that it was about the English Henry IV. My chagrin was great. But what could I do? We all sat down. I put my son beside me. He's only three, but I thought it would be good for him. A prince cannot be too young to learn how to be bored.' He gave them all an ironic look.

'And so, my friends, the play began. I will not say I understood it all, but it had a big, fat character in it called Falstaff who seemed to be quite amusing.

'And to my astonishment, my little boy seemed to be enjoying it more than anybody. He was fascinated by this Falstaff. I have no idea why, but he was. We came to the end of a scene. We applauded. There was a silence. And then, suddenly, my little boy stood up, pointed at the actor who was playing the prince and shouted: 'Off with his head!' Just like that. 'Off with his head!'

'Everyone turned to look at him. I could see the actors were alarmed. They obviously suspected the French were monsters. 'You really want me to cut off his head?' I asked. '*Oui, Papa*,' he says. 'Off with his head.'

'I did not know he was so bloodthirsty,' laughed one of the ladies.

'Nor did I, madame,' confessed the king. 'But it was then that I made my great mistake. I looked at him severely, and I said: "You must wait. We never execute an actor until the play is finished." And that was that.'

'You mean he was quiet after that?'

'Not at all, madame. I mean that the actors absolutely refused to continue. They begged the ambassador to save them. Nothing would persuade them to give us another line.' He turned to one of the gentlemen. 'Bertrand, you were there. Didn't it happen just like that?'

'Exactly, sire.'

They all burst out laughing.

'You did not command them to continue?' asked one of the ladies.

'Well, to tell you the truth,' King Henry admitted, 'I was getting quite bored by then, so I called for refreshments instead.'

His anecdote done, he seemed about to engage in conversation with one of the ladies. Robert longed to reach out and grab him by the arm, but could not. Was this chance of helping Alain slipping away from him as well?

The king was murmuring something to the lady. But then, abruptly, he turned back to Robert.

'Walk with me, de Cygne,' he said kindly, 'and your brother too, of course. I think best when I am walking.'

They moved along the path that ran parallel to the great gallery.

'Tell me,' King Henry said to Alain, 'are you a young man who likes adventure?'

'I am, sire,' Alain replied.

'The greatest adventure in the world is in America, at present,' King Henry declared. 'I am thinking in particular of the northern region we call Canada. A huge wilderness, unimaginable in its size and, perhaps one day, its riches. A vast territory to be explored and settled. During your lifetime, it could become a huge colony, a new France. Might that be of interest to you?'

Robert looked at King Henry in horror. Was he trying to send his beloved brother away into the wilderness? Where he might never see him again?

But Alain's face had lit up.

'Under what terms might I go, sire?' he asked.

'I gave the trade monopoly and settlement to the Sieur de Mons. He has a number of talented men with him. There's Du Pont, the explorer. There's a young fellow named Champlain. He comes from a family of mariners, knows how to explore the great rivers and how to survey land. He seems to have talent. We have both Catholics and Protestants, all working together. Hardly any nobles. If I ask de Mons to find a place for you, he will. But after that, it will be entirely up to you how you impress these men, and what you make of it. There's not much ceremony in such circumstances. But plenty of adventure. You'd learn a lot.'

'I am ready to learn, Your Majesty.'

If Alain seemed eager, Robert had taken note of something else the king had let fall. There were hardly any nobles out there. If Alain did well enough, then later on, once the settlements grew to be colonies under royal rule, he would have an advantage. He could even finish up as governor of a province some day. And his family in France would certainly make sure that his name was remembered in the royal court. He could see the cleverness of the king's offer. But what a distance.

'So,' the king asked, 'am I to take it that you are interested?'

'Most assuredly, sire.'

'I am afraid your brother will never forgive me.' The king gave Robert an understanding look. 'It seems that he is fond of you.'

'My brother is the best man I know, Your Majesty,' said Alain with feeling.

The king turned back to Robert.

'Sometimes, de Cygne, to get on, we must make compromises. Even sacrifices. But remember this: France is full of ambitious nobles. Many have families far more powerful than yours. But across the ocean, a man can make a name for himself more easily.' He paused, and nodded. 'And there is so much land . . .'

The king now signified that the interview was over, and that they should withdraw. As they did so, he called out: 'Long life, Alain de Cygne.'

'To Your Majesty also,' Alain replied.

King Henry looked thoughtful, but said nothing.

As the two brothers made their way back into the Marais, they were both rather quiet. Finally Robert said: 'I had not thought of you departing.'

'I know,' Alain answered. 'Nor had I. But it's an opportunity. A big adventure. And with a letter of recommendation from the king . . .'

'But Canada . . .'

'I shall write to you, brother.' Alain put his arm around Robert's shoulder. 'With every ship that crosses the ocean.'

Simon Renard was just a quarter mile ahead of the two brothers as he turned into the street that led to his house.

At just past forty, he was quite a handsome man, with only a few grey hairs. A year ago his wife had died, leaving him with three children. He was still getting over her loss.

On reaching his home, he found the house quiet. There was a single servant in the kitchen, who told him that his daughter had taken the younger children to the market with one of their friends, but that the friend's mother would be coming by to pick up her child.

Simon was glad of the chance to make up his accounts in peace for an hour, and was about to go out to the storehouse in the backyard when he heard a knock at the street door and, on opening it, saw a pleasant, dark-haired woman who was obviously the mother of the child to be taken home.

'Come in,' he said. 'I'm afraid the children went to the market, but no doubt they'll be back soon.' It was annoying to have his work interrupted, but he hoped he didn't show it.

She stepped in and glanced around.

'You have always lived here?' she inquired.

'Yes. It was my parents' house. I enlarged it some years ago.'

'Ah.' She nodded. 'Your parents are still living?'

'No. I lost them in the plague of '96.'

The plague had returned to Paris twice since his childhood. Once in 1580, then again in 1596. The first time it had missed this little enclave of the city. The second time, he had been away in Lyon on business and returned to find both his parents gone.

Simon tried to think of something to say. His children had many friends, and he didn't always remember the details of all their families.

'I forget how many children you have,' he said.

'Just three.'

'Ah yes. The same as me.'

They had stepped into the parlour. It was well furnished. There was a pair of square, upright walnut armchairs with panels of Brussels tapestries across their backs, and a carved trestle table. There was a Turkey carpet on the floor, and a tapestry hanging on the wall. Simon was rather proud of it. So he was pleased when the woman glanced around admiringly and remarked that he had a very handsome parlour.

'I see your business prospers,' she remarked with a smile.

Unlike his father, Simon had not refused to accept any help from his relations. When Guy's father had offered to put him in the Italian trade, importing silk and leather gloves, he had gladly accepted, and the results had been excellent. Indeed, he could have increased his fortune more had he wished to. But he didn't. He'd enlarged the house. His family wanted for nothing. But that was enough. He was a member of a guild, but he took no part in its politics. He did not want to impress anyone. He hoped his children would marry into solid, honest families, but not more than that. He had never moved from the quiet spot at the end of the alley which remained a haven of peace and quiet in a stormy world.

His visitor was smiling at him.

'You do not remember me.'

'Forgive me.' He gave her an embarrassed look. It was no use pretending. 'My children have so many friends . . .'

'The fault is mine. You are clearly expecting someone. The mother of some child your children know. But I am someone else. I was last in Paris thirty-two years ago. I did not even know your name. But I came here to see if you still lived here, because I owe you thanks. When I was a little girl, you saved my life. Do you know me now?'

He stared at her in amazement.

'My God. You are the little Protestant girl. You are Constance?'

'I would have sent you a message years ago, but when your father left me with my relations in La Rochelle, all those years ago, he would not even tell them his name. He just hurried away.'

'I didn't know that.' Simon nodded thoughtfully. 'I suppose that in those days, when it was dangerous even to help a Protestant, he might have thought he was protecting our family that way.'

'I think so too. And if I ever knew your family name, I certainly forgot it. I was only five. But I always meant to thank you. So when I arrived in Paris the other day, I set out to find the house. I thought I could remember it.'

'And you did.'

'Yes.' She smiled. 'Well, after wandering around looking for an hour. I wondered if you would still be living here, and I had no idea if I'd recognise you if you were. But when you opened the door, I thought it was you. And then before I could say anything, you asked me in.'

'But this is wonderful.' He nodded to himself as he remembered. 'When my father came back from La Rochelle, he told us you were safe. Then not long after, the royal army came to take La Rochelle. The Protestants held out there so strongly that the army gave up. But we heard that many people had died during the siege, so I had no idea whether you had survived. And here you are. You must bring your husband and children to meet my children.'

'We are still Protestants, you know.'

Simon shrugged.

'It's legal, now,' he said.

The truth was that, though a Catholic himself, Simon Renard didn't much care what religion people followed any more. Even now, he could still remember his sense of shock as a boy that Christians could murder innocents in the street in the name of their faith, and

363

his sense of disappointment when Uncle Guy had seemed to condone it. He had joined that large body of moderate Catholics who felt – no matter what the pope said – that such horrors were against the Christian spirit.

'Well, I should be happy to bring my children to meet your family,' she said. 'But alas I cannot bring my husband. He died two years ago. I have come to Paris with my brother-in-law and his family. Our children have grown up together. And when some friends of his urged him to come and join the Protestant church here in Paris, we decided we'd all come together.'

'Then you shall all come,' said Simon. 'We shall have a reunion.' And he was about to tell her that his own wife had died, but for some reason he decided not to. Not just yet.

So it was agreed that they should all meet the following Saturday afternoon. Then Constance left.

After she had gone, Simon went back to attend to his business. But for some reason, he found it hard to concentrate.

Did Constance remember that in those far-off days when they were both little children, he had taught her the alphabet? Perhaps. He must ask her. Did she remember that when she was about to leave with his father, he had declared he would marry her? Probably not.

That was certainly out of the question. King Henry might have made peace, but Catholics and Protestants didn't marry.

He realised that he had never even been inside a Protestant church. He had no idea what one of their services was like.

Perhaps he'd ask Constance and her brother-in-law to take him to one. There could be no harm in that.

Chapter Twelve

1898

It was a cold January afternoon when Roland brought Marie to Versailles. The trees were bare, and the sky was grey. The palace was closed to visitors that day, but he'd arranged a private tour, and he acted as her guide.

If the lunch at the Blanchards' apartment had been marred by the unpleasantness concerning Dreyfus, there would be no sign of that today. Roland had felt ill at ease on the boulevard Malesherbes, but at Versailles he felt he was on his own turf. And he did the thing in style.

Indeed, he rather enjoyed the situation. It was pleasant to be able to show his guests that he could arrange a private tour like this. Moreover, his family had been at the court of Versailles in its heyday, and passed down plenty of anecdotes with which he could amuse and impress his guests. He was determined to be charming.

He met them at the station with a large carriage that would hold them all – Marie, her brother Marc, Hadley the American, and Fox the English lawyer. This was just the right amount of company to give him the chance to observe Marie carefully, without it being too obvious.

After all, he reminded himself, that was the point of the exercise: to find out whether Marie might be a possible wife. With a little luck, he'd be able to discover that by the end of the afternoon.

It did not occur to him that he had competition.

He noticed one thing straightaway, before they even reached the entrance to the palace: he liked the way she sat and walked. She had a perfect upright posture. Roland didn't like women who stooped.

He'd always supposed that his wife would be elegant. Marie might not be elegant in the way of the slim, fashionable women one saw in

Paris drawing rooms, but she was undeniably pretty. She was also one of those fortunate women who would get even more attractive with age. He could see her in middle age, and beyond, far more attractive than some of today's elegant women would look by then. In old age, her posture would ensure that she was always dignified. So he might be giving up a little elegance with Marie, but he'd get something even better in return.

Before entering the château, they surveyed the vast courtyards around which the palace was spread. With its huge extended centre and wings, Versailles was certainly breathtaking in its scale.

'I have visited this palace since I was a little boy,' he remarked to Marie, 'yet even now I confess that it takes my breath away.' He glanced at Hadley, who had never seen the place before, and wondered what the best introduction would be. But the American made that easy by laughing pleasantly and remarking:

'Call me provincial, but I still haven't got used to the size of your great houses. All this,' he spread his arms, 'just for Louis XIV and his family?'

'Ah, my friend,' Roland responded, 'you would be right. And it started, you know, as quite a modest hunting lodge. But this huge assembly you see here was built not just for a family, but for the entire court. The royal family had apartments within the palace, but from around 1680 until the French Revolution – over a century – Versailles was the administrative capital of France. All kinds of people had to be lodged here: the administrators, the most powerful nobles, anyone who had business with the king. When foreign ambassadors arrived, Versailles impressed them with the might of France. The king insisted that almost everything in it was of French manufacture, like the Gobelins tapestries and Aubusson carpets he promoted – so it was like a sort of permanent trade exhibition. It was quite practical.'

Now Marie gently joined the conversation.

'I have heard,' she said to Hadley, 'that one can still see the original hunting lodge within the palace building.' She turned to Roland. 'Is that true, Monsieur de Cygne?'

Roland smiled to himself. He suspected that Marie knew the answer to her own question perfectly well, but that as he was acting as guide, she was being careful not to intrude upon his territory.

'You are exactly right, mademoiselle,' he said. 'The very centre of this huge facade contains the original hunting lodge. Just a modest house with a few bedrooms. But they preserved it and then built outward in every direction.' He turned to them all. 'Shall we go in?'

As they started to move towards the entrance, he heard Marc murmur to his sister, 'You knew where the hunting lodge was. Why didn't you just say?' But Marie ignored him.

So Roland had been right. He remembered a conversation with Father Xavier, years ago. 'When you marry,' the priest had said, 'before you take any action, think first how it will feel to your wife. Consider her feelings before your own. If you and your wife both do this for each other, you are on the road to a happy marriage.'

Roland wanted a marriage like his parents'. He wanted to love and be loved. 'I will try to do as you say,' he'd answered the priest.

'I am glad to hear it,' Father Xavier had replied with a smile. 'So let me add one word of caution. However much you may fall in love, do not waste that love on a woman who is not considerate in return.'

Marie's act of good manners was only a small sign, but an encouraging one. It suggested that she was thoughtful about others.

As they approached the entrance, Hadley had another question.

'Why did he move from Paris?' he asked. 'He had the Louvre Palace, which is big enough.'

'Some say he hated Paris,' said Marc.

'That may be so,' Roland said. 'But he still built Les Invalides, and some of the first boulevards in the city. The truth is, nobody knows for certain. But I think it was part of a larger process. France had been brought together as a single country, but it was still very hard to govern, with great nobles controlling huge regions. In the time of his father, Louis XIII, the great Cardinal Richelieu tried to bring order to the land by making the monarchy absolute. When Louis XIV came to the throne, he was only five years old, but all through his childhood, Richelieu's successor, Cardinal Mazarin, followed the same policy. And once Louis XIV took power, with the help of his finance minister, Colbert, he continued to centralise the administration of France. What better way to control the nobles than to have all the powerful ones in one place, where he could keep an eye on them. Over two generations he became so clever at making them dance to his tune at the court of Versailles that he completely neutered them. He couldn't have done that in Paris. It's too spread- out.'

'And hard to control,' Fox added.

'Impossible. Always full of places for people to hide, and breed dangerous ideas.' Roland smiled ruefully. 'Paris gave us the Revolution.'

Now he turned to Marie. Partly it was politeness. Also a little test. 'But what do you think, mademoiselle?' he asked.

Marie considered for a moment.

'Everything you say seems correct, monsieur,' she answered carefully, 'yet I would add one thing.' She glanced at Hadley. 'Monsieur Hadley may know that during the boyhood of the king, perhaps as a reaction to the autocratic policies of Cardinal Mazarin, there were two terrible revolts, known as the Fronde. One night, the Paris mob broke into the Louvre and came into the king's bedchamber. He was still only a child. He pretended to be asleep while they came around his bed, inspecting him. Imagine the scene. It must have been terrifying. Nobody could have stopped them if they'd wanted to murder him. And I suspect, monsieur, that the memory of that night stayed with the king all his life. His head may have dictated the move to Versailles, but I believe that, in his heart, even as a grown man, Louis XIV never felt safe in the Louvre.'

Roland looked at her admiringly.

'I think your woman's wisdom comes closer to the mark than all my calculations,' he said with respect. And though he did not say it aloud, he added to himself that it would be a lucky man who had her by his side.

At the entrance, a guardian let them in. After that, they had the place to themselves. No footfalls, no voices but their own disturbed the silence of the huge marble halls, the gilded chambers and endless galleries.

They went through the King's Apartment, stately, sombre and impressive.

'Each reception room is named after one of the classical gods,' Roland explained. 'The throne room is for Apollo.'

'It's curious, isn't it,' Marc remarked, 'how our Christian monarch showed such a taste for comparing himself to pagan gods. He wasn't called the Sun King for nothing.'

Here and there, Roland pointed out paintings and decorations, all by French artists like Rigaud and Le Brun as they moved through the stately sequence of high, cold rooms. The culmination was the War Salon, a temple of green and red marble, massively ornamented with gold, and dominated by a huge oval relief of the godlike Sun King, mounted on a horse that was trampling upon his enemies.

'Everything depended upon the king,' Roland remarked. 'His control was complete. The ritual was endless.' He gave Fox and Hadley an amused look. 'Everything that the English and the American political systems wanted to avoid.'

And with that he led them through the doorway into the most famous room in France.

The Galerie des Glaces, the Hall of Mirrors. Nearly eighty yards long. Great windows down one side, gilded mirrors opposite, a tunnel-arched ceiling from which the massive row of crystal chandeliers hung in galactic splendour. The almost endless polished expanse of parquet floor gleamed like a lake under the sun.

'This is where everyone waited for the king to pass on his way to chapel,' Roland remarked.

'I've read that the court etiquette was pretty stifling,' Hadley said.

'It was. But I think the women had the worst of it,' Roland told him. 'Somehow a fashion evolved where the women were supposed to take tiny steps very quickly – you couldn't see it of course, under their long dresses – so that it seemed as if they were floating.' He turned to Marie. 'What would you say to that, mademoiselle?'

A mischievous glint came into Marie's demure eyes.

'Do you mean like this, monsieur?'

And then, to the astonishment of the four watching men, she set off up the Hall of Mirrors. Her dress was long enough so that one could not see her feet. And the effect was astonishing. It was, indeed, as if she were floating away up the gallery. With the pale light coming in through the windows, her floating form passed like a ghost from mirror to mirror so that one could almost have imagined she were passing into some other age until, turning some hundred feet away, she glided back to them and to the present.

Finally, when she stopped the gentlemen burst into a little round of applause.

'Where did you learn that?' asked Marc in amazement.

'I had a dancing teacher who could do it. She showed me how.'

'*Formidable!*' cried Roland enthusiastically. 'More than that. Exquisite. You must have been at the court in another life.'

'A remarkable performance,' said Fox. 'Wonderful.'

'It's quite tiring,' said Marie with a laugh. 'I'm glad I don't have to do it every day.'

They moved into the Queen's Apartment. Redecorated several times in the eighteenth century, these had a lighter air.

'Your family were at Versailles, Monsieur de Cygne?' Marie asked.

'Yes. In fact, it's rather a romantic tale. Back in the days of Louis XIV, my family almost came to an end. There was just one de Cygne left. He was getting old, and he had no heir. But then, here at Versailles, he met a young woman, of the D'Artagnan family. And despite the great difference in age, they fell in love and married.'

'D'Artagnan like in *The Three Musketeers*?'

'Exactly so. Dumas used the name in his novel, but it was based on a real family.'

'And they were happy?'

'Very happy, I believe. They had a son.' He smiled. 'Otherwise I wouldn't be here.'

'I think that's charming,' said Marie.

As he guided them out of the Queen's Apartment, Roland announced that he would show them the chapel, which lay across the courtyard. As they walked across the courtyard, Marie turned to him.

'I was interested by the story you just told us,' she said quietly. 'I always supposed it would be very difficult to have a happy marriage when there is a great difference between the husband and wife.'

'A difference of age, you mean?'

'Of age. Or other things.'

A delicate question, he thought, but sensible. She was right to raise it. After all, he was an aristocrat, and she, though rich, was a woman of the bourgeoisie. Such a difference in traditional France was still huge.

'I think that if there is affection, mademoiselle, and mutual respect, and if people have interests in common, then the differences can be solved as long as both parties make compromises. And compromise comes from affection.'

She nodded thoughtfully. Then she smiled.

'What you say seems very wise, monsieur.'

The chapel was a baroque masterpiece, dedicated to the medieval king Saint Louis.

'In the latter part of his reign,' Roland remarked, 'the Sun King became increasingly religious.'

'And this was entirely thanks to his second wife, Madame de Maintenon,' Marie added cheerfully, 'who was a good moral influence on him.'

Roland laughed.

'She's quite right, of course,' he told Fox and Hadley. 'No doubt every man needs a wife to give him moral guidance. But Louis XIV certainly did!'

Fox, however, did not seem to share their amusement. He nodded thoughtfully, but pursed his lips.

'You must forgive me if I can't be so enthusiastic about the religious feelings of Louis XIV. It was those feelings that made him kick my family out of France.'

Roland looked at him in surprise.

'You're a Huguenot?'

'We were.' Fox turned to Hadley to explain. 'You've probably heard of the Huguenots, as the French Protestants were often called. We lived in France protected by an act of toleration known as the Edict of Nantes. But then in 1685, Louis XIV revoked that protection and told the Huguenots to convert. About two hundred thousand escaped, many of them going to England. My family was one of those.'

'But you haven't got a French name,' Marie said.

'No. Some of the English Huguenots kept their French names. But others translated them into English. A family called Le Brun, for instance, became Brown. And Renard translated to Fox.'

'Your name was Renard?' said Roland with sudden interest.

'Yes. It's quite a common name.'

Roland looked thoughtful for a moment. He knew that his family had married a Renard heiress once, a woman of the merchant class – a girl like Marie Blanchard, perhaps. That had been centuries ago, hardly worth thinking about. But it was conceivable that his family could be distantly linked to that of the English lawyer. Did he wish to investigate further? No, he didn't want to be related to Fox.

'It's true,' he agreed, 'there are many Renards.' And he let the matter drop. 'But now,' he announced, 'the carriage will take us down to the end of the park where we can look at the charming little ensemble of the Trianons.'

Anyone who knew James Fox would have said that, when he decided to marry, his choice of wife would be wise, and that he'd make an excellent husband. He'd already been a little in love with several women, and recently he'd wondered if it might be time to settle down.

But he'd never experienced the thunderclap of a grand passion, the *coup de foudre*. Until last Sunday.

And now he was in love. And his love was impossible.

He'd always assumed he'd need a wife who spoke French. The family firm had begun in London, but the Paris office was an important part of the business. He and his father were liked and trusted by the British embassy, and he expected that he'd be moving between the London and Paris offices for the rest of his professional life.

Finding an English wife who spoke French should not be too difficult. Ever since the might and prestige of the Sun King had made French the language of diplomacy, it had been *de rigueur* for ladies of the upper and upper-middle classes to speak French – at least in theory. Indeed, most middle-class girls would learn a smattering of French at school.

But what about a French wife? The idea was quite appealing. In France, it could only help. And in London, so long as she could speak passable English, it would be thought rather elegant.

Either way, James Fox might hope to marry well. True, from the point of view of an English bride, his position as a solicitor lacked the social cachet of the barrister who appeared in court. But the Paris connection, the fact that James and his father were invited to embassy receptions and had dealings with the aristocratic world of diplomacy, added to his status. A young woman who hoped to marry a diplomat might settle for a life in glamorous Paris with a professional man of solid family fortune. With the French, his position was even better. The British Empire was at its zenith; it had a monarchy, which many

French secretly craved; and the British pound sterling bought a great many French francs. Less aware of minor English social distinctions, the French saw only a prosperous English gentleman. Even a rich family like the Blanchards might have considered him.

Except, of course, that he was Protestant.

Every week he attended St George's Anglican Church near the Arc de Triomphe, or sometimes the nearby American church of the Holy Trinity, just south of the Champs-Élysées, where the cousin of J. P. Morgan the banker had been rector for decades. Some of the Foxes' French friends were Protestant, but the majority, naturally, were Catholic. As his father had told him since his early childhood: 'Many of our dearest friends are Catholic, James. But although there's no need to talk about it, always remember that you are a Protestant.'

So on Sunday, when James had found himself staring at the fair curls and blue eyes of Marie Blanchard, and known, instantly and irrevocably, that this was the woman he wanted to marry, he had also realised that it was madness.

Monsieur Blanchard would almost certainly forbid it. His own father would not take kindly to the idea at all. There would be the inevitable wrangle about the children's religion. As a lawyer he knew only too well how even the nicest families could be broken apart, wills altered and worse, the moment one crossed the religious divide.

And besides even that, it was very clear that there might be an offer from de Cygne, a rich aristocrat of impeccable religion.

He was wasting his time even thinking about Marie.

But James Fox was a patient man. He didn't give up easily.

The Trianon where the Sun King would retreat with Madame de Maintenon from the formality of his court was a charming country house built of stone and pink marble. The nearby Petit Trianon of his successor Louis XV was a doll's house by comparison.

'This is where we are reminded that the Bourbons were humans after all, and not gods,' Roland remarked. 'And also that they were vulnerable. For this tiny palace of the Petit Trianon became the favourite retreat of poor Queen Marie Antoinette in the years before the Revolution.

'And now, my friends, if you will permit me, I will offer you this reflection upon the meaning of Versailles. Consider first: it was almost entirely built by Louis XIV with additions by his successor Louis XV, in variations of the classical style. Architecturally, it has unity. Second, let us remember an astonishing fact of French history. The Sun King lived so long that he saw his son and grandson die before him. As a result, it was his great-grandson, a little child, who succeeded him. From 1643 until 1774 – over a hundred and thirty years – France was ruled by only those two kings, Louis XIV and XV. Add the quarter-century of the next reign – that of Louis XVI and his queen Marie Antoinette – and you are at the French Revolution. From the seventeenth century until the Revolution, with very little interruption, France is ruled not from Paris, but from the court of Versailles.

'But now let me tell you why, for me, Versailles has a certain melancholy. Think of the Sun King, so anxious to bring order to France, aided by the Catholic Church, which is fighting back with all its baroque power against the Protestant Reformation. He seems to succeed, he makes France the greatest power in Europe. But he overreaches himself, becomes involved in ruinous wars, sees his family die and instead of a secure succession, leaves a half-ruined kingdom to another child, just as he was. Imagine what his grief must have been.

'The new century sees a gilded age, and the Enlightenment, to be sure. But also financial difficulties, the loss of France's colonies in Canada and India to the British, and ends with the Revolution, when the Paris mob forces poor Louis XVI and Marie Antoinette to return to Paris, and the guillotine. With this, the age of Versailles comes to an end. Everything its builder had hoped for has been utterly destroyed.

'Yet perhaps that is why Versailles is so haunting. It is an entire world that suddenly ended, and remains in all its perfection, frozen forever, just as it was when they dragged the king and queen away to their deaths.'

There was one last site to visit. It was quite close by. While Roland walked ahead with Marie and her brother, Fox followed with Hadley.

Fox liked this intelligent American friend of Marie's brother. They chatted briefly about their visit. 'De Cygne's an excellent guide,' said Fox.

'Yes.' Hadley gazed at the three people ahead of them. 'They make a handsome couple, our aristocrat and Marie, don't you think? Blond, blue-eyed . . . He'd be quite a catch for her, wouldn't he?'

'I suppose so,' said Fox calmly. 'Has he made any declaration?'

'Not yet. Marc would have told me, I'm sure.'

'What about Marc?' Fox inquired. He asked partly to make conversation, and partly because, if he was going to have any chance in his hopeless quest for Marie, he'd better discover everything he could about the family.

Hadley chuckled.

'Not exactly. My friend's in a rather different kind of trouble.'

'What's that?'

'Do you keep secrets?'

'Every day of my professional life.'

'Well, Marc's got himself in a bit of trouble with a girl. Hardly uncommon. But his father's so angry he's cut off his allowance.' And he gave Fox a brief account of the circumstances.

'It's unfortunate, but hardly a scandal,' Fox remarked when Hadley had finished. 'As a lawyer, I see something similar almost every week.'

'It's the choice of family, I think. Marc's father feels bad about that. And that the girl's family are going to throw her out. Blanchard feels responsible for her.'

'I commend him for it. Plenty of rich men wouldn't. Have they made any plans for the girl, and the baby, assuming it's born?'

'Not yet.'

Fox was thoughtful. It might be that Hadley had just told him something rather useful.

And now they had come to the one little corner, among all the huge palaces and formal spaces of Versailles, that was completely eccentric.

'*Voilà!*' cried de Cygne. 'The Hamlet.'

Marc had heard of the artificial village where Queen Marie Antoinette liked to dress up in a simple muslin dress and a straw hat and play at being a peasant woman. With its mill, and dairy and dovecote, the little hamlet was her private domain where no one could enter without permission.

'It was just a toy village to amuse a poor little rich girl, wasn't it?' he said.

'History is not fair to Marie Antoinette,' Roland replied. 'In fact the hamlet – it's a model Norman village in fact – really functioned and provided food for Versailles. Plenty of people dream of a private retreat, especially if they're trapped in a formal world like the court of Versailles. It's got a rustic charm. But it wasn't built until 1783. She hardly had six years in which to enjoy it before the Revolution brought her life to an end.'

It was certainly a charming spot to walk around. Hadley and Marc had strolled to one side with James Fox, so Roland took his chance to question Marie a little further. He asked her if she had enjoyed the visit, and she said she had.

'I could see that you're well acquainted with the history of Versailles. I hope my commentary for our friend Hadley didn't bore you.'

'Not at all. I enjoy historical places and family stories. But I really don't know so much.' She smiled. 'My aunt Éloïse says I should read more.'

'There is no need,' he said firmly. 'But what do you enjoy doing?'

'The usual things in the city. We go to the opera. I have asked Marc to take me to the Folies-Bergère, but he hasn't yet. I think my parents may have brought me up too strictly.'

Roland smiled. It was a charming little flirtation.

'Your parents are quite right. I go to the Folies-Bergère myself, however.' Would he take his wife to the Folies-Bergère? He could imagine Marie persuading him to do it, and the thought was quite delightful. His bride, of course, must be pure. But from all he had seen today, he felt sure that when her husband taught her the ways of love, this demure and charming young woman would be an eager pupil.

'You spend time in the country as well?'

'We have a house in Fontainebleau. I go riding in the forest there.'

'You like to ride?'

'I enjoy it, but I only ride occasionally. I should like to ride well.'

'It takes a little hard work.'

'I don't believe one can do anything well if one isn't prepared to work at it, monsieur.'

'This is true.'

'But apart from this, monsieur, my relationship with the country-side is too like that of Marie Antoinette at the Hamlet. I only play at it.' She paused. 'We do own a vineyard that my father bought, however, where I always go down for the harvest. I work with the women picking the grapes. It's not very elegant, but I love to do it. I think perhaps I am happiest at the vineyard.'

Ah, thought Roland, she was not just a rich bourgeoise, then. She had a feel for the land. An aristocrat should be elegant in Paris, but know how to run an estate. He thought he could see Marie learning these dual roles.

The four men wanted to take a brief turn in the ornamental gardens before they left. It was only a short walk to the Grand Canal in the centre of the park, and Roland led the way. As they reached the Grand Canal, he let them wander about, and for the first time since their arrival he found himself momentarily alone and able to observe them.

The January afternoon would be closing in soon. The clouds were so high that it seemed they had scarcely moved at all since the place was built. The Grand Canal ran down the centre of the lower gardens. Louis XIV and his court liked to gather there for boating parties. But the canal was empty now, grey as the sky. Only Marie and her brother, Fox and Hadley stood like shadowless statues by the stony water's edge, and all around them the vast formal terraces, geometric gardens, the endless parterres and distant fountains – all empty, all silent.

And it came to him with great force that if he married Marie, he would be bringing into his life a warmth and comfort that was not to be found in these huge, echoing spaces where the hand of man clipped hedges with geometric precision, and the eye of God, hidden behind the grey-ribbed clouds, saw all and judged all, against the pattern of His greater and still more fearful symmetry.

The life of the French aristocrat was full of ghosts – of kings, and ancestors and great events all moving about like shadows in an echo-ing garden. Like all ghosts, they were strangely cold, and the posses-sion of them set him apart in ways he could scarcely explain himself, and which Marie Blanchard would neither share nor probably wish to share. She would bring him the warmth he needed. But could he tolerate that warmth? And would she tolerate the cold ghosts that he must also live with? He did not know.

To his surprise, he suddenly had a great desire to ask his father what he thought. He'd talk to him as soon as possible.

It was ten days later that Jules Blanchard was surprised to receive a visit from James Fox, who asked if he might speak to him alone.

Sitting down in his little library, the polite Englishman opened the conversation carefully.

'In our work between London and Paris, monsieur,' he began, 'we often find ourselves asked for advice on family matters of all kinds. And we are always glad to be helpful whenever we can. Some of these are private matters requiring discretion. Others are relatively simple.' He paused only briefly. 'At the moment,' he continued, 'I have two clients in England who have asked for help. One is a very straightforward matter. There is a nice, respectable family in London who would like to find a nanny for their children. They want the children to grow up speaking French and so they are looking for a Frenchwoman to act as nanny and governess until the children go to school. You have such a huge acquaintance that I thought I would ask if you might know of anyone.'

'I'm not sure,' said Blanchard. 'I can ask my wife. What's the other matter?'

'The second is much more private, and requires discretion. But having had dealings with you, and having the pleasure of meeting your family, monsieur, I feel I may confide in you – with your permission.'

'Certainly.'

'This concerns a family who live outside London, clients of our firm for two generations now. Sadly, after some years, this couple have been unable to have children, and they want to adopt a child. They do not mind whether it is a boy or a girl. It's easy enough, of course, to obtain a child from one of the many orphanages, but they would like to find a baby whose parentage is known, and one who is likely to be able to benefit from what they have to offer. And that is a great deal. The father is a banker, and the mother, whose own father was a professor, is a lady of considerable artistic talent. Our

London office has no suggestions at present, but asked me if I could help. Unfortunately, I don't myself know of anybody who might have an appropriate baby needing parents. But given your huge acquaintance, I thought I'd ask if you might discreetly let this be known on the grapevine.' He spread his hands. 'Whoever their adopted child finally is, he or she will be fortunate. They live in the most pleasant circumstances.'

This was followed by a long silence.

'I see,' said Jules Blanchard.

Fox said nothing.

'And you don't know of anyone in Paris who might fit the bill?' asked Blanchard.

James looked him straight in the eye.

'No,' he said.

'Liar,' said Jules quietly, and smiled. 'But I am grateful for your discretion. So you are offering me a wonderful solution to two problems that I have. Will this cost me something?'

'I don't see why it should. A ticket on the ferry to England perhaps.'

'You've gone to a lot of trouble. Why?'

'Both families are clients of the firm.' He looked thoughtful. 'Priests often arrange these things. They have the information, and the judgement. And it's well that they do. But I like to think that lawyers can sometimes make a contribution too.'

'If this works out,' said Jules, 'I shall be in your debt, Monsieur Fox.'

'Then you will pay me a compliment,' said James, 'by knowing that I do not consider that any debt has been incurred at all.'

It was nicely said, even if it wasn't quite true. He just needed Marie's father to be grateful to him.

Roland de Cygne arrived at his father's house early that evening. Just before leaving the barracks, he'd heard news which pleased him.

Émile Zola, that tiresome writer who'd made such a nuisance of himself over the Dreyfus affair, was about to be arrested. The rumour was that he'd got wind of it and was already on his way to hide out in England.

'Just so long as he stays out of France,' one of his brother officers had remarked. And Roland agreed with him.

He'd written to his father soon after the visit to Versailles. Without being specific, he'd told him he'd like to ask his advice about a personal matter. The vicomte had written back at once. Knowing that Roland's regimental duties made it difficult for him to take time off so soon after a period of leave, he'd informed his son that he intended to take the train up to Paris that day, and offered him dinner at the house. It was good of him to make the journey, Roland thought with affection. He was looking forward to their meeting.

The train his father took normally arrived late in the afternoon. The coachman had been sent to the station to meet him. They hadn't got back when he arrived at the house, but he'd been quite content to sit with his old nanny in the meantime. An hour had passed quite pleasantly, but then the old lady had looked at the little clock on her mantelpiece and remarked that either the train was very late, or that the vicomte had missed it. Dusk had already fallen, but there was another train arriving two hours later. No doubt the coachman would wait at the station for that one.

This was quite annoying for Roland. It meant that the time he'd planned to discuss Marie with his father would be greatly curtailed. But there was nothing to be done about it. He poured himself a whisky.

Another half hour passed. Then there was the sound of the bell being pulled at the front door. Without even waiting for a servant, Roland went into the hall and went to the door himself, ready to welcome his father.

Buy it wasn't his father. It was his friend the captain. He'd come from the barracks.

'My dear fellow,' he said. 'A telegram came for you to the barracks. I wasn't sure how urgent it might be, but knowing you were here, I thought I'd bring it around to you myself. I think it comes from your family's château, by the look of it.'

'How very kind of you. Won't you come in?'

'No. I must get back in a moment,' the captain said. But Roland noticed that he didn't move to go at once.

He opened the telegram.

It was brief. It announced that his father had suffered a seizure that morning. And that he had departed this world soon afterwards.

He bowed his head and handed the telegram to the captain, who read it in silence.

'I am so sorry,' the captain said. 'If you need to stay here, I'll take care of everything at the barracks.'

'I hardly know what I should do,' said Roland.

Chapter Thirteen

1898

Love was not eternal. Human love, at least. Only the love of God was eternal, and ever-present. Marie knew this.

Love might come suddenly, unsought, from a place not looked for, and stay for a while before departing into the distance, to a place where it cannot be reached.

Or so it said in novels, plays and stories.

But life was not like that for Marie Blanchard, or anyone she knew. She would marry someone from a family like her own. He might be a man like her father, or a banker, a lawyer, a doctor, someone from a family with money. He might be one of their neighbours on the boulevard Malesherbes, like the Prousts. Or he might be from one of the big families in Fontainebleau with their fine houses in and around the town, and their big apartments in Paris. He might come from one of the wealthy shipping families in one of France's ports, or one of the regional insurance families. His family might own a newspaper in the provinces, or even in Paris. He would be a few years older than herself.

They would live surrounded by a network of cousins, and have children and grandchildren. And one day, when she departed this life, Marie would have the satisfaction of knowing that, though she would be gathered into the arms of the Almighty, here on earth she would live on through the ever-broadening family she left behind, and be remembered by them.

It was quite simple. It was what she knew, or thought she knew.

The first thing that she noticed about him at the Sunday lunch was how handsome he was. She was careful not to stare at him. The demure manners of her strict upbringing prevented her from making a fool of herself.

She had not met anyone quite like him before. He came from a different world. That had made her curious about him at once. So she listened, and watched.

And she had been glad that they were to meet again so soon.

The day after the lunch party, her father called her into his little library and told her to sit down.

'Tell me, Marie, you and your brother are going to Versailles with Monsieur de Cygne this coming Saturday, are you not?'

'Yes, Papa.'

'And why is that, do you think?'

'Monsieur de Cygne was kind to offer a tour so that we could show the palace to Marc's American friend.'

'That is true. But it is also an excuse. I think de Cygne is taking you all to Versailles so that he can discreetly get to see more of you.'

'Do you know this?'

'No. But I think it is likely, and so does your mother. I think, quite simply, that he wishes to get to know you better. Have you any objection?'

'No, Papa.'

'Do you like him?'

'He was rather severe about Captain Dreyfus.'

'A lot of people are getting far more angry about this Dreyfus affair than he was. Do you find him agreeable in other ways?'

'It is too early to say, Papa.'

'That is fair. You and he may find you have nothing in common. But if you do come to know each other better, and if one day he were to make a proposal, you would have to consider carefully. It would be a marriage which, socially, many people would envy. But I do not wish you to consider that at all. There should be no question of your marrying a man for whom you do not feel affection. You would also have to consider that his way of life and his attitudes are different from ours. I know and like his father, who is a charming man. But he is an aristocrat. In a sense, he is apart from even a rich family like ours. He does not consider himself the same kind of human being as a Blanchard. Under the charm and good manners of almost all the aristocrats I know, there is a certain snobbishness, even a coldness towards the rest of humanity. Not always, but often. Keep these thoughts in your mind and use your judgement. No one can do this for you.'

'Yes, Papa,' she said.

Versailles had been a success. She felt that she'd done herself credit, and she was fairly sure that de Cygne had been impressed with her. And the little walk in the Galerie des Glaces had been a triumph.

She only did it because of him. He must find me very strait-laced, she thought. They say the women in America are much more free in their manners than well-brought-up women are in France. I'm sure he thinks me dull.

So she'd seized the opportunity to do something a little unusual. De Cygne and Fox had certainly admired her performance. He hadn't said anything. She'd hoped he would, but he hadn't, which was vexing.

So she'd have to try something else to get his attention, next time they met. But when would that be? She wondered if she could suggest some expedition to Marc, without letting him guess her purpose of course. That would be too embarrassing. But she hadn't seen Marc for over a week. There seemed to be a coldness between Marc and her father, though she had no idea why.

She found a book on America in her father's library, and read that. It was all about great spaces, and railways across the plains, and the huge opportunities for the continent's future trade. She read it all, and she made notes of questions she could ask the American when they did meet. Questions that would show that she wasn't just a pretty rich girl without a thought in her head.

Once her father came upon her reading the book and asked her with surprise what she was doing.

'When I met that American friend of Marc's,' she said, 'he seemed quite nice, but I couldn't think of anything to say to him, because I know almost nothing about America. I found the book in your library.'

'Well, it's a good book, but hardly women's reading,' he remarked with a smile. 'If we go to the bookshop, I'm sure we can find you something more amusing.'

'You could buy me a book and surprise me,' she suggested. 'But there's no hurry.'

After all, it wasn't as if she was going to marry Hadley. That was quite impossible.

It wasn't often that Éloïse Blanchard received a message from her brother asking for her advice. Naturally, she came at once.

'What do you think of Roland de Cygne?' he asked, as they sat alone in the salon.

'He's all right in his way. I haven't much in common with him, myself.'

'And if he married Marie and made her happy?'

'I should try to like him – if he made her happy. Why? Is he going to?'

'Not at present, it seems. I have just had a letter from him, with the sad news that his father suddenly died. There will be something in the newspapers tomorrow, he thinks.' Jules paused a moment. 'Given my friendship with his father, I might have expected to receive a *faire-part* announcement in due course, but he was under no obligation to write to me like this.'

'Perhaps, with Marie in mind . . .'

'The thought occurred to me. Including her in a party to visit Versailles hardly constitutes a declaration of interest, but the letter suggests that he wishes me to know his situation. He writes that for the moment, he will be in mourning – which might go on for some time in an aristocratic family like that. He also has to decide whether to resign his commission and take over the running of the family estate – to settle down in the country, as he puts it – or to continue his military career.'

'If he settles down, he'll want a wife. If not, he may stay single.'

'Ah. You think so. That's how I read it as well.'

'Jules, he has committed himself to nothing. He merely indicates that Marie should wait and see what, if anything, he decides to do. I think it's arrogant.'

'You're a little harsh. He is risking that Marie could marry someone else in the meantime. I think he is quite honest. The poor fellow's not sure what to do.'

'You would say that. You're a man.'

'Well, we shall have to wait and see. I am writing to him at once to express my condolences. His father was a good fellow. But this brings me back to Marie. I have a small problem, and I need your help.'

'Ask it.'

'James Fox, the lawyer. He's being very helpful about this trouble with Marc. He may have found a position for the girl, and a couple to adopt the baby. Both in England. Well out of the way.'

'Excellent. He seems discreet.'

'Entirely. He's a good man. He's proposing to include Marie and Marc in a little cultural expedition, like the one de Cygne organised to Versailles.'

'Do you object?'

'Not in the least. Whether de Cygne will want to join them now seems unlikely. But I need a chaperone for Marie.'

'Isn't Marc going? He was her chaperone at Versailles.'

'That was different. At that time, neither de Cygne nor Fox had any idea about the scandal. But now Fox does, and I expect the American may know too. It will lower our entire family in their eyes to think I'd send Marie out with such an unfit person as chaperone.'

'Has Marie herself any idea about Marc's little problem?'

'Of course not. Even Marc would not tell her, I am certain.'

'Of course not. As you say.' Éloïse sighed. 'Why is it, my dear brother, that people of our class bring up their young women in such complete ignorance until they are married? Don't you find it absurd?'

'Perhaps. But you know the rules. If I don't bring her up that way, she won't find a husband. At least, not one we'd want. She must be pure.'

'One can be pure without being ignorant.'

'That has never been proved,' her brother answered, wryly.

'So you want me to be her chaperone?'

'You wouldn't mind?'

'When?'

'The second Saturday in March.'

'Ah. Then I can't. You know I will do anything for Marie, but I have promised to spend that weekend with friends at Chantilly.'

'In that case, either her mother or I will have to go.'

'Is that so bad? It might be a pleasant outing.'

'No doubt. But I do not wish to spend an afternoon with Marc.'

'My poor Jules,' said Éloïse. 'You'll have to forgive him one day.'
Her brother did not answer.

Frank Hadley was enjoying Paris. Every morning, as soon as there was enough natural light, he would start work – sometimes drawing, painting or studying. By mid-morning he was usually working with one of several artists in their ateliers. Three days a week, after a light lunch, he spent a couple of hours with a student who gave him French lessons. In the evenings he went out to meet his growing circle of friends. No matter how difficult it was at first, he spoke nothing but French, and tried to read as much as possible in French too. As a result, his French was improving rapidly. His greatest friend remained Marc Blanchard.

There had been one awkward moment.

'Did you tell Fox about my problem with Corinne Petit?' Marc suddenly asked him one day.

'I did. When we were at Versailles. I apologise, Marc. I don't know why I did it. I'm an idiot.'

'Just don't do it again.'

'I certainly won't.'

'As it happened, you did me a favour.' And he told Hadley what Fox had done.

'Why would he do that?'

'Simple enough, I should think. He's helping three of his family's clients in one transaction. I dare say he reckons that the more he shows my father he can trust him, the more of my father's business may come their way.' He smiled. 'As for our family's little secret, I'm sure it's nothing compared to some of the stuff he knows about his clients.'

Hadley nodded.

'By the way,' Marc continued, 'you won't ever mention this business to Marie, will you?'

'Of course not. Never. But you don't think she might hear?'

Marc shook his head.

'Not a chance. In the same circumstances, would an American girl know?'

'Girls from respectable families are brought up with very strict morals. But they're not shrinking violets. They usually have some idea of what's going on.'

'If my parents have anything to do with it, not a word of this will ever be spoken in front of her. She will be totally innocent.' He grinned. 'But don't worry, Hadley, I can introduce you to plenty of girls who aren't so respectable.'

Frank Hadley considered.

'So tell me,' he said quietly, 'where does Mademoiselle Ney fit into all this respectability?'

Sometimes, Marc had to admit, his private life was getting too complicated. Women found him attractive, he told himself. That was the trouble. Apart from two models and the banker's wife who'd sat for him, and Corinne Petit, of course, there had been numerous casual encounters.

Hortense Ney, however, was a very different matter.

At first, he had hardly known what to make of her. Though she was not yet married, it was clear that she had long ago reached the age of independence. She spoke little, yet was very much in control of herself. When he asked her to sit down across from the window and look across to the wall on his left, so that he might study her for a while and see how the light fell across her face, she sat very still, her expression unsmiling and quite immobile. She was slim, her face pale. She wore a long skirt, and an elegant jacket closed tightly up to her neck, the sleeves with a small, fashionable puff at the shoulders. The ensemble was topped off by a little hat with a feather. Everything was neat, controlled, buttoned up.

So that it was hardly surprising that Marc experienced a growing curiosity to discover what lay underneath this cool, closed perfection.

'Were you expecting to be painted sitting down?' he asked after a while.

She did not turn her face towards him, but her shoulders moved just enough to suggest a shrug.

'I suppose so.'

'I am going to ask you, if you please, to stand up and this time to look towards me. If I move about, do not turn to look at me, but stay in the same attitude.'

He did move about. She kept perfectly still.

'If I asked you to stand like that for an hour or two,' he asked, 'do you think you could do it?'

'Yes.'

'I shall provide you with a chair to stand beside. I should like you to come next time wearing a dress, something that you might wear in the evening, open at the neck. Naturally, your hair will be coiffed as though you were going to a dinner party. Please also bring a fan.'

'As you wish, monsieur. That is all for now?'

'Yes. I have made some quick sketches of you. Now I have to study them.' He smiled. 'Most carefully. It will take me many hours.'

'Oh.' Her face, just, registered surprise.

'You only have to return,' he said pleasantly, 'but I have to begin to understand you, and I have much to learn.'

It was a line he had used a few times already. It usually worked.

She had come for her sittings once or twice a week. He had discovered gradually that, though she didn't talk much, she was well-informed. She saw all the exhibitions, went to galleries, plays, and sometimes the opera, although music interested her little. She attended charity events and was even a trustee for one or two. It seemed that she knew a good deal about her father's legal practice, and Marc soon realised, from small remarks Hortense let fall, that she had a sharp eye for making money.

But she had never given any hint of interest in sex. Hadley came by one day during a sitting and afterwards remarked: 'That's a cold, prim woman.'

It might be so, but to Marc, there was something about her, something contained yet erotic, that made him all the more curious. By the third week, he started making small moves, delicate suggestions, to see if he got any response.

He didn't. She observed him calmly with her brown eyes, but gave him nothing for his pains.

A month had passed before one afternoon he found it necessary to rearrange the line of her dress over her breasts. Stepping forward to do so, he paused a moment longer than he need have.

'Are you trying to make love to me, monsieur?' she quietly demanded.

Taken aback, he hesitated.

'Why do you ask?'

'I have had that impression for some time.'

389

'I am sure it would be interesting,' he said.

'Perhaps. There is only one way to find out.'

'Assuredly.'

It was a week later, coming to see his friend, that Hadley had found her at the studio wearing only a sheet she had hastily draped over herself. He had beat a hasty retreat, but later Marc had confessed to him: 'It's quite amazing. I just can't get enough of her.' He'd nodded thoughtfully. 'Or she of me.'

'And she seemed so cold. Is this her first adventure?'

'No. Her first was a long time ago. In Monte Carlo. She's very careful. Has adventures when she's away.' He grinned. 'I am the first in Paris.'

'Congratulations.'

As Fox looked at the party going to Malmaison, he knew he was lucky. But he was nervous as well.

He was lucky because he'd got exactly whom he'd wanted. Marie and her brother, of course, and Marc's friend Hadley. He was glad to have the American there, both because he was a nice fellow, and also because he provided cover. But luckiest of all, he'd got both Marie's parents as well. And in its way, this was even more to his purpose than having Marie herself.

Part of the reason both Jules and his wife came, he supposed, was his choice of venue. When he'd told Jules, the older man had been most intrigued. 'No one's been there for years. I didn't know one could even get in.'

'I just wrote and asked,' said Fox blandly. He did not say that his letter had also mentioned the fact that he'd like to show the place to the family of the owner of the Joséphine department store.

De Cygne had not been able to come, so there were six of them altogether in the big landau Fox had hired.

They were joined by one, tiny additional passenger. For a week ago, Jules Blanchard had given his wife a charming present: a brown-and-white King Charles spaniel, to which she was already devoted, and who came with them on the trip.

It was a jolly party. If Jules Blanchard was barely on speaking terms with Marc, one would never have known it. The puppy, a tiny, fluffy ball of life, kept them all amused as they rolled pleasantly along.

But James Fox was nervous, and with good reason. The more he had thought about his strategy, the more correct it had seemed. But even without de Cygne – who could reappear any day – his chances were not good. Any attempt to court Marie, to declare his interest openly, and he could be quite certain that her family would make it impossible for him to see her again. They might like him, but he was a Protestant. His only hope, therefore, was to become so much a part of their family that they would make an exception for him. He must become like a brother to her.

Could he manage to conceal that he was in love with her? His English manners helped. With perfect self-control, he could become her best friend without giving himself away. But he still needed to see her regularly.

How to accomplish this? He could see her father on business more often. That was a start. But it didn't get him into Marie's company. And he certainly couldn't invent an expedition like this every week.

Today gave him the chance to work on both her parents. He must watch for opportunities somehow. He had to find a way into their house on a regular basis.

So he wasted no time in pleasing Madame Blanchard.

'As an Englishman, madame, your choice of puppy gives me particular pleasure,' he pointed out. 'This breed originated in England a couple of centuries ago. Although,' he smiled, 'there are certain perfidious persons who say that they were brought to England by the French princess who married our King Charles.'

'They're becoming very popular,' said Marie.

'Yes. But let me tell you something. People have been breeding these little spaniels with pugs, thinking this will make them even neater-looking. And the results are not entirely successful. Whereas I can see that the dog you have comes from the pure old breed, which I think is better.'

'He's quite right, you know,' said Jules. 'That's exactly what the breeder told me.'

As for his wife, she gave Fox a smile that told him that he'd scored a point.

'There's a dog exactly like that in an early painting by Manet,' Hadley remarked.

'He knows everything,' Marie cried delightedly.

'He certainly does,' said Marc with a grin. 'Soon, Hadley, you'll know more about France than we do.'

'You're setting me up for a fall, I see,' Hadley answered amiably. 'And by the way,' he added, 'I know almost nothing about this place we're going to.'

Marie was impressed. They had scarcely arrived at the gate before a balding, middle-aged man came hurrying out to meet them. After briefly greeting Fox, he turned at once to her parents.

'Monsieur and Madame Blanchard? I am the private secretary of Monsieur Iffla, and he asks me to present you a thousand apologies. He had particularly hoped to meet you. But then this morning he had word that his niece was sick, and so he was obliged to go back into Paris to see her. But he hopes you will enjoy your visit here. I am to show you anything you wish.' He bowed and smiled. 'Monsieur Iffla and his nieces are great admirers of the Joséphine department store,' he continued, 'and it is a great honour to welcome you to the house of the Empress Joséphine who, I understand, inspired your choice of name for your store.'

'Monsieur Iffla is very kind,' said Jules, and one could see that he was flattered.

What a good man Fox was, thought Marie. What trouble he had taken to ensure a fitting reception, and to give her parents so much pleasure.

For if Jules Blanchard was rich, Monsieur Iffla's wealth was on a completely different scale. Born in Bordeaux, of a Moroccan Jewish family, he had taken a Christian wife, and emerged from a career in banking and investment one of the richest men in France. Not only his wealth, but his magnificent acts of philanthropy had earned him the nickname Osiris – the Egyptian god, the Lord of Life.

And if it weren't for Osiris, this charming national treasure of Malmaison would probably be in ruins.

It was a manor house, really, whose elegant proportions earned it the title of château. Or, since it lay not four miles west of the Bois de Boulogne, one might almost call it an intimate suburban palace.

It was a few years after the French Revolution when Joséphine de Beauharnais had bought the little estate after marrying the rising young general Napoléon. By the time he returned from his campaign in Italy, the young conqueror found that Joséphine had already spent far more than he could afford on improvements to the place. But in the end Joséphine's extravagance had produced a delightful retreat, where she'd lived herself until her death. Since the days of Napoléon, the house had had several owners until it had been occupied and stripped by the military in the war of 1870, from which it had not recovered.

But now Osiris was taking the place in hand.

'It will still be years before we have entirely restored the place,' the secretary explained, 'but Monsieur Iffla has a fine collection of Napoleonic objects which will find a natural home here. He is a great admirer of the emperor.'

'What does he admire in particular?' Marc inquired.

'Many things. But especially that Napoléon gave the Jews religious freedom.'

As they walked through the house, their guide pointed out the music room; the fine dining room in the Pompeian style; the council chamber which had been decorated to look like the inside of a lavish military tent; and the library, which might have belonged to a Roman emperor. These were full of Napoleonic character. But Marie and her mother preferred the rich but charming room of Joséphine with its canopied bed.

'One must always remember,' their guide remarked to her, 'that Joséphine became elegant, but she was also a little exotic. She was brought up amid plantation life in the Caribbean. That was perhaps what fascinated Napoléon: that she was different.'

'I have never travelled anywhere,' Marie remarked.

'You have plenty of time, mademoiselle,' he said kindly. 'Plenty of time.'

One of the last rooms they visited was the Salon Doré – a salon that had once been beautifully gilded, but was now in a state of terrible disrepair.

'This was horribly damaged in the war,' the secretary remarked. The curtains had been torn to shreds, he explained, the furniture had had to be thrown out, even the gilt panelling had been smashed.

At one side of the room, on a table, were various items that had been salvaged. These included a rather nondescript chess set, which caught her father's eye. He smiled.

'I have read that the emperor Napoléon was an indifferent chess player,' he remarked. 'Too impatient. Perhaps Joséphine was better.'

'Papa took up chess recently,' Marie told them all. 'But he doesn't practise.'

'I'm so bad that no one wants to play with me,' her father said. 'And Marie refuses to learn.'

She noticed Fox looking thoughtful.

'Do you play, Monsieur Fox?' she asked.

'Funnily enough, I'm in the same situation as your father,' he replied. 'Perhaps we should play occasionally?' he suggested to Jules.

'My dear Fox,' her father replied, 'this is a stroke of fortune. Why don't you come around one evening? What about Thursday?' He glanced at his wife.

'I hope you will dine with us,' she said to the Englishman. 'Just *en famille*. Then you two men can play chess afterwards.'

Fox bowed.

'You're very kind. I should be delighted,' he answered.

Marie gave him a smile. She liked the way he made her father happy.

The little park outside was delightful. Marie walked between Fox and her father, while her mother was accompanied by Marc and Hadley. Marie was quite content, but she quite often glanced at the American and wished that she, and not her mother, was beside him. Their guide, meanwhile, was explaining the challenge that the park presented.

'The empress Joséphine kept all kinds of exotic animals here. Ostriches, zebras, even a kangaroo. This we cannot replicate.' He smiled. 'The original park was larger. The real question is, what can be done about the plants?'

And now Marie's mother gently intervened.

'The empress had an orangerie with all kinds of rare plants, from around the world. And her rose garden changed the history of gardening.'

'My wife knows a great deal about gardens and plants,' Jules said proudly.

'Then you will know, madame, that the empress Joséphine's huge collection of roses was wonderfully recorded by the artist Redouté.'

'And her lilies too,' Marie's mother corrected. 'I have several prints at Fontainebleau.' She looked about. 'A garden takes much longer to build than a house. I think you'll have to leave the rose garden until later.'

It was this little exchange that gave Marie the chance to bring the American into the conversation.

'What sort of gardens do you have in America, Monsieur Hadley?' she asked. 'Are they anything like our European gardens?'

'Not as good, I have to say,' he answered easily. 'The traditional garden of Colonial America is usually not large, but somewhat formal, with clipped box hedges, quite geometric. A modest version of what you find in some French châteaus, or old English gardens, I think. My parents have a garden like that at their house in Connecticut.' He smiled. 'Our houses are quite modest. My parents' house is typical.' And he briefly described the pleasant white clapboard house his parents occupied, with its picket fence and quiet old trees.

'It sounds enchanting,' Marie said.

'It is. But it's not at all French,' he said.

'Why so?'

'Because I have noticed that in Europe, people put walls around their houses if they can. They defend their privacy as if they lived in a little fortress. And the bigger houses are set up to suggest the social status and power of their owners. The big plantations in the south have some of that character, but up in the north-east, our tradition is more democratic. There was never a lord of the manor. Equal citizens got together to elect their local officials. Our houses, big or small, have low fences. It's all about being a good neighbour.'

'These are the ideals of the French Revolution,' Jules remarked.

'Tell me, sir, your house at Fontainebleau is a château?'

'Not at all. It's in the town. But it has a very nice garden.'

'And what encloses the garden?'

Jules laughed.

'A high wall.'

'Perhaps Monsieur Hadley should see the garden,' suggested Marie, 'to judge for himself.'

'We'll arrange it some time,' said her father.

'The truth is,' said Marc, 'that most Frenchmen know only two things about America: Lafayette and Buffalo Bill. I think we should all come to America to visit you, Hadley.'

'You'd be more than welcome,' Hadley replied. 'My parents would be glad to repay some of your hospitality. Come in the summer and we can all go up to the cottage in Maine.'

'A cottage,' said Marie. 'That sounds even more charming. Does it have a thatched roof?'

'When Americans like Hadley speak of a summer cottage,' her brother explained, 'they mean something different. I've seen a photograph of the Hadley summer cottage. It's a huge shingle house on a rocky coastline, with the sea on one side and a lake on the other.'

'It's a pretty nice place,' Hadley admitted. 'The sun comes up over the sea and sets over the lake. It's wild but comfortable.'

'Do you row on the lake?' Marie asked.

'I do.'

'He rowed for his university,' Marc told them. 'You can see he's built to be an oarsman.'

The conversation turned back to the delights of Malmaison after that. But on the way back, though she tried not to look at him, Marie to her surprise found herself imagining Hadley rowing across the wild American lake, his shirt open, and his thick mane of hair blowing in the wind.

One other member of the party was also lost in thought on the journey back, but his concerns were very different.

He was thinking that he now had four days to learn to play chess.

Fox's first evening visit was a great success. Before the meal he chatted easily with Marie and her mother, and played with the puppy just as if he were a member of the family.

At dinner, he talked delightfully about his childhood in England and holidays up in the wilds of Scotland. The conversation turned serious for a little while when he and her father discussed the latest vicious quarrels in the newspapers over the Dreyfus case. But he then told a story of two brothers getting into a fight over Dreyfus and suing each other, which was so absurd that they were all in fits of laughter.

Afterwards, he and her father had their game of chess. It was a close thing, they both agreed, but in the end Fox prevailed. This pleased her father even more than if he'd won.

'I want my revenge next week,' he demanded.

'I could manage Wednesday or Friday, but not Thursday,' Fox replied. 'On Thursday I go to the opera.'

'Wednesday, then,' said Jules, with a quick glance at his wife.

'Dinner will be at eight,' she said with a smile.

Two days later Marie was amused to see her father reading a chess manual.

Marie went to see her aunt that weekend. Unlike the rest of her family, Aunt Éloïse chose to live in a quarter that was not fashionable. The apartment lay just south of the university Latin Quarter near the Luxembourg Gardens, but it was large and light, and the walls were hung with paintings, mostly of the Barbizon school and the Impressionists that had followed it, all of which she'd bought herself over the years. She was delighted to see Marie and wanted to hear all her news.

'What of Monsieur de Cygne?' she asked.

'We have heard nothing recently. My father says that he took extra leave to deal with his father's affairs and the family estate.'

'And what do you feel about him?'

'It is flattering that he may have taken an interest in me.'

'And that he may again.'

'He is very agreeable, but I hardly know him. That is all I can say.'

'You have no other prospects at present?'

'If I have, nobody has told me. Aunt Éloïse,' she went on, 'will you please tell me if my father and Marc have quarrelled.'

'What makes you think they have?'

'Marc never comes to the apartment any more, and Papa doesn't want me to visit his studio.'

'You'd have to ask them if they've quarrelled. I might not know. Perhaps your father doesn't think you should disturb Marc in his work.'

'But I never see him.'

'Well, you can certainly meet him if he comes here, or if I take you both out. Your father cannot object to that.' She paused. 'If we go out, I may ask him to bring his American friend. I think he's a good influence on your brother. Would you mind?'

Marie's heart missed a beat.

'I don't mind. Monsieur Hadley seems nice enough.' She shrugged. 'As far as I can tell.'

In the coming weeks she met Marc several times at her aunt's. He was usually with Hadley.

She noticed that Hadley's French was getting very fluent now. Not only that, he was picking up all kinds of the idiomatic expressions the French love. Instead of saying, 'To return to the subject', for instance, he'd say: *Pour revenir à nos moutons*, 'To return to our sheep'. He might say, 'He bores me stiff.' But he might also say *Il me casse les pieds*, 'He breaks my feet.' And this new confidence with the language made a difference in their relationship.

He began to converse with her.

He'd talked before, of course. But when he sat down on the sofa beside her at Aunt Éloïse's apartment and turned to her, and looked into her face seriously with his handsome eyes and asked what she thought of the Dreyfus affair, or some other piece of current news, or whether she liked a particular painting by Manet, and why, she experienced two reactions.

She felt short of breath. It wasn't the questions. It was the fact of his presence, so close to her, the fact that her heart would palpitate, she hardly knew why. She managed never to blush; she was grateful for that. She made herself concentrate very hard on everything he said as if he were a teacher in a classroom, and made herself think hard before she replied. That got her through.

'You look a bit distressed sometimes, when you're talking to Hadley,' Marc told her. 'But you mustn't mind him. It seems the American girls are used to discussing all kinds of things and having their own opinions in a way that men wouldn't care for here.'

But the other reaction she experienced was even stranger to her.

It was a thrill of a new kind of excitement. She felt uplifted, as if this stranger from another world was taking her into a new and larger life. To a place where she could grow, like an exotic plant, become a person she had never dreamed of being before.

So when Marc asked her if she was still finding his friend a little difficult, she replied: 'No. He's American, but I'm getting used to it.'

★   ★   ★

Early in May, Aunt Éloïse announced that she and Marie were coming to visit Marc in his studio. They came late in the afternoon. The light was good, and it looked as if Marc had tidied the place up before their coming. Against one wall was a settee and chair where visitors could sit, and a low table on which he'd set out some refreshments. His easel stood about twenty feet away, with a low dais and chair for a sitter. Stacked against the far wall were two sets of canvases, one set face out, the other reversed. Beside them was a plan chest for drawings, a roll of canvas and a pile of stretchers.

'This portrait,' – he showed them the painting on the easel – 'is almost complete. What do you think?'

The picture showed a slim, pale woman in a long dress, her unsmiling face half turned towards the viewer. The effect was one of conventional formality, yet there was a hint of ambiguity in the depiction, as if it were the frontispiece of a short story that the audience was waiting to be told.

'Who is she?' asked Marie.

'Mademoiselle Ney, the daughter of a lawyer. Father got me the commission, which was good of him.'

'There is something hidden yet sensual about this woman,' Aunt Éloïse remarked.

'Really?' Marc looked at her. 'How interesting you should say that. I can't see it myself. She is highly respectable, I assure you. And her father is paying handsomely for it.'

'No doubt,' said his aunt, drily. 'May we see some more?'

For ten minutes or so he showed them paintings, drawings, sketches, of people, landscapes, animals, some finished, others not.

'Well, Marc, I can see you've been working. And I am very glad of it. Are you happy in your work?'

'I am.'

'And what of those?' Aunt Éloïse indicated the stacked canvases.

'Oh. Things I've abandoned. Canvases I'm going to paint over.'

'May we see them? You never know, Marc, artists are not always right about their own work. There may be something good in there.'

'Absolutely not.' He gave his aunt a hard look. 'There's nothing there that I wish you and Marie to see.'

Aunt Éloïse bowed her head.

'I understand, Marc,' she said. 'An artist must always protect his reputation.'

Aunt Éloïse seemed well pleased with the visit, Marie thought. As for herself, she was delighted.

As they were leaving, she noticed Aunt Éloïse slip a roll of banknotes into Marc's hand. Her aunt thought she wouldn't see, but she did.

'Why did you give Marc all that money?' she asked after they had left.

'Oh,' said Aunt Éloïse, with scarcely a moment's hesitation, 'I owed him for a painting he bought for me.' But Marie wasn't sure that this was true.

It was two weeks later that her father told Marie he had received a letter from Roland de Cygne.

'He writes that after much consideration, he has decided to rejoin his regiment and devote himself to his military duties. I think that means he has decided not to settle down and take a wife just yet. At all events, we shall not be seeing him for a while. His regiment has been posted to eastern France.'

'I am sorry not to see him, Papa, but I am not hurt,' Marie replied. It was always agreeable, she supposed, to know that such an eligible man might be a suitor; so she could not help feeling that she had lost something. A little status, perhaps.

'I must confess, I'd rather hoped he might have pursued you,' her father said frankly. 'And until I knew whether he might, I didn't look too hard for other candidates.'

'We'll both keep a lookout, Papa,' she said.

'And he'll be a lucky man,' he replied, and kissed her.

'Marie,' her aunt told her the following week, 'I have a very important errand. Your brother's friend Hadley wants to meet Monet. Marc tells me he's quite set his heart on it.'

'But they say he never sees anyone nowadays,' Marie objected, 'unless he already knows them.'

It was years since the great painter had retreated to the quiet village of Giverny, some fifty miles out from Paris, on the edge of Normandy. For a time he'd known peace there. But gradually, young artists had started making pilgrimages to Giverny to see him. A regular artists' colony had developed. Nowadays, in self-preservation, Monet had been forced to close his doors, in order to get any work done.

'There is someone in Paris who may be able to give me a special dispensation,' her aunt said with a smile. 'I'll pick you up tomorrow.'

The rue Laffitte was hardly a ten-minute walk from the family apartment: across the columned front of the Madeleine, past the Opéra, and then the rue Laffitte was on the left. It was a straight, narrow street. On its modest journey northwards, it encountered other, larger thoroughfares with famous names: the boulevard Haussmann, the rue Rossini, the rue de Provence, rue La Fayette, rue de la Victoire. But humble though it was, the rue Laffitte contained some of the best art galleries in Paris.

They had just crossed the Boulevard Haussmann when, ahead of them, they saw Marc and Hadley waiting. Moments later, they were in the gallery.

Monsieur Paul Durand-Ruel was already in his sixties, though he looked ten years younger. He was a dapper man with a small moustache and kindly eyes, and as soon as he saw Aunt Éloïse, those eyes lit up with pleasure.

'My dear Mademoiselle Blanchard. Welcome.'

Aunt Éloïse quickly made the introductions.

'My niece Marie has been here before, Marc I think you know, and this is Monsieur Hadley, our American friend who is studying art in Paris for a while.'

There was no particular show at the gallery at that moment, but a selection of gallery artists hung on the walls. As they went around together, Durand-Ruel chatted amiably.

'Your family still has the house near Barbizon?'

'At Fontainebleau, yes.'

'Back in my father's day,' the dealer explained to Marie, 'your aunt was buying members of the Barbizon school from us. She has two Corots, I think. And then, when I began to promote the Impressionists, as we call them now, your aunt was one of our first supporters.'

'Tell them how that adventure began,' said Aunt Éloïse.

'Our first exhibition of Impressionists was not in France at all,' Durand-Ruel explained. 'During the German siege of Paris, in the war of 1870, I managed to get out and go to London. Monet, Sisley and others were painting there at that time. I made their acquaintance, and was so excited by their work that I organised a show in London, on New Bond Street. Then in the seventies, we started Impressionist shows here in Paris. And people laughed at us. They said we were mad. But your aunt saw the light. She was one of the few. She bought Manets, Monets, Renoirs, Pissarros, Berthe Morisot, the American Mary Cassatt . . .'

'It was you, monsieur, who single-handedly brought the Impressionists to New York,' Hadley interposed.

'You are very kind,' said Durand-Ruel. 'And may I congratulate you on your excellent French. It is true that we opened a New York gallery, and also that the American collectors were wonderfully receptive to the Impressionists, far more so than the French at that time, I must say.' He turned to Aunt Éloïse. 'But you must have a remarkable collection yourself by now. Wherever do you put them all?'

'In my apartment,' said Aunt Éloïse, simply. 'But they are scattered about in every room. Most people don't even know what they are.' She paused. 'This reminds me. I have a favour to ask of you.'

'Ask it.'

'Our friend Hadley here would like to visit Giverny, and I thought we might all go up there. I know that Monet is besieged by people wanting to take up his time, but I wondered if you might give us an introduction . . .'

'With the greatest pleasure. I shall tell him that you were one of the first to acquire his work – he likes to sell, you know! – and that you have the work of all his friends. He will be delighted to receive you. If you care to look around the gallery, I'll write the letter straightaway.' And he disappeared into his office.

Marie was fascinated. She had always known that her aunt was cultivated and that she bought pictures, but she had never realised quite how far this went.

'I must look at the pictures in your apartment more carefully,' she whispered to her.

Meanwhile, Marc and Hadley were moving from picture to picture. After a few minutes, she noticed that Hadley had remained in front of one in particular for some time.

'Let us see what Monsieur Hadley is looking at,' she said to her aunt.

It was a painting of the Gare Saint-Lazare. Clouds of steam were rising from the railway tracks, as seen from behind a bridge above. The thing had an extraordinary life, and Hadley was gazing at it with rapt attention.

They were standing beside him admiring the painting when Durand-Ruel came back.

'This should do,' he said, as he handed Aunt Éloïse the letter. He looked at the painting. 'You like it?' he asked Hadley.

'I love it,' Hadley replied.

'Many artists have painted the Gare Saint-Lazare, including Monet, but this is by a painter named Norbert Goeneutte. He painted at least three of Saint-Lazare in different lights.' He paused. 'I'm sorry to say that he died, about four years ago. He was hardly forty years old. A considerable talent, lost.' He paused. 'It's for sale.'

'I'd love to buy it,' Hadley said frankly. 'But my father gives me an allowance to study, and I don't want to ask him for more. Perhaps later – though I'm sure you'll find a buyer for such a fine work long before I can buy it.'

Durand-Ruel did not press the matter.

And it was then that Marie had her wonderful idea. But she didn't say a word.

They set out early from the Gare Saint-Lazare. The train took them fifty miles down the broad valley of the Seine to the small town of Vernon. From there, it was only a four-mile ride in a cab, crossing the river by a long, low bridge and following the curve of the stream up to Giverny.

As the train puffed through the delightful countryside, Marie felt a great sense of happiness. Her little plan had worked.

Five days ago Aunt Éloïse had bought the Goeneutte painting for her. It was a private matter between themselves, and nobody else knew about it. Aunt Éloïse had the painting now, safely in her apartment, but it was agreed that when Marie could, she would buy the painting from her at the same price that Aunt Éloïse had paid the gallery. There was only one other aspect to the business, that even Aunt Éloïse did not know.

One day – she did not know when, or under what circumstances – Marie was going to give the painting to Frank Hadley.

The Seine was broad and very peaceful at Vernon that June morning as the *fiacre* clipped across the bridge. Here and there they passed small houses, or an old mill, with their charming, half-timbered Norman frames and tiled roofs. Everything seemed wonderfully green. It was late morning when they passed the church and came to the centre of Giverny, leaving them time to have a pleasant walk about the village before having lunch at the inn. After that, they were to call upon the great painter.

'There's something strange about this place,' Marc suggested. 'Does anyone notice what?'

'No,' they said.

'Then I'll show you.'

They had gone only fifty yards, and were walking by a small orchard, when they encountered a pleasant young fellow carrying a folder and wearing a wide-brimmed hat.

'Excuse me,' Marc said in English, 'but could you recommend where to get a drink?'

'Why certainly,' the young man answered, in an accent that suggested he came from Philadelphia. 'I'd recommend Monsieur Jardin's little café, where you can get an aperitif. Or of course, there's the Hôtel Baudy. I'd say that's the best place in the village.'

'Thank you,' said Marc.

A few moments later they saw a couple approaching. 'Go on,' he told Hadley. 'You ask this time.' And sure enough the couple responded the same way, in English.

'Where are you from?' Marc asked.

'New York,' they said.

'All right,' Hadley laughed. 'You've made your point. The place has been overrun by my countrymen.'

'I doubt this village has more than three hundred French inhabitants,' Marc said. 'And there must be another hundred American artists living here as well.'

'A gross exaggeration.'

But as they passed an old mill, they heard American voices within. And seeing a handsome old monastery on a slight rise, Marc asked a local French villager whether it was still a religious house and was told, no, a charming couple called MacMonnies had just moved in there.

Yet it had to be said, the invasion of artists seemed to have brought no harm to the village. The Americans were evidently quiet, and an easel propped up at the edge of a field, or by the riverside, did nothing to disturb the natural economy.

But if the rest of the village had absorbed the visitors without fuss, one family had seen its opportunity and seized it.

The Baudy family owned the stout inn of geometrically patterned brick that bore their name, in the middle of the village. And their enterprise was obvious as soon as the little party reached the building.

'Look at that!' Marc cried, as they approached.

For there, on a grass plot just opposite the hotel entrance, were two well-maintained tennis courts.

'Tennis courts, in the middle of rural Normandy! Those have certainly been put there for the visitors. I doubt that the villagers even knew what they were.'

Entering the hotel, they at once found notices which announced that the hotel had stocks of all kinds of art supplies, of the best quality – paints, brushes, canvases, stretchers – everything that a resident artist might need. In the spacious dining room they found the walls covered with paintings by its many patrons.

Sitting down, they were offered all kinds of drinks, including whisky.

'Whisky for the Americans, eh?' Marc commented cheerfully.

'Perhaps, monsieur,' the waiter answered, 'but Monsieur Monet always likes to drink it.'

They enjoyed a pleasant lunch. Everyone was conscious that they were about to meet a great artist, but Marc filled in a little more background for them.

'He may surprise you. He was poor for a long time, but he had a patron named Hoschedé, who owned a department store. When Hoschedé became bankrupt, the two families lived together, and finally after both Monet's wife and Hoschedé had died, Monet and the widow married. Monet is an artist, but he's determined not to be poor again, and a part of him wants to be a rich bourgeois. He's been

405

like a paterfamilias to both families for years.' He grinned. 'You'll find him very solid.'

'How do you rate him as an artist?' Hadley asked.

'You know what they say of him? He is the great eye. He may not think as much as some artists, but he sees, perhaps more than any man living.'

And then it was time to see the master himself.

Marie noticed his clothes first. Though it was quite a warm day, Monet was wearing a three-piece suit, the long jacket fastened by a single button over the chest, the other buttons left open, so that the jacket fell comfortably loose. He sported a folded white handkerchief in the breast pocket. But she knew enough to see at once that the coat was made of the finest cloth and had been made by a first-rate tailor.

His hair was cut short, and brushed forward. He had a full, rich beard. His face was large-featured and strong, the eyes luminous, but powerful. Had she met him in the garden of the family house at Fontainebleau, she might have taken him for the owner of an industrial enterprise, or possibly a general.

His wife, a stately, matronly woman, seemed to be of a similar type.

He welcomed them to his domain, addressing himself especially to Aunt Éloïse.

'I was so delighted, madame, to receive the letter of Durand-Ruel, which gave me and my wife the opportunity to welcome you to our house after all these years.'

He suggested that they might like to visit the garden first, and speak in the studio afterwards. And putting on a large, broad-rimmed straw hat, he led them outside.

The main building was a long, low farmhouse with green shutters, set close to the lane, its walls pleasantly covered with flowering plants and creepers. On the garden side of the house, in the centre, stood a pair of yew trees, between which a broad path led down through the garden.

But there all resemblance with any garden Marie had seen before came to an end.

The garden was not a wilderness. Far from it. For a start, everything was divided into carefully planted flower beds, though they were placed so close together that one could hardly walk between them. There were fruit trees and climbing roses. But having placed them, Monet left the plants to develop a life of their own. The result was a richness and profusion that was astonishing.

'I plant for colour,' he explained. 'I have daffodils and tulips, hollyhocks and daisies, and poppies. Sunflowers. All kinds of annuals. In late summer the nasturtiums appear and cover the path. And then friends bring me all kinds of things, rare plants from all over the world, and I find a place for them all.'

This rich riot of colour filled over two acres.

'I should have brought my mother,' Marie exclaimed.

'Bring her another time,' he said kindly.

If she ever took him up on the offer, Marie thought, she'd better find some quite amazing and exotic plant to bring.

They wandered about very contentedly, chatting about the garden.

'I paint plants,' he remarked genially to Marc and Hadley. 'I sell the paintings, and with the money I buy more plants. It's a harmless kind of lunacy, I suppose.' He turned to Aunt Éloïse. 'Would you like to see my pond?'

'By all means.'

For this it was necessary to leave the garden by a small gate at the bottom that gave on to a little local railway line.

'There's no station here,' he explained, 'but once in a while a train comes by, so we take care as we cross the tracks.' And he gave Aunt Éloïse his arm.

Once across the tracks they entered another enclosure, entirely different from the first.

'We rented the house for years before I was able to buy it,' Monet explained. 'Then, five or six years ago, I was able to buy this plot across the tracks, where there was a small stream, and this enabled me to create a pond. And here,' he said proudly, 'is the result.'

If the main garden was a paradise of plants, this new domain was like a dream.

Willows and delicate bushes fringed the pond. Water lilies floated upon its surface. And at a certain narrow point, a local craftsman had constructed a curved, wooden Japanese bridge over the water. Up by the house, one looked at flowers. Here one looked at lilies floating in a watery world, and at the reflection of branches, leaves, flowers and the sky and clouds above, in the soft, liquid mirror of the pond. They walked on to the bridge and gazed down, in silence.

'We started the pond in '93,' Monet said. 'But one has to wait for things to grow. Nature teaches us patience. I didn't start to paint a thing down here until '97.'

'I think it could become an obsession,' said Marc.

'I have always painted light striking objects – a building, a field, a haystack. This is different. The colour is different. And you are right. Water draws one in. It's very primitive. Mysterious. I think I shall be painting these lilies for the rest of my life.'

They walked slowly back. As they came to the railway line, Monet again offered Aunt Éloïse his arm. And following suit, Hadley offered his arm to Marie, who took it. And as she did so, never having touched him before, she felt something suddenly run through her so that she involuntarily trembled.

'You all right?' he asked.

'Yes. I'm just afraid of trains. I used to have dreams of getting stuck on a train track when I was a little girl.' What was this nonsense she was talking? Did she sound like an idiot?

He took her arm firmly.

'It was grizzly bears for me.' He grinned. 'No trains coming. Tell me if you see a bear.'

Safely across the tracks, he let go of her arm, and she gave a little gasp.

'You're that relieved?' he said in a friendly voice. 'We'd better keep you off the tracks.'

As they made their way back through the garden, she felt the sun beating upon her head.

Monet's house had two studios. The first had formerly been a small barn, and he showed them some work there, including one of the Japanese bridges he was working on. The second studio was larger. In here, he turned to Marc and remarked: 'You were saying that the pond could become an obsession. I will confess that recently I have been haunted by a dream for a huge project. It would be a huge room, circular, with enormous panels of lilies, floating in the water, and a hint of cloud perhaps. One would be completely surrounded by this great essay in blue light. I say blue, but of course

I mean a thousand colours, mixing and reacting like the plants in the garden. For when colours interact, they create new colours, that one has never seen, or known that one has seen with the eye before.'

'Such an obsession would be a life's work, monsieur,' said Marc appreciatively.

Monet nodded. Then he glanced at Marie. By chance, she was standing beside Hadley at that moment. His eyes took them both in.

'So, this handsome American gentleman is your fiancé?' he asked.

'My . . .' She was completely taken off guard. She had not been prepared. She felt the deep blush coming into her face and it was no good, there was nothing she could do to stop it. 'No, monsieur,' she stuttered.

'Ah,' said Monet.

'I've no such luck, monsieur,' said Hadley cheerfully, and glanced at Marie in a friendly way. But she could not look at him.

Then Aunt Éloïse said something to Monet, and he answered her, and the conversation moved on, and nobody seemed to notice her any more, for which she was grateful.

A few minutes later, it was time to leave. As they were moving towards the doorway, Hadley turned to Marie and remarked quietly, 'I hope Monet didn't embarrass you by thinking we were engaged.'

'No,' she said. 'It was nothing.' And she wanted so much to say something else. Something to make him think of her. 'I'm sure you've got prettier ladies to consider,' perhaps. Something. Anything. But she could not.

As they waited on the platform for the train at Vernon, Marc and Hadley were deep in conversation, while Aunt Éloïse and Marie quietly chatted.

'I think that was a very successful visit,' said Aunt Éloïse.

'Yes. Monsieur Monet was really glad to see you. And I think he was glad to show off his garden.'

'It's a marvel,' said Aunt Éloïse. 'A marvel.'

When the train came they all got in. Soon they were clattering back towards Paris.

'Well,' said Marc, 'Hadley and I have come to a decision.'

'And what is that?' asked his aunt.

'I'd thought of spending time down in Fontainebleau during the summer, but' – he gave his aunt a look – 'that may not be possible just at the moment. So Hadley and I are going to take lodgings up at Giverny for the summer. We shall paint up there.' He smiled. 'We'll see you all at summer's end.'

'Oh,' said Marie.

There was an ancient peace at Fontainebleau. The Royal Château and its quiet park were older by far than Versailles. The place had first been used by King Philip Augustus, back in the twelfth century. But the main inspiration for the present palace came from the French Renaissance, in the time of François I and Leonardo da Vinci. And though Napoléon had used it as his personal Versailles, old Fontainebleau, with its shaded alleys, and huge forest nearby, retained a settled, quiet air that the stark magnificence of Louis XIV's huge palace entirely lacked.

As for the town, it was quiet, and conservative, and full of cousins.

It was a pity, Marie thought wryly, that none of her cousins was the right age. Then she could just have married one of them and everyone would have been happy.

'At least when you marry a cousin,' one of them had truly remarked, 'you know what you're getting.'

So she walked the puppy, and visited her cousins, and took riding lessons because she might as well improve her skills. 'In case another aristocrat comes along,' she told her mother with a smile.

But she did not find much peace.

Where was he? At Giverny. What was he doing? Painting out of doors, sketching, eating and drinking with the other artists there.

Was he still speaking French? Or was he relapsing into English with the American colony in the village? Was he with a woman? Had he met a charming American girl, an artist perhaps, from a good family like his own? Would Marc write and mention casually that his friend was engaged?

She imagined him, in this situation and that. Her imaginings did not fade away. They grew stronger, worse, as the days went past.

And she had no one to share her troubles with. She could not tell her parents. She loved her cousins, but none of them was a confidant.

She was a little afraid even to tell her aunt Éloïse. And the one person she might have confided in, Marc, was Hadley's friend, so that was impossible. As the days of July went by, apart from her physical and social activities, she read, or pretended to read, and took up desultory needlework, and tried many times, with indifferent success, to sketch the puppy playing in the garden.

Her brother Gérard came down with his family twice to stay the weekend. Her father had left the business largely in his care for the summer, and he would come down and sit with his father on the big veranda, and give him reports that were generally satisfactory. Once Gérard had taken her aside.

He knew she didn't like him. But he was trying to be nice. She understood this. He was doing his best. But his best wasn't very good.

'I'm sorry that things didn't work out with de Cygne,' he remarked.

'They never really started,' she said.

'I know. All the same, that would have been something . . .'

'He might have turned out to be a bad character.'

He shrugged.

'We're going to look out for someone. We have more friends than you think. God knows, you're pretty, and you're going to have an excellent dowry. Really excellent. It's amazing that you're not married already, but you're an excellent catch.'

'That's a comfort.'

'But you've got to look out for a husband, Marie. Do you know what I mean? It's not about waiting for a knight in shining armour. It's about seeing what's out there, and making some choices. One's just got to be practical.'

'And that's it?'

'It is.' He smiled encouragingly. 'That's the wonderful thing. It's all quite simple. Well, it is if you've got money.'

'Is that what your wife did?'

'Absolutely.'

'And you're both happy?'

'Yes. We're very happy.' He gave her a look that was surprisingly full of affection. 'Totally happy.'

And she realised that he was.

'Thank you,' she said.

*   *   *

She was relieved when her father invited Fox down for a weekend. At least he didn't talk to her about marriage. As always, he was easy company. And he liked the family house.

The Blanchard house at Fontainebleau was typical of its kind. In structure, it was a smaller and provincial version of an aristocratic mansion. One entered from the quiet street through a pair of high iron gates into a cobbled courtyard with a pavilion wing on each side and the main house in the centre. The main entrance was up a broad flight of steps, the house being raised over extensive cellars. Above this was a floor of bedrooms, with attics above that. The salon, on the left of the front door, was large and extended all the way through, giving on to a broad veranda which ran the length of the central house and overlooked the gardens.

Seen from the garden, when the family gathered on the veranda, it looked exactly like a picture by Manet.

If the big salon, with its classical, First Empire furniture, had a Roman simplicity and repose, the garden had a character of which both Marie's parents were proud.

'Why,' Fox exclaimed when he saw it, 'you have an English garden.'

It was very long and divided into two parts. Close to the house, it was laid out with gravel paths, a small ornamental pond and fountain, flower beds of lavender, roses and other plantings, and a lawn. After fifty yards, a high, neatly clipped hedge formed a screen, with a wicket gate in the middle, through which one passed into an orchard. At the far end of the orchard, behind other screens, was a garden shed and compost heaps.

'My wife is in charge of the plants, and I am in charge of the lawn and the orchard,' Jules explained. 'Do you approve?'

'I certainly do,' said Fox. 'I could almost be in England.'

'Almost?' Jules nodded. 'My lawn isn't quite right. It's mown, but I have had difficulty in obtaining a roller. An English lawn would be rolled. How long does it take then, to get a truly English lawn?'

Fox looked at the two Blanchards, then at Marie, and gave a broad smile.

'Centuries,' he said.

They took him around the old château and walked in the forest and had a delightful weekend. And perhaps because he was not a threat to her emotional life, and because he was so clearly a nice man,

Marie felt more contented during his stay than she had for some time, and was sorry to see him depart.

Later in July, Aunt Éloïse came down for a few days. She enjoyed that. While she was there, a letter came from Marc. He and Hadley were getting along famously. They were both very productive, he reported. And the company was excellent.

What did he mean by that? Who was Hadley seeing? She could only wonder.

'Do you think we should pay them a visit?' she asked Aunt Éloïse.

'It means going to Paris first and then up to Normandy.'

'That's not so far.'

'I'll think about it. Perhaps I can arrange for you to see Marc without going to Normandy,' she said. But this was not quite what Marie wanted to hear.

In the month of August, all the inhabitants of Paris who were able to do so deserted the city. Jules announced that he would spend the entire month at Fontainebleau.

It was a week into August when he informed them that Fox was coming by.

'He wanted to stop on his way down to Burgundy. Naturally I said he's welcome.'

They were all glad to see him, but the manner of his arrival took them by surprise. For instead of a cab from the station, it was a cart that trundled through the iron gates into the courtyard. While the driver and his assistant went to the back of the cart, Fox got down looking pleased with himself.

'Are your bags so heavy?' Jules inquired.

'Not exactly. I have something for you.'

And then, down a ramp from the back of the cart, manhandled with some difficulty by the driver and his mate, there came a garden roller.

'*Mon Dieu!*' cried Jules. 'I can't believe it. Look at this,' he cried to Marie and her mother. '*Mon cher ami*, where the devil did you get it?'

'From England of course. I had it shipped.'

Marie laughed out loud. One had to love him.

And he insisted on giving them a demonstration of how to use it.

'If you do it right,' he explained, 'it's wonderful for strengthening all your muscles and stretching the back.'

It was half an hour later, entering the empty salon while Fox and her father were on the veranda, that Marie heard a few words of conversation that she did not understand.

'Everything is fine. Our young friend will soon be installed in London. As for the banker and his wife, they are delighted. Their daughter is a lucky girl.'

'Should I meet them? I feel I should like to.'

'I strongly advise against it.'

'You're right. I am very grateful to you.'

'Our firm is there to provide service to all our clients. But I think the business has gone well.' He paused. 'I must catch a train shortly. May I have the pleasure of calling in on you on my return? I shall want to inspect the lawn.'

'We look forward to it.'

After he had gone, Marie asked her father if Fox had also come to transact business.

'Yes. A piece of English business I had, as it happens. He's a good man.' He didn't elaborate further, and she didn't ask.

She did not hear a murmured conversation between her parents in their bedroom that night, however.

'I like Fox,' said Jules. 'It's a pity he's a Protestant.'

'So do I,' agreed his wife. 'But he's Protestant, all the same.'

'Yes. It's a pity, though.'

Nor did she hear a conversation a few days later when her aunt arrived to see her father.

'My dear Jules, it's time to forgive your son.'

'Why?'

'The Petit girl is installed in England. Her daughter is safely born and she has been adopted by a charming family like our own. Our troubles in this matter are over. The Petit family have disowned their daughter, which I consider an abomination, but sadly it's what many others would have done. The conventions of society are cruel. But Marc has been punished enough. God knows he has done nothing worse than many other young men of his age.'

'He hasn't been punished at all.'

'Of course he has.'

'He seems to live quite well, after I stopped his allowance.'

'He gets commissions.'

Jules looked at his sister affectionately.

'How much are you giving him, Éloïse?'

'If I were, I wouldn't tell you.'

'He's not suffering at all.'

'He is suffering by being deprived of his father and mother.'

'It must be killing him.'

'More than you know. He loves you.'

'I'll think about it.'

Marc and Hadley arrived at Fontainebleau for the last ten days of August. For Marie, it was a magical time. Sometimes they would go into the forest to sketch, and she would go with them, taking a book and a sketch pad herself, to keep them company. She and her mother conducted Hadley around the château, which he preferred to Versailles. In particular he liked the old tapestries that showed the courtly hunting scenes in their deep, rich colours.

In the evenings everyone would sit out on the veranda. Her father would often read the paper then, and Marc and Hadley would chat, while she quietly listened. At Marc's prompting, Hadley would talk easily about his childhood, of tobogganing in the snow, of his rowing days at university, or his year of ranching. Sometimes he would mention little things. 'When I was eighteen, my father gave me a pair of wooden hairbrushes. Dark hickory, with my initials carved on the back. I always take them with me. Some people have fancy ivory brushes, but I wouldn't change the hickory brushes my father gave me for anything in the world.'

He talked of his parents also.

'If I like to travel, I dare say I get it from them,' he remarked once. 'My father usually had spare time in the summer. Before I was born, they went to Japan, to England, to Egypt. And they'd take us children to all kinds of places too. When I marry,' he added easily, 'I hope my wife will want to travel with me. It's a wonderful thing to share.'

She listened to these and other things until, she thought, she knew everything about him.

One evening on the veranda, after they had spent the afternoon walking through the forest to nearby Barbizon where Corot had painted, Hadley threw back his head and closed his eyes.

'You know, I feel as if I've entered a beautiful, unchanging world,' he confessed to them. 'There's a softness in the light, a sort of echo everywhere in the landscape. I can't really put it into words.'

'Everyone is seduced by the French countryside,' said Marc. 'But you should also understand that we French are so conscious of our history – it's everywhere around us – that we all feel as if we have lived many times before.' He smiled. 'This may be a delusion, but it's a rich one, and it gives us comfort.'

'We also find comfort in the Church,' his mother added.

'Same wine, same cheeses,' said Jules pleasantly. 'Once a Frenchman, always a Frenchman.'

'French life has so much charm,' said Hadley with a contented sigh. 'I could imagine living here.'

Could Hadley really live in France? Marie wondered. She tried to imagine him living in the house in Fontainebleau. She thought of his sketches on the wall of the passage that led to the kitchen; the picture of the Gare Saint-Lazare she would give him, in the salon perhaps; and his hairbrushes, on the table in her father's dressing room.

Or would he live in America, and travel like his parents? He could have a house in France, she thought, and spend every summer here. Why not? His children could be bilingual.

One afternoon, Hadley and Marc were painting in the garden, and she came out to look at what they were doing. Hadley was painting a flower bed which contained some magnificent peonies in full bloom. So far, his painting looked like a glowing, almost formless sea of colour.

'I see what it is, but I'd never have thought of it like that,' she said.

'The difficulty isn't putting the paint on the canvas,' he answered quietly. 'It's seeing what you're painting. I mean, looking at it without any preconceptions about what it's supposed to look like. If you think you know what a peony looks like, then you'll never be able to paint it. You have to look at everything with fresh eyes, which is difficult.'

'I can understand that in painting and drawing, I think. I don't think it works for other arts, does it?'

'There are some writers who are trying to do something similar. Especially in France. The symbolists like the poet Mallarmé. And there are political revolutionaries too, who say we should start all over again and decide what the rules of society should be. After all, they were doing that when they destroyed the monarchy and attacked religion back in the days of the French Revolution.' He smiled. 'I dare say people have always been changing the rules ever since the Greeks invented democracy or man invented the wheel.'

'So do you want to change the world?'

'No. Because the world's been pretty good to me. But I like to try to discover the truth about how things look.'

She left him to his work and went back to the shade of the veranda. Then she took out her sketch pad. She started a drawing of the puppy. It wasn't any good, but if anyone asked what she was drawing, she'd have that to show them. Meanwhile, as her father buried himself in his newspaper, she turned to a fresh sheet underneath the drawing of the puppy, and she started to draw Hadley.

She tried to do exactly as he said, and just look at exactly what she saw. At first it didn't seem right, but gradually she realised that by concentrating her eye, she had produced exactly the line of his jaw, and his powerful neck, and the way his hair tumbled down in its strong, unruly way. And she found herself smiling as she realised how perfectly she knew him.

Later she and her mother went into the kitchen, and she helped the cook prepare the evening meal. And she insisted that the strawberry flan, which she knew Hadley loved, should be made entirely by her own hand.

Just before the end of August, James Fox called in on his return from Burgundy. One could see he'd been out in the open air. He looked fit and well.

Since the whole family was planning to return to Paris the following day, they suggested he should stay the night so that they could all go back together.

They had a large lunch that lasted until three in the afternoon. Then, rather than doze on the veranda, the whole family went for a walk to the old château – the two Blanchard parents, Marc and Marie, Fox, Hadley, and the puppy too. They walked about in the park for a while. It was hot. The little puppy was running about excitedly, but in the end even he got tired and sank contentedly into the slow lethargy of the August afternoon.

As they returned, the dusty streets of Fontainebleau seemed half asleep. The roadway glared in the sun while the houses, some stone grey, some brick, were shuttered against the brightness, getting what coolness they could from the sharp shadows falling from the eaves. As they reached the road that led to the house, they were the only people in the street, apart from a coachman dozing in a trap, drawn by a single horse, that was waiting outside one of the houses for someone to come out.

'The puppy's on his last legs,' Marie remarked to Fox. 'I'd carry him if we weren't so close to home.'

The little spaniel had been dragging his feet for some time. But curiosity had given him the energy to inspect a small bundle lying in the roadway. Marie glanced back and shrugged. The road was quiet.

It was a second later that they heard the loud bang of a shutter that someone had opened carelessly. Obviously they had opened the window as well, for there was a sudden flash as the glass caught the sun.

It was nothing. But it was enough to spook the horse in the waiting trap. Throwing its head up, it plunged forward, and before the dozing coachman could gather his wits and fumble for the reins, the trap was surging down the street.

The puppy did not see the trap coming up behind him. If he heard it, he took no notice. He was interested in the bundle, and its curious smells.

Marie screamed. Everyone turned to look.

She would never have believed that Fox, who was a tall man, could move so fast. Racing towards the puppy, he dived, scooped up the tiny dog in one hand, went into a roll and as the trap missed him by inches, emerged lying on the roadway with the puppy held above his head.

'*Mon Dieu*,' gasped Marc. A half second's error and the Englishman could have been seriously injured.

'Nice move,' called Hadley admiringly.

Fox stood up. He was dusty and one of his sleeves was torn.

'Cricket,' he said. 'Fielding practice.'

'Ah, Monsieur Fox,' cried Marie's mother gratefully.

But Marie was ahead of her. She ran up to Fox and kissed him on the cheek.

For just a moment Jules frowned. Not that he was shocked, but Marie wasn't supposed to do that.

Fox saw it.

'Well,' he said to them all, with great good humour, 'if I'd known I was going to get a kiss . . .' He strode across to Jules and handed him the puppy. 'Would you be so kind, monsieur, as to place this puppy in the road, so that I can do it again!'

Jules laughed, and relaxed. But his wife was looking at Fox's arm.

'You are bleeding, my dear Fox,' she said.

'It's nothing. I'll get cleaned up as soon as we're back.'

The letter was waiting for him in Paris on his arrival back at his studio. The next day, when Hadley came around, Marc showed it to him.

> *Mon Chéri,*
>
> *Welcome back. I long for you. Every time we make love, I only want you more, and I believe it's the same for you.*
>
> *But now, chéri, the time has come to make a decision. Is it going to be better than this with someone else, for you, or for me? I don't believe so.*
>
> *I want to have your babies. There is still time. You know that I am a woman of fortune. Why not make your life more easy? Why not have babies with a wife who loves you, instead of these mistresses who have children you have to hide?*
>
> *But if you decide that this is not what you want, if you don't want to marry me, then although I love you, chéri, I am leaving you to find someone who will give me what I want, and what I deserve.*
>
> *Think about it. Je t'aime,*
>
> *H*

As he passed the letter to Hadley, Marc shrugged.

'She wants to marry me.'

'Evidently.'

'What do you think?'

'You could do worse. How do you feel about her?'

'She never bores me. There is always something new. She has . . .'
– he searched for words – 'a ruthless intelligence.'

'Ruthless?'

'It fascinates me. And I also get a lot of work done when she's
around.'

'Marry her.'

'She's older than me.'

'That's not everything. She looks as if she'll age well.'

'I don't know. I don't know what my parents would think.'

'If you marry a woman with a small fortune and stay out of trouble, Marc, I suspect they can live with it.' Hadley shook his head.
'You'll have to make a commitment, that's all.'

'But I've never made a commitment in my life,' Marc objected.

'You could start.'

'I don't know.'

'You'll lose her. I don't think it's an idle threat. She'll go.' He stared
at Marc. 'I guess the question is, can you live without her?'

'I can live without everybody.'

Hadley sighed.

'Spoken like a true artist.'

Marc looked at him in surprise.

'You think so?'

'They say that most artists are monsters. Not all. But most.'

'I meant, do you think I'm a true artist?'

'Oh, I see.' Hadley smiled. 'Well, at least you're a monster. Be
grateful for that.'

He handed the letter back to Marc, who put it on the table.

'By the way,' said Marc, 'I promised Marie that we'd meet her at
rue Laffitte. We'd better get going. I'll think about Hortense on the
way.'

The Vollard gallery was just up the street from the older Durand-
Ruel gallery. Its owner was a gruff fellow. Unlike Durand-Ruel, he
did not support artists. 'He churns out work, buys a lot cheap and
sells it quickly. But he has the most interesting shows, all the same,'
Marc had told Hadley. 'In '95, he had a big show of Cézanne, who
most people had never heard of, and made quite a name for himself.'

They waited awhile for Marie to arrive, but as she didn't, they made themselves known to the owner.

Vollard was a large, sharp-eyed, bearded man. Marc asked to see a Cézanne. 'He'll deliberately ignore what I asked for and bring something else,' he whispered to Hadley, and sure enough Vollard returned a few moments later with a painting by Gauguin, a scene from Tahiti.

They gazed at the strange, exotic colours.

'It's powerful. Astonishing,' said Hadley.

'Come back in two months,' Vollard told them. 'I'm having a big Gauguin show.'

'What else would you like to show us?' asked Marc.

'What about this?' Vollard produced a small painting of the French countryside, the Midi somewhere, by the look of it. In some ways there were hints of similarity with the Gauguin painting. But there was a strange nervousness, a sort of cosmic urgency and fear in the work that was hard to define.

'Who's this?' Hadley asked.

'He died nearly a decade ago. His brother was a dealer. Small-time, but good.' Vollard shrugged. 'I bought some. Still got a few. They're not expensive.' He didn't sound very enthusiastic. 'Van Gogh is the artist's name.'

'I haven't heard of him,' Hadley confessed.

'Not many people have,' said Marc. 'Buy one if you like it.' He smiled. 'Just don't expect to make any money from it.'

They looked at some more work, hoping that Marie might still appear, but she didn't. After half an hour, they left. On the way back to Marc's studio, they stopped for a drink.

Marie was so annoyed with herself. She'd been shopping with her mother and mistaken the time. When she reached Vollard's gallery, he told her she'd missed her brother by ten minutes.

It was hardly a fifteen-minute walk from the gallery to her brother's studio, so she thought she'd go over there to apologise.

When she got to the street door, she found it open, so she mounted the stairs. At the door of the studio, she knocked and listened, but heard no sound. She tried the door. It opened.

'Marc?' she called.

Silence. Obviously he hadn't got back yet. She wondered whether to leave again, but thought she might as well wait a little while. Then, if he didn't appear, she could always leave him a note.

She moved around in the studio, looked out of the window, glanced at the stacks of paintings. She was quite tempted to look at them, but thought that he wouldn't like it if she disturbed them.

She sat down to wait. Twenty minutes passed. Perhaps he'd gone somewhere else, and it would make more sense to leave him a note. She looked around for some paper and something to write with. There was a letter already lying on the table. Idly, she picked it up. *Mon Chéri*, it began. A private letter, obviously. She shouldn't read it. She left it alone. She glanced at it again. She read it.

Then she heard steps coming up the stairs. Marc's voice. Hadley's too.

She quickly sat down again and tried to look unconcerned. But she was very pale.

Marc was surprised to see Marie sitting in his studio, but he smiled.

'We missed you at Vollard's!' he cried. 'Did you think we were meeting here?'

'No. It's my fault. I was shopping with Maman. I got there just after you left. I came round to apologise.'

Something wasn't right. She looked pale. Her voice sounded unnatural. He glanced at the table and saw the letter from Hortense.

He thought quickly. Personally he didn't care what Marie knew, but his parents did. Whereas if his American friend had been a naughty fellow, it wouldn't matter to anyone. Casually he picked up the letter, and handed it to Hadley.

'You shouldn't leave things lying around, *mon ami*,' he murmured.

Thank God Hadley had a quick brain. He read the situation at once.

'Ah,' he said quietly, folded the letter, and put it in his pocket.

They chatted for a few moments. It was hard to tell whether Marie had read the letter or not, and Marc certainly wasn't going to ask her. Then, after apologising again for missing them at the gallery, Marie said that she had to get back home.

After she'd gone, Marc turned to Hadley.

'Thanks for getting me out of that one,' he said. 'Have I ruined your reputation forever?'

Hadley handed him back the letter.

'Your sister's well brought up,' he said. 'I don't suppose she even read it.'

Half an hour later, Aunt Éloïse was most astonished when Marie arrived unexpectedly at her apartment. She was looking distraught.

'Whatever's the matter?' Éloïse asked.

Marie sat down on the sofa. For a moment she couldn't speak.

'Something terrible,' she cried. 'About Hadley. He has a mistress.'

Her aunt smiled.

'My dear little Marie,' she said gently. 'Hadley is a handsome young man. If he has a mistress, it wouldn't be so surprising, you know.'

'She wants to marry him.'

'This also is not unknown.'

'And he's already the father of a child. Quite recently.'

Éloïse frowned.

'How do you know this?'

'There was a letter. He left it on a table at Marc's. I read it.' She shook her head. 'It was terrible.' She started to cry.

Éloïse gazed at her.

'Do you mind so much what Hadley does?'

Marie did not reply. And now her aunt understood.

'My poor Marie. What a fool I am. I didn't think of it. You're in love with Hadley.'

'No. No.'

'Yes you are. Why shouldn't you be?'

'You must not tell,' cried Marie. 'Promise me you will not tell.' And then she wept as though her heart would break.

The note Aunt Éloïse wrote was very short. It was an order. She gave it to her housekeeper with precise instructions. Then she went back to looking after Marie.

She made her drink a little tea. She sat with her and talked quietly about the loves of women for talented men. She spoke of Chopin and George Sand, the woman writer who had loved him. And of Wagner, and how his last wife, Cosima, had left her husband to marry him instead. In truth, there was no particular plan in Aunt

Éloïse's conversation, other than to suggest how the nobles and best women might fall in love with men who had great gifts. Her main purpose was just to keep Marie's mind occupied until the house-keeper got back. At last, after nearly an hour, she did, and gave Aunt Éloïse a meaningful nod.

'Have a little more tea, my dear, and I shall rejoin you in five minutes,' her aunt told her as she left the room.

Down in the street, she found Marc waiting, as instructed.

'You are to tell me the truth at once,' she commanded. 'Marie read a letter. Was it addressed to you or to Hadley?'

'We thought it best to let her think it was addressed to Hadley. You know what Papa and Maman feel. Marie's not supposed to know anything like that . . .'

'I know. It's what I suspected. She thinks badly of Hadley, that's all.'

'Does it matter?'

'No,' his aunt lied. 'It doesn't matter in the least. Except that I am sorry Hadley should have to assume responsibility for things he hasn't done. It's not a nice way to treat a friend, who's a guest in our country.'

'That's true. I feel ashamed. What do you want me to do?'

'Nothing. Absolutely nothing. I'll deal with Marie.' She paused. 'I'm bored with all these lies, Marc. I'm just bored, that's all. Now go home.'

She gave Marie a glass of brandy first.

'If I tell you the truth, are you prepared to keep a secret? You must not tell your parents that you know. Will you promise me that?'

'I suppose so. Yes.'

'Good. Well then, I think it's time for you to be treated as an adult.'

'Oh,' said Marie when she'd finished. 'Marc has been very wicked, then.'

'My dear child, by the time you reach the end of your life, you will know so many men – and women – who have done the same or worse, that you will be forgiving.'

'And Hadley . . .'

'Was not the person to whom that letter was addressed. And so far as I know, he has not had an illegitimate child with anyone either – which your brother certainly has.'

'Then Hadley assumed the guilt for my brother. He's a saint.'

'No, he is not a saint!' cried her aunt with momentary irritation. 'And a good-looking boy like that has probably had a mistress or two by now.' She paused. 'So Marie, you love Hadley. Does he have any idea of this?'

'Oh no. I don't think so.'

'And if he wanted to marry you . . .?'

'I don't think Papa would allow it . . .'

'He comes from a very respectable family, as far as I know. Is he Catholic?'

Marie shook her head.

'I have heard him say to Marc that his family are Protestant.'

'And he will probably live in America. Can you imagine yourself living in America, far from your family? You'd have to speak English. It would be very different, Marie. Did you ever consider this?'

'In my dreams, I have,' Marie admitted.

'And?'

'When I am in his company, I am so happy. I just want to be with him. That's all I know.' She shrugged. 'I want to be with him, all the time.'

'I cannot advise you. Your parents will not wish to lose you, I am certain. But if you and Hadley truly wish to marry, and they believe you could be happy, then it's possible they would agree. I can't say.'

'What should I do?'

'In the first place, I think you should let Hadley know that you like him. It might turn out that he likes you more than you think. If he does not return your feelings, it will be very hurtful for you, but at least you will know not to waste your time.'

'How will I do that?'

Her aunt stared at her.

'I see,' she said, 'that I had better take you in hand.'

Hadley was rather surprised, a week later, to receive a message from Aunt Éloïse that she wished him to call upon her, but naturally he did so. When he got there, she welcomed him warmly.

'You've never really seen my little collection, have you?' she said. 'Would you like to?'

'I certainly should.'

It was quite remarkable what she had. Corots, a little sketch by Millet and country scenes by others of the Barbizon school. She had more than twenty Impressionists, a pretty little scene in a ballet school by Degas, even a small van Gogh that she'd got for almost nothing from Vollard.

Then, suddenly, he stopped in astonishment.

'I wanted to buy this painting,' he cried.

'The Goeneutte of the Gare Saint-Lazare?'

'Yes. But I couldn't. So you bought it.'

'Not exactly. Marie asked me to buy it for her. She's going to buy it from me when she can. I didn't know you liked it too.'

'She has good taste,' he remarked. 'Well, I guess if I can't have it, I'm glad it's gone to one of your family.'

'Marc has talent, of course. How much remains to be seen. But Marie has a very good eye. She'll have her own collection one day, I'm quite sure.'

'That's interesting.'

Aunt Éloïse smiled.

'Marie has been brought up to be quiet. But there's more to her than you think.'

They talked of his time at Giverny and the work he was planning for that autumn. It was all very pleasant. She didn't seem to have any other object in inviting him to visit her, but he was certainly glad that he had come.

He heard a sound at the outer door. Then the maid announced that Marie had arrived.

'Ah,' said Aunt Éloïse as Marie came into the room. 'My dear, you couldn't have arrived at a better moment. Look who I have here. Our friend Hadley.'

'So you do,' said Marie, and gave him a delightful smile.

'Come and sit down,' said her aunt.

Hadley gazed. Something had changed about Marie. He wasn't sure what, but she was different. She was looking wonderfully well, but there was a little glow of confidence in her manner. In some undefinable way, the girl with the blue eyes and the golden curls had suddenly become a confident young woman.

426

She hadn't got married in the last week. And he was quite sure she hadn't been having an affair. But whatever it was, he suddenly realised that Marie was intensely desirable. Had she changed her scent?

'It seems Hadley wanted your picture of the Gare Saint-Lazare,' Aunt Éloïse remarked.

'Perhaps we should give it to you,' said Marie.

'Oh no. You must enjoy it,' he said quickly. 'But I shall be content to envy you.'

Aunt Éloïse mentioned a few of the other paintings in the apartment that Hadley had liked. Then she rose.

'I must leave you with Marie, Hadley,' she said. 'I have something to attend to. But I shall be back in a moment.'

They sat in silence for a few seconds.

'Your aunt has a wonderful collection,' said Hadley, still trying to make out what had changed in Marie.

'Yes.' Marie paused. 'Hadley,' she said, 'I think I had better tell you, I know all about Marc.'

'Oh?'

'The letter, the woman and the baby.'

'Oh.'

'My aunt Éloïse decided it was time I grew up.' She smiled. 'But don't tell my parents that I know.'

'No.'

'I think in America, it's different. American girls are not so sheltered.'

'It's not that different.'

'Well, my aunt thinks it's absurd. I'm quite old enough to be married.'

'Yes.'

'But I'm kept in a state of idiotic innocence. So that's over. Perhaps you disapprove.'

'Oh, no.'

'It was very nice of you to take the letter from my brother, the way that you did. I think you're a very good friend. Though I don't think he should have done it.'

'I'd have done the same in his place,' he lied.

'Are you telling me you have a mistress who's trying to marry you, and an illegitimate child as well?'

427

'No.' He laughed. 'Not at all. Neither.'

'That's good,' she said.

Aunt Éloïse reappeared.

'Shall we have some tea?' she asked.

'I must go,' said Marie. 'I'd like to stay, but I'm on my way to the Rochards'. I only looked in to deliver a message, Aunt Éloïse, that you are invited to lunch on Sunday. And as I have found you, Monsieur Hadley, would you please tell my brother he should also come? You are invited too.'

'That's very kind.'

'Until Sunday then.' She kissed her aunt, and was gone.

After tea, Hadley rose to leave. He thanked Éloïse for a delightful time.

'I'm glad you like my pictures,' she said.

'Very much.' He paused at the door. 'I was rather amazed at the change in Marie.'

'Well, it's time she married. So it's not too soon for her to . . . wake up. She's a lovely young woman. Don't you think?'

'Yes.'

'Perhaps.' She spoke very quietly, but he was sure he heard her say: 'Perhaps you should wake up too.'

Aunt Éloïse was pleased. The family lunch was going well. Everyone seemed to be getting on very well. Even Gérard was being pleasant. Marie was looking radiant. And if she was not much mistaken, Éloïse thought, Frank Hadley was watching her niece with more than usual interest.

All that was needed was an opportunity for them to spend some time together. It presented itself during the dessert.

They had been discussing the statue of Charlemagne. Jules had been rather pleased with the results of his committee. 'We raised all the funds we needed,' he remarked. 'I'm sorry that the Vicomte de Cygne didn't live to see it, because he'd have been pleased. We even got an excellent contribution from that lawyer, Ney, whose daughter you painted.'

'Talking of sculpture,' remarked his wife, 'I hear there's a scandal about Rodin the sculptor in the newspapers. Is this right?'

'Rodin's *Kiss* and his *Thinker* have even become quite famous in America, you know,' Hadley remarked. 'I didn't know there was a scandal, though.'

'It's not exactly a scandal,' said Marc. 'Nearly ten years ago, he was commissioned by the author's society to do a big statue of Balzac. As most people think he's our greatest novelist, something monumental was called for. And Rodin's been at it ever since. He's had to ask for fifty extensions to complete the work. And now they've seen it, they've rejected it.'

'Why?' asked Marie.

'I heard it was a monstrosity,' said Gérard.

'*Ah non*, Gérard,' said Aunt Éloïse.

Marc laughed.

'Actually, he's right. It is a monstrosity. But a magnificent one. Faced with such a heroic task, Rodin attempted to depict the soul of the writer, rather than the literal man. The result is a shape like a tree trunk wrapped in a cloak, with this great head, with a neck like a bull, bursting out of it. They were all horrified. So Rodin's taken the plaster model back to his studio. Perhaps it will never be cast.' He smiled. 'Personally, I'd have preferred it if they'd put it in Père Lachaise instead of that rather boring head that sits over his grave at present.' He turned to Hadley. 'You remember the one I mean?'

'Do you know,' said Hadley, 'I've never been to the cemetery of Père Lachaise.'

'You haven't?' Aunt Éloïse was astounded. 'My dear Hadley, you must go there.'

'You should,' agreed Jules. 'Certainly worth a visit.'

'I propose,' said Aunt Éloïse, seeing a beautiful chance, 'to take you there myself. Marc and Marie, you must come too. I insist. We shall go this very week, while the weather is still so mild.' She looked at them all.

'Why not?' said Marc.

And Aunt Éloïse was feeling quite pleased with her cleverness when Gérard intervened.

'I think that's a wonderful idea. We should love to come too.'

'We should?' said his wife, looking puzzled and not especially pleased.

'My dear Gérard,' said Aunt Éloïse, 'I think you might be rather bored.'

'Not at all,' said Gérard. 'We're coming.'

It seemed to Hadley that Marc was looking a little pale when he came by to collect him.

'Something wrong?' he asked.

'Hortense,' said Marc.

'You spoke?'

'You could call it that.'

'You broke up with her?'

'I did.'

Hadley gazed thoughtfully at his friend.

'I guess you know what you want,' he said.

'She wasn't too pleased.'

'I don't suppose she was.'

'She called me a lot of names.' Marc sighed, then shrugged. 'However, I'm used to that.'

'I'd imagine you are.'

'Let's go to Père Lachaise,' said Marc.

It was such a perfect afternoon. The weather was still pleasantly warm. The leaves were on the trees. But there were hints of gold in some of them, and now and then, as a light gust of wind made them tremble, a few leaves floated down to the ground.

The two men, Aunt Éloïse and Marie shared the Blanchard carriage. Gérard and his wife were meeting them at the cemetery.

But it wasn't Gérard and his wife they found waiting for them.

'She couldn't come,' Gérard explained. 'The children needed her. So I have brought a friend of mine instead. May I present Rémy Monnier.'

He was a well-dressed man of about thirty. Medium height. Alert hazel eyes. Hair cropped very short, rapidly balding. But there was a brisk, almost dynamic energy about him that was quite impressive. He seemed like a man who shaved close and knew all the markets.

He bowed in a friendly way to them all, and immediately paid his addresses to Aunt Éloïse, as good manners demanded.

Meanwhile, Gérard was murmuring to Marie.

430

'Rémy is a very good man. The family's rich, but he has several brothers. So he's determined to make a fortune of his own. And he will. He's in banking, has a huge talent for finance. And he's not Jewish.' He nodded. 'I think you'll like him.'

Marie said nothing.

'Oh,' Gérard continued, 'and he knows his wines. Collects pictures, too. Old Masters mostly. Loves the opera. Very cultivated. God knows what he's read.'

'Poetry?' she asked, not that she cared.

'Probably. All sorts of stuff.'

Marie gazed at the banker. Not that she knew about such things, but she imagined that Rémy Monnier was also an accomplished lover. He would have seen to that.

It was pleasant enough visiting the famous cemetery. They showed Hadley the monument to Abelard and Héloïse. They found the grave of Chopin, and of Balzac, with its impressive if rather conventional bust. They saw graves of Napoléon's marshals and they went to the Mur des Fédérés, where Aunt Éloïse explained the tragedy of the last days of the Commune to Hadley.

The banker came and made himself agreeable to her as they walked along. He asked her about how she had passed her summer, spoke interestingly about the château of Fontainebleau, which he knew well. They talked about the grape harvest.

'I usually go down for the *vendange* on our little property,' she told him, 'which will be quite soon. But I haven't decided whether I'll go this year.'

'Not to be missed,' he said. 'I shall have to be in Paris, but I'd much rather join you and pick grapes.'

She also noticed that when she told him where the family vine-yard was, he guessed at once exactly which grapes they harvested, and how they made the wine. He knew his subject thoroughly.

And although she wished he were not there, and that she could talk to Frank Hadley instead, she could see that the supremely competent Rémy Monnier would be very interesting indeed to many women.

When they had seen all they wanted of Père Lachaise, Aunt Éloïse announced that she and Marie were going to the charming Parc des Buttes-Chaumont nearby.

'You and Marc will come with us, of course,' she said to Hadley.

'We'll follow in a cab,' said Gérard.

'So, Hadley,' said Aunt Éloïse with a smile, as the carriage rolled away, 'you have been working hard at your painting in France for many months now, and I have never asked you: Are you satisfied with your visit so far? Are you finding what you hoped for?'

'Thanks to this fellow here' – Hadley indicated Marc – 'and the kindness of his family, I've been more fortunate than I could have dared to hope. Many people come to France and see it from outside, but by getting to know a family, I've already learned far more about France than most people do.'

'This is probably true in any country,' said Aunt Éloïse, 'but it is especially true in France. And tell me – honestly, I beg you – how you like it here.'

'Oh, I'm in love with it,' Hadley said simply.

'You are?' said Marie.

'I don't mean that France has no faults. I find people a little too obsessed by their history. But the culture has so much charm, that's understandable. And nobody can call France old-fashioned. A little slow to adopt mechanical inventions, maybe. But all the new artistic and philosophical ideas are happening here. That's why all the young American artists come piling in.'

'And what of your own painting?' asked Aunt Éloïse. 'Are you making progress?'

'Some.' He hesitated, then smiled a little ruefully. 'Not enough.'

'You have talent,' Marc assured him.

'A little, Marc. But not enough. That's what I've learned. I shall study painting all my life, but I'm not going to be a painter. That's what I needed to find out, and I've seen so much already that I know my limitations. I'm not disappointed. I just needed to know.'

'Too soon to give up,' said Marc. 'Tell him so, Marie.'

'I watched Hadley working in Fontainebleau and I was very impressed,' said Marie. 'But I'd rather know what he thinks.'

'I've decided that I want to live a life more like my father's. I don't want to go into business, as I'd thought I might. I want to live in the same world that you and your aunt do, Marc. If I apply myself, there will be positions I could take in art schools or universities in America.

That would allow me free time to do my own work and travel in the summer. I mightn't get rich, but I'm fortunate. I'll have enough private income to get by.'

'You could have a house in France and spend your summers here,' said Marie.

'I could certainly do that,' said Hadley. He smiled. 'Sounds a pretty good idea.'

They had reached the gates of the Parc des Buttes-Chaumont.

'Marc, wait here for Gérard and his friend,' said Aunt Éloïse. 'Then take them up to the little temple at the top of the park, where we shall meet you.' And with that she swept Hadley and Marie away.

It was warm and it was quiet. There was scarcely a soul about as they wandered along the winding path that led down to the small lake. In the middle of the lake, the island rose up steeply to the tiny temple far above.

'This way,' said Aunt Éloïse. And she led them around the edge of the lake until they heard the sound of a waterfall. 'It's one of the wonders of the place,' she explained to Hadley. 'This was the entrance to an old gypsum quarry, but they turned it into a grotto with an artificial waterfall and stalactites.'

They entered the grotto together. It was empty.

'I'll just see where the others are,' said Aunt Éloïse, and left them.

The water cascaded down delightfully. The stalactites that hung in huge spikes from the roof of the cave gave it a magical air. Standing together, they looked up the waterfall to a patch of blue sky in the roof, far above. Marie stepped back into the cave, under the festoons of stalactites, and stood watching Hadley as he inspected the area around the waterfall.

She had never been entirely alone with him before. She felt her heart beating, but she kept still. He walked back to her.

She was looking up at him. She was almost trembling, but still she held herself under control, forced herself to be calm.

'It seems my chaperone has deserted me,' she said softly.

He gazed at her, uncertain.

'Obviously,' he said with half a smile, 'she trusts me not to behave like Marc.'

She gave a hint of a shrug, and smiled, still looking up at him.

'Why?'

As he looked down at Marie, with her face upturned and her lips slightly parted, Frank Hadley felt a great wave of desire. And perhaps, even then, he might have held back; but the fact that she knew about her brother, and had told him so, had somehow removed the awesome barrier of her innocence. In his mind, she was a woman now. He bent his head down, and kissed her.

And suddenly Marie found herself receiving his kiss, with her head thrown back, and she felt his arm around her waist drawing her up, and her hands reached out, clasping his neck, his body, needing to hold him, and she thought that she would swoon.

Until a voice interrupted, and brought the sky crashing down.

'In the name of God,' cried Gérard, 'what are you doing?' And as they sprang apart: 'Marie, are you insane?'

Gérard took charge. For once, they all had to do what he said. Not a word, he ordered. Not a word to anyone, not even to Marc.

At least, thank God, Rémy Monnier had no idea what had happened. Not only would it have ruined Marie's chances with him, but a few words from Monnier and the news would have been all over Paris.

Even Aunt Éloïse, who had so shamefully left them alone, had to keep quiet. It only confirmed Gérard's opinion that his aunt was an irresponsible fool. If he hadn't decided to come down to see where they were, and taken a different path from the one where she was standing guard, she might have got away with this nonsense. And where would that have left everybody?

As it was, they all trooped up calmly to the little temple, Marie walking with her aunt and he with Hadley, and they all admired the little temple and the view. And Monnier declared it was a delightful afternoon.

When they got back to the entrance to the park, Gérard suggested in the most natural way that the others should take the family carriage and drop Rémy Monnier at his house, which was almost on their way home, up near the Parc Monceau, while he conveyed Hadley back: 'Because I never get a chance to talk to him.'

So Rémy Monnier found himself in the carriage with Marie, and Gérard went off with Hadley.

★   ★   ★

434

Gérard wasted no time. But to Hadley's surprise, he could not have been more friendly.

'My dear Hadley, please forgive me, but I have to protect my sister's reputation – which my aunt entirely failed to do. In my place, you'd be obliged to do the same.'

'The fault's mine, not hers . . .' Hadley began, but Gérard wouldn't hear of it.

'That grotto's a romantic place, and my sister's . . . well, in my opinion, she's everything a man could want.'

'I wouldn't disagree with that.'

'You kissed her. Any of us might have done the same. That's what chaperones are for.'

'There was no disrespect, I assure you.'

'Of course there wasn't. We know you're a good fellow. My brother, Marc, whom we all love, is not a good fellow. His family know it, and I'm sure you know too. In fact, my parents thought you were a good influence on him. But tell me, Hadley, what are your intentions? Are you wanting to marry my sister?'

'It hadn't quite come to that,' answered Hadley truthfully. 'It was all a bit sudden. But I reserve the right.'

'Hadley, we like you very much,' declared Gérard. 'But you can't marry Marie. It's out of the question. Think about it. You'll go back to America. Would you take her away from all her family? Would she be happy there? My parents wouldn't consent to the marriage, and I'd oppose it strongly, for those reasons. Besides, you're a Protestant. Marie's a Catholic. Are you planning to convert? Because she isn't going to.'

He didn't belabour the point. But when he dropped Hadley off, he added one thing.

'Do you think Marie has fallen in love with you, Hadley?'

'I couldn't say.'

'Well, nor could I. But if she has, then the best thing is to leave her alone. Don't raise hopes which can't be fulfilled. That would be unkind.'

And the trouble was, Hadley thought, as he mounted the stairs to his lodgings, that although he didn't like Gérard, what he said might be true.

*   *   *

435

The next day, he made his decision. His reasons were straightforward.

Professionally, he'd achieved his purpose in France. He was ready to return to America and start his career.

If the circumstances had been different, he thought, he might have spent more time in Marie's company, and he might have offered to marry her. The idea of living in Europe and spending summers in France was delightful.

But if there was going to be implacable opposition from her family, what was the good of that, for either of them? There was only one sensible and decent thing to do.

The next day he sent a cable to his father. Having done so, he went to see Marc.

'My father's sick. I have to return to America at once.'

'My dear Hadley. Just when we were getting used to you. I'm heartbroken.'

'I'm sorry to go, but there's nothing to be done.'

Then he called on Marie and her parents.

Jules and his wife had no reason not to accept his explanation at face value, and urged him warmly to come straight to their house whenever he returned. 'And if you ever come to America,' he said in return, 'my parents and I will be so delighted if you will stay with us.'

'If we come, my dear Hadley, you'll be the first to know,' said Jules.

His interview with Marie was not so easy.

'It's my fault you're going, isn't it?' she said.

'No it isn't. Not at all.'

'What did Gérard say to you?'

'Not much. He was quite friendly, in fact. But he wants to protect your reputation. Rightly so.'

'Your father is really sick?'

'I'm afraid he is.'

'Will you come back when he is well?'

'I haven't even thought of anything, except getting to him as quickly as I can.'

She nodded, and held out her hand.

'Good-bye, Hadley,' she said.

After he had gone, she told her parents that she was going to take a little rest. Then she closed the door and quietly locked it, and pushed her face into her pillow to muffle the sound and, knowing that she had lost him, wept for over an hour.

Two days later, she departed for the family vineyard, to take part in the *vendange*.

It was a week after her return to Paris that James Fox came to see Jules Blanchard.

'I have come on a personal matter,' he explained.

'My dear Fox, what can I do for you?' Jules replied.

'I have to tell you something which you may not like. I am entirely in love with Marie, and I wish to ask your permission to let her know that this is the case.'

'Has she any idea of it?'

'To the best of my knowledge, none. I came to see you first.'

'You certainly behave well. But that is no surprise. How long have you loved her?'

'Since the first day I met her. It was a *coup de foudre*. But since then I have come to know her and to love her for all her qualities of character and mind. Otherwise I should not be here to ask for her hand.'

Jules considered.

'Fox, we like you, and it is my opinion that you would make a very good husband. I do not know what Marie's feelings might be about your proposal, and that will be for her to decide.'

'I have not the least wish to marry a woman who doesn't want to marry me.'

'Of course. But I must tell you that there is the problem of religion.'

'It is a problem for me as well. I have had a long discussion with my father, whose wish is that I should marry a Protestant.'

'Ah. That's the thing.'

'However, my father is a realist, and because he understands the strength of my desire, he has made a concession which may shock you, but which is the only way that I can hope to marry, without causing deep distress to my own family.'

'I'm listening.'

'I should myself remain a Protestant, while my wife remains a Catholic.'

'That might be acceptable. But what of the children? That's the question.'

'In France, society is mainly Catholic. In England, naturally, people normally belong to the Church of England, and if the truth is told, there is still in many quarters a certain suspicion of Catholics. Therefore my father proposes that if we live in France – as we surely would for the time being – the children should be Catholic. However, if in later years the family business should require my presence in London, then the whole family would worship at a Church of England church. The nearest church to our London house, as it happens, is so High Church, as we Anglicans put it, that visiting Catholics often mistake it for one of their own.'

'There is a degree of subterfuge, even dishonesty in this.'

'Precisely.'

'I wonder what Marie would think of it. She would have to be told.'

'Yes.'

'My wife would not like it.'

'That would be up to you to tell her.' Fox paused. 'It wouldn't be obvious.'

'No. In France there would be no problem at all. Not, of course, that I have ever had secrets from my wife.'

'Indeed.'

'Come back in a week. Let me speak to Marie, and my wife . . . Then I shall give you my answer.'

'That is all I ask.'

Jules Blanchard smiled.

'Whatever my answer turns out to be, my dear Fox, I am honoured by your proposal.'

Two days later, Jules told Marie the entire conversation.

'Fox is a very nice man,' he said to her, 'and it seems he is truly in love with you. So I want to be careful that we respond clearly.'

'I should not be unhappy. I am sure of that, at least,' Marie said. And that is far better, she thought, than what I have now. 'But I only considered him as a friend before.'

'Friendship may be the best way to start,' her father suggested.

'Yes. Can you give him permission to court me?' she asked, quite cheerfully. 'Aunt Éloïse can always be my chaperone. Then I can see how he does.'

Chapter Fourteen

1903

It was some years since Adeline had suggested to Ney, soon after Édith's mother had died, that Édith and her husband, Thomas Gascon, should move into the big house with their children.

'The arthritis in my hand is slowing me down a little, monsieur,' Adeline had explained, 'so I really need more help from Édith. If she could be on call at all times, it would be much better.'

'And where would they live?'

'There are three or four unused rooms on the attic floor. Thomas is good with his hands. He would renovate them at no charge to you.'

The arrangement worked well for everyone. Édith continued to work for the same wages, but lived rent-free. Thomas had his own work, but gladly undertook small tasks as a handyman when needed. 'If they do not disturb the residents, the children will bring a family spirit into the house,' Monsieur Ney had declared.

It seemed to Édith that Monsieur Ney had mellowed as he grew older. She had four children now: Robert, the oldest; Anaïs; a second boy, Pierre, now five years old; and little Monique, the baby of the family. And since he had no grandchildren of his own, the stiff old lawyer had unbent into a grandfatherly figure to her children, bringing them chocolates, and treats, and little presents from time to time.

For Hortense had still not married. Around the turn of the century, she had told her father that her doctor had prescribed that she should spend her winters in a warmer climate, and she had been in Monte Carlo most of the time since then.

The portrait of Hortense by Marc Blanchard, however, was in the place of honour in the hall. Though Ney had originally intended that it should grace his own house, he was so proud of the picture that only the splendid architecture of the hall with its noble staircase seemed worthy of it.

As the years had gone by, Thomas Gascon and his family had come to think of the curious old mansion as their natural home.

It was a cold March day when Monsieur Ney arrived looking rather pleased with himself. Having distributed some bonbons to the children, he summoned Édith and Aunt Adeline, and made a surprising announcement.

'In going through some old papers, I have made a surprising discovery. Do you know the age of Mademoiselle Bac?'

'She might be over ninety, I think,' Aunt Adeline suggested.

'She will be a hundred this summer. I have the papers to prove it.'

'It is a tribute, monsieur, to the care you have always lavished upon her,' said Adeline.

'Indeed. And we shall have a party to celebrate. Mademoiselle Bac shall participate, even if she is not aware of the circumstances.'

'You are kind, monsieur.'

'But more than that. Have you considered the favourable publicity this will generate? Few places indeed can boast of a resident of such an age. We shall be in the newspapers. The finest establishment of its kind in Paris.'

Édith had never seen him so excited.

'Will you tell Mademoiselle Bac?' she asked.

'I think I shall. I shall do it this very moment – even if she does not understand.' And he hurried out.

They did not see him again for half an hour.

It was Édith who found him. He was lying in the hall, in front of the painting of Hortense. Whether he had been suddenly overcome on his way up to see Mademoiselle Bac, or whether he had already performed that mission when he was struck, she could not tell. But it was clear that he had suffered a massive stroke, and he was already quite dead.

When Hortense arrived from Monte Carlo, she made the necessary arrangements. She was quiet and efficient. At the funeral, she ensured that there were two dozen clients, and various people who had been involved with his charitable works, including even Jules Blanchard. It was a dignified gathering that would have gratified her father very much. In the funeral address, which was given by the priest who attended the home, the facts of Ney's ancestry were rehearsed – including even a hint that he might have been related to Voltaire – as well as his indefatigable efforts to secure the comfort and happiness of all those in his care.

Not the least of Ney's achievements, it was now discovered, was to have secured a grave in the cemetery of Père Lachaise. Not quite in the avenue where his distinguished relation's grave had been placed – among other great Napoleonic military men – but within sight of it.

Soon after the interment, Hortense departed for the south again, having instructed Adeline and Édith to run everything exactly as usual until her return in May.

It was not until the second week of May that Hortense came back from Monte Carlo. To their surprise, she arrived in the company of a very handsome olive-skinned gentleman named Monsieur Ivanov who, she explained, was her financial advisor.

'Ivanov: that's a Russian name, isn't it?' Aunt Adeline asked him.

'It is Russian,' he replied, 'but my mother was Tunisian.'

Monsieur Ivanov had sleek black hair, brushed back, and his clothes were perfectly tailored. He said little, but he was always at Hortense's side.

Hortense stayed in her father's house for a month. She looked in at the home most days. Aunt Adeline told her that her father had desired to have a celebration when Mademoiselle Bac was a hundred, but Hortense said she was very busy and that it would have to wait.

One day she came by with a middle-aged couple and spent two hours looking over the building, inspecting every room.

It was the middle of June when Hortense called in one fine evening. Thomas and Édith were sitting with Aunt Adeline in her room, after putting their children to bed.

'I have news for you,' Hortense said. 'I am returning to Monte Carlo immediately. The home has been sold. The new owners have no need of any help, however, so you will all have to leave. The new owners will take over tomorrow, but you can stay another two weeks.'

'But we have nowhere to go,' Thomas protested.

'You have two entire weeks.' She shrugged. 'That should be plenty of time to find something. At least temporary.' She turned to Monsieur Ivanov. 'There is a picture of me in the hall. Take that. It belongs to me. I have to go and say good-bye to one of the residents now.'

While Aunt Adeline, Thomas and Édith sat in stunned silence, and Monsieur Ivanov went to take the portrait down from the wall, Hortense made her way upstairs. Édith went with her. She wasn't going to accept this without a protest.

'Surely, Mademoiselle Hortense, you can give us more time, at least. I have four children.'

'You will have to think of something. I will give you a reference.'

'My aunt and I have served your father many years. Did he not remember us in any way?'

'No.'

Hortense did not pause on the main floor, but continued up to the attic. While Édith stood in the doorway, she entered the room of Mademoiselle Bac. It was silent.

'Mademoiselle Bac,' she said clearly, 'can you hear me?' No sound came from the iron bed. 'Monsieur Ney is dead.' Hortense paused. 'The place has been sold, and everyone has gone. You are all alone.' She paused again, to let this sink in. 'It is time to die now,' she said. Then she left.

They went down the main stairs. Down in the hall, Monsieur Ivanov was holding the painting.

'What did you tell the old lady?' he asked.

Hortense shrugged.

'The truth.' She opened the big front door. 'Let's go.'

And Édith was left alone in the hall, wondering what to do next.

Chapter Fifteen

1907

Roland de Cygne could hardly believe his ears. He was Captain de Cygne these days, and his friend the captain was now a commandant. Yet for all his respect for his mentor, he thought the commandant must be mistaken.

'I assure you, *mon cher ami*, that it's true,' his mentor continued. 'I didn't tell you at the time, because thanks to that waiter at the Moulin Rouge – to whom you owe your life, by the way – the fellow was frightened off. But we were all watching out for you. After your father's death, you will recall, the regiment was posted away, and there was less to worry about. But now that we are to return to Paris, I feel obliged to mention it to you.'

'And the name of this lunatic, or villain – I don't know what to call him?'

'Jacques Le Sourd. I know nothing about his whereabouts, but no doubt he can be found. Whether he would still like to kill you . . . who knows?' He smiled. 'Just watch out, if you go visiting any of the courtesans of Paris again!'

'I think,' said Roland, 'that I'll pay a visit to the waiter. What's his name?'

'Luc Gascon.'

Luc was easy to find. He had his own bar these days, just off the Place Pigalle, a quarter mile east of the Moulin Rouge.

He was stouter than before, but just as charming. And when Roland told him who he was, he nodded.

'I thought I recognised you, Monsieur de Cygne. I knew that your regiment had been away. Welcome back to Paris.'

Roland briefly explained how he had found out about Le Sourd.

'You understand,' he said, 'that until recently I had no idea of the service you had rendered me.'

'I know, monsieur.'

'I should like you to accept this, to show my gratitude,' said Roland, and handed him an envelope, which Luc quickly inspected.

'You are more than generous, Monsieur de Cygne,' he said. 'I could open a restaurant with this.'

'Just don't spend it at the races,' Roland said with a smile. 'But the question now is, what should I do about Le Sourd? Do you have any idea why he wanted to kill me?'

'*Non*, monsieur. I never discovered.'

'I should like to talk to him. Do you know where he is?'

'Give me a day, and I shall find out, monsieur. But it might be dangerous for you to interview him.'

'I'll take a pistol,' said Roland.

It was good to be back in the family house again. Now that he was based in Paris, he thought he might use the house, as far as his regimental duties allowed. Most of the rooms were under dust covers, but his old nanny was still living there with a housekeeper and a maid to keep the house going, and he spent a pleasant evening talking to her.

Most of the time, when he was away on his regimental duties, Roland did not need to reflect on political matters. But finding himself back again in his family's old mansion, in the great historical centre of France, he could not help being struck by the mutability of the past and present.

The ancestors who had lived in this house had doubtless considered England their traditional enemy, as she had been for so many centuries. Yet now all that was changed. Bismarck's German Empire had arisen. France had suffered the humiliation of 1870, and the loss of AlsaceLorraine. When he was a boy, who had his teachers at the Catholic lycée along the street told him were his enemies? The Germans of course. His generation's duty? To avenge France's dishonour.

And who were France's allies now against the kaiser's German threat? The English, linked to France by the Entente Cordiale, together with the Russians, who feared the kaiser too.

Wherever one looked in the streets of old Paris, from the ruins of the medieval walls to Notre-Dame, to the bleak grandeur of Les Invalides, it was always the same story: Men called to glory, or to defend *la patrie*; men killed, in many thousands. The struggle for power, and, intermittently, the attempt to find a balance of power among the nations, until the peace broke down once again.

Would his own generation do any better? he wondered.

Luc Gascon was as good as his word. He came by during the evening with the address of Le Sourd's workplace, a printer's on the edge of Belleville, and even the days of the week when he might be found there.

Roland set out late the following morning. His plan was simple. He would have lunch at Maxim's. After that, he would go and interview Le Sourd. The late afternoon and evening he left open. If things went wrong, Le Sourd might have killed him by then. Or he Le Sourd. In either case the evening might be disrupted. No point in making plans one might not keep.

Before he set out, he discovered a small problem. His service revolver was not easy to conceal. Although it fitted into the deep pocket in his outer coat, it might be discovered when he took off his coat at Maxim's. The alternative was to put the gun in an attaché case.

But this presented a social difficulty. For just as no gentleman in Europe would be seen carrying a parcel if he could avoid it – there were servants, or in worse cases women, for that – even an attaché case, in the mind of Roland de Cygne, made one look too like a businessman, instead of an aristocrat. Had he been in uniform on his way to a staff meeting, that would be an entirely different matter; but he was going to Maxim's for lunch.

It took him several minutes to think about it. If he'd taken his own conveyance, he could have left the revolver there. His father's jaunty carriage was still in the coach house, though without horses or coachman, and Roland had been thinking of buying himself a handsome motor car, a Daimler perhaps. But until he did so, he had no transport, so he'd have to take a cab. Once he got to the restaurant, he'd leave the case at the hat and coat counter, of course, and with luck no one he knew would see him arriving with it. He wondered whether, after lunch, he could discreetly remove the revolver, slip it into his coat pocket, and leave the case at Maxim's to be picked up later. For if Le Sourd by any chance killed him, the thought of the newspapers reporting that his body had been found with an attaché case was highly irksome.

Yes, he decided, he'd try to do that.

Yet despite the probably dangerous business that lay ahead, Roland was in a cheerful mood. It was a bright October day. He was happy to be back in Paris, and eager to investigate the changes that had taken place there since he had been away.

He'd already been struck by the motor cars in the street – there were not many among the horse-drawn vehicles, but certainly more than one saw in the provinces. More surprising was the presence of the Métro. For if Paris had been slow to adopt underground trains, when it finally happened, the network grew fast. Above all, he'd been struck by the elegance of the serpentine, Art Nouveau entrances to the Métro that appeared down all the boulevards. They were really very pleasing.

He soon found a cab, and told the driver to continue a little way along the Seine, until they were level with Les Invalides. For there were three more additions to the city he could look at as they passed. The first was a bridge.

The Pont Alexandre III had also been completed while he was away. Named for the recent Russian tsar who'd become France's ally against German aggression, it was a flamboyant affair, a pair of golden winged horsemen supported on pillars at each end, and other emblems linking Paris with St Petersburg. It might be a little gaudy, Roland thought, but on the whole it was magnificent.

Immediately across the bridge he encountered the other two. On his left, the Grand Palais, and on his right, the Petit Palais.

If the great fair of 1889 had bequeathed Paris the Eiffel Tower, the next fair at the turn of the century had left these two magnificent pavilions: a facing pair of exhibition halls that started as handsome stone museums and, as they rose, turned into soaring Art Nouveau glass houses. They were like opera houses made of glass, he thought, and flanking the short avenue to the new bridge, with the trees of the Champs-Élysées just behind them, their setting couldn't have been more delightful.

The cab turned into the Champs-Élysées. Moments later they were at the Place de la Concorde, turning up to La Madeleine, and there was Maxim's on the left.

Maxim's: it had been a struggling new bistro the only time that Roland had been there before, back in the nineties. But now it was a palace.

The location, of course, had helped. Set in the broad street between the Place de la Concorde and La Madeleine, it lay at the very epicentre of the city for the rich Parisian or visitor alike. Its facade was discreet. But it had been the transformation of the interior that had raised Maxim's to the height of fashion. And as he entered, Roland was astonished.

White tablecloths, deep red carpet and banquettes along the walls: rich, discreet – all the plush comfort he might have expected for the enjoyment of haute cuisine. The genius however came from the decoration. Carved woodwork, painted panels, lamps, even the great painted glass ceiling – all Art Nouveau. It was softly lit, yet stunning; it was the latest thing, yet from the moment of its creation it seemed as if it had always been there. Like all great hotels and restaurants, Maxim's was not just a place to eat, it was a theatre. And a work of art.

He had only a light lunch of a fillet of sole with a single glass of Chablis. He allowed himself a small chocolate pastry and a sharp coffee. He wanted to keep his wits about him.

He hadn't seen anyone he knew, which perhaps was a sign that he had been away too long. And he was about to leave when a passing gentleman stopped, and then addressed him.

'Monsieur de Cygne?'

It was Jules Blanchard, a little more portly than when they'd last met, but quite unmistakable. Roland rose at once and greeted him.

They had a pleasant chat. Roland learned that Marie and Fox had married and gone to London, where James was to take over from his father. Marie's English, her father proudly informed him, was already perfect.

But all the same, her parents hoped her absence would not be too long – especially since she now had a daughter, Claire. 'My granddaughter will speak English perfectly,' her grandfather predicted. 'But she'll always be French, of course.'

'I missed my opportunity to marry her myself,' said Roland politely. 'Alas, it was the time of my father's death . . .'

Meanwhile, he made Jules promise that he and his wife would come to his house to dine with him.

'I shall open up the house for that, at least,' he said.

Assuming, of course, that he was alive.

Apart from one or two visits to Père Lachaise, Roland had never been anywhere near Belleville. The printer's was in a small industrial space between a builder's yard and a dingy office building.

He put his hand in his coat pocket as soon as he had stepped down from the cab, and kept it there resting gently on the pistol.

Entering the printer's, he found an outer office with piles of recently printed materials – posters, broadsheets and business advertisements – on the floor, and a stained wooden counter manned by a small, bald-headed man in shirtsleeves. The smell of paper and printer's ink was so sharp it almost made his eyes water.

'I am here to see Monsieur Le Sourd.'

The bald man looked surprised.

'He's working. Is he expecting you?'

'Kindly tell him that an old friend from the past has arrived in Paris and is anxious to see him again.'

Rather unwillingly, the man went through a door behind him, and returned a minute later with a message that Le Sourd was not expecting anyone.

'Tell him I will wait,' replied Roland. But there was no need: for a moment later, drawn by curiosity, Jacques Le Sourd appeared in the doorway.

At the sight of de Cygne, he froze. So, thought Roland, he knows me. But after a brief hesitation, Le Sourd regained his composure.

'Do I know you, monsieur?'

'Captain Roland de Cygne.' Roland gazed at him evenly.

'I have nothing to say to you, monsieur.'

'There I must disagree. You can help me solve a mystery. It will only take ten minutes of your time. After that we may each of us return to our business. Or I can wait here until you are free at the end of the day.'

Jacques Le Sourd looked at the bald man, who shrugged. Then he signalled Roland to follow him into the street.

A hundred yards to the left there was a small bar. Apart from the owner, it was empty. They moved to a table and Roland ordered two cognacs. As they waited for the cognacs to arrive, Roland kept his right hand in his coat pocket. Le Sourd noticed it.

'You carry a gun,' he remarked.

'Merely a precaution, in case I am attacked,' Roland answered calmly. 'I have a dinner engagement this evening, and it would be impolite not to appear.'

The cognacs arrived. Roland raised the small glass with his left hand, took a sip and put it down.

'And now, Monsieur Le Sourd – of whom, until recently, I had never heard in my life – be so good as to tell me: Why do you wish to kill me?'

Le Sourd's face was impassive.

'Why do you think that I do?'

'Because some ten years ago you waited for me with a pistol in the rue des Belles-Feuilles. I have no idea why, but you can hardly blame me for being curious.'

Jacques Le Sourd was silent. For a moment it looked as if he in turn might ask a question. Then he seemed to think better of it.

'We are not far from the cemetery of Père Lachaise,' he said finally. 'There is a wall there called the Mur des Fédérés, where a number of Communards were shot.'

'So I have heard. What of it?'

'They were shot out of hand, without trial. Murdered.'

'They say that the last week of the Commune saw many terrible deeds, by both sides.'

'My father was one of the men shot against that wall.'

'I am sorry to hear it.'

'Do you know the name of the officer who directed that firing squad?'

'I have no idea.'

'De Cygne. Your father.' Le Sourd was watching him carefully.

'My father? You are sure of this?'

'I am certain.'

Roland gazed at Le Sourd. There was no reason for him to invent such a thing. He stared away, into the middle distance.

Was it possible that this was the reason his father had always been unwilling to discuss that period in his life? Had the memory of the execution haunted him? Might it even have caused him, ultimately, to resign his commission? If so, his father had taken that secret to the grave.

But even if such thoughts entered his mind, Roland was far too proud to share them with Le Sourd.

'And this would give you the right to murder me?'

'Tell me, Monsieur de Cygne, do you believe in God?'

'Of course.'

'Well, I do not,' said Le Sourd. 'So I have not the luxury of imagining that there is an afterlife. When your father murdered mine, he took away everything he had. Everything.'

'Then I am glad I believe in God, monsieur. And I assume, not being a Christian, that you believe in revenge.'

'Isn't it true that many Christian officers, men of honour, believe their duty is to avenge the loss of Alsace–Lorraine?'

'Some.'

'What's the difference? Call my wish to kill you a debt of honour.'

'But you have not come out into the open and done it, as a man of honour would.'

'I will not put more important matters at risk just to secure your death. You are not significant enough.'

'How fortunate,' said Roland drily. 'I assume that the important matters you speak of are political in nature.'

'Of course.'

'Yet in the last thirty years,' Roland remarked, 'the radical parties have achieved so many of their aims.' He ticked some of them off. 'There is little chance of either a monarchy or a Bonapartist military government. Every man has the vote. There is free public education for every boy and girl – I may not see the necessity, but it is so. And education is in the hands of the state, not of the Church. Even the traditional independence of the ancient regions of France, it seems to me, is being eroded by your bureaucrats in Paris. As one who loves France, this also saddens me. But all these changes are not enough for you?'

'They are a beginning. That is all.'

'Then perhaps you are part of the Workers' International.' It was two years now since the left wing of France's conventional radicals

451

had formally split away to form the French section of the Workers' International. 'You will only be content with a socialist revolution, whatever that may mean.'

'You are correct.'

Roland looked at him thoughtfully. Le Sourd was dedicated to everything he despised. He would oppose him and his kind in every way he could. Yet to his surprise he did not hate him. Perhaps the very fact that the fellow wished to avenge his father's death made him seem human.

'If you believe that your presence is essential to world revolution, monsieur,' Roland said, 'then I advise you not to try to kill me again. For your desire to murder me is now well recorded, and if something happens to me, you will be immediately arrested.'

Le Sourd gazed at him. His eyes, set so wide apart, were certainly intelligent. They conveyed no emotion.

'I am glad that we have had this meeting,' Le Sourd said calmly. 'For centuries your class and all you represent have been an evil force. But I see that we are making progress. For you are almost an irrelevance, and soon I think you will be an absurdity.'

'You are too kind.'

'When the opportunity comes to kill you, I shall take it.' He stood up. 'Until then, Monsieur de Cygne.' He bowed and left.

Before returning home, however, Roland had another idea. There was one other person he needed to see.

'Take me across the river,' he ordered the taxi driver. 'You can put me down at the church of Saint-Germain-des-Prés.'

The church wasn't far from the family mansion in that aristocratic quarter, but his object, first, was an old presbytery near the church that housed half a dozen elderly priests. In particular, it was now the home of Father Xavier Parle-Doux.

Father Xavier was there, and delighted to see him.

'Your last letter said that you would be back in Paris. But with all the things you must have to do, I did not expect to see you so soon.'

They had always written to each other every month or two, and so it did not take them long to exchange their recent news. Roland told Father Xavier how delighted he was with Paris, which he found more elegant than when he had left it. 'But I thought you would be

452

interested to hear that I have just met a man who is trying to kill me,' he announced.

'Evidently he has not succeeded yet. Tell me all,' said the priest.

When he had finished the story, Roland had one question.

'Did my father ever express to you any regret about this business? I am wondering if it had any connection with his decision to resign his commission.'

Father Xavier paused.

'Had your father ever said anything about this in the secrecy of the confessional, I should not tell you. But it is not a secret that he considered the war of Napoléon III against the Germans to have been a foolish adventure, and that the necessity of Frenchmen killing each other at the time of the Commune was distressing to him.' He looked at Roland curiously. 'Do you wish to inform the police about this Jacques Le Sourd?'

'No. His attempt upon me ten years ago would be hard to prove. And . . .' – he shrugged – 'it's not my style.'

'Personally, I do not think you are in immediate danger from this Jacques Le Sourd,' said the priest. 'Though morally I consider him a madman, I do not think he is a fool. If his socialist revolution comes about, however . . .'

'They will probably kill me anyway.'

'I have always felt,' confessed Father Xavier, 'from your infancy, that God was reserving you for some special purpose. One should not seek to guess the mind of God, but I felt it nonetheless. It has seemed to me that the wonderful birth of your ancestor Dieudonné, at the time of the Revolution, was a sign that God had a special love for the family de Cygne. Perhaps we should just await His plan and not concern ourselves too much about the ravings of this atheist.'

'I am glad you say that, *mon Père*. It was my feeling too.'

'Speaking of your family,' said Father Xavier pleasantly, 'isn't it time that you got married? We need another generation, you know.'

Roland smiled.

'Perhaps you are right. I'll think about it.'

'Don't wait too long. I should like to see your children.'

Roland gave him a quick look. The priest was thinner than when he last saw him. Was he unwell? Seeing his look, Father Xavier smiled. 'I am not sick, Roland, but none of us is getting any younger. Besides, I have already decided how to die.'

'Really?'

'I think that I shall know when it is approaching. And at that time, I intend to go to Rome.'

'Why?'

'Where else to die,' said the priest with a wry smile, 'if not in the Eternal City?'

Chapter Sixteen

1911

It was a quiet Sunday morning in September, and Édith and the girls were at Mass when Luc came to his brother's lodgings.

'Can you give me some help this evening?' he asked. 'We'll need that handcart of yours. I have some furniture to shift.'

'All right. Shall I bring Robert?' His eldest son was a strong young fellow.

'No. I want to talk with you in private.'

'What about?'

'I'll tell you later,' said Luc. 'I must go now. Meet me with the handcart at the restaurant this evening. Six o'clock.'

Thomas Gascon shrugged.

'As you like.'

He'd owned the handcart for half a dozen years now, and it had been a good investment.

The loss of their lodgings at Monsieur Ney's establishment had been a great blow to the Gascon family. There was rent to pay, and with her six young children, Édith hadn't been able to earn much. Thomas had been ready to move up on to Montmartre, on the edge of the Maquis, but Aunt Adeline and Édith wouldn't hear of it. When Aunt Adeline had found work as a housekeeper near the Pigalle district however, they had moved to lodgings close by.

This brought them into the vicinity of the Moulin Rouge and the foot of Montmartre – hardly a respectable area, and frequented in the evenings by ladies of the night. But Édith wanted to be near her aunt, and Thomas, at least, was not unhappy to find himself near his brother.

As a foreman, Thomas earned good wages. But there had been two more girls born since then, and so money was often tight. Sometimes Aunt Adeline had to help them with the rent.

One weekend, an old carrier living nearby had asked Thomas if he would help him on a Sunday. He did all kinds of odd jobs carrying furniture and delivering goods in the area. After helping him a few times, Thomas realised that this could be a useful way of supplementing his earnings. Soon, complaining of a bad back, the old man had given up his trade, and Thomas had bought a new handcart for himself, which he kept in a local stable yard. Before long, anyone in the area who wanted a piece of furniture moved, or some sacks of flour, or a load of firewood, would probably ask Thomas Gascon if he'd be free on a Sunday afternoon.

When Édith got back from Mass, she wasn't too pleased to hear about Luc.

'I hope he's going to pay you,' she said.

'He will if I ask,' answered Thomas.

'Be careful what he wants you to carry. It may be stolen goods.'

'No it won't.'

'Just make sure it isn't the *Mona Lisa*.'

It was hardly a month since Leonardo da Vinci's famous painting had been stolen from the Louvre. Apollinaire, a writer thought to be an anarchist, had been arrested; and then a friend of his, a young painter no one had ever heard of, named Picasso. But though they remained under suspicion, no proof against them had been found so far. Nor was there any sign of the painting.

'You always think the worst of my brother, for no reason,' Thomas complained. Some years back, a grateful client had given Luc enough money to expand his bar into a restaurant. 'He must have stolen the money,' Édith had declared. 'He saved the man's life,' Thomas assured her. But she only sniffed. 'So he says,' she said. 'You can believe it. Not me.'

Her unreasonable dislike of Luc was one of the few sources of friction in their marriage. If she ever regretted her hesitant acceptance of Thomas that magical evening after the Wild West show in the Bois de Boulogne, she had never shown it. If she'd wished she had married a man with a little money – and how she must have wished that, after they suddenly lost their lodgings – her only reaction had been to apologise to him. 'I never thought that could happen. We had always counted on Monsieur Ney.'

After ten pregnancies, with six healthy children, she still had a good figure. You couldn't say that of many wives he knew. Whatever her faults, he counted himself lucky to have married Édith.

After lunch he took all but the youngest two children for a walk up the nearby hill of Montmartre. There was a funicular, nowadays, that ran up the left side of the steep, high slope, but one had to pay. Besides, as he told Monique when she complained, they wouldn't get any exercise if they didn't go up the steps.

The sun was out, catching the soaring white domes of the church of Sacré Coeur. High on its hill, it gleamed over the huge oval valley of Paris.

'Most of my life,' Thomas remarked to his children, 'this hilltop was just a huge field of mud and wooden scaffolding. I used to wonder if I'd ever live to see the church finished. They didn't take the scaffolding down from the big dome until you were born, Monique, when I was thirty-five.'

'And you were even more pleased to see me than the church,' she insisted.

'Except when you misbehave,' he answered genially.

The transformation of the site was almost complete. The platform, upon which the great Byzantine shrine stood, had been laid out as handsome terraces and flights of steps, like hanging gardens. A splendid statue of Joan of Arc gazed out over Paris from beside the church door. And though not visible to the eye, a subtler change had also occurred.

As four decades of republican government had gradually weakened the power of the Church, even the message of Sacré Coeur had been altered. Men like Father Xavier and Roland de Cygne remembered that it proclaimed the triumph of a conservative Church over the radical Communards. But most Parisians who nowadays gazed up at the shining white temple on the hill supposed that it was a memorial to the Communards' heroism – a view which radical governments were glad to encourage.

Since living in Pigalle, Thomas Gascon usually brought his children up here a couple of times a year, and the ritual was always the same. They would wander over the top of the hill, visit the Moulin de la Galette where their uncle Luc had started work, visit the Maquis to view the house where their father had been brought up, and then complete the circle of the hill, walking by the little school where Thomas had learned to read and write.

For the first five years, the tour had always ended with one dramatic moment in front of Sacré Coeur before they descended.

Pointing across the rooftops of Paris to where the Eiffel Tower soared into the sky, Thomas would cry out: 'Take a good look at the tower, my children, and remember. For it won't be there much longer.'

Everyone had known. In 1909, the twenty-year licence that Gustave Eiffel had been granted would be up. The city authorities would then order the tower to be dismantled. Even if he couldn't be the foreman, Thomas had wanted to apply to work on that job. 'I put that tower up, and I'll take it down,' he used to say. But it would break his heart to do it.

So a chance meeting early in 1908 had brought him great joy. He'd been working on a project to the south of the Eiffel Tower, and if the weather was fine he would walk past the tower at the end of the day. One evening, he saw Monsieur Eiffel just ahead of him in the dusk. He couldn't resist going up to him to pay his respects; and to his pleasure, Eiffel recognised him at once.

'Well, Gascon, it's good to see you again.'

'It is possible, monsieur, that you may see more of me next year. For I shall certainly apply to dismantle the tower, although it is a terrible shame to do it.'

Eiffel smiled at him.

'Then I have good news for you, my friend. I have just concluded an extension of the contract, until 1915.'

'Another six years. That is something at least, monsieur.'

'And I have other plans too. Do you realise the usefulness of the tower, my dear Gascon, for radio communications?'

'I had not really thought of it.'

'Well, I can assure you that the tower is the finest radio mast in the world. And I have a few other things up my sleeve. Trust me, my friend, and I believe I can save our tower. Just give me a little time.'

And some time later Thomas had read in the newspaper that the army and navy had declared that the tower was essential for their military communications.

Once again, the genius of Eiffel had triumphed. The tower was now sacrosanct. It was part of the defence of France.

So today, before they returned home, Thomas Gascon could pause, point to the Eiffel Tower and tell his children: 'That tower is so well constructed, it will stand as long as Notre-Dame. And always remember,' he added proudly, 'that your father built it.'

Luc was waiting for him at the restaurant. The restaurant didn't open on Sundays, so the shutters were closed.

It was strange for Thomas to realise that his brother was a man in his thirties now. He hadn't changed that much. His pale face was a little more fleshy. Thomas's short brown curls had thinned, but Luc had exactly the same dark hair falling handsomely over his forehead. He looked like an Italian restaurant owner.

And his small restaurant, though it wasn't making him rich, was undoubtedly providing him with far more income than Thomas could ever earn in manual work.

He still hadn't married. But Thomas had seen his brother with a succession of handsome women.

The object to be moved turned out to be something more mundane than the *Mona Lisa*. It was just a carpet.

'I thought it would be a good idea when I put it down,' Luc confessed, 'but it wasn't, and we're tripping over the edges. I'm going back to a bare floor, and I'll use the carpet for my own house.' The tables had already been moved to the side and the carpet lay rolled and tied in the centre of the floor.

'It's heavy,' said Thomas as they began to drag it out to the cart.

'It's good quality,' said Luc. 'That's why I'm taking it for the house.'

They had quite a job getting it on to the handcart, and a section stuck out at the back, but Luc supported it and pushed while Thomas pulled the cart from the front.

'We need Robert,' said Thomas.

'We'll be all right,' said Luc.

It was a long, slow climb up the streets towards Luc's place. Years of manual work had given Thomas the strength of an ox, but he was grunting, and Luc was sweating profusely. Finally, however, they reached their destination.

Luc's house lay at the end of a narrow street that was nestled against the hillside of Montmartre. It had belonged to a builder before Luc bought it. There was a small yard at the front, with bushes on one side and trees on the other. Behind the house lay a small garden. On the left rose the steep slope of the hill covered with shrubs. At the end, a wall. On the right, another wall, and the back of a shed belonging to another house. Against the slope, there was a wooden hut containing a privy, with a small garden shed adjoining it.

They got the carpet into the house, down the narrow hallway and into the main room. At the end of that, they needed a break.

'I'll get you a beer,' said Luc, and Thomas nodded gratefully.

As Luc poured their beer, Thomas said, 'The carpet's too big for this room, I think.'

'I'm going to cut it down.'

'Do you want to open it out and see? I don't mind helping you.'

'Not now. I'm too tired.'

'What was it you wanted to talk to me about, then?'

'Oh. I just wanted to know if you needed any money. I have quite a bit put by.'

'That's kind of you, Luc. But we're all right. If I'm ever in trouble, I'll tell you.'

'Just so long as you let me know.'

They drank their beers in silence, until Luc got up to use the privy.

Thomas measured the carpet with his eye. He wondered how much too big it was. It suddenly occurred to him that if there was a spare strip, he might take it for the passage in their lodgings. Taking out his knife, he cut the string that was tied around the carpet, and began to unroll it.

Then he stepped back, and stared in horror.

Luc gazed at him sadly.

'Why did you do that?' he said.

Thomas did not answer.

'I was only gone for a moment.' Luc sighed. 'I never meant you to see. I didn't want you to know.'

'What happened?'

'An accident. It was awful.'

460

'Didn't you get the police?'

'I couldn't. They mightn't have believed it was an accident.' He shook his head. 'It didn't look right.'

'You killed her?'

'Of course not.'

'People will look for her.'

'I don't think so. She was just . . . a young lady of the night. If they asked me, I could say that she left. But I don't think they'll even ask. I just have to get rid of the body.'

'Why did you kill her?'

'I didn't. I swear it. There was an argument . . . She fell. It was an accident. That's all.'

'*Oh mon Dieu!*'

'You mustn't tell anyone, Thomas. Not even Édith. Especially Édith.' He paused. 'Unless you want your brother . . .'

Executed. Or at least in prison.

'And now I'm party to it,' said Thomas.

'You opened the carpet. I never meant that to happen.'

'How will you dispose of the body?'

'That's a secret. Unless you want to help me.'

Thomas was silent. He had two choices. One was to go to the police at once, and betray his brother. The other was not to betray him. If the latter, then he wanted to be sure the body was never found. The poor girl was dead anyway.

He weighed the options.

'I never knew what was in the carpet. You understand? If you're ever caught and it's discovered I brought the carpet up here, I had no idea what was in it.'

'That was always my plan.'

'How will you hide her?'

Luc glanced out of the window. Dusk was already falling.

'You'll see soon enough,' he said.

It had been a year ago, Luc explained, that he'd been in the privy and heard a sound of rock and earth falling just behind him. Investigating afterwards, he'd discovered that there had been a little landslide on the slope. And as he probed further, he realised that a small fissure, a few inches wide, had appeared. When he pushed a stick through, he

461

found a cavity. The rock was quite soft. Widening the fissure, he was soon able to step into the cavity, and the next thing he knew, he was in a tunnel.

'It wasn't a great surprise. You know the hill of Montmartre is riddled with old gypsum mines.'

'So did you explore?'

'Oh yes. There's a network of tunnels in there.' He nodded thoughtfully. So I rebuilt the privy with a shed beside it. The back of the shed slides open. The opening's just behind it.'

'Did you tell anyone?'

'Not a soul, except you.'

Although the little garden wasn't overlooked, Luc waited until darkness had fallen before he led Thomas out to the privy. He gave Thomas a covered lamp to carry. While Thomas waited, Luc entered the little shed beside it, and Thomas heard a wooden partition slide open.

'Bring the lamp,' Luc whispered. Thomas stepped into the shed and felt Luc's hand guiding him through into the tunnel. 'Turn left,' Luc whispered, 'and walk twenty paces. Then you can uncover the lamp.' The surface under his feet felt stony.

When he uncovered the lamp, Thomas saw that he was in a high passage, about six feet wide, that led away into the distance. The walls were quite smooth and it was dry.

'Leave the lamp here,' Luc said. 'Nobody can see the light from outside. We'll go back for the girl now.'

She clearly had been in her early twenties. A fair-haired girl. She'd been hit in the face, but that hadn't killed her. More likely the blow to the back of her head had done that. She must have fallen hard against something. Thomas wanted to ask, 'How did it happen?' but he decided the less he knew the better.

There hadn't been too much blood, and Luc had wrapped her tightly in several large tablecloths to keep it from spreading. The blood there was dry and black.

'You'll have to get rid of the cloths. And the carpet might be stained,' Thomas said.

'I know,' said Luc. 'If there's a stain on the carpet, I'll cut it out. Use the good bits. Burn the rest. No one will ever see.'

It was completely dark when they took the girl's body out. They used straps to carry the corpse, which made it easier. It was a little tricky getting her into the shed and closing the door behind them, but they managed. Once they were in the passage, Luc closed up the entrance. After that, walking along the tunnel was relatively easy. When they reached the lamp, they put the body down. Thomas picked up the lamp and retraced their steps. He wanted to see if there were any drops of blood on the ground. He couldn't find any.

'Where to now?' he asked.

Without a word, Luc looped the strap over his left shoulder and, holding the lamp in his right hand, led the way. They made three or four turns down similar passages before coming to a larger, higher one. It was hard work and they paused several times. Thomas wasn't sure of the distance, but he thought they must have walked nearly three hundred yards.

'Are you sure people don't come in here?' he asked.

'They can't. I've explored it all. This part of the old mines has been sealed off for decades. The little landslide behind my house opened the only way in.'

'Then why are we going so far?'

'You'll see.'

At last they came to a high chamber, almost like a cave.

'This is it,' said Luc. They put the body down. Then he raised the lamp high. And Thomas let out a cry of fear.

For they weren't alone.

All around the walls, the skeletons lay. Some of them were propped almost in a sitting position, staring at them in their tattered clothes, as though at some final supper in the dark.

'Do you know who they are?' asked Luc.

'No.'

'At the end of the Commune, forty years ago, there was the famous last fight of the Communards at Père Lachaise. But before that, a party of Communards at Montmartre retreated into the gypsum mines. And instead of going in to finish them off, the army dynamited the entrance of the mine. They knew there was no way out of this section. I found other skeletons in the passages, but I think these fellows made a compact and decided to shoot themselves all together.' He turned to the corpse of the girl. 'Help me get her clothes off, then we'll drag her over to the wall.'

It wasn't pleasant work, but they did it. At one moment, Thomas gave a little gasp, and Luc said, 'What?' and Thomas said, 'Nothing.' When they had her propped naked against the wall, Luc carefully removed the tattered remains of a Communard's coat and wrapped it around her.

'In a year or two, she'll be a skeleton like the rest of them.'

'If anyone ever examines the shed . . .'

'I thought of that. I can cover the side of the hill up again. Close the entrance. It should be all right.'

Thomas frowned.

'Just one thing I don't understand. Why did you ever make the arrangement with the shed and the tunnel in the first place?'

Luc paused.

'I thought it would be a good place to hide things. That is, if I ever wanted to.'

'Oh,' said Thomas.

When they got back into the house, Luc said that Thomas should go.

'I'll be lighting a fire in the grate tonight,' he explained. 'Got to burn the clothes and the tablecloths. Then I'll check the carpet. You need to be well away before I start.'

'I delivered a carpet, that's all. I've got a family to support,' said Thomas.

'I know.' Luc looked up at him. 'When I was a little boy, you came and saved me from the Dalou gang. And you fought for me. I never forgot that, you know.'

Thomas shrugged.

'You were my little brother. That's all.'

'You just saved my life tonight.'

'I won't do it again,' Thomas warned.

'I'll never ask you.' He looked at Thomas with sad eyes. 'Do you still love me, brother?'

Thomas didn't answer.

'Well,' said Luc quietly, 'I love you.'

Thomas left.

As he took the cart back down the hill, he reflected on all that he'd seen. It seemed Édith was right about his brother. If he wanted a secret hiding place, then he was probably a receiver of stolen goods, and possibly a thief, just as she'd suggested.

Even worse was something else he'd noticed. As they were stripping the girl in the lamplight, he'd suddenly realised that there were bruises around her mouth and nose that didn't look like the bruising from being hit. Only one thing he knew of produced bruises like that.

If someone was deliberately suffocated.

His brother may have hit the girl. She may have banged the back of her head. But her death hadn't come from that. Luc had suffocated her.

His brother had just made him a party to murder.

For three days he wondered whether to go to the police. But the risk was too great. What might they do to him?

A week later, Luc came by to see them, but only briefly. As he left, he signalled to Thomas to walk down the street with him.

'The police came by. Asked me if I'd seen the girl. I said I thought she'd come by late in the week, and I had an idea she spoke of leaving town. But I've heard that before from these girls, I told them, and they usually show up again. They asked me if I knew where she came from. Not a clue, I said. They weren't very interested in her, I can tell you.'

'I don't know what you're talking about,' said Thomas quietly.

'Don't worry,' said Luc, 'nor do I.'

And as the weeks went by, they heard nothing more. Winter came, and the girl was forgotten. Just before Christmas, snow fell, covering all that was dark beneath the streets of Paris; and on the day after Christmas, the sun came out, and the snow gleamed as white as the church of Sacré Coeur, high on the hill of Montmartre.

Chapter Seventeen

1637

It was a December evening when it happened. Or did it? Something happened then, or close to that time. That was not in doubt. But what? Did the eyes of Charles de Cygne deceive him? There was no way of knowing, although the kingdom of France was at stake.

It began in an anteroom where he'd been waiting. Through the window, by the lamplight, he could see the bare boughs of a small tree bending in the December wind. Then the door opened, and a lackey's head appeared.

'His Eminence wants you.'

Charles de Cygne stepped out into the passage. A moment later he was in a high hall with a stone staircase.

Cardinal Richelieu's palace was magnificent. He had decided to build it just north of the Louvre, to be close to the king. And that was clearly convenient since, for nearly two decades now, it was Cardinal Richelieu who effectively ruled France.

People feared Richelieu. Perhaps a ruler needed to be feared, Charles thought. But he was a good master. Charles was thirty, with a young family. One day he'd inherit the family estate from his father, Robert. But in the meantime, the rewards that Richelieu had given him for his services provided income for which he was more than grateful.

Charles liked to think that he and Richelieu understood each other. They were both French aristocrats. But he had quickly learned what Richelieu valued. Speed, accuracy and, above all, discretion. Richelieu saw everything that passed in France. His spies were everywhere. Working for him, Charles had seen much private information. But whatever he saw, he kept to himself. Sometimes people would ask him about his work – people he knew and thought he could trust. They might be enemies of Richelieu, they might have an interest in some matter before the cardinal, or they might be spies, sent by Richelieu to test him. Who knew? But not one of them had ever got a word out of him. Not a word.

He started up the stairs. Reaching the top, he turned into a reception room.

Charles liked the Cardinal's Palace. With its big courtyards and delightful arcades, it had an Italian air. On its eastern side, work had begun on a handsome private theatre.

There were a few people waiting to see the cardinal in the reception room. He walked to the door at the opposite end, which was immediately opened for him. Aware of the envious glances from the men waiting behind him, he passed through into another salon. This one was empty. But now through a small door in the far corner, a single figure emerged.

He was nothing much to look at. A simple monk, well into middle age. In fact, Charles thought, he looked pale and unwell. He saw de Cygne, and a faint flicker of the eyelids indicated recognition. But nothing more.

Father Joseph, the *éminence grise*, who stood like a shadow beside the cardinal. A walking conscience. A man of silence. A man whose very mysteriousness made him feared.

Father Joseph and the cardinal had one enormous project upon which they agreed. They must weaken the influence of the Hapsburg family. With Spain to the south, the Holy Roman Empire and the Netherlands to the east, all under Hapsburg family control, France was boxed in. The interest of France must therefore be to weaken the Hapsburg threat.

One might like Richelieu, or not; but no one could doubt his devotion to France. It was one of the reasons de Cygne was proud to serve him. Father Joseph, however, was another matter. The ageing monk was against the Hapsburgs for another reason. They did not want to go to war with Turkey. That was not so surprising. Turkey was on the borders of their empire. Why should they want to stir up trouble so close to home? But Father Joseph wanted all Christendom to proclaim a new crusade against the Moslem Turks. It was his obsession. First weaken the Hapsburgs, then let France lead the West, as in olden times, against the Moslem power. Privately, Charles considered the idea of a latter-day crusade the height of folly and certain to bring ruin upon his country.

Once he had been summoned into the room by Richelieu when Father Joseph was with him, and the cardinal had remarked with a smile: 'Father Joseph wants France to lead a new crusade against the Turks, de Cygne. What do you think?'

Thank God that he'd already learned the rules of survival by then. With a low bow to the monk he had replied: 'My ancestors were crusading knights, Eminence. It is even believed that we descend from Roland, the companion of Charlemagne, who died fighting the Moslems of Spain.'

A clever answer. It seemed to say everything, and in fact said nothing. It appeared to satisfy the monk, anyway, and Richelieu smiled.

Rule number one of survival: never, never tell anyone what you really think.

This evening, therefore, he bowed respectfully to the ageing monk as he passed. Father Joseph really didn't look well. Perhaps he was going to die. That wouldn't be a bad thing, thought Charles.

He went through the small door from which Father Joseph had emerged, and found the cardinal writing a letter in his office.

'Sit down, my dear de Cygne,' he said quietly. 'I shan't be long.'

Charles sat quietly. The room was high and handsome without being sumptuous. Shelves of leather-bound books lined the walls – for Richelieu was a great book collector. It might have been an office in the Vatican. Patron of the new Académie Française, connoisseur of the arts, subtle diplomatist: Richelieu was a Frenchman, but he was more like an Italian prince of the Church.

From his chair, Charles surveyed the great man. Tall, elegant, a handsome, finely drawn face, his small beard neatly pointed, his eyes always thoughtful. As so often in times past, thought de Cygne, God had given France exactly the right person in her hour of need.

When that likable old rascal King Henry IV had been killed by a lunatic back in 1610, his heir was only a little boy, and Henry's widow, Marie de Médicis, had ruled the Regency council for young Louis XIII. It was strange, Charles thought, that an Italian Médicis should be stupid, but the Queen Mother certainly was, and she'd ruled badly. Indeed, as far as Charles de Cygne was concerned, she'd done only three good things for France: She'd been the patron of the great artist Rubens, she'd built a delightful little palace for herself, called the Luxembourg, about half a mile south of the river, and west of the university. And she and her council had first brought Richelieu into the royal government.

It had taken young Louis XIII a while to get power away from his mother. But though he dealt quite effectively with some rebellions, the daily administration of his kingdom seemed to bore him, and he'd entrusted more and more administration to Richelieu. It was the best thing he could have done. For nearly two decades they had made a wonderful team.

The cardinal finished his letter. Before sealing it, he carefully read it over. He looked tired.

As Charles gazed at him with admiration, he wondered: What would happen when the cardinal left the scene? Not that he was old. He was only in his early fifties, but his health was not good. Something he'd said the other day had indicated that he himself had his earthly end in mind.

'You know, de Cygne, I have already left this palace to the king in my will. It seemed the sensible thing to do.' Then he sighed. 'We have achieved much, but there has never been time to tackle the country's finances properly. That is the great task for the future.'

Yet who could take his place? There was no obvious candidate yet, but the man who had impressed the cardinal most in recent years was a young Italian with a gift for diplomacy. Mazarini was his name, though he'd changed it to Mazarin now, which sounded more French. He wasn't noble. It was even rumoured that he was partly Jewish. But it was his intelligence that impressed Richelieu, who considered him a future statesman.

It turn, Charles had noticed, Mazarin seemed to model himself on the cardinal, cutting his hair and beard in exactly the same way. He had his own personality though. He liked to gamble. He had already made himself popular with both King Louis and his wife.

Would Mazarin be his next master? Charles de Cygne had no idea, but with all his heart he wished Richelieu long life.

Richelieu folded the letter, dripped a little sealing wax on to the paper and gently pressed his signet ring down upon the hot wax.

'My friend,' he said softly, 'I want you to walk across to the Louvre. You are to ask, in my name, to be taken to the queen. Please give this letter into her hands – and her hands only. When that is done, and she has it, there is no need to wait for a reply, but be so good as to return here and let me know that this little mission is accomplished.' He smiled. 'I entrust this errand to you personally because the subject of the letter is exceedingly sensitive.'

Leaving the palace, Charles wrapped his cloak about him tightly. A cold rain was falling with the gusting wind. Foul winter weather. He crossed the square in front of the cardinal's palace. Ahead of him, the long mass of the Louvre's north side loomed dark and solemn. Through the rain, he could see the dim lamps by a side door.

He announced his business. The sentries knew him. A young officer conducted him along the dimly lit stone halls and galleries towards the queen's apartments.

As he walked along in silence, he had time to reflect.

Anne, the daughter of the Hapsburg king of Spain, had married King Louis XIII of France when they were both fourteen. It was the usual dynastic marriage, on this occasion to lessen tensions between her Hapsburg family and the kingdom of France.

What had it been like for her? Charles wondered. It couldn't have been easy.

For by the time they met, Louis XIII of France was exhibiting a very rare medical condition: a double set of teeth. Perhaps because of this, or perhaps for other reasons, he had a terrible stutter. If the girl found this off-putting, what agonies, Charles wondered, had the fourteen-year-old boy suffered?

When they were both eighteen, they conceived a child, but it was stillborn. The same thing happened again, three years later, then another four years after, then another five after that, in 1631. And then, nothing. It was said that when they did sleep in the same bed, his wife kept a bolster between them.

Charles felt sorry for the king. People complained that he was constantly off hunting. Poor devil, he thought, it's probably to get away from them all. He seemed to have no mistresses. Was that piety, lack of inclination, or the fear that women found him repulsive? Who knew?

'He's bedded one or two young men,' the king's hunting companions told him. Perhaps that was what Louis preferred. Or perhaps he'd turned to men because he'd given up on women.

Whatever was going on in the king's mind, or in the heart of his wife, France had no heir.

That wasn't quite true. There was the king's younger brother Gaston. But what a disaster he would be. Constantly plotting against Louis and Richelieu, unreliable, untruthful, disloyal and still without any male heirs of his own in any case, Gaston was the last person that any responsible courtier wanted to see on the throne of France.

No wonder, as he felt his own health failing, that Richelieu had been secretly doing all he could to provide France with an heir. Some time ago, he had persuaded the royal couple to resume their marital relations, and they'd done so. Such things could be known, and Richelieu knew. But nothing had come of it yet.

One could only pray.

They were at the queen's apartments. He was told to wait. Then the door was held open.

She received him in an anteroom. Her bedroom was just beyond. She was wearing a nightgown. It seemed she was already retiring to bed. But she smiled at him pleasantly as he bowed.

'Good evening, Monsieur de Cygne. I'm sorry if you got wet coming to see me. You have a private letter from the cardinal?'

Despite her strict Spanish upbringing, there was a gentle playfulness in her manner that was entirely pleasant. She was certainly a good-looking woman, Charles thought. Her hair had a natural hint of red, her eyes were large and brown. She was full-breasted, her skin perfect, her hands especially beautiful. For just a second his face may have given away that he was thinking how delightful it must be to share her bed, but he quickly lowered his gaze. If she noticed, she probably didn't mind.

'I was to deliver it personally, Majesty, into your hands alone.'

'Then I thank you, monsieur.' She smiled again. 'Good night.'

'Your Majesty.' He bowed again and began to withdraw.

It was as he did so that the door of the queen's bedroom beyond slowly swung open, allowing him a glimpse into a large, high room, softly lit with candles.

And then he saw the man. It was only a fleeting glance, since he instantly looked down, pretending to have seen nothing as he backed out of the anteroom. A moment's vision of a man in the candlelight.

It could have been King Louis. He thought the king had gone away hunting, but it could have been King Louis, certainly. Only, in that brief glimpse, he could have sworn it was another face he knew.

Mazarin. The Italian. It had looked like Mazarin.

He'd been away in Italy recently, and on his return, Richelieu had sent him off on another commission. Charles had not thought that Mazarin was in Paris.

Ten minutes later he was back in Richelieu's office.

'It is done, Eminence. I spoke with the queen and gave her the letter myself.'

'Good. Did you see anything else?'

Charles hesitated, just a second. What did the cardinal know? What answer did he want? If in doubt, discretion.

'The queen had just retired. She came out and received me in the anteroom. Having delivered the letter, I withdrew. That is all I can say, Eminence. I had the impression that she was about to go to sleep.'

'And so you should yourself, de Cygne. Go home to your wife and son. How old is young Roland, now?'

'He is seven, Eminence.'

'I am glad you have a son. It is a fine thing for a man to have a son.' The cardinal paused. 'Let us hope the king will have a son, before too long. That's what we need.'

Charles stared at him. But the great man had already started to write another letter, and he did not look up.

So Charles remembered that strange evening, nine months later when, to general rejoicing, King Louis XIII of France and his wife had a son, to whom he gave his own name, Louis. Everyone said the birth of the child was a gift from God, and so no doubt it was.

Thus Louis XIV was born, a strong and healthy baby. Richelieu was relieved.

And Charles de Cygne said not a word.

1665

The Pont Neuf was a curious place. When Henry IV had built it, he had wanted a fine, simple bridge, uncluttered by houses, that spanned the entire river from Right Bank to Left, with the Île de la Cité serving as a central platform, a station, as the new bridge strode across the water. He wanted something handsome.

But then humanity came flocking, from every alley, every tavern, every dark cavity of the city. And instead of a jostling narrow thoroughfare squeezed between houses, like the other bridges, it found a broad open platform, delightfully set over the busy river, where there was ample room to play.

Singers, dancers, musicians, acrobats, jugglers, women selling love potions, cutpurses, preachers – they all gathered on the Pont Neuf. Anyone crossing the bridge on a sunny day was certain to find something to claim their attention and make them late for their meeting.

And not the least among these entertainers and villains was a large man, quite a handsome fellow really, with a mop of dark hair, who wore a red scarf around his neck, who made extemporary speeches from which he would continuously break off to insult any passerby. The richer and more important they looked, the more vigorous and more pointed his insults. It would have shown a lack of Gallic spirit if his victims had not thrown him a coin or two for insulting them – so long as it was done with wit. But there was always the possibility that someone would not see the humour of it, and try to punish him. And this would cause merriment as well, for he was not only large but exceedingly strong.

'I was born a huge baby,' he would declare. 'So my father called me Hercule, after the hero Hercules. My mother, after giving birth, called me Salaud. And I have been both ever since.'

His speciality was logic. He would take any proposition – it might be supplied by his audience, the more absurd the better – and then with extravagant logic, with indefatigable reasoning, and with asides insulting anyone who caught his eye, he would prove that the insane proposition must be true.

'I am the modern Abelard,' he would shout. 'But I am superior in three ways. My logic is better than his. And I have two balls.' And then, to the nearest pretty woman, irrespective of whether she was a streetwalker or a fashionable lady in her carriage: 'Permit me, madame, to furnish you with the proof, the absolute proof, of my assertion.'

If anyone crossed him, however, they could expect no mercy. When a young noble passed by him with a look of scorn, Hercule Le Sourd's revenge was to call out instantly:

> *'He will not pay me for my wit,*
> *This noble in his fine outfit*
> *Fine clothes, monsieur – a perfect fit*
> *On a piece of SHIT!'*

And when the young man made as if to draw his sword: 'He draws his sword. By day he wears it at his side. By night, between his legs. After all, he needs something to get his hands on.'

When he wasn't holding court on the Pont Neuf, he made a living as a shoemaker. That was his craft. But this he did at his own little workshop, and at his own pace. Whenever the weather was fine, he came out on to the Pont Neuf, and picked up quite as much money by exercising his wit as he ever made from his proper trade.

Once a young dandy, refusing to take his wit in good part, had drawn his sword and wounded Le Sourd badly in the arm. Le Sourd could have had him arrested, but he didn't.

'I never resort to the law,' he explained to his audience. 'I am a philosopher.' Six months later, the young dandy vanished.

But today, on a warm afternoon in the summer of 1665, Le Sourd the philosopher had a slight feeling of unease.

It was the fourth time the carriage had stopped near him on the bridge.

The carriage was closed. It evidently belonged to someone with money, but there was no coat of arms or other marking to identify the owner. It was driven by a coachman without grooms in attendance. As before, it stopped at a short distance just south of him on the bridge, but close enough to hear his speeches through a narrow opening in the door. There was a thin curtain across the slit, but he had the feeling that he was being observed as well.

Observed by whom? Some aristocrat who found him amusing, but who did not wish to reveal his identity? Possibly. A spy? Also possible.

Cardinal Mazarin always had many spies. They'd have been in the crowd, no doubt, but if their reports had made the great man curious . . . One never knew.

But the person in the carriage couldn't be Mazarin himself. Four years ago, after governing for as long as his mentor Richelieu, he also had died in harness, before the age of sixty. It might be some other powerful figure though. It could even be . . . he trembled slightly at the thought of it . . . the young king himself.

So was he going to change his tune? Was he going to watch his language, or be careful not to insult the government – just in case?

No. He was Hercule Le Sourd. Let them arrest him if they dared. This was the Pont Neuf, and he was its philosopher king.

He ignored the carriage and began a tirade about the vices of the nobles, adding, for good measure, that if young Louis XIV were a man, he'd hang most of them from the nearest lamp. He glanced at the carriage as he said it, but there was no sign whatever from within.

The carriage was still there when he finished almost an hour later. He started to walk across to the Left Bank, which meant he would pass the carriage. As he drew level, the coachman touched his shoulder lightly with his whip and called down to him: 'Get in.'

'Why?'

'Someone wants to speak to you.'

'Who?'

At this moment, the carriage door opened. And Hercule Le Sourd looked up in surprise.

Geneviève d'Artagnan had always understood her situation in life, from the time she was a little girl. Her family was noble, but they were out of money.

For her brother, the choices were clear. He could marry an heir-ess. Even if she wasn't noble, he would still be, and so would their children. Or he could become a big success in the world and recoup his fortunes that way. Of course, he couldn't engage in trade of any kind. That wasn't something a noble was allowed to do. But he might become a soldier, or serve the king in some capacity that would bring him fame and fortune, and marry a rich wife too.

For girls like her, it was different. She must marry a noble and preferably a rich one.

For if she married a man who wasn't noble, then she lost her own nobility at once, and her children would be baseborn too. Her husband might be rich, but she would have no social standing. Society's doors would be closed to her and her descendants, and if those descendants wanted to achieve any high position in the king's service, it would be almost impossible for them without noble status. It mattered. It was everything.

And yet, in France, there was a way around this problem. The king might ennoble one's husband for his services. But that could take a lifetime. There were also numerous official positions which carried with them a title of nobility. Or, simpler still, one could buy a title.

Over the centuries, noble families often acquired many titles. Often the titles came with estates they had been granted or had acquired. And they were allowed to sell those titles. It was perfectly legal. So a rich man could buy his way into the nobility. And if his wife came from a noble family herself, with relations who were only too anxious to keep the family status up, then her children would slide so easily into the noble title their bourgeois father had bought that few people would even remember that they had nearly slipped out of the class to which their mother belonged.

Geneviève's sister Catherine had married a rich merchant. But he had shown no interest in getting himself ennobled. This had caused Geneviève and her brother some grief, but it seemed there was noth-ing they could do about it. Geneviève had married a noble.

Perceval d'Artagnan came from a cadet branch of the ancient family of Montesquiou d'Artagnan, which, long ago, had gone their own way and chosen to be known by the simpler appellation of d'Artagnan.

When Geneviève married Perceval, she had done well. He had enough money to maintain both a pleasant château on the edge of Burgundy and a house in Paris. He was proud of his ancient lineage, which went back over seven centuries to an ancient ruler of Gascony. In this century, however, a distant relation had also taken the name of d'Artagnan, and this had not pleased Geneviève's husband.

'The fellow's just a spy and general stooge for Mazarin,' he'd told her dismissively when they first married. But recently this d'Artagnan had risen so far in the royal service that he'd become head of the king's prestigious Musketeers, and favoured at court. From this time, Geneviève noticed, her husband started referring to him as 'my kinsman d'Artagnan, the Musketeer'.

It might be said, then, that Geneviève had everything she wanted. She had comfort, and status, and after a dozen years of marriage she had two children living, a boy and a girl, both of whom were strong and healthy. There was only one problem.

She had a husband who did nothing.

He had always been a man of strong views. The chief of these, from their earliest days together, had been the importance of the old aristocracy.

'It all began with Richelieu,' he'd complain, 'a nobleman who should have known better: this constant undermining of the old feudal privileges. They want to make the king into a central tyrant. As for the upstart Mazarin . . .' His disgust for the lowborn Italian cardinal was complete.

The two Fronde rebellions that came just before their marriage had brought matters to a head. First the lesser nobles and Parisians had rebelled against paying new taxes; then the old princely families had done the same. The mob had entered the Louvre. Mazarin had been driven out of Paris.

But order had been restored. Supported by the young king's mother – who was now so close to the cardinal that they seemed like man and wife – Mazarin ruled once more. The boy Louis XIV, whom Mazarin treated like a son, had come of age; in 1661, when the cardinal died, he had taken the reins of power into his strong young hands.

And if one thing was clear, Geneviève thought – whether her husband liked it or not – it was that young Louis XIV, having loved

Mazarin like a father, and seen the chaos of the Fronde, had no intention of leaving France in the hands of the old feudal nobility. He meant to rule them with a rod of iron. Her husband could huff and puff as much as he liked, but he was living in the past.

And doing nothing. He spent time on his estate. He hunted. He went about in Paris. And that was it. His sole occupation was being an aristocrat, and it never occurred to him that this was not enough do with one's life.

'You know, Catherine,' she remarked to her sister once, 'I some-times think you were right to marry a merchant. At least he has something to do.'

'He works because he has to.'

'That may be. But he works. A man should work. I respect him.'

'You don't respect Monsieur d'Artagnan?'

'No. Not any more. It makes things . . . difficult.'

'I'm sorry.'

'Perhaps you could lend me your husband now and then.'

Her sister laughed.

'What would Monsieur d'Artagnan say to that?'

Geneviève shrugged.

'At least it keeps it in the family.'

'Well, I'm afraid you can't borrow my husband, and please don't try.'

'I won't.' Geneviève sighed. '*Mon Dieu*, Catherine, I'm bored.'

Hercule Le Sourd stared. It was a handsome, fair-haired woman inside the carriage. An aristocrat by the look of it. She motioned for him to sit opposite her. He hesitated. Then, out of curiosity really, he complied.

'Close the door,' she said.

He did so, and immediately the carriage started to move.

'I have been listening to you, several times,' she said.

'I noticed. But I assumed it was a man. A government spy, perhaps.'

She laughed.

'I suppose I could be a government spy. No doubt some of them are women. How exciting.'

'What do you want?'

'You are quite clever, monsieur. If you weren't clever, the things you shout would merely be rude, and vulgar. But your speeches are very witty. Do you rehearse them?'

'There are parts I have composed. But I invent things as I go along. As the spirit moves me.'

'Can you read and write?'

'A little.'

'You sound quite learned. All that philosophy.'

'I used to go into the Latin Quarter and listen to the students talking in the taverns. I picked it up. I suppose it interested me.'

'What else do you do?'

'I make shoes.'

'And what is your name?'

'Hercule Le Sourd.'

She laughed.

'It's a funny combination. Half hero, half robber, perhaps.'

'I've never had to steal. What is your name?'

'I shall not tell you, monsieur.'

'As you like.'

Le Sourd looked at her thoughtfully. He already knew what she wanted.

He'd been married when he was younger. His wife had died three years ago, leaving him with a five-year-old son. He and his sister's family lived in the same street, just south of the university quarter, near the Gobelins factory where the tapestries were made. With his son and his sister's children almost forming an extended family, Le Sourd had felt no immediate pressure to provide himself with another wife. The personal magnetism he displayed on the Pont Neuf made him attractive to women, and for the last couple of years he'd enjoyed a series of romances while retaining his independence. His conquests had included the wives of several well-to-do merchants. But this aristocratic lady was something entirely new.

He decided to wait and see what she did next.

'You must be hungry after all your efforts,' she said. 'Would you like to dine with me?'

'If the food is good,' he answered.

*   *   *

479

The coachman seemed to know where to go. They had crossed on to the Right Bank now, east of the Louvre. Soon the carriage turned left, towards the Marais. The thought crossed his mind that this woman could be a lunatic of some kind. He was big and strong enough to overpower her and the coachman too. But what if she decided to poison him?

She seemed to read his thoughts.

'Life is full of risks.'

'Are we going to your house?' he asked.

'No.' She was watching him carefully. 'I dare not. Tell me about yourself.'

He shrugged. He had nothing in particular to hide. He told her about his family, poor craftsmen mostly. 'They say we descend from quite an important criminal, who was hanged, a long time ago.'

'You think it's true?'

'I expect so. We've tried not to get caught since.'

He told her about the loss of his wife and that he had a son.

'But you haven't married again.'

'Not yet.'

'You prefer to be independent.'

'What makes you think so, madame?'

She smiled.

'Have you heard yourself ranting on the Pont Neuf?'

Through the thin curtains, he could see where they were now. They had come into Henry IV's Place Royale, in the heart of the Marais. There they stopped. He heard the coachman descend. The door opened.

'We shall dine,' she said to the coachman. And turning to Le Sourd: 'If you step out for a moment, he will set up the table.'

The coachman went to the back of the carriage. From a compartment he removed a narrow table with legs that swung down, like a trestle. To his surprise, Le Sourd realised that this was going to be inserted inside the carriage. While the coachman busied himself with this task, he looked around him.

There was no doubt that the square was the most delightful place in Paris. With its four equal sides of perfectly matched brick and stone, the terraced mansions gazed softly down upon the rows of clipped green trees inside which lay the four lawns. At the street level, the arcades with their rounded arches turned the ensemble into a huge cloister.

Unsurprisingly, everyone soon forgot that King Henry had meant these houses to be tenanted by honest working families. The rich, seeing the quality of the place, had taken it over for themselves. But ordinary folk could still enter its quiet arcades and enjoy the intimate peace of the great square.

Having inserted the table inside the carriage, the coachman drew out a wicker basket from the same compartment and proceeded to lay the table. When he had done that, he took a wooden pail, went to a nearby pump and filled it so that the horse could drink. It was clear that he was now supposed to go off to a tavern and leave his mistress and her guest to their meal.

'Come,' she called to him quietly. 'Let's dine.'

It was really a most convenient arrangement. The table took up the space where he had been sitting. But by sitting beside his hostess, there was plenty of room to eat very comfortably.

'My husband invented the table and had a carpenter make it,' she informed him. 'This is my husband's one contribution to civilisation.'

'And it works,' Le Sourd pointed out, in fairness to the absent gentleman.

Haricots, pressed duck, an excellent wine, several cheeses, fruit. It was a perfect little meal. Without giving away her name, or where she lived, she talked in general terms about her family and the château where her husband now was to make it quite clear that she was exactly the aristocrat he had taken her to be.

Did she do this regularly? he wondered. The coachman, whose discretion she clearly trusted, seemed to know exactly what to do.

'I feel I am taking part in a ritual,' he remarked.

'A ritual, monsieur, that takes place very rarely. Only when the heavens are aligned in a particular way.'

'Then I am honoured indeed.'

'If you aren't happy, you are always free to leave.'

'I prefer to stay.'

When they had finished, she asked him if he had observed how the table and the basket fitted into the compartment behind. He said he had. 'Then perhaps you would be so kind as to return them to their place.' He easily repacked the basket. It took him a moment or two to master the catch that released the table, but soon he had that outside. It took him only a couple of minutes to stow everything safely in the back.

He glanced around. It was a quiet, sleepy evening. Hardly anyone was moving about in the square.

He stepped back into the carriage and closed the door.

She had removed her gown. He could see that she had a splendid body. She reached out her hand to pull him towards her.

The coachman did not return for over an hour.

It was October when Geneviève told her sister.

'Does your husband know?' Catherine asked.

'I told him.'

'Does he think the baby could be his?'

'No. It's impossible.'

'Tell me what happened.'

Geneviève told her everything.

'You're insane!' cried Catherine.

'I know.' Geneviève shook her head. 'I can't believe I did it.'

'Why? Was it the risk? The danger?'

'Yes. That made it exciting. I was so bored. I wanted something . . . exciting to happen.'

'Does Perceval know what you did? I mean, going out into the streets like that and . . .?'

'No. I lied to him about that. He thinks it was something that suddenly happened . . . a moment's madness . . . you know.'

'What's he going to do?'

'Preserve the honour of the family name, of course. What else?'

1685

Perceval d'Artagnan gazed at his daughter Amélie. He was a medium-sized man with a pot belly, and the long wig that was the fashion of the day disguised the fact that he was entirely bald. Whoever Amélie's real father was, d'Artagnan thought, he seemed to have bequeathed her a fine head of dark brown hair. In other respects, she looked very like her mother.

Amélie herself, of course, had no idea. She thought he was her father. She loved him as a father. So he found himself torn.

How could he not love the pretty little child who would come running up to him in total innocence and put her hand in his? The child whom he carried on his shoulder and taught to ride? She was sweet-natured, truthful, everything he could have desired in a daughter. He loved her for herself.

And only sometimes, when he was quite alone, did he secretly allow himself to feel the black rage, the hatred that was in his heart – not for the child herself, but for his wife.

Geneviève had not been unfaithful to him again. She had sworn an oath and he'd been sure she would keep it. For the last twenty years they had got along together as well as most married couples. Some affection had grown up between them, especially because of his kindness to little Amélie. But during those years he had learned another sad truth: small wounds are healed by time; but time can only bandage great wounds, which continue to bleed in secret.

And now Amélie was in love. She was not yet twenty. Her mother had discovered the state of her feelings the day before, and had asked him to talk to her.

'My child,' he said, firmly, but as kindly as possible, 'you can't marry this man, you know.'

She stared at him miserably.

'Is he intending to ask for your hand?'

'He loves me. I am sure he loves me.'

He smiled at her fondly and shook his head. The whole business was absurd, but he knew that didn't make it any easier for Amélie.

If only Geneviève's sister hadn't married a tradesman, none of this would have happened. In all likelihood, Amélie would never have met Pierre Renard. But of course, when she went to see her cousins, she met all sorts of townspeople like him, whom she would not have been familiar with in her own home.

Pierre Renard was a pleasant, handsome man in his late twenties. He was a younger son, but his family were modestly wealthy. Any young girl might have fallen in love with him.

But he couldn't marry Amélie.

In the first place, he was a Protestant. Until late in the reign of Henry IV, his forebears had been good Catholics. But then his grandfather had married a second wife who was Protestant and converted himself. Pierre's father had built up a considerable fortune, but never returned to the Catholic faith. Whether nineteen-year-old Amélie, seriously in love for the first time, imagined that she could convert her husband back to the true faith, or whether she planned to become a heretic herself, d'Artagnan did not know. He didn't even need to find out.

For a second objection overrode even the religious one. Pierre Renard was not noble.

'I couldn't let you lose everything that your nobility gives you, my child,' he told her. 'When you are older you will thank me for saving you and your children from such a terrible and permanent blow.'

It was true that he was saving her from herself. But there was another thought, equally important, in his mind. Whatever the circumstances of her birth, she bore his name. His family honour was at stake. No one bearing the name of d'Artagnan was going to marry out of the nobility.

'You must put this young man out of your thoughts, Amélie, and you must not see him again.'

As she left the room, he could see that she was about to weep, but there was nothing else to be done.

His eldest son and daughter were both married, quite happily, into noble families like his own. He'd known that it was time to find a husband for Amélie too. This little incident was a reminder that he'd better make a start.

The letter he had received that morning came at an opportune moment, therefore. He decided to reply to it at once.

The following days were hard for Amélie. When she had confessed to her mother that she was in love, she hadn't told her everything.

The crisis had begun after she confided her feelings for Pierre Renard to her cousin Isabelle. Isabelle had told her brother Yves, who'd discovered from Pierre that he was in love with Amélie, but that since she was both noble and Catholic, and he couldn't abandon his Protestant faith, he thought there was no hope. Isabelle had passed this information back to Amélie.

'If he asked me, I'd probably elope with him,' said Amélie.

'But what about his religion?' Isabelle had objected.

It was certainly true that in the last few years, life had become much more difficult for the Huguenot community. Louis XIV believed the old adage: 'The people follow the faith of their king.' He liked order. Protestants in a Catholic country meant disorder. And he could point to the earlier troubles in France and in many other countries to prove his assertion.

King Henry IV's Edict of Nantes had protected the Huguenots for more than eighty years. But nowadays, the Sun King was putting more and more pressure on them to convert. He'd even started quartering cavalry troops in Protestant households, making the owners' lives a misery. And there was every sign that the persecutions were likely to get worse.

'You'd have to be mad to become a Protestant now,' Isabelle told her.

But Amélie was too much in love to care.

She didn't care that he wasn't noble either. When she looked at the lives of her cousins, they seemed quite happy, living without the social burdens and prohibitions that were the price to be paid for a noble's pride and tax reliefs.

Wisely, she didn't say any of this to her parents.

But she thought of Pierre. She thought of him constantly. She yearned just to be in his presence. If only she could talk to him.

What a fool she'd been to confess her secret to her mother. She had little doubt that her cousins would have let Pierre know her feelings for him by now. If she'd just kept her mouth shut with her mother, she and Pierre might have met at her cousins' house, just as they had before. She could have given him an opening. They might have reached an understanding. Even if he'd told her that love between them was impossible, that would have been something. He could have told her that he loved her all the same.

Instead of which, she was left in doubt. Her parents were keeping her away from her cousins, so there was no news from them. She kept hoping, foolishly, that he would appear, that he'd come to the house to see her father and ask for her hand. He might be refused, but the fact that he'd come would have meant the world to her. She knew it made no sense. Her father's house lay a short way west of the Cardinal's Palace – the Palais Royal as it was called now – and she'd stare out her window moodily into the rue Saint-Honoré, in case he should go by. If he'd come to the window with a ladder, she'd have scrambled on to it. An even more absurd idea. But she couldn't help it. These were her sad daydreams.

It was on a Friday in mid-October that her mother came into her bedroom and gave her a strange look.

'There is news that you should know, Amélie. Yesterday the king took a great decision. He is revoking the Edict of Nantes. It will become law on Monday.'

'What will that mean for the Protestants?' Amélie asked.

'They will all be forced to become Catholic. The king is sending troops to all the main routes out of the kingdom to stop the Huguenots from escaping.'

'Then Pierre Renard will be a Catholic.'

'No doubt.' She looked at her daughter sadly. 'It won't help you, Amélie. He still won't be a noble.'

On Monday, the Revocation became law.

On Wednesday, her aunt Catherine came to the house, accompanied by Isabelle. Amélie anxiously took Isabelle to one side to ask if there was any news of Pierre Renard.

'You haven't heard?'

'I've heard nothing.'

'Pierre Renard has vanished.' Isabelle took her by the arm. 'You'd better forget him, Amélie. The whole family's gone. Nobody knows where they are. But I don't think he'll be coming back.'

All over France, a similar pattern could be found. Some families acted at once, others waited for months. But the Edict of Fontainebleau, as the king's order was called, had just made their lives impossible.

All Protestant churches were to be destroyed and any Protestant religious meeting, even a small group in a private house, was illegal. The participants would have all their property seized. Any child born to a Protestant parent was to be baptised Catholic and sent to Catholic schools. Failure would mean a huge fine of five hundred livres. Protestant ministers had two weeks to renounce their faith or leave France. If caught after that, they'd be sent to the galleys. Ordinary members of the Protestant congregation trying to leave France would be arrested. Men to the galleys, women stripped of all their possessions.

It was totalitarian. It was comprehensive. A century before, the Massacre of Saint Bartholomew's Day had been a horror. But the machinery of Louis XIV's centralising state was far more thorough. The Protestants were smashed. Large numbers, having no other option, converted to Catholicism. Perhaps a million converted in this way.

And yet, miraculously, hundreds of thousands managed to leave. Taking quiet roads, walking through woods, hiding in wagons and barges, hundreds of thousands of them managed to slip over the borders into the Netherlands, Switzerland or Germany. Others got out through Huguenot ports before the king could block them. They ran huge risks in doing so, and they had to be careful. But for all his power and all his troops, the Sun King could not stop them. France was too big, the Huguenots too many. Like the mass migration of Puritans from England to America, fifty years before, about two per cent of the population, including some of the most skilled, were lost to their country, and gained by others.

The Renard family, by acting swiftly, had shown much wisdom. Without a word to their friends and neighbours, they discreetly vanished. A month later, they arrived in London, where the existing Huguenot community soon grew to many times its size.

A week after the Edict of Fontainebleau, Perceval d'Artagnan called Amélie to him for a talk.

'My child,' he announced, 'I have good news for you. A great opportunity has arisen – one that may change your life entirely.' Madame de Saint-Loubert, a distant kinswoman of the family, well connected at court, had recently written to him, he explained, to let him know of a position that might be of interest. He had written back. 'And now it's all arranged.' He smiled. 'You're to go to Versailles.'

'To Versailles, Papa?' Amélie looked astonished. 'I thought you hated the court.'

She was right, of course. During the last twenty years, d'Artagnan had watched the Sun King's grip on France get tighter and tighter. If Cardinal Richelieu had been the mentor of Cardinal Mazarin, Mazarin in turn had left the king with a trained successor, the super-intendent of finances, Colbert. For twenty years Colbert had built up a bureaucracy of plain men who quietly took more and more of the administration of France into their hands.

As long as the court remained in Paris, the process hadn't been too noticeable. The king had made improvements to the Louvre, and started building the splendid hospital of Les Invalides for army veter-ans. That was welcome. Social life had continued as usual. The aris-tocrats had their mansions. Corneille, Molière and Racine had filled the theatres. And if bureaucrats increasingly attended to the tiresome business of running the government, the aristocrats still provided the army officers. Theirs was the honour of battle. They could fight and die for their king, in the old-fashioned way, pride themselves on their valour, win glory like the heroes of feudal times and look down upon the bureaucrats and merchant classes alike.

Until the court moved to Versailles. It had happened only three years ago, but the transformation had been complete. Anyone who wanted office and preferment now had to abandon Paris and live under the king's supervision there. Even valiant soldiers, having campaigned in the summer – for war, thank God, was still an affair of gentlemen, to be conducted in the summer season – still needed to spend the winter in lodgings in Versailles so that they could catch the eye of the king and get a command the following year. And they had to hang about there all the time. They could visit their estates when necessary, but if they slipped off to Paris for a week without permission, the king would notice and their chance of a command would be gone. D'Artagnan disliked the king and his methods, but he could see his cunning. Louis now had everyone under his thumb.

'It's true that I don't like Versailles,' he confessed to Amélie, 'and I don't want to go there myself. But it's still a wonderful opportunity for you. The position that's on offer is beyond anything we might have hoped for. You'll be one of the maids of honour to the dauphine, the daughter-in-law of the king himself.' He smiled kindly. 'And I think the change of scene will do you good.'

The matter was decided in any case. Three days later, Amélie found herself on her way to the court at Versailles.

As Roland de Cygne looked at the letter, he knew that he must answer it. But he didn't want to.

It was some months since he had communicated the sad news of his wife's death to his cousin Guy in Canada. It was the first time he'd written to him in years.

In the early part of the century, his grandfather had corresponded with his brother Alain regularly. They were devoted to each other, and the three thousand miles of ocean that lay between them could not alter that. For a long time Robert had hoped that his younger brother would cover himself in glory in Canada, achieve a great position and the wealth that came with it and return to France to found a second branch of the family. This dream perhaps never died until the day that Robert himself departed.

But things hadn't worked out that way. Not that Alain had done badly. He'd received some quite substantial land grants. But they required his attention if they were going to be worth anything. In due course he'd asked his brother to find him a wife of noble family, but who would not mind sharing the hardships of the frontier. That had not been easy. It had been quite impossible to find a girl with any fortune. But in the end Robert had found the youngest daughter of an impoverished nobleman who was reduced to a state hardly better than a small farmer, and she had been willing to take on the nobleman with his tract in the wilderness. After her arrival in Canada,

Alain had written back that his brother had made an excellent choice, and that they were very happy together.

The next generation had continued the correspondence. Roland remembered his grandfather speaking of his Canadian cousins as if this was a part of his family that he would surely meet one day. And after his grandfather had died, his father Charles had kept the connection alive, out of family duty. Roland and his second cousin, Guy, sent letters to each other from time to time, especially concerning any important family event.

Guy de Cygne in Canada, therefore, had known that Roland and his wife had only one daughter who lived to adulthood and that she was long since married to a noble in Brittany. He had known that her two sons had both died as infants, that Roland was now fifty-five years of age and that he was a widower. It could hardly be thought that he was likely to marry again and start a fresh family.

Though Guy de Cygne was aware that his cousin in France had once been wounded in battle, he had no knowledge of the details of the wound, and so he was unaware that Roland's nose had been split and that his face was quite unsightly, making it even less likely that he would obtain another wife at this late stage of his life.

All he knew for certain was that as things stood at present, upon the death of Roland, his own son Alain would be the only male de Cygne left, and presumably heir to the family estate.

The letter before Roland now came not from Guy, but from his son Alain, a young man of twenty, containing the sad news of Guy's demise, and asking Roland de Cygne whether he wished him to come to France.

It was a fair question. If the young man was to be the representative of the family in France, then he would have much to learn, and Roland should summon him to his side at once.

But he couldn't bring himself to do it. A deep, primitive voice inside him urged him to fight. He would not give in. I may not be much to look at, he thought, but I still have my name, and my health. I have another ten years. More than that, perhaps.

Madame de Saint-Loubert was a middle-aged woman with a long face and very large blue eyes. Her mother and d'Artagnan's mother had been cousins. Her husband, the count, had a modest position as a superintendent of mines, but hoped for more, and to help him accomplish this, she had made friends with a large number of people at court. They had a small house in the town, where Amélie spent her first night. The very next morning, Madame de Saint-Loubert announced that she was taking Amélie to court.

'You are not due to see the dauphine until tomorrow. You needn't worry, by the way. I happen to know that you are the only person under consideration at the moment, so you only have to be polite and the position will be yours. But it will be a good idea for you to get an idea of the court before you meet her. So just stand beside me and watch.'

It took hours to dress. Amélie's gown was charming. An under-petticoat of watered satin trimmed with bands of silk. A hooped skirt gathered at the waist, divided, looped at the sides and then flowed back to end in a short train behind her. It was made of a heavy silk, but with a light brown colour, shot with pink, that suited her very well. Her tight bodice was decorated with charming ribbons tied in bows. French lace at her wrists and neck. It was the most feminine thing imaginable. Madame de SaintLoubert's hairdresser spent another two hours on her hair, arranging it with ringlets and ribbons in the style then current. She was relieved that her dress passed muster. 'It's better than many of the ladies of the court. Not everyone here is rich, you know. You look very well. Come along.'

The first thing that surprised Amélie as they approached the vast palace was how many people seemed to be crowding around the entrance. 'Who are they?' she asked.

'Anyone who wants to look at the king.'

'Anybody can walk into the palace?'

'Yes. And they do.'

Just then a closed sedan chair was carried in past them.

'Who is that?' Amélie asked.

'Hard to know. All the sedan chairs are hired. Only the royal family are allowed to have their own.'

They went up the great staircase and came into the huge Galerie des Glaces. It was crowded with people, from aristocrats to trades-men. 'We'll stay back a little,' said her guide. 'We aren't trying to catch the king's eye – which most of the people here are. I just want you to observe.'

They waited awhile. Amélie gazed around. The vast mirrored hall stretched so far that, with all the people there, she could not even see the ends of it, but only the long succession of crystal chandeliers hanging from the painted ceiling high above.

And then suddenly a silence swept along the huge hall. Footmen were approaching and other court officials. The great throng miraculously parted, like the Red Sea, withdrawing to the sides and leaving a broad path down the centre.

Down which, a moment later, came the royal entourage.

'The king goes to Mass at exactly this hour every day,' Madame de Saint-Loubert whispered. 'You can set the clock by his movements.'

The king came first. He was certainly an impressive figure. Wearing a large black wig and magnificently embroidered coat he moved down the gallery at a swift but stately pace. His face was aquiline, the nose a little hooked, his eyes half closed. But Amélie had the good sense to realise that under their half-closed lids his eyes were observing everything. She also noticed something else. The king's height owed something to the high heels of his shoes. She whispered this to Madame de Saint-Loubert.

'He wears high heels to make himself seem taller. He always has,' her guide whispered back.

'He does not seem so terrifying.'

'Do not ever make that mistake, my dear. The king is the politest man in France. He even touches his hat to the scullery maids. But his power is absolute. Even his children are terrified of him.' She indicated a man in the robes of a Jesuit priest walking just behind him. 'That's his confessor, Père de La Chaise.' Amélie noticed that people were smiling at the priest. 'Père de La Chaise is kind to everyone,' said her friend. 'If the king is the most feared, La Chaise is the most loved man at the court.'

Next came a large, blond man, with a pleasant, Germanic face, and the first signs that his impressive physique might run to fat.

'That is the king's eldest son, the dauphin. We call him le Grand Dauphin, because he's so tall. It's his wife you'll see tomorrow.

'Ah. And behind him you see the Duc d'Orléans, the king's brother, and his wife.'

A handsome woman, dressed very simply and wearing a diamond cross, passed by.

'Since the queen died, the king's friend Madame de Maintenon has so taken him over that the rumour is that they have secretly married. But nobody knows.'

Then came a lady who clearly had once been very beautiful. Her face still contained traces of beauty, but it was clear from the way she walked that her legs had puffed up.

'Madame de Montespan, the king's most important former mistress. She gave him a number of children, and he's legitimised them all.'

'He can do that?'

'I'm surprised you didn't know. He can do what he wants. Well, almost. You know he chooses the French bishops. He doesn't let the pope do it.'

After the cortege had passed, her friend decided to give Amélie a tour of the palace and grounds. 'Over there,' she indicated, 'is the north wing where you'll have your room, assuming the dauphine accepts you. But we can look at that tomorrow.'

Madame de Saint-Loubert could see that Amélie's ignorance of the court was far greater than it should have been for an aristocratic girl, and she hoped that she hadn't made a mistake by suggesting that she come to Versailles. However, others had come there with far less breeding and good manners than Amélie and done very well, so she set to work to explain some of the principal characters at the court, how they were related and where they stood in the pecking order.

The list was long, and the relationships were so complex that it made Amélie's head spin. There were the children of the king by the late queen, and then his children by his mistresses. Then there were the children of other branches of the royal family, both legitimate and illegitimate. And of course, the many descendants of branches of royalty, legitimate or otherwise, going back for centuries. Usually the offspring of the king's mistresses were married into the greatest noble families, sometimes even into the legitimate royal family.

'Don't worry,' Madame de Saint-Loubert told her, 'the pattern will soon emerge if you just keep paying attention.'

When it came to the pecking order, she had to explain a most important principle.

'The princes of the blood are closest to the king in rank, and so the precedence is usually easy to follow. But rank and power are completely different. The king's eldest son and the king's brother are at the top of the tree. But they have no part in the government. Louis won't even let them attend meetings with him.'

'But why?'

'To keep all the power in his hands. No chance of rivals, I should think. Wouldn't you?'

'I hadn't thought of it.'

'If you need a royal favour, then go to the mistresses. It's a general rule that his mistress usually has more influence on a king than his wife.'

'What about his old mistress, Madame de Montespan? Is she important?'

'He visits her every day. He's fond of her. But you know there was a big scandal – well, you were too young. Anyway, it was said that she used poison to get rid of another mistress. Nothing was ever proved. I'm sure it's not true. But there's always been a cloud over her since.'

'I feel as if I've walked into a dangerous labyrinth.'

'All courts are like that.'

As they returned from the palace, Amélie could not help feeling a sense of misgiving.

The next morning they returned to the palace to see the dauphine. Amélie knew her story. 'She is not one of the court beauties,' Madame de Saint-Loubert had told her, 'yet she seemed to please the dauphin. They've had three children. But the last birth, this year, took a toll on her health, or so she says.'

The apartment of the dauphin was large, bright and airy. But that was not where they found his wife.

Although it was morning, the small back room was dark, the windows covered. An Italian maid let them in. The wife of the large, hearty-looking prince Amélie had seen yesterday did not seem well. Though Amélie knew that she was only about twenty-five, she had the impression that the sickly figure before her was much older. The dauphine was sitting in a *fauteuil*, and she summoned Amélie, telling her to sit on a small gilt chair. Her gesture was rather listless.

Only as she got close did she realise something else about the dauphin's wife: She was astonishingly ugly. Her skin was blotchy. Her lips were pale as an old woman's, her teeth were rotten, and her hands were unnaturally red. But most striking of all was her big, bulbous nose.

The poor lady's looks were so unprepossessing that it was lucky Amélie had been prepared for them. She kept her face a mask.

First the dauphine offered her a piece of cake. Since it would have been impolite to refuse, even though she didn't want it, Amélie ate the cake while the dauphine watched her.

'Despite her physical ugliness, the dauphine is most fastidious when she eats. She cannot bear to have women near her who eat messily,' Madame de Saint-Loubert had forewarned her. 'But don't worry, your table manners are excellent.'

As she didn't drop any crumbs from her mouth or spill anything on the floor, this seemed to satisfy the dauphine.

Could she read and write? Had she a good hand? The Italian maid brought her a pen, ink and a piece of paper and she was commanded to write a few lines of any verse she knew.

Amélie obliged with some elegant religious verses from Corneille. The choice, and her handwriting, seemed to do.

'The dauphine is well read and speaks three languages well. She won't expect this from you, however,' her mentor had also informed her.

Then the conversation turned to her family.

Who were her parents? Amélie named them. And her grandparents? Amélie named them too. And her great-grandparents? These she also named. And their parents? Amélie named all sixteen.

'They are all noble?' The dauphine sought confirmation. Amélie confirmed that they were. 'This is good. This is important,' said the dauphine.

'You must understand,' Madame de Saint-Loubert had explained the night before, 'that if you think your father is concerned with ancestry, this pales into insignificance compared to the attention paid to the subject by German royalty and, as I hope you know, the dauphine by birth is a Bavarian princess. She might take you if you weren't of sufficiently pure blood, but she'd give you a terrible time. She even treats Madame de Maintenon like a servant because her ancestry is imperfect.' She smiled. 'I had already checked with your parents, or I wouldn't have brought you here. It would have been too cruel.' She paused. 'By the way, I wouldn't say that you are close to your cousins who lost their nobility, if I were you.'

And did she have cousins in Paris? the dauphine asked, quite pleasantly. And Amélie was just about to answer happily that she had indeed, her mother's niece and nephew of whom she was so fond, when, by the grace of the Almighty, she remembered and avoided the terrible trap.

'I must confess with shame that one of my mother's family made an unfortunate marriage,' she answered quietly, 'and I believe there are children, but I know nothing about them.' With this monumental lie, her dear cousins Isabelle and Yves miraculously disappeared.

'Many families suffer misfortune. Your family has behaved quite correctly,' the princess told her. She turned to Madame de Saint-Loubert, who had remained standing quietly in a corner near the door. 'I think she will do very well,' she said. 'Will you show her where her rooms are?' Then she addressed Amélie. 'Come to me tomorrow morning, my dear, after Mass. By the way,' she added, 'as I never go out, there is nothing for you to do. But you won't mind.' This last, it seemed, was an order. They quietly withdrew.

'You didn't tell me she was quite so ugly,' Amélie protested to Madame de Saint-Loubert. 'I almost made a face. However did her husband find her attractive?'

'Well, he did. There's no accounting for tastes. Let's go to see your room.'

The north wing was given over entirely to the quarters of the many aristocratic folk with duties of one kind or another in the palace. There were also some impoverished aristocrats who, if they'd ever had any duties at the court, were now too ancient to perform them, together with a few relics of former courtiers. Some of the grander courtiers had quite elegant quarters there. But large though the place was, the need for lodging had already outgrown the space available. And what with subdivision and doubling up, the higher floors had in no time turned into the most aristocratic tenement in the world.

Having climbed the stairs to the highest floor below the attic, they made their way along a passage until they reached a door that had been cleverly cut in half and divided so that the left half swung one way, and the right the other.

496

'Yours is the left-hand side,' said her guide, and as they opened it, 'I'm afraid the right side got the window.'

It was the size of a small room. Big enough for a little bed and an armoire for her. It was airless. And pitch-black.

'It's not very nice,' said Amélie.

'It's a start,' said Madame de Saint-Loubert firmly. 'We'll go and get a candle and some other things.'

'You don't think,' suggested Amélie, 'that the wife of the Dauphin of France would want her maid of honour to have a window?'

'It's hard to know,' said Madame de Saint-Loubert, 'since she seems to like sitting in the dark herself.'

As they went down the stairs again, her mentor tried to comfort her a little.

'You must understand,' she explained, 'that the main thing is to be here. Everything comes from that. Once you're here, who knows what wonderful things may happen? But if you're somewhere else, nothing will ever happen. That's the point.' She gave Amélie an encouraging smile. 'You're quite nice-looking. You're noble. Just be polite to everyone and make friends. That way, with a little luck, you'll find yourself a suitable husband.'

'Is that what my parents want me to do?'

'Every important and eligible person in the kingdom comes here. What would you hope for if you were a parent?'

The next day, Amélie arrived at the appointed time. She was told to sit quietly, which she did for an hour. Then the dauphine asked her to take a letter to the Duchesse d'Orléans, and Amélie set off.

She got lost only twice. She delivered the letter, and on being told that there was no reply, she made her way back. She was nearing the dauphine's door when out of his apartment stepped the dauphin. She stood to one side and curtseyed, but instead of striding past, he stopped, looked down and with a very pleasant smile asked her who she was.

'My wife's new maid of honour? Well then, welcome. Tell me about yourself.' And on learning her name: 'A relation of the famous Musketeer?'

'The connection is distant, monseigneur, but it exists.'

'Splendid. I shall look forward to learning more of you another day.'

After this very pleasant conversation with the future king himself, Amélie felt quite elated, and passed the rest of the day sitting on a chair in the half darkness quite pleasantly.

The dauphine had informed her that, owing to the peculiar regime she kept, she would not normally require her presence in the evenings, and so it was agreed that a little before dusk each day, Madame de Saint-Loubert would walk in a certain part of the gardens so that Amélie could find her there if she needed any help or advice. Thinking that her mentor would be pleased to learn of this pleasant interview, she met her there that evening.

Madame de Saint-Loubert did not smile, but received the news thoughtfully. Then she gave Amélie a strange look.

'The dauphin is a handsome, vigorous man, wouldn't you say?'

'Certainly.'

'He started an affair with his wife's last maid of honour.'

'Oh.'

'Of course, it was the best thing that could have happened to her.'

'Why?'

'The king and Madame de Maintenon didn't approve. So the girl was immediately found a husband from one of the greatest aristocratic houses of France.' She paused. 'I suppose the same thing could happen to you.'

'Certainly not,' cried Amélie. 'My parents would be appalled.'

For a moment or two, Madame de Saint-Loubert was silent. Then she spoke quietly but firmly.

'My child, your parents were entirely aware of the business with the dauphin before they sent you to Versailles.'

'Dear God, is this how one gets married?'

'It's one way.'

She did not see the dauphin for another week. Most days he went out hunting early and did not return until late.

Keeping the dauphine company was not quite as bad as she might have thought. Her children appeared from time to time. The baby was with a wet nurse, the elder two cared for by others, but their occasional visits provided a change. Madame, the Duchesse d'Orléans, would come to see her. The two ladies liked to talk and Amélie was usually sent out of the room at these times. But since the dauphine would talk to her later, she often picked up, indirectly, the court gossip that madame had brought.

She learned that the king had been in a bad temper ever since the Revocation of the Edict of Nantes, how the young bloods of the court had been allowed to go off to fight against the Turks, who were troubling Eastern Europe, and how this man or that had pleased the king with his deeds of valour , or angered him by something that he had written in a letter.

'The king's servants read everyone's letters,' the dauphine remarked to her one day. 'So be careful what you write, because the king will soon know of it.'

After a few days, Amélie began to feel that, though she still had much to learn, she was unlikely to see anything that would surprise her. She was wrong.

It was an afternoon. She was passing near the king's apartments. Ahead of her, another lady-in-waiting of about her age was standing in a hallway when the king suddenly appeared. He did not see Amélie, but he did see the other girl.

It happened so fast that Amélie could scarcely believe her eyes. The king put his arm around the young woman, signalled by a nod that she was to raise her skirts, and after some brief but practiced fumblings, had her pressed against the wall with her legs around his body while he pressed home his advantage.

Terrified, Amélie managed to shrink behind a pillar. She wanted to run away, but did not dare, for fear of being seen. She did not have to wait very long. She heard a door open and close, peeped out to see the girl rearranging herself, and fled. When she got back, the dauphine glanced up and remarked that she looked as if she'd seen a ghost. She assured the dauphine that she hadn't.

'Well, you are not to do so,' said the dauphine tartly, 'because I don't like them.'

That evening, however, she confided what she'd seen to Madame de Saint-Loubert. But if she imagined that her mentor would be shocked, she was quite wrong.

'Really?' that lady said. 'How interesting. He used to do that when the dear queen was still alive. But since he's been with Madame de Maintenon he's renounced the sins of the flesh, more or less.' She thought for a moment. 'He visits Madame de Maintenon twice a day, which is more than she wants really, though she does her duty, as she would say. Perhaps he's going to stray a little.'

'But madame, what about the young lady?'

'What about her?'

'I mean, to be used like that . . .'

'He's the king. He can do what he wants.'

'It's disgraceful.'

'Power is an aphrodisiac, both for the man who has it, and for the women who are attracted to him. It has been so since the days of Babylon. I dare say it will always be so. Women come here to be close to power, and to profit by it.'

'But . . . a man who just takes whatever he wants . . . It's childish, contemptible.'

'Powerful men become like children, because they can do what they want. But it's no good despising them. This is how things are. It's more intelligent to work with it.' She stared at Amélie severely. 'Don't look for purity in palaces, my child. You won't find it.'

'But it could have been me,' Amélie protested. Her mentor did not reply.

In the days that followed, it might have been foolish, but she couldn't get the memory of the incident out of her mind. Nor had Madame de Saint-Loubert offered her much comfort, beyond saying that it was probably a small aberration and she doubted that the king would return to his former ways.

As she walked down the marble halls, past the rich, dark tapestries and sumptuous pictures of the royal family dressed as classical gods, Amélie felt more and more that she had entered a huge, echoing world in which, though the cross of Our Lord was carried before the king like a trophy, it was the pitiless pagan sun god, in league with the solemn ruler of the underworld, who reigned at Versailles.

If only she could find a way to escape.

She had gone out into the huge formal gardens one evening, to the place where she usually met Madame de Saint-Loubert. But her friend was not there that day. She waited in the hope that she might still appear, but she did not. Still unwilling to return to the château, Amélie began to walk down a long alley.

She was quite alone. The light was fading. The yellowed leaves that had fallen from the trees were turning to grey. It was a quiet, ghostly time. The alley was empty.

And then, a hundred yards ahead of her, a single figure turned into the alley. It was a large, powerful man, also alone. And even in the fading light, she recognised him at once.

It was the dauphin.

She stopped. Hoping he would not see her, she was about to press herself against a tree at the side of the alley. But before she could, he caught sight of her.

And then Amélie did a foolish thing. She panicked. She panicked, and began to run.

She couldn't help it. The memory of what she had seen the king do was too fresh in her mind. She was alone and quite defenceless. What if the dauphin behaved as his father did? What would she do? Plead her virginity? Scream? She had no idea. She ran away up the alley.

But glancing back, she saw that he had started running too. He was large and powerful. She thought she heard him laugh. What did that mean? A laugh of amusement or of triumph? He was a large man. He was bounding along.

She tried to increase her pace. She came to another alley on her left, rushed into it.

And saw, facing her, not thirty feet ahead, another figure. And this one was horrifying. For if the body was that of a man, the face seemed distorted like a classical grotesque, with a split nose. In her terrified state, she screamed. Trapped between the two threats, she looked for escape, saw a curving path between hedgerows to her right, fled into it. And found herself a moment later in a dead end.

She was panting, trembling and trying to make no sound at the same time, as she heard, only a few yards away, the dauphin's heavy footfall arrive and suddenly stop.

'Monsieur de Cygne. It's you.'

'It is, monseigneur, at your service.'

'Did you see a young lady just now?'

'Certainly. But before I had the chance to introduce myself, she ran past me towards the palace.'

'Ah. I think she thought I was chasing her.'

'If that is the case, monseigneur, I assume that she will allow herself to be caught if you continue towards the palace.'

'Thank you. Good night, de Cygne.'

After this, she heard the sound of the dauphin walking swiftly away. Then silence. It seemed that the grotesque was saving her for himself. She prepared to scream. But nothing happened until, after a long pause, the voice she'd heard before spoke.

'Forgive me for addressing you without an introduction, young lady, but I know that you must be close by, since there is no exit from the little hedgerow into which you have run.' The voice was kindly. 'I am Roland de Cygne, a poor widower who was wounded long ago in the wars, which is why, though my wounds were honourable, I think it more pleasant for others that I should take my walks at dusk. I can tell you that the dauphin has departed towards the palace. I doubt that he meant you any harm, for that is not his reputation. I shall now continue on my way, but if you wish me to conduct you safely back to your quarters, I shall be happy to do so.'

She heard him move on. She waited, then, emerging cautiously from her hiding place, she looked to see if the coast was clear. It was getting quite dark. Who knew if the dauphin was lurking out there? She looked into the long alley and saw the back of Monsieur de Cygne, already fifty yards away.

'Monsieur,' she called softly. 'Monsieur, if you please.'

By the time he got back to his house that night, Roland de Cygne was in love. It hadn't taken him long to discover who this young lady was, but when he tried to discover why she was so afraid she became reticent, and he didn't press the matter. God knows what the innocent girl might have seen in the corridors of Versailles.

But by the time they reached the north wing, he had discovered enough about her to know that she was honest as well as kind.

'I am sorry that I gave you such a fright out there,' he ventured.

'It was just the shock of running into you when I was already so frightened.'

'My face can be a surprise, I'm afraid.'

'Since it was not the dauphin's face, monsieur, I can assure you that for me it was nothing but a relief.' She gave him a wry look and smiled. 'I spend all my days with the dauphine, monsieur.'

He laughed quietly.

'The king likes everyone to look beautiful if they can. Most of the people at court are handsome. But though I seldom come to court myself – for I need no favours from the king – he is always polite if he sees me. The only thing he cannot tolerate is cowardice in battle, so my war wounds are in my favour.'

'And why did you come to Versailles, monsieur?' she asked.

'For my dear wife. It gave her pleasure to be at court. And since her death two years ago, I have remained here. I have a little house in the town. I come and go as I please and spend most of the summer down on my estate. I've grown used to Versailles, I suppose. But I don't love it.'

'I do not think I shall ever get used to it, monsieur. I do not belong here. But I fear that my parents would be very angry if I returned home,' she confessed.

As soon as he got back to his house in the town, Roland de Cygne ate a light supper, as was his usual custom. After that, having told his groom to be ready to leave for Paris in the morning, he sat down to write a letter.

Ten days had passed since this incident when Amélie received word from Madame de Saint-Loubert that she should come to her house that evening. When she arrived, she found to her delight that her mother was there. Not only that, but her mother embraced her warmly and congratulated her.

'You have done very well, my dearest child. Both your father and I are delighted.'

'I have? I just sit in a dark room with the dauphine all day and talk to her when she wants.'

'I don't mean the dauphine, Amélie. I am speaking of your marriage to Monsieur de Cygne.'

'My marriage?'

'He didn't tell you?'

'I met him only once.'

'Well it's all agreed. Your father is very pleased. I shall meet Monsieur de Cygne tomorrow, but he is from a very old family, he's entirely respectable and his estate is actually larger than ours. It's quite splendid. And so quick. I can't believe it.'

'Have you seen him, Mother? He's an old man with a split nose.'

'He was wounded, I know. But he needs an heir. Madame de Saint-Loubert says he is a good and kind man too. You don't think he'd mistreat you, do you?'

'No. That wasn't my impression. But I hardly know him. I do not love him.'

Her mother looked at her for just a moment as if she were stupid, and then changed the subject.

'Of course, since you are at court, the king will have to give his permission, but there's no reason for him to withhold it.'

'Mother, I do not consent to marry Monsieur de Cygne. And I am very unhappy here at Versailles. I beg you to let me return to Paris with you.'

'That is not possible, my child. The king would probably refuse his permission, unless the dauphine says she doesn't want you. And your father would not take you back. Not after refusing such an offer.'

'I cannot believe he would be so cruel.'

Her mother looked at her sadly.

'You do not know,' she said quietly, 'how kind he has already been.'

And then, after asking her hostess if she might be left alone with Amélie, Geneviève d'Artagnan gently told her daughter the truth.

When she had finished, Amélie was silent. She just stared ahead in shock.

'So I am not my father's daughter,' she said at last. 'Not a d'Artagnan.'

'No.'

'Who is my father, then?'

'I shall never tell you.'

'Was he noble?'

'No. But your father has given you the d'Artagnan name, which makes you noble, and you must honour it. You are fortunate. But you must also consider your father's position. He is providing a dowry for you, but it is only a small one. If your father were very rich, it might be different, but as things are, although he loves you, he does not feel he can give away too much of the family inheritance in order to provide for you. Monsieur de Cygne has a fine estate and needs an heir. He is prepared to accept a small dowry. But it might be hard to find another suitable husband who would. You must consider your father as well as yourself. You should not take money from him when there is no need.'

'I could just marry a poor man who isn't noble.'

'No. You cannot dishonour the name you have been given by your father. That is not fair to him either. If you marry Monsieur de Cygne, however, then everything is solved. It's your duty to do so, Amélie, and I believe you may be happy too. He seems to like you very much, by the way. He writes like a man in love.'

'Mother, I shall return tomorrow to discuss this with you further,' said Amélie. 'I am feeling very tired.'

And without even bestowing the usual kiss upon her mother, she left.

The following day, explaining to the dauphine that her mother had arrived to see her, she received permission to leave a little early. So the afternoon was still light as she walked into the town.

It had not been difficult to discover where Monsieur de Cygne lived.

Having seen her mother that morning, Roland de Cygne was rather surprised that Amélie should arrive at his house unaccompanied, but he received her in his elegant salon. The walk from the palace had brought a freshness to her cheeks.

Amélie noticed the elegance of the house. In the hall was a portrait of Roland de Cygne as a young man, before he had received his wound, looking very handsome. In the salon, over the fireplace, was another portrait, of a lady of the court with a pleasant, kindly face. This evidently was his late wife.

Seen by the light of day, Roland de Cygne looked exactly what he was, a middle-aged aristocrat whose handsome face had been marred by a slashing sword. It appeared that he was a man who had been happily married and who, no doubt, was now a little lonely. If he seemed very old, it was also clear to her that he had kept himself fit and that for all his modest manners, he was not a man to be trifled with.

'Monsieur de Cygne,' she came straight to the point, 'I have understood from my mother that you have done me the honour to ask for my hand in marriage. Is that still the case?'

'It is, Mademoiselle d'Artagnan.'

'You have seen my mother today?'

'I have.'

'And what has she told you of the circumstances of my birth?'

He looked mildly surprised.

'That you are the youngest child. Your brother will inherit the estate. Your sister is well married.'

'Then I must tell you, monsieur, that you have been deceived. I am not my father's daughter. I do not know who my real father is, but he was not noble.'

Roland de Cygne looked at her thoughtfully. He had been a little surprised at the smallness of the dowry offered, and had assumed that this was because his own bargaining position was so weak. An older man with an ugly face, in desperate need of an heir, cannot demand a high price for marrying a fellow aristocrat's good-looking daughter. This new information was no doubt a further reason for the smallness of the amount.

'When did you discover yourself, mademoiselle?'

'Last night, monsieur.'

He nodded thoughtfully.

'It came as a shock to you, therefore.'

'It did, monsieur.'

And why is she telling me? he wondered. Because she thinks I will break off the marriage agreement? Is she so anxious not to marry an ugly old man? Yet at the same time, he thought, she was taking a terrible risk with her own reputation. With her small dowry and her dubious origins, she was ruining herself in the marriage market. Did she realise this?

She was young, and upset, and a little foolish. That was clear. But he decided that she was also honest and courageous. And he loved her for being so.

He also needed an heir.

'Mademoiselle, I honour you greatly for coming to me in this way,' he said. 'You did not wish to deceive me, and you have trusted me with a secret. And now, for my part, I wish to tell you that I did not ask for your hand because of your name. I already have a name, of which I am proud. Nor did I ask for you because of the charms of your person, though those charms were evident even in the dark, and are even more to be admired in the light of day. But I asked for you because of those qualities of goodness and honesty which I at once perceived in your character.'

'You are kind, monsieur.'

'I hope so. Your case – even if you are correct, and there has not been some misunderstanding – is not as rare as you may suppose. Therefore, for your own sake, and for your parents' honour, I ask you to say nothing of this to anyone for a few days. I need a day or two to reflect, myself. Would you do this for me as a kindness? Afterwards, we can all decide what to do.'

'If that is your wish, monsieur, then I will do as you ask.' It would have seemed churlish to refuse.

After she had gone, Roland de Cygne thought for some time. He was annoyed, certainly, by the news. Amélie's looks and manners were entirely aristocratic, but the thought of base blood entering the noble family of de Cygne was repugnant to him.

But then a memory caused him to pause.

It had been a few months before he had died that his father had confided to him a strange scene he had witnessed in the Louvre. 'You were only seven years old at the time,' Charles had told him, 'and I had to take a letter to the queen, our present king's mother.' And then his father had told him about the strange figure in the bedroom. 'They say that the king returned and spent a night with the queen at that time, and it may be so. But I tell you, Roland, I could have sworn it was Mazarin that I saw in there.'

Roland de Cygne sighed. What if his father was right? In subsequent years, after Louis XIII was dead and Mazarin was running the kingdom, there was no doubt that the queen and Mazarin were so close that people wondered if they were secretly married. If Mazarin was the true father of the present monarch, then the Sun King was descended from a base-born Italian whose ancestors may even have been Jewish.

But he was still king of France.

And whoever the real father of this honest young girl was, she bore the name of d'Artagnan. That was enough for the honour of his family.

One other consideration also came into his mind. He had not been without conscience, or misgiving, about forcing such a young

507

woman into marriage with him. But given these new circumstances, there was no question that, in the long run, it was for her own good. Her chances of making a good marriage on such a small dowry were slim. And if her parents had hoped that she might do well for herself by becoming a royal mistress of some kind, he was sure that they had misjudged the girl. That wasn't her character at all.

If she married him, however, she'd have rank, security and a comfortable life. And after I am gone, he thought, she'll be well placed to make a second marriage more to her liking.

He made up his mind. It was time to take action. He was going to secure the heir his family needed, and to protect this young woman from her own foolishness.

The king liked brave men. And he'd never asked for anything before. He'd seek an audience with him in the morning.

Two days later, as Amélie was sitting in the dauphine's dark room, both she and the dauphine were astonished when a courtier came to inform her that the king himself desired her presence.

'I can't imagine why,' Amélie said. 'I'm sure I've done nothing wrong.'

'Nor can I, but you must go at once,' the dauphine told her.

She knew that, when not in council, the king conducted most of his business with a very few advisors. But she was quite surprised to find herself ushered into a salon in which the king was sitting on a *fauteuil* quite alone. Beside him was a table, covered by a rich cloth on which there were a number of papers. She curtseyed deeply as the door closed behind her.

She had never been in the intimate presence of King Louis before. He was wearing a coat of deep red velvet trimmed with gold, a lace cravat and a large wig that reproduced the magnificent dark brown hair of his youth. He face was sensual, a little fleshy now, but every line proclaimed that he was used to being obeyed. His eyes were smaller than she had realised, as dark brown as his wig, and sharp and cynical as the world that he commanded. In his usual fashion when seated, his left leg was tucked back and his right, impressively muscular in its white silk stocking, was stuck out proudly.

'You are young, Mademoiselle d'Artagnan,' he said calmly. 'You bear a fine name.'

'Yes, Your Majesty,' she said. She felt rather frightened.

'It is my wish that you should honour the name of d'Artagnan that you are so fortunate to bear. I am sure you understand me.'

'I think so, sire.'

'Whatever you may believe about your birth, you are never to speak of these doubts again. Never. If you do, you may be sure that I shall hear of it.'

'I merely try to be honest, Your Majesty,' she ventured.

'That is often commendable. But in these circumstances it is ill-advised and would bring pain to others and to yourself. You will therefore do as I wish.' He looked at her to make sure she had understood.

She bowed her head, and said nothing.

'You have the opportunity to render a great service to a family who have served France for many centuries, and to bring happiness to a brave and honest man. I am speaking of course of Monsieur de Cygne.'

'He did me the honour to propose marriage, Your Majesty, but he may have changed his mind.'

'On the contrary, he is quite determined to marry you, Mademoiselle d'Artagnan, and it is my wish that this marriage should take place.'

'I wonder, Your Majesty . . .' she began desperately, but the king signified that she should cease speaking at once.

'I wish it,' he said bleakly.

Le Roi le veult: the king wishes it. The final word against which there could be no argument and no recourse. She fell silent.

And then she discovered why even the princes of the blood trembled in the presence of the Sun King.

'It is best for everyone that you do exactly as I say, mademoiselle,' King Louis quietly continued. 'You must trust my wisdom. You will never question your birth again, you will marry Monsieur de Cygne and one day you will be glad that you did.' And now his voice suddenly became harsh. 'But if you fail in the slightest degree to follow the instructions I have just given you, then you will regret it.' He picked up a sheet of paper from the table. 'Do you know what this is?'

'No, Your Majesty.'

'It is a *lettre de cachet*, mademoiselle. With this, I can send you to the Bastille or any prison of my choosing. I can place you in solitary confinement, and give instructions that you are never to be seen again. I do not have to supply any reason for my action. It is entirely within my power. I have sent young women to prison in this manner before. And I am quite ready to sign this letter now, and find Monsieur de Cygne another wife. The guards outside the door will convey you to prison at once. In one minute from now, mademoiselle, you will vanish forever.'

Amélie felt herself shivering. A terrible cold descended upon her. She had never known such fear before.

'I will do as you command, Your Majesty,' she said hoarsely.

'Do not at any time disobey me, mademoiselle, in the smallest particular. I shall hear of it if you do. And then, even Monsieur de Cygne will not be able to save you.'

'I shall never disobey you, sire,' she swore, 'as long as I live.'

'I shall come to your marriage,' he said, and dismissed her.

A year later, Amélie de Cygne gave birth to a baby boy. Her husband wrote to his young cousin in Canada to announce the fact. He did not write to him again.

1715

It was quite a common sight, in the early years of the eighteenth century, to see the old man on the Pont Neuf, especially when the weather was warm. His grandson would bring him there in his cart.

Some people could still remember him in his prime.

'You should have heard him then,' they would tell the younger folk. 'The greatest mouth in Paris.' And strong as an ox. For look at how long he had lived. Nobody was sure of his exact age, but he must be over eighty. He still wore a red scarf around his neck, under his white beard.

If people came up and spoke to him, he would answer them briefly, and when he did so it could be seen that he had two or three teeth, which was remarkable for such an aged man.

When he appeared in the summer of 1715, Hercule Le Sourd had not been seen for months, and the previous winter had clearly taken its toll. His face was gaunt, and his clothes hung upon him loosely. But he got out of his grandson's cart and walked stiffly across to the middle of the bridge. And was seen there every week or so after that.

One day his grandson took him along the Left Bank of the river so that he could gaze down the huge southern sweep to the cold facade of Les Invalides, to which King Louis had added a splendid royal chapel with a gilded dome. 'I've seen pictures of St Peter's, Rome,' his grandson told him, 'and this looks exactly the same. Paris is the new Rome.' Another time, they went to the northern part of the city where King Louis had demolished parts of the old city wall and built handsome boulevards there instead. 'The king's made France more glorious than she's ever been before,' the younger man declared confidently.

'That may be,' Hercule said, but he was too old to be easily impressed.

Yes, he thought, King Louis had added to the glory of Bourbon France. The great nobles obeyed him. The country was better run. Across the ocean in the New World, French adventurers had just made good their claim to the territory centred on the vast Mississippi basin and called it Louisiana.

In Europe, the power of the mighty Hapsburgs of Austria and Spain was waning. By force and clever bargaining, the Sun King had grabbed rich border territories like Alsace out of Hapsburg hands and into his own. By marrying his heirs to Hapsburg princesses, King Louis had done even better. For when the inbred Hapsburgs couldn't even provide an heir for Spain, one of his grandsons had inherited the Spanish throne. True, the Bourbons had to promise the rest of Europe that France and Spain would never be ruled by a single monarch, but it was a friendly Bourbon, rather than a rival Hapsburg, who now lay over France's southern border.

French culture was the fashion. All over Europe, French was becoming the language of diplomacy and the aristocracy.

I, myself, as a Frenchman, am proud of all this, Hercule admitted.

Yet the Bourbon glory had come at a cost. The Sun King's ambition had alarmed his fellow rulers, especially the Protestant ones. When he'd attacked the Netherlands, he'd gone too far. And the last two decades had seen a long-drawn-out war in which the great English general Churchill, now Duke of Marlborough, had smashed the French army several times, proving to all the world that mighty France was not invincible. The war had left the Sun King's treasury depleted, and France with few friends. Was that so good?

And yet beyond that, it seemed to Hercule, there was something else. Something intangible, like a cloud obscuring the sun.

The ancient Greeks told it as the tragedy of hubris. A king grows too proud, and the gods punish him. Medieval men spoke of the wheel of fortune, which never ceases to turn. Or perhaps God, for His own good reasons, had turned His face away from the King of France.

Whatever the cause, one thing was clear to Hercule Le Sourd: in the last few years, King Louis XIV had run out of luck.

It wasn't only the grim cost of his wars. Everything had gone wrong. The harvests had failed – the surest sign of divine displeasure.

Disease and famine had struck the countryside. And now his heirs had started dying. The dauphin, heir to France. The dauphin's son. The dauphin's elder grandson. Was there a curse on the family? One had to wonder. And now the king was old, and his health was beginning to fail, and his heir was his younger great-grandson, a little boy of five.

After all of King Louis XIV's dynastic efforts, the kingdom of France would shortly be back where it was before: financially ruined, and with a helpless child upon the throne.

The sun was being extinguished. The darkness was closing in.

It was almost the end of August when the strange thing occurred. Hercule Le Sourd had asked his grandson to take him to a different place that day: the stately square of the Place Royale in the Marais quarter.

When they got there, he directed his grandson to a particular spot, and then got out and stretched his legs a bit.

'Why do you choose this place to stop?' his grandson inquired.

'Something wrong with it?'

'No.'

'Then mind your own business,' said his grandfather.

What had happened to that strange woman? he wondered. Probably dead by now. And no doubt I'll be following her soon myself, he thought. And it occurred to him that in every corner of Paris there must be places where people had made illicit love – people who were long since turned to skeletons and dust. And if they were all to be resurrected in the body at the same time and in the act of love, what a strange panting, and moaning, and grinding of bones there would be. And in the warm, thick air of that August afternoon, it seemed to him that just for a moment, he could sense all those vanished bodies like spirits all around him, but as spirits with substance, however light. Was it possible that memories, and souls, could take a vaporous form and float about? If they could do it anywhere, it would surely be in the sultry warmth of the intimate, arcaded brick-and-stone enclosure, on a silent August afternoon.

It had not happened only once. The lady had come back for him the next day, and the one after that. Three times they had made the journey from the Pont Neuf to the Place Royale. Three times they had made passionate love. He had been young then, and vigorous.

Then she had disappeared, and he'd never seen her again. He did not know who she was, and made no attempt to find out. What would be the point? He was left with three strange, magical memories, as if he'd been transported like a knight in a romance, into another world.

He stayed there some time. Then he said he wanted to go home.

The cart had just started up when he turned to his grandson and remarked: 'Look at that.'

'What?'

'Over there.' Hercule pointed to a spot just in front of the arcades, about fifty paces away, where a figure was standing.

'I don't see anything.'

'The small man, the old one, dressed in red.'

'There's no one there, Granddad.'

And then Hercule understood.

'You're right,' he said. 'Trick of the light.' But he gazed down at the little red man as they passed him, and the red man stared back.

So that was him, Hercule thought. Usually it was kings and great men who saw the red man, just before some terrible event – often their own death. But he'd heard stories of ordinary people seeing him.

What did the red man's presence mean this time? The death of the king, like as not. Perhaps his own as well.

'I wouldn't be surprised,' he said aloud.

'What?' asked his grandson.

'Nothing.' If he was about to die, Hercule thought, he was glad he'd come to this place of memories today. 'The best three fucks I ever had in my life,' he said aloud.

'What?'

'I don't think the king's going to live much longer.'

'Well, he'll die knowing he left his mark on history,' the younger man remarked.

Hercule Le Sourd nodded thoughtfully. No doubt that was true, so far as it went. But what that mark on history would be was still hidden behind the dark clouds.

'No man ever knows his legacy,' he said.

Chapter Eighteen

1914

On the seventh day of September, 1914, one of the strangest sights ever seen in the history of warfare took place in the city of Paris.

Thomas Gascon, his younger son Pierre, and Luc were standing at the top of the Champs-Élysées to witness it, at almost exactly the place where, a quarter-century ago, Thomas had watched the funeral cortege of Victor Hugo. But the procession today was of a very different kind. And it was not the figure of Édith that he was straining to see, but that of his son Robert.

For the French army was going to war.

In taxis.

In the summer of 1914, Europe had been at peace. If France had been watching her neighbour Germany with alarm, as Germany's army and navy swelled, she had not been idle. Indeed, her battle plan if hostilities with Germany ever resumed was to race eastward and recapture Alsace–Lorraine. Attack: that was the word, and the inspiration. Attack and avenge the honour of France. But so far, the tense peace of Europe, held together by her complex network of alliances, had remained unbroken.

And then, out of the blue, an Austrian archduke was murdered in Sarajevo. What had this to do with Germany and France? On the face to it, nothing. But when Austria declared war on the Serbs, Russia defended their fellow Slavs. Germany, allied with Austria, was obliged to declare war on Russia. Russia was allied with France. To avoid a war on two fronts, Germany resolved to smash France quickly. The German High Command already had a detailed blueprint, the Schlieffen Plan, for how to do it.

Would not this bring out the army of the huge British Empire to defend France, to whom she was bound by the Entente Cordiale?

Perhaps. But the Entente was rather vague about hostilities. The British might fight, or they might not.

Except for one thing.

Little Belgium. Set up when Europe was being reorganised after the fall of Napoléon. A constitutional monarchy with a modest king and queen. A small, comfortable kingdom, whose neutrality was universally recognised as inviolable by all the countries of Europe.

The large French forces, poised to attack, lay south of the Belgian border. The German army had no wish to go up against them. But if the German army crossed Belgium, it could walk straight into France unhindered. Diplomatically it was impossible. Morally unthinkable. Militarily, obvious.

In August the Belgian king and his government received a note from Germany. It was couched in the most diplomatic terms. But its message in plain English was clear as day:

We're going to need to walk through your country and occupy it for a while. When we're done, you can have it back again. Hope you don't mind. We'll be coming in a couple of days.

But the Belgians did mind. They said they'd fight. It had not occurred to the German High Command that this comfortable little kingdom would be so valiant.

And Britain had a treaty with Belgium. A cast-iron treaty, to defend it if Belgium was attacked. Britain, therefore, entered the war at once.

Thus, in the first days of August 1914, all the tottering structures erected to preserve the peace of old Europe came crashing down. No one could have foreseen that it would happen this way.

By the first days of September, Thomas Gascon was in a quandary. Though delayed by the tough Belgian resistance, the German army was in France, its advance guard less than fifty miles from Paris. And every Parisian knew what that meant.

'It'll be 1870 all over again. Paris will fall. Get out while you can.'

The government got out. Leaving the capital in a hurry, they all headed south for Gascony and the great port of Bordeaux, hoping they might be safe down there.

Thomas Gascon had watched in disgust as the motor cars of the officials sped past the wagons and handcarts of the poor.

'Even if we leave,' he said to Édith, 'I don't know where we'd go.'

And then a remarkable thing happened. It was his eldest son, Robert, who brought the news.

At the age of sixteen, Thomas's younger son Pierre was already taller than his father. A handsome boy, with a freckled face a little like his mother's. But when people saw Thomas and Robert standing side by side, they smiled with amusement. For Robert was a perfect reproduction of his father. 'I have more hair than you,' Robert would point out to Thomas cheerfully, but his uncle Luc would tell him not to expect this difference to last. 'You look exactly the way your father did when he was working on the Statue of Liberty. So in twenty-five years, you can expect to look the same way he does now,' his uncle said. Thomas and Robert had the same physical toughness, the same love of work in the open air, even the same sense of humour. Since Robert was grown up, father and son enjoyed nothing more than going out for a drink in a bar together.

At the age of eighteen, Robert had been conscripted. Now he was part of the reserve.

'General Joffre is regrouping. He refuses to give up,' he told his family excitedly. 'The British are with us on our northern flank. Joffre thinks we can drive them back at the Marne. We're all being called to the front for an attack. Will you come and see me off tomorrow?' He grinned. 'There's transport laid on for some of the boys. But personally I'll be taking a taxi.'

It was an extraordinary manoeuvre. Ten thousand reservists were being called to the front. The army had transports for only four thousand. The solution? Taxis.

A decade ago they would have been horse-drawn – and there were still plenty of horse-drawn vehicles in Paris, as in every other part of the Western world. But the Renault company had produced a sturdy and excellent motor – the Renault AG – that now served as the favoured taxicab in the city. Six hundred of them had been put in service for the patriotic task. They'd have to make the journey two or three times.

The Renault AG was a cheerful little vehicle. It looked as if the passenger cabin of a horse-drawn cab had been placed on smaller wheels, and a motor attached to the front. On that warm day, most of the soft roofs on the backs of the cabs were folded down.

The first fleet of taxis was circling the Arc de Triomphe to the applause of the crowd before they turned, two, three, four at a time, and scuttled down the Champs-Élysées towards the Louvre and then, eastward, towards the front.

How splendid the young men looked in their kepis, their blue coats and red trousers, hardly changed since the glorious days of Napoléon. With what gallant panache they waved and saluted from their taxis as they passed. It was so colourful, so stylish, so French. If the Parisians had been terrified and ready to flee just days before, this cheerful, mad parade of courage and daring seemed to put new heart into them. When a dozen taxis broke out from the Arc de Triomphe and careered down the Champs-Élysées all together, the cheers turned into a roar.

All the time Thomas was watching intensely. Robert was in one of the taxis, but heaven knows which one. He'd told him where he planned to stand, so he'd be looking out, as long as he was able to get in the right side of the taxi.

Several times he reached out to take Pierre's arm, thinking that he'd caught sight of him, and Pierre got ready to wave, but each time Thomas had shaken his head; and he could tell that, although Pierre naturally wanted to wave to his brother, he was starting to get bored.

But then at last he saw him. He was sure he did. Robert was sitting in the back of the taxi looking out.

'Robert!' he cried, so loudly that surely one would have heard it from the avenue de la Grande-Armée. 'Bravo, Robert!' And he waved wildly from the edge of the street, and Pierre and Luc waved too. And it seemed to them that the figure in the cab raised his hand in acknowledgment as best he could, for he was probably pressed rather tightly in the cab, and then a moment later the cab had passed.

'I think it was him,' said Thomas.

'Certainly it was,' said Luc.

'Did he see us?' asked Pierre.

'I'm sure he did,' Luc answered.

It was clear that he and Pierre were ready to go.

'You go on,' said Thomas. 'I'll just wait a while.' He was still watching the cabs going by.

'Are you sure?' asked his brother.

'You know,' said Thomas quietly, 'just in case it wasn't him.'

'It was him,' said Luc. But Thomas didn't answer. So Luc and Pierre left, but Thomas Gascon remained where he was, staring into every cab that passed. Because he wanted to be sure that Robert didn't come by and see nobody waiting for him. After all, you never knew what was going to happen, out there at the front. Several times he waved at cabs where he saw someone who resembled his son.

And though the crowds began to thin, he remained there another hour until, at last, a cab went by with a single old gentleman in a top hat, whoever he was, and then there were no more.

When he got home, Pierre gave him a message that Luc wanted to see him at his restaurant, so Thomas went round there.

Luc was sitting alone at a table, and he motioned his brother to sit down and poured him a glass of wine.

'I've been thinking, brother,' Luc said. 'This big offensive out at the Marne. It's quite a gamble, you know.'

'I suppose so.'

'If it fails, the Germans could be here in less than a week. What will you do then?'

'I don't know. What will you do?'

'Serve them dinner.' He shrugged. 'What else does a restaurant do?'

'I hadn't thought about it like that.'

'But what if we hold them at the Marne, or somewhere out there in eastern France? Everyone thinks this war will be a short affair, one way or the other. If they're right, there's nothing to do but wait. But what if it isn't so short? What'll happen then?'

'Pierre might have to fight.'

'Not only boys like Pierre. There'll be a general conscription. I've heard army officers talk about it in the past. You're over fifty, a bit too old. But I'll probably be called up.'

'You think so?'

'I do. So I've made a decision. I'll wait a little while, but if we hold the Germans, I'm going to volunteer.'

'Why?'

'You probably get better treatment, have a better chance of finding yourself a good billet, if you're a volunteer. People who wait to be conscripted, and forced into the army, don't do so well. That's usually how these things work.' He gave his brother a thoughtful look. 'If that happens, Thomas, I want you and Édith to take over the bar and restaurant.'

'But that's not what I do.'

'Thomas, if the war drags on, life might get very hard. I don't think people will be building much. And anyway, you're not getting any younger. There could be food shortages. Think of the siege of Paris back in 1870. People were starving. With the bar, you stand a better chance of getting by than most people. And then after the war, whoever wins, you'll still have it.'

Thomas looked doubtful.

'I don't know, Luc. It's not my style. And Édith . . .'

There was no need for Thomas to finish the sentence. But it wasn't only that Édith had never liked Luc. Ever since the terrible secret of the murder had come between them, there had been a distance between the two brothers as well. Nothing was ever said, but they both knew it. Even in Luc's absence, Thomas was reluctant to become involved in his brother's business. And he certainly didn't want to join him as any kind of partner.

'Don't worry,' said Luc, wryly, 'I'll probably be killed. I wouldn't be the first,' he added quietly.

But to Thomas's surprise, when he spoke to Édith about the subject that night, she was enthusiastic. 'As long as Luc's not there,' she stipulated.

'I thought you would not want it,' he said.

'Why? It's better than what we have.'

'Luc thinks he might be killed.'

'Make sure he leaves the business to you. Make sure there's a proper will.'

This wasn't Thomas's way of doing things. But the next day when, with embarrassment, he mentioned what Édith had said to his brother, Luc smiled and remarked that she was quite right. 'Give this to your wife,' he said, and handed Thomas a copy of his will, together with the name of his lawyer.

*   *   *

It was not long before news started arriving about the great battle on the River Marne. It had been the small band of gallant aviators in their flimsy biplanes who had brought the French command news that the German forces outside Paris were split. French and British troops, reinforced by the Parisian troops who'd come in by taxi, were poured into the gap.

The fighting was desperate, the casualties huge. But in less than a week, the Germans had pulled back north-eastward to the line of the River Aisne in Picardy and Champagne. There they started a massive line of trenches, and dug in. Paris was saved.

But the news of the casualties was terrible. In that one week of battle, France alone had a quarter of a million casualties, of whom eighty thousand were dead. In such extreme circumstances, it was not always possible to make precise tallies, nor, at first, to inform all the families of the dead.

A week after the battle was over, when there was still no news of Robert, Luc Gascon went to volunteer. He'd taken his decision carefully.

It was clear that Germany would not be able to overrun France as planned. Not only that: the kaiser would now be forced to fight a war on two fronts – on the plains of France and Flanders to his west, and in Russia to the east. The war might be brief, but Luc suspected it would not. More recruits would certainly be needed, and soon.

The recruiting station was a collection of quickly erected wooden huts near the Gare de l'Est railway station. There he found a small crowd of men, waiting in groups and chatting together before they joined the short line filing in at the doorway. As he certainly wasn't in a hurry, he paused and surveyed the scene.

There were all sorts of men. Most seemed to be in their thirties. The younger men, he surmised, had been more recently conscripted and were probably already in the reserve. A few were labourers and factory hands, but more of them looked like clerks or shop assistants, mostly in suits, some sporting straw hats or trilbies. And he'd been watching for a couple of minutes when he saw a face he thought he knew.

Who the devil was it? A face from long ago. He was sure of that. And Luc prided himself on never forgetting a face. But it still took him a little time before he realised who it was.

The strange fellow who'd lain in wait that night, long ago, on the rue des Belles-Feuilles. The man who'd wanted to kill that army officer, Roland de Cygne. The man he'd shaken down so successfully in the Bois de Boulogne. Now he remembered the fellow's name: Le Sourd. That was it.

Luc was wondering whether to hide himself when he remembered that the fellow might not even have known for sure what part he'd played in that little drama. And he never even saw me, Luc thought, except in the Moulin Rouge. It was Luc's nature to be curious, and he wondered what sort of man Le Sourd had become these days, and why he'd come to the recruiting station. So, cautiously, he drew closer so that Le Sourd could see his face.

It was just as he thought. No reaction. Not a glimmer of recognition.

He went up to him and nodded.

'Taking the plunge?'

'Yes.'

'The rumour I heard,' said Luc amiably, 'is that when they start the general call-up, it'll be everyone up to age forty-five.'

Le Sourd nodded.

'I heard that too.'

'And what age might you be, if you don't mind me asking?'

'Forty. And you?'

Luc did a quick sum in his head. Whatever Le Sourd's real age, it had to be nearer fifty than forty. Evidently his desire to fight was strong enough to make him lie about his age. That was probably why he'd decided to volunteer rather than wait for the call-up. For when the general call-up came, they'd be checking everyone's papers carefully, and they might reject a man who was over the age limit. Whereas at present, Luc guessed, they'd take anyone who offered, as long as they were fit enough, with no other questions asked.

'I'm thirty-nine. Tell me,' he continued, 'since I had to think about it myself, I'm curious to know what made you decide to volunteer?'

Le Sourd shrugged.

'I'm a socialist. If the German kaiser wins the war, that won't be good for us.'

This was certainly logical. The conservative German emperor had far more authoritarian instincts than the left-leaning French government. Most of the French trade unions and socialist organisations had come to the same conclusion and backed the government at once. As an expression of national solidarity, several socialists had immediately been given important government positions.

'You're like me, then. I'm a patriot, but a socialist too,' said Luc. It wasn't true, but years behind the bar had taught him two things: if he agreed with a man, that man would believe him, because he wanted to; he'd also be far more talkative. And he could have defended his socialism with ease. Men had confided every political position to him, so many times that he could reproduce those views exactly as he'd heard them. 'I was a Jean Jaurès man myself.'

Jean Jaurès, the working men's leader. A figure of towering decency, beloved by every socialist and even many conservatives too. Murdered by a right-wing fanatic that summer, and generally mourned. A safe choice that carried immediate conviction.

Jacques Le Sourd nodded, and continued.

'I've seen so many of my young comrades – good union men, socialists, even anarchists – going to the front, that . . . I felt embarrassed to remain behind, to tell you the truth.'

Luc glanced at him. He'd heard so many stories down the years that he could usually tell if a man was lying. If he was any judge, Le Sourd was telling the truth.

'Any family?' he asked.

'A wife. I married late. But I have a little boy.'

'Did that hold you back?'

'Yes. I lost my own father. He was a Communard. It's not good, to lose a father. But then I thought, what if my son has to live under the kaiser because I refused to fight?'

'That's it. I've nephews and nieces. I feel the same way.'

Was it possible this married man was still pursuing his strange vendetta against de Cygne? It seemed improbable. Nor could Luc see how the war would make it any easier to accomplish. Even if, by some fluke, Le Sourd appeared in the same company or regiment as the aristocrat, de Cygne would soon come to know of it. He discarded the idea.

'Shall we enlist, comrade?' said Le Sourd.

'Why not?'

When they got to the desk, a young officer was taking down their details. He looked like a child. Le Sourd gave his age as forty, and though the officer gave him a quick look, he either didn't care, or he was so young that anyone over thirty-five seemed equally old to him.

With Luc, for some reason, the officer took more care. Searching through a huge dossier on the desk he found his name.

'The doctors will check you out,' he said, and he waved him on.

> *Dear Maman and Papa, and all the family,*
>
> *I am alive and well. I have been digging trenches since the big battle, which you'll have heard about. Please send me strong gloves if you can, because I may be in this trench for some time.*
>
> *Thank you for seeing me off, Papa. I saw you waving like a lunatic in the Champs-Élysées, but I was too embarrassed to wave back.*
>
> *My love to you all.*
>
> *Your son,*
>
> *Robert*

Marc Blanchard had not expected the proposal from his brother, nor was it welcome. Though he was forty-five, he'd been wondering whether to enlist.

'What about Father?' he said. 'He could do it far better than me.'

'He doesn't want to,' Gérard answered. He gave a wry smile. 'I already asked him.'

It was more than five years since Jules Blanchard had finally retired to Fontainebleau. He still kept the big apartment on the boulevard Malesherbes, but he went there less and less.

'The store manager and two of my best clerks have all gone to fight. I couldn't stop them,' Gérard continued. 'I need help, and I want someone in the family. If anything happened to me . . .'

'You look pretty robust.'

'That may be. But all the same . . .'

'James could do it. He's a lawyer, and far more competent than I.'

'Your sister and brother-in-law are in England. They can't come over.'

'You've already asked them?'

'Of course. I knew you wouldn't want this. You have your own life – though that may be somewhat curtailed while this war lasts, I imagine.'

Marc's career had been moderately successful. Every year he got a commission or two for a portrait. When a gallery put on a show of his work, a large and fashionable crowd turned up and the paintings would sell. He had talent, but not genius. Had he wanted to, he could have become the director of a museum or an art school, or he could have run a gallery, but he disliked administration. Instead, while carrying on his own work, he became a critic and promoter of the work of others, a respected fixture on the art scene and a man with many friends. Now that the war had started, he had wondered whether to offer himself to the government as a war artist.

And now his brother wanted him to come and help run the family business.

'I could be called up,' Marc objected. 'I'm probably just young enough.'

'I already have an exemption for you,' Gérard told him. 'The wholesale business is part of the war effort, you know. We're already supplying food to the troops.' He paused. 'I need you to understand the wholesale business, but your main task would be to keep the store going – if we can.'

'Joséphine? You'd close Joséphine?'

'I know you like the store. It would break Father's heart if we had to close it. But if the war drags on, fashion goods are going to be tough to sell. It may be hard to keep Joséphine going. I know I wouldn't be able to do it. I haven't got the talent. But perhaps you could succeed.' He glanced at his brother with mild amusement. 'Funnily enough, if you put your mind to it, I think you'd run Joséphine rather well.'

Marc gave his brother a long look.

'But I'd have to work for you.'

'We'd work together. But yes, I'd make the final investment decisions.' Gérard gazed at him calmly. 'People are going to sacrifice their lives, Marc. This would be your sacrifice. You may dislike the idea, but it wouldn't kill you. And I want to preserve the business for the next generation.'

'I'll give you my answer tomorrow,' Marc told him.

He was at his aunt Éloïse's apartment within the hour. She wasn't surprised to see him.

'I assume that Gérard has spoken to you,' she remarked.

'You'll support me when I refuse, won't you?' he said.

'Not at all,' she answered firmly. She smiled. 'I love you, Marc, but you are selfish. And we're at war. You must accept at once.'

Chapter Nineteen

1917

Father Xavier had been buried in Rome a month ago, in May, and Roland was glad that they'd never meet again. For he had no wish to tell the priest he thought that God was dead.

He'd seen too much in the last three years.

As for the terrible mission he must undertake now, Roland de Cygne felt only disgust and shame. But he would do his duty. What else was he to do?

Swiftness and secrecy were paramount. People in Paris had no idea what had happened. The British were largely in the dark. As for the Germans in the opposite trenches, not a hint of it must ever reach them.

Not the faintest whisper on the wind.

When they paused to rest the horses, he took out a cigarette and lit it. Before putting the lighter back in his pocket, he gazed at it thoughtfully.

It was nearly three years since he'd been given that lighter. On the eve of the battle of the Marne.

How proud of themselves his regiment of *cuirassiers* had been. They'd made one concession to the modern world. Realising that their shining metal breastplates might attract enemy fire, they had covered them with cloth. And there they were, entering Europe's first mechanised war as if it were still the age of Napoléon.

He'd come upon one of his troopers fashioning the lighter out of the shell casing of a rifle bullet. Duras was the trooper's name, a genial young fellow, good with his hands. The lighter fuel went in the shell casing, then the wick and a small flint striker were fitted on the top. A simple mechanism, but sturdy and reliable.

'Do you often make these, Duras?' he'd asked.

'*Oui, mon colonel.*'

He'd just been promoted to lieutenant-colonel the week before, he remembered, and he'd still been getting used to the appellation.

'Would you make one for me?'

'I will give you this one, *mon colonel*,' Duras had replied, 'as soon as it is finished.' And a short time later he had brought it to him and shown him, neatly incised on the side of the casing, his initials: R de C.

'What shall I pay you?' he'd asked.

'A bottle of champagne when the war is over?' the young fellow suggested.

'Agreed.' Roland had laughed.

And he'd kept the lighter with him ever since, perhaps as a talisman of those last days, when war had still seemed to belong to a world he'd thought he knew.

A week later, on the orders of a well-meaning captain, Duras and a troop of more than 150 other *cuirassiers* had ridden over a low ridge and charged down upon a German force they hoped to clear from the area. There had been a sustained rattle of machine-gun fire, followed by silence. Half a dozen of the horses had returned, without their riders. The rest of the horses and all the men were dead, every one.

His *cuirassiers* had ceased to be a regiment in anything but name, soon after that. Sometimes they operated as mounted infantry, using their horses to cross terrain before they dismounted to fight with carbines on foot. They helped bring supplies. They escorted prisoners. No one even thought of a cavalry charge nowadays.

If only it had been the cavalry alone who were ill-prepared. What of all the infantrymen in their blue coats and bright red trousers – a uniform hardly changed in a hundred years? A uniform that guaranteed they were instantly visible to an enemy whose dull combat dress blended with the landscape. Madness. A quarter of a million brightly dressed soldiers killed or wounded in a single week upon the Marne. It had been months before the French army learned the simple art of camouflage.

Even their arms were inadequate. The Saint-Étienne, the Hotchkiss and the Chauchat light machine guns were hopelessly unreliable. It was the second year of the war before the troops had the more reliable Berthier, and there still weren't enough of them.

Almost a million Frenchmen had been killed in the first three years of the war – five per cent of the entire male population of France, from cradle to grave. And that was before the recent catastrophe.

Why did my country fail to learn from the conflicts of recent decades? he asked himself. The British had changed their uniforms, learned camouflage and flexible cavalry tactics from the Boer War in Africa. The Germans had studied these lessons too. And they had better arms.

If he'd been on the staff himself, Roland thought, wouldn't he have been wiser? Or would he have succumbed to the terrible French habit of arrogance, just as everyone else had? France was the best, the most cultivated, the most intelligent nation in the world, so went the refrain. Therefore she had nothing to learn from the boorish Germans and the crude Anglo-Saxons, or anybody else.

But alas it was not so, and now she had a million dead to prove it. Brave troops, who'd fought like lions. The finest attacking troops in the world, in Roland's opinion. The British soldiers said so too.

It is we who let them down, he thought. We who prepared our army so poorly. We who misjudged the German plan, so obvious in retrospect. We who arranged a European world that could not avoid this war. We the rulers, with the power to destroy all that we love, and the stupidity to do it.

And now, it seemed, the army command had finally gone too far.

General Nivelle's offensive that spring had been bold, yet strangely unimaginative.

'We'll smash through the German line on the River Aisne, and win the war,' Nivelle declared.

To Roland the plan seemed little different from the strategy that had already cost countless lives already.

'We're going to break through at the section known as Chemin des Dames,' his commanding general told him, 'and roll up the German line. And here's the clever thing,' his general continued. 'We're going to use a tactic that we tried out at Verdun, but on a huge scale.'

'What is that, *mon général*?'

'A creeping barrage. The artillery will fire just ahead of our troops as they advance. We lay down a stupendous shelling on the enemy trenches. What's left of the men there will be entirely disoriented. And then our men will be able to race in behind the barrage and overwhelm the trenches before the enemy can even see them coming.'

'Won't a good many of the shells fall short and hit our own troops?'

'Yes, but not too much, we hope. And it's a lesser price to pay, if our men can sweep into the trenches almost unopposed.'

Roland had his doubts, but he knew it was pointless for him to say anything.

'What about tanks?' he asked. Personally, he thought of the new metal chariots as mechanical knights in armour. Partly for that reason, he believed they were important.

'Lots of them,' the general said. 'We know what we're doing.'

Nivelle's offensive had succeeded in taking some points on the German lines, despite appalling weather, and the incompetent failure of the tank attack. But the German front did not collapse. And the losses of Frenchmen had been terrible.

'It wasn't our fault. It was poor intelligence, my dear de Cygne,' his general had told him. 'Who could have guessed the Germans were making their trenches like that?'

As the French troops advanced, taking huge casualties from their own artillery, and finally reached the German trenches, they did not find the Germans smashed and disoriented at all.

For the German trenches were not like the French ones in the least. To the French soldier, a trench was just a temporary, makeshift cover, from which to attack. To the Germans, a trench was a system.

Many of the German trenches had the advantage of high ground, but above all, their construction was entirely superior. The Germans dug far deeper. They fortified. They even had shelters underground. When the French laid down their huge bombardment, the Germans waited it out in the relative safety of their deep redoubts, and when the French troops finally raced towards the line, they found the Germans waiting for them, freshly supplied with first-rate new machine guns, with which they mowed the Frenchmen down.

The Nivelle offensive did not smash the German front. It hardly made a dent.

Its profound effect was not on the German army at all, but on the French. That was the tragedy.

And it was the reason for Roland de Cygne's secret mission that day. A terrible mission he had never dreamed in his life that he would ever have to perform.

For unbeknownst to her allies and her enemies, right across the Western Front, the brave army of France had mutinied.

If Roland de Cygne was the guardian of a secret that June day, Marc Blanchard was guarding three. Two he had possessed since a week ago. They had caused him great agony of mind. This evening, he was going to talk to his Aunt Éloïse before making the decision about what to do.

The third he had learned that morning.

The meeting was so secret that it had not been held in any government office, but in a private apartment in an undistinguished street north of the boulevard des Batignolles. There were several government men, an important building contractor, an Italian lighting engineer named Jacopozzi, and several others. He wondered why they had invited him. Perhaps because, these days, they thought of him as both a designer and a businessman. Whatever the reason, he was flattered that they trusted him.

They gathered in the dining room of the apartment. It was a representative of the prime minister himself who opened the meeting.

'Messieurs, we are here to consider a most important project, and I must ask you never to divulge what we are going to discuss.

'Today we believe that Paris may face a new and terrible threat. It is a threat that London has already faced, and it is a threat that will only grow with time. I am speaking, naturally, of aerial bombing.' He paused for effect. 'In the three years since this war began, many aspects of the military effort have altered; but the transformation of war in the air has been astounding. When we began, there were a few planes, mostly for reconnaissance, and if bombs were used, they were usually grenades or adapted shells dropped by hand by the pilots or co-pilots of those small open planes.

'Now, however, the German Gotha bombers are large, they carry a payload of over two thousand pounds, and they can fly at over twenty thousand feet where it is hard, if not impossible, for our fighters to attack them.

'I need not tell anyone here the supreme importance of Paris – its history, its art and its culture, for France and for the world. Paris must be protected. But we are not so far from the German lines. Fleets of Gotha bombers, making night raids, night after night, could do appalling damage – for let us remember that we are speaking not only of the explosions, but of the fires that may follow them. We can fire up into the sky. Our gallant fighters can go up to tackle the bombers, but all the evidence so far suggests that large bombing raids would be hard to stop. And so, if we cannot stop them, we must deceive them.'

'Deceive them?' Marc was puzzled. So was everyone else, except the Italian Jacopozzi, who was grinning. And now it was the turn of another of the officials to unroll a large map of Paris on the dining table, and to address them.

'Aviators at night cannot see much on the ground. If there is a little moonlight, however, they can usually catch the glimmer reflected on a river, and they often navigate by this means.' He took a pointer and indicated a point on the map. 'Here you can see the River Seine. And I direct your attention to a place about three miles north of the city. As you see, the Seine here displays a series of curves which closely mimic those it makes as it passes through Paris. As you also see, much of the area here is open fields. It would be much better, therefore, if the German bombs fell up here rather than on the city. Our intention is to invite the Germans to do exactly that.'

'Invite them?' Marc was confused.

'Even so, Monsieur Blanchard, and in the simplest way possible. Paris will miraculously move.' He smiled while his audience waited. 'Messieurs, we are going to institute a total blackout in Paris itself, and then we are going to build a second Paris, a fake Paris, just to the north.'

'You're going to build a fake city? The size of Paris?'

'Big enough to be mistaken for Paris at twenty thousand feet, yes.' The man spread his hands. 'I am speaking of a stage set, messieurs. A Potemkin village, but a thousand times larger than anything the Russians ever dreamed of.'

'Made of what?'

'Wood and painted canvas, mostly. And lights.' He indicated the Italian. 'Thanks to Monsieur Jacopozzi, thousands of lights.'

'You're going to copy big buildings?'

'Naturally. Buildings that the enemy will be looking for. Buildings that they can see. The Gare du Nord, for instance.'

'And the Eiffel Tower?'

'Yes. That should really fool them.'

'I can precisely copy the lights of the Eiffel Tower,' Jacopozzi said enthusiastically. 'You'll never be able to tell the difference. They will see an illuminated city.'

'You're insane,' said Marc, shaking his head. 'This would be the most daring theatrical deception in the history of war.'

'Thank you,' the prime minister's man said. 'We thought that you might like it.'

Marc laughed.

'It's daring. It has style,' he agreed. And then, after a little reflection, he paid the project the highest compliment that a Frenchman can pay: '*Ça, c'est vraiment français*: that is truly French.'

A general discussion ensued after that. There were all kinds of practical questions to consider. But it was agreed that he and Jacopozzi would look at the overall design together, and come up with further specific recommendations.

When the meeting ended, he decided to walk the short distance to Place de Clichy, past some of his old haunts, and then down to the office from there. Since he'd become involved in the family business at the start of the war, he hardly ever went up that way.

Passing a bar he used to know, he went in and ordered a coffee. The waiter who brought it to his table was a young man. Marc noticed that he hobbled slightly as he walked. Marc gazed around the bar.

Wartime Paris was a curious place. For the last three months of 1914, when so many people had fled, and the government itself had briefly left for Bordeaux, he had wondered if it would turn into a ghost town. But once the two armies had settled into their trench warfare, the government and most of the people had returned, and Parisian life had resumed, albeit quietly. Food was often short, but Les Halles and the local street markets were still supplied. Bars and restaurants still opened, and night-time entertainment too.

Paris had three main functions now. From the military headquarters in Les Invalides, it directed the war. It was also the place to which the vast number of casualties were taken. All the great hospitals of the city were full, aided by the American Hospital out at Neuilly, where American volunteers had taken over the entire local lycée as well, to provide beds for the French wounded.

And of course, it also provided rest and relaxation for the troops on leave from the front.

That meant large numbers of men, not only from every part of France, but from all over her colonies too. There were the colourful Zouave troops from Africa. Tirailleurs from Senegal, Algeria, Morocco, even Indochina. Men of every colour, giving Paris a more international look than it usually wore.

In the far corner across from him, Marc watched two Zouaves talking quietly. It was a pity, he thought, that like everyone else, the dashing troops of France's army of Africa had been obliged to abandon their bright uniforms and baggy trousers for duller khaki, but there was still something romantic about them as they smoked their long pipes.

He'd heard rumours of trouble in the army. The word was that a division or two had even refused to go back to the front line without some changes in their conditions, and that the army might be granting more leave. If so, there would be still more troops visiting Paris. The ladies of the night would have more work to do.

He turned his thoughts back to the fake Paris. Would it really work? Could the secret of it be kept from the Germans? He was just pondering this when the patron came over from the bar, and addressed him.

'Monsieur Blanchard? Do you remember me?'

Marc looked up at his face. It was familiar, but he couldn't place it at once. Then he did remember.

'You were the foreman when we were building the new rooms at Joséphine. You'd worked on the Eiffel Tower.'

'*Oui, monsieur.* I am Thomas Gascon. It's my brother who owns this bar.'

'Dark-haired. Am I right? I used to come in here. Where is he now?'

'In the army.'

'At the front?'

'Not exactly. He's in the quartermaster's department. Supplies. He's good at that.' Thomas did not add that he and his family had benefited from the army's food supplies now and then, on Luc's visits to them.

'You were a good foreman, I remember. Do you ever do any work of that kind now?'

'Not recently, monsieur. Not much on offer.' He grinned. 'Unless someone's wanting to build another Eiffel Tower.'

You have no idea, Marc thought, how close to the truth you are. But when work began, Thomas Gascon might be a good foreman to use. He'd remember him.

'You have a family, I think.'

'My wife and daughter are next door, in the restaurant. My son Robert, with the wooden leg, served you coffee.'

'Any other sons?'

'I had. Pierre was my younger son. We lost him at Verdun.'

'I'm sorry.'

'And your family, monsieur?'

'My parents are down at Fontainebleau, getting old. My sister is well. But my elder brother died three months ago.' He smiled sadly. 'That is why I must go to the office now – like you, to keep the family business running.'

Thomas Gascon wouldn't take any money for the coffee. Marc made a mental note to go to the restaurant some time, and leave a tip.

Gérard. Dead. Even now he could scarcely believe it. He'd been in the office when it happened. A clerk, ashen-faced, had come into his office and led him down the passage to Gérard's. His brother had been sitting at his desk – almost as he usually did, except that he was leaning back at a strange angle in his big chair. The stroke had obviously killed him quite suddenly. There had been no warning at all.

And Marc had been obliged to take over in his place.

Looking back, it seemed to him that from the first day Gérard had asked him to join him, his brother had had an inkling of what was coming. He'd taken care that, little as it interested him, Marc obtained a good idea how the wholesale business worked, who the suppliers were, how to treat them and the workings of the distribution process.

535

Though Gérard controlled the finances, including those of the department store, Marc understood how all the accounts were put together and where all the information was kept. He was quite surprised to discover, after the first shock of Gérard's death, that he knew exactly what to do.

For the last three months, he'd kept everything in good order. Not only that, he'd made his own investigations into every corner of the businesses, just to make sure that some aspect of them didn't suddenly take him unawares.

That was how, last week, he had made the two awful discoveries that had been haunting him ever since.

Gérard had known he'd discover those, too. In fact, Marc realised, he'd wanted him to.

He wondered what Aunt Éloïse would say when he told her.

She had changed remarkably little down the years. She used an ebony stick when she walked, but didn't always bother to do even that. Her face remained smooth. She was as elegant at seventy as she had been at forty.

He'd offered to take her out to dinner, but she preferred to have a delicious little supper served in her own apartment. They dined under a small Manet and a Pissarro. He waited until the dessert before he told her.

'I have two pieces of bad news. The first is that I made a discovery in the accounts. It went back to early 1915, but I happened to find it when I was going through the records of one of our suppliers.'

'We owe money?'

'Not exactly. Worse. Gérard had dealings with a wholesaler up on the north coast. Dunkirk to be exact. They were supplying shipments of food to the French army.'

'What of it?'

'A huge shipment – potatoes, flour, all kinds of essentials – went missing. Apparently the Germans took them. But Gérard was paid all the same.'

'There's nothing wrong with that.'

'Except that he sold them to the Germans.'

'Are you sure?'

'There can be no doubt. But the Germans didn't get them. He told them that the French army had captured the shipment. So the Germans paid him to get some more.'

'Which he delivered?'

'No. He said that the French had captured them too.'

'So who got the supplies in the end?'

'The French. But they had to pay for them. He sold the same goods four times.'

'At least we got them in the end.'

'But it's criminal.'

'By Gérard's standards, one might say it was patriotic. The Germans paid twice and got nothing.'

'God knows what else he did that I don't know about. The question is, what do I do? I'd like to do something for the French.'

'The first thing is that you must not say a word about shipments. Not a word. It will never be discovered now, and does nothing but bring his memory and our name into disrepute. Think of his widow and his children. You should burn the records straightaway. Give them to me and I'll burn them. Then forget about it. By all means find any way you can to contribute to our war effort. You will be thanked, and that is good. After all, you had no part in the business, and I know that you would never have done such a thing.'

'I'm just shocked.'

'You said there were two items of bad news. What is the other?'

'Joséphine. The store. It's losing money. In fact, it has been since the war began. Gérard always told me that we were breaking even. But he was lying. I was running it, but I left the financial side to him. I feel a fool.'

'I'm not surprised in the least. A war isn't the best time to sell fashion goods. Money's tight.'

'We still made sales. Dropped our prices, changed the merchandise, operated only part of the store. But it seems we lost money. Why didn't he tell me?'

'It was the price he thought he needed to pay to keep you in the business. Thank God he did. We need you there now.'

'I don't know what to do.'

'Yes you do. Sell it or close it.'

'But that's terrible. Think of Father. It would break his heart.'

'He's a businessman. He'll understand. All he wants to do now is enjoy his old age in Fontainebleau.'

'But I can't run a wholesale business.'

'You must. Gérard has two daughters and a son, who will be conscripted any minute. You must do it for them. It's your duty.'

'But my talents . . .'

'Will have to wait. I love you, Marc, but you must continue to be unselfish. Your family has given you all the good fortune you have. You said you wanted to pay your country back for Gérard's theft. Good. And you must pay the family back for your good fortune.'

'I don't particularly like Gérard's children.'

'I couldn't care less. Marc, when I depart, I have always intended that you should be my heir. Who else would I leave all these paintings to? But if you won't do what you should, then you are no better than your brother, and I shall leave everything to a museum.'

'I thought you were more spiritual.'

'I am very spiritual. Others are dying at the front. Be grateful that your duty is, by comparison, so easy.'

Marc sighed.

'I was afraid you'd say something like that,' he said.

Le Sourd had no doubt about his fate. He was going to be shot. He'd written two letters to his son. One which the censors might see. The second, of which he made three copies, was given to three men in the regiment that he trusted.

The letter explained what he believed in and why he had acted as he did, but it did not enjoin his son to follow in his footsteps. It told him to make up his own mind what course to follow when he became a man, and to think only of his mother and her welfare until then.

He'd never made any secret of the fact that he was a socialist. There had been no need. There were plenty of good trade union men in the army, and most of them had socialist leanings, at the least.

'We need to fight the German Empire,' he would tell his comrades, 'but it was the capitalist class that got us into this mess, and when the workers sweep them away, the need for wars will end.'

Since he was older than the other men, they began to call him Papa. Even the sergeants called him that sometimes. His job in the printer's and his reading had left him more literate than most. If a young fellow was struggling with a letter home, he'd often come to Le Sourd to help him straighten it out grammatically, or provide the words he was searching for. Sometimes, he would do more. When young Pierre Gascon was killed at Verdun, along with his lieutenant and captain, it was Le Sourd who wrote a letter to his parents about the young man's valour and his other good qualities.

But he never lost sight of his ultimate goal, and he watched for opportunities. Indeed, the war itself, with its massive casualties, was an opportunity. If this senseless carnage and destruction were the result of the present world order, didn't that show that it was time for a change? Wasn't the capitalist world demonstrating that it was a heartless consumer of lives, whose inherent contradictions would lead it to destroy itself? He had brought quite a number of the men around to his point of view.

He suspected that he'd even got through to an officer once. 'Well, Papa Le Sourd,' the captain had remarked to him in a friendly way, 'you think the workers of the world could organise this war better?'

'The question, *mon capitaine*,' he'd replied, 'is whether they could do worse.'

The officer had laughed, and said nothing more. But Le Sourd suspected that, in secret, the captain didn't disagree.

By 1916 he'd been promoted to corporal. His captain had once asked him if he'd like to be a sergeant, but he'd said no. That would be yielding to the system too much.

Meanwhile, he'd been receiving literature regularly from Paris. Some were permitted newspapers, others were more private communications.

And then, in 1917, had come the electrifying news from Russia. The army had mutinied. It was a revolution.

The socialists were astonished. The revolution was supposed to begin in the industrialised countries, where there was an urban proletariat, not in backward Russia. Evidently the war had been the catalyst. And if in Russia, why not elsewhere? A stream of literature began to reach Le Sourd from Paris. All along the Western Front, other men like himself were being alerted. For the committed men of the Left, a new excitement was in the air.

And then, at the end of May, after the disaster of the Nivelle Offensive, the news had come. The authorities might be able to keep it hidden from the outside world, but they couldn't stop the rumours spreading along the front. They spread like wildfire.

'There's a mutiny. Whole regiments are leaving the front.' Ten, twenty, thirty thousand men had marched to the rear and refused to go back to their posts. The conditions were terrible. The direction of the war was completely incompetent. The slaughter was senseless. All along the line, troops that had been in the towns behind the line were refusing to obey orders. Just after the start of June, an entire regiment had taken charge of itself and marched back to occupy the little town Missy-aux-Bois, which it was holding for itself.

An infantry brigade had looted a supply column and was returning to Paris. A motor convoy had been taken over as well.

They had been here at the front when the mutiny had come to their regiment. It had started with a small incident. The enemy trenches had a number of outworks at that point in the line, and a sniper had taken possession of one of them. During the last few days he had managed to wound one fellow and kill another. It wouldn't be a bad idea to take him out, if possible. So one of the lieutenants had gone to the section of trench just beyond Le Sourd's, and told a corporal and a few of his men that he'd lead them on a reconnoitre that night, to see what could be done about the sniper.

And whether he'd been planning to, or whether it just came to him at that moment, the corporal had said no.

'Don't refuse an order,' the lieutenant had said to him quite kindly. But it hadn't done any good.

'I refuse. I've had enough,' the corporal replied, and the private beside him had ceremoniously laid down his rifle and said, 'Me too. No more orders. It's finished.' There had been a murmur of assent from all the men around.

And that was it. A mutiny.

Le Sourd had wasted no time. Within minutes, he was distributing leaflets down the line. In his own section of the trench, he had the men singing 'The Internationale'. One young man improvised a red flag and hoisted it over the trench.

'The mutiny is just a start,' he told the men. 'It will be nothing unless it leads to something with real meaning. France led the world with its Revolution. That was the beginning. But now we have the chance to take the next great step forward. This war has shown the absurdity of the capitalist world. Now is the time to join your fellow workers in Russia and all over the world. We want revolution and nothing less.'

For a few days, he thought it might work. Other units across the front also raised the red flag. If the mutiny had been complete, if the troops had turned and converged upon Paris, then who knew what might have happened?

But the French troops still loved their country. And the government for once acted wisely. Nivelle lost his command. And in his place they put a very brave and clever man.

Pétain.

General Pétain acted swiftly. Word went out at once to all the troops. Their grievances would be heard. Their tours of duty at the front were to be shortened, and there was to be more leave, forthwith. Last but not least: 'The Americans will be with us soon. There shall be no new offensive until we have the support of American arms and men.'

With this promise, the mutiny of the French army was calmed, and everyone sat down to talk.

But the mutiny could not be ignored. Discipline must be restored. The chief culprits must face a court-martial. And each regiment where there had been a mutiny was told: 'Choose the ringleaders only, and they'll have a fair trial.'

Commissions were sent out to give guidance to each regiment, and to escort the culprits to trial.

Le Sourd was quite clear that he would be chosen. He was guilty of more than inciting mutiny. He'd encouraged the troops to overthrow the government itself.

And if he'd had even the faintest doubt on the outcome of the business, it vanished immediately as soon as he saw the leader of the commission ride up to the line.

It was Roland de Cygne.

Roland didn't catch sight of Le Sourd. His mind was on the business at hand. When he'd been given his mission, his general had been extremely clear with him.

'My dear de Cygne, this must seem a wretched mission I am giving you, more suitable to a hangman or a jailer.'

'That is true, *mon général.*'

'Yet in fact, it is a mission of the utmost delicacy and importance. So first I am going to tell you a little secret. Pétain has been to see Haig, the general commanding the British forces. He has informed Haig that there have been some small mutinies, quickly contained, and that they only touched two divisions of the French army. Do you know how many divisions have in fact been affected?'

'No, *mon général.*'

'More than fifty.'

'Fifty?' Roland was thunderstruck. 'That's half the entire army.'

'Exactly so. The whole business is top secret. All the papers are being classified and will be under embargo. With luck, nobody is going to have any access to the truth for fifty years. Meanwhile, we are going to have to tread very carefully, or there won't be an army at all. If the Germans find out . . .'

'I understand.'

'We have to do two things. One is to reassert military discipline. Many senior officers believe we should have immediate, large and summary executions. Pétain does not think it wise, nor does the prime minister. What do you think?'

'My opinion is altered by what you have just told me about the size of the mutiny. I think the numbers should be as small as possible.'

'Good. When we've got them all rounded up, we shall have trials and give the death sentence to very few. Then we shall shoot fewer than that. Probably fewer than a hundred.' He paused. 'For the second thing we have to do, even more important, is to restore morale. Each time you reach a regiment or division – some are up at the front line, many are farther back – you are to ensure that when the officers and NCOs select the men to be sent for trial, they send troublemakers, that is, people who may start up this business again, and if possible, men who are not too popular with their comrades. We want as few martyrs as possible, and we don't want to damage morale. Use your judgement.' He gave Roland a firm look. 'Now you see that I am paying you a compliment by entrusting this mission to you.'

Roland understood. But it didn't mean he liked the mission any better.

*   *   *

They met in the officers' tent. The colonel of the regiment was there, a short, bristling man, together with a captain and three lieutenants.

'We've got ten men for you,' said the colonel. 'Though I could let you have at least fifty who deserve to be shot.'

'I'd rather have five,' said Roland. 'This wasn't a very large disturbance.' Then he explained what Pétain was trying to achieve. 'The minimum that will preserve discipline while encouraging morale.'

'If we chose only the men who first initiated the mutiny, the ones who refused a direct order, then I think it would be five,' suggested the captain.

'And that devil Le Sourd,' said the colonel. 'That makes six.'

Roland noticed that the captain and one of the lieutenants looked awkward.

'Describe this Le Sourd to me,' said Roland.

'He's a big fellow,' said the captain. 'He must have been over the age limit when he volunteered. The troops call him Papa.'

'He's a communist agitator, a revolutionary,' the colonel said furiously. 'He had a red flag up, told the men they'd march on Paris and take down the government. He deserves to be shot more than any of them.'

'Black hair, and eyes wide apart?' asked Roland.

'That's the man. Do you know him, sir?'

'He may be a fellow I came across once. The politics sound like him.' Roland thought for a moment. 'You say the men call him Papa. Does that mean they like him?'

'Yes,' said the captain. 'He helps them with their letters, you know, that sort of thing. He's a good soldier,' he added, with an uncertain glance at the colonel. 'Just believes in world revolution, that's all.'

The colonel gave a snort of disgust.

'I need to know one thing,' said Roland. Did he commit an overt act of mutiny? Did he refuse an order to fight?'

'Not really,' said the captain, with another apologetic look at the colonel. 'His advocacy of revolution came after the mutiny began.'

'What the devil does that matter?' cried the colonel.

'He committed an act of revolution, but not of mutiny,' said Roland.

'Are you mad?' cried the colonel.

'There are men in the government at this moment,' Roland said quietly, 'who probably believe in world revolution. And after the war, *mon colonel*, if you wish to take up arms against them, I will fight at your side. I am the Vicomte de Cygne, and I am a royalist. But the instructions I have, which come directly from Pétain, oblige me to counsel you that this Le Sourd is not a mutineer – at least, not the kind we want at present.' He looked at them all severely. 'I shall leave you for a short while now, messieurs, and when I return, I shall expect to receive from you the names of the men we are to take for court-martial.'

He walked away from the tent. He wasn't sorry to be alone. This was the first time that his mission had taken him to the front line. The officers' tent was just behind a small stand of trees. He walked through them. A short way in front of him he saw some breastwork made of mud and wicker. There was no one there. He could see an observation post thrust somewhat farther along the line.

He looked over the breastwork. It was strange to think that the enemy lay only a few hundred yards away, presumably quite unaware of the crisis taking place across the no-man's-land between them. He stared ahead gloomily.

War had always been bloody, he thought. Nothing new there. But this war was different. Was there really a place for a man like himself – or for any human being, come to that – in this terrible world of machine guns, barbed wire, shell hole and trench?

Men used to speak of the glory of war. Perhaps that had been a lie. They'd spoken of honour. Perhaps that was only vanity. They'd spoken of grief. Yet there was hardly even grief any more. Grief had been numbed.

For war was industrial now, like a great iron-wheeled engine of destruction that compressed flesh and broken bone alike into the endless mud of the killing fields. And for what purpose? He could scarcely remember.

So if ordinary men said that he and his kind had brought them to this nightmare, to this meaningless wasteland, he would have to acknowledge that they were right. And that perhaps their mutiny, for which they were to be shot, was the only sane act of the last four years.

And when it was all done, what story would be told? He did not know. Would tales of glory be invented? Or would there be a great silence? Men who have been tortured do not wish to speak of it. They close the memory in a lead-lined box and leave it in the cellar of the mind. Perhaps it would be like that. Or perhaps there would be a revolution.

He heard the sound of a rifle bolt behind him. Then a voice.

'If you reach for your revolver, I shall fire.'

He turned slowly.

'Le Sourd. I heard you were here.'

'We are quite alone. Did you know that there is a German sniper out there? I thought I would shoot you before he did.'

'I should have thought of that. It has been a long time. Aren't you running some risk yourself?'

'I could say I went forward to warn you about the sniper, but that he got you. Then I could shoot some rounds towards the German lines.'

'You might get away with it. You might not.'

'I shan't bother. They're going to shoot me anyway as a mutineer, so I have nothing to lose.'

'Perhaps they will not charge you with mutiny.'

'I think they will.'

Roland de Cygne gazed at Le Sourd. He could have told him that he wasn't going to be charged, but that would have looked as if he were trying to curry favour, a weakness for which Le Sourd would have rightly despised him. Roland was too proud for that.

'Perhaps,' he said calmly, 'when you have shot me – and I advise you to stick with the story of the sniper, it's worth a try – you will do me a small favour. In my pocket, you will find a lighter that a trooper once made for me. It's just a little thing. You can send it to my son, and tell him that I asked you to do so. I should like him to know that I was thinking of him. That is all.'

'You are asking me to do you a favour?'

'Why not? With my death you have avenged your father. Matters between us are settled. You have no reason to refuse a small kindness to my son.'

Le Sourd gazed at him.

'Even in death, the aristocratic pose. I am not impressed, Monsieur le Vicomte. You are merely playing a role. Here in the middle of this desert of the spirit, you act out a part that belongs to . . .' – he searched for words – 'a great illusion. It's absurd. Perhaps you imagine that, in the afterlife, God is going to tip His hat to you in courteous recognition, like the Roi Soleil.'

Roland de Cygne said nothing. Even if he had agreed with Le Sourd, he would not have told him.

Le Sourd aimed. Roland waited.

'*Merde*,' said Le Sourd. And instead of firing, he turned and walked away through the trees.

Chapter Twenty

1918

James Fox looked thoughtfully at the young woman who sat across the desk from him.

It was a November day. As usual, the offices of Fox and Martineau, of which he was now the senior partner, maintained an almost sepulchral quiet. Occasionally a sound from the narrow alley off Chancery Lane intruded through the window, but seldom enough to challenge the soft hiss of the coal fire in the grate.

The young lady had arrived a little while before, without appointment, and asked to see the senior partner. He had no meeting at that moment, and when he'd heard her name, and realised who she must be, he'd told his clerk to usher her in.

She was quietly, almost severely dressed – a white shirt, a simple pearl choker, dark grey coat and skirt, her dark hair swept up and pinned under a sensible hat. Appropriate, for the country was still at war. But the material was expensive. One could tell that she came from the well-to-do upper-middle class.

Her face was rather beautiful, he thought. Her eyes large, almost violet in colour. There was a certain elegance in her movements. Was there something French about her, or did he just imagine it because of what he knew? Her name was Louise.

'How can I help you?' he asked.

'You are the family lawyers,' said Louise. 'I believe you always have been.'

'That is certainly true. It began with my own father and your grandfather.'

'So if I were adopted you would know.'

He did not move a muscle of his face.

'We might, or might not, I should say.'

'I think you know.'

He did not answer.

'My mother told me I was adopted. She told me when I was sixteen.'

'Did she?'

'She didn't want to tell me, even then. I never had any idea until one day I overheard two of my parents' friends talking about our family, and one of them said that I was adopted but that I didn't know. What do you think of that, Mr Fox?'

'If clients ask us, we generally recommend that they should tell children when they are adopted. Some do not. But even if you had been adopted, I don't know why you'd come to see me.'

'When I asked my mother about it, and I told her what I'd heard, she wasn't very pleased. Then she told me that she and my father had adopted me because they loved me, but that my real parents didn't love me, and didn't want me. I was quite upset by what she said at the time. It was a new thought for me, you see, that my real parents had rejected me. But now I think my mother said it because she wanted me to love her, and not the parents I never knew.'

'I believe you have had a happy childhood and a good home. Is that correct?'

'Yes, it is.'

'And your parents loved you as they should?'

'Yes, they did.'

'Parents need to be loved too, you know. Even if everything you say is correct, I think you should consider your mother. Perhaps she was afraid you would love her less. You surely do not wish to hurt her.'

'But I'd like to know if she was telling me the truth.'

'Quite often people have children that they can't look after, for all sorts of reasons. It's not lack of love, but circumstances that force them to act. Whoever your parents were – assuming you are correct – it's clear that they went to great lengths to ensure that you had a wonderful home and upbringing, probably one they could never have given you.'

'Shouldn't one always want to know the truth?'

'Speaking as a family lawyer of thirty years' experience' – he smiled – 'sometimes I wish people knew the truth, and sometimes I wish they didn't. So if you have come to me for advice, then I advise you to be kind to the parents who gave you a home, and to forget the rest.'

'I didn't come to you for advice.' She looked at him steadily. 'I asked my mother who my real parents were, but she wouldn't tell me. Then a bit later, I overheard my parents talking. And I heard my father say, 'Only Foxes know.' The only Foxes I could think of were your firm, the family lawyers. And it seemed logical that the family lawyers might know, wouldn't you say?'

'I can see you might have thought so. Do you always listen at doors?'

'No, but I did that day. Hardly surprising.'

Fox considered. 'If I have understood you correctly, this conversation must have taken place some years ago. Why the long wait before coming to see me?'

'I couldn't very well come waltzing into your office at the age of sixteen, could I?' Louise paused. 'There's another reason. You know the terms of my father's will. Don't worry, I'm not asking you for anything. He has told me that he intends to provide a dowry for me when I marry, but that the rest of his money will be used to provide for my mother, and that after that, the residue will go to some blood cousins. So being adopted isn't quite the same, you see. The point is that I'm not an heiress.'

'You surely are not seeking to discover your real parents in the hope of monetary gain?'

'Not at all.' She gave him a quizzical look. 'Are you good at mathematics, Mr Fox?'

'Moderately.'

'Well, here is a very simple proposition. When this war is over, I'm sure everyone will be wanting to get married. But there's a difficulty. The casualties have been so terrible that there won't be enough men to go around, especially young men of my class. We all know that the casualty rate among young officers has been appalling. I dare say the heiresses will find husbands, unless they're terribly ugly. And lots of girls will marry men they wouldn't have looked at normally. The rest will have to remain spinsters, or become governesses if they haven't the means. A few independent-minded women will find ways to fend for themselves.'

'I have the impression that you fall into that last category.'

'I think I probably do.' She smiled mischievously. 'I am well aware, Mr Fox, that to call a woman independent-minded is not usually a compliment.'

He smiled in turn. It seemed to him that any young man who didn't want to marry this spirited young woman would be a fool. But she had a point.

'I don't think you need despair of finding a husband,' he replied. 'But you may have to be a little careful not to frighten them. Though there are some men,' he added, 'interesting men perhaps, who find independent women attractive.'

'Well, my parents assume that I shall marry, anyway, and that then their work will be done. The idea of my earning a living is unthinkable to them. I know there's been a lot of war work, but after things get back to normal . . . It's not what people of our class do, is it?'

'Marriage isn't so bad, you know.'

'Oh, I'm not averse to marrying, Mr Fox, but I have to allow for the fact that I may not. And I think I want my life to be more of an adventure. Perhaps I can become a photographer, or go to America, or something like that.'

'And you have discussed these ideas with your parents.'

'A little. They are not enthusiastic, but I can't help that.'

'I can't think of any parents I know who would want their daughter's life to be an adventure,' said James with perfect truth. 'You have not quarrelled, I hope?'

'No. But there's trouble brewing. I can feel it.' She nodded thoughtfully, and he wondered what else had been said. 'So if I am to lead my own life, Mr Fox, I'd like to know who I really am. And I want you to tell me. Who were my parents?'

James shook his head.

'Even if all your surmises were correct, I could tell you nothing. Your father is my client, not you. I have never divulged a client's private business in my life.'

'Couldn't you tell me anything? Just a hint. Something to work with.'

'No, I could not. Nor do I admit any knowledge of the subject at all.'

'I really wish . . .' she began, when there was a noise in the street. She turned and frowned.

Fox was looking towards the window too. The noise from Chancery Lane seemed to be turning into a roar. He saw faces appearing at the window of the lawyer's office across the alley. Then there was a shout from the alley itself. Moments later, footsteps came rapidly up the stairs. His own office door burst open without even the courtesy of a knock, to reveal his elderly clerk, suddenly flushed and with his half-moon spectacles not quite straight.

'Excuse me, sir,' he said, 'but the war is over.'

Everyone had believed that it must come soon. But the day London heard that the Great War had truly ended and that the Armistice was signed was like no other before or since. Four years of slaughter, done with. From street to street, from smokestack to steeple, from grimy terrace to stucco mansion, there was not a household, an office, a congregation that had not lost at least a friend. Thanks to the food shortages, there was not a child who had had enough to eat.

And now at last the great cloud over their lives was about to be lifted. The bleak, seemingly endless nightmare was over. The loved ones would be reappearing over the horizon.

As the news was heard, as the realisation took hold, an extraordinary thing occurred. Spontaneously, like some huge chemical reaction, people started pouring into the streets. From shops, from offices, from department stores, even from Harrods itself, they came out. People were cheering, smiling, weeping with relief. All work stopped. People who had never seen each other in their lives embraced.

Outside the offices of Fox and Martineau, the sedate little alley was filling with the workers from legal offices. Twenty yards away, the traffic in Chancery Lane had already halted. The roadway was suddenly full of lawyers, clerks, typists, stationers, even wigmakers.

Louise went down the staircase with James Fox, whose tall figure was soon moving through the crowd outside, shaking hands to left and right. He let his old clerk pump his hand, and put his long arm around a secretary who had burst into tears.

Louise stood close to the door. She smiled and murmured kind words to at least a dozen strangers, but not knowing anyone, she had no reason to delve into the throng.

And then an idea suddenly occurred to her.

The passageway inside the door was empty. Everyone seemed to have gone into the street. She went back up the stairs to Fox's office, and looked in through the open door. It was quiet. Her eyes scanned the room. Apart from his desk, three leather chairs and a low table, there was no other furniture to speak of, apart from the bookcases on the walls. No sign of any filing cabinets.

She went to the next door along the landing. This was a secretary's room. A large typewriter on a desk, some files, but only a few. Perhaps they kept the files in another part of the building, down in the basement perhaps. She tried the next door.

Files. Shelves of files. Some in boxes, some tied with ribbons, all rather Victorian, but clearly in order.

'Can I help you?'

She started. A young woman of about her own age. She smiled and tried to look relieved.

'I was seeing Mr Fox. I was looking for a lavatory.'

'Of course, miss. This way.' She led her downstairs and towards the back, to a small room containing a water closet and a washstand.

'We're quite modern,' the girl said proudly.

'Thank goodness I found you.'

'Shall I tell Mr Fox you're waiting?'

'It's all right. We were in the middle of our conversation when all this happened. We went down into the street.' She smiled. 'I'll just wait. I'm not in the slightest hurry. What a day.'

'Yes, miss. Is there anything else?'

'I should go outside if I were you. Everyone else seems to be there.'

She went into the washroom, waited a minute, then looked out again. The coast was clear. She went quickly upstairs again.

The files were in alphabetical order. It took only a minute to find her father's files. They were contained in two boxes.

There were quite a lot of papers. Letters in connection with some property he'd purchased a few years ago. Various deeds. His will, revised not long ago. She didn't bother to read it. She went right through the first box but found nothing. She opened the second. The top papers in this box were ten years old. She began to peel though them. Fifteen years ago, eighteen. She was nearly at the bottom of the box.

ADOPTION. A sheaf of papers wrapped in a ribbon. She opened it. A summary sheet. Child's name: Louise. Chosen by the birth mother, agreed to by the client. The birth was in Sussex, the mother's name Corinne Petit. An unusual name. Unless the mother was not English. French, perhaps, or Swiss?

Father's name: Not given. She searched through the other papers to see if she could find it. There was no clue. Until she came to a note. It was from the firm's Paris office. It was not long. It thanked the then partner in the London office for his discreet handling of the business and remarked that his client Monsieur Blanchard was most grateful. It was signed: James Fox.

He knew then. He knew everything.

'You realise that I could probably have you arrested.'

His voice. He must be standing behind her in the doorway. She did not turn.

'I doubt that you could. Or that you would. So you actually arranged my birth, and my mother was Corinne Petit. Was she French?'

No answer.

'And who is Monsieur Blanchard? My father, I assume?'

She heard him sigh.

'Corinne Petit is dead. She was a nanny for some years. Then she married and, sadly, died in childbirth. I promise you this is true. Her family had turned her out when she became pregnant. She had nowhere to go. She was very young. I have no hesitation in saying that I did the best thing possible for her and for you. It was sheer luck that I had heard from our London office about your parents, who wanted a child and couldn't have one of their own.'

'And my father?' Now she turned. 'Monsieur Blanchard: Is he dead too?'

'You are assuming he was the father. He might have been helping a friend with a completely different name.'

'You won't tell me.'

'Certainly not. Are you going to raise this with your parents?'

'I don't know.'

'Then I shall have to tell them how you came by the information. Otherwise they might suspect me of a breach of confidentiality.'

'I shan't tell them. It wouldn't get me anywhere even if I did.'

'I am sure you are right. Will you promise me that? I must defend myself.'

'Yes. I promise.'

'To save you more wasted effort, I closed our Paris office at the start of the war. There is nothing for you to find in that quarter. As for Blanchard, it's a common name, and the father you seek may not have that name at all. I should be sorry if you wasted your life looking for someone whom you would never find.'

'Is he alive?'

He paused, and chose his words carefully.

'It's years since I was in France.' He shook his head sadly. 'Their war casualties have been worse than ours, you know. Far worse.'

'Well, anyway,' she said brightly, 'the war's over, and it seems I'm French.'

'Personally, I'd have said you were English.'

But being French sounded more of an adventure to her.

'No,' she declared, 'I'm French. Good-bye, Mr Fox. Do I owe you a fee for this consultation?'

'I'd settle for an armistice,' he answered with the hint of a smile.

After she'd gone, he sat at his desk for a while. Then he laughed. He wondered whether to tell Marc that he'd met his daughter. He supposed that would be a breach of confidentiality. Could he tell Marie about it? No, he thought. Better not. Her family wouldn't like it.

Chapter Twenty-one

1920

Marie Fox had certainly not expected to become a widow when she did. But in the spring of 1919 she'd lost her husband, James.

The great influenza epidemic of 1918 and 1919 – the Spanish flu, as it was called – did not enter the popular imagination of the age. Yet it killed more people than even the Black Death nearly six centuries before. In Britain, a quarter of a million people died; in France, nearly half a million; in Canada, fifty thousand; and in India seventeen million. Around the world, of those who caught the flu, between ten and twenty per cent died. The death toll was especially high among the young and fit. It was not only a human tragedy, but a huge statistical event. In the United States, as a result of the flu, life expectancy fell by ten years.

But there were plenty of deaths among the middle-aged as well.

The flu came in great waves. In England there had been two waves in 1918 and a third in March 1919. It was the third that carried off James Fox.

He became sick one afternoon. That night the aches and fever of flu began. All through the next day he grew worse, and during the night it seemed he was developing pneumonia. The following afternoon, as Marie watched, he began to turn a strange, pale shade of blue. And not an hour after teatime, she heard the rattle in his breath, and he left her.

Marie was holding his hand when he died. Despite her protests, Marie wouldn't let their daughter, Claire, into the room. 'Those are the doctor's orders, and it's what your father would want.' Marie was lucky not to catch the flu herself. Claire did not catch it either.

For the rest of that year she and Claire remained in London.

For Claire, at least, London was her home. She had gone to the Francis Holland School, near Sloane Square. This suited her parents' religious compromise, for though Church of England, the school was so High Church that its observances could almost have been mistaken for Roman Catholic. Its academic standards were unsurpassed. French at the school was even taught by a Frenchwoman – a concession that lesser schools might have viewed as rather suspicious, but which Francis Holland could carry off with aplomb. Since Claire's parents had always made a point of speaking French in the home, she always came out top of the class in that subject.

But her friends were English. The games she played, the entertainments she went to, the music she loved were all English. And her mother was content for this to be so. Marie had been happy with James in London.

As the months went by after James had gone, however, Marie could not help feeling a little lonely. She missed her own family in France. And towards the end of the year, she began to think that perhaps she should take Claire to see her family in Paris for a while.

'I should like you at least to know your French family a little better,' she told her. Matters were brought to a head in December 1919, when she received a letter from Marc to say that her aunt Éloïse was not well, and that he thought she should come over before too long.

A month later, she and Claire crossed the Channel. They had no particular plan.

Even in the depths of winter, the simple charm of the family house at Fontainebleau with its welcoming courtyard and its long garden brought Marie a sense of peace and restoration she had needed more than she realised. Her father was in his eighties now, rather smaller than she remembered him. Her mother was remarkably unchanged, except that she walked stiffly, and her hair formed a sort of fluffy, snowy white aureole around her head.

They were delighted with Claire, especially pleased that she still spoke near-perfect French.

'But it's *formidable* how she resembles you,' her mother remarked to Marie.

It was true. Claire had the same golden hair and blue eyes. Was her face just a little longer than her mother's? people might ask themselves. Perhaps. She was certainly an inch taller.

Claire was delighted to find herself with the old couple. She hadn't seen them since before the war when she was a young girl. Now she had all sorts of questions she wanted to ask. She was delighted to learn that Jules's grandfather had bought the house a century ago, and that he had been present in the French Revolution and known Napoléon.

'Can we stay here awhile?' she asked.

After two days, Marc brought Aunt Éloïse down to stay for a few days.

In many ways Marie found her aunt remarkably unchanged, but she did notice that she looked thinner, and that she was rather weak. That evening Aunt Éloïse took her aside.

'My dear Marie, I am very glad you came when you did. I'm perfectly all right, I am very fortunate to have lived in quite good health for so long. But the doctor tells me that I shall be leaving you in a little while.'

'How long?'

'About six months. So I shall be able to see the summer in. I love it so much when the chestnut trees blossom in May. But I shall be glad to go by August, when it becomes much too hot – unless, of course, *le bon Dieu* is planning to send me somewhere even hotter.'

'I'm sure He isn't,' said Marie, with an affectionate smile.

But that decided her. She discussed it the next morning with Claire, who entirely supported her decision.

'Marc,' she said, 'Claire and I will stay in Paris at least until the month of August. Will you help us rent an apartment? Somewhere near Aunt Éloïse, I think.'

'I was hoping,' he said, 'that you'd do that.'

For the next six months, they lived in a delightful apartment just north-west of the Luxembourg Gardens, near the great baroque church of Saint-Sulpice.

Marie had never lived on the Left Bank before, and she found that she liked it. Two minutes' walk northwards and she was in the aristocratic Saint-Germain district. If she continued northwards up the rue

Bonaparte, in less than five minutes she was at the river, looking straight across at the Louvre. If she turned eastward, on the other hand, along the boulevard Saint-Germain, in five minutes she'd be in the heart of the university Latin Quarter, where she could cross to the Île de la Cité under the elegant spire of the Sainte-Chapelle.

Marie saw Aunt Éloïse every day. Meanwhile Marc arranged for Claire to take a course at the École des Beaux-Arts, at the top of the rue Bonaparte.

Marie and her daughter had always had an easy relationship. Towards the end of her school days there had been the usual moments of friction to be expected between a mother and a daughter of that age; but the huge consciousness of the war, with its daily tragedies and privations, did not leave much space for family strife.

. The sudden death of her father had matured Claire, as well. She knew that her mother needed company, and made a point of being her friend as well as her daughter. They often went out together and if, as sometimes happened, a stranger wondered if they might be sisters, she was both amused and happy to see her mother's pleasure at the compliment.

Claire soon made friends in Paris. She liked the company of people her own age. But she also enjoyed exploring the city together with her mother, and most weekends she and Marie took the train down to Fontainebleau.

At least one day a week, Marie would go over to the Right Bank, where she would meet Marc for lunch and then spend the afternoon with him in the office. 'For as you're here now, Marie,' he had remarked, 'you may as well know something about the business. When our parents die, you're going to own a part of it, after all.'

Though it wasn't how he really wanted to spend his time, Marc had been conscientious in managing the family's affairs. Gérard's son, named Jules after his grandfather, was taking an active part now. 'He works hard, and he's absolutely determined to run the business successfully,' Marc told her, 'but he's still in his twenties. I oversee what he does, and I watch over the finances like a hawk. Two or three years more and I hope he won't need me.'

Marie rather liked the young man. He reminded her a little of her father, except that he was slimly built and he was going prematurely bald. He worshipped his father's memory – and even if she couldn't share his enthusiasm, she found it rather touching. His sisters were already married, so he regarded himself as the future head of the family, and protector of his mother.

Marie hadn't a lot to say to Gérard's widow. She was a perfectly pleasant woman with plenty of friends and not a lot to do except shop and pay calls. A year after Gérard's death she had dyed her hair with henna. 'A mistake,' said Marc laconically, 'but it may be a signal that she hopes to find another husband. We invite her to all family gatherings,' he continued, 'and she gives no trouble. You should go shopping with her. She'll be quite happy if you do that.'

So that's what Marie did. It was agreeable enough, just the same as shopping with one of the mothers she'd known in London. Their tastes were different. Once or twice Marie tried to lure her sister-in-law into art galleries or exhibitions, without success. She'd rather look for bargains in a department store. But Marie discovered that her brother's widow had a weakness for jewellery and high fashion. They would spend a happy hour or two in the area north of the Tuileries Gardens, around the elegant Place Vendôme, looking in the showcases of Cartier and the other jewellers, or in the new couturiers like Chanel. After that, Marie would arrange for Marc to give them lunch at the nearby Ritz Hotel, before she went off to spend the afternoon with him at the office.

And it was thanks to a chance remark of her sister-in-law's that Marie came to a realisation that was to change her life.

'You should stay in Paris, you know,' she told Marie one day. 'You have your family here, and you could have a pleasant life just like mine.'

It was perfectly true, Marie thought. She could find plenty to interest her in Paris for the next thirty or forty years, become a grandmother no doubt, devote herself to some good causes perhaps, and in the end die quietly, in Paris or in Fontainebleau. She could do all that and count herself a very lucky woman.

But rather to her own surprise, she realised it wasn't what she wanted. She needed something more. She just didn't know what that something might be.

She was chatting with Marc in the office one afternoon in May, when he'd remarked what a blow it had been to close down Joséphine. 'It was the right thing to do. It was draining money,' he said. 'But I wish in a way we'd held on until the war was over, because I think it could be a viable business now.' He laughed. 'The lease was taken up by an insurance business, but they've just moved on, so it's available at this moment. I haven't got the energy to start it again, though, and young Jules couldn't possibly do it, and wouldn't want to.'

And then, almost before she knew what she was saying, Marie had asked: 'So why don't I do it?'

Marc had looked at her in astonishment.

'My dear Marie, you've never been in commerce.'

'No, but I've been learning a bit recently. You could help me.'

'You're also a woman.'

'The widow Clicquot ran her champagne business for decades and made Veuve Clicquot the most famous label in the world. Chanel is a single woman. She seems to be doing all right. I'm in her store almost every week.'

Marc laughed.

'It's not a boutique,' he said. 'It's huge.'

'I wouldn't take the whole space. Just the Art Nouveau part that you designed.'

'I'm flattered.' He smiled. 'I suggest, my dear sister, that you sleep on the idea. You may have been in the sun too long today. When you wake up in the morning, no doubt you will have regained your sanity.'

'No,' she said. She suddenly saw everything very clearly. 'This is my plan. I am going to devote my time entirely to Aunt Éloïse as long as she's alive. But if she says she's going to die in August, then she probably will. After that, if the lease is still available, I want you to get it for me.'

'I've never seen you like this,' he said.

'Well, you have now,' she answered. 'Joséphine is going to be reborn.'

In the spring of 1919, when Louise had said she wanted to learn French, her parents had been surprised.

'You learned it at school,' her mother said. 'Are you sure you need more than that, dear?'

'I learned schoolgirl French at school,' said Louise, 'but I couldn't really have an intelligent conversation with anybody. You never know,' she continued, 'it might come in useful. I might marry a diplomat, or something.'

Her father was quite agreeable to the idea. The war had only just ended. The world was still at sixes and sevens. There could be no harm in his daughter acquiring such a useful accomplishment.

'As long as you work at it properly,' was his only stipulation.

So a French teacher was found and Louise began to work with her.

After six months, her teacher was astounded. 'I have never had such a pupil,' she declared.

Louise had never worked so hard in her life. She attacked her studies with a passion. By the end of three months she knew many of the *Fables* of La Fontaine by heart. They even began to tackle the novels of Balzac together, despite their huge and complex vocabulary.

Her father was pleased with what he took to be signs of a new maturity. At the end of a year, Louise announced: 'Mademoiselle says it would be a good idea for me to spend a few months with a French family,' Louise told her parents. 'Total immersion, she calls it.'

Her mother was not so happy about this idea. Though she was quite accomplished artistically, she was a conventional woman of her class, and she felt it was unseemly for a girl to have too many intellectual attainments.

But her kindly, round-faced father was more amenable.

'It's not as if she wanted to go to university,' he remarked. 'No man wants to marry a girl who does that.' He paused. 'But going to France, it's more like a finishing school really, isn't it?'

And so she was sent to stay with a suitable family, who lived in a small *manoir*, a farmhouse really, in the valley of the Loire, not far from the Château de Cygne. Her hosts were a retired official from the colonial service, who was from the *petite noblesse*, the minor nobility, and his wife. Their children were all grown up, their son in Paris. And for more than six happy months Louise had lived with them like a daughter. By the end of 1920, although she might not be up to date with some of the latest idioms used by the young, Louise spoke perfect French.

Chapter Twenty-two

1924

Claire was happy to be in Paris. 'I'm just a wide-eyed girl,' she would say with a laugh, 'whose mother took her to the most exciting place in the world.'

But it was her uncle Marc who really opened her eyes.

'The whole of Europe is devastated after the Great War,' he liked to say, 'but in Paris, we are recovering with style.' Certainly for a struggling artist, a poor writer or a young person like Claire, Paris was heaven on earth. And nobody knew more about what was going on than Marc.

After Aunt Éloïse died, and left everything to him, Marc moved into her apartment. He kept all her pictures, adding his own, so that the walls were wonderfully crowded. More than once he had given Claire a guided tour, explaining where each picture came from, and something about the artist. One day, when she'd admired a painting of the Gare Saint-Lazare, he told her, 'That picture really belongs to your mother. She can take it any time she wants.'

But when she asked her mother about it, Marie told her: 'Aunt Éloïse bought the painting for me, but I never paid for it.'

'What made you choose it?' Claire asked.

'That's a little secret from long ago,' her mother replied with a smile. 'Anyway, it looks very well in the apartment where it is. Let it stay there.'

Her uncle would tell her about the artists he'd met.

'I'd love to take you to Giverny to see Monet, but he's getting so old now that I don't like to trouble him,' he remarked.

'The last survivor of Impressionism,' she suggested.

'I'd say he's lived right through it and out the other side,' her uncle replied. You have the post-Impressionists like van Gogh, Gauguin, and the Expressionists – people who created a world that seems almost more vivid, urgent, even violent than real life – though they're all tending towards abstraction – Cézanne especially, I'd say. But Monet's gone on for so long that those pools of water lilies and screens of willows he does have turned into a sort of dream world of colour that's almost pure abstraction.'

'Have you met Picasso?' she asked.

'Yes. He's a brilliant draftsman, you know,' he said. 'He could have been a pure classical artist. He has incredible facility. Instead of which, he decided to break every rule of art.' He smiled. 'Naturally, if he was going to invent Cubism, he did it in Paris.'

They talked about Surrealism, which was all the rage just then. And Diaghilev's Ballets Russes. 'They operate mostly in Paris, but they're going to Monte Carlo for the winter now,' he explained. Her uncle had been at the stage scandal of *L'Après-midi d'un faune*, and the riot which took place when Stravinsky's *Rite of Spring* was first performed.

'But what you must understand,' he would impress upon her, 'is that all this excitement in Paris isn't just about painting, music and ballet, interesting as they all are. It's deeper and broader than that. We've just had a war. The German Empire, the ancient Hapsburg Empire in Vienna and the creaking old Ottoman Empire of the Turks are all broken. The Russian Empire has undergone a Bolshevik revolution. The old world order has gone. We've seen warfare on an industrial scale that's not only killed millions but may even call into question our society and the nature of man himself.

'Naturally, most people assume that the comfortable old life with its solidity, its stratified classes, its masters and servants will gather itself together again. The world that is good to people like us.

'But the avant-garde are looking to the future with fresh eyes. These artistic movements you read about – the Constructivists in Russia, the Vorticists in England, or Futurists in Italy – they're artistic movements certainly, each with their manifestos – but they're reacting to this new reality, where the old certainties of humanity are all called into question, and the destructive industrial machines we've created seem almost to have taken on a fearsome life of their own. And if you want the best expression of that uncertainty, then read this.'

He gave her a slim book of verse: *The Waste Land*, by T. S. Eliot.

'It's just published. Eliot's an American in London – I suspect he may turn into an Englishman, the way Henry James did. His friend Pound, an American who's been living in Paris, gave it to me.'

On other occasions, he spoke of some of the French authors – Apollinaire, the modernist and anarchist. He told her delightedly how Apollinaire and his friend Picasso were briefly arrested, for reasons known only to the bureaucratic mind, when the *Mona Lisa* had been stolen. 'Turned out it was a crazy Italian who wanted to return the *Mona Lisa* to Italy. They found it in his lodgings.'

Most important of all, however, he introduced her to the novels of Proust.

'The Prousts were our neighbours on boulevard Malesherbes,' he told her. 'We just thought Marcel was a show-off and a dilettante. So did everybody. Who would have guessed he was hatching this work of genius in his head?'

'Does he still live there?'

'He moved just a block up the street and around the corner on boulevard Haussmann – only five minutes' walk from Joséphine. He lived there until just after the war. But they say he's dying now, and his brother may have to finish his work.'

The following year, Proust had died. But by then Claire had finished *Swann's Way*; now she was halfway through *Sodom and Gomorrah*.

She'd never read anything like it before. Proust's search through his extraordinary memory, his re-creation of every detail of the passing world, his ruthless portrayal of every aspect of human psychology, were fascinating to her.

'I'm delighted to see you taking such an interest in literature,' Marc said. 'I'm only sorry you can't share it with Aunt Éloïse any more. She'd read everything. But don't forget,' he added, 'people like Eliot and Proust are writing radically new work, but they are still quite conservative politically. They're looking for meaning at the end of the old world. Many of the avant-garde have a very different outlook.'

'They believe in revolution, don't they?'

'Paris has always prided itself on being home to revolutionary thought. Ever since the French Revolution, we believe that all radical ideas belong to us. And people with radical ideas have always come to Paris to discuss them. A lot of radical Paris believes that only world revolution will solve all these new problems. Now we've had a Russian revolution, they think the rest will follow – or should. I'm sure Picasso's a communist, for instance.'

But if Claire was excited by the cultural ferment of Paris, most of her time now was spent working on a grand commercial enterprise.

Joséphine. When her mother and Marc had reopened the family store, they had asked her to come and help just to give her something to do. But that was two years ago. She was an integral part of the operation now. 'I don't know,' her uncle was kind enough to say, 'how we'd have done it without you.'

Of course, her mother was the central figure upon whom everything turned. She had a wonderful way with all the people working there. She was always calm, sympathetic, but very firm, like a mother in control of a large family. She inspired loyalty.

Marie controlled all the day-to-day running of the operation, and dealt with the biggest and most important suppliers – couturiers like Chanel, and others. But she soon delegated a smaller but very important task to Claire.

'I want you to find new designers and clothes makers. The ones who are going to attract girls of your generation. You find them, then you bring them to me, and we'll see if we can make a deal.'

She had found them – in Paris, sometimes in the provinces, in Italy. And she would sit in on the meetings they had with her mother, and see how quickly and cleverly her mother discovered the strengths and weaknesses of their operations.

'How are you so good at business?' she asked her mother once. 'You never did it before this.'

'I don't know, to tell the truth. I suppose it must be in the blood.' Her mother smiled. 'Do you think I'm good, then?'

'You know very well you are.'

Two years of working together had changed their relationship in subtle ways. They really were like a pair of sisters now. Sometimes they disagreed about whether to take on a supplier, or how to price the goods. When they did, they argued it out, and although Marie had the final say, she always respected Claire's opinion and her intellect.

But they would both have agreed instantly on one thing. The Joséphine store could never have succeeded without the guiding hand of Marc.

'Our greatest competition is the Galeries Lafayette. They are just along the boulevard from us. They are much bigger. The business is well run and constantly innovating. There's no point in trying to mimic all their departments, like haberdashery. We compete, as we always did, on fashionable goods at the best price. So we have to make people come to us because of the way we sell the goods, and because we always have the latest style, almost before it's arrived! We must follow the old French military maxim: *Il nous faut de l'audace, encore de l'audace, toujours de l'audace.*' We need audacity, more audacity, always audacity.

'You make it sound like a theatre,' Claire laughed.

'But that's it, exactly,' cried Marc. 'A great store is not just a useful place. It's an experience. It needs drama and surprise, like a theatre.'

And he proved it. The Joséphine store was a constant surprise. Mannequins were being used in store windows now. But the windows at Joséphine didn't only show off the dresses. They told a story, like a painting. Marc also had a gallery inside the store, where new artists' work was shown. Every month something happened at Joséphine, something that was talked about, something that one had to go and see before it disappeared. It was a sensation.

The beauty parlour and the hair salon were huge successes too. Joséphine was the best place for young women to get the new, short, boyish haircut, the gamine look.

By the spring of 1924, Marc was running with a new theme for the summer.

The Olympics.

It was quite remarkable really. The ancient sports festival had been revived only in 1896. Appropriately, the first games had been in Athens. With one gap during the war, the games had continued every four years. Paris had been the venue in 1900, followed by St Louis in America; then London, Stockholm and Antwerp had all had their turns. But now the games were returning to Paris again: proof indeed, the French thought – as if any were needed – that the capital of France was the finest city in the world.

Already Marc had his plans for windows with themes like track events, swimming, boxing, cycle racing. The store's theme that summer would be sportive, with sportily cut tweeds and jaunty little cloche hats lined up for the months of September and October.

It was going to be a spectacular year. All three of them – Marc, Marie and Claire – had been working harder than ever, and enjoying every minute of it.

Only one thing was missing from their lives.

'It's time you girls got married,' he remarked to Marie and Claire one day.

'I have been married, and very happily,' Marie replied.

'It's you who ought to get married,' Claire told her uncle.

'I'm too old,' he said with a smile.

'He's too selfish,' Marie observed to her daughter.

'Unfair,' said Marc. 'Look at all the things I do for you.'

'I can't imagine Uncle Marc allowing any wife to rearrange the pictures in his apartment,' said Claire.

Marc considered.

'She could do what she likes in the kitchen,' he said. 'And maybe the bedroom. I have my dressing room, after all. But seriously' – he turned to Claire – 'your mother was wonderfully fortunate in marrying your father, but it's nearly five years since he died. Don't you think your mother should marry again?'

'If she wants to,' said Claire. 'If she finds a man she really likes.' She looked at her mother. 'I think you should.'

'I haven't the time,' said Marie.

And they were all certainly going to be busy as the month of May approached, when the Olympic Games officially began.

By July, Roland de Cygne would normally have been in the country at his château for the summer. This year, however, he had lingered because of the Olympics. Not that he was interested in most of the proceedings, but there was a week of polo at Saint-Cloud at the start of the month and the equestrian events were taking place towards the end. So he'd decided to stay for them. As he would still be in the city then, he'd bought a couple of tickets for the ballet at the Opéra right at the end of the season and told his son, despite the boy's protests, that he'd take him. 'It will be good for your education,' he said cheerfully.

As compensation, however, he'd taken him out to the stadium on the western outskirts of the city where the track events were being held, and they'd seen some thrilling races, culminating in the hundred-metre final when a British athlete named Abrahams had taken the gold.

'One doesn't think of a Jew being an athlete,' he'd remarked mildly to his son. 'There was once a famous boxer named Mendoza, mind you, but he was a Spanish Jew, which is different.'

Today, he'd made sure to be back in his house by early evening so that he could attend a small social event. Yet as he set out to walk from his house towards the Luxembourg Gardens, he wondered if he was making a mistake.

He'd been at a charity event the other evening when he and Marc Blanchard caught sight of each other. Though they moved in different circles, he'd been reminded of Marc from time to time when articles by him appeared in the serious newspapers. They were reviews of exhibitions or books, usually, and read more like little essays than jobbing articles – as befitted an established cultural figure with an independent fortune.

Politeness dictated that they should greet each other, and Roland asked after Marc's parents.

'They are both quite well for their age. My father still takes an interest in life, though he is a little forgetful. It's many years since he retired to Fontainebleau. And you, Monsieur de Cygne,' Marc inquired, 'your father had a house near the boulevard Saint-Germain, I seem to remember?'

'I have it still. After the war, I retired from the army to look after my estate and my son.'

'I heard that you had married.'

'Yes, but sadly I'm a widower now. My father adored his wife, lost her and was left with an only son. I never imagined that exactly the same thing would happen to me. But *le bon Dieu* evidently decided that, having established this pattern with our family, He would continue it.'

Marc expressed his sorrow for de Cygne's loss.

'And are you married?' the aristocrat asked.

'Not yet,' Marc confessed. 'At present I've too much else to do. During the war my brother died, and I had to step in and run the family business. It's not what I wanted, but someone had to preserve it for the next generation. I'm still doing it now.'

'This does not prevent you marrying,' de Cygne gently observed.

'My sister says I'm too self-centred.'

'I remember your charming sister well. She married the Englishman, Fox, your father told me.'

'She did. They were quite happy and had a daughter. Sadly Fox was one of the victims of the flu epidemic. My sister and her daughter returned to Paris for a visit three years ago, and I'm delighted to say that they stayed.'

'Ah. I had no idea.'

'As it happens,' Marc said after a pause, 'I am having a few people over for a drink next week in my apartment. I took over my aunt Éloïse's apartment near the Luxembourg Gardens when she died. Marie and her daughter will both be there. You are most welcome to join us, if you would care to. Wednesday evening.'

'I shall check my appointments when I get home,' Roland said. It was always wise to leave oneself a graceful way out. 'But if I am able to come, I should be delighted.'

So Marc had given him the address, and they'd left it at that.

And for several days he had been uncertain whether to go or not. He was quite sure that Marc's friends would not be to his taste. On the other hand, he couldn't help being curious to see what Marie looked like these days. He remembered how he'd imagined she would be like by now, when he had considered marrying her all those years ago.

There was no particular reason he shouldn't satisfy his curiosity, he told himself. He only had to be polite and friendly, and then he could leave.

He felt in his pocket for his lighter.

It was foolish, no doubt, but he'd always thought that the little lighter in its shell casing might have saved his life. Had it touched the heart of Le Sourd when he'd asked him to send the lighter to his son? Was that why Le Sourd had failed to shoot him that day at the front? Who knew? Perhaps, when the moment came, he wouldn't have pulled the trigger in any case. But it seemed to Roland that the lighter had brought him luck, and he nearly always kept it with him, like a talisman.

Not that he needed any luck this evening. There was nothing to be lucky about. He certainly wasn't in the least excited about the prospect of seeing Marie again, he told himself, as he walked the short distance from his house to Marc's apartment.

Marie Fox was in a sunny mood as she and Claire went across to her brother's. One never knew who was going to be at one of Marc's parties. One time Marie had found herself talking to Cocteau the writer; the next time she had even found herself chatting with the American novelist Edith Wharton. Everyone came to Paris these days, and Marc seemed to know them all.

When she'd first started work at Joséphine, Marie had wondered if she should return with Claire to the area of the old family apartment, so that she would be near the store. She had hesitated for two reasons. First, she wasn't sure she wanted to go back to a place where she lived before. Somehow, it seemed like a retreat. Second, Claire didn't want to go there.

'It's so boring,' she said.

For Marie, the main attraction of their present apartment was the charming Luxembourg Gardens, just nearby. For when King Henry IV's widow, Marie de Médicis, had wanted a little Italian palace to remind her of her native Florence, she had unwittingly given future generations of Parisians their most delightful park. Sixty acres of gardens surrounded the building, with a big octagonal pool where children now sailed their toy boats, a puppet theatre, a grotto, leafy alleys in which to stroll and lawns where one could sit and catch the sun. From the middle of the gardens there was an elegant view south towards the Sun King's handsome Observatory.

But for Claire, it was the area just to the south of the park that was the attraction.

Montparnasse. Mount Parnassus. A place for the gods. And if the gods who lived in Montparnasse now were mostly very poor, they were surely touched by the divine. Artists, writers, performers, students – Montparnasse in the 1920s was like Montmartre the generation before, with one difference: Montparnasse was international in a new way. Italians, Ukrainians, Spaniards, Africans, Americans, Mexicans, Argentinians, a colony of artists from Chile – they all crowded into Montparnasse, and made it their home. They

were international Parisians, and they were rapidly forming a sprawling cultural club that would spread from Paris to Buenos Aires,
London, New York and the Orient.

Marc decided the issue.

'Both of you – Claire especially, but you too, Marie – need to live
in contact with the avant-garde. The people running Joséphine need
to be elegant, chic and absolutely up to date with everything that's
happening. We sell our goods to the bourgeoisie, near La Madeleine,
but we need to know what's going on in the Latin Quarter and
Montparnasse.'

It was quite convenient. Marie had considered using a motor car
and chauffeur to get to work, but she often found it easier to walk
the short distance to the Sèvres-Babylone Métro station; a few
minutes later she'd be at La Madeleine. Marc had been right. So far,
she hadn't regretted staying on the Left Bank.

Marc's parties were always well judged – plenty of people, but
never a squash. Claire had found a young designer to talk to. Marie
had been chatting to a couple of writers she knew for five minutes
when she saw the tall, aristocratic figure enter the room. His hair was
grey now – it set off his blue eyes very well, making them seem
brighter – but there was no mistaking Roland de Cygne. He came
over to her at once.

'Madame Fox, I think. Indeed, I am certain, for you are quite
unchanged.' He made a slight bow. 'Roland de Cygne.'

'Monsieur de Cygne.' She smiled. 'We are all changed a little. You
have grey hair, but it suits you very well. What a pleasant surprise.'

'Your brother did not tell you he had invited me?'

'He never says who's coming.'

'Ah. First, madame, may I express my regret: Marc told me you
had lost your husband – whom of course I remember well. You may
not know that I married a few years before the war, and sadly my
wife died two years ago, so I understand what it is to lose someone.
You have a daughter, I believe.'

'I have, monsieur.'

'And I have a son.'

They talked easily about their children. She explained that Claire
was in Paris now and working in the family business. His own son
was still only a boy, the aristocrat explained. 'I was without a mother

571

myself,' he said, 'and I am very sad that the same thing should have happened to my son. I do my best, as my father did, but it worries me. I am so afraid that in my own blindness I shall repeat the mistakes of the past.'

He had mellowed, she thought, and she liked his honesty. She found his worries about his son rather moving. And they continued chatting about her time in England, and his estate, and life in Paris, so that they hardly realised that a quarter of an hour had passed.

'I go to the opera from time to time, madame,' Roland said finally, 'and I wonder if you would do me the honour of accompanying me one evening.'

'That sounds delightful,' Marie said.

'As it happens, I have seats this coming Saturday for the ballet. I told my son that he is to accompany me for his education. I don't imagine you would be free at such short notice, but he would be eternally grateful if you would take his place.'

She thought for a moment, and smiled.

'The appointment I had can easily be changed.'

'Then I shall collect you at your house.'

Marc now joined them, and their conversation turned to the war. Marc gave de Cygne an amusing account of his efforts to build the fake model of Paris to deceive the German bombers.

'Construction was already well under way, you know, when the armistice came. Had the war lasted into 1919, I dare say we should have had a dummy Eiffel Tower in the sky.'

Roland was fascinated.

'We were quite unaware of all this at the front,' he remarked.

'It was a huge secret. Of course, it would only have taken one German plane flying over the place in daytime to see the two towers. The whole scheme was probably insane.'

'Talking of secrets,' Marie remarked, 'there was a rumour in London that some of the French army had mutinied, but that it had all been hushed up. Did you ever see or hear anything of that, Monsieur de Cygne?'

Roland did not hesitate. Amazingly, the truth about the mutiny had never reached the press, or the history books. Those involved preferred to forget it, and the army was determined to help them.

'I did know about that business, as it happens,' he said calmly. 'One prefers not to speak of it – even a hint of mutiny is embarrassing – but it was very limited, you know. A handful of incidents in a couple of divisions. The whole thing lasted only a day or two. Most of the army never even knew about it.'

'That's what I heard,' said Marc. 'Now I'll tell you,' he went on cheerfully, 'where there will never be a mutiny. And that is in the Joséphine department store. Thanks to my sister. She rules the entire staff with a rod of iron, yet they're all devoted to her.'

Roland looked slightly confused. Marc saw it.

'Marie didn't tell you that she runs Joséphine?'

Roland shook his head.

'She's the big boss,' Marc continued with a laugh. 'I often think she's got the best business head in the family.'

Roland looked at Marie with astonishment.

'I had no idea you were so terrifying, madame,' he said with a smile, but she could tell that he was shocked as well as surprised.

'Does this mean, monsieur, that the invitation to the opera is cancelled?'

'Not at all. Of course not.'

No, that would be rude, she thought, but I bet you wish you hadn't made it.

She was glad that at that moment Claire came to join them. She was always proud of her daughter, but Claire was looking particularly elegant today, and she saw that de Cygne noticed it.

'I've just had an idea for the store,' Claire announced. She hesitated, and glanced at Roland de Cygne uncertainly. Marc laughed.

'Monsieur de Cygne knows how to keep a secret. Continue.'

'Someone's just been telling me about a book called *The Phantom of the Opera*. And I suddenly thought, couldn't we make it a theme for a set of window displays one day? You could do all kinds of things with a theme like that.'

'I don't know this book,' said Marie. 'Do you?' she asked Roland.

'I have heard of it, but never read it,' he confessed.

'I think that you are right about the possibilities, but wrong about the windows,' said Marc. 'The story's based on a very famous book called *Trilby*, where a girl is turned into an opera star by hypnosis. The hypnotist is named Svengali. That was a huge success in its day.

The Phantom story features a monster who lives under the opera house, where the secret lake is. It was a serial originally, then a book. But it didn't sell many copies. So I don't think it's well enough known, at present, to be a store feature.'

'That's a pity,' said Claire. She turned to de Cygne. 'You see, monsieur, all my life, nothing but rejection.'

'I cannot imagine anyone rejecting you, mademoiselle,' he responded gallantly.

'Isn't he nice?' Claire said to her mother, who laughed.

Marc took de Cygne away now. 'I've got a charming old historian, who's writing about the ancient families of the Loire. He'd very much like to meet you.' Claire went to talk to a young painter. Marie began to make her way through the groups of guests, nodding or smiling to those she knew, but feeling a little disengaged from the proceedings.

How strange it had been to encounter de Cygne again. It was quite agreeable, but it took her mind back to those days at the turn of the last century, just before she'd married, and for a moment or two, she found herself almost transported back to those days, and the people around her seemed to dissolve into the background.

She soon pulled herself together. There were people to meet, people who might be useful to the store. She looked around. As she did so, she noticed someone looking intently at the painting of the Gare Saint-Lazare by Norbert Goeneutte – her painting. The man had his back to her, but she was sure she knew him. He turned.

It was Hadley. The realisation was so sudden that it made her gasp. Not only that, he was completely unchanged. If anything, he looked even younger. The same tall frame, the same mane of hair, the same eyes, gazing straight at her. Dear God, he was more handsome than ever.

Her heart skipped a beat. She felt the need for air. It was as though, by some strange magic, she was a girl of twenty again.

How was it possible? Had the meeting with de Cygne opened some mysterious corridor between the present and the past? Had she, in the middle of this party, unwittingly taken a journey in H. G. Wells's time machine? Was she hallucinating?

His eyes were on her. Now he started to come towards her. Dear heaven, she was blushing. This was ridiculous. And yet, strangely, there was no light of recognition in his eyes. Had she turned into a ghost? No, he was going to introduce himself.

'*Je m'appelle Frank Hadley.*'

His French accent left much to be desired.

'Frank Hadley?' She said the name in English.

'Junior. My father . . .'

Of course. Everything suddenly made sense.

'You can speak English to me, Mr Hadley. I am Marie Fox, Marc's sister. I remember your father from many years ago. He knew my late husband too. You look just like him.'

'Oh.' He smiled broadly. 'My father told me to contact Marc when I came to Paris, but he thought you lived in England, so I didn't imagine we should meet. You fit the description my father gave me exactly.'

'Really.'

He smiled.

'He said you were very beautiful.'

She stared in surprise, but there could be no doubt about it. He was flirting with her. The cheeky monkey. He was looking straight into her eyes now, and she realised that his own eyes were rather beautiful, and full of life. To her embarrassment – but she couldn't help it – she felt herself going weak at the knees.

This was ridiculous. She could be his mother. She managed an entire department store.

'I'm going to be in Paris for some months,' he said. 'My father gave me very clear instructions. He told me to learn French, and not to come back until I was fluent.'

The hint wasn't blatant, but it was quite unmistakable. He was telling her that he had come to learn French, and that he was available if she cared to teach him.

They looked at each other. A couple of seconds passed. And then, suddenly, Marc appeared beside them, with Claire.

'Ah, Frank, *mon ami*,' he said, 'I see that you have met my sister. Now let me introduce you to her daughter, Claire.'

Luc Gascon had started smoking during the war. It was the thing to do. Every *poilu* in the trenches seemed to have a packet of Gauloises in his pocket. The little blue packets and the strong, Turkish aroma of the cigarettes suggested comradeship. And they were supposed to steady the nerves. If a man were taken to a field hospital, like as not, the first thing the orderlies or the nurses would do was give him a cigarette. Luc had started smoking mainly because he was bored.

And he had just been smoking a Gauloise when he met Louise. It was at the cinema. As usual, it was his genius for making himself useful that enabled him to pick her up.

The Louxor wasn't just any cinema. It had only just opened then, in 1921, but it had instantly become one of the exotic landmarks of Paris.

Sitting splendidly on its corner site on the boulevard de Magenta, a short walk east of the Moulin Rouge, the Louxor was a mock Egyptian palace worthy of the pharaohs or of Cleopatra herself. With its Egyptian pillars, its golden ornaments and richly painted walls, it reminded Luc of those fantasy Oriental rooms in some of the most expensive brothels – if, that is, the brothel were on the scale of the palace of Versailles.

The cinema was often sold out, so Luc had not been surprised, arriving early one evening, to find twenty or thirty young people being sorrowfully turned away at the doors.

Why had she caught his eye? Because of her looks, of course. And she was alone. That was intriguing. But there was something else about her that aroused his curiosity. Something different. He decided that he needed to find out.

There are many kinds of womaniser. With some it is vanity or a sense of power, with others greed. With Luc it was that purest of all motives: endless curiosity.

'I am sorry you could not see the film, mademoiselle.'

'Yes. It's annoying.' She was polite, but cautious. He had a sense that if he made one wrong move, she would freeze him out. But he also noticed her accent. Very pure. The best French, not even the slightly pointed enunciation of the Paris sophisticates. She might be from a very high-class French family, or she might be a foreigner who had learned the language in that environment.

'I haven't got a seat either, but I am still going to see the film.' He smiled. 'My nephew is the projectionist. I'm going to watch it with him, up in his little box.'

'Really?' She looked amused. 'Then you are fortunate indeed, monsieur.'

He smiled, bowed, and started to walk away. Then he hesitated and turned. She was still watching him.

'Mademoiselle, I think there is room for one more person up there. If it would amuse you.' He shrugged. 'You will be quite safe, I promise. And should my nephew, who is a good boy, be distracted from his duties by your beauty, one scream and the entire audience will turn around, while the management comes running.'

She laughed, gave him a quick, careful look, and evidently decided that he was respectable.

'Very well, monsieur, I accept the adventure. But if the film frightens me, I shall also scream.'

'Then thank God it is Buster Keaton,' he replied.

The girl's mind was quickly set at rest when the man at the door greeted him politely: '*Bonjour,* Monsieur *Gascon.*'

'My nephew's up in the projection room? I'm going to take this young lady up there, if that's all right.'

'Whatever you wish, Monsieur Gascon.'

When they got up into the projection room, and Louise encountered a most surprised young man of about her own age, who he informed her was his nephew Robert, Luc did not permit her to introduce herself at all, raising his hand and declaring: 'This young lady is an angel who has come down to earth to watch the movie. When it is over, Robert, she will fly back to the heavens – though we may hope for her benediction before she goes.'

The evening's entertainment consisted of two Buster Keaton movies. As the projection room was not very comfortable, Luc was glad that they weren't watching one of the new epics – for he knew that Abel Gance in France, and von Stroheim in America, were both producing movies that would run for seven hours or more. The girl seemed to be enjoying herself, anyway.

When it was over, it was time for young Robert to go off duty, so Luc said he'd walk home with him as soon as he was ready to leave. Meanwhile, he escorted Louise down to the entrance, and said he hoped she'd enjoyed the show.

'Very much, monsieur. I'm not sure if I thanked your nephew properly.'

'I will do it for you.'

'He seems to have a limp.'

'He has a wooden leg, mademoiselle. He came by it honestly, serving his country in the war. He was working in the family restaurant, but I could see his leg was troubling him, so I was able to get him this job instead. I happened to know the manager of this cinema.' He paused. 'We are going to have supper at our restaurant now, in fact, just along the street. If you would like to join us, please be our guest. We can find you a taxi to take you home afterwards.'

'I mustn't be too late. It would upset the elderly lady with whom I live.'

'Not a problem.'

A quarter of an hour later, Luc had her comfortably installed in the restaurant, eating a *croque monsieur* and *haricots verts*. Business was fairly quiet that evening. Édith came by to chat for a few minutes. 'This is my sister-in-law, the mother of Robert,' he explained. 'And how should I introduce you, mademoiselle?'

'Just Louise,' she said.

'Mademoiselle Louise, then.' He smiled. 'Who speaks a French so elegant and so pure, that either she comes from a château or a manor house in the Loire Valley, or she was sent there by her parents to perfect her French.'

Louise laughed.

'The latter, monsieur. I am English. But I have French family connections.'

'All is explained, mademoiselle. I will guess that through your parents, perhaps on the advice of the consul or someone in the embassy, you lodge in the apartment of a widow, whose husband was a civil servant, perhaps, so that you can live respectably protected, while you study here in Paris. However, since you were alone this evening, it would seem that for some reason you have not chosen to make many friends among your fellow students.'

Louise laughed.

'I attend several classes which interest me, monsieur, but as I'm not following a particular course, I'm not thrown together with the same group all the time.' She shrugged. 'I have made a few friends, all the same, but sometimes I prefer to be alone. Everything else you said is correct, however, in every detail. I don't know how you knew all that.'

'Uncle Luc knows everything,' said Robert.

'He thinks he does, anyway,' Édith remarked. She gave Louise a thin smile that might have been friendly, or might, Louise thought, have contained a hint of warning.

'It was an easy guess,' said Luc easily.

Louise turned to Robert.

'You are fortunate that your family owns a restaurant,' she said with a smile.

'It's my uncle Luc who owns it, really,' he said between mouthfuls. 'But he lets my parents run it. He looks after everybody.'

And Louise was just deciding that Luc must be a very nice man when he cut in swiftly.

'My nephew is making me out to be better than I am, mademoiselle. It's true that I started the bar next door, where Robert's father is now. And a stroke of luck enabled me to acquire this little restaurant. But my brother and his wife kept them going for me during the war, and after that I didn't really want to do it.'

'My parents are happy, that's for sure,' said Robert. Louise liked the way he was determined not to let his uncle escape the credit for his kindness.

'Your mother is happy. She likes to run the restaurant. My brother would rather be out of doors on a building site. But he's getting a little old for that, and your mother prefers him to be safely at home. He runs the bar very well.'

'And what about you?' Louise asked.

'I have what I want, mademoiselle. I take a share of the profits, I eat here for nothing whenever I wish. And I'm free to engage in a few small businesses that interest me.' He shrugged and smiled. 'I don't like to be tied down.'

He had been watching her more carefully than she realised. Her long, dark hair was quite striking. Her features were regular, but there was something interesting about her face, a muselike quality that was hard to define. Her body was slim. If she cut her hair in the short gamine style, there would be something both feminine and boyish about her. She would photograph well, he thought.

And what kind of girl was she? She had class, that was obvious. Intelligent. Sexually innocent, so far. Lonely. He could tell that she was lonely, but whether that was a passing mood, or something deeper, he'd have to find out.

It crossed his mind that this girl could even be useful to him. She had all kinds of potential. But it would take careful handling. Very careful. Finesse. A challenge.

'Tell me, mademoiselle, have you ever modelled – I mean modelled clothes for a serious couturier?'

'No, monsieur. I'm sure I wouldn't be nearly chic and sophisticated enough. There's a special walk, isn't there?'

'It can be learned.' He paused. 'I certainly cannot promise you anything, but I have an idea . . . If you come by this restaurant in a week's time, I shall leave a note for you with my sister-in-law. It may be nothing, but there might be an introduction for you. We'll see. Would you be prepared to do that?'

'I suppose so. The evening has been full of surprises.'

'Good. Now I shall find you a taxi. What quarter of the city will you be going to?'

'Near Place Wagram. Not far. I could really walk.'

'Absolutely not,' he said. And a few minutes later he returned to tell her that the taxi was at the door, and that the driver had been paid to take her to that quarter of the city. 'Perhaps we shall meet again, mademoiselle, and perhaps not. But there will be a note for you in a week's time.'

Louise had lied. She quite often did with strange men – for her own protection. It was better that they should think that she was a respectable young woman with a family to protect her.

And it was mostly true. She was a respectable girl, studying in Paris. And she was living in the apartment of a widow who had been recommended by the British consul.

But she was not being watched over, even from a distance, by her parents. Because her parents were dead.

It had happened soon after her return from the Loire. She'd been feeling so pleased with herself. Back at the big, Edwardian house behind its high hedges, the world had seemed so secure. She'd rather shocked her parents by telling them that, until such time that she found a husband, she'd like to teach French in one of the better London schools. They didn't approve, but she was quite determined to be independent.

And then suddenly the world had changed. It had been such a foolish business, really. Her father had a Wolseley motor car of which he was very proud, and he liked to drive it himself. He and her mother had gone out one misty day. There weren't many cars driving on the lanes near the house.

But the big tractor coming towards them had been too much even for the solid Wolseley. And suddenly Louise hadn't any parents any more.

Mr Martineau, the senior partner at Fox and Martineau now, had been very helpful. Her father had left her an inheritance in trust. Enough to tempt a prospective husband, perhaps, though not enough to keep her in the style to which she'd been accustomed. She'd get the principal when she was thirty and only a modest income until then.

So what was she to do? Become a French teacher in London, perhaps? Or something more adventurous?

She had no one else to please. No one to approve or disapprove. She was of age. She could do exactly what she wanted.

And the British pound went a long way, in postwar France.

So she had gone to Paris. She could live quietly there, take some courses, and continue to lead a genteel student life for as long as she wished. Or until something interesting turned up, of course.

After all, she was French really, whoever and whatever her parents were.

Chanel. She was to present herself at 31 rue Cambon, just behind the Ritz Hotel, where the *maison de couture* had its sublime headquarters. Chanel: of Paris, of Deauville in Normandy, where the racing set gathered, of Biarritz on the Atlantic coast in the south where the rich Spanish liked to holiday. Chanel, who lent her Paris house to Stravinsky, and underwrote the production of *The Rite of Spring*. Louise couldn't believe it.

Madame Chanel herself was there, just back from the south of France. It seemed to Louise that she exuded an elegant sexuality. Dark-haired, very simply dressed, she had the eyes of a watchful panther.

'So, you are the one Luc Gascon found. Turn around. Walk forward. Turn, and walk back. Tell me about your education and upbringing.'

Louise did so.

'So you speak elegant French and English. That is rare. You could do very well, depending on how you wish to live. How many lovers have you had?'

'None, madame.'

'If you wish to succeed in life, you should do something about that at once. Choose wisely. My lovers made me rich. The rest comes from my talent and hard work. Are you ruthless?'

'I don't think so.'

'The English bring their children up not to be ruthless. It is all a lie. Those who succeed are just as ruthless as the rest of us. This we call English hypocrisy. Are you a hypocrite?'

'No, madame.'

'Good. Hypocrites soon become boring. That is their punishment. Nobody wants to talk to them. Find a rich lover and become ruthless. The girls will show you how to walk. I shall pay you a little. Maybe more, later, if you are any good.' And with brief instructions to one of her assistants, she waved Louise away.

In the succeeding days, Louise learned how to walk, and much else besides. As to the rich lover, she decided she would have to think about that.

It was a week later that, sitting in the restaurant early in the evening, Luc Gascon saw Louise approaching. He rose politely to greet her, and she accepted his offer of a little food.

'Just a salad.' She smiled. 'I am slimming.'

'I have a bottle of Beaune, as you see. A glass can do you no harm.' He poured.

'I came to thank you. I am doing a little modelling for Chanel. You seem to know everyone in Paris, monsieur.'

'Not everyone, mademoiselle.'

'She is paying me. I feel I should owe you a commission. A present at least.'

'It always gives me pleasure to help people discover their destiny. That is my art, if I may say so. And you are giving me a charming present by finding me here and sitting at my table.'

They chatted for a while. She liked Luc, she thought. He was so easy to talk to. She liked the faint aroma of Turkish cigarettes that he carried with him. He gave her his complete attention, asked what she thought of all sort of things and seemed to take her opinions very seriously. It was nice that a mature man should treat her with such respect.

She decided that he was quite handsome, in his way. In a former century, she supposed, she could imagine him as one of a powerful Italian family like the Médicis, made a cardinal at twenty and enjoying the fleshly delights of Rome until he became pope. But perhaps not, she thought. The lock of dark hair that fell so elegantly over his broad brow seemed better suited to a *maître d'hôtel* than a priest, though she couldn't say exactly why. Anyway, she could see that he knew how to charm the girls, and good luck to him.

'Forgive me, Mademoiselle Louise,' he remarked after a while, 'but although you have this new excitement in your life, it seems to me that, nonetheless, there is a certain sadness about you.'

'Oh,' she said. How had he detected that? 'It's nothing.'

'A lover giving trouble, perhaps?'

'No.' She laughed. 'None of those yet, monsieur. Madame Chanel told me to find a rich lover, but I wouldn't know how. That's not how I was brought up.'

'I am glad to hear it,' he said, with a fine insincerity.

'The truth is,' she confessed, 'that I was not entirely frank with you when we met. One has to be careful. My parents died not long ago, leaving me an orphan. I live very respectably and study, but it is sometimes a little lonely.'

'I am sure you have friends in England, mademoiselle,' Luc said kindly. 'You can always go back when you tire of Paris.'

'Yes,' she said, 'I know.' But then, because she felt the need to confide in someone, she added: 'The trouble is, it's more complicated.' And then she explained about her adoption.

She did not tell him everything. She did not tell him how she had got the information about her mother, nor did she give him any names. He might be a sympathetic ear, but he was still a comparative stranger. She protected her privacy.

Luc listened, and now he understood. This was the key he had been searching for.

'So you believe that you are French.' He nodded thoughtfully. 'Do you want to discover your French family? Have you any information at all?'

'I am not sure. I have my mother's name. That's all.'

'There are records. In every town hall. They're not always open to the public. But I know a lawyer who specialises in searches. He's quite reasonable.' He took out a little notebook, wrote down a name and address on a page, and tore it out. 'There. You can always see him if you want.'

She waited two weeks before she went to see the lawyer. Monsieur Chabert was a compact, grey-haired man with a quiet voice and very small hands. He agreed to start a limited inquiry.

'I shall begin in Paris, mademoiselle. Most likely the Corinne Petit you seek was a young woman when this happened, and was sent out of the country to have the child. If that is the case, I should have a list of possible candidates quite soon.' He mentioned an amount that would use up the spare cash she had after a couple of small payments she had just received from Chanel. 'I shall keep within that budget, mademoiselle. Before incurring any extra expense, I shall ask your permission. Come to see me again in ten days.'

When she returned, he greeted her with a smile.

'The search was quite simple. I found three girls born in Paris who would have been under twenty-five at the time of your birth. Keeping within your budget, I was able to check all three of them. One married and went to Lyon, the other resides in Paris. The third, however, came from a family who are still to be found in the Saint-Antoine quarter. They have moved from their old address, which actually made it easier for me to seek information about them from old neighbours. In one evening I was able to discover quite a bit. It seems that Corinne found a position with a family in England and never returned. After her departure, the family never spoke of her. I cannot promise you, but I think it is very likely that this is the family you seek. What do you wish me to do?'

'Nothing more at present, monsieur. But I thank you.'

'A word of caution, mademoiselle. If you go to see them, they may not welcome you.'

'I understand, monsieur.'

But she didn't.

*   *   *

She took the Métro to Bastille. To reach the address the lawyer had given her, she only had to walk eastward down the rue de Lyon and into the avenue Daumesnil. But when she emerged from the Métro, she found that the pale sunlight of the afternoon had given way to a dull, listless grey, and suddenly feeling that she wasn't prepared for her encounter, she turned southward instead.

From the Place de la Bastille to the Seine, a line of wharfs ran down the side of one of the northern canals as it widened into a long basin, where the barges unloaded their cargoes. For a quarter of an hour she wandered there. Then a yellowish peep of sun seemed to signal that she should proceed, and so she crossed the water by the lock near the Seine and made her way eastward again.

The avenue Daumesnil was long, straight and grim. Immediately behind it ran a large, high viaduct that carried the railway trains out to Vincennes and the eastern suburbs beyond. She walked down the avenue. There were motor cars and buses in the roadway, but here and there a horse-drawn cart carrying coal or timber lumbered sadly by. Twice, a train from the viaduct let out a prolonged rattle that gradually died away behind the eastern rooftops.

The street she sought lay on the right. It was narrow. The storefronts on the street level mostly had shutters and their windows informed the passers-by, with seeming reluctance, what might be found within. A selection of hammers, copper pipes and boxes of screws, accompanied by a familiar, metallic smell from the open door, announced the hardware and ironmonger's emporium. Another window contained rolls of wallpaper, only one of which had deigned to reveal its pattern. And halfway down the street, a window containing a well-made table and bookcase, and a faded gold sign above the door saying PETIT ET FILS, told Louise that she had reached her destination.

The young man who emerged and stood behind the desk at the back of the little showroom was about her own age. He had brown hair and blue eyes. Nothing special. Did he look like her? Not really.

'May I ask,' she said politely, 'if your family name is Petit?'

'Yes, mademoiselle.' He spoke respectfully. His accent belonged to the streets. She hadn't thought of it, but she realised that, of course, whether in English or in French, she spoke in the accent of a different class from that of her real family.

'It is possible,' she said, 'that we have a family connection.'

'A connection?' He was polite, but obviously puzzled.

'Through Corinne Petit.' She watched him a little anxiously.

'Corinne?' He looked mystified. Clearly the name meant nothing to him. 'There is no one of that name in this family, mademoiselle. I have never heard it. It must be another family.'

'She went to England.'

'My uncle Pierre and his family went to Normandy once on holiday. That's as close as anyone has been to England.'

'Is your father here?'

'He will be back tonight, mademoiselle, but not until late.' He looked apologetic, but then brightened. 'My grandmother is here, if you would care to wait a minute.' He disappeared into the workshop behind.

His grandmother. My grandmother, perhaps, she thought. After a long pause, the older woman appeared.

She was slim. When she was younger, she would have had a figure very similar to her own, Louise realised. Her hair was grey, frizzed in the fashion of an earlier time. Her eyes were just like her own. But they were hard, and angry. She stared at Louise in silence for a moment.

'Mademoiselle?'

'I was asking your grandson . . .' Louise began.

'He has told me.'

'I am the daughter of Corinne Petit, madame.'

She watched the old lady's eyes. There was recognition. She was certain of it.

'There is no one in this family of that name, mademoiselle.'

'Not now. But I believe there was once. She led a respectable life in England, married and died. I never saw her. I was adopted by a banker and his wife.'

'You are fortunate, then, mademoiselle.'

'Perhaps. I was curious to know something of my French family, madame. That is all.'

'And why did you suppose you would find them here?'

'A lawyer made researches for me. He found three families with a daughter of that name born in Paris at the right time.'

'Perhaps your mother was not born in Paris, mademoiselle.'

'It is possible, madame, but I suspect she was.'

'I should know if I had given birth to a daughter named Corinne, mademoiselle. And I did not. You have come to the wrong place.'

She was lying. Louise knew it instinctively. She was certain of it. This old woman was her grandmother. Was the scandal really so terrible for the family, back then? Was her grandmother still implacable? Perhaps it was because the boy was there.

'I am sorry you cannot help me, madame,' she said sadly. She suddenly felt an urge to cry.

'I may be able to help you,' the old lady said. Was there a hint of pity, of kindness, in her voice? She paused. 'My late husband had a cousin. They never spoke. There was a family quarrel – he never told me what it was about. But he had two daughters. One went to live in Rouen, I believe. The other, I don't know. She could have been called Corinne. It's possible. If you could find her sister in Rouen . . .' She turned to the young man. 'Jean, I forgot that cake in the oven. Run upstairs to the kitchen, and take it out for me.'

The young man disappeared.

'I think you are my grandmother,' said Louise. 'Was my mother so terrible that you have to lie?'

But now, with her grandson gone, the old lady changed abruptly. The look she gave Louise was venomous. When she spoke, it was quietly, almost a hiss.

'How dare you come here? What gives you the right? The person you speak of has been dead to us for more than twenty years. You want to come here with your stupid quest, and disgrace the next generation as well? We didn't want her and we don't want you. Now get out, and never show your face here again.' She went to the door and opened it. 'Get out! Live your life elsewhere. But stay away from us. Forever.' She reached for Louise's arm, seized it with surprising force and shoved her out into the street, slamming the door behind her.

Louise looked back at her grandmother through the glass. There was no hint of mercy in the old lady's face. It was pale, and cold, and hard.

It was still early evening when Luc came by the restaurant. He'd been on a business errand.

Sometimes he told himself that he should work harder, but the twenty or thirty clients to whom he discreetly supplied cocaine provided him with all the ready cash he needed. Years ago when he was operating the bar before the war, he had run a few girls as well, acting as a protector mainly. But he'd given that business up. It was too much trouble. People had sometimes asked him if he could supply them with a nice girl. 'If I find someone, I'll let you know,' he had always told them. But so far he hadn't come upon a good prospect.

He was carrying quite a quantity of cash, and was going to put it in the small safe he kept in the office behind the restaurant. Then he was going to have a meal, walk up to his house, and go to bed early.

When he got to the restaurant, Louise was sitting quietly at a table. 'She's been sitting there two hours,' Édith told him. 'Waiting for you, I suppose.'

He sat down opposite her.

'Have you eaten?' he asked.

She shook her head. He ordered for them both.

'I met my grandmother today,' she said. 'She told me never to come there again.' She gave him a sad smile. 'It seems nobody wants me.'

'You must eat,' he said.

As they ate, Luc did not try to comfort her too much. But he did try to explain. He pointed out that it was natural for the old lady to act as she had. 'I dare say that's how your mother was treated all those years ago when they threw her out. Plenty of families would have done the same. They do it to protect themselves. So when you appeared and threatened to upset the apple cart, she must have been terrified.'

Louise listened. She understood what he was saying, but she was still all alone in the world.

When they had finished their meal he asked her quietly if she would like to come with him, and she nodded. After they had left the restaurant, he put his arm around her shoulder, protectively, and she smelled the aroma of Gauloises in his clothes, and she felt comforted. Then they walked up the hill of Montmartre towards his house.

*   *   *

The affair between Luc and Louise lasted several months. At first, they would meet in the afternoons at his house. But after a little while, he found her an apartment. 'It belongs to a businessman I know and it's in a good quarter of the city, just north of the Palais-Royal and near the stock exchange, the Bourse. That'll be convenient for getting to Chanel as well.'

'Won't it be expensive?'

'No. He's a rich man. His daughter was using it, but she's left and he hasn't decided whether to sell it or let it. For the time being, he'd be glad to have a respectable person there. Assuming he thinks you're respectable, he wouldn't charge you any rent, but you'd have to leave if he wanted the place back. That ought to suit you rather well.'

She'd met the man, a middle-aged stockbroker with a respectable family, who had been suitably impressed by her background. Sometimes Luc would join her there for the night, and sometimes she would go up to his house on the hill of Montmartre.

She quite liked the house. It was a little masculine, as one might expect, and it was permeated by a faint aroma of coffee and Gauloises, like a bar, but it was comfortably furnished with pieces that he had probably found in sales over a period of time. The salon contained a large sofa in the Directoire style, some Second Empire chairs, prints of Napoleonic soldiers on the walls and a thick carpet which, he informed her, he had laid himself. The bedroom contained a large bed made of the best African mahogany and handsomely inlaid. The kitchen contained a gas cooker and a fridge. He was a good cook, on the rare occasions that he took the trouble, but she liked to cook for him.

Luc was a wonderful lover. He was skilful, strong and considerate. In later years, she would say simply: 'It was the right time for me.'

They met several times a week. Often they would explore the city together. She had thought she knew Paris fairly well, but soon she began to see it not as a big city but as a series of communities. She shared his memories of characters who had lived their eccentric lives in every corner of the city. She discovered ancient street markets, the places along the river where she could buy good flowers cheaply; he showed her where to eat the food of Normandy, or Alsace, or Provence; he showed her where the licenced brothels were, and where the old prisons and gallows had stood. He paid for everything, for he always seemed to have cash, and since she was living free, she could save not only her modest allowance but the small sums she got from modelling as well.

One benefit of working for Chanel was that, once in a while, she might be given small items of clothing. But most of all, she found that she was developing an eye for fashion. And with the advice from the other models, and information from Luc, she was able to assemble a little wardrobe that was getting quite chic.

It also amused her that, though he did not always say anything, Luc's eye missed nothing. A grunt of approval meant that he had noticed the new blouse she was wearing. And once in a while, if she was carrying some elegant little bag she'd picked up somewhere, he'd ask sharply, 'Where did you get that?' For he didn't like to think that there was any bargain in the city that he didn't know about. And she would say, 'I shan't tell you. A girl has her secrets.' And then, on and off, he might question her: 'Was it one of those second-hand shops behind the rue Saint-Honoré, or that Moroccan dealer on the rue du Temple?' And even if he guessed right, she would always deny it. And though he would pretend to be annoyed, she knew he liked the challenge of these little games, and others that she learned to play, to tease him.

Yet despite all the time they spent together, she never discovered anything about his business. If he was out, he was out. That was it.

'Never ask a man his business,' he told her. 'He'll either get his whip or get bored.'

'Bad alternatives,' she said with a laugh.

'*Voilà.*'

She had the impression that he might be part-owner in other bars and clubs, and that there might be properties from which he collected rents, but that was all she knew.

Meanwhile, she was happy in the new quarter where she found herself. With the stockbrokers and financial men around the Bourse, the area was less residential than most other quarters of the city. But it had a feature of particular charm – a whole network of glass-covered arcades and halls, some of them more than a century old, that housed all kinds of stores and places of refreshment. She would often walk about these intimate malls, exploring happily for an hour at a time.

Only once during all this time did she glimpse another side of Luc – and even then, it was hard to say what she had seen. It happened at dawn, on a summer's day, up at his house on the slopes of Montmartre.

She was suddenly awoken by a cry beside her. Luc was thrashing about wildly in the bed. Before she could do anything, his hands encountered her, and then suddenly seized her by the throat. She tried to pry them off, and scream, but his grip was so strong that she couldn't even breathe. She was completely in his power, and he was still asleep. She hit out wildly, slapped his face as hard as she could. His eyes opened. He looked startled and confused. His grip relaxed.

'Luc, what are you doing?' she gasped.

'A nightmare.' She could see that he was still struggling into consciousness.

'Evidently. But you almost throttled me.'

'*Chérie*, I am so sorry.'

'Who were you trying to strangle?'

'A dog.'

'A dog?'

He propped himself up on one elbow and stared at her.

'A dog. I can't explain. It was a crazy nightmare. Without any sense to it.'

And then he gave her a strange look.

'Did I cry out anything?'

'No.'

'A name?'

'You mean the dog had a name? What's he called? Fido?'

'I didn't call anything out?' He was fully awake now, and he was watching her in a strange way. She'd never seen him look like that before, and she found it disquieting.

'Nothing. You were thrashing around in the bed. That woke me up. The next thing I knew, you were strangling me.'

He continued to look at her. Then, apparently satisfied, his expression changed to one of tender concern.

'I hardly ever have nightmares. It must have been something I ate. Are you all right?' He kissed her softly on the forehead. 'You had better hold me. I was afraid.'

They lay together for a little while. She held him. His fear subsided, and his courage grew. But just when she thought he was going to start making love, he got up from the bed, and went to the window. Opening the shutter, he looked down into the little garden behind the house. His eyes seemed to be fixed on something.

'What are you looking at?' she asked.

'Nothing. I was listening to the dawn chorus. One could be in the middle of the country.'

'Come back to bed.'

'In a minute.'

And soon he did, and they made love, and everything was back to normal.

But she couldn't forget the strange expression on his face when he was questioning her, even though she had no idea what it meant.

The girl. It was a long time since that vision had troubled him. Luc knew it was said that murderers revisit the scene of the crime, but he had never gone down into that cave again. The girl must surely be whitened bones by now. Even her name was forgotten. After all, it was more than ten years since she'd disappeared. A world war had come and gone. Millions had died. Bushes had grown across the hidden entrance behind the little shed in his garden. One would have to cut them down even to get into the caves now. There was no reason to give the girl a thought.

Nor did he, during his waking hours. But sometimes, in his sleep, her face rose up before him. Her pale face, her eyes angry and accusing. And he would know that she was a ghost, and be afraid.

But that night the dream had been different. He had seen her skeleton, in among the others in the cave. But a strange plant had been growing from the bones, sending out long shoots. And one of the shoots had turned into a long stalk that had started winding its way along the passage, yard after yard, until at last it found its way to the entrance hidden behind the shed in his garden, and somehow it had managed to creep around the back of the shed and out on to the grass where it lay, apparently exhausted by its efforts to make its way out of the darkness into the light. And from the end of the green stalk, now, small flowers like lilies began to grow.

Perhaps the plant might have remained there, doing no harm, had it not been for the dog that suddenly appeared. Luc had no idea where the dog had come from, but it seized the plant, and began to pull on it. Luc took the dog by the collar and tried to drag it away, but the dog would not be dissuaded from its task. It pulled on the long stalk and dragged it several feet. Then it leaped forward and grabbed the stalk farther up, and pulled that out from the tunnel too. Far underground, the skeleton of the girl began to move, and now Luc realised that if the dog kept pulling, it would pull the dead girl all the way up until she was back in his garden. He must stop the dog, before it dug her up again.

And it was then, in his dream, that he had grabbed the dog by the throat, and started to throttle it, squeezing harder and harder, to choke the life out of the animal.

Luc waited a month before he suggested to Louise that it was time for them to part.

It was not because of the dream, though that perhaps had shown him that she was getting too close to him. Too close.

He had always intended that, when his work was done, their relationship should move into a different phase. He led up to it gradually.

'*Chérie*,' he said kindly to her one afternoon, 'will you promise me one thing: when our affair comes to its natural end – as it will – we shall remain friends. It would pain me very much if, when you left, you were no longer my friend.'

'I have no plans to leave at present.'

'That is good to hear. But one day you will. It's only natural. You will go forward with your life. But I shall be left with wonderful memories, the best of my life. And those will make me happy, as long as we remain friends.'

'The best of your life?'

'Absolutely, I assure you.'

'I was very ignorant.'

'You are not at all ignorant now. Not in the least. You are wonderful.'

'If so, I have you to thank.'

'I could only bring out what was already there. The gardener does not create the flower.'

There was a pause.

'Are you trying to get rid of me?'

'You're getting too cynical.'

'I learned that from you.'

'Only for your own protection. I'm protecting myself as well, you know, by being realistic.' He smiled. 'I am a middle-aged man of no importance. You should move on, get yourself a rich lover, as Madame Chanel told you.'

He had let her think about it for a couple of weeks, then told her that he had to leave Paris on business for a little while. It was quite true, as it happened. He had to go to Amsterdam for a week. 'When I get back,' he said, 'we shall be friends.'

'Oh. I see.'

'Always ask me for help, whenever you need it, whatever you need.' And seeing her look doubtful, he added: 'Remember, I should be hurt if you did not.' He smiled a little sadly. 'My only fear is that you will never need me any more.'

She did not see him again for over a month. She was sure he was back from Amsterdam, and several times she was on the point of going around to the family restaurant to ask after him. But her pride held her back. He had told her she wouldn't need him. She'd show him he was right.

And finally, it was he who came to her. He turned up at her door one evening.

'I came to see how you were.'

'I am well,' she said calmly, but she didn't invite him in. If he was hoping to crawl back to her, she was going to make him crawl a long way for a long time.

'Is there anything you need?'

'No, thank you.'

'Would you like to make some money?'

'Why? How?'

He shrugged.

'Let me give you a meal and I will tell you. It's an opportunity that came my way. It may be of no interest to you. It's something . . . diplomatic.'

And because she was curious, she agreed to meet him that evening at a brasserie nearby.

It was interesting to observe him because, after a number of inquiries about her welfare which were practical and thoughtful, he became rather businesslike.

'There is an ambassador I know. He's from a small country, he's rich, and unusually for a diplomat in that position, he's unmarried.'

'How do you come to know such people, Luc?'

'It does not matter. He is a nice man, he knows everybody of importance in Paris, he is very cultivated, and he is . . . fastidious.'

'And so?'

'I think you should get to know him. He would like you.'

'And do you propose to introduce me to this person?'

'I have told him all about you. He's quite interested to meet you. In fact, he'd like to take you out to dinner.'

'Let me understand. Is he looking for a wife?'

'No.'

'A mistress?'

'Let us say, an occasional mistress.'

'Luc, are you asking me to be a prostitute?'

'He would not be interested in most prostitutes. He is very fastidious, as I have told you. You would see if you liked each other over dinner. If not, there is no obligation whatever. But if you liked each other, then perhaps . . .'

'He would pay me?'

'Certainly. He would pay fifteen hundred francs each time. You would give me half. If you had any difficulties, I would take care of them. But I am quite certain that you would not. This is a very civilised man. You are the only person I have ever known who I should dream of recommending to him, and he is the only person I should think of recommending to you. But as well as the money, he might be a good friend for you to have.'

'I can't believe you would treat me in this way.'

'One must be practical.'

'This makes me a prostitute and you a pimp.'

'The situation is more specialised. As for the money . . . Why don't you think about it for a little while? Remember, he has offered you dinner without any obligation at all. You might like him.'

She was silent for a little while.

'What you are really thinking,' she said quietly, 'is that I might like the money.'

*　　*　　*

When Marie had a problem, she often liked to walk in the Luxembourg Gardens to work it out. The gardens were classical in their outlines, but they were simple, and friendly, and sensible. By ten o'clock on the Saturday morning after her brother Marc's party, she was walking there.

It was still quiet. A few children were already sailing their model ships in the big basin. Some elderly men had begun a game of boules on the gravel beside one of the statues. Marie walked to the bottom of the park and back, thinking hard. For today she had a very big problem indeed.

What was she going to do about Frank Hadley Jr? They were going to meet later that morning.

Marc had started the business by inviting them all to join him at the Ballets Russes that evening. Young Frank Hadley and Claire had wanted to go. She couldn't herself, she'd explained, because she'd agreed to go to the opera.

Then Frank had asked if anyone would like to accompany him to the Olympics. 'I'm going to watch the boxing with an American friend and his wife on Saturday afternoon,' he'd explained. Claire had wanted to go, Marc could not.

Was Claire attracted to the young American? It had looked as if she was, and it would hardly be surprising. In any case, Marie had told herself that she couldn't possibly leave her daughter alone with a young man who had such a glint in his eye, so she'd declared firmly that she and Claire would both accompany him.

And now she considered the day ahead. It was one thing for the young American to flirt with her, seriously or otherwise. She was a widow, after all, who could certainly take care of herself. Claire, however, was another matter. Her daughter might be grown up, and the world might not be the same as it was before the war. But the rules of society hadn't changed so much; and the human heart, not at all. Claire still had to be protected. She didn't want her daughter being compromised, and she didn't want her being hurt.

So she was going to be practical. Very practical. If necessary, she supposed, she might have to send Frank Hadley Jr away with a flea in his ear. Unless, of course, she decided to take the young man in hand herself.

*   *   *

596

The bookshop where they were to meet Frank's friends was only a short walk from their apartment. They arrived there punctually at noon.

If the area from the Seine into the *Quartier Latin* had been the home of the bookstall for centuries, it was the recent arrival of two eccentric bookshops on the rue de l'Odéon, both run by women, that had turned that little area into the literary capital of the world. The first was the French literary bookshop of the warm-hearted Adrienne Monnier. The second, almost across the street, had been named Shakespeare and Company by its owner, Sylvia Beach.

Claire was better acquainted with the bookstores than her mother.

'The French writers go to Monnier and walk across the street to Sylvia Beach, and the English and Americans start with Sylvia and then explore Monnier as well. They're both such nice women. Best of all, they fell in love with each other. They actually live together now.'

'Oh. Is anyone shocked?'

'I don't think anyone cares.' She smiled. 'Shakespeare and Company's like a sort of club. As well as selling books, Sylvia also has a lending library. She supports authors, too. About a year ago, she even published *Ulysses* for James Joyce, the Irish writer, at her own expense, when the manuscript was virtually banned in Ireland and England. She even lets people sleep at the place. Everyone loves her.'

And indeed, when they arrived, Frank introduced them at once to the owner, who turned out to be a bright, friendly woman in her mid-thirties, who soon remarked to Marie that around the time she and James Fox had left Paris for London, she'd been arriving in Paris for the first time with her father, who was taking up an appointment as assistant minister at the American Church.

'I've hardly a single ancestor in a century who wasn't either a pastor or a missionary,' she informed Marie with a wry smile, before she left them to attend to business.

Frank's friends were an American journalist who wrote articles for a Canadian newspaper, and his wife. The wife was the first to arrive, a broad-faced woman in her early thirties with intelligent eyes.

'This is Hadley,' Frank explained, and grinned. 'We're not related. Hadley's her first name. The match with my family name is pure coincidence.'

'And here comes my husband,' said Hadley, indicating an approaching figure.

He was a muscular-looking fellow, somewhat younger than his wife, but his impressive appearance seemed to make up for the difference. He was six feet tall, with a broad regular face and a moustache, and eyes set wide apart and square. Despite the warm July weather, he was wearing a sturdy tweed suit which, Marie guessed, served him for all occasions, and a pair of equally sturdy brown shoes – that let one know at once that he was a sportsman and an outdoorsman. She thought he looked like a young Theodore Roosevelt, without the politics or the glasses. From the way he carried himself, she guessed that he wrote fine, clean prose about where he'd been and what he'd done, and how it felt.

'This is Hemingway,' said Frank.

To Marie's surprise, Hemingway turned to her at once and said that he'd seen her before.

'You like to walk in the Luxembourg Gardens,' he explained. 'We live just south of there, beside a sawmill in the rue Notre-Dame-des-Champs on the edge of Montparnasse.' He grinned. 'The poor district. Sometimes I sit quietly in the Luxembourg Gardens, and I see you. But I'm usually keeping my head down, and when no one's looking I grab a pigeon.'

'Whatever for?'

'To eat, madame. I kill it quick, tuck it under my coat, and head for home. The Luxembourg pigeons are well fed, so they cook up nicely.'

'I don't believe you are so poor, monsieur,' said Marie.

'Sometimes we are,' he said.

'None of the French can believe that any American is short of money,' Frank remarked with a laugh. 'Especially in the last couple of years, with the French franc falling like a stone against the dollar. That's why so many of us are flocking over here. They say there are thirty thousand Americans in Paris now.' He looked at his friend, who was shaking his head. Then, excusing himself, Hemingway and his wife stepped outside for a moment to look at the shop window.

'Actually,' Frank continued quietly to Marie, 'Hadley has a small income from a trust fund, but they lost some of it recently, and Hemingway quit his job with the newspaper to write his fiction. So they're sometimes a little short. Hemingway can write articles to make money if he has to, but his short stories are already attracting notice. Ford Madox Ford has started publishing them in the *Tribune*.'

As they went out to rejoin Hemingway, it was Claire who spotted the volume in the window.

'Look,' she said to her mother. The volume was very slim and its cover was very simple. It was titled, in lower-case letters, *in our time*.'

'Those are Hemingway's,' said Frank, with almost as much pride as if they had been his own. 'Short stories. How many has Sylvia sold?' he asked the author.

'Nearly twenty already.'

'Not bad,' said Frank cheerfully. 'It's not just the numbers, but the quality of the readers.' He grinned. 'A novel or two and you'll be rich.'

'Come on,' said Marie.

The boxing was taking place in the covered winter cycling track, the Vélodrome d'hiver, that lay on the Left Bank just downstream from the Eiffel Tower. They walked westward along the boulevard Saint-Germain until, at the intersection with the boulevard Raspail, they found a taxi and all piled into it.

During their walk, Marie discovered from Hemingway's wife that they already had a baby boy, not yet a year old. They also learned that Frank had been out at the open stadium outside the city during the track events ten days before.

'The British did very well,' he informed them. 'Their man Abrahams even beat our Charley Paddock to take the hundred-metre gold. But the finest thing I ever saw was the Scotsman Liddell. He'd pulled out of the hundred metres months before the games because the heats were being run on the Sabbath. So he trained for the four hundred instead, although nobody thought he had a chance. Then he ran like a man inspired. Covered the first two hundred at a speed no one thought he could possibly keep up, and just kept going. Running for God. And God gave him the gold. Almost a whole second faster that our man Fitch. It was a magnificent sight.'

In many ways, Marie could see, Frank and Hemingway were similar. Both were clearly athletic fellows, although Hemingway was more of a showman. Hemingway was only a couple of years older, but Frank treated him as a mentor. Maybe because Hemingway was already a married man, but more likely because he'd served in the war. That was the great dividing line in the younger generation, she'd noticed – whether you'd been in the war or not.

Hemingway, for his part, treated Frank very much like a brother, and one he respected. 'I know you're a good oarsman, Frank,' he remarked, 'but you should try boxing. I know a good trainer here. I'd be glad to spar with you.'

He also told them that Frank was writing short stories, and was quite surprised they didn't know.

'I hope to learn a little about writing while I'm here,' Frank confessed. 'But I shall go home like my father, in due course, and become a teacher.' He smiled. 'That's a good enough life for an honest man.'

'It certainly is,' Hemingway agreed, 'but you could make a name as a writer. It may surprise you, but it won't surprise me.'

Claire seemed intrigued by Frank's literary interests and wanted to know more, but Frank was keeping his cards close to his chest.

'I'll tell you one thing, though,' he said. 'The best advice I ever had came from Hemingway here.'

'Tell us,' Claire said.

'Everyone who tries to write anything should know this,' said Frank. 'What Hemingway told me is that he never stops a day's work until he knows exactly what's coming next. Stop then, and you'll be able to get back into rhythm when you start writing again. If you don't do that, you'll probably get stuck at the beginning of every day's work.'

'So don't come to the end of a section and put down your pen and say, "That's done, now I'll stop for the day." '

'Exactly. Natural reaction, but fatal error.'

'I like that,' said Claire. 'It's good to know practical things.'

Marie watched. A flirtatious young man can be attractive, but when he shows he has a serious side as well, and skills that he values, he becomes even more intriguing. She wondered what else Frank was going to say to get her daughter's interest.

The Vélodrome d'hiver was a big covered stadium. For the cycle races, a wooden track would be set up, and the spectators would crowd into the centre area of the track as well as the steep tiers of seats around the sides. Hemingway told them that he loved to come to the cycle races, but that all the terms were French and it was hard to write about them in English.

For the boxing, however, the stadium had been turned into a huge auditorium with the ring in the centre, and an array of powerful lamps hanging from the metal rafters high overhead.

They watched several bouts. Both Hemingway and Frank seemed to be well informed. The United States looked set to take the most medals, but the American strength was in the lighter weight classes. The British dominated the middleweights. The Scandinavians were strong in the heavyweight class.

The two men discussed the boxers with some knowledge. It seemed that Hemingway sparred in a gym quite often, and Marie asked him if he went to boxing matches in America.

'The last I went to, I saw the finest fighter in the world.'

'Who's that?'

'Gene Tunney. Light heavyweight champion. If he could make the extra weight and fight as a heavyweight, I think he could beat Jack Dempsey.'

'I thought no one could do that.'

'Tunney might. That's a man I'd like to meet.'

Frank grinned.

'What would you say to Tunney if you met him, Hemingway?'

'I'd ask him to fight me.'

Marie laughed, but Hemingway's wife, Hadley, shook her head.

'You don't understand,' she said. 'He really would.'

Frank laughed.

'Tell them the Pamplona story, Hadley,' he said, with a sideways glance at his mentor.

'Last year,' said Hadley, 'when I'm pregnant with Jack, I am told that I must watch a bullfight in Pamplona because the sensation of it will be good for my unborn child. You know. Toughen him up before he's even born.' She looked at Hemingway fondly. 'I am married to a crazy man.'

Soon after four o'clock, Marie and Claire left their new friends and returned to their apartment. Frank was going to join Claire at her uncle's in the evening. On their way back, Marie asked Claire what she thought of the day so far.

'I love Shakespeare and Company.'

'And the Hemingways?'

'They seem very much in love. He means to be a figure in the world.'

'I agree. A showman,' said Marie.

'They say his short stories are really fine, though.'

'And Frank Hadley?' She made it sound casual.

'Were you interested in his father?'

Marie laughed.

'He was Marc's friend, rather than mine. Your father and I were already courting at that time. I think the son's a bit of a flirt. Not to be trusted.'

'He seems serious about his writing. He denies it, but I think he is.'

'That may be. Avoid him if he has any talent.'

'Why?'

'Because all artists are monsters.'

'Tell me about Monsieur de Cygne. Is he an old flame?'

'No. His father and your grandfather were friends. He was always away with his regiment. But he was nice, the few times we did see him.'

'You're both free now. You could be a vicomtesse.'

'Better than that, *chérie*. I can be seen at the opera with him. It's quite respectable, and chic.'

'Is that so good for you?'

'You're missing the point, my child. It's good for the store.'

She enjoyed the evening. It was the very end of the ballet season, after which the Opéra would close until September. The opulence of Garnier's opera house, the magnificent, gold Corinthian columns, the sumptuous decoration, the gilded balconies and tiers, and the rich, velvety red seats recalled the Belle Époque of her youth so strongly that she gave a light laugh as they sat down.

Roland gave her a quizzical look.

'It's so preposterous,' she said happily.

'You find it vulgar?'

'Can an overstuffed cushion be vulgar? It's a kind of heaven, like a huge gâteau.'

He chuckled.

'I can imagine my dear father looking down from the balcony with the same ironic pleasure you feel.'

'And my father too. They smoked the same cigars, you know.'

'We share similar memories.'

'Mine are more bourgeois, Monsieur de Cygne.' She smiled. 'Complementary, perhaps.'

'That's it exactly,' he said with a nod.

During the interval, they sat and talked. She asked him about his son.

'He's at the same lycée that I went to,' he told her, 'and I don't know if I did the right thing or not. It was always very conservative, and it still is. I wonder if I should have sent him to a place where their ideas are more modern. On the other hand, I feel I can help him better because I understand the school.'

'Is he happy?'

'He says he is.'

'I think you did right. If you felt out of sympathy with the school, uncomfortable with the teachers, then you'd feel off-balance yourself. Children don't have to agree with their parents, but they like it when their parents are comfortable with themselves, if you know what I mean.'

'I'm so glad you say that.'

She could see that he said it with some emotion. Yes, she thought, you're a good man.

She wanted to go straight home after the performance, but when he asked if she might care to go to the opera when the new season began, she smiled and told him: 'After such a delightful evening at the ballet, monsieur, I cannot imagine why I should not want to go to the opera with you.'

'I go down to my estate in a couple of days,' he said, 'but you may be sure, madame, that I shall look forward to taking you to the opera as soon as I return in September.'

The apartment was quiet when she returned. Claire was still not back. After she had prepared for bed, Marie told her lady's maid that she and the other servants should go to sleep and that she'd let her daughter in herself.

She was looking forward to hearing about the Ballets Russes from Claire. Diaghilev and his company had decided to stage *Le Train bleu* for the Olympics, and it had opened just four weeks ago at the Théâtre des Champs-Élysées, which lay below the great avenue, near the river. All Paris knew about the huge front cloth that Picasso had painted for it, of two strangely ungainly women running on a beach.

Claire could be relied upon to give a vivid description of the performance.

An hour passed. Marie supposed that her brother had either taken the young people out to a restaurant, or was giving them a drink at his apartment. She decided to telephone him.

When he picked up the receiver, he sounded half asleep.

'I was looking for Claire,' she said.

'Oh. They went for a drink with friends. Americans.'

'Where?'

'How do I know?'

'You let Claire go out with a young man, to God knows where, in the middle of the night?'

'Look, Marie . . . She's a young woman now.'

'She's a respectable young woman. Do you remember what they are like?' she shouted down the line. 'But I was forgetting,' she added bitterly, 'you never knew any respectable girls in the first place.'

'What do you want me to do?'

'Look after her. Return her to me. Not let her go off with a young man in the middle of the night. You have no sense of responsibility,' she cried in exasperation. 'You never had.'

'Well, there's nothing I can do now, anyway.' He sounded guilty, but bored as well, which only infuriated her more.

She hung up.

And then she waited. After a while, she opened the window of the salon, which gave out on to a small balcony where she could see up and down the street. Paris was silent. Now and then someone appeared in the lamplight, but it seemed that the city had gone to sleep.

Were they in a bar or nightclub? The night was warm. Were they walking along the Seine, or out on one of the bridges? Was young Frank's arm around Claire? Was he kissing her? Or worse, had they gone back to his lodgings? Would he do such a thing? Of course he would. He was a young man.

She wanted to run into the street and save her daughter. And perhaps she might have gone out, if she had any idea where they might be.

She pictured Frank Hadley, his tall frame and unruly mane of hair, so exactly like his father. She imagined his eyes in the darkness.

And then, despite herself, she was assailed by a terrible sensation. It caught her by surprise and took hold over her before she even knew it was happening.

She wanted Frank Hadley.

Was it young Frank, or his father? She could hardly say. The other evening at her brother's it had seemed that the Frank she knew had suddenly walked in from the past. Now it felt as if her old self had reappeared, as if the layers that made up her personality had been peeled back to the girl she'd been a quarter of a century ago, who had now emerged, hardly changed from what she had been before.

The shock she had felt when she saw Frank had now turned into something else. A terrible longing.

Desire. Jealousy. She wanted him for herself.

Could one be two people at the same time? It seemed she could. As a mother, she wanted to protect her daughter from Frank Hadley. But when she thought of them together, she wasn't a mother any more. She was a woman whose rival is trying to steal her lover. She felt ready, almost, to physically attack her. But first, she had to know.

Was Claire her rival? And how far had it gone?

She was sitting on the sofa in this confused state when she heard a sound at the door. She moved quickly to the hall. The front door opened. It was Claire.

'Are you all right?'

'Yes, I'm fine.' She looked pale. 'I drank too much.'

'It's so late. I was worried about you.'

'I'm fine.' Claire closed the door.

'You came home alone?'

'No. They brought me to the door.'

'They?'

'Frank and his friends.'

Was she telling the truth? Marie wanted to run back to the balcony to see if they were down in the street, but didn't feel she could.

'So long as you're all right,' she said.

But the next day she warned her daughter that she must be more careful with her reputation and that her uncle shouldn't have let her wander off with Frank as she had. She was quite relieved when Claire made no objection.

The month of August was quiet for the Joséphine store. Most Parisians were out of town, though foreign visitors to the city came in. The whole Blanchard family based itself at the house at Fontainebleau, and Claire and her mother took turns going into Paris for a day and a night each week to keep an eye on things.

Jules Blanchard and his wife had retired into one of the pavilions beside the courtyard now, leaving the main body of the house for the family. Gérard's widow and her children were there, as well as Marc, Marie and Claire, but there was still room for guests, and so there were usually a dozen people sitting out on the broad balcony looking over the lawn on any August afternoon.

Claire was always happy to be at Fontainebleau. She loved her grandparents. Her grandmother had become a little confused lately, but old Jules, though somewhat forgetful, still liked to sit out on the veranda and chat, and she would ask him questions about the days of his youth, and he would describe the old people he could remember who had lived through the French Revolution and the age of Napoléon.

During those long, easy summer days there was only one shadow over her life. A cloud of uncertainty. Did Frank Hadley have any interest in her?

Perhaps it was because her parents had come from different countries that she was hard to please. As a girl being brought up in London, she liked the English boys she knew, but always felt that there was something lacking. It wasn't only that they didn't speak French. She was used to seeing things through her mother's French eyes as well as her father's. And indeed, her father had lived in Paris so long that, English though he was, he also saw the world in larger terms than most of his neighbours. True, there were English people – many of them – who had served the British Empire in far corners of the world, and whose imaginations had large horizons. But most of them still saw that larger world in imperial terms, secure in the knowledge that, at the end of the day, British was best. English people who had lived on the continent of Europe were a much rarer breed.

Similarly, when she returned to France with her mother, she found Frenchmen interesting, and seductive – yet even while she was catching up with the cultural excitement of France, the Frenchmen she met began to seem a little less fascinating. They too, she realised, were part of a crowd – a different crowd, but still a crowd.

And almost without realising it, she began to wish that she could find a different sort of man. A free spirit. A man for whom life was an open-ended adventure. He might be English, he might be French, he might come from any nationality. An explorer perhaps, or a writer, or maybe a diplomat . . . She really didn't know.

And where did one find such a man? It had taken her a little while to discover that there was a community in Paris to which people of that sort were drawn.

The Americans.

Why was that? She soon came to realise that there were many reasons. Freedom was in their blood. It was their birthright. But almost to a man, these expatriates felt that the mighty engine of America was still too young, too raw to have developed the rich culture they were looking for. Whereas Europe had over two thousand years of culture, from Greek temple to English country house, or Parisian nightclub, all there for the taking. The Americans came, not arrogant, but eager to learn. They meant to have it all.

And so it was that Gertrude Stein and Sylvia Beach from America, and Ford Madox Ford the Englishman, and the Spaniard Picasso, and Diaghilev and his Ballets Russes, and French writers like Cocteau, and young Ernest Hemingway could all find each other in the bookshops and bars and theatres of Paris on any day of the week – and did.

So when her uncle Marc asked her casually one day what she thought of the Americans in Paris, she answered: 'I wouldn't want to marry Hemingway, but I like his adventurous spirit.'

'Perhaps you could find yourself a younger version and share your adventures. Though you may have to work to get him the way you want him.'

'That sounds like a challenge.'

'Don't you want a challenge?'

Perhaps she did.

So what did she have to do to get Frank Hadley Jr to notice her?

He was friendly. He was easy to talk to. That evening after the Ballets Russes, they'd gone back across the river with her uncle Marc, and then walked down the long boulevard Raspail into Montparnasse where they'd met his friends, and she'd felt so easy in his company. He'd seemed to enjoy her company too. He'd laughed at her jokes. When they walked her home, there had been a party of six of them, walking along empty streets, and they'd all linked arms. Frank had been next to her, so that she'd felt his tall, warm body against hers, and they'd all kissed each other on both cheeks, in the usual French manner, before she went into the building where she lived. But she hadn't been able to tell whether he was interested in her or not.

She'd seen him once again, at the very end of July. She'd agreed to meet him and the Hemingways early one evening at the big Dôme Café bar, where all the artists and writers gathered. 'Lenin used to come here too, when he was living in Paris,' she informed him. 'Uncle Marc told me.' It had been very pleasant. Hadley Hemingway had informed them proudly that Ernest had written maybe a dozen stories already that year, and then Hemingway had turned to his wife and asked if she'd seen any of Frank's writing. Frank frowned, and she said, No, she hadn't.

'You should show her your stuff,' said Hemingway to Frank. 'She'd be a good judge.' But Frank just looked awkward and said it wasn't good enough yet, and probably never would be.

'You need to stay in Paris for a good while,' said Hadley. 'We think it suits you.'

'That's right,' said Hemingway.

'Don't go disappearing on us, like Gil,' said Hadley.

'Who's Gil?' asked Claire.

'Oh, he was a nice young American that we all thought had promise,' said Hadley. 'And then suddenly he wasn't there any more. Disappeared without a word.'

'I won't do that,' said Frank.

After that, he'd walked her back, and he'd talked about his home in America, and asked her all kinds of questions about Joséphine and the plans for the store. He seemed quite interested in what her mother did there as well. In fact, he seemed rather fascinated by her mother. Then he told her that he was going to spend part of August in Brittany. So she hadn't expected to see him again until September.

It was the third week of August when Marc, after an absence of a few days in Paris, returned not alone, but with Frank. 'I'd just looked in at the Dôme to meet a man, and there he was. I told him to come down to Fontainebleau with me.'

Since the house was almost full, Marie told Claire that she'd better let Frank have her room.

'There's the little boudoir beside my room,' she told her daughter. 'We can put a bed in there for you.'

Frank seemed a little embarrassed that he might be inconveniencing everybody, especially Claire; but Marie assured him that it was a family house and everyone was used to making room for friends.

And indeed, Marc soon made Frank into a family project.

'This is a wonderful opportunity for you,' he declared. 'Here you are in the middle of a French family, and we shall teach you how to be French.' He smiled. 'An even better Frenchman than your father was.'

Every morning, Claire was to spend an hour teaching him to speak French. Then he'd spend another hour with Marie. She might take him to the kitchen and show him how all kinds of dishes were made. Or she might take him to the market to shop. She simply involved him in whatever activity she was employed upon at the time, and gave him a running commentary. As for Marc, he would take Frank and anyone else who wanted to come to the old château, or across to the village of Barbizon, or show him books in the small library and talk of French history and culture. In ten days of this regime, Frank learned an astonishing amount.

One lunchtime, Frank confessed that he had still not fully understood how Paris was organised geographically. And here everyone had something to tell him.

'First,' Marc explained, 'you must understand how Paris has grown from a modest Roman town to a medieval city.' And he told him how the city had expanded, like a growing egg, as he put it, enclosed by a series of walls taking in further suburbs each time.

'So we have, for instance, the ancient Île de la Cité, and the Montagne Sainte-Geneviève where the university is, which was once a Roman forum. Across the river you have the Temple area, once a suburb where the Templars lived, and near it the Marais, so called because it was once a marsh. Most of the other quarters keep the names either of former villages or churches. And each has its own character – though many smaller quarters practically disappeared when Baron Haussmann knocked them down in the last century.'

'But what about the arrondissements?' Frank asked. 'That's where I get confused. They have numbers, but there seem to be two sets. And they also seem to have their own reputations, don't they?'

Marc turned to Gérard's son, young Jules.

'To be precise,' Jules told him, 'soon after the Revolution the inner parts of Paris were divided into twelve arrondissements – and people sometimes still refer to them as the old arrondissements. But in 1860, the whole of Paris was divided into a new set of twenty arrondissements. They start with the Louvre area and the western part of the Île de la Cité: that's the First Arrondissement. Then they continue in a clockwise spiral, the first four on the Right Bank. The Third contains the Temple, the Marais is mainly in the Fourth. Then you cross the river to the Fifth, which is the Latin Quarter, the Sixth, which is the Luxembourg Gardens area, and the Seventh, which is maybe a little cold, but rich, and includes Les Invalides and the Eiffel Tower. Back across the river, you're in the huge area that runs south to north from the river right up to the Parc Monceau, and west to east from the Arc de Triomphe, right down the Champs-Élysées to the Madeleine and the Opéra. That's the Eighth. It's socially grand.

'Then you go around the city again. The Ninth to the Twelfth Arrondissements are on the Right Bank – the Twelfth runs out from the Bastille, along the rue du Faubourg-Saint-Antoine to the old Vincennes gateway. Then to the Left Bank: the Thirteenth, the Fourteenth, which is Montparnasse, and the Fifteenth.

'Across the river again for the last five. The Sixteenth is long and runs right up the west side of the city to the Arc de Triomphe and the avenue de la Grande-Armée. The Bois de Boulogne lies beyond it. There are old villages like Passy, where Ben Franklin lived, in the

Sixteenth, and the avenue Victor Hugo. It has a reputation of being smart and international. Above that, on the north-west edge of the city, is the Seventeenth, with the old village of Neuilly to the west of it. Neuilly is chic. The Seventeenth is respectable but dull.'

'The Seventeenth is not so bad,' said his mother.

'But it's boring,' Claire whispered to Frank.

'The Eighteenth,' continued young Jules, 'you might say is the top of the city. It contains Clichy and Montmartre. Then on the outer north-eastern edges of the city are the Nineteenth, which contains the Buttes-Chaumont park, and the Twentieth, which is the working-class district of Belleville, but also has the Cemetery of Père Lachaise.'

'Normally,' said Claire, 'though old people don't use the arrondissements so much, if someone asks you where you live, you'll say "in the Fifth" or "in the Sixteenth", unless it's a special quarter or place of interest. If you lived on the hill by Sacré Coeur, you might say you lived in the Eighteenth, but you'd probably say you lived in Montmartre. Same with Montparnasse. Or the Île de la Cité, or the Marais.'

'But if you lived in Pigalle,' added Marc with a smile, 'which contains the Moulin Rouge and some far less savoury places, you might say "in the Ninth", which could mean you lived more respectably near the boulevard Haussmann.'

'I get it now,' said Frank. 'I'd better study a map.'

'By all means study a map,' said Marc genially, 'but personally, I recommend that you live in Paris.'

The afternoons passed easily. Everyone would sit out on the long veranda, and old Jules would read his newspaper, and Marie would walk about in the garden or rest, and Frank was left to write in his notebook without anyone inquiring what he was doing or asking to see it.

On Sunday, of course, the women went to church in the morning, and the whole family, except for Claire's grandparents, would go for their traditional walk in the Forest of Fontainebleau.

But despite their being often together, and despite the fact that he was slightly flirtatious with her mother, Frank never made the slightest move towards Claire. He was friendly, like a brother, but nothing more. Nothing at all.

Sometimes she observed him while he was working in the afternoons. As long as he could be observed he would sit there looking quite contented, and making a note or two, apparently just as casually as if he were reading a newspaper. But sometimes the veranda would be empty, or the people there would be dozing; and if she looked out through a window, or watched him from the small arbour at the side of the garden where the roses grew, and where he could not see her, his face would become concentrated, and intense, and she would know that he was on some quest that he kept hidden from the world, and that there was a force driving him, and that behind the handsome young man with the sometimes flirtatious manner there lay a man who was very fine, and serious. And she wished that she could share his private world.

She wasn't going to throw herself at him. Sometimes she would say something to make him laugh. At other times she would engage him in a conversation that would show him she could be serious, and that she thought about the world. But it didn't seem to do her any good.

They were all going back to Paris in two days. The August afternoon was hot, the long garden filled with sun, dappled here and there by shade from the trees along its edges. There was scarcely a breath of wind and, apart from the occasional creak of a cart easing its way along the street, the only sound was the quiet hum of the bees visiting the roses and the warm, dry lavender bushes beside the lawn.

Uncle Marc had put a record on the gramophone in the salon, leaving the French doors open so that the sound of Debussy's 'String Quartet' wafted out on to the veranda where he was sitting with a book.

He was pleased with the record. 'It's played by the Capet Quartet. They're just starting a whole series of recordings. I got it from a friend,' he added with some pride. 'It's not even on sale yet.'

Apart from her grandfather, who was dozing, Marc was the only one on the veranda when Claire came out.

'Where's everybody?' she asked her uncle.

'Frank wandered down the garden. I think your mother's somewhere in the house. Don't know about the others,' he replied.

She was going to sit down, but then she thought she'd take a turn round the garden herself, so she started to walk along the lawn.

The music followed after her. The quartet had just reached its slow movement. How soft and sensuous it was, like the faint hum of the bees in the sun. She felt a bar of shade steal across her face, and then the sun touched her hair again.

The music was just rising to its first small climax, like a sudden, urgent whisper in that lazy afternoon, as she came to the hedge at the end of the lawn where one passed through an arch of privet into the green space beyond where there was a small tree, and roses, and red poppies, and blue cornflowers grew in a bed beside the grass.

And there she saw her mother standing with Frank. They were standing close. Her mother's face was turned up to his, and he was looking down, and there could be no doubt, she was sure there was no doubt, that Frank was about to kiss her mother, and that her mother wanted him to, the way she was smiling, with her face turned up.

And then they saw her, and they did not spring apart, but Frank half turned towards her to make it look as if they had just paused for a moment while they were talking, and he said something to her but she did not seem to hear what it was he said.

'I just wondered where everybody was,' she said, and looked at the flowers for a moment as though nothing had happened. 'Don't you love Uncle Marc's record?' she said, and then she went back through the privet hedge and made her way down the lawn. Uncle Marc glanced up at her, then down at his book. And when she was getting closer she saw him glance behind her and guessed that her mother and Frank were walking down the lawn too, talking as though nothing had happened. She didn't stop on the veranda, but went into the house. She would have gone to her room, but it was Frank's room at the moment, so she went into the courtyard instead, and out through the iron gateway into the street, and walked in the street for ten minutes before returning.

When Marc suggested to Frank that they go for a stroll the following morning, Frank was quite agreeable. They walked along to the château, talking of this and that, and Marc remarked that despite all the long royal history of the place, it was always the image of Napoléon, bidding farewell to his guards in the courtyard, before he left for exile, that came into his imagination each time he approached it.

'Tell me,' he suddenly said as they reached the gates, 'did your father give you any warnings before you came to France?'

'He gave me all sorts of advice. Things to do, things not to do.'

'What did he tell you to do when you met respectable young Frenchwomen?'

Frank looked a little taken aback.

'Well,' he answered cautiously, 'he told me to be careful to treat them with the same respect I would an American girl from a family like ours. We're pretty conservative, you know. But he said the French were even more so.'

'A girl like Claire, for instance.'

'Yes. Well, she's quite English, but it's the same.'

'You wouldn't want to make an enemy of her family.'

'No, I wouldn't. You don't think I've behaved improperly towards her, do you?'

'Not at all. I shouldn't have let you wander off into the night with her, but I'm sure no harm was done.'

'Absolutely none. I promise you.'

'I believe you. You realise she's in love with you?'

Frank looked astonished.

'Claire?'

'She watches you when you're not looking. You fascinate her.'

'Oh.'

'You like her?'

'Very much.'

'But you are being careful.'

'Very.'

'Whereas my sister's different.'

'I'm not sure what you mean.' Frank looked awkward.

'You couldn't shock me if you tried, my friend. Most young men think it would be fascinating to have an affair with an older woman, and my sister's very attractive. She's widowed. She can look after herself. No difficulties with her family, no complications. I think she quite likes you. You remind her of your father, obviously. You're very young, of course. She wouldn't want to make a fool of herself. But . . . who knows?'

Frank said nothing.

'But if by any chance you decide that you wanted to court Claire

– in a respectable way, of course – then you cannot sleep with her mother. It would be a very bad idea, and I will not allow it. Do you understand?'

'Yes.' Frank looked a bit shaken. 'I hadn't been thinking of . . . courting. I mean, I had no idea she was interested.'

'And you were afraid to flirt with her. Which left her mother.'

'I wouldn't put it like that. Her mother is remarkable . . .'

'I didn't say you shouldn't have fallen in love with an older woman. It's quite usual, you know.' Marc nodded to himself. 'France is a sensuous place, especially in summer. The warmth of the Mediterranean travels north, where it is diffused and softened. It's all in the music of Debussy, I should say.'

'I think I understand.'

'Well,' Marc ended cheerfully, 'choose one woman or the other, but not both. Let's get back for lunch.'

It was the end of the first week of September that Luc asked Louise if she'd like another client. She had three so far. One man she saw once a week, the others every two weeks. All three were middle-aged, respectable and rich. The first, the diplomat, lived in a handsome apartment in the broad avenue that led down from the Arc de Triomphe to the Bois de Boulogne. The second lived in the somewhat austere, fashionable quarter between the Eiffel Tower and Les Invalides. The third in an elegant apartment on the rue de Rivoli that interspersed modern, chic comfort with pieces that might have come from Versailles.

By spending two or three nights a week with interesting men in impressive surroundings, she now had all the spending money she needed, and was saving more than a thousand francs a week. It wasn't a fortune, but it was more than she could have made in any full-time employment. And Luc, who was getting the same, must be saving even more from her activities.

She understood now why girls became whores. If you could get the right clientele, the money was good, very good, and it was nice to have it.

'If you add this man, who's a charming fellow,' Luc pointed out, 'you'll almost double your savings.'

'Where do you find them?' she asked him, not for the first time.

'I've built up so many contacts over the years,' he answered with a shrug. 'And you're a great success. You have class, which is hard to find. People are talking about you.'

'One more is all I want, Luc.'

'Understood. The arrangement will be as usual. No names. At least, not at first. You'll meet for dinner. After that, it will be up to you.'

'And him. He may not like me.'

'He will. By the way, this man knows about a lot of things. You could learn from him.'

They met at the Café Procope, just off the boulevard Saint-Germain. He looked in his fifties, but well preserved. Greying temples. Above medium height. Quite slim. An intelligent face. He looked artistic, but she suspected he might be lacking the pugnacity of a creative artist. An intellectual of some kind. But one with money, clearly.

'I hear you're English,' he said pleasantly.

'Half English, half French,' she answered.

'Well, I don't know about your English, but your French is very good. And you model for Chanel?'

'Yes. It's quite interesting. And she is remarkable.'

'Indeed.'

She had a feeling he probably knew Chanel, but she wasn't going to ask. He'd tell her if he wanted her to know. The art was to be discreet.

They made light conversation. The Café Procope, with its gilt mirrors and pictures, was like stepping into the eighteenth century. She said she liked it.

'It was founded back in the seventeenth century. It's funny to think that Voltaire himself ate here, and it probably looked much the same. What other restaurants do you like?'

She wondered if he was expecting her to name some expensive places.

'Places with character.' She smiled. 'I'm just as happy in a bistro if it's interesting.'

'Really?' He looked at her thoughtfully. 'There are plenty of interesting places to eat if one knows where to look. By the way, do you know the origin of the word "bistro"?'

'I don't think so.'

'After Napoléon fell, and the Russians briefly entered Paris, the Cossacks were camped up on Montmartre and went into the little restaurants, and when the service was slow they kept shouting "bistro", which is Russian for "quick".' So the French started calling these informal restaurants bistros.' He shrugged. 'Well, that's the story anyway. It probably isn't true.'

They talked of many things. He was clever and amusing. By the time they'd finished the main course she was sure that she liked him. So much so that, for once, she even ventured to ask him a question or two.

'Luc is very discreet, monsieur, and so am I. But he told me that you were not married. And I am surprised that someone as charming as you doesn't keep a mistress.' She smiled. 'Unless you already do.'

He laughed.

'No, mademoiselle, I don't. Though I have done so in the past. But in my life at present, if I can find a suitable person – I mean someone like yourself, which is hard to find – then it's better for me to have an evening a week, let us say, to look forward to, than to have a constant companion.'

'Less personal commitment?'

'Not only that. I do so many things. I have a family business that occupies some of my time. I have many other activities. Often I go out on social engagements in the evening and then return home to work at night, or to read. I haven't room for a companion, to whom I should otherwise feel bound to give my attention. You may think this selfish, but it is the only way I can get things done.'

'Are you an artist, or a writer? I do not mean to pry.'

'I was an artist at one time. I prefer to write about these things now.'

'I have one other question, monsieur. Might I ask how it is that you know Luc?' She shook her head and smiled. 'I've never been able to work out how he knows so many people.'

He looked at her cautiously.

'You do not know?'

'No. I have always been curious.'

'Are you going to repeat what I tell you?'

'Absolutely not.'

'It is cocaine, mademoiselle. Luc has supplied cocaine to people for God knows how many years. Everyone. It is always pure. Everyone trusts him. He supplies . . . all sorts of people. And sometimes they ask him for other things.'

She stared at him. Of course. Everything made sense now. How could she have been so naive, and so stupid, not to have guessed? Was that how he knew Chanel? God knows. It was none of her business.

'He always has money,' she remarked, 'but I don't think he's rich.'

'The people like him are not the ones who get rich in that business. Often they become addicts themselves.'

'I don't think Luc uses the drug.'

'He doesn't. He's rare. I seldom use it myself. Sometimes, if I have too many things to accomplish, it helps me work through the night. That sort of thing.' He smiled. 'So, mademoiselle, I have answered all your questions. May I ask now if you'd be interested in seeing where I live?'

'I should be delighted, monsieur.' She meant it, and he could see that she did.

As they left the restaurant, she linked her arm in his. It was only a short walk to his place near the Luxembourg Gardens. On entering, they took the small elevator up to the third floor and entered his apartment. It seemed to be empty.

'I have only two servants that live in,' he explained. 'And they are up in the attic quarters for the evening. So we have the place to ourselves. Would you like a drink? I'm having a little whisky.'

'The same. Thank you.'

The apartment was impressive. She'd never seen so many paintings in a house in her life. She saw Manet, Monet, van Gogh . . .

'Turn on any lights you want,' he said, as he handed her a tumbler of whisky. 'I'll be back in a moment.'

She sipped her whisky and looked around. The salon was large. There was a grand piano in one corner with some framed photographs on it. She went across to look at them, turning on a table lamp to see them better.

They were not photographs designed to impress the visitor, but family photographs by the look of them. A number of them featured a tall, elegant woman. One was a wedding group. She saw her companion at once. He was a young man then, but quite unmistakable. She looked at the bride and groom.

And froze.

The groom was James Fox. The London lawyer. There was no mistaking him. Not a shadow of a doubt. She stood there staring at it.

Behind her, she heard him come back into the room. He came and stood beside her.

'That's you, isn't it?' She pointed to him in the group, trying to sound casual. 'Family wedding?'

'Yes. That's my sister in the middle, the bride. And that's her husband. An Englishman as it happens. But of Huguenot origins. They were called Renard, and anglicised it to Fox.'

'Interesting. The wedding looks French.'

'It was. At Fontainebleau. Her husband died, sadly. A very nice man. The flu, you know, after the war.' He pointed to the elegant woman in another picture. 'My aunt Éloïse. She had this apartment before I did. A remarkable woman.'

'She looks it,' said Louise, trying to sound interested.

Her mind was working fast. Fox. His Paris law office. The adoption. Blanchard. She turned back to the wedding group.

'So these would be your parents?'

'Correct. And that's my brother. He was the respectable one – in those days. I was the artist.'

'In your twenties.'

'Yes.'

'Very handsome.' She considered a moment, and chose her words. 'It looks the perfect bourgeois wedding. If you don't mind my saying so.'

He chuckled.

'That describes the Blanchard family, all right.'

'Would you excuse me a moment?'

He indicated a passage. 'Down there on the right.'

It took her a minute or two to collect herself. James Fox had married a member of the Blanchard family. It was too great a coincidence. This must be the same Blanchard family who knew who her father was. Probably one of themselves. And if her father was a

Blanchard, then the obvious candidate was just a few feet away from her.

And then, suddenly, she wanted to cry. So it had come to this: she'd almost found her father after all. But either it was this man, who now knew, or someone else whom he would tell, that she was a whore, and that Luc the cocaine dealer was her pimp. This was her life. What sort of welcome was that likely to earn her?

She sat very still. She did not allow herself to weep. But she saw her situation with icy clarity. If she didn't do something, she was about to sleep with a man who was probably her father.

She had to get out of there. Fast.

It was the first conflict Claire had experienced with her mother. But the conflict was silent, unspoken, never acknowledged. How could it be?

In the first minute, as she had walked down the lawn away from Frank and her mother, she had experienced only cold shock. By the time she'd entered the house, she was shaking. But as she wandered in the street, another sensation gradually began to take over.

Anger. Rage. How dare her mother try to steal her young man? She wasn't going to let her do it. She was young. She had good looks. She'd show her mother. She'd take Frank Hadley from her.

But powerful though the feeling was, it didn't last for long. By the time she passed the local parish church, it changed to a sense of hopelessness. Frank Hadley didn't belong to her. He'd made no sign that he wanted her at all. It seemed he wanted her mother, and perhaps he was going to get her.

There was nothing she could say. So she said nothing.

And her mother didn't say anything either. She carried on calmly, as if nothing was happening at all. If she'd raised the subject, she knew what her mother would say: 'He's flirting with me.' She'd shrug. 'It's amusing, I suppose.' And what could she say in return? Protest that it was disgusting? Then her mother would guess that she was jealous, that she wanted him for herself, but that he didn't want her. Why should she expose herself to that defeat?

So she gave no sign. She felt misery, resentment, humiliation. But she gave no sign at all.

As soon as they were back in Paris, they were both busy at the store. She watched for hints of Frank hanging around her mother. He didn't seem to be.

She was quite surprised, therefore, a week after her return when Frank telephoned her at Joséphine.

'I thought you might be interested. There is a whole crowd of us going up to Montmartre this evening. The Hemingways, some artists, some people from the Ballets Russes. If you're free, I thought you might want to be there. Hemingway told me to tell you to come.'

She had nothing special planned. And he was right, this was the sort of gathering she should be at.

'I'm wondering if my mother would like it,' she said.

'This is really a younger crowd.'

They met at the foot of the hill. There was a group of a dozen people waiting there when she arrived. Frank greeted her with the usual two kisses, but it seemed to her that there was a new warmth in his manner. Nothing obvious, but something.

A moment later the Hemingways arrived and they all cheerfully piled into the funicular cabin and rolled up the steep tracks. As the rooftops of Paris began to fall away below them, Frank, who was pressed quite closely beside her, whispered, 'I get vertigo in these things, but don't tell Hemingway.'

'He wouldn't mind,' she suggested.

'No, but he'd put it in a book.'

At the top, they walked across from the funicular to the steps in front of the great, white church, and looked across Paris as the early evening sun turned the rooftops into a golden haze, and the Eiffel Tower in the distance was like a soft grey dart pointing at the sky, and below them on the broad, steep steps that flowed down the hill, the people and the benches threw their lengthening shadows eastward.

Frank was standing beside her. He pointed towards the Bois de Boulogne that lay under the sun, and his hand rested on her shoulder as he did so. She experienced a tiny shiver and he asked her if she was cold, but she shook her head.

After they'd all stared at the view for a while, they went along the narrow street to the Place du Tertre and sat at a long table under the trees.

It was a good-humoured gathering. Claire knew some of the people. She thought she recognised a couple of the dancers from the Ballets Russes. Frank told her he thought Picasso might be coming, but there was no sign of him yet. There was a charming Russian with a kindly, pointed face sitting almost opposite her, in his mid-thirties she guessed, who told her in accented French that he'd lived in Paris before the war. 'I was in Russia again for a couple of years until I returned to France recently,' he explained. He smiled. 'Paris is the place to be these days.'

'Where did you spend the summer?' she asked.

'Brittany, some of the time,' he answered.

'Frank was up there too.' She indicated Hadley.

'I'm afraid I missed you,' he said to Frank, with a twinkle in his eye.

His name was Chagall, she discovered, but despite his years in Paris, he certainly wasn't among the names one had to know. Her uncle had never mentioned him. But he said he knew Picasso.

Frank already knew about him, however, and while Chagall was speaking to someone else he told her: 'He paints beautiful, intimate work, especially about his childhood in a Jewish shtetl. It's strange, almost surrealist stuff. Wonderful colours.'

'I heard that Vollard is arranging a show for you in America next year,' he said to the artist at the next break in the conversation. And Chagall nodded modestly. 'Will you go over for it?' Frank asked, but the Russian shook his head.

'Can't afford it.'

Claire was impressed that Frank was already ahead of her with this information. Obviously she'd better keep an eye out for Monsieur Chagall in the future.

They discussed Paris for a while, and all the exciting people in it.

'It's funny,' Claire remarked. 'If I listen to my uncle Marc, who's been at the centre of everything going on here for three or four decades, he talks of Paris as a French city, full of French culture. But you all see it as something else. As a place where all the artists come to play. So which is the real Paris, I wonder?'

Hemingway reached over and poured her some wine.

'Maybe it's in the eye of the beholder,' he said. 'Paris has always been proud of being a cultural centre ever since the university was set up. Now it's become the place that people come to from all over the world. So it's just a more international version of what it always wanted to be. A city's a huge organism. It can be all sorts of things at the same time. History may or may not remember the recent French presidents, but it's going to remember the Impressionists, and the Ballets Russes, and Stravinsky, and Picasso I suspect, all together. So what will Paris be? The memory of all those wonderful things. We remember Napoléon, the Corsican, and Eiffel, who was Alsatian, and most of us also remember that Ben Franklin lived here. That's Paris.' He grinned. 'Paris became an international city, so now it belongs to all of us. Everyone in the world.'

They started ordering food after that. And then Hemingway and Frank got into a friendly argument about Paris and New York, because Frank said that after Paris he wanted to go and live there.

'You stay here,' Hemingway told him. 'At the moment, at least, Paris is the only place to be.' He turned to Claire. 'Don't you agree?'

'For painting, dance, and fashion, everyone says it is,' said Claire. 'Though I love London theatre. What about music, though?'

'Stravinsky's here,' said Hemingway. 'What more do you want?'

'I want jazz,' said Frank. 'I want all that fresh rhythm and excitement and improvisation of jazz. That's in New York. And by the way,' he turned to Claire, 'I know London theatre has the best tradition in the world, but amazing things are happening in New York now. Eugene O'Neill will have five plays running on Broadway this season.'

But Hemingway wasn't having it.

'If you're going to write for the stage, Frank, then maybe. But none of the good writers of books and poetry want to be in New York. They're all in London and Paris. Eliot, Pound, Fitzgerald. Everyone's in Europe.'

'Not true. There's a crowd of writers in New York. They hang out together at the Algonquin Hotel every week.'

'A bunch of old women,' Hemingway retorted.

'They're not old women. They're bright, and they're young.'

'Give them time.'

It was obviously no use arguing with Hemingway, so Frank didn't try. Soon they were all eating. The waiters put small candles on the table as the sun went down.

By the end of the main course, a certain mellowness had descended upon the table. Claire noticed that Chagall had taken out some crayons and was quietly doodling on the paper tablecloth. By the candlelight, it looked like a goat in a green space and a lady in a flowing dress flying through a deep blue sky.

But then Hemingway rapped on the table and said he was going to read from something. And she supposed it might be one of his latest stories, and she was eager to hear it, but it wasn't his own, he told them.

'This is something I was shown in Shakespeare and Company the other day, and I liked it and thought you'd enjoy it too. It's the opening to a story that's still being written.'

Hemingway had a good voice for reading. It was a light baritone, unaccented, straightforward, like a correspondent reporting from a faraway place, and when he descended into the wide trench of the open vowels, his tone became somewhat gravelly.

But the place he was describing now, as he read from some sheets of typewritten paper, was not a war zone, nor was it an American forest, nor a big river or a mountain somewhere, but a long garden, and a wide French house, quite simple and provincial, with shutters on the windows, and a bed full of lavender and cornflowers where the bees hummed, and a veranda where an old man sat reading a newspaper, with his old wife who could no longer remember who he was, sitting by his side, and a pretty girl going into the house and past the kitchen where there was still a smell of oil and vinegar from a salad bowl that had been left on the wooden table.

And Claire realised that it was the house at Fontainebleau, and she stared at Frank, who was looking both embarrassed and pleased.

When Hemingway stopped, she whispered to Frank that he had written it, and he whispered back that he didn't know Hemingway was going to do that, and he shouldn't have shown it to him.

Then Hemingway said that he'd never read anything which conveyed the sounds and smell and feel of a place so well and so simply, and that it really made one want to know more about the characters, and especially the girl, who was still – he glanced towards Claire with a grin – tantalisingly mysterious. And he nodded to Frank, so that everyone understood he was the author.

Later that evening Frank took her home, and when he left her at the entrance to the building, he kissed her on the cheek, but he pressed her arms lightly as he did so.

'Hemingway really likes you,' he said. And she knew this meant that he did too.

When Marie thought back to the last days in Fontainebleau, she could almost have cried out in vexation.

When Marc brought young Frank Hadley to the house, and she had given him Claire's room, and put Claire in the boudoir beyond her own bedroom, she had told herself that it was not only a simple solution, but it protected Claire from the young man during the night. The only door to the boudoir led into her own room. No one could slip in or out of the boudoir during the night without crossing her bedroom, and she was a light sleeper.

So her daughter was safe. And of course it also followed – she admitted it freely to herself – that, with her daughter denied him, Frank was more likely to turn his thoughts to herself.

And why not? Why shouldn't she? If he was discreet. If she'd let the father slip through her fingers, why not the son?

It hadn't been difficult to interest him. Showing him things in the kitchen or about the house, taking him to the market and walking about the town with him, introducing him to the rich, sensuous world of provincial France in summer. She'd kept her figure. If her face contained lines, they were interesting ones. As a Frenchwoman, she walked with a poise and lightness that was different from the frank, easy movement of an American girl. All this was heady stuff for any young man looking for adventure.

As for herself, after the years of being alone, it made her feel young in a way that she had never thought she would again. As she looked at her face in the glass in the soft lamplight in the evening, and shook her hair loose, she thought the face she saw wouldn't look bad on a pillow. One night, when Claire was asleep, she'd slipped out of her nightdress and surveyed herself naked in front of her long mirror, and had been pleased to see that her breasts still looked so firm, and that she hardly had to pull her stomach in. When she turned to look behind, she saw only a few dimples, nothing much.

Day by day she had seen his interest growing. And when it had culminated that sensuous afternoon, at the end of the garden, she thought he was hers. Another moment and they would have kissed. It would have been enough to hold him. Perhaps they might have made love at Fontainebleau. It would have been difficult. They might have gone for a walk in the forest and kissed more passionately, at least. And then, another day or two, and once back in Paris, anything could have been arranged.

Just another moment, if Claire had not arrived.

But the next day, something had happened. He seemed suddenly to draw back. At least, he made no further move. There were two occasions when they found themselves alone in the house, once in the salon, once in the hall, but he did not come close either time. She wondered why. What had happened? Did he suddenly find her unattractive? Did she seem old? Was he afraid?

Frank was going to take the train back to Paris a day before the family left, and Marc said he'd drive him to the station. While Frank was waiting by Marc's car in the courtyard, Marie had come out and stood with him. They were almost as close as they had been in the garden, and she looked up at him and smiled, and he smiled too. But there was nothing else. Nothing at all.

'You said the other day that you'd never been to the Jardin des Plantes,' she said.

'I haven't.'

'This is a good time of year to go there. It's rather dull in winter. Telephone me, and I'll take you there.'

'Thank you. I will.'

A week passed. Then another. But he had not called.

Claire saw him. Marie and Marc were talking in the office one day when Claire put her head around the door and asked her uncle if he'd ever heard of an artist called Chagall. He hadn't and asked her why.

'He may be someone to watch. I met him the other night, in a crowd of people up at Montmartre.'

'Was anyone there that I do know?' Marc inquired.

'Hemingway.'

'Was Frank Hadley there?' asked Marie.

'Yes. I said hello, but I hardly spoke to him. He and Hemingway were arguing about something or other.'

Marie said nothing. Perhaps she should call him herself. Perhaps not. She hadn't heard a word from Roland de Cygne yet, either, though he was sure to be back in Paris by now.

She was feeling rather deserted when, a few days later, Claire came into her office and asked if Frank had got through to her on the telephone.

'He was trying to reach you, but he got me instead. He said you'd offered to take him to the Jardin des Plantes. Why don't we all go this Saturday?'

'Ah,' said Marie, and shrugged. 'If you like.'

They all had lunch at the Brasserie Lipp: Marc and Marie, Claire and Frank. Marc chose the Brasserie Lipp because it was conveniently close on the boulevard Saint-Germain, and Frank hadn't been there before. 'It's an institution,' Marc explained. 'You can't make a reservation. It doesn't matter who you are. But if they say you'll have a table in ten minutes, then you will.'

The brasserie specialised in German and Alsatian food. Marc and Frank ate sausages, and sauerkraut, washed down with German beer; the women ate *cassoulet*, and drank the dry Riesling of Alsace. When they had all eaten and drank too much, they came out of the brasserie and made their way eastward along the boulevard a little way before turning right into the big curving slope of the rue Monge.

'This is part of the hill of Roman Lutetia,' Marc reminded Frank. 'If you haven't seen it, the old Roman arena's coming up on our left in a few minutes.'

They walked slowly, Marc and Marie side by side, Frank and Claire a little ahead.

'They make a handsome couple, don't you think?' Marc said quietly to his sister.

'I was a little nervous about him,' Marie said. 'But I don't think they're interested in each other.'

Marc glanced at her.

'I wouldn't be sure of that,' he replied. 'She's certainly in love with him. I saw that at Fontainebleau.'

'You did? When she saw him up at Montmartre, she said they scarcely spoke.'

'What if he were serious about her? What if he wanted to marry her?'

'And take her away to America? A Frenchwoman in America?'

'She's half English, for a start. Would you have gone at her age, if you'd been asked?'

Marie did not answer. She frowned. Her mind was in a whirl. Was Marc right? Was that why Frank had suddenly drawn back? Was Claire closer to Frank than she realised? Was her daughter deceiving her? She was still lost in these questions when they came to the site of the old Roman arena.

'Paris was always supposed to have had a Roman arena, but nobody even knew exactly where it was until about sixty years ago,' Marc told Frank. 'They started building a depot for tramcars on the site and came upon the remains. We're still excavating, but as you see, the arena itself was a circle, with a semicircle of stone seats around one side of it. So they could have put stage plays on here as well.'

'It's a fair size,' Frank remarked.

'You could imagine between fifteen and twenty thousand spectators. About right for a significant Roman town.'

Claire was staring at the open central space. It was grey and dusty. There was a blank wall of an apartment building overlooking it.

'There seems something bleak about it,' she remarked. 'Did they have gladiators? People were killed here?'

'Of course,' said her uncle. 'This was the Roman Empire. Our classical tradition is splendid, but it was always harsh.'

Frank walked out into the centre of the big circle and looked around it thoughtfully. Claire went to stand beside him, and linked her arm in his. It was just a friendly gesture.

Marie was standing just beside one of the entrances to the ring that went into a tunnel under the stands. She supposed that the gladiators, and the sacrificial victims, passed through this way. She thought she could imagine how they felt. She glanced at Frank and Claire. Frank was looking across the ring the other way, but Claire was looking straight at her. And there could be no mistaking the little smile of triumph in her eye.

You want him, it said, but I have taken him from you, and now he is mine.

Then her daughter turned away.

*　　*　　*

It was a long time since Marie had been in the Jardin des Plantes herself, and she had almost forgotten how magnificent it was.

'The place was started by the king's doctors, back in the days of the Three Musketeers,' Marc told them. 'Then the Sun King brought in a team of the world's finest botanists, and they expanded it. And now . . .'

The sky was clear. The sun was still quite high, and if not quite so warm as at Fontainebleau, two weeks before, it was only the first tinges of yellow in the leaves of some of the trees that warned of autumn approaching.

They toured the long alleys, they admired the great cedar of Lebanon, brought from Kew Gardens in London, and looked at the little royal zoo, taken from Versailles after the Revolution. They visited the charming little Mexican hothouse. Marc and the two young people were clearly enjoying themselves. Marie smiled pleasantly.

But she scarcely saw what they were looking at.

Of course, she thought, how foolish she had been. What was her sudden passion for young Frank – an attempt to re-create a lost time with his father? Yes. An attempt to rekindle something in herself that she had not expected to feel again? That too. Was it normal? She didn't know. Was it absurd? No doubt.

She'd had her time. Indeed, she'd been lucky. James Fox had been a good husband. It was her daughter's turn for love now. Claire might be lucky or unlucky. That was for the Fates to decide. But young Frank belonged to Claire. And I am in danger, she realised, of making a fool of myself.

She glanced up at the sun. It was warm, but it was bright. No doubt it was picking out, stencilling, every wrinkle on her face. How harsh the sun was, how terrible.

And suddenly she was overwhelmed by a feeling of desolation, as if life had passed her by and, long before she was ready – for she was ready, never more so than now – fate and that terrible sun had sentenced her to exile. To a barren waste, and autumn cold, and emptiness.

They walked into the circular maze on its little hill. The winding path and the clipped hedges seemed like a prison to her.

Then Marc led them to the centrepiece of the Jardin, the vast exhibition hall of the Grande Galerie de l'Évolution. They paused outside for a few moments, gazing down the long grass esplanade in front of it.

She stared, but hardly noticed that Frank was standing by her side.

'By the way,' he said, 'I forgot to mention that I had a letter from my father yesterday. He told me to give you his best wishes.'

She nodded, and managed a smile.

'Please return mine to him, when you next write,' she said.

'Actually, you'll be able to give them in person,' Frank continued. 'His letter says he's coming to London next month. Unfortunately my mother isn't able to accompany him, which is a shame. But after that, he's coming to see me in Paris. I think he may stay here awhile.'

'Your father is coming to Paris?'

'Yes.'

'Oh,' said Marie.

As Louise approached the office of Monsieur Chabert the lawyer again, she wondered what he had found. She'd gone to him the very next day after the incident with Blanchard.

Luc hadn't been too pleased about her walking out on a customer. He'd come straight around to her place that night.

'Are you all right? I got a call to say you walked out.'

'I felt a little dizzy.'

'Did he do something bad to you? Was there something you didn't want to do?'

'Nothing like that.'

'So are you sick? He liked you. He was worried about you.'

'I can't see him.'

Luc went very quiet.

'You can't act like that,' he said. 'You have to tell me why.'

'I can't, Luc. But it won't happen again.'

He didn't reply for a moment. He seemed to be considering something.

'Make sure it doesn't,' he growled finally. 'I couldn't tolerate that.'

She didn't like the way he said it.

'I thought you were my friend.'

'I am, *chérie*. But think how this makes me look to him. I look like a fool. And it's bad for your reputation too.'

'I understand, Luc. It really won't happen again.'

He left after that. But there was tension in the air.

There was no tension today, however, with Monsieur Chabert. The little lawyer beamed at her.

'Mademoiselle, you gave me a very easy task. The gentleman concerned is Monsieur Marc Blanchard.' He gave her a quick summary of the family, of Gérard, Marc and Marie, the Joséphine store and the house at Fontainebleau. 'Interestingly, it is Marc's sister who married Fox the Englishman, who now runs the store. Marc was an artist. His work is considered talented, if not of the first rank.'

'Thank you, monsieur. This is exactly what I wanted.'

'If this family was involved directly with your mother, then there are two obvious possibilities. She might have been a servant in the house. Or possibly an artist's model.'

Louise thanked him, took the little dossier he had prepared and went home to consider it.

The next day she went to Joséphine. Explaining that she was a model for Chanel, it was easy to strike up a conversation with one of the young women working in the store, who had soon pointed out both Marie and her daughter to her. She obtained a good look at each of them.

Two days later, she took a train to Fontainebleau. When she reached the address Monsieur Chabert had given her, she entered the courtyard and went up the steps to the front door, where she rang the bell. A maid soon answered it. Might she speak to Monsieur Blanchard, she asked? 'My name is Louise Charles,' she added. It was a common name she'd chosen at random.

After a couple of minutes she was ushered into the salon, where she found an elderly man, looking a little puzzled.

She'd prepared a simple story. Her father, who had retired to the south, had once had a friend called Gérard Blanchard, whose family came from Fontainebleau. Hearing that she was visiting the town, her father had asked her to find out what happened to his friend.

'Mademoiselle,' the old man said, 'I regret to inform you that my son died during the war. His widow lives in Paris, however, as do his brother and sister.'

She explained that it was really Gérard that her father knew, but took his widow's address when the old man insisted on writing it down for her. She refused any refreshment, but thanked him for his kindness.

Out in the street, she walked a little way to the small square by the local church, where she sat down on a bench.

Had she just met her grandfather? She'd liked the old man. She hoped it might be so.

And if she had met Marc in some other circumstances, if she was still the person she had been before Luc had introduced her to her present life, she might have gone back and told the nice old man her story. If she could have convinced him that she hadn't come to cause trouble, he might have been persuaded to tell her who she was. And, if she was lucky, to say a word of kindness to her.

But she couldn't. Not now.

At least, she thought, if he really is my grandfather, I shall have met him and known what he was like.

So now she knew the Blanchard family. What could she do next?

The gallery was in the rue Taitbout, only a short walk from her apartment. She'd gone to several of the best galleries – Vollard, Kahnweiler and Durand-Ruel. She quite enjoyed her quest. It was educational. They all knew Marc Blanchard, but it was the assistant at Durand-Ruel who knew where his work was to be found.

'It's a small gallery, quite new. The Galerie Jacob,' she was told.

The gallery was certainly small, and Monsieur Jacob turned out to be a young man, only a little taller than herself, with delicate features.

'My grandfather has an antiques business, and my father helps him, so I wanted to do something different,' he explained. 'I'm delighted if you are interested in the work of Marc Blanchard. He was very helpful to me in getting started, and I represent him. If you stay in the gallery, I'll bring some of his work for you to see.'

They spent quite a while looking at canvases. Though she didn't know much about art, it seemed to her that the work was good. Several were portraits, and she told him she'd like to see more of them. He had almost a dozen.

'Do we know who any of these young women are?' she asked him.

'Most are studio models, or people he happened to meet. They tend not to have names. The commissioned works are nearly all in private collections, though there are sketches for many of them. He has more work that he keeps himself. I could always ask him. Would you like to meet him?'

'No,' she said. 'That won't be necessary.'

One picture in particular intrigued her. It was a nude. A young girl with a very pretty body and long hair. It seemed to Louise that she looked a little like herself.

Was she looking at her mother?

'Again,' said Jacob, 'no name.'

'I should like to come and look at some of these again,' said Louise. 'If you can find out the names of some of the sitters, that would also interest me.' She smiled. 'It would be a present for my husband. He likes to put names to people.'

'And your own name, if I may ask, madame?' said Jacob.

She reached into the little bag she was carrying, as if to take out a visiting card, and frowned. 'I have left my cards at home. I am Madame Louise. I shall call in again in two or three weeks.'

She wondered whether it would turn out that any of the models was named Corinne.

The note from Roland de Cygne early in October was profuse in its apologies, and rather touching. During August, down at the château, his son had become ill – so much so that at one point the doctor had feared for his life.

All was well now, however. Father and son were safely back in Paris, where the boy was to convalesce for a month.

Sure enough, a few days later, he telephoned to ask if she would like to go to the opera. As it happened, she could not go on the evening he suggested. But wanting to be friendly, especially after his troubles with his son, she made a countersuggestion.

'I met the manager of the Gobelins factory the other day, and he offered to give me a private tour of the place. On the last Monday of October, in the morning. I wonder if you and your son would like to join me. Perhaps it might amuse him.'

The offer was accepted at once.

*   *   *

633

Why was it, Marie would sometimes ask herself in later years, that of all the many discussions she had, during two turbulent decades, about the destiny, even the survival, of the world she knew, the one she most remembered was a short and unplanned conversation with a boy?

The Gobelins factory was in the Thirteenth Arrondissement, about half a mile south of the Jardin des Plantes. The manager gave them a delightful tour of the collection of buildings.

'As you see, we have returned to making tapestries, just as we did in the time of Louis XIV,' he explained, and showed young Charlie de Cygne the working of the looms. 'Some of these are the original seventeenth-century buildings. They were set up beside the little River Bièvre, which runs into the Seine near the Île de la Cité, so that the river could provide water power when it was needed. But do you know what else was made here?'

'You made furniture for quite a while,' said Roland.

'Indeed, monsieur, that is correct. But we also made statues.' He pointed to a couple of buildings. 'They were foundries. We supplied most of the bronze statues in the gardens of Versailles.'

'Has the works been going continuously since Louis XIV?' young Charlie de Cygne asked.

'Almost. As you may know, the wars of the Roi Soleil were so expensive that he ran out of money once or twice. We briefly had to close in the 1690s, then for about a decade after the Revolution. And then, unfortunately, during the Commune of 1871, the Communards burned part of the factory down, which interrupted our work for some time.'

It was clear that the manager was no lover of the Communards, and he glanced at de Cygne, clearly hoping that the aristocrat would express his distaste for them, but Roland said nothing.

The visit was a success. After they came out, it being almost the lunch hour, Roland asked if Marie would like to eat something.

'Why don't we just go into a bistro?' she suggested.

It seemed to Marie that Charlie de Cygne was a nice fourteen-year-old, rather shy, who resembled his father and had manners of respectful politeness that only someone like Roland de Cygne could have taught him. It also seemed to her that he was perfectly well and ready to go back to school again. His father, however, was still showing lines of worry. He'd lost weight. She felt a strong maternal urge to feed him.

'You'll have a steak with me, won't you?' she asked, although she would much rather have had a salad. And when he had finished that, she persuaded him to eat a strawberry flan with Chantilly cream. Getting young Charlie to eat, of course, was not a problem.

They took their time, chatting of nothing in particular, but being careful to ask Charlie what he thought of the Gobelins factory, and making him part of the conversation.

As she and Roland had coffee, he asked her if he might smoke a cigar, and she was fascinated when, instead of an elegant lighter, he pulled a strange little object made of a shell casing out of his pocket. 'I always carry this with me,' he explained with a smile, as he laid the lighter on the table. 'It brings me luck.'

And it was then that Charlie asked a question.

'The man at the Gobelins factory said that the Communards burned the place down. That's not so long ago. Do you think something like that could happen again?'

Marie and Roland looked at each other.

'Yes,' said Roland.

'I don't know if you heard about it, Charlie,' said Marie, 'but just this weekend, Zinoviev, who's an important man in Communist Russia, wrote a letter to one of the British Labour leaders outlining how they should work together for world revolution. That's what they want.' She nodded firmly. 'The whole of England's in an uproar. There's a general election in two days, and this will probably put the Conservatives back in power.'

'Today's paper says that Zinoviev claims it's a forgery,' Roland remarked.

'But he would say that, wouldn't he?' Marie answered.

'This is true.'

'But are there many Frenchmen who really want a communist revolution,' asked Charlie, 'like in Russia?'

'Certainly,' said his father. 'You and I would both be killed, my son. And Madame Fox too, I'm afraid.'

'You know such men, Father?'

Roland picked up the little lighter and looked at it thoughtfully.

'Oh yes. I have known such men. And there are many of them.'

'People at school say that the Jews are behind the revolutionary movements,' said Charlie. 'Do you think it's true?'

'No less a person than the great Lord Curzon, who's the British foreign secretary, has just made a speech about the Zinoviev letter,' said Marie, 'where he reminds us that most of the inner ruling circle of the Bolsheviks are Jews. So he seems to think there's a connection.' She shrugged. 'He would know more than we do. I have a few Jewish friends who I'm quite certain are not revolutionaries.'

Slightly to her surprise, the aristocrat wasn't content to let it go at that.

'Lenin himself, of course, was not Jewish in the least. In fact, he was technically a Russian noble, you know. To the surprise of his audiences, his revolutionary speeches were made in a highly aristocratic accent.' He smiled at the irony of this truth. 'But you must be very careful, my son,' he continued. 'Your school friends are partly thinking of the famous Protocols of the Elders of Zion, a document which outlined a Jewish plan to take over the world. It was a complete forgery. We know this for certain now.'

'Lots of people still believe in it, however. Especially in America,' Marie pointed out.

'*Oui, madame.* But that is partly because Henry Ford, the motor manufacturer, is obsessed with it and tells all the world it's true. But it's still a forgery.' He paused a moment. 'I am sensitive to this because, as you will remember, I myself was entirely persuaded of the guilt of Dreyfus when I was a young man. I thought he was a traitor because he was Jewish.'

'So did half of France.'

'That in no way excuses me. It is now absolutely established that he was innocent.'

'So you do not think the Jews are behind the revolution, Father?' His son wanted clarity.

'There are many Jews who are in the revolutionary movement, especially in Germany and Eastern Europe. It may also be true that, because Jewish families have historically been more mobile, that there is a Jewish network that will operate, along with other networks, in spreading international revolution. Many people think it, but I do not know if it is so or not. For there are plenty of revolutionaries who are not Jewish. There are also many Jews who are not revolutionaries. You must be guided by the evidence, my son, not by rumour or prejudice.'

'But you do think that there is a danger of international revolution spreading from Russia around the world.'

'I am quite certain that is true.'

'So what should we do, Father?'

'It remains to be seen. The revolutionaries are ruthless. Perhaps the democracies of the free world are strong enough to defend themselves against them. I hope so. But it may be that the free world will have to adopt some of the tactics of the revolutionaries to counteract them. Beat them at their own game.'

'What sort of organisation are you thinking of?' Marie asked.

'I'm not sure. Perhaps some kind of order, like the crusading orders of long ago. Perhaps military governments. We shall need strong leaders, certainly, and we don't have them now.'

'It sounds a little frightening.'

He smiled.

'Not as long as we have good people like you, madame, and I hope myself too, to keep us all sane.'

'And what do you think, Charlie?' she asked the boy.

'I'm ready to fight,' he said. 'Father tells me I may have to.'

'And who will you fight?'

'The communists, I suppose, madame.'

So the conversation ended. The two de Cygnes returned home. She went across the river to Joséphine. But she never forgot it. They had said nothing out of the ordinary. Any conservative, and even some liberals, in both France and Britain would have expressed the same sort of views. She, too, had thought them natural, at the time.

The arrival of Mr Frank Hadley Sr at the end of October was marked by a gathering at Marc's apartment. All the Blanchard family were there, except for Marc's parents. But Marc was going to take the Hadleys down to Fontainebleau for lunch the following week.

He'd asked Roland de Cygne, who had said that he'd be delighted to see the American again after so many years, and asked if he might bring his son. There were also a couple of art historians and one or two dealers, including young Jacob – all people whom Hadley might enjoy meeting.

He was standing beside his son, talking to young Jacob, when Marie entered the room. And he recognised her at once and smiled, and she went towards him to greet him.

But she was ready for him now. She was prepared. She'd seen a recent photograph that young Frank had shown her, so she knew that there were some strong lines creasing his cheeks nowadays, and crow's-feet from a quarter of a century of smiling pleasantly at his students. And she knew that he was still just as tall and athletic as before, because regular exercise had toned his body and preserved his figure. And she knew that there was a little greying at the temples. But the photograph, being black and white, could not convey the healthy youthfulness of his complexion, and the rich colour of his hair; and so although she was well prepared and totally in control of herself, and greeted him as an old family friend, she was all too aware of the little gasp, the intake of breath that caught her unawares, despite all her preparation, as she crossed the room towards him.

They chatted easily. Roland de Cygne came and joined them.

'I am sorry that your wife could not come with you,' Marie said.

'So am I. But her sister lost her husband recently, so she wanted to spend a little time with her. And she doesn't really like to travel.'

'Hates the sea,' said his son. 'She won't come sailing with us.'

'And where are you staying?' asked Roland.

'I thought I'd stay a month, revisit old haunts, that kind of thing. So instead of a hotel, I took an apartment in the Eighth, overlooking the Parc Monceau. There's a housekeeper who comes in each day. It suits me very well.'

'I should like to give a dinner for you,' said Roland de Cygne.

'That would be very kind.'

'Have you retired from teaching, to be away for so long?' Marie asked.

'I'm not ready to retire for a long time yet,' Hadley answered. 'But I took a sabbatical. With my son in France, it seemed a good time. I'm doing a little monograph on the Impressionists in London.' He smiled. 'Did you know that when he did all those paintings of the Thames, and the London fog, Monet was staying at the Savoy Hotel? Painted looking out of the window. He stayed at the Savoy for weeks. So much for the struggling artist!'

'I hope a stay at the Savoy formed part of your own research,' said de Cygne.

'As a matter of fact,' Hadley answered cheerfully, 'it did.'

He still spoke excellent French. As she looked at young Frank, watching the little group with Claire, she thought how nice it must be for him to have a father he could feel so proud of.

The next ten days were busy. Marc, she and Claire took the two Hadleys for an evening in Montparnasse, starting with a drink at the expatriate Dingo Bar, and ending with a long meal at La Coupole. The Hadleys went on a long afternoon tour from the Louvre, across to Notre-Dame and ending with a meal at a bistro in the Latin Quarter, but she was too tied up at the store to join them. For the same reason, she couldn't go down to Fontainebleau with them, though she would have liked to. But she did attend the dinner for Hadley at the mansion of Roland de Cygne.

It was an interesting evening. He had invited both the Hadleys, a French diplomat and his wife, who had recently spent some years in Washington, together with their daughter, who was young Frank's age. There was also a rich American lady who lived in a palatial apartment on the rue de Rivoli, and the daughter of a French count, whose family had an art collection, and being only seventeen, was obviously there as company for young Charlie, who had been allowed to join the grown-up party.

It was interesting to watch. At the drinks beforehand, Roland introduced everyone with charming grace, and they all seemed to find plenty to talk about. The diplomat and his wife were old hands at this sort of thing, but it was clear that Hadley was no stranger to smart social gatherings, and he and the rich American lady soon found people they both knew.

They sat ten at dinner, and Roland asked Marie to act as his hostess. Since the dinner was being given for Hadley, he was on her right, and the French diplomat on her left. Conversation was easy. Halfway down the table, young Charlie de Cygne, despite his strict upbringing, was staring in open-eyed admiration at the aristocratic young girl on his right, who was exceptionally pretty. Marie noticed, and so did Roland. Their eyes met, and they silently shared their amusement.

Only a certain number of people in Paris could give an aristocratic dinner of this kind. The setting, the family silver and china, the footmen behind every chair – hired in to be sure, but looking entirely in place in such a house – the wonderful food and wine: Was Roland, by putting her at the head of the table opposite him, showing her what he had to offer any potential wife? He might be.

Meanwhile, however, Hadley was sitting beside her, looking impossibly handsome, and she knew she was looking her best herself. It occurred to her, with a little frisson, that if she was going to make a discreet pass at Mr Hadley Sr, then this would be a good moment to do it. If she could do so, that is, without it being visible to his son, or her daughter, or Roland de Cygne.

But how? Making light conversation with him was certainly easy. During the last quarter of a century, Hadley had acquired a rich fund of amusing stories, which made him a delightful dinner companion. She watched his friendly eyes, to see if they were indicating that he was also finding her attractive. It was hard to tell. More promising, he was fascinated that she ran a business.

'Since the war,' he said, 'a lot of young American city women are going to work. But they never get to run anything. Is it different now, in France?'

'I think it only happens in family businesses,' she said. 'But it wasn't forced on me, and I must say I enjoy it.'

He asked her all sorts of questions about how she ran Joséphine, and her answers seemed to impress him.

'I think you are remarkable,' he said, and she could see that he meant it. Good, she thought. She intrigued him. That was a start.

She asked him one or two innocuous questions about this wife of his, who didn't like to travel. But she received only innocuous answers. Mrs. Hadley was a good wife and mother. She liked tennis. She had a talent for flower arranging. This was all information that might have been said about any wife, but it was not accompanied by any of the slight inflections that a man sometimes uses to hint that his wife is boring him. She suspected that, even if he were dissatisfied at home, he would never show it. But that was hardly to her purpose.

She reminded him of their visit to Giverny long ago, and he became quite enthusiastic about the subject. She caught a certain light in his eye as he remembered that summer day, but whether it was engendered by herself or by the garden she wasn't sure.

She also learned that he would be remaining in Paris for another three weeks before taking the liner back to America. So if she was going to spend time with Mr Hadley while he was in Paris, she had better do it soon.

'Would you like to look over the store?' she suddenly suggested. If he was intrigued by the idea of her business, that seemed a promising venue. Taking him around the offices and the storerooms opened up all sorts of possibilities for moments of private intimacy.

'Yes,' he said. 'If it's not too much trouble, I should.'

'Then telephone me at my office tomorrow,' she said. 'I need to check my appointments, but we can arrange a time.'

She felt decidedly pleased with herself. Whether he had understood her design and was complicit she wasn't sure. It didn't matter. She just needed to get him to herself.

A new course was being served. With a charming smile, she turned to talk to the diplomat on her left.

The next day she casually asked Claire if she had any plans for seeing young Frank that week, and learned that she was taking him to a fashion show at Chanel the following day.

'It's a small afternoon show for some of her customers, but he's never been to such a thing.'

Perfect. With Claire and Hadley Junior otherwise engaged, she would have his father entirely to herself. She smiled at her daughter kindly.

'Enjoy yourselves.'

So she was more than a little surprised and vexed, an hour later, when instead of a call from Mr Hadley, she received a visit from her brother.

'Hadley just called me. He's asking if he can see us. Just you and me. Privately. He wonders if we could meet at his apartment. It's not far.'

'I suppose so. When?'

'Tomorrow afternoon.'

The apartment was on the third floor, in a big, ornate mansion block. It had a handsome double salon whose windows looked over the leafy, well-tended walks of the Parc Monceau. It was furnished in the rich style – heavy carpets and hangings, gilded ornaments, Louis XV furniture – so favoured by the great banking families of the late nineteenth century. Not quite Hadley's style perhaps, but he seemed to be enjoying it as a place to stay.

As soon as they'd sat down, he came straight to the point.

'We know each other well enough to be completely honest with each other,' he said, 'so I want to ask you both. What are we to do about my son and Claire?'

Marie sat up sharply. She looked at Marc, who seemed quite unfazed.

'Are you suggesting they've . . .'

'No. My son assures me not, and I believe him. But he's falling in love with her.'

'Have they really had time to be so much in love?' Marc asked.

'I don't know. But the first thing Frank told me when I arrived was that he's glad I've come, because he thinks he's found the girl he wants to marry.'

'I'm against it,' said Marie.

'Why?' asked Marc.

'Because I don't see young Frank in France for the rest of his life, and I don't see Claire in America.'

'You've never been to America,' Marc pointed out. 'By the way,' he asked his sister, 'has Claire talked to you about this?'

'No. She hasn't.'

'I'm surprised,' said Hadley.

'The young are strange,' said Marie crossly. 'I don't understand them.'

'What surprises me,' Hadley remarked, 'is that neither of you have mentioned the question of religion. My son is not a Catholic.'

Marc shrugged. He didn't care.

'Claire's life has been a little unusual. One could say that she has been brought up to be both,' Marie said. And she explained the bargain that James Fox had originally struck with her father.

'I had no idea,' said Hadley.

'We must also remember that Claire has been brought up in England rather than France,' Marc added. 'The cultures are closer than France and America.' He turned to Hadley. 'You haven't expressed your own view.'

'I haven't got one,' said Hadley. 'I know your family.'

'All too well,' said Marc drily.

'I've also had a chance to get to know Claire a little, and I like her very much.'

'Your son's a good boy too,' said Marc. 'None of us has anything against him.'

'Your son does you credit,' Marie agreed.

'The point is this,' said Hadley. 'If my son wants to propose, and if Claire wants to accept him – which it seems none of us knows – what are we all going to do? Are we going to forbid it?'

Marc indicated that he wasn't worried personally. Marie was silent.

'You know,' Hadley added quietly, 'I can stop it. I could put my son on a boat to America tomorrow if it's necessary.'

'You realise, don't you, that if they marry, your son will probably take my only child three thousand miles away across the ocean, where I shall never see her, or my grandchildren. Quite apart from the fact that I need her at the store.'

'Then perhaps I should act,' said Hadley.

Marie shrugged.

'Let her decide for herself,' she said miserably.

The next few days were not easy for Marie. It was as though a spell had been cast over the last three months. The shock of the first encounter with Frank Hadley Jr, then the excitement of his father's arrival, had blinded her to the cold, grim reality that if her daughter fell in love with young Frank, he would take her away forever and she would be alone for the rest of her life. And when she thought of that, she cursed the young man's coming.

She asked Claire what she thought of young Frank the next evening, when Claire was reading a magazine, and Claire looked up and said he was nice enough, which was clearly an evasion.

'Well, don't go falling in love with him, unless you want to find yourself cut off from everything you love, in America – which all the Americans seem to be trying to get away from,' she said, as though she were joking, but they both knew she wasn't.

'I'd like to see New York,' said Claire, casually, turning back to her magazine. And Marie wanted to continue the conversation, but realised that it was no good, and silently cursed the fact that the little scene in the garden at Fontainebleau had left her, forever, in a false position with her daughter.

She wished there was someone to comfort her, but Marc was no real support, and she didn't want to share her thoughts with de Cygne. And Hadley didn't call.

It was three days after the meeting that she went to Hadley's apartment. She really hadn't meant to. She hadn't planned it at all.

She'd had a lunchtime meeting with a designer who had a little studio on the rue de Chazelles, just above the Parc Monceau. As she came out, she saw that despite the fact that it was November, it was a bright afternoon with a wintry sun in the sky, so she decided to walk through the park, as she had done so many times as a child, and continue down to the boulevard Haussmann and across to her office.

And having decided that, it was only a very small detour to ring the bell of Hadley's apartment, in case he'd like to walk with her in the park.

He was in. He came straight down.

The park was such an elegant little place, with curling walks, and statues discreetly placed upon lawns or under trees. In the morning, nannies wheeled prams there, and rich little children played, but it was nearly deserted now. There were still golden leaves on many of the trees.

'I'm glad you came,' he said. 'I almost called you. I realised afterwards what a terrible thing it must be for you that my son might take your daughter away, and I wasn't sure what to do.'

'I shall feel very lonely. But . . . It's her life, not mine.'

He offered his arm. She took it. They walked a little way.

'Our families have seen a few things together,' he said.

'Have we?'

'I was thinking of the time, all those years ago, when Marc got in trouble with that girl about the baby . . .'

'The baby was adopted in England by a very good family, so she's all right,' Marie remarked. 'She's probably a happily married Englishwoman by now.' She smiled. 'That's one bit of the past that can be left to rest in peace. I never even knew her name.' She sighed. 'It's amazing what we don't know.' She walked on with him in silence for a little way. 'Talking of the past, did you know I was in love with you in those days?'

He hesitated.

'I thought that, maybe a little.'

'It was more than that.'

'Oh.'

'Do you mind?' She looked up at him.

'No. I'm very flattered.' He paused. 'You probably didn't know that Gérard warned me off.'

'He what?'

'Well, you know, wrong religion, America not where the family wanted their only daughter, and all the rest. He was perfectly nice about it. I never liked him much, but he didn't accuse me of seducing you or anything. Well, not quite. He found us in the grotto in the Buttes-Chaumont, if you remember.'

'Gérard.' She shook her head in mystery. Gérard, who'd been betraying her since she was a child. She might have cried out, 'May he rot in hell!' though she did not. But she stopped walking for a moment, and stared at the ground. Hadley put his arm around her to comfort her, and neither of them moved. Then she indicated that they should walk on, and he offered his arm again, and this time she clung to it so that her head rested against his shoulder.

'You know,' she said, 'I always felt that I missed my chance. So if Claire wants to go away to America with Frank, I can't stand in her way. I don't want her to miss hers.'

'I'm sorry I caused you pain,' he said quietly. 'I don't know if I would have proposed. But I might have.'

'It's nice of you to say so.'

'It's true,' he said simply.

They had crossed the park now, to its eastern corner, where there was a pond, partly enclosed on one side by a charming Roman colonnade. It was a romantic place.

Marie straightened herself and turned her face up to him.

'You know,' she said with a smile, 'we could make up for lost time. While you are here in Paris.'

He stared at her.

'Are you suggesting . . .?'

'It's nice to close unfinished history.'

'No doubt.'

She could tell from the way he said it that the idea was not at all unattractive to him. That was something, at least.

'I'm a married man.'

'You're in Paris. Nobody will know.'

'There are things to think of,' he said.

'One can think too much.'

'One can think too little. And what about my son and your daughter? If they were to marry?'

She shrugged.

'It's good to keep these things in the family.'

'Only a French person could say that.'

'We're in France.'

He sighed and shook his head.

'Marie, I swear to God I'd like to. But I can't.'

'Let me know,' she said, 'if you change your mind.'

But he never did.

In May 1925, Mr Frank Hadley Jr and Mademoiselle Claire Fox were married in Fontainebleau. The bridegroom's father came across the Atlantic to attend the wedding. He could stay only a few days. But everything went off very well.

The following week, Marie received a visit from her friend the Vicomte de Cygne. He was looking very spruce and handsome in a pale grey suit, with a flower in his buttonhole.

He asked her to marry him. She asked for a little time to consider.

Chapter Twenty-three

1936

All sons are wiser than their fathers. And as Max Le Sourd looked at his father, Jacques, he felt concern. Max wasn't thirty yet, his father was past seventy. But there were things his father did not understand.

And Max was wondering: Was he going to have to tell him?

Early afternoon. A weekday in June, in a fateful year.

From all over the world, athletes had already started making their way towards a new Olympic Games, to be held in Berlin, and hosted by Germany's Nazi regime. Russia was not attending, but despite individual protests, other nations were.

In Spain, the election of a Popular Front of leftist parties had left the old conservative forces furious, and summer arrived, and left- and right-wing forces eyed each other tensely, there was danger in the air.

And in France . . .

On any normal day, there should have been cars in the Champs-Élysées, and people crowding the broad walkways under the small trees. But there were almost no cars, and few people. It was eerily quiet. As they gazed down towards the distant Louvre, it seemed that all Paris had fallen strangely silent.

Jacques Le Sourd turned to his son.

'I thought I wouldn't live to see it,' he confessed.

Once before, he'd thought it had begun. There had been that moment during the war, when the army had mutinied. He'd thought it was starting then. But he'd been premature. France had not been ready.

Russia had been ready, though. The Russian Revolution had succeeded. And with that massive example before all Europe, it had seemed inevitable to Jacques Le Sourd that now it would spread. The question had been: Where next?

By the mid-twenties, all eyes had fallen on Britain. France might be the cradle of revolution, but Britain was also a logical choice. Wasn't Britain the first home of capitalism, colonial empire and exploitation? Wasn't London where Karl Marx had written *Das Kapital*?

The Zinoviev letter of 1924, forgery or not, might have frightened the British middle classes into electing a Conservative government, but the Labour Party and the unions were soon ready to show their power. And in 1926, a huge general strike had brought Britain to a standstill.

Was it the beginning of a revolution? All Europe had waited. If the British Empire fell to the workers, then the rest of the capitalist world could crumble.

But once again, the phlegmatic British had displayed their lack of interest in ideas, their endless capacity to muddle through and compromise. The British bourgeoisie had come out, manned the buses, taken over the essential union jobs. Professional people, students, retired army officers were found driving trains. And they'd been allowed to get away with it. Jacques had even heard stories of an opposing line of strikers and British policemen organising a football game between each other. He sighed whenever he thought of it. What could you do with people like that?

For another decade, France had drifted. With a weak franc – good for the British and American visitors, but bringing inflation to the French themselves – the weak liberal governments of the Third Republic had tottered on, still opposed by the old guard of monarchists, conservative Catholics and military men. When America's Great Depression hit Europe, French jobs were lost and wages fell.

Jacques Le Sourd had known how to use the time, however. Endless quiet campaigning with the Socialist Party, writing and distributing pamphlets, talking with union men, visiting small works and large factories: this had been his life.

'When the new revolution comes,' he would tell his son, 'Paris will be the key. Not only because it's the political and spiritual centre of France, but because of the industrial workers here. When I was a young man,' he'd explain, 'most manufacturing around the city was done in workshops and small plants. But now we have huge factories, producing things like cars, that didn't even exist before.' More than once he had taken Max down to the suburb of Boulogne-Billancourt, which lay in a great loop of the river south of the Bois de Boulogne, and taken him through the gates into the Renault works. 'The men here,' he told him, 'will one day have the destiny of France in their hands.'

Though Jacques always reminded his son that he was just one of many good socialists giving the lead, it pleased young Max to see how, in the huge car works and in smaller plants all over the city, his father was respected.

And two years ago, the work of Jacques Le Sourd and his friends had been rewarded.

At the start of 1934, the old guard had occupied the parliament and tried to stage a coup. Within days, the socialists and the communists of France cooperated in a general strike. Millions put down their tools. In Paris, the workers filled the streets. The country came to a standstill. The old guard were kicked out.

'Now's the time to play politics,' Jacques had urged. 'All our efforts will be for nothing unless we can win political power.'

A grand coalition had been formed. First the two great trade unions – the moderate CGT and the communist-led CGTU – had come together. Cleverer still, the political parties had come to a subtle agreement. His own Socialist Party and the French Communist Party had arranged that the communists would give silent support to the socialists, but take no part in any government, so as not to frighten off the bourgeoisie. With this reassurance, and a promise to respect private property and not to nationalise the banks, the left had been able to form a coalition with the bourgeois radical and liberal parties of the centre.

'Call it the Popular Front,' Jacques said, 'and we could win an election.'

He'd been right. By the start of 1936, the Popular Front was ready to fight an election. A month ago, at the start of May, the Popular Front had won, and Léon Blum, the Jewish leader of the Socialist Party, was prime minister of France.

When Le Sourd had been asked if he'd like any government job, Max had assumed he would accept. But his father had surprised him.

'There's something more important for me to do,' he'd said. And despite his age, he'd thrown himself into another, feverish round of activity. Meetings with important union men, visits to factories: for three weeks Max hardly saw him. But when he did, his father always said the same thing.

'Now is the moment, Max. Strike while the iron is hot. Everything is possible, if we act fast.'

His father was right. All over France, from plant to plant, strikes started breaking out as workers, bolstered by the thought of having a socialist government, began demanding all rights: a forty-hour week, paid holidays, wage increases. As Jacques had also predicted, the key was Paris, and by late May he could point out triumphantly: 'Thirty-two thousand workers have occupied the Renault factory at Boulogne-Billancourt. Every big engineering works around Paris is out on strike now. That's another hundred thousand men. The workers of the Bloch aircraft factory out at Courbevoie are with us.'

A few days ago, there were two million Frenchmen out on twelve thousand separate strikes.

The part of the Champs-Élysées where they were standing lay less than halfway down from the Arc de Triomphe, just above the Art Nouveau glass houses of the Grand and Petit Palais. The triangle of streets that lay between this section and the River Seine was becoming known as the Golden Triangle, the Triangle d'Or, for as well as the American Cathedral church and the recently built Hotel George V, it was home to some of the richest people and most elegant enterprises in the city.

It wasn't an area that Jacques Le Sourd would normally care to visit. But today he had come there, for the satisfaction of seeing it all shut down.

They crossed the Champs-Élysées. As they walked between the trees on the avenue's northern side, Jacques glanced at his son with affection.

If he'd taken a long time to find a wife, his marriage was a happy one. He'd met Anne-Marie when he was forty and she was twenty-five, when she had come to work for the Socialist Party. He hadn't thought of her as anything but a young colleague at first. But as he'd come to know her a little better, he'd been astonished by her

650

direct and uncompromising mind. He'd never known any woman like her.

She was southern, with straight black hair and pale skin. Her father was a worker from Marseille, her mother a devout Catholic from the countryside of Provence, and she spoke with a Provençal accent. But everything else in her life she'd decided for herself. When he asked her if she was religious, she replied simply: 'No one has ever given me any useful proof that God exists, so obviously I can't believe in Him.' The idea of faith without proof didn't make any sense to her.

In the same way, socialism wasn't a passion or a religion with her – as it was for so many in the movement. She'd just decided that capitalism was unjust, and socialism was more logical. After that, she couldn't see the point of arguing about it.

He had been fascinated by this strange girl from Provence. He found himself spending more and more time in her company. After a year had passed, they had become inseparable. 'We may as well live together,' she'd remarked one day, 'since we're never apart.' When she became pregnant with Max, they'd married.

Max looked very like his father, but he was not quite so tall, and his face was finer, more Mediterranean. And though he had his mother's talent for logic, his reactions to life were those of his father. They shared jokes, and even when they argued, they would often finish the other one's sentences. Jacques was never more comfortable than when he was in his son's company.

For some years now, Max had written for the communist paper *L'Humanité*, which was read across the nation. And he'd joined the Communist Party.

They reached the Place de la Concorde and stared across at the Tuileries Gardens and the Louvre.

'The site of the guillotine,' Jacques remarked wryly to Max. 'In the first revolution, we took away the nobles' lives. The second revolution is kinder. We take away the capitalists' money.' He shrugged. 'It's more practical.'

They walked past the Hôtel de Crillon, a short way along the rue de Rivoli and up into the Place Vendôme, where Napoléon's great column graced the centre.

'In the Commune,' Jacques reminded his son, 'we knocked that column over.'

'Why?'

'I forget.' He smiled. 'Do you see what I see?'

On their left, the Ritz Hotel had a shuttered look, like someone pretending to be asleep. Around the rest of the square, small groups of men were standing, some with placards, in front of the closed doors of the shops.

'*Mon Dieu*,' said Max, 'even the jewellery store workers are on strike.'

In high good humour the two Le Sourds continued up through the rue de la Paix, across Saint-Honoré with its chic boutiques, through the heartland of fashion, finding everything on strike. Once or twice Max glanced at his father, wondering if he might not be getting tired, but the tall seventy-year-old was striding like a young man.

They left the world of fashion, passed through the Ninth Arrondissement, then up past the back of the Gare du Nord, and into a little poor district known as the Goutte d'Or, where, finding a small bar run by an Algerian, they finally sat down.

'A good journey,' his father remarked. 'From the Triangle d'Or to the Goutte d'Or.' He ordered cognacs and coffee to celebrate what they had seen. 'Today, the world changes,' he announced.

'It's certain that Blum's government are going to offer a huge package of reforms,' Max agreed. 'It will transform the life of every worker in France.'

'Of course,' said his father, 'but that's not what I mean. It will go much further than that. All we have to do now is keep the strike going, and power will pass into the hands of the workers. It has nowhere else to go.'

'But we already have an elected socialist government,' Max pointed out.

'Exactly. And as Marxists, they will see the inevitability of the situation as it unfolds. The Popular Front has served its purpose. Now as the workers take power, everything else will crumble away. Give the strike a month and I tell you, a new state will be born.'

And it was now that Max looked at his father and wondered whether it was time to break the news to him. He didn't want to do it, but he felt that he must.

It was only when they had finished their drinks, however, and Max had insisted on buying a second round that he plucked up the courage.

'You know, Father,' he said quietly, 'in another couple of days, the strike is going to end. It's already been decided.'

'By whom?'

'By us, Father. By the communists.' He paused while his father stared at him in stupefaction. 'We don't want to upset the capitalists. We need them.' He smiled sadly. 'Those are the orders.'

'Orders? From whom?'

'From Russia.'

Max had been a boy when fascism began, in Italy, where the former socialist Mussolini decided that authoritarian nationalism worked better. If Il Duce was supposed to be like some ancient Roman Caesar, it was harder to know what to make of the next Fascist Party when it had suddenly sprung up in Britain a few years ago, and he'd read the accounts with fascination.

A genuine English aristocrat, of ancient lineage, was leading huge rallies of men in black shirts against his own British establishment.

It seemed to Max, however, that Sir Oswald Mosley was far closer to the military men of the French right who were fearful of the communists and socialists, and disgusted with the liberal weakness of their governments. 'If the left wants revolution and will use force to get it, then the only defence is to beat them at their own game.' Mosley doubtless considered that he was fulfilling the role he was born to, as a forceful leader of national regeneration.

When there were scenes of violence at a big rally at Olympia, however, the placid British public turned against him and the movement fell apart.

But Germany was another matter.

Max found it easy to understand why the German fascists had arisen so rapidly. During the twenties, with the miseries that followed the war compounded by the crippling demands of reparations from the Allies, and a runaway inflation that wiped out everyone's savings, the Weimar Republic had been brought to ruin and despair. It did not surprise him that people were looking for a strong leader who could hold out the promise of hope and regeneration.

'Unfortunately,' his father had remarked, 'Adolf Hitler is a messianic speaker, but he's also a lunatic. There's an imperfect French translation of his book *Mein Kampf* and I've actually read it. The most turgid stuff. But it sets out his whole plan. He seems to believe Germany's problems are caused by the Jews, and he plans to conquer France and Eastern Europe. The whole thing is evil, but it's also insane.'

'Yet people don't treat him as a lunatic.'

'No. And I think I know why. He's anti-Semitic. So are most of the ruling class in the Western world, and most Catholics, too. Think of our own Dreyfus affair. Or the recent Stavisky scandal. A French Ukrainian financier defrauds a huge number of people and everyone says it's because he's Jewish. It's absurd, yet everyone does it.'

'But there's a difference, surely,' Max had objected. 'People aren't saying that the Jews should be attacked.'

'I believe you're missing the point.'

'Which is?'

'As long as they don't see it, Max, they don't care. If a Jew is mistreated they think: Well, he probably asked for it. If a Jewish community were to say that women and children had been rounded up and shot, those same people will say: 'These Jews are probably lying.' They may think Hitler and his Nazis are extreme, but at the end of the day, they don't want to know.'

'And if he says he'll conquer Europe?'

'He's against the communists. That's his attraction to them. It's the ancient principle: the enemy of my enemy is my friend. The bourgeoisie of Europe fear communist Russia. Hitler is a buffer between Russia and the West. They think he's defending them.'

'Until he attacks us.'

'They don't believe he will.'

'Why – when he says he's going to?'

'Because they don't want to. They can't bear to think it. The memory of the Great War is so terrible that no one wants to believe it could ever happen again. So if Hitler prepares for war but says he wants peace, they tell themselves it must be true.' His father had shrugged. 'The bourgeoisie will always choose comfort over reality.'

Max reminded his father of that conversation now.

'Stalin's no bourgeois, Father. He sees Hitler for the threat he is.

Look at what happened this spring. Hitler marched into the Rhineland. Admittedly the demilitarised zone, but he was still breaking the German treaty with the Allies after the last war. Nobody seemed to think it mattered, but the message is clear. Hitler can't be trusted, and he means war. Stalin knows that to protect Russia from Hitler, he needs strong allies in the West. So for the time being, at least, Russia needs bourgeois friends. That's why the party doesn't want a revolution here. We need to reassure the bourgeoisie, here and in other countries.'

'But if the workers form committees in every factory, we can push straight through to a Marxist state. Then Russia will have a true, Marxist regime in France as her ally, instead of a bunch of timorous bourgeois.'

'I know, Father. That's what Trotsky is saying. But he's wrong. It's too risky.'

'Revolution is about taking risks.'

'Yes. But Russia is the only Marxist state at present. We have to protect her.'

'And we're to betray the workers for this?'

'Blum is offering them almost everything they want. It will completely transform employment conditions in France. That's revolutionary.'

'But it's not revolution. They're prepared to stay out on strike. Believe me, I know. They want complete change.'

'Yes, but they can't have revolution. Not yet. The union leaders are going to tell them to take the deal, and go back to work. All the Communist Party boys are being mobilised to back the union leaders up.'

'I haven't heard this.'

'It's only just been decided.'

'Where? By whom? Why don't I know?'

It was time to break it to him.

'They knew what you'd say, so they didn't ask you.'

'It seems that you knew about this,' his father said quietly.

'I work for *L'Humanité*. That's how I heard.'

'You may find,' his father said coldly, 'that some of the workers refuse to obey orders.'

Max looked down at the floor, and said nothing. His father stared at him for a little while.

'So what else haven't you told me?' Jacques said at last.

The unkindest cut of all. But it couldn't be avoided. Max took a deep breath.

'Blum has troops gathering outside the city.' Max paused. 'I'm sure they won't be needed. But just in case . . .'

He saw his father's head fall. The tall man's body seemed to shrink.

'Troops. Against our own people . . .'

'It's only a precaution.'

Jacques Le Sourd did not speak for a little while. He stared up towards the domes of Sacré Coeur high on the hill above them, but whether he even saw the basilica's pale form it was impossible to say.

So it had come to this. Full circle. It seemed to Le Sourd that his entire life had suddenly become an illusion, an irony, an evaporation into the blue sky.

At last he spoke.

'Sixty-five years ago,' he said quietly, 'in the Commune of Paris, we began the rule of the people. And it was actually working. But the government sent the army into the city, and they were too well armed for the ordinary Parisians, and the Communards were smashed.' He nodded to himself. 'My father was a Communard. In the last, terrible weeks, a great many Communards were shot. Many were shot up there on the hill of Montmartre. My father – your grandfather – was shot in Père Lachaise. I vowed to revenge myself on the family of the man who did it, and when I had the chance, I failed.' He shrugged. 'So much for me. But I have dedicated my life to completing my father's work.' He paused. 'The men who smashed the Commune, our enemies, had at least this in their favour. However mistakenly, they believed they were right. The man who shot my father probably thought he was fighting for God and the honour of France. His son, whom I failed to kill, was an aristocrat and a bour-geois lackey, and history should have swept him aside and thrown him into the fire. But he was brave, and proud, and honest, and he had a son he loved. That's why I didn't shoot him.'

He stood up, and looked down sadly at his son.

'But now, when we have the chance again, a better chance by far than we have ever had before, I find that it is not the monarchists and the bourgeois who are bringing in the troops, but the socialists, and the communists – our own side. And having spent my life trying to honour the memory of my father, I find that my own son is with the traitors. So perhaps if I can find some brave men to stand with me, I can defy your troops, and your treachery, and you and your Russian friends can watch them gun me down.'

And with those last bitter words, he turned and walked away. And Max knew that there was nothing he could do but watch his father go, and wonder if, having hurt him so much, he had lost him.

By 1936, L'Invitation au Voyage was a very special establishment. It was named after the famous poem in Baudelaire's *Les Fleurs du mal*, whose refrain expressed everything the place hoped to be.

> *Là, tout n'est qu'ordre et beauté*
> *Luxe, calme, et volupté*

Order, and beauty, luxury, calm. And sexual pleasure. There were two further things for which the house had gained a reputation: It was spotlessly clean. And it was always changing. In fact, it was a work of remarkable imagination.

The imagination of its owner, Madame Louise.

The French government had a very sensible attitude towards brothels, Louise always thought. It regulated them. The laws went back to the time of the great emperor Napoléon.

Not that regulation had been a new idea in Europe, even then. Back in the Middle Ages, the many brothels along the south bank of London's River Thames were supervised by their feudal lord, the bishop of Winchester, who drew up the regulations.

In Paris, however, it was not the Church but the civil authorities who licensed the brothels. There were regular inspections and twice-weekly medical checks for all the women employed there. It was pragmatic, logical and responsible.

It was six years now since Louise had opened her brothel.

Perhaps, if she'd been colder, a little more ruthless, Louise could have followed in the wake of Coco Chanel – whose lovers, like the Duke of Westminster, included some of the richest men in Europe. But Louise had been too slow to understand the lesson that a woman's fortune depended entirely on the circuit in which she moved. On the arm of a man who was very rich, she would meet other equally rich men, who cared very little for the rules of society, because they could make the rules for themselves.

True, in France – where it was well remembered that at the court of Versailles, a royal mistress might have more power and prestige than a queen – a mistress might be a highly fashionable woman, and not a person to be hidden away and looked down upon, as in many other countries. But even so, a well-to-do Parisian was unlikely to give her the social protection or the money she would need to progress beyond a certain point.

So Louise lived quietly, and she did not become rich, but nonetheless, by the time she was thirty, she had been the kept woman of several men who could afford to be generous, and together with the capital sum from her father when she reached that age, she had enough money to stop being dependent on others and to go into business for herself. That was when she had opened L'Invitation au Voyage.

Luc had helped her find the place. There were many areas where brothels were to be found. Apart from the red-light district of Pigalle near the Moulin Rouge, there was the ancient rue Saint-Denis that ran up the edge of the Second Arrondissement just east of Les Halles. For male homosexuals, there were the bath houses on the Left Bank in the Luxembourg quarter; the best lesbian house was even grander, in a private mansion on the Champs-Élysées. Louise didn't like the rue Saint-Denis. The girls who walked the street there were prostitutes of the lowest sort. Though she was sorry for them, and for their sad, degraded lives, she wasn't going to have them on her doorstep. But Luc found a place a little to the east on the edge of the Marais quarter, on the old rue de Montmorency, where Nicolas Flamel, the medieval magician, had owned a neighbouring house.

Luc had also been useful at the start in helping her find the girls. And Louise had wondered if he would want her to make him a partner, which she didn't want to do. But when she offered him a salary instead, for these and other services, he seemed quite content, and she realised that, even in middle age, he was happier with the freedom of the streets than the responsibility of a business. He still supplied cocaine to his large network of clients, and in its first year, he provided more than a dozen valuable customers to the brothel.

But he and Louise had one understanding. None of her girls were allowed to take drugs of any kind, especially cocaine. It was a rule she had made right at the start, and she never deviated from it.

'I've seen too much of what cocaine can do,' she told Luc. 'I want all the girls to look wholesome. I won't have them getting skinny and rattled, no mood swings, no girls without septums in their noses, no lying. Girls in other places may be like that, but not here.'

Luc had understood. All the girls were clean.

When Louise received the note from Jacob, one morning early in September, she decided to go to his gallery that very afternoon. Every so often, when he had something that he thought she might like, Jacob would send her a little note. His judgement was usually excellent, and down the years she'd bought a number of paintings from him, including one by Marc Blanchard – a small landscape of the very street in which her establishment was situated.

She'd often thought about the portrait of the girl who might have been her mother. But she'd never bought it. She'd developed an aversion to false hopes, and disappointments. Had she discovered for certain that the girl in the painting was her mother, she'd have wanted it. But she preferred to ignore the picture altogether rather than invest her emotion in a possible delusion.

She liked Jacob. It was clear that he loved the work he was selling, and once he got to know her, he would give her frank advice. His prices were always sensible. She looked forward to seeing what he had to show her.

First, however, there was the daily business of the establishment to be attended to.

Every morning the house was cleaned. Though they were always kept shuttered on the street side, all the windows were opened, the bedclothes were completely changed. Every tile and bathroom was washed, scrubbed and disinfected. By noon, the house smelled as if it had just been fumigated, and Louise inspected it with the thoroughness of a strict hospital matron. Not until teatime would little sprays be used to perfume the rooms again.

At one o'clock, a potential new girl arrived for an interview, and Louise saw her in the little office on the upper floor where she had her own apartment.

The girl was the cousin of Bernadette, one of the most reliable of the twenty girls who already worked for her. During the last couple of years, most of the new girls had come to her in a similar way. Indeed, the two that Luc had found had proved to be unsatisfactory, and she had been obliged to send them away.

At first sight, the girl looked promising. She was fair-haired, slim, elegant. Her manners were excellent, she was well-spoken, but her face had a cool distance that was intriguing.

The interview was thorough. Beyond the official medical tests, Louise explained, she would insist on the girl visiting the doctor that she used for an even more thorough screening. She also asked in detail exactly what her experience was, and what she was not prepared to do. But this was by no means all. She made the girl walk about, so that she could study her deportment, she made her read aloud, she asked her questions about clothes and fashion and she wanted to know if she had ever acted.

By the end of the interview, she had decided that the girl was certainly a prospect. Well worth a trial.

'Come with me now,' she instructed, 'and you can see some of the rooms.'

At this, the young woman's calm face lit up.

'I've heard about the rooms, madame,' she said. 'I'm quite excited.'

There is nothing new under the sun. Certainly not in a brothel. But it could truly be said that, of its kind, L'Invitation au Voyage was exceptional. And if it was, Louise knew, the inspiration for her work hadn't come from a house of pleasure.

It had come from the Joséphine department store.

She'd gone in there so many times. Her only concern had been that she might encounter Marc Blanchard. It was possible of course that he might not recognise her, but she preferred not to take the chance. And having learned from the shop assistants that he almost never went into the store in the morning, she went then, and had never seen him.

But she had seen his work. And it was spectacular.

She was fascinated by the way that the store was like a changing stage set. There was always something new, to dazzle or surprise. Even the mannequins in the windows or the floor displays seemed to be engaged in some action in which, perhaps mysteriously, they had been suddenly frozen.

Though she avoided Marc, she had on one occasion talked to Marie, who had come up while she was engaged with one of the assistants. Louise had complimented her on the way the store was run.

'That's very kind of you,' Marie replied. She seemed genuinely pleased. 'We do our best. Sadly, however, my daughter, who married a charming American last year, is going with him to America shortly. She's the one who scouts for talent and keeps us up to date. It won't be easy to replace her.'

'I wish I could help you,' Louise said on impulse, 'but I don't know enough.'

She realised her folly as soon as the words were out of her mouth, but saw a light of interest in Marie's eyes.

'What do you do?' the older woman asked.

'I study art, and model for Chanel.'

'Really?' Marie looked quite thoughtful. Louise knew the impression she made on people. Her clothes, her manners, and her elegant French always impressed them. 'I wonder if you should talk to my daughter and my brother,' Marie mused. 'You're the right sort of age . . .'

'It's a charming idea,' Louise said quickly, 'but not possible, I'm afraid. I wish you luck, though, madame.'

Marie was still looking at her curiously as she beat a hasty retreat.

Whatever her exact relationship to Marie might be, Louise liked and admired her. And she was quite taken aback when, a year later, the Joséphine store suddenly announced that it was closing.

The statement to the press was remarkably frank. The owners felt that, after years of brilliant success, they were in danger of getting stale. Rather than see the business descend towards mediocrity, they were going to close it. They hoped that Joséphine would be remembered as a work of art. After her initial shock, Louise decided that the choice was rather admirable. How many stores and restaurants lived on the reputation of their past, when they would have done much better to close?

The space was soon rented to another enterprise. Two months later, Louise saw a small notice in the newspaper that Marie had married the Vicomte de Cygne.

So when she opened L'Invitation au Voyage, Louise tried to follow a parallel course with her own business. Several of the best Paris brothels had exotic rooms and some staged erotic entertainments, but in Louise's house, every room had a theme. Some, she realised, should not change, because customers asked for them again and again. But seven of her rooms were changed at regular intervals. She not only had an English room, a Scottish room, even a Wild West room, but she would decorate the rooms to evoke particular moments in history. She began to deal in fantasies of every kind, and it amused her to think of fresh ones with which to surprise the men who came there. I should ask Marc Blanchard to help me, she thought wryly. He'd be good at it.

But she didn't really need any help. She was discovering a rich imaginative vein in herself that she'd never knew she had.

She spent considerable sums on every redecoration, but she kept a sharp eye on the profits and the cash, and found that she could charge more for the quality of service she was providing. As for the girls, they loved dressing up to suit the part, whether Egyptian princess, Roman slave or any of the many roles that fantasy, light or dark, might demand.

There was always something new at Louise's brothel, and it was done with style. She hoped that her Blanchard family, if they had known, would have been pleased.

After the prospective girl had gone, telling her staff that she would not be back for several hours, Louise left for Jacob's gallery. It was less than a mile and she decided to walk. She walked west to the Place des Victoires, crossed behind the Palais-Royal, and up through the district near the Bourse that she knew so well. She was in a good mood as she entered the rue Taitbout.

Monsieur Jacob was delighted to see her. His wife was visiting the gallery. Her plain dress and pale skin suggested that, as Louise had always supposed, the Jacob family were strictly observant. She had a baby girl with her, of whom Jacob was obviously very proud.

'Your first?' she asked with a smile.

'*Oui, madame.*' He beamed.

'Her name?'

'Laïla.'

'A beautiful name.'

She suspected that Jacob himself knew what she did. He might have told his wife, or he might not. The younger woman seemed a little reserved, but that might just be her manner. She did not touch the baby, but she congratulated both parents on having such a pretty child. Then mother and daughter left.

'So what have you for me?' she asked Jacob.

'Something different, madame. Drawings.' He went to a plan chest and returned with a portfolio containing a number of charcoal and pencil sketches on thick paper, which he placed on a table. 'I remembered that you had taken an interest in the work of Marc Blanchard,' he continued, 'and I was at his place the other day.'

'Ah. He is well?' She was careful not to sound too interested.

'He is getting old, madame. But I asked him if he had any other work for me – for I have sold a number of his paintings, you know. And he told me that the only thing he had was a portfolio of drawings that he hadn't looked at in years, and that I was free to take it away and see if there was anything of interest.'

He showed her three. One was a rough sketch of Paris seen from the hill of Montmartre, not especially interesting. Two others were very incomplete life drawings, one of a man, the other of a middle-aged lady in a hat.

'They're all right . . .' said Louise, without much enthusiasm.

'I agree,' said Jacob. 'I don't find them interesting. But then I came upon something else.' His small face gazed at her seriously. 'Do you remember that you once made an inquiry about a portrait of a girl? Quite good, we both thought. You asked the identity of the sitter, and I did inquire, but the artist did not tell me.' He produced another sketch. This was a pencil drawing, quite detailed, and he laid it in front of her. Louise recognised it at once.

'It looks like a sketch for that portrait.'

'Exactly, madame. I still have the portrait and I placed them together. There is no question. As a collector, you will well understand that to possess both the portrait and the artist's sketch is highly desirable. I should certainly wish to sell the two together.'

'Naturally. Though we still don't know the sitter's identity.'

'No, madame. At least, not quite.' He reached into the portfolio. 'But there is a third item, madame, a charcoal sketch, unquestionably for the same picture, and on this there is a name – as you see.' And he placed the charcoal sketch on the table. At the bottom, quite clearly, the artist had written a single name.

Corinne Petit.

Louise stared. And then, quite suddenly, she felt her throat contract, and before she could do anything about it, tears came into her eyes. There could be no further doubt. The coincidences were too many. Marc was her father. And she was looking at her mother.

She kept very still, hoping the little dealer had not noticed.

He stood up.

'I will bring the portrait in, madame, if I may,' he said, moving to the door at the back. 'It's interesting to see all three pieces together.'

He was gone for several minutes. By the time he returned, she had fully recovered herself. But she felt sure that he had noticed, and that his absence was tactful kindness.

'You see, madame.' He hung the portrait on a blank wall, and adjusted the lighting. Then he held up the two sketches, one in each hand, beside the portrait.

'A set of three,' she said. 'They look wonderful together.'

'I hoped you might say that. I think so too.'

'The painting was for someone else originally,' she lied. 'But I might take them for myself. I remember you quoted me a price for the painting. But that was some years ago. What would it be now, with the drawings as well?'

'The same, madame. You are an excellent client.'

'You are kind, Monsieur Jacob.'

'If you will permit me, madame, I should like to get the drawings framed, and then we can arrange delivery.'

'Excellent, monsieur. Meanwhile, I shall choose a suitable place to hang them.'

When the transaction was complete, she prepared to leave.

'There is just one thing, madame,' Jacob said. He was gazing at her kindly. 'The artist may ask me who bought the painting.'

'Just tell him that a private collector has the work.'

'You are sure, madame? He might like to meet you.' His voice was very soft.

He had guessed. She was sure of it.

'No, monsieur, I do not wish to meet the artist.'

664

'As you wish, madame.' He opened the door and bowed, as she stepped out into the street.

She took a taxi back. She was eager to spend a little time alone in her apartment thinking about the best place to hang the picture and its accompanying drawings.

She also couldn't help reflecting that it was sad that she couldn't make herself known to her blood relations – to Marie, whom she liked, and Marc who, whatever his faults, had talents to be admired, and to her dear old grandfather down at Fontainebleau. Might she and Claire, whom she'd seen only from a distance, have become friends? Or would they have rejected her, as her mother's family had done? She didn't intend to find out.

But unknown to them all, with the purchase of the portrait, she was piecing together her family, her true identity, reconstituting a past and a truth that would otherwise have been lost.

For a few moments, her thoughts turned to Luc. He was the one who had set her upon this path that put a moral and social barrier between herself and her real family. Most people would say he had corrupted her. But if she felt a resentment over the fact, she told herself that it was useless. She had chosen her path too. Had she chosen another, she might have found a respectable husband. Perhaps. But then she'd have had no freedom. There were no other paths to fortune that were open to a woman. Whereas, after a few more years of this, she'd be able to retire as a lady of independent means.

Only one thing was missing from her life now.

A husband? Truly, she wasn't sure she wanted one, and certainly not the kind of man who'd want to marry a brothel keeper. But she would have liked a child. And time was passing on. She was thirty-six.

It could be arranged. She could surely find a rich lover again, a man of some interest, perhaps. She needn't tell him her intention. If he wanted to help the child, good. If not, she could provide. Perhaps, she thought, as the taxi reached the rue de Montmorency, this would be the next step forward in her life.

She paid the cab and went swiftly up to the door, letting herself in with her key. The hall was empty, as was the salon on her right, but from the morning room at the back, some low voices told her that one or two girls had already arrived. She was just about to mount the stairs when she heard a man's voice, speaking softly. She frowned. Surely this wasn't a customer. They were always kept in the salon. Then she realised it was Luc's voice. Perhaps he had wanted to see her.

She went quietly to the door of the morning room, and opened it.

The two figures sprung apart. It was Luc and Bernadette. The girl went pale. But they weren't breaking from a lovers' embrace. She could tell that at once. It was something else. The girl was holding a small handbag. She had clipped it shut as she moved back. Louise came into the room and closed the door behind her. She ignored Luc, but went straight towards Bernadette.

'Open your bag,' she commanded.

'But those are my things, madame,' the girl protested.

'Give it to me.' She didn't wait. She took it from the frightened girl before she could resist. She opened it, looked in and saw what she had suspected at once.

Two little packets of cocaine. She took them, satisfied herself that it was what she thought and handed the bag back to Bernadette.

'Madame . . .' the girl began, but Louise cut her off.

'You know the rules. Get out.'

'Madame?'

'Don't come here any more. Tell your cousin we can't use her either. Now get out.' She turned, opened the door and indicated the way out. The girl looked at Luc, expecting him to intercede.

'But it's not necessary, Louise . . .' he began.

'We always agreed,' she answered. 'You can't go back on it now.' She turned to the girl again. 'Go,' she commanded. And this time Luc was silent.

After the girl had gone, Louise turned to Luc. She was no longer angry, but she was sad.

'How could you betray me?' she asked.

'It's not so important.'

'It is to me. How many others were there? I need to know.'

'Only Bernadette. She has been using cocaine for years. She's not addicted. She's all right.'

'So you've lied to me for years.'

666

'It's only Bernadette.'

'I can't trust you, Luc.'

'You can trust me.'

'No.' She shook her head. 'I can't.' She sighed. 'Don't come here any more, Luc. Don't come near my girls.'

'Don't talk to me like that, Louise. You need me.'

She paused. She didn't need him at all, but she didn't say it.

'Whatever I owed you was paid long ago,' she said. 'You have hurt me very much. I don't wish to see you any more.'

'Just don't forget to pay me,' he said quietly.

'I'm not going to pay you any more.'

She saw his hand go towards his side. She remembered that he sometimes carried a stiletto. But his hand did not go farther, and she decided it was just an automatic reaction when he was crossed.

'You pay me,' he said, 'or you will regret it.' Then he left.

Now, she thought, she had two new girls to find.

After the rapid ending of the strikes in June, Max Le Sourd and his father had seen little of each other. Through the long summer and into the autumn, they had each gone about their business. Each Sunday afternoon, Max would look in at his parents' apartment in Belleville. His mother would be there, but his father would always go out. In due course, Max supposed, he'd find his father there, but it hadn't happened so far.

For Max it was a painful time, not only because he felt the separation from his father, but because by the time that summer was over, it was beginning to look as if his father had been right.

True, at first, the party strategy had seemed to be wise. The strikers had accepted the terms of the government's settlement, and gone back to work. Even the employers had praised the parties and the unions for showing such responsibility. Moreover, the new working conditions were a huge improvement. 'This is historic progress,' the unions could claim. They had won respect.

But would it last? Within weeks, the employers started to whittle back the benefits the strike had won. As he looked forward, it was clear to Max that he would soon see more of the same.

Outside France itself, the Spanish military and Catholic right had launched a massive counterattack on the leftist government in July.

Spain was now in a state of civil war. Fascist Italy and Germany were sending support to the military. In France, Blum's socialist government was dithering over what to do. Was Spain about to fall under a fascist regime?

And in the month of August, the Nazi regime in Germany had staged the Olympic games with a magnificence that the whole world had watched and applauded. A token German athlete with a Jewish father had been allowed to take part. But while all the world's press and thousands of visitors had only to look around them in Berlin to see what the Nazi regime was really like, the splendour and beauty of the games had overpowered their imaginations. As his father had perceived, they didn't want to know. Hitler's fascist regime had scored a huge propaganda success.

So what had been achieved? Max asked himself. The answer: nothing. The Marxist cause had been betrayed, the chance of revolution lost, its enemies stronger than ever.

He had been wrong. His father had been right. The question was, what could he do now?

On the first Sunday of October, the fourth day of the month, Max went as usual to his parents' apartment. His father was not there, so he talked to his mother as usual. But instead of leaving at the end of the afternoon, he remained there.

It was six o'clock when his father came in.

'Oh,' he said, 'you're here.' But he didn't leave.

'I came to say good-bye,' said Max. 'I didn't want to leave without saying good-bye to you.'

'Leave?' His father frowned. 'Where are you going?'

'They're recruiting international brigades to fight against Franco and his fascists in Spain.'

'I've heard.'

'I went for an interview on Friday. Paris is the main recruitment centre, as you know. Being a Communist Party member, I was accepted at once. All the others have to be interviewed by a Russian intelligence officer.' He grinned. 'I would have enjoyed being grilled by the NKVD, but it was denied me.'

His father registered faint disgust at the mention of Russia, but made no other comment.

'Why don't you go as a war correspondent, for *L'Humanité*?' his mother asked.

'Not needed. Anyway, I want to fight.'

His mother said nothing. He turned to his father.

'I have to go, you know.'

'I know.'

'This summer, I was wrong. You were right.'

'There was nothing you could have done yourself, in any case. It wasn't your fault.'

'No. But all the same . . .' Max shrugged. 'I wanted to say I was sorry.'

His father gave a brief nod. Then, rather stiffly, he hugged him.

'Come back,' he said.

Chapter Twenty-four

1794

It was the age of hope. The Age of Reason. The dawn of Freedom, Liberty, Equality. The time for all men to be brothers.

And now it was the time of the Terror.

In France, when the eighteenth century began, that grim, magnificent autocrat the Sun King still sat upon the throne. The long reign of his successor, Louis XV, had brought a financial collapse, it was true, but there had also been a gilded luxury that would be remembered with pleasure for centuries to come.

And the Enlightenment, and the Romantic spirit: these too, Frenchmen could say – for they claimed both Voltaire and Rousseau as their own – had been born in France during that mighty century. Voltaire had taught the world to love reason; Rousseau had taught the natural goodness of the human heart.

Hadn't these ideas inspired the American Revolution? Hadn't French support, and French arms, made possible the independence of the grand new country in the huge New World?

Now, in the reign of Louis XVI and his not-very-popular Austrian wife, Marie Antoinette, France itself had begun its own revolution. But where the American Revolution had promised an honest freedom from oppression, this French Revolution would be something altogether more radical, more philosophical, more profound. After all, it was French.

In France, a new world age would be born.

First they had stormed the Bastille. Then they had taken the king from Versailles to Paris, and made him obey their will. And when he had tried to flee, they had cut off his head. And after that?

After that, the world had turned against them, and they had argued among themselves.

And now, it was the time of the Terror.

*　　*　　*

The Terror had already continued for many months that sunny afternoon, when the widow Le Sourd, after crossing the Pont Neuf, arrived with her daughter, Claudie, on the Left Bank of the Seine. She was on her way to visit an old acquaintance who lived below the Luxembourg Gardens.

She was walking down the rue Dauphine when she saw the young couple.

As they turned into a side street, she saw them only for a moment before they were out of sight.

A casual observer might have supposed the man was a young clerk or attorney, out walking with his wife. But the eyes of the widow were not so easily deceived.

It was the seventeenth day of July in the year of Our Lord 1794 – but not in France. For the last two years, since the proclamation of the Republic in the autumn of 1792, France had used a new calendar. The twelve months had been renamed. Gone were the pagan gods of the old Roman calendar, and in their place, the seasons of the year. Winter thus contained the month of snow: Nivôse. Autumn had Brumaire, the month of mists. Spring contained months of germination and flowers: Germinal and Floréal. Summer boasted months of harvest and heat: Messidor and Thermidor.

The date that day in Paris was therefore the twenty-ninth day of Messidor, in the Year II.

The widow Le Sourd was a big-boned, black-haired woman. Her ten-year-old daughter, Claudie, was thin, and pale, and had stringy hair, and walked with a slight limp ever since breaking her leg as a child. But she got about the place with astonishing speed.

'Come,' she said to her daughter. 'I want to see where those people are going.'

When she and Claudie reached the corner, the young couple were still less than a hundred yards away. The widow stared after them.

There was no doubt as to what they were, despite their pitiful attempt at disguise.

She could always spot aristocrats, no matter how they tried to conceal their identity. Those fresh-faced people with their dainty ways. Aristocrats, untouched by sun or rain, who'd never done a day's work in their lives. Aristocrats, who thought themselves superior. She could smell them. She despised them.

But they could be dangerous.

Ever since the storming of the Bastille, the logic had been inescapable. The enemies of the Revolution would never give up. When the king had been dragged from Versailles to Paris, he had promised to be a constitutional monarch. But then what had he done? Tried to flee the country with his wife, to raise an army in Austria that would restore the rotten old autocracy to France again. He'd been caught, and rightly executed, and his Austrian queen as well. But had that been enough? Of course not.

Were the other monarchies of Europe going to tolerate a revolutionary republic in their midst? Never. They were preparing to attack her even now. Would the Catholic Church and the many aristocrats in exile accept the new regime? They were dedicated to destroying it. Those aristocrats remaining were constantly plotting in secret. The Terror was uncovering new conspiracies all the time. Even the peasants in some areas couldn't see that the Revolution was for their own good. Down in the Vendée, that huge, traditional region spreading out from the lower reaches of the Loire, the ordinary peasantry had been in armed insurrection – a virtual civil war – because they wanted their medieval Church restored, and refused to be conscripted into the army to defend the new regime. Many had been massacred. But even while the Vendée region smouldered, Brittany, Maine and Normandy had broken out into another revolt.

One couldn't even trust the Convention. There were backsliders and traitors there, who had to be rooted out.

For there could be no doubt: once the Revolution had begun, there could be no turning back. Either the business must be carried through to its conclusion, or everything would be lost.

Sometimes it seemed to the widow Le Sourd that it was the women who were the true guardians of the Revolution. In its early days, it had been the women who led the march down to Versailles. Women were the practical ones. Men made fine speeches, but women got things done. She'd lost her own husband to sickness three years ago. So she was head of the family now. And she was going to make sure that her daughter Claudie and her little son Jean-Jacques received the inheritance of Liberty and Equality that was now their birthright.

She kept her large eyes constantly open, to protect the Revolution.

So here was the question. Who was this pair of young aristocrats, trying to disguise themselves, and walking the streets of Paris? Why were they there? And what were they up to?

In the small chapel of Saint-Gilles, Father Pierre was still shaking. He had witnessed so many terrible things. Who had not, in these recent godless years? But the sight he had witnessed today had shocked him deeply.

He tried to pray.

At least he was lucky to have a chapel where he could do so. For most of the churches of Paris were closed. Some were used as barns. The great cathedral of Notre-Dame had been horribly abused and turned into a Temple of Reason. But his little chapel on the Left Bank was so insignificant that no one had bothered to do anything about it.

Not that it was obviously a house of God any more. No bell was rung. No crucifix was to be found under its dark old arches. Even the few brave souls who were his congregation came there quietly, surreptitiously, to join together in their secret prayers.

Was it legal? The priest himself wasn't quite sure. When the Revolution had passed its terrible statutes, seizing the Church's property, forbidding monasteries and stopping all payments to Rome, it had made the priesthood one concession. Priests might continue to reside in France, if they gave up their duty to the pope and became salaried officials of the state. If they refused, they must get out of France at once, or face prison and possibly the guillotine.

Most of the clergy had refused. But some in Paris had reluctantly accepted, thinking it was better to serve their congregations as best they could, rather than abandon them entirely.

Father Pierre was one of these. He was not proud of himself. He did not know whether he had made the right choice or not.

He had been praying for some time when he rose to his feet. He felt stiff. He was getting old. He was also a sociable man. He loved to talk to people, and it was hard for him to be so often alone as he was nowadays. He went towards the door which gave on to the street.

* * *

It was a long time since Étienne de Cygne and his wife, Sophie, had dared to go out. And they would not have done so now, except that it was Sophie's birthday, and the weather was so fine, and she had confessed that she would so love to see the river and look across to the noble pile of Notre-Dame again.

They'd taken great care, gone by quiet streets. None of the people they had passed seemed to take the least notice of them. And they had held each other's hand and gazed at the old river, and the cathedral's Gothic towers. And they had been glad that they had done it.

Now they were returning with equal circumspection. And they were right to be careful. For they had lost their protector, and they were not safe any more.

Étienne Jean-Marie Gaston Roland de Cygne was thirty years old. His wife Sophie was twenty-five. And they loved each other very much.

Étienne was just above average height, slim, fair, blue-eyed. His features were perfectly regular, and his expression soft. Seen away from his wife, he might have been called pretty. But when seen together with his wife, an inner strength appeared: one could see at once that he would defend her with his life.

They had been married five years, and their only regret was that, after two miscarriages, God had not yet granted them a child. But they still had hope. For their faith was strong.

They were also enlightened.

It was quite the fashion of their generation. After the pleasure-seeking luxury of the old court, many of their friends had taken the ideas of Liberty and Reason to their hearts. Young ladies had begun to favour simpler, classical dress, like the women of Republican Rome. Men spoke of reform. Glamorous heroes like the Marquis de La Fayette, who'd gone to seek glory with Washington when the American colonists had sought their independence, spoke of the honest, natural virtues of the New World. Perhaps, some had said, France should combine the best of the traditional and the new, and change its creaking old autocracy for something more modern, like the constitutional monarchy of Britain.

Having come into his father's estate at the age of twenty, it had seemed to Étienne that he should use his good fortune to make the world a better place.

He loved the old family château and the people who lived and worked there, and they liked him. When he went to Paris and encountered a larger world, he realised that he was full of love for all his fellow men.

He was sorry that he had been born too late to take part in La Fayette's American adventure. But perhaps some great advancement of the human spirit was about to begin in France, and if so, he hoped that he might play some modest part in it.

With all of this, his young wife was in perfect agreement. Sophie had a round face, rosy cheeks, red lips, and big brown eyes. Her hair was dark. Her father had been a general; and although Sophie had never harmed anyone in her life, when she believed a thing was right, she would dig in and defend her position with a determination her father would have been proud of.

For Sophie, it was all about justice. It couldn't be right, she declared, that her own class had so many privileges, when ordinary people had none; or that poor people could starve in the rich land of France. One of the first things that had made her fall in love with her husband was his desire to do good. Her dream was that one day the ordinary people of France should elect men to a parliament and, perhaps with a kindly king as figurehead, the elected parliament would rule the land. She felt quite sure that the people in the area around the family château would gladly elect her handsome husband to represent them, and she was probably right.

So it was hardly surprising that when, in July of the year 1789, news came that the Bastille had been stormed, and the French Revolution had broken out, the young de Cygnes were excited.

They had been spending the midsummer months down at the château. Étienne had immediately gone to Paris, passing through Versailles, to discover all he could.

'Nothing is decided yet,' he told Sophie on his return. 'La Fayette and his friends believe there will be a constitutional monarchy.'

'And the king and queen?'

Étienne had shrugged. There had been scandals at the court in recent years. Most were invented by mischief-makers, but his opinion of King Louis XVI and Marie Antoinette was not high.

'They mean well,' he said, 'but I don't think they know what to do.'

It had seemed to both Sophie and Étienne that they should return to Paris as quickly as possible.

'We don't want to miss anything,' Sophie had said excitedly.

How naive they had been, Étienne thought, as he looked back now. Many nobles had fled the country right at the start. Étienne knew of plenty of men whose property had been confiscated, and who'd been condemned to death in absentia. But he and Sophie had believed in the ideals of the Revolution, and had faith that a workable new government could come out of it.

And perhaps a transition to limited monarchy or to a republic might have been possible. But it seemed to him now that none of the parties in France were ready. Perhaps Europe itself wasn't ready.

So they had stayed, and endured five years of increasing misery. Five years of confusion, failed governments, intrigues, invasion from the angry monarchs of Europe, the king and queen executed, even risings in parts of rural France itself. And now, driven by fear of all these enemies, within and outside France, the Convention had approved a fearful purge, the witch hunt of the Terror.

It was the most radical of the Jacobins who had conceived it. Robespierre, their guiding spirit. They had vowed to destroy one category of people. But it had turned out to be a large category.

Enemies of the Revolution. They were all sorts of folk. Aristocrats were suspect first, of course. Their servants, too. Tradesmen. Peasants. Conscientious Catholics. Members of the liberal Girondin faction, who had opposed the radical Jacobins in the Convention. Even other Jacobins, who'd fallen out with Robespierre and his clique.

No one was safe. Anyone might be accused. And if the Tribunal judged that they were guilty, then execution followed rapidly, by the guillotine.

Month after month, using several guillotines in different parts of the city, the huge bloodletting had continued. Nor were there any signs that it would cease. It seemed that Robespierre and his friends were determined to purge France of every enemy and every error.

So what chance had a well-meaning young aristocrat who had believed in justice, and kindness, and compromise? Probably none.

Could they, even then, have escaped? Virtually impossible. All the ports were watched. To be caught in the attempt would mean instant execution.

By the previous autumn, Étienne and Sophie had been expecting to be thrown in jail on any day. And perhaps that would have happened, if it hadn't been for the help of a wise friend who had shown them how to survive.

How innocent they were, even about that. For whatever its horrors, Étienne had still assumed, somehow, that the new republic would be different from the governments of the old regime that had gone before.

But Dr Blanchard had known better. He'd shown them how to save their lives.

He was a sturdy, kindly figure. If Blanchard was successful, it was not only that he was a good doctor, but that his patients trusted him. They felt safe in his care. He'd been the family's physician for a decade now, and had become a trusted counsellor and friend.

'You need a protector,' he'd explained. 'And I have the perfect man for you.' He'd smiled. 'He's a patient of mine too, and I know him quite well. Would you like me to arrange something?'

Danton, the giant. Danton the Jacobin. Danton the hero of the *sans-culottes* in the streets. Danton, whose stentorian voice carried all before it in the Convention. Danton, who set up the Committee of Public Safety.

'You mean he'd help us?' Étienne asked in astonishment.

'Yes. Probably. For a price.'

'Danton the Jacobin takes bribes?'

'His loyalty to the Revolution is total, I assure you,' Blanchard continued. 'But he has huge appetites. And no self-discipline.' He grinned. 'The poor fellow's always in debt.'

'How do we go about this?' Étienne asked.

'I'll tell him you're a good fellow. No threat to anyone. You're not planning to threaten anyone, are you?'

'Heavens, no.'

'He'll give you protection. He'll put out the word you're not to be touched, and that should do the trick. Then you give him a present. Make it a good one. I'll guide you, if you like.'

'I wish you would.'

So Danton had received his money, and all through the previous autumn and winter, Étienne and Sophie de Cygne had received no harm.

Then, in March, came the blow.

The fall of the mighty Danton had been sudden and spectacular. He'd fallen out with Robespierre. Suddenly, he was accused of being an enemy of the Revolution. It was asserted that his management of the finances was chaotic and that he had taken bribes – both probably true. He was a popular man and he defended himself, but Robespierre had outmanoeuvred him. And to Étienne's horror, Blanchard had arrived at his house to warn him.

'They are taking Danton to the guillotine. You have lost your protection.'

'What can we do?'

'Stay out of sight. They may not even remember you. Above all, stay away from anyone who could get you into trouble. Remember, they're looking for conspiracies.'

Since then, Étienne and Sophie had lived almost like hermits. They stayed mostly indoors. They had liked to go discreetly to Father Pierre's little chapel of Saint-Gilles, but they stopped doing even that. Apart from the housekeeper and a few old retainers in the house, who'd known them all their lives, they saw no one. To all intents and purposes, for the last four months, Étienne and Sophie de Cygne had disappeared.

They came to a crossroads. They had been meaning to go straight on, but a small crowd had gathered outside a house ahead of them. It looked as if someone was being denounced. They turned off down another street. It was only when they had gone a dozen yards that they realised this route would take them past old Father Pierre's little chapel to Saint-Gilles.

All the same, they hadn't expected to find the old priest at the chapel door. Seeing them, he insisted that they step inside. With a quick glance up and down the street, they followed him in. It would have been discourteous and unkind not to do so.

The widow Le Sourd watched. She had only just come to the end of the little street. When the young couple glanced furtively back, she did not think they had noticed her.

A priest. It might mean nothing. Or it might be a conspiracy. She turned to Claudie.

'Go into that chapel down there. Pretend to pray. See if you can hear what the priest and those people are saying. Can you do that?'

Claudie nodded. Claudie was good at doing things like that.

Father Pierre was so glad to see the two de Cygnes. He had wondered what had happened to them. Of all the loyal Catholics who came to his little chapel, these two were his favourites.

He had gone to their house a couple of months ago, and the housekeeper had told him that they were away in the country.

'I am so delighted to see you,' he cried. 'But what terrible events are happening all around us. Have you heard about the Carmelites today?'

They hadn't. And he was just about to inform them when a skinny young girl with a limp came in. Moving to a bench only feet away, she sat down, and seemed about to pray.

Father Pierre looked at her. No doubt she was harmless, but in the awful world in which they were living now, one had to be careful. He moved to her side.

'Are you all right, my child?'

'Yes, Father. I was passing, and I came in here to pray.'

'Ah.' He smiled. 'It is a house of God. Do you pray often?'

'Each day. I pray that my leg may get better.'

'And what caused you to come into this chapel?'

'I cannot say.'

'Did you know that this chapel was dedicated to Saint-Gilles?' As she looked uncertain, he continued. 'Saint-Gilles, my child, is the patron saint of cripples. You have chosen well to pray here.'

He turned back to the de Cygnes, and they moved a few feet away.

'Did you hear?' he murmured to them. 'The child was passing, and did not know that this is the chapel of Saint-Gilles, nor that he is the patron saint of cripples. *Voilà.* Even in such times as these, the providence of God is manifested. Perhaps the saint himself summoned this child to his church.' But now he turned to the matter in hand. 'Oh, my dears,' Father Pierre began, 'what terrible news I must share with you.'

∗   ∗   ∗

Claudie listened carefully. The priest was very upset. Sixteen women from a Carmelite religious house had just been executed today, near the Faubourg Saint-Antoine. They had refused to obey the Clergy Law. They had declared that they would sooner be martyred for the faith.

'They went to the guillotine chanting,' the old priest declared. 'They were martyred, every one.'

'Martyrs indeed,' said the man, and the young lady agreed with him. And they both said it was a disgrace, and that it should not have been done.

Then they asked the priest to come home with them for a little while. The lady said the old man needed a hot drink. 'Laced with brandy,' said the young man.

Claudie went back to where her mother was waiting, and told her exactly what she had heard.

'Follow them, Claudie,' said her mother. 'I'll keep a little way behind you. Let's find out where they live.'

Following them was easy. The old priest couldn't walk very fast. The place they went into was a mansion with a courtyard in front of it, in the Saint-Germain quarter. A regular aristocrat's palace, her mother said.

After that, it had taken only a few inquiries along the street to discover who lived in the mansion. A tavern keeper said that the family owned a château in the Loire Valley, down in the west.

'That is interesting,' her mother said. 'You go home now,' she told Claudie. 'I'll be back later.'

The widow Le Sourd walked swiftly. She had not far to go. Back to the Pont Neuf, across to the Right Bank, then northwards up to the rue Saint-Honoré. For that was where the man she sought was living.

The house that the widow Le Sourd was seeking belonged to Monsieur Duplay the cabinetmaker. But it was not Maurice Duplay that the widow sought. It was his long-time lodger. As she had hoped, he was at home.

The room was not large, but pleasant. There was painted panelling on the walls and a small chandelier. He was sitting, very straight, at a table. She had heard that he had not been in the Convention for three weeks. Some had wondered if he might be sick. Others believed he was preparing an important speech. He looked perfectly well, so she concluded that it was probably the latter. They had met only a few times, but he had evidently remembered her and knew that she was loyal.

'How can I be of service to you, *citoyenne*?' he asked.

Some people said that he was ugly. But the widow Le Sourd didn't think so. His broad brow suggested a fine and quick intelligence. His jaw protruded slightly, but that told her that he was tenacious.

He was small, but wonderfully upright. She liked that. Truth to tell, the large-boned woman had a secret desire to scoop him up and take him home with her.

But above all, as the whole of France knew, he was incorruptible. He was pure. He was unyielding. Men like Danton might have been impressive, spoken louder and been more loved, but the lonely figure of Maximilien Robespierre was superior to them all.

It did not take her long to tell him about the old priest and the young de Cygnes. It was evident from what they had said in front of Claudie that they were enemies of the Revolution.

'I'm only surprised,' she said, 'that they have not been arrested already.'

'I have heard the name of de Cygne before, *citoyenne*,' Robespierre replied. 'I think Danton answered for them.' He shrugged. 'Perhaps he was paid.'

He said nothing more for a moment, and seemed to be thinking. Could it be, she wondered, that the evidence she had brought was not enough for him?

'There is more,' she continued. 'He told the old priest that he had encouraged the peasants on his estate to join the insurrections in the Vendée. His estate is close to the Vendée, as you may know.'

It was a lie. Yet she felt no guilt at making it. The two de Cygnes must die. She was quite persuaded of it. The lie was merely the vehicle – like providing a cart to take someone to their destination.

And in telling it, she was just doing her duty. Wasn't she a guardian of the Revolution, after all?

'Ah.' The eyes of Robespierre fixed upon her. Did he know that she was lying? She wasn't certain, but she thought that he probably did. He nodded slowly. Then he spoke. 'You know, *citoyenne*,' he said in his high-pitched voice, 'when the great debate took place about whether the king should be executed, I reminded the assembly of a very important fact. We were not there to try the king, I said. We were not there to decide if he was guilty of this, or of that. We were there for a greater cause, which was the cause of the Revolution. And it had become abundantly clear by that time that the Revolution was in danger, both from forces inside France and outside, so long as the king lived. Therefore, it was simple logic that the king must die. There was really nothing else to discuss.'

'You were right, Citoyen Robespierre,' she said.

'And now the case is the same again. The Revolution is in danger. And until these nobles are eliminated, it will remain in jeopardy. By themselves, the de Cygnes are perhaps not important. But their existence is a threat. That is the point.' He took out a sheet of paper. 'Will you oblige me, *citoyenne*, by taking this note to the Committee of Public Safety?'

'At once, *citoyen*,' she said proudly. 'At once.'

After Father Pierre had gone, young Étienne de Cygne paced restlessly. His wife had taken up a piece of needlework. She did not interrupt him.

The de Cygne mansion was very quiet these days. Étienne and Sophie used the big old salon in the summer months, when it did not require heating. In winter, they used a smaller sitting room. Most of the other rooms were under covers so that the housekeeper and the handful of servants could keep the place running.

'It was wonderful to walk with you today,' he suddenly said.

'I am happy we went, too,' she answered.

'It's difficult being cooped up,' he remarked.

'But we have our occupations,' she reminded him.

Had they not still been so much in love, this close proximity, with little to do, might have become irksome indeed. But fortunately, quite early in the Revolution, as social life fell away, they had each found projects to keep themselves occupied; and these had been most helpful during their recent seclusion.

Sophie and the housekeeper had decided to take every piece of linen and lace in the house, to mend and embroider it all. This, as she told her husband, was a task that might possibly go on forever. For two hours a day, she practised the piano, mastering it in a way that she had never dreamed of doing before.

Étienne, deciding that he would attend to the furniture, had gone to a local restorer to learn how the fine old tables and *fauteuils* from the reign of the Sun King should be properly cleaned and waxed. Having learned that, he decided to try his hand at carpentry. His first efforts were clumsy enough, but by now, he could make quite a creditable kitchen table or chair, and he was amazed to discover the sense of achievement and peace this simple craftsmanship brought him.

'I can do things,' he laughingly told Sophie. 'I'm not an aristocrat any more.'

And during the long summer evenings, they would sit together very contentedly, and read to each other, as the sinking sun made the polished wood of the old chairs and tables gleam softly, like ancestral friends, in the high salon.

But one other thought was troubling Étienne that evening.

'Sometimes, you know,' he said, 'I wonder if I made a mistake. Perhaps we should have gone down to the château long ago, instead of staying here in Paris. At least we could have walked in the park.'

'I don't think we made a mistake. I think we are safer here, Étienne,' Sophie replied.

'Why?'

'The château is too near the Vendée. At the moment the rebellions there have mostly been crushed, but they could start again. What if the fighting came to the château? I think the local people would all join the rising. They love their religion. And they don't hate us. Then we'd either have to oppose our own workers and tenants, or be called traitors to the Revolution.'

'That is true. All the same . . .'

'We are quiet as mice.'

'I feel we are alone.'

Sophie held out her hand.

'At least,' she said sweetly, 'we have each other.'

And so it was that evening that they sat together quietly. But before the sun sank, as the room filled with a warm, red light, Étienne put his arm around his wife, and in no time at all they were in a close embrace, only disengaging from each other enough to reach their bedroom, where their embrace became complete.

The battering at the outer door soon after dawn took them completely by surprise.

Dr Émile Blanchard rode along the edge of the big open square. In its centre stood the guillotine. The Place du Trône was just one of several sites where guillotines had been set up. Or to be precise – since the Revolution had changed the name of the old ground to the Place du TrôneRenversé – the square of the overturned throne. Its guillotine had devoured sixteen Carmelites the day before, and the grim blade had been kept busy for weeks. Thirty, often fifty, heads a day had fallen to its rattle and thud.

Ahead of Blanchard lay the cheerless prospect of the rue du Faubourg-Saint-Antoine, like a long stone furrow, leading westward from the poor quarter towards the distant Louvre.

Blanchard urged his horse forward. There was no time to lose. The only question was: Might he already be too late?

He'd gone out early to visit a craftsman in Saint-Antoine. The fellow had been one of his first patients when he began.

Émile Blanchard was an ambitious man. In the early days of the reign of Louis XV, when the financial affairs of France had unfortunately been entrusted to the hands of a clever Scotsman named John Law, the country had suffered a financial collapse quite as terrible as the South Sea Bubble in England. Émile's grandfather had lost the family's modest fortune, and his father had become a bookseller on the Left Bank of the Seine, whose liberal ideas had grown ever more ambitious as his means had grown less. Determined to set himself up in a more solid existence, Émile had studied medicine.

Since starting modestly, he'd done well. He had numerous wealthy patients like the de Cygnes, who paid him handsomely.

The old man he'd gone to see that morning couldn't afford to pay him much, but Émile was proud of the fact that he had never dropped a patient because they were poor. And he had just been finishing his visit when his son had arrived with the message.

'The de Cygnes have been arrested. Their housekeeper came to the house looking for you.'

'Where have they been taken?' There were many prisons in Paris housing enemies of the Revolution.

'To the Conciergerie.'

'The Conciergerie?' This was grave indeed. No wonder the doctor rode swiftly.

He had a particular fondness for the young couple. The lovebirds, he privately called them. He knew how much they longed for a family together and it had pained him to attend Sophie when she suffered first one, and then another, miscarriage. But as he had assured the two young people on several occasions: 'I have seen so many couples suffer in the same way, and go on to have a large and healthy family.'

The question now, however, was very different. Could he save their lives at all? He doubted it. He doubted it very much. But he continued to think, as he rode along.

Ahead of him lay the remains of the old Bastille. He'd gone by the place, on that famous day when the mob had stormed it. They'd gone there, he knew, because, having got arms from Les Invalides, they needed the gunpowder that was stored in the old fort. But for some reason, nowadays people claimed the aim had been to liberate the elderly prisoners, mostly forgers, who lived in the place.

If they'd stormed it a few weeks earlier, he thought wryly, as he rode past it, they could have liberated the Marquis de Sade.

From the Bastille, his journey led him westward past the Hôtel de Ville. Beyond that was the Louvre.

How many happy evenings he'd spent in that area, during the delightful final decade of the old regime. Just north of the Louvre, to be precise, in the welcoming gardens of the Palais-Royal.

The king's liberal cousin the Duc d'Orléans, who resided there, had turned its huge courtyards and colonnades into an open camp for all those who believed in enlightenment and reform. Philippe Égalité, everyone called him, some mockingly, others with admiration.

What had Orléans really been up to? Some had thought he wanted a republic, others that he wanted the throne for himself. You could discuss anything you liked in the cafés and taverns under those colonnades. His princely protection had allowed revolutionary literature to be printed in the presses there. Half university, half pleasure ground, the Palais-Royal had been the happy seedbed of the Revolution.

But it hadn't done the Duc d'Orléans any good. A few years later, the revolutionaries meeting in their great hall, only yards away, had sent him to the guillotine, just like his royal cousin.

He was lucky to be a doctor himself, Blanchard considered. His own politics were republican. But he was a moderate. He could have lived with a constitutional monarchy if he had to. But where would he have sat in the Assembly and the Convention which succeeded it? Not with the monarchists, certainly, who were still there at the start. With the Girondins probably, the majority of liberal republicans. Not with the extremist Jacobins. He was sure of that. And if so, as the Revolution became more and more radical, he would have been sent to the guillotine himself, by the Jacobins who had bullied their way into power. And now, these Jacobins were even executing each other.

Politics was a slippery and dangerous business. Even La Fayette himself had not been able to weather the storm. A hero of the Revolution when it began, and given military command, he and the Jacobins had fallen out, and he had been forced to flee from France.

No, Blanchard did not think he would have survived in politics.

But as a doctor, as long as he kept his head down, he was outside the fray. He had treated Danton, and many others. They seemed to like him.

And that fact, he realised – as he turned down towards the river to cross to the Île de la Cité – that fact might give him the one chance of saving his young friends.

Well, not both of them. One of them, perhaps.

But it would take cool nerves.

Was any building in Paris more fearsome than the grim old prison of the Conciergerie? Sophie didn't think so. It stood beside the lovely Sainte-Chapelle, but there was nothing gracious about it. Its bulky turrets and massive walls housed the waiting rooms and dungeons where prisoners were finally brought before their trial and execution. Upon any day, there might be more than a thousand prisoners housed in the Conciergerie somewhere. And few of them had any hope.

Sophie already knew that she was going to die.

The trial, if trial it could be called, had lasted scarcely minutes. They had been taken from the heavy stone halls of the Conciergerie into the Gothic old Palais de Justice next door. There, two large, bare rooms had been set aside as special courts. And they were special indeed.

She had wondered if they might be summoned together, but they were not. Étienne went in first. The big door closed, and she heard nothing of what passed behind it. After a long, cold silence he came out, looking ashen. He tried to smile and moved across to kiss her. But the guards would not let him, and pushed her through the door into the courtroom, and she heard the heavy door thud.

They took her to a wooden rail, upon which she could rest her hands, and told her to stand behind it. Opposite her was a table at which several men were sitting. In the middle was a small man with a pointed face and sharp eyes, who reminded her of a rat. On each side of him were others. These were the judges, she supposed. At the end sat a tall, thin man, all in black, who looked bored. Several men were sitting at another table. She supposed they were the jury. At one side of the room there was a row of chairs. One of these was occupied by a large, ugly woman with black hair, whom Sophie had never seen before.

Now the small man at the centre of the table spoke. It seemed he was the principal judge.

'Citizen Sophie Constance Madeleine de Cygne, you are charged under the Law of Suspects with treason, as an enemy of the People and of the Revolution. How do you plead?'

'Not guilty,' Sophie said, as clearly as she could.

Now it was the turn of the tall man. He did not bother to get up, but asked her whether she had been in the company of the priest known as Father Pierre the day before.

'I was,' she replied, wondering what this could possibly be about.

'Call the witness,' he said.

The big, black-haired woman at the side of the room now rose and stood before the judge's table.

The widow Le Sourd was soon established by the tall prosecutor as a citizen of good character, and she told her tale. With horror, Sophie heard her harmless expression of shock at the death of the Carmelites turned into an attack on the Revolution. But then, to her astonishment, she heard that she and her husband had told their labourers and tenants to join the rising in the Vendée.

'Your daughter was in the chapel with them when she heard these words?' the prosecutor asked.

'She was. She has a perfect memory, and she told me at once.'

'But this is absurd,' cried Sophie. 'Let me call Father Pierre and he will tell you I said no such thing.'

'The prisoner will be silent,' said the judge.

'I may not be defended?'

'By the law of 22 Prairial, enacted by the Convention this year,' the judge intoned, 'those brought before this court are not allowed any counsel for their defence.'

He turned to the jury.

'How do you find?' he asked.

'Guilty,' they said all together.

He nodded and turned back to Sophie.

'Citizen Sophie de Cygne,' he announced, 'you are sentenced to death at the guillotine. The sentence may be carried out at once.'

And that was the end of the matter.

She had been sitting in a cell with Étienne and four other unfortunates for two hours when Dr Blanchard appeared. The guard let Blanchard in and he embraced the de Cygnes warmly, but his face was grave. He knew already what the sentence of the court had been, and he told them that there was a priest visiting the prison, and that he would arrange for the priest to come to their cell, if they would like to see him.

Then Blanchard took Étienne to one side and whispered to him earnestly for a minute or two. Sophie could not hear what they were saying, but she saw Étienne nod. After this, Blanchard told her that there was another, empty cell nearby, in which he wished to see her alone, and calling the guard to open the door, he motioned her to follow him. Étienne told her she should go. So, still rather puzzled, she accompanied him.

Then he told her that he wished to examine her.

It was a long shot. He would have to be convincing. And it was not certain that the Tribunal would take any notice. But there had been a number of examples recently when they had cancelled or deferred the execution of women who were pregnant. Even a stay of execution would be something. A delay might bring another chance of life, at least.

After returning Sophie to her cell, Blanchard went quickly out of the Conciergerie and across to the Palais de Justice. He had to wait an hour before the Tribunal would see him.

He knew how to speak to them. His tone was respectful, but professionally firm.

'I must inform you at once,' he told the presiding judge, 'that the de Cygne woman is pregnant.'

'How do you know?'

'I have just examined her.'

'It seems suspicious.'

'I don't think so. She is a young married woman.'

'In these cases, Doctor, we normally send the women to our old people's home, where they are examined by the nurses.'

'As you wish. But forgive me if I say that my diagnosis is more likely to be correct than that of some old midwives. I have made this a particular field of study.'

'Hmm.'

The judge was considering his decision when Blanchard heard the door opening behind him and saw the judge's eyes look up alertly, and then saw him bow his head. Then a high-pitched voice cut through the quiet.

'I sent two aristocrats to you. Named de Cygne.'

'They are already dealt with, citizen,' said the judge.

And Blanchard turned, to find himself staring into the face of Maximilien Robespierre.

What a strange, enigmatic figure he was, Blanchard thought. Most men feared him, and with good reason; but as a doctor, he found the incorruptible Jacobin an interesting study.

Most of the Jacobins were atheists. If they worshipped anything, it was Reason; if they were impelled by any emotion, it was probably as much a hatred of the old regime as a love of Liberty. But not Robespierre. He believed in God. Not the old God of the Church, to be sure, but a new, enlightened God, that he had invented: a Supreme Being whose vehicle was the Revolution, and whose expression would be the new world of free and reasonable men.

He was quite open about it. Just recently, on the great open space of the Champ de Mars south of the river, he had organised a huge

Festival to the Supreme Being which thousands had attended. Some found it pretentious, even laughable, but as Robespierre had given his long and grandiloquent speech, it was clear that this extraordinary Jacobin was not just a soldier of the Revolution, but a visionary, a high priest.

Perhaps this was his strength. Perhaps this was what made him so ruthless, so unbending. The servant of a Supreme Being has little fear of hurting mortal men.

Yet he was still a mortal himself. He could be jealous, even petty.

'There is a problem, however, citizen,' the judge continued.

'What problem?'

'This doctor says the woman is pregnant.'

Maximilien Robespierre looked at Émile Blanchard calmly. His face gave nothing away.

'Do I know you?' he asked at last.

'I attended you once,' said Émile, 'at the request of your own doctor, Souberbielle, when he was indisposed.'

'I remember you. Souberbielle thought highly of you.'

Blanchard bowed.

'You say she is pregnant?'

'I do.'

Robespierre continued to stare at him.

'Was Danton one of your patients?'

'Yes. For a while.'

The question was obviously dangerous, but it would be unwise to be caught out in a lie. Robespierre seemed to be satisfied.

'Is there room at the Temple prison?' he asked the judge, who nodded.

'De Cygne has been sentenced to death. Let it be done at once, then. I think his wife should go to the Temple . . . for the moment.'

Blanchard saw the judge make a note.

Robespierre turned to leave. Then he seemed to think of something.

'Citizen Blanchard: You have said that you are sure this woman is pregnant. Very well. In a little time, we shall see.' He paused, and raised his hand in admonition. 'But, should it turn out that you have lied, that you have made this claim in order to pervert the course of justice, then you yourself will go before the Tribunal. I shall see to it myself.'

He turned, and left the courtroom without another word.

Later that afternoon, Dr Émile Blanchard stood in the huge open square between the Tuileries Gardens and the great avenue of the Champs-Élysées. The Place Louis XV, it had been named, but now it was called the Place de la Révolution. And in its centre stood the guillotine.

He knew the route that the tumbrils followed. From the Conciergerie, across the river and around the streets where the crowds could watch, and curse, or mock, as they chose. The tumbril which bore Étienne de Cygne was the last of the day. Blanchard caught sight of his young friend as he entered the square.

The crowd made little sound as the tumbril entered, probably because they did not recognise its occupants. And perhaps, Blanchard supposed, they could even be growing tired of the endless bloodletting enacted before them each day. However that might be, Étienne entered the Place de la Révolution with no particular indignity. He was staring towards the guillotine, high on its scaffold, and looking very pale.

It was ironic, thought Blanchard, that the great engine of death should have been invented by a medical man – the good Dr Guillotin – as a more humane way of executing criminals. For as the great blade fell, death was instant, and clean. And for that reason, many had objected to its present use, saying that the enemies of the Revolution should be made to suffer more, and that they should be torn apart as traitors in the good old way, to give the virtuous onlookers more pleasure.

But as he watched, Blanchard was filled by another, terrible realisation. In a month or two, or three at most, he himself would be passing that way.

Robespierre had seen through him. In his desire to save a life, he had diagnosed a pregnancy that was not there at all.

Sophie herself had not wanted to accept this subterfuge. 'I will die with you,' she told Étienne. But he would not hear of it, and told her that she must at least take the chance that Blanchard had provided. 'If you do not,' he told her, 'you make my death still harder for me to bear.'

So she would live a short while more, in prison. Then the truth would be known, and she would be executed anyway. And Blanchard, too, would be taken before the Tribunal and placed on a tumbril, and brought, like as not, to this very place, and go under this same terrible blade. And his wife and his children would be left without a protector.

A single act of kindness, a single act of folly. A well-meant but horrible miscalculation that would cost him his life. How could he have done such a thing? He cursed his stupidity. And it seemed to Blanchard, at that moment, that there was no justice, no purpose in the world at all, but only the operation of strength and caution, speed, concealment and chance, to cheat extinction for a little while, no different from the animals in the forest or the fishes in the sea.

So he watched, both with sorrow, and pity, and great fear, as they took Étienne de Cygne up on to the scaffold, and laid him down flat, far under the fearsome diagonal blade which, in no time at all, rattled down.

He saw Étienne's head fall down into a basket below. And then he saw a big, black-haired woman, standing below the guillotine, reach into the basket, seize the head and, holding it by the hair, raise it high, in triumph.

The week that followed was hard for Dr Blanchard. Sometimes, because he always shared everything with her, he wanted to tell his wife. Part of him was too ashamed to do so. What would his poor family feel when they discovered that he had so carelessly given up his life, their home and their security? Had he given no thought to them, before he put everything at risk for Sophie de Cygne? What kind of husband and father was he? Even worse: the gesture was completely useless. Sophie was going to die anyway. It was all for nothing. He was a fool.

So he said not a word.

He told himself that he was protecting them. Why plunge his family into despair months before it was necessary? Let them all enjoy the time remaining before the world came crashing down around them. He would dedicate himself to making these the best, the happiest, months of their family life.

And up to a point, he thought he was succeeding. On the very first evening, when his daughter asked him to play cards – and when he would normally have told her that he had work to do – he had sat down and played the foolish game for over an hour. When his son had carelessly torn his best coat, he had smiled sympathetically and told him it could have happened to anybody. With his wife, he was loving and solicitous. After three days, he was feeling quite proud of himself. Whatever his faults, he considered, he was at least showing grace under pressure, and in the terrible times to come, this would be remembered. So he was rather taken aback that very evening when, once they were alone, his wife turned to him and asked: 'What's the matter?'

'Why, nothing,' he answered. 'Why do you ask?'

'You seem tense. You look unhappy.'

He had almost broken down and told her everything that moment. But instead he had cried: 'Not at all, *ma chérie*. These are difficult times, certainly. But my greatest comfort is my wife and family.' And he had redoubled his efforts the following day.

Another day had passed, and another. Each day more instigators of plots, real or imagined, were brought to trial, and the tumbrils rolled. But Dr Blanchard continued on his way, maintaining his outward cheerfulness, and concealing his private hell.

Nearly ten days had passed since the execution of Étienne de Cygne when news came from the Convention. After a month's absence, Robespierre had returned to speak. But instead of the usual rapturous reception of his every word, an extraordinary thing had occurred. Blanchard heard it from a lawyer who had witnessed the scene.

'They shouted him down,' the lawyer told him excitedly. 'They'd had enough of him. He's gone too far. It's got to the stage that nobody knows who he's going to turn upon next. After he presided over the Supreme Being Festival, some of the Convention are saying he thinks he's God. And Danton had a lot of friends, you know. They didn't dare speak before, but they've never forgiven Robespierre for destroying him.'

'All the same,' Blanchard cautioned, 'Robespierre's a formidable opponent. The people who shouted him down may live to regret it.'

But he was wrong. For the next day came news that was even more startling. Someone with a grudge had tried to shoot Robespierre and wounded him in the face.

And then it happened. Perhaps the resentments that had been secretly brewing would have burst out soon in any case. Blanchard didn't know. But now, seeing Robespierre defied and then wounded, like a pack of wolves turning upon their leader when they see him falter, the Convention suddenly turned upon him with an animal ferocity. It was the speed of the savagery that was so breathtaking. He had been denounced and sentenced. Then, his jaw tied up and bleeding still, the indomitable, the incorruptible, the Jacobin High Priest of the Revolution was taken in a tumbril, as so many of his victims had been before, and guillotined on the Place de la Révolution while the crowd roared.

Within a day, dozens more of his closest followers had gone the same way.

The guillotine had claimed the Terror itself. The Terror was at an end.

But what does that mean for me? Émile Blanchard wondered. Sophie de Cygne was still supposed to be pregnant. When it was finally discovered that she was not, would they carry out the execution to which the Tribunal had sentenced her? Would his own role be remembered? There had been witnesses, after all, to Robespierre's probing questions, and his threat. Might he still be arrested? It was hard to guess.

He went about his business quietly. Nobody was bothering him yet. He visited Sophie in her prison, and brought her food each week. Even three weeks after the execution, she told him that she was still troubled by nightmares, and shaking fits, and indigestion. 'Nothing seems to be right with me,' she told him mournfully. But he explained to her that these symptoms were only to be expected after such a terrible shock and that in time they would pass.

And he was confident that they would. She was a healthy young woman. What the future might hold he still could not foresee, and he took care not to speak to her of such things. During the next month, each time he visited, though she still suffered various small complaints, she seemed to have grown a little calmer.

The prison in which Sophie was kept was a curious old place. Long ago, it had been the tower of the Knights Templar in their great compound on the city's edge. Some of the royal family had been held there too. Sophie was lucky because her cell was high enough above the ground to give her a view of the city and the sky through a narrow window.

It was a fine day in early September when Dr Blanchard went up to the Temple. By now he had made friends with the prison warders. A few small presents, the speedy and effective lancing of a boil from which the chief warder was suffering, for which Blanchard refused any payment, and the good doctor was greeted with smiles. No objection was made to the small posy of flowers he brought Sophie that day, as well as the usual sustaining provisions – and a bottle of brandy for the warders themselves, of course.

But he found Sophie in a somewhat distracted mood.

How did she feel? he asked.

'You remember I was still a little nauseous last week,' she said, 'and you gave me a potion for it.'

'Indeed. Is it better?'

She shook her head.

'There is something else. You remember I said that nothing seemed right with me at first, and you told me these things would gradually pass. And it is true that I am better. But something is still not right.' She paused. 'My time of the month has not come. This is the second time.'

He stared at her.

'I will examine you,' he said.

Some doctors and midwives swore that they could tell from a woman's urine. He would make the inspection if the patients seemed to want it, to keep them happy. But Blanchard was never entirely convinced by this test. If a woman had missed two periods, however, he considered it highly likely that she was pregnant. False pregnancies could occur, occasionally. But he had developed an instinct, which he could not explain himself, which he had come to trust. A few minutes later, therefore, he told her:

'It seems, Madame de Cygne, that after all, you are going to have a child.'

The months that followed were strange times. The moderate Girondins were in the ascendant now, the Jacobins reviled. Even when gangs of gilded youths, some claiming to be royalists, attacked Jacobins in the streets, no one seemed to care.

True, the Committee of Public Safety and the Tribunal were still in existence, but their power was much muted now. Some of the unfortunates that the Jacobins had thrown in jail remained under lock and key, but others were released. Even some aristocrats who had fled abroad were allowed to return.

And as 1795 began, some of the churches – so long as they rang no bells and displayed no crosses – were being allowed to operate discreetly again.

They were times of confusion, and contradiction. But at least they were not the Terror any more.

And so it was, in March 1795, when to add to all this chaos there was a shortage of bread on the Paris streets, that Dr Blanchard was able to obtain permission to remove Sophie de Cygne from the Temple tower into his safe keeping, in order that she might safely have her child. After all, as he pointed out, it was one less prisoner to find bread for. And when the boy was born, no one bothered to object when he removed the baby and his mother quietly to the family château in the valley of the Loire.

Sophie called the baby Dieudonné – the gift of God. And truly, it seemed to Blanchard, that was what the baby was.

For a time, in the years that followed, Émile Blanchard and Sophie kept in touch. He was rather proud of the fact that it was he, Blanchard, to whom the noble family of de Cygne owed their continued existence. For her part, she was determined to bring up her son away from Paris, which she had come to fear. And this the doctor could well understand. Dieudonné de Cygne was brought up in the quiet of the country, therefore, and there could not possibly, Blanchard thought, be any harm in that.

Not that life in Paris was so bad. The Revolution had learned a lesson from the Terror. Gradually, a legislature with two chambers emerged, themselves subject to election and law. There were problems. Members of the Convention dominated the legislature. There were riots, effectively put down. But for four years, the new system, with a small Directory acting as a cabinet government, brought some order to the land.

Émile kept meaning to go down and visit Dieudonné and his mother, but somehow other business always intervened.

For his own life in Paris kept him very busy indeed. His practice thrived. He treated a number of politicians and their families. But perhaps the most important patient he ever acquired was a charming lady, a widow with two children, who was the mistress of Barras, one of the members of the Directory.

In itself, this was a most useful contact, but it was to lead further than Blanchard could have imagined.

For when Barras decided that it would be a good idea if Joséphine transferred her attentions to a rising young general, who was proving most useful to him, and who was clearly fascinated by her, Blanchard found himself the friend of young Napoléon Bonaparte.

'And from then on,' he would tell the younger members of his family in years to come, 'I never looked back.'

For whatever the faults of the future consul and emperor of France, Napoléon was a loyal friend. Having decided that the doctor attending Joséphine was an honest and capable man, he sent patients to him throughout his reign. Often they were powerful and rich. Blanchard was well rewarded.

By the time that the emperor Napoléon's extraordinary reign of conquest, imperial grandeur and tragedy was finally brought to an end in 1815 at the Battle of Waterloo, Dr Émile Blanchard was a wealthy man and ready to retire to the pleasant house he had purchased in Fontainebleau.

Not that the fall of the emperor affected him professionally. He was secure, he was fashionable. The restoration of the monarchy brought him more aristocratic patients than he could possibly accept.

It also caused him, quite inadvertently, to do a final good turn to the family of de Cygne.

In the year 1818, one of his noble patients asked the good doctor if he'd like to be presented to the king. Naturally, Blanchard was happy, and somewhat intrigued, to accept.

He found the king much as he'd expected: very corpulent, but with a certain nobility and dignity in his face. When the nobleman told the king that Blanchard had treated such people as Danton, Robespierre and others in the days of the Revolution, Blanchard was a little taken by surprise.

He was afraid that this information would not make him a very welcome visitor with the king, and he would hardly have blamed him. But not at all. The king was rather curious, and asked him to tell him about them. Then he asked what had been Blanchard's most memorable experience from that time. And Émile was just wondering what to say when he remembered poor Étienne de Cygne and his son – whom he hadn't thought about for several years.

He told the king the whole story, start to finish.

'And so this lie you told, that the lady was pregnant, not only saved her life, but turned out to be true?'

'Exactly, sire. Conception must have been a day or two before, I think.'

'It was a miracle.'

'The boy was named Dieudonné, sire, since he was clearly a gift from God. Thanks to his birth, the family continues.'

'A family, my dear doctor, who have served my own for many centuries. I had not known of this wonderful circumstance.'

He seemed quite delighted.

'Well,' he suddenly declared, 'if God shows such favour to the de Cygnes, then so should their king. I shall make the boy a vicomte.'

And it gave Dr Blanchard great pleasure, soon afterwards, to write to Dieudonné and his mother to congratulate them on this happy addition to the family's ancient honour.

Chapter Twenty-five

1936

When Roland de Cygne had first proposed to her, Marie had made a mistake. She'd refused.

'I'm very honoured,' she told him, 'and very touched. But you need a wife who can devote herself to you, and your estate, and your son. And with Joséphine to look after, I can't do that. I wouldn't be any use to you.' She had smiled. 'If it weren't for all that, I think I should say yes. But I know it wouldn't be fair to you.'

'I did not make any conditions in making my offer.'

'I know. But that doesn't change the circumstances.' She had put her hand affectionately on his arm. 'I should like it very much if we could be friends.'

'Of course.'

'And I think you are right. May I say it? You should marry. God knows, there must be any number of charming women in Paris who would leap at the chance.'

'But it was you I was asking,' he pointed out.

'There are many better choices all the same.'

'Well then,' he said crossly, 'if you are so certain about it, you'd better find me a wife.'

'You want *me* to find you a wife?'

'Why not? You tell me you are my friend, and that although you can't marry me yourself, there are all these other women I should marry instead. Very well. Show them to me. I trust your judgement. You choose the wife, and I will marry her.'

She had laughed. But as she was growing fond of him, she did select one or two women, introduced them, and sent him out with them.

The first one he told her frankly was beautiful, 'but there was no spark between us'.

The second he liked better. But she was 'just a little too stupid'.

'Ah,' she cried, 'you are *difficile*!'

'Perhaps, but I must ask you to try again.'

The third took her a month to find. The woman was aristocratic, amusing, elegant – perfect in every way. He took her to the opera and to dinner. To her surprise, he turned up without warning at her apartment the following evening.

'Well,' she asked, 'how was this one?'

'No good.' He shook his head.

'What's the matter with her?'

'She's too intelligent.'

Marie burst out laughing. 'You're not *difficile*; you're *impossible*.'

He made a face. 'What can I do?'

She took his coat by the lapels, pretending to shake him. And whether she was taken by surprise when he held her and kissed her, or whether she was not, they had become lovers that evening.

'I shall be your mistress, but only until you find a wife,' she declared.

But then Claire had left for America. She hadn't realised what an effect that would have. Life at the Joséphine store was not the same. They tried to replace her, but none of the replacements worked. Before long both she and Marc came to the same conclusion. They weren't having any fun. The store was still doing well, yet they could both foresee that it would slide into mediocrity. They'd decided to close it.

So now she had nothing to do. And she was lonely.

She had no right to be lonely, she told herself. She had her brother and her aged parents, and even Gérard's widow and children. She had many friends. She had a lover.

But her only child – and her grandchildren, when they came into the world – would probably remain three thousand miles away. The store which had filled her days was no more. She hadn't enough to do.

Roland, reading her mood, had proposed again, and this time she had accepted. Cleverly, he had pretended that his affairs were in less good order than they actually were. And the château, he assured her, needed a thorough renovation. She had a project now, to keep her busy. She felt a sense of purpose again.

And indeed, there were all kinds of decisions to be made. The first was what to do with the mansion in Paris. For ample though de Cygne's resources were, the place had become drainingly expensive to maintain. 'The sensible thing would be to live in the country, and to maintain an apartment in Paris,' she told him.

'I wouldn't know how to live in an apartment,' he complained. But she guessed that he knew very well that this was what he ought to do, and that her role, as the new wife from the upper-middle class, was to organise the business while he told his aristocratic friends that she had made him do it. Since many of those friends had long ago done the same thing, Roland could still claim that he was one of the last hold-outs from the old regime. For the truth was that, apart from a few industrialists, or the great Jewish families like the Rothschilds, who had a magnificent mansion above the Champs-Élysées, and a handful of Sephardic families near the Parc Monceau, few people could maintain such houses now.

But Marie had thought of a clever compromise. For two seasons, the de Cygnes had entertained brilliantly in the mansion. This had given Roland a chance to show off his wife to all his old friends and many new figures she was able to entice to the house. With her practice at organising and her knowledge of the fashionable world, Marie made these parties memorable. They culminated in a magnificent party for Roland's son.

In the summer of 1929 they sold the house for a huge sum. Three months later, the Wall Street crash came. The next year, for a fraction of the proceeds from the house, they acquired a splendid apartment on the nearby rue Bonaparte. Into this went the best of the furniture from the house. The effect was breathtaking.

Meanwhile, without disturbing the rustic charm of the château – which might have been considered an act of vulgarity – Marie was able to redecorate a salon in the eighteenth-century part of the house, create a magnificent dining room and improve several of the bedrooms with furniture left over from Paris.

Her relationship with the château was particularly happy. Before they married, she had asked Roland for his advice about how to approach the people on the estate, whose workings would be new to her.

'When you started Joséphine,' he said, 'it was your own creation, so you were the boss from the start. But the estate has been there for centuries. It's like joining an old regiment. I'd advise you to ask everyone how things are done. Let them adopt you, before you make any changes.'

It had been sound advice and she had followed it. Everyone at the château knew that she was a rich and powerful woman, and they had been bracing themselves for the new regime. So they were charmed when she came to them so modestly and showed herself so ready to learn.

And the life she encountered there was, indeed, new to her. In the château's ancient, vaulted kitchen and larders, she found hams, sides of beef, churns of milk, as well as, naturally, the produce of the fruit and vegetable gardens, which had all come from the estate. Her husband would walk out into his woods in the early evening and return with pigeons he had shot as they returned at dusk. For the first time in her life, she was in the real, rural France, where man and nature existed side by side as they had for thousands of years. And chatelaine though she was, she was quite determined to learn how to do everything, including skinning a hare and plucking a pheasant. It was not long before her husband, passing by, heard laughter from the kitchen and guessed that his wife was with the cook in there.

Perhaps her happiest day was when Roland asked her parents to spend a long weekend with them during the summer. Her mother had become so vague in her mind that she was no longer up to it, but her father came.

Roland could not have behaved better. Dinner was becoming a little too taxing for old Jules, so Roland gave a luncheon party to which he invited a number of his neighbours, and made a most gratifying speech welcoming Jules not only as his father-in-law but as the dear friend of his own father.

'Indeed,' he added gallantly, if not quite truthfully, 'had it not been for my father's sudden and unexpected death, and my regiment's posting to the east of France, I might have asked for your daughter's hand many years ago. But before my battle dispositions were made, another lucky man stepped in and married her.'

Despite his age, old Jules was quite lively. He took a great interest in the estate, and she discovered that he knew more about farming than she had realised. Before he left, he told her: 'I was so pleased and proud when you took on Joséphine. But now I am happy to see you here.' He'd smiled. 'You did not know, in the days when you were a little girl, how much pleasure I used to take in visiting the farms with whom we used to do business. For it's the countryside – the farms and villages as well as the estates like this one – where every Frenchman belongs. This is the true France.'

Marie also took up riding in earnest. Roland gave her instruction, and she soon made progress. Each morning she would ride out with the head groom, and in no time she was taking small fences. There was an enthusiastic hunt in the local forest: mostly stag, sometimes boar, were hunted. The riding itself was not arduous, and though it was mostly men taking part, a few of the women rode. One day Roland suggested that Marie might like to ride with him at the next meet, and with some uncertainty she agreed. But when the head groom asked anxiously if she was still intending to hunt, she went to Roland and asked him if he thought the groom was trying to suggest that she should not. To her delight, Roland only chuckled.

'It's the other way around,' he said. 'He's so proud of you that he's been boasting about it to all his friends. He's only terrified you won't show up.'

'How do you know?' she asked.

'Because he told me.'

Having organised the decorating of the house, Marie had turned her attention to the library. It contained some fine old volumes from the eighteenth century, but almost nothing since. So she set to work. 'You're indefatigable,' he laughed, as she imported the classics from the nineteenth century and some of the more interesting productions of modern literature – none of which he had any intention of reading. But he didn't stop her.

Of more interest to Roland was another, longer-term project Marie undertook.

The de Cygne family archives were not in good order. 'My father meant to sort them out,' Roland told her, 'but he died before he got very far.'

There were boxes of letters tied with ribbon in cabinet drawers. There were trunks of unsorted documents in the attic, and lead-lined strongboxes of parchment, going back to the sixteenth century.

'It's probably a treasure trove,' Marie informed him, 'if we can ever sort it out.'

'It will keep you occupied for years,' he replied with a grin. 'And future generations will bless your name.'

These researches were not only significant because anything relating to one's ancestors was important to an aristocrat. One day Marie even discovered that the family owned some quite valuable fields a few miles away that, during the confusion at the time of the Revolution, they had forgotten that they possessed. Roland was both proud of the fact that his noble family could forget such a detail, but equally delighted when Marie managed to recover the fields for him.

And then there had been the evening when she had come into the old hall carrying a small box of letters and asked him: 'Did you know that your family went to Canada?'

'No.' He frowned. 'In fact, I'm sure they did not.'

'Well, there are a whole collection of letters here, written with great affection, from the brother of a former owner of this house. They date from the early seventeenth century. He'd gone out to Canada and settled there. It's clear that the two brothers were in quite regular correspondence. I wonder if there were descendants.'

Roland was silent. For some reason she didn't understand, he looked awkward.

'I seem to remember hearing from a Canadian once,' he said. 'But I don't know that he had anything to do with this seventeenth-century fellow.' He shrugged. 'I may have written him a rather unfriendly letter.'

'You could always write again.'

'It's all a long time ago,' he muttered. And since the business seemed to embarrass him, she didn't bring it up again.

Meanwhile, she continued to archive the material, and see if she could find any more hidden treasure for her husband.

She was enjoying being chatelaine of the estate, and she believed that she might be getting quite good at it.

In fact, she only had one regret. She wished, now, that she had married Roland a few years earlier. Not because of Roland himself, but because of his son. She would have liked to be more of a mother to Charlie.

Everyone called him Charlie. The serious boy she'd first met at the Gobelins factory had still been at school when she'd married his father. He was already a tall, good-looking young fellow by then, though still a little gangly. He looked quite like his father, except that his hair was dark where his father's had been fair, and Marie suspected that before he was thirty, his hairline would be receding. Like many boys, he'd been a little unsure of himself, and occasionally with-drawn, but she had been very straightforward and friendly with him, and he seemed to like that. She'd never pressed him to confide in her, but she'd ask him what he thought about all sorts of things, and freely shared her own thoughts about everything from politics to marriage. She hoped she'd made his home a warm and comfortable place for him.

But they'd only really got to know each other for about a year before it was time for him to do his military service.

The liberal French governments of the twenties had no great wish to build up the military, which had always been their enemy. So Charlie's military service had lasted only one year. But that had been long enough to transform him from a gangling boy to a strong, athletic young man. The experience hadn't awakened any desire to follow a military career, however, nor did his father encourage it. Charlie had begun to study law at the Sorbonne, though he didn't study very hard. But that didn't mean that he had no ambition. Indeed, his ambition soon became absolutely clear.

He wanted to be a hero.

It was only natural, Marie supposed. He was a young aristocrat, heir to a fine estate. He'd fallen in with a crowd of young men who obviously expected him to play a certain part. And he'd found he could do it.

He already rode well, and hunted. The first winter after his return, he took up skiing. And his father let him buy an open-top Hispano-Suiza in which he drove about in great style.

He and Marie continued to get along famously. They'd hunt together with his father. He'd drive her at breakneck speeds through the countryside, on condition that she never tell his father how fast they went. In 1934 he had replaced the open-top with something rarer – one of the latest, aerodynamic Voisin C-25 coupés, whose powerful, American-designed engine and elegant Art Deco body was a wonder to behold.

In Paris, she had shown him the things a man might need to know about women's fashion, and dropped gentle hints – about what made a man attractive to women, and what they liked – that might be useful to him in life. He learned these lessons quickly. He was seen with beautiful women on his arm at the fashionable race meetings at Longchamp and Deauville. He went to shoot on the estates of rich men and nobles. He was everything a young aristocrat should be. His father was proud of him, and it gave Marie pleasure to see her husband so happy.

She was also there to observe him acquire a new passion.

His father had always been partial to musical entertainment. From the Folies-Bergère of his youth to the Casino de Paris in the years after the war, he'd always gone to revues. 'I wish I could take you to see Maurice Chevalier and Mistinguett performing together,' he told Charlie, 'but Chevalier's gone to Hollywood now, and I doubt that he'll come back.'

But Charlie had discovered jazz.

They called it rag at first. The earliest performers had started to trickle across the Atlantic when Charlie was still a boy, but during the twenties, a stream of black performers had come to Paris. To their amazement they found that the French made little distinction over race. The segregation they were used to in New York, even in places like the Cotton Club, was unknown in Paris. Soon Montmartre became known as a second Harlem. Charlie became an habitué of the area. Since the jazz scene would go on into the early hours, there were cafés up there which served breakfast twenty-four hours a day, and Charlie would often be out until dawn.

And supreme above all the black entertainers was Josephine Baker. She danced almost nude. She sang – so well that with training she could even triumph in light opera. In America she was a black performer, who could be refused entry to a hotel or restaurant. In Paris she was a diva, welcomed as a star wherever she went. Charlie went to see her perform in nightclubs. Marie was taken by Roland to her more sedate performances. Charlie had even got to meet her, given her flowers and received a photograph.

There was only one thing missing from Charlie's life. Something that would be even more glamorous than his car: he wanted to fly an aeroplane.

And his father refused to buy him one.

'I have to refuse Charlie something,' he told Marie, 'or he'll end up spoiled.'

Marie stared at her husband. Surely he must be joking. His son was already spoiled – charmingly, but massively.

Yet Roland wasn't joking at all. And this reminded Marie of a very great difference between her and her husband.

She hadn't realised it at first. Roland had all sorts of quirks about the way he did things: small prejudices – things one didn't say, or wear, or do – which belonged to his class. As a man of the world, her father had shared some of these, but Roland had others that she had not encountered. She found these amusing, and he had no objection if she teased him about them, since they were all signs that he was an aristocrat.

But behind them lay something more fundamental. And this she found harder to understand.

Despite his heroic social life, there were still times when Charlie was moody. And during those periods, he could still seem a little lost, and vulnerable, like an adolescent boy. Marie assumed that it was partly just his character to be this way. But she could not help thinking that if he had more to do, Charlie might be happier.

It used to astonish her how little he accomplished in a day. If he spent the morning being fitted for suits by his tailor, Charlie thought he'd had a fruitful day. When she considered how much she had crammed into a day when she was running Joséphine, she found the pace of his life almost comical. Not that he was inherently lazy. If, for instance, there was some new agricultural method that might be useful for improving the estate, he would throw himself into it wholeheartedly. When he and his father decided they might grow mushrooms, Charlie turned himself into an expert on the buildings for the mushroom beds, and on the entire process, and the ensuing business was a big success. But when that was all set up and running, he immediately returned to his social life again.

'I suppose, being a bourgeois, that deep down I feel that a man should go out to work each day,' she remarked to Roland one evening. 'He should have a job, an office, an occupation.'

'The noble tradition – at least in France,' he replied, 'is that we are there to lead in battle. To fight and die for our king, or our country. And when we aren't doing that, we manage our estates, and dress up to look elegant. This last is very important.'

'It's not the way most people see things.'

'We are not most people.'

'You're not ashamed of not working at a regular occupation. A job.'

'On the contrary. I'd be ashamed if I had a job.'

'Ordinary work is beneath you.'

'I suppose so.'

'And by cutting a handsome figure in the world, of course, Charlie is bringing honour to the family name.' She nodded. 'This is what it means to be an aristocrat.'

'Not only an aristocrat, I think. It's the same with a matador, a great opera star, or a sporting hero. It's a human instinct.'

'That is true,' she acknowledged.

But aristocrats were more imbued with the idea than other classes, all the same. She remembered a conversation at the dinner table with a visiting aristocrat who was descended from La Fayette, and whose family still had the sword that George Washington had given him. 'La Fayette certainly found a way to make a name for himself,' the aristocrat said proudly.

'But he was driven by a passion for freedom and democracy, wasn't he?' Marie asked.

Her guest looked doubtful.

'It's true that he came to believe that a constitutional monarchy, like the English one, would be best for France,' he answered. 'But he wasn't searching for freedom in America. He was searching for glory.'

Of course, she thought. Nothing had changed since the Middle Ages. Heroes went in search of honour and renown. War, crusade, America: it made no difference.

So what could a young French aristocrat do in the decade after the horrors of the Great War? Become an explorer? Perhaps. Charlie could do that. In the meantime, however, even the fastest motor car did not look daring enough. No wonder Charlie wanted an aeroplane.

The first time Louise set eyes on Charlie was in 1937. Some friends had brought him to L'Invitation au Voyage. He was standing in the hall. He was a little taller than his companions, both of whom had been there before. He was very handsome, she thought.

The three men were ushered into the salon. They sat down. Champagne appeared, and she sent three girls in to chat with them. From the doorway, she noticed that although he observed the girls and quickly noted their good points, there was an air of detachment about him.

Curious, she stepped into the salon herself and went over.

'You have never been here before, monsieur.'

'*Non, madame.*' The faint surprise in his voice told her that he had noticed her elegant manner and accent. 'But I had heard of it by reputation, and my friends here were kind enough to bring me here to see for myself.'

'Louise,' one of his companions now cried out, 'I haven't introduced my friend to you. This is Charlie de Cygne.'

She bowed her head politely. If this was the case, she thought, then he must be the stepson of Marie. But her face betrayed nothing.

'Allow me to welcome you then, monsieur. I am Madame Louise, the owner. Most of the girls are quite amusing to talk to. You are free to enjoy their company in the salon.'

Then she left him.

Even in an exclusive establishment like L'Invitation au Voyage, people would appear without any introduction to spend an hour or two; but the majority of the men who came there were regulars, or soon became so. And before any new patron of her establishment sampled the goods, it was Louise's custom to invite him to her office for a discreet conversation. This would not only ensure that all financial matters were taken care of, but she would also do her best to ensure that her girls wouldn't pick up any infections. 'I run my house rather like an English gentleman's club,' she would explain. 'The other members are your friends. And of course, if you break the rules, your membership will be revoked, permanently.'

She waited twenty minutes before she sent a servant to ask him to come upstairs.

She observed him carefully as he entered. She liked the way he moved. He was elegant, but strong. As he reached the chair, he had to turn slightly, so that she could see his body in profile. She noted everything about that too. Perfectly formed, she thought. As he sat down, he smiled. Good smile. He seemed quite relaxed. Confident in himself. His eyes looked slightly amused.

She stared at him for a moment or two.

'You haven't come here for the girls at all, have you?' she remarked pleasantly.

'Why do you say that, madame?'

'I don't mean that you won't sample the goods. But I think you came out of curiosity. Because of the rooms.'

'It's the total experience, perhaps.'

'You don't want it said, when history is written, that in the Paris of his day, Monsieur Charles de Cygne missed out on L'Invitation au Voyage.'

He laughed.

'I confess.'

'Well, monsieur, I am very flattered that my house should qualify as such an attraction.'

'It is becoming a legend, madame.'

She inclined her head. Then she stood up.

'One moment, monsieur.' She walked past him to a small filing cabinet, opened a drawer, closed it and returned past him to her seat. As she passed him, her keen sense of smell picked out the faint lemony smell of the pomade he used for his hair, receding a little, and the lavender balm he applied after shaving. Behind that, she could just discern the natural smell of his body with which these scents interacted, flesh and follicle, in a way that was pleasing.

She made up her mind.

'Very well.' She smiled apologetically. 'The truth is, monsieur, that your arriving without an appointment this evening has placed me in a small difficulty. I don't think I have a girl for you. But I should like to offer you something in recompense. On Sundays we are closed. That is my rule. If you care to come by on Sunday afternoon, I will show you all the rooms. Then,' she smiled, 'you will be able to say that you have seen something that very few men have ever seen.'

He stared at her in amazement.

'You would really do that?'

'I would.'

'Then I accept, madame, with pleasure.'

'You are to come alone, monsieur. I am not turning my house into a public gallery.'

'Of course, madame,' he said. 'I understand.'

She wondered if he really did.

He arrived promptly at four o'clock the following Sunday afternoon. Apart from herself and a couple of servants still cleaning the house, the place was empty.

It took her some time to show him all the rooms. He was quite curious. Two of the rooms were Belle Époque and very plush. Another might have come from the eighteenth century, shortly before the Revolution. She had a Napoleonic room. 'At least three of our regulars,' she told him, 'I am certain, imagine they were the emperor Napoléon in another life.'

The English Tudor room with its heavy oak four-poster bed also contained two Elizabethan portraits that caught his attention at once.

'They look genuine,' he remarked.

'They're seventeenth-century copies, and heavily restored,' she told him. 'But I got them through an English dealer I trust. They look well, don't they?'

This caused him to ask if she had English connections, and she smiled.

'My parents were English, in fact. Highly respectable. My father was a banker. Fortunately they can't see me now.'

'So that's why your French is so pure. You learned it.'

'I did. In the valley of the Loire.'

Were her parents still alive? he asked.

'They were killed in a car accident, I'm afraid. Driving in the mist.' She shrugged sadly. 'A long time ago.'

She could see he was intrigued by her creative efforts. She showed him the Wild West room next. Then a room draped as if it were a tent, with a low bed and many cushions.

'It's like something from the Valentino movie, *The Sheik*,' he cried.

'Of course. It's quite popular. We have one man – he comes once a week, always the same girl, always this room. He's tall and hand-some. They're both into role-playing. They really get into it.'

Charlie admired the Oriental room, and the Spanish room. Recently, Louise had created a German room, modelled after the romantic castle of Neuschwanstein. 'I wanted music for this room,' she said. 'You know: Wagner. It's difficult to arrange it short of having a full orchestra in the house. I tried a gramophone playing *Carmen* in the Spanish room, but it didn't really sound right.'

By the time she had shown him all the rooms, almost half an hour had passed.

'That's everything?' Charlie asked.

'There was a girl who wanted to make a dungeon in the cellars. You know, chains . . . everything. But I said no.' Louise shrugged. 'Perhaps I'll change my mind, one day.'

Did she ever take on any of the customers herself? he ventured to ask.

'Absolutely not,' she answered firmly. 'In fact, I haven't had a lover for quite a while. It would have to be someone who interests me.'

'And may I ask what your next design is going to be?'

'I've got a girl – very beautiful – from Senegal. I want to make an African room for her. But I haven't yet decided how to do it.'

He accepted her offer to take a little tea, in the English manner, in her apartment. She asked a few questions about his life. He was intrigued to know how she came to make such a transition from upper-middle-class England to being a madam in Paris.

'The transition was not as great as you might think,' she said. 'I was sent to France. I liked it. I modelled for Chanel. I became the mistress of a rich man, then another. I inherited a little money.' She shrugged. 'But I didn't marry. And I wanted a business.'

'But you hadn't lived the life of the streets.'

'No. I had a friend – he's not a friend any more now – but he knew everything there is to know about Paris, from the richest houses to the low life of the streets. He was very helpful to me. But as you know very well, a business like this is as far removed from the poor prostitutes in the rue Saint-Denis as your own house is from a slum.'

'I've often seen them. Can't say I ever felt any attraction.'

'Don't go near them. But most of those girls are just trying to survive. Put food on the table. They can't charge much, so to make any money at all they have to do maybe ten tricks a day. To do that you have to turn yourself into a machine, just to survive. And it's physically dangerous too.' She shrugged. 'Paris is the romantic capital of the world. But there's nothing romantic about the underside of any great city.'

He nodded.

'Funnily enough, you remind me of my stepmother,' he remarked.

'Why?'

'She ran a business, with a lot of imagination. She's very capable.'

'Stepmothers have an evil reputation.'

'Not this one. I love her. And she makes my father happy.'

'I'm glad to hear it.'

'I have another question. I noticed a picture when I came in. It looked a bit like you.'

'It does, doesn't it? That's just a coincidence, though. I bought it from a dealer because it came with two preparatory sketches, which you don't often find.'

Louise stood up and went to the window. It was an October afternoon. The sky was clear; the sun was still shining over Paris. She loved the autumn season, yet she often felt a strange melancholy on Sunday afternoons.

'Would you like to go for a walk?' she suddenly said.

They walked down the old rue du Renard, crossed the big open space in front of the Hôtel de Ville and then crossed the Seine to the Île de la Cité. The sun was in the west, the light on the Seine was golden, but there was a certain coldness in the air over the water that made her shiver. They paused in front of Notre-Dame.

'It's too early to eat, but I'm hungry,' she said.

They found a bistro nearby. There were only a few tourists there, and the place was quiet. They ate a light meal and talked of all sorts of things. She could see that he was becoming even more intrigued by her than he had been before. Then she said that she wanted to go home, and he insisted on walking her back, as she knew he would.

Their affair began that evening. It was conducted, usually, on a Sunday. Sometimes he would drive her somewhere in the Voisin. Sometimes they would stay in and she would cook for him. They always found things to talk about.

By the end of the year, they had made love in every room in the house.

They were not seen together socially. She suspected that he had not told his father and stepmother about her existence. She didn't mind in the least. She had her own plan for the relationship.

And the plan worked very well. Before Easter 1938, she told him she was pregnant.

'It must have been the Wild West room,' she said.

Chapter Twenty-six

1940

When Marie looked back, she wished that she could have done more herself, but she understood that she could not. And she wished that Charlie had not hurt his father – though she knew he never meant to.

But what was the use of wishing? It was a time of trial, when everything was changed.

It was not that the French had been unprepared for war. The huge Maginot Line of fortified defences along France's eastern front was virtually impregnable. Six years ago, whatever Hitler's grandiose plans, the French army had outnumbered and outgunned him. Had he attacked even three years ago, she thought, he might still have been crushed.

Back in 1936, when Hitler occupied part of the Rhineland, and the Western powers had agreed to it, Marie had told herself it was for the best. In 1938, when he'd taken a bite out of poor Czechoslovakia – and France and Britain, despite their treaties with the Czechs, had accepted Hitler's assurances at Munich that he meant only peace – she had felt uneasy.

But it was meeting an Englishman at a cocktail party in Paris soon afterwards that had really alarmed her. He was a ramrod-straight, somewhat peppery British officer, on secondment from the British army to the French Staff College, where he was teaching military intelligence. Was he worried about the situation with Hitler? she asked him.

'Of course I am, madame.' He spoke excellent French.

'People always say that it would take Germany twenty years to be ready for war,' Marie suggested.

'Yes, madame. That is the received wisdom. And the original estimate was probably accurate. Unfortunately, it was made just after the Great War – nearly twenty years ago.'

'You do not think Hitler's intentions are peaceful?'

'Why should I, when *Mein Kampf* says explicitly that he wants war, and when he is rearming Germany at a fantastic rate?'

'Is this a widespread belief?'

'My brother-in-law is the military attaché in Poland. He tells me that everyone in Eastern Europe knows exactly what Hitler is up to. Our air attaché in Berlin told London that all the new commercial and private airports Hitler is building in Germany could be converted to military airfields in days. He was recalled home in disgrace for saying it.'

'I lived for years in England, you know, and I always follow the British Parliament. Mr Churchill makes the same warnings about rearmament, but he seems to be almost a lone voice.'

'He's only saying what the whole diplomatic corps and military intelligence know to be true. The conference at Munich was a farce.'

'It's hard to believe that anyone would want another war.'

'Hitler does.'

'The French defences are still strong.'

'The Maginot Line is magnificent, madame, but the cost of building it has been so great that it doesn't go all the way north to the sea. The Germans could come across the north, and if we mass our armies there, that still leaves a convenient gap between the Maginot Line and the northern plain.'

'But that's the Ardennes. It's all mountain and impenetrable forest.'

' "Impenetrable" is a big word, madame. Come through the Ardennes and you're in the open fields of Champagne with a clear run to Paris.'

'Our army is still large.'

'It is, madame, and your men are brave. Moreover, you actually have more tanks than the Germans. But the tanks are scattered all over the place, whereas the Germans have a large, concentrated force of tanks with the proper air cover which can advance with devastating speed. There's a thoughtful officer in the French army who advocates tank formations like the German ones. His name's de Gaulle, and you've probably never heard of him. He's not senior enough to get the general staff to listen to him. But he's absolutely correct.'

Marie told Roland about the conversation afterwards.

'I've never heard of de Gaulle either,' he said, 'but your Englishman may be right.'

For Marie and Roland, the rest of 1938 and the first half of 1939 passed quietly. Charlie was spending the month of August with them at the château when the news that stupefied all Europe arrived.

'Russia and Germany have made a pact?' cried Marie. 'I can't believe it. They're sworn enemies. They hate each other. How can they be allies?'

Roland had little doubt.

'It must mean war,' he said. 'The logic is inescapable: Stalin has seen that his Western allies are too weak to help him against Germany, so he's done a deal with Hitler. And why's Hitler done it? Russia has raw materials he needs. But above all he wants to neutralise the Soviets while he attacks the West. He doesn't want a war on two fronts.'

'You think he'll attack soon?' asked Charlie.

'Probably.'

'I'd better get ready to fight, then.'

August had scarcely ended when it came. And with a speed that was breathtaking.

Blitzkrieg. Hitler's armoured columns swept through Poland and crushed it. France and Britain declared war and began a naval block-ade of German shipping. But they were powerless to save poor Poland, which Germany soon divided up with her new ally, Russia.

As for Charlie, he didn't even wait for the call. He went straight to Paris to offer himself to the army.

It was a sunny day when he departed. As he was leaving his Voisin at the château, Marie and Roland saw him off at the train station.

How handsome he looked, waiting on the platform. It seemed to her that she felt just the same pride, and secret fear, as if he'd been her own. Then the little steam engine puffed and clanked its way up the line towards them, and the railway cars slowed to a halt, and he prepared to swing himself up.

'One small thing, *mon fils*,' his father said. And he reached into his pocket. 'This little lighter, as you know, was made for me by a trooper in the Great War. It's nothing much to look at, but it brought me luck. Take it, and perhaps it will do the same for you.'

Charlie looked at the little shell casing, slipped it into his coat pocket and grinned.

'I shall keep it with me at all times.' He embraced his father. After stepping into the carriage, he turned to look out of the open window. As the train moved off, he waved to his father and blew a kiss to Marie. She and Roland stayed on the platform until he was out of sight.

'I'm sure he'll be all right,' she said.

The months that followed were a strange time. The French army was deployed. A large British force had come to northern France. Yet nothing seemed to happen. Hitler made no further western move. October and November passed. Then Christmas. Still nothing. 'The phony war,' the British called it. The funny sort of war, said the French: *la drôle de guerre*.

As usual, they spent most of the months of winter and spring in Paris. And during this time Marie was interested to observe a new mood setting in. By year end, their friends were starting to talk about what they might do in the summer. In January, a fashionable neighbour who also had a son in the army remarked that it was high time her boy had some leave. 'I dare say this war will fizzle out soon enough,' her neighbour concluded. 'The Germans won't dare attack France.' It seemed to be the general view.

Marie couldn't share it. To her clear mind, this attitude was evidence of how quickly human nature will take a temporary reprieve from disaster as a sign that the threat can be discounted.

Yet as it turned out, the development that would change everything for the family was one she hadn't foreseen at all. It happened late in March.

She had just returned to the rue Bonaparte from a visit to her brother Marc when a telegram came from Charlie. It was addressed to her, rather than his father. It told her his leg was badly broken, and ended with the single plea: HELP ME.

'Why the devil did he send it to you and not me?' asked Roland, puzzled rather than angry.

Marie didn't tell him, but she had guessed at once.

In Roland's aristocratic world, a man might have the best of everything, but when it came to being injured at war, then you took whatever the army doctors offered and you didn't complain. Charlie hadn't actually been wounded in battle, but he'd fallen and been struck by a tank during manoeuvres, and broken his leg in several places.

'The military doctors know what they're doing,' Roland told her. 'If he walks with a limp, he walks with a limp. No dishonour in that.'

Marie said nothing. She went straight to the telephone. Within an hour, she'd discovered the best surgeon for that kind of injury in Paris, spoken to his office, and made all the arrangements. She'd even spoken to Charlie's colonel in person. Using the combination of her rank and wealth, and the skills she had developed running Joséphine, she both intimidated and charmed the colonel. By that evening, somewhat sedated and strapped to splints, Charlie was being whisked in a private ambulance to Paris. Having discovered that the surgeon operated not only at one of the great Parisian hospitals, but also at the American Hospital at Neuilly, she had also got the surgeon to admit him there.

'Charlie will be more comfortable at Neuilly,' she said firmly.

'Women shouldn't interfere in these things,' Roland grumbled, though Marie suspected he was secretly amused.

The spring of 1940 was beautiful and surprisingly warm. Each day, on her way to see Charlie at the hospital, Marie would tell the chauffeur to take a route through the quiet boulevards and avenues of Neuilly – boulevard d'Inkermann was her favourite – so that she could see the soft lines of horse chestnuts putting on their leaves and breaking, early, into their white blossoms.

The operation had been a great success. With luck, and careful treatment, Charlie would be able to walk quite normally. 'But you must be patient,' the doctor told him. 'This will take time.' By mid-April, it was agreed that, rather than go to a convalescent home, he should return to the apartment on the rue Bonaparte where Marie made arrangements for a private nurse to be in attendance.

A string of friends came to see him, and he seemed to be constantly on the telephone. His father would read the paper with him each day and discuss the news. Marie would play cards with him. He seemed to be cheerful enough. Only one thing irked him.

It started as a joke. One of his friends pretended to believe that his injury was a skiing accident. Within a day, the idea had gone around all his friends in Paris. It was meant as a harmless bit of teasing, yet it had to be confessed that behind it lay the perception that Charlie was the rich, athletic aristocrat who could do anything he liked.

And Charlie would probably have taken it in good part if it hadn't been for the circumstances.

For in April, Hitler had been on the move again. Scandinavia this time: Denmark and Norway both fell, their monarchs unwillingly forced to acknowledge a German overlord. In England, the more pugnacious Churchill replaced Chamberlain as prime minister.

'I should be back on duty, ready to fight,' he moaned. 'And everyone is going to say I wasn't there because of a stupid skiing accident.'

'No one seems to believe that France will even have to go to war,' Marie said to comfort him. And it was perfectly true. Even now, as the warm days of May began, Parisians were starting to sit outside the bistros and cafés to enjoy the sunshine as if Hitler and his armies belonged in another universe.

'But you think we're going to war, don't you?' Charlie replied. And she couldn't deny it.

To Roland she confessed: 'I'm just relieved he isn't on the front line.'

Roland, of course, would never admit to such a thing.

'The boy can't fight on crutches,' he muttered, 'and that's all there is to say.'

It came on the eighth day of May. Blitzkrieg. Straight through Belgium, the Netherlands, tiny Luxembourg and the Ardennes. The German armoured divisions poured through between the end of the Maginot Line and the French and British forces guarding the northern coastal plain.

It happened so fast that, in later years, people would say that the French collapsed and gave up in face of the onslaught. It was not so at all. The French fought heroically. But, just as had happened in the Great War before, the high command had not adapted to the latest modern warfare. That essential combination of tanks operating with air cover, on a large scale, was lacking. Even the tank division bravely commanded by Colonel de Gaulle was forced to retire in the face of overwhelming air attack from German Stukas.

In the space of days, France lost a hundred thousand men – not casualties, but killed.

By early June, the British forces, together with a hundred thousand French troops, were trapped against the coast at Dunkirk, while Paris lay open before the German divisions.

In Paris, Charlie was beside himself.

'I'm sitting here doing nothing to defend my country,' he cried.

But his father was more realistic.

'There is nothing useful you could have done,' he told him grimly. 'The war is already over. The British are about to be annihilated at Dunkirk, and that's it.'

He was right – and, miraculously, wrong. Hitler, having just won the war, didn't realise it. Fearful that his lines were overextended – they were, but the Allies had no armour to throw at them – and trusting mistakenly in the Luftwaffe to finish the British army on the huge beaches of Dunkirk, he hesitated. And thanks to this God-given but astounding military error, Paris learned days later that nearly a third of a million British and French troops had been ferried across the English Channel to safety.

But France itself could not be saved. France was lost. By the tenth of June, people were evacuating. Roland told Marie and Charlie that they must all go down to the château. 'The Germans will occupy Paris,' he said. 'If they take over the apartment, so be it. But at all costs we must try to save the château.'

They set off at dawn, but the lines of people along the roads were so great that they did not reach the château until nightfall. The following day, they heard that Paris had been declared an open city, rather than have the Germans perhaps destroy it. Five days later, the elderly General Pétain, the hero of the Great War who had secretly brought the mutiny to an end, took over as premier of France.

'That's good,' Roland declared. 'Pétain has judgement. He's a man one can trust.' And when, the very next day, Pétain declared an armistice with the Germans, Roland only shrugged and remarked that he didn't see what else the old man could do.

It had always been a source of some amusement to Roland and Charlie that Marie insisted on listening to the BBC on her wireless. The signal was not strong, but she could still pick it up at the château.

'You spent too many years in England,' Roland would tell her with an affectionate kiss. 'You believe that only the English news can be trusted.'

But it was thanks to Marie's prejudice that the family listened to a broadcast, arranged at short notice, that very few people in France ever heard.

It was late afternoon on the very day after Pétain had announced the armistice that Marie called to Roland to come to the wireless at once. Charlie was already in the room, sitting with his leg stretched out on a stool.

'There's going to be a statement from a French officer who has just flown to London,' she told him urgently.

'About what?'

'I have no idea.'

The voice that came across the airwaves was deep, sonorous and firm. It announced, in total defiance of Pétain, that France had not fallen, that France would never surrender, but that Frenchmen outside France, in England and in France's colonies, with the help of others including the Americans across the ocean, would restore France. And it urged all men under arms who were able to do so to join him as quickly as possible.

The message was startling. The language in which it was delivered was as magisterial as it was simple. The voice declared that, in the meantime, though he had only just been promoted to the rank of general, he was declaring himself the legitimate government of France, in exile, and that he would broadcast again from London the following day.

The name of the general was de Gaulle. 'That's the man who wanted more tanks,' Marie said. 'The one that the English officer told me about after Munich.'

'He's mad, but magnificent,' Roland remarked.

Charlie said nothing.

But the next day, he told Roland and Marie what he proposed to do. And Marie's heart sank.

History gives no precise date for when the French Resistance began. In his three broadcasts of June 1940 – on the eighteenth and nine-teenth, and a longer broadcast, heard by many more people, on the twenty-second – de Gaulle called all military forces to the aid of their country, but made no mention of any internal resistance movement. Little of significance seems to have happened before 1941.

But there was one man in France who believed he could say precisely when, and where, the Resistance began. And that was Thomas Gascon.

Because he started it.

Thomas Gascon's defiance of Hitler and his regime began on the morning of Saturday, the twenty-second day of June, 1940. Hitler himself was hardly thirty miles to the north of Paris that day, at Compiègne, signing the new armistice in the very same railway carriage that had been used to sign the old armistice of 1918, so humiliating to Germany, that ended the Great War.

'He will come to Paris,' Thomas remarked to Luc as they sat at a table outside the little bar near the Moulin Rouge.

'We don't know that.'

'Of course we do. He's just won the war. Paris is at his feet. Obviously he'll come.'

'Perhaps. But when?'

'Tomorrow.' Thomas looked at Luc as if his brother was foolish. 'He's a busy man. He's here. He'll come tomorrow.'

'And what of it?'

'He'll want to go up the Eiffel Tower.'

'Probably.' Luc took out a Gauloise and lit it. 'Most people do.'

'Well, he's not going up. He may have kicked our asses, but he's not going to look down on Paris as if he owns it from the top of Monsieur Eiffel's tower. I won't allow it.'

'You won't?' Luc chuckled. 'And how are you going to stop him?'

'I've been thinking. It can be done. But I'll need your help. Maybe a few other men too.'

'You want me to attack Hitler?'

'No. But if we can cut the elevator cables, then he can't go up. Unless he wants to walk up, which would be humiliating, so he won't do it.'

'You're nuts.'

'I'm telling you, it can be done.'

'Well, I won't help you.'

'I helped you once,' said Thomas, quietly.

There was a moment of silence. In almost thirty years, Thomas had never made any reference to that terrible night when they had carried the girl's body into the hill of Montmartre. Luc gazed at his brother, surprised, a little hurt, but cautious.

'You saved my life, brother,' he answered softly. 'It's true. But why should I repay it by getting you killed?' He reached out and took his brother's arm. 'You're not young any more, Thomas. You're over seventy-five, for God's sake. If you don't fall and break your neck, you'll probably get arrested. And then the Germans will shoot you.'

Thomas shrugged.

'At my age,' remarked Thomas with a shrug, 'what does it matter?'

'Think of Édith.'

It was amazing really, Luc thought, how little Thomas and Édith had changed. They both had grey hair, of course – not that Thomas had much hair left, just a few crinkles – and many lines on their faces, and some stiffness in the joints now and then, but his sturdy brother still took a two- or three-mile walk every day and insisted on managing the little bar, which he still did so well. Édith had given up running the restaurant some years ago, but with ten grandchildren to keep her busy, she was always on the go. She relied on Thomas though, in every way.

Luc could imagine Thomas climbing the tower. He'd probably get some way up before he tired, or something went wrong. And he was quite sure his brother was entirely serious about his hare-brained scheme. But he certainly wasn't going to encourage him.

'Even if there were time to organise such a thing, I'd say forget it,' he told him. 'The answer's no.'

He went indoors for a few minutes. When he came back, Thomas had gone.

It was quite a while since Thomas had walked into the Maquis. The whole of Montmartre had become more and more built-up. Many of the old establishments were still there, even little bars like au Lapin Agile. But more and more they were turning into curiosities for visiting tourists. A little while ago, some enterprising fellows had taken a vacant lot on the backside of the hill and turned it into a vineyard, to commemorate the ancient vines and winemaking that had graced Montmartre in the centuries before. The wine they made, so far at least, was quite undrinkable. But nobody cared. They had a very jolly time harvesting the grapes each autumn, and celebrating in the usual manner.

Even the Maquis was becoming somewhat respectable. Well, insofar as that was possible when some of the old families still resided there.

As he passed an open window, Thomas heard the unmistakable sound of Édith Piaf's voice singing, and he smiled. He'd seen her perform in a nightclub once – a tiny, sparrowlike girl, who sang with the accents of the street. He knew she'd made one or two records before the war. But if she wanted to make a living now, she'd have to sing for the Germans.

Well, he thought, the voice of the streets was going to fight back.

He found the collection of shabby little tenements that housed the extended Dalou family, and asked for Bertrand.

He still had a mop of greasy hair, but he walked with difficulty. He'd put his back out years ago, and never recovered. Thomas nodded to him.

'You know who I am?' he asked.

'I know. What do you want?'

'I need help.'

'Go screw yourself.'

'I'm going to kick Hitler in the balls.'

'Go and do it then. I hope he cuts yours off.'

Thomas produced a bottle of brandy he'd taken from the bar.

'Let's talk,' he said.

'You really think it's possible?' Bertrand said, ten minutes later.

'I know the tower like the back of my hand,' Thomas replied. 'As for the elevators, I understand how they work. Give me a little time and I can disable them all.'

'It's the shortest night of the year.'

'There's enough time. But I need help.'

'What about your own family?'

'My son's missing a leg. As for Luc . . . He thinks it's a bad idea.'

'He's a rat.' Bertrand Dalou shrugged. 'Why come to me?'

'I need a tough son of a bitch. You came into my mind.'

This answer seemed to please Dalou.

'I'm no good since my back gave out. But I've a couple of grand-sons.' He turned and called out: 'Jacquôt! Michel! Come here.' And a moment later two swarthy and disreputable-looking young men appeared. 'You're going out tonight,' he commanded them.

There were five of them in the end. Michel had a friend called Georges, a small, wiry man who was a steeplejack. That was helpful. Georges had brought his mate.

'We're going to need a couple of big cable cutters,' Thomas had told them. 'The biggest we can get.' A supplier called Gautier, at the bottom of the hill, had them, he explained, but Gautier closed at lunchtime on Saturdays, and he hadn't been able to get in.

An hour later, Michel and Jacquôt had returned with the very cable cutters he needed. He didn't ask how they got them.

They decided to approach separately and rendezvous beneath the tower at midnight. There were thin, high clouds in the night sky that obscured some of the stars, but it was only two days since the full moon, and they had all the light they needed. The great tower was deserted. A solitary policeman patrolled under it from time to time, before descending to the quays along the river and making his slow round again.

While he was out of sight, they climbed over the barrier and into the stairwell. Thomas needed a little help from Michel and Jacquôt, but he was pleased to find that he could manage pretty well.

The first task was to place a lookout. Since Jacquôt wasn't sure about his head for heights, Georges the steeplejack took him up to a vantage point about sixty feet up, from which he had a good view in both directions. His signal was a low call like an owl's hoot.

In the tower's early years, there had been elevator systems in all four of its legs, but the elevators, operated by huge hydraulic pumps below, were just in the east and west legs now. It took only a few minutes for the men to climb up and get out on to the tracks above the car in the western leg. Six stout wire cables ran up there. They had to be careful as the greased tracks were slippery. The cables, grouped three and three, were easy enough to see in the moonlight, as they ran up the great, curving tracks, passing guiding sheaves here and there, until they disappeared into the soaring tunnel of girders in the sky.

'The pump below powers it,' Thomas whispered. 'These metal cable ropes go from the pump all the way up to the big block, which is like a great wheel, about four hundred feet up there, above the second platform, then down to the car, which gets lifted. So, cut through the cables and it's disabled.'

The cables were thick, though. He could only just get the big cutters around them. He checked to see that the cables were well greased. They were. That would make the job easier and quieter. But it was still going to be hard work. Taking one of the two cable cutters, he showed them all how to cut through a cable.

'It's just like scissors or wire cutters,' he explained, 'but you have to work at it. The cable is spun from a lot of wire strands. But it's big. Very big. So you'll just have to keep on working and cutting until you can take a final bite at the central core. Be patient. Take turns.'

It took him ten minutes to get through the first cable, while they all watched. After that, he kept Michel with him and sent Georges the steeplejack and his mate across to the eastern leg, while he and Michel worked on the rest of the cables. 'After you've finished,' he told Georges, 'go up the stairs to the second floor. We'll meet up there.'

They had just started on the third cable when a low hoot from Jacquôt above them warned that the policeman was approaching. Thomas motioned Michel to press himself against the girders by the track. They kept very still. He hoped that Georges had heard the signal too.

The policeman passed under the tower. They waited. He disappeared from view. A low whistle from Jacquôt signalled the all clear.

When they were done, he and Michel clambered across into the stairwell. Thomas gave Michel the cable cutter to carry, and they started up the stairs.

It was a long climb. At the first platform, Thomas rested a little. Then they continued on up towards the second platform. Halfway up this section, Thomas had to rest again. His legs were aching and he felt a little short of breath. He saw Michel looking at him nervously.

'How's your head for heights?' he suddenly asked the younger man.

'Fine.'

'Good. It'll need to be,' he added gruffly. That made him feel better.

When they got up to the second platform, they had to wait only a couple of minutes for Georges and his mate to appear.

'All done,' Georges said with a nod. 'No problem.'

'This is where it gets more interesting,' Thomas told them.

The elevator system in the top section of the tower was quite different. There were two passenger elevators, linked by cables over the usual pulley wheels up above the third platform, so that they hung, counterbalancing each other. That reduced the amount of extra power needed to raise and lower them. A pair of hydraulic rams under the elevators provided power, raising each car halfway up the ascent. The passengers then got out, walked across a gangway, and entered the other car for the final ride to the top. It was an efficient system, making use of gravity to do much of the work.

There was a little service elevator as well. Georges quickly climbed on top of it and cut the cables. Then he and Thomas had a quick conference.

'I want to make sure they can't repair this without replacing the entire length of the cables,' Thomas told him. 'So I'm going up to the gangplank halfway up. I don't want to cut right through the cables, or they'll fall down two hundred feet and make a hell of a noise. But I'm going to weaken them. It'll be easier for me to fray them if they're tense. So can you cut almost through the cables on top of the car at this level, but don't make the final cut until I've finished up above?'

'Understood. No problem,' Georges replied.

To reach the highest level they had to mount a narrow spiral staircase. It was hard to carry the long-armed cable cutters for two hundred feet up the metal stairs' thirty-inch spiral. But eventually Thomas and Michel came out on to the gangway. Looking up, through the soaring girders, they could see the dark square of the topmost platform two hundred feet above them.

They walked across to the closed elevator doors, behind which lay the empty shaft. Two hundred feet below them they could just hear the faint scraping sound of Georges working on the cables above the elevator car.

'We've got to climb into the shaft,' said Thomas quietly. They had plenty of light from the moon up there, but it took them a couple of

728

minutes to work out the best way of climbing over the caging that fenced in the gangway. Once over that, they had to ease their way carefully along a girder until they came to the edge of the big open drop of the shaft. The car cables hung in the middle, just out of reach.

'Now what do we do?' asked Michel.

Thomas looked for an upright metal strut.

'Get your leg around that, and one arm too,' he said. 'Can you do that?' After a few moments of fumbling, Michel did it. 'Now,' said Thomas, 'with your free arm, grab hold of my leather belt, right in the middle of my backside. Got a good grip?'

'I reckon so.'

'I'm going to lean out over the shaft, so I need you to hold on.'

'All right.'

Thomas leaned out. Stretching the heavy cutters at arm's length, he could just get the cutter blades around the first cable. He knew his arms would be aching soon, but he could make a start. Carefully, he clamped the cutters tight and started to work them, sawing and cutting at the cable. After a minute, he paused.

'You all right, Michel?'

'I need a rest.' Michel pulled on his belt, Thomas returned to the vertical, and he took a step back. Just then, a soft owl hoot from far below told them the policeman was coming.

Five minutes later, they began again.

'It's funny,' Thomas remarked as he leaned out, 'I was hanging just like this the first time I saw my wife. From a balcony on the Champs-Élysées.'

'Eh?' said Michel.

'Doesn't matter,' said Thomas. 'Just hold on.'

He spent five minutes on the next cable. Rested a bit. Then the same on the third.

'We'll have to move around to the other side for me to reach the others,' he said.

That took another five minutes. Far below, the scratching sounds ceased. Obviously Georges had done his work. But Thomas was determined to finish his self-appointed task up here. He was just about to start when another hoot from Jacquôt told him to wait.

This time, when they were ready to start again, Michel had a question.

'I've been thinking,' he said.

'What?'

'You know what you said about the two elevator cars balancing each other?'

'Yes.'

'So these cables we're sawing at, they go right up to the top, over a drum, and down to the roof of the car on the other side.'

'Right.'

'So if you keep weakening the cables, they might give way, and if they do, then won't the other car fall down?'

'Go on.'

'Well, if the other car falls all the way to the bottom and smashes, it'll make a hell of a racket.'

'Go on.'

'People all around will be calling the police. We'll get arrested.'

'Could get shot, I reckon, if you're right.'

'Then this isn't a good idea.'

'At my age,' Thomas told him with a shrug, 'I don't care.'

'But I'm not your age.'

'I know. But I'm not worried, because I don't care if you get shot either. Hold tight.' And Thomas leaned out again.

'*Salaud*,' said Michel.

Fifteen minutes later, after Thomas had cut more than halfway through all the cables, while Michel watched in the greatest misery, they were back on the gangway again. They paused for a moment. Thomas pointed up to the platform high above them.

'Can you make out the bottom of the elevator car hanging up there?'

'I think so.'

'Well, ever since the American Monsieur Otis invented this kind of elevator, nearly a century ago, they've had automatic brakes. They can't fall.'

'Oh.'

The view from the gangway was truly wonderful. They could see all Paris bathed in the moonlight below. Thomas gazed up at the moon, gleaming against the backdrop of stars.

'You know what?' he said. 'If Hitler wants to go up this tower, he's buggered.'

Down on the second platform, they found Georges and his mate waiting patiently on top of the elevator car.

'All ready,' said Thomas.

They heard the cable cutters snap – once, twice . . . six times – and it was done. The elevator was disabled.

The descent from the second platform took twenty minutes. Five of those were a welcome rest while the policeman passed underneath. As they climbed out on to firm ground and Jacquôt joined them, they all shook hands and decided to split up into three groups. Thomas and Michel proceeded together towards the river, taking the cable cutters with them. The bridge was empty. As they walked across, they tossed the wire cutters over the parapet and heard them make two soft splashes, like a pair of divers, in the waters of the Seine below.

'Can I ask you something?' said Michel, when this was done.

'Of course.'

'You know up there you told me the elevator couldn't fall because it had safety brakes?'

'Yes.'

'When Georges was cutting the cables finally, I saw you staring up towards the top elevator, and when he cut the final cable, I saw you flinch.'

'Did I?' Thomas nodded. 'I was pretty certain,' he admitted, 'but' – he shrugged – 'I could have been wrong.'

For Louise, the second half of 1940 was a strange time. In the first place, after the beautiful spring and the sudden, terrifying month of war, everything seemed normal.

France still had a French government: Marshal Pétain himself, military hero, in his eighties now, but with all his faculties. France had fought bravely and lost a hundred thousand men. Like Poland, Belgium, the Netherlands, she had been unable to withstand the German blitzkrieg. If Marshal Pétain addressed them as Frenchmen and told them to cooperate with the German occupiers, who needed to argue? It wasn't as if there was an alternative.

True, the lone voice of de Gaulle spoke from London. But in practical terms, he had nothing to offer. The British army had completely collapsed when they tried to fight the Germans, and been sent scurrying back home. Only the narrow waters of the English Channel had saved the British from being overrun at the same time as France. Their turn would come soon enough.

Meanwhile, the Germans had left France with her honour. Pétain's French government was still in charge.

Well, more or less. Pétain himself was based in the south, in the town of Vichy, whose pure waters made it such a pleasant spa. The Mediterranean coast, Provence, the Midi, the deep central countryside of Limousin and the huge open hills of Auvergne were all in the Vichy zone. But the north of France, roughly from the Loire valley to the English Channel, was under German military occupation, for which the French government had to pay. So was the western, Atlantic seaboard, from the Spanish border up through Bordeaux, the mouth of the Loire and into Brittany. Within these northern and western occupied zones, the Pétain government was technically in control, and French police maintained law and order, but the presence of German troops reminded everyone that France still had a German overlord whose will would prevail.

Yet Louise had to admit that, so far at least, the Germans had behaved politely. They had occupied certain buildings, of course. The Luftwaffe had taken over the charming Luxembourg Palace. Göring himself liked to live at the Ritz where, Louise soon heard, he liked to wear jewellery, and dress up in silk and satin dresses – though his tastes, it was soon confirmed, were not for men but for women, with whom he was regularly supplied. Other German generals were looking for mansions they could use. It was clear that the orders of the day for the German occupiers were simple: Don't annoy the natives, and enjoy yourselves.

As for the Parisians, after the initial exodus, the city was filling up again. Life had to go on. Pétain the patriot had told them so. For many on the old military, monarchist right wing, and some of the bourgeoisie too – who, like Pétain himself, had never been so enamored of democracy in the first place – the new regime was not so bad. On the left, the communists had been ordered by Moscow to collaborate with the Germans because, since the new pact, Hitler was now Russia's ally.

True, Hitler had come to Paris for a few hours on a Sunday in June and found that he couldn't go up the Eiffel Tower because the elevator cables had been cut. But no one knew for sure who'd done it. The rumour was that some fellows from the Montmartre Maquis area had been behind it. But the old shanty town had a vow of silence. No one would ever get to the bottom of that business.

The question for Louise had been, what should she do?

She had formed her plan even before the baby was born. She didn't want to bring the child up inside a brothel. So she had taken a modest but pleasant apartment not far away, opposite the Musée des Arts et Métiers. She engaged a nanny, and here the baby slept. She spent as much time in the new apartment as she could, but continued to use her apartment in the rue de Montmorency house to supervise that establishment.

By the time the little boy was ten, she estimated that she would have paid off all her debts and accumulated enough money to retire from business and eventually leave him a good little inheritance. That was the plan.

She had named him Esmé, the old French name meaning 'Beloved'. He was going to have everything that she had been denied. She had deliberately brought him into the world, she was never going to desert him and he was going to know that he was loved.

When she had first told Charlie she was pregnant, Louise had explained very frankly what she'd done.

'I chose you to be his father,' she said, 'but I want him for myself. You're free. I can look after him.' It was her pride that she could say this. And it was her absolute determination that no one, not even Charlie, was ever going to part them.

She also made one other stipulation.

'I don't want you to tell your father or your stepmother about Esmé. That's going to be a secret between you and me. I want you to promise me that.'

Charlie thought this second stipulation rather strange, but he'd agreed. The rest he accepted easily enough. Though she had never told him the story of who she really was, he could see that it was important to her. Most men in his situation, he supposed, would have been grateful to escape responsibility for an illegitimate child. But he still wanted to do something for his baby son. He knew this wasn't virtue on his part. It was easy to be generous if you were rich.

'Come and see us,' she said. 'Just don't ever try to take him away.'

But she hadn't foreseen the German occupation.

What was she to do now? She had no wish to provide the hospitality of L'Invitation au Voyage to Hitler's henchmen. Could she afford to retire? Could she even sell the business in the middle of the occupation?

Before the end of July, the situation was made even worse for her when, to her surprise, she received a telephone call from Coco Chanel. Some years ago, the great mistress of fashion had decided to live in a luxurious suite at the Ritz, and she was calling from there.

'I just wanted you to know, Louise,' she said, 'that the Ritz is simply swarming with the German High Command. I've told them all that you're my friend, and that L'Invitation au Voyage is the place to visit in Paris.'

'Oh.'

'They all have masses of money, you know.'

'I know.' It was already a sore point with the French that the money they had to pay for the support of the occupying Germans was calculated in German marks, using an exchange rate that hugely favoured them. As a result, the Germans could afford anything they wanted in Paris.

'I told them they can trust you,' Coco continued. 'Don't let me down.' Then she rang off.

Louise was still struggling with her conscience a day later when Charlie came to call.

When Charlie had told his father and Marie what he wanted, Roland had been doubtful.

'There's no network to join,' he pointed out.

'Then I'll have to build one.'

'It's a pity we've lost so many men,' his father said.

It wasn't just the loss of a hundred thousand, killed in May and June. By the time the fighting was over, the Germans had taken a million French troops as prisoners of war. Sadly, even the French troops evacuated at Dunkirk had been sent back to France by the British, who probably didn't know what to do with them, and most of those had finished up in German prisoner-of-war camps too.

'As far as I can tell,' Marie had remarked, 'most of the people of our sort would rather follow Pétain anyway.'

'That's exactly why I'm not likely to be suspected,' Charlie told her. 'And you can help me by providing cover. If we just act the part of conservative aristocrats, the Germans will suppose we're on their side.'

The opportunity had come only two weeks later, when a large car with two outriders had drawn up at the château, and a smartly dressed German colonel and two young staff officers had alighted. At the door he had politely introduced himself as Colonel Walter, and explained that he was looking at châteaus which might be requisitioned for army use.

He spoke excellent French, and Charlie suspected that he might be taking a look at the occupants of the château as well as the building itself. When Marie asked if he could stay to lunch with his staff, he readily accepted.

As they toured the house, it was quickly established that both the German and Roland de Cygne came from military families. Charlie was still walking with a stick and the colonel asked if this was a wound.

'No, *mon colonel*. I broke my leg quite badly in an accident. So I missed the fighting.'

'You had good doctors, I hope.'

'Very. At the American Hospital.'

The colonel nodded, and Charlie supposed that the information would probably be checked. Colonel Walter's attitude was made apparent, however, when he turned to Roland and remarked: 'The French army fought with gallantry, monsieur. But your High Command did not prepare correctly.'

'That is what I think,' Roland answered. 'It is gracious of you to say it.'

But the defining moment came a few minutes later. They were in the old hall where the lovely tapestry of the unicorn hung on the wall, and they all stopped to admire it.

'Truly beautiful,' Colonel Walter remarked. 'A jewel in a perfect setting. Has it always been here?'

And then Roland, remembering the circumstances of his father's purchase, had an inspiration.

'As it happens,' he replied, quickly rearranging the facts to suit, 'it was my father who bought this tapestry. The price was a little high, but he discovered that if he didn't buy it at that price, it was going to be acquired by a Jew. So he paid.' He gave the colonel a glance, accompanied by a faint shrug. 'We felt that it belonged here.'

'Ah.' Colonel Walter inclined his head. 'A good deed.' Charlie could see the two staff officers visibly relax.

The lunch was pleasant. The German officers were correct in their behaviour, but it was clear that, as far as they were concerned, the family of de Cygne were just the kind of people they wanted to encourage.

As they were leaving, Roland did murmur to Colonel Walter that, should the army need to requisition the château, he hoped he might receive a little notice.

'Of course,' Walter replied, and smiled. 'Look after that tapestry.' Charlie was pretty sure that his family would not be troubled further.

He was still walking with a stick, but looking otherwise well, on the Sunday afternoon when he turned up to see Louise. It was the first time he had been to her apartment since the previous autumn, and although she had come to the hospital once, she had been reluctant, because of her fear of meeting his family.

Under his arm, so that anyone could see it, he was carrying a book by Céline, the darling of French reactionaries, whose anti-Semitism left even the Nazis awestruck.

As he approached, Charlie wondered what would happen between them. Thanks to the war, it had been a year since he and Louise had been alone together. She had the child she wanted, and she had made her desire for independence very clear. Would she still want to continue the affair? And did he want to continue it himself? He didn't really know. He thought he probably did, but he decided he'd just have to see how things developed when they met.

In the meantime, he realised that he was quite excited to see his little son.

They stood in the salon of her apartment opposite the museum.

'We should celebrate your return,' she said. 'Champagne?'

They were face-to-face, just a little apart.

'I'm still a cripple,' he said.

'So I see.' She smiled.

How wonderfully attractive she was. Nothing had changed. Nothing at all. He was about to take her in his arms when she gently held him back.

'Wait. You have somebody to see first.'

She led him across the small hall and into the second bedroom, which was arranged as a nursery.

How quickly little children grow, he thought. The baby he remembered had turned into a little boy. Only two years old, but a child who walked, and talked – and who resembled him. He picked Esmé up and held him so that the little fellow looked straight into his eyes. He smiled.

'Do you know who I am?'

'My papa.'

'Yes. Your papa.'

'Will you stay here?'

'Not all the time.'

'Maman belongs to me.'

'I know. But I shall see her sometimes. Whenever I see you.'

The tiny boy gazed at him thoughtfully.

'You are my papa.'

'Yes.'

And then Charlie suddenly had an urge to stay with this woman and with his son. And he hardly cared that she was much older than he was, and that she owned a brothel, and that he was the future Vicomte de Cygne. And he wanted to marry Louise, even though he knew that he would not.

He stayed half an hour with his son, playing with him. Then the nanny came in to take Esmé for a walk, and Charlie and Louise retired to her bedroom and made love.

It was early evening when she told him about her dilemma. Should she keep L'Invitation au Voyage open – in which case she'd have to cater to the occupying German officers – or should she try to close the place down?

'You dislike the Germans?' Charlie asked.

'Occupation is occupation.' She shrugged. 'But perhaps you like them, Charlie. Most of the fashionable people seem to. And you turned up here with a book by Céline under your arm.'

'A German colonel and his staff paid us a visit at the château. They are well satisfied that the Vicomte de Cygne and his family share their views on life. That suits me very well, and I mean to keep it that way.'

'Are you telling me to do the same?'

'Tell me,' said Charlie after a pause, 'what's the most important priority in your life?'

'To protect Esmé.'

'Then do so. Carry on as normal. Entertain the Germans. What else can you do?'

'I don't know.'

'France is occupied, Louise,' he said earnestly. 'De Gaulle sets up his headquarters in London, and hopes that the French colonies and the Americans may drive Hitler out. But it's just a dream. More likely, London itself will fall.' He paused. 'However, just suppose that one day things were to change, that there was a real chance that Hitler could be driven out.' He gave her a steady look. 'If, in those circumstances, you had senior German officers spending their time here, you might hear all sorts of things that could be useful, if you wanted to pass them on.'

'I see.' She gave him a curious look. 'Are you up to something, Charlie?'

'Absolutely not.' It was a lie, and meant to be seen as such. 'I'm cooperating like everybody else. I have passages of Céline by heart already,' he added cheerfully. 'By the way, may I come and see you and Esmé next Sunday?'

'Of course,' she said.

It was at the end of September that Louise received a visit from Jacob. He came to the door of L'Invitation au Voyage without any forewarning and asked to see her. She took him straight up to her office, and asked what she could do for him.

'I have a favour to ask,' he said. 'Have you seen the new ordinances for the Jews?'

Louise knew that the community had been swollen by Jews fleeing the harsh German rule in the east. Now the Germans were cracking down on the Jews in France as well.

'I haven't read them,' she confessed.

'We all have to register with the authorities, both our families and our businesses, so they know exactly where to find us. If there are food shortages – and that always happens in time of war – we aren't allowed to stand in the food lines. We can't even use public telephones.' He shook his head. 'But the word is that they're going to start taking over our property.'

'I'm sorry,' said Louise. In truth she was disgusted, but she didn't want to say it. 'But why have you come to me?'

'Would you store some of my pictures?' He looked at her earnestly. 'You see, Madame Louise, you already have quite a few. No one would have any reason to doubt you if you said that they belonged to you.'

'You know that the German officers are starting to come here?'

'Yes. I think that makes it even safer. The last place they'd suspect would be right under their noses. Some you could put on the walls, some you could store . . .'

She hesitated. She imagined it was illegal. On the other hand, there was no reason for anyone to know. She could put some in the bedrooms, whose decorations were always changing. Others could go into the apartment nearby.

'Twenty,' she said. 'More than that might attract attention.'

He looked disappointed.

'Could you manage twenty-five? And some drawings?'

'All right. But not more. Perhaps you can find other people to help you. But one thing, Monsieur Jacob. Nothing in writing. You will have to trust me.'

'I trust you, madame,' he said gratefully.

After he had gone, Louise shook her head. It seemed that, unexpectedly, her private resistance to the occupation had just begun.

As Marie looked out at the world, she couldn't help being glad that her daughter was in America. From the BBC broadcasts she was able to gather news that was fairly reliable. In the late summer and autumn of 1940, she had listened day after day as the Luftwaffe tried to destroy the Royal Air Force. Miraculously, by the end of October, it was clear that Hitler had not succeeded. Germany was mighty, but not invincible. For another half a year Hitler had tried to bomb the British into submission, but by May 1941 he'd had to give up. In other theatres too, Britain was pushing back against the fascist enemy. In Africa, Hitler's Italian allies had retreated under British attack, and Hitler had been forced to send German troops there to hold the line.

And France herself was still fighting. Admittedly, the Vichy government was supplying troops to the German side. But the Free French Naval Forces had brought fifty ships and nearly four thousand men to serve with the British navy. And if there had been Polish airmen in the Battle of Britain, there were soon French pilots flying Spitfires too.

In London, de Gaulle's government in exile had taken the great, double-barred Cross of Lorraine – the region from which Joan of Arc herself had come – as its symbol; and as de Gaulle had hoped, French colonies like the Cameroons, French Equatorial East Africa and New Caledonia had sided with him, with others likely to follow. In the Middle East, Free French forces had joined the fight in Syria and Lebanon.

In Paris, however, life had continued quietly. The de Cygnes and the Blanchard families were not troubled at all. Indeed, the German authorities seemed positively anxious to court them. Marie saw an example of this early in the new year.

Since the German occupation, Marc had retreated into private life. He still turned up for cultural events from time to time, but mostly lived in dignified isolation. She doubted whether the Germans thought that a liberal intellectual like Marc was a supporter of the authoritarian government; but he was getting too old, and was too self-centred to give them any trouble.

In fact, it was the Germans who tried to coax him into more activity. Marie became aware of it one evening in February.

It had been months since Marc had invited them to a social gathering at his apartment, so she and Roland both went, and took Charlie with them. There was a crowd of people there, mostly from the world of the arts, but she was surprised to see a couple of German officers in uniform. A moment later, all was explained, as Marc signalled them to join him.

'Allow me to present my sister and her husband, Vicomte and Vicomtesse de Cygne, and her stepson, Charles – the German ambassador.'

Whatever one might think of Hitler and his inner circle, they could be clever when they wanted. The appointment of an ambassador to France at all was a well-calculated gesture to preserve the fiction that France was still a sovereign state ruling herself – with a little help from her German friends. But their choice of ambassador was inspired. Otto Abetz was urbane and cultivated, and he had a French wife. His job was to reassure the French and help them accept German rule.

Abetz was quite young, only in his late thirties. He was immaculately tailored, and might have stepped straight from a Parisian salon. With his appreciative bow and greeting to Roland and his son, he conveyed in an instant that he was well aware of who they were, and that they were considered as aristocratic friends of the regime who shared its values and, still more important where trust is concerned, its prejudices. To Marie, he then turned with practiced charm.

'Madame, I hope you will help me persuade your brother to take a more active role in Paris life again. We all need him. He was good enough to accept an invitation to the embassy' – as if he could refuse, she thought – 'and I begged him to let me come to see his wonderful collection of pictures. My wife has already read two of his monographs, which she says are as elegant as they are scholarly, and I have them by my bedside to read myself.'

Marie could tell that even Marc, who had seen more winters than most in the art world, was not entirely immune to this flattery.

'It has not been easy to persuade him from his retirement for a number of years,' she offered, 'but I always tell him that if he does not take exercise, he will grow old.'

'*Voilà!*' The German turned to Marc with a broad smile. 'I do not ask you to listen to me, my friend, but you should listen to your sister, who is wiser than either of us.'

The following month, Marc was seen again at a reception Abetz gave for the cultural and academic elite of the city. He still didn't go out much, but no doubt Abetz was content that he served the German purpose well enough.

Despite the ambassador's charm, there were still plenty of reminders that an iron fist lay behind the velvet glove. German street signs directed one to all the new German buildings. Even the Hôtel de Crillon on Place de la Concorde was now the huge and threatening offices of the security services. Cars with loudspeakers circulated to remind everyone that troublemakers would not be tolerated. There was a strict curfew at night. Food rationing began in earnest.

'It's all right for us,' Charlie remarked. 'We only have to go to the château and there is food. I can always go out into the woods and shoot a pigeon. But the poor people of Paris are not so lucky.'

And what was Charlie up to himself? Marie had been able to do one great thing for him, in the autumn of 1940. But once that was done, she had been careful not to interfere. Sometimes he would disappear for days at a time. She never asked him where he had been or what he was doing. She was fairly sure he had a woman somewhere, and it would have been strange if he had not. But as to his other, perhaps more dangerous, activities, she could only guess.

If there were resistance groups forming, it was still hard to see at present what they could usefully do, since the German control of northwestern Europe appeared to be complete.

But as the summer of 1941 began, two events gave a hint that the German supremacy might begin to falter. For in May, Germany's mighty battleship the *Bismarck* was sunk. And then, at the end of June, came the astonishing news that Hitler had suddenly turned on his new friend Stalin, and invaded Russia.

'He must be mad,' Roland remarked. 'Doesn't he know what happened to Napoléon when he invaded Russia back in 1812?' He shook his head. 'Perhaps Hitler thinks he's a better general.'

'And what do you think?' Marie asked Charlie.

'I think,' said Charlie, 'that this changes everything.'

For Max Le Sourd, it brought relief. The last year had been especially difficult for him.

With the French Communist Party joined in lockstep with Moscow, the journalists at *L'Humanité* had been obliged to follow the party line.

'We have to advocate collaboration with the Germans,' he told his father. By the end of 1940, he was adding: 'I'm not sure how much longer I can do it, and nor are many of my communist friends.'

But his father had never made any comment at all.

Since Max's return from the Spanish Civil War, the relationship between them had been perfectly friendly. Both regretted equally that Franco and his right-wing army had prevailed, and that Spain, for all its Catholic trappings, was really a fascist regime. His father accepted that Max had fought bravely and that his heart was in the right place.

'But he doesn't trust me,' Max said sadly to his mother.

'You mustn't take it personally,' his mother told him. 'But with the communists on the Germans' side . . . he can't.'

Was his father in a resistance movement of some kind? As the months went by, Max often wondered. His father was well into his seventies, but with his tall, lean frame he seemed hardly changed. He'd still walk from Belleville to the Bois de Boulogne without seeming tired.

It was no use asking him. Once, in the spring of 1941, Max told him frankly that he was ready to start working against the Germans. But his father made no comment at all, and never referred to the subject again. Max understood, though he still found it hurtful.

Only at the end of June, when Hitler invaded Russia, did the situation change.

'We're organising a communist resistance movement,' Max told the older Le Sourd. 'I don't know details yet, but I shall join it, of course.' He gave his father a careful look. 'Unless you have any other suggestions.'

And this time, though his father didn't say anything, he put his arm around Max's shoulder and gave a gentle squeeze. A few days later, on a warm day in July, he suggested: 'As it's a beautiful day, let's go for a picnic, you and I.'

'As you like. Where do you want to go?'

'The Bois de Vincennes,' said his father. 'We can bicycle out there, together.'

Max hadn't been there for years. Not that it was so far away. He'd forgotten how delightful the old forest was.

For if Parisians could enjoy the open spaces of the Bois de Boulogne on the western side of the city, on the eastern side the Bois de Vincennes was just as fine. The old royal forest still contained an ancient château that kings had used until the days of Louis XIV, but people mostly came to walk in the woods.

They found a pleasant, deserted spot and set out their little meal of bread, pâté and cheese. Max had provided a bottle of *vin ordinaire*, and as he looked at his father stretched out so comfortably on the grass, he felt a great wave of affection. They ate and drank for a little while before his father broached the subject that was on his mind.

'You were serious about working in the Resistance?'

'Yes.'

'Do you want me to tell you something about it?'

'I do.'

His father nodded thoughtfully.

'You know that, as a socialist, I've always believed it's of paramount importance to be organised. Random acts of violence are useless. The thing is to have an organisation well prepared so that, when the time comes, one is ready to seize the initiative. It's the same with any resistance movement. Especially when you are dealing with a ruthless enemy like Hitler.'

'That makes sense.'

'Now that there's an eastern front, we could make enough trouble to tie up troops here. That might cause Hitler some difficulties. One day, perhaps, if America comes into the war, it may even be possible to liberate France. A big Resistance network could be crucial in providing information and sabotage prior to an invasion.'

'You'll need good links with de Gaulle in London, then.'

'Up to a point, yes. But don't forget the bigger picture. In the event that French and Allied troops can liberate France, we need to be completely organised so that the France they liberate belongs to us. By the time they get to Paris, it will be a Commune.'

'The old dream.'

'It's a hundred and fifty years since the French Revolution and we still haven't made good its ideals. But maybe this time it can be done.'

'That's what you're fighting for?'

'Yes. I want the Nazis out, of course. But my ultimate goal is to complete the Revolution, for France to reach her true destiny. And I hope it may be your goal as well.'

For the next ten minutes he gave Max some details of the networks as they were emerging. It was evident to Max that his father was telling him far less than he knew, but it was clear that, both in Vichy France and in the occupied north, they were extensive.

'The cells are linked, but also separate. Only a few key individuals know much outside their own cell. That's for security.'

'What will your role be?'

'Propaganda. I'm getting a little old to run around blowing things up. But we need a newspaper. We may revive *Le Populaire*, which was suppressed. Underground of course. I'll be helping with that.'

'I want to do something more active. My time in the Spanish Civil War taught me a good deal.'

'I know. And that's the point. I've gathered together a bunch of boys, and I think I should turn them over to you and your friends. They all want action.' He grinned. 'Do you know, I even found the fellow who cut the elevator cables in the Eiffel Tower? He's about the same age as me, but he's still going strong. And we have some villains from the Maquis. In fact, I have all sorts of fellows. Are you interested?'

'Absolutely,' said Max.

His father drank a little more wine and stared through the trees. He seemed to see something that caused him to nod, but when Max glanced around, he saw nothing.

A couple of minutes later, a tall, handsome man suddenly came into the little clearing where they were, hesitated, and apologised for disturbing them. To Max's surprise, his father turned to the stranger and remarked: 'You are not disturbing us at all, my friend. This is my son, Max.'

The stranger, who was in his late twenties and had a decidedly aristocratic air, bowed and said that he was delighted to meet him.

'Max,' his father continued, 'this is my good friend, who is known as Monsieur Bon Ami. Please remember his face so that you will know him when you meet again.'

The two younger men gazed at each other and smiled. Then Monsieur Bon Ami slipped away through the trees as quietly as he had come.

'Who the devil was that?' asked Max.

At first, when Charlie had thought about how to make himself useful to de Gaulle, there had been one great obstacle. Who to talk to, and how to find them? So many of his own contemporaries had been among the million prisoners of war taken into the German work camps. Others might have been amenable to doing something, but they had no idea how to make contact with the Free French across the water.

Of his father's generation, even the most patriotic military men all seemed to be following Pétain.

It was Marie who made a clever suggestion. After a few telephone calls, she found an instructor in the Staff College who'd been close to the English officer she had met before the war. Her approach to him was subtle. Was there any way that he was ever in contact with the Englishman, she inquired?

'I doubt that such a thing is possible, madame,' he replied. But she noticed that he did not say that it was out of the question.

'I should be grateful if you would not mention this to anyone, because my husband and his son are ardently for Pétain, and would not wish me to have any contact with the Englishman at all, but before he left Paris, he left some prints with me and asked if I could dispose of them for him. I did so, and I have the proceeds. If you ever think of a way of my discreetly letting him have his money, I should be glad. That is all.'

'It will probably have to wait until the cessation of hostilities, madame,' he told her. 'But I will make inquiries.'

A month passed. Charlie kept busy. For a start, he got a list of all the officers who used Louise's brothel on a regular basis, found out their duties, everything he could about them. He also constructed a list of people who, if they could be persuaded to help the cause, might be useful. Given his social position, and his family's reputation as German sympathisers, he was often a guest at the receptions that German generals were giving in the mansions they had requisitioned.

'It's remarkable,' he said to Marie once, 'apart from a German host and a sprinkling of German officers, I seem to see just the same people at all these parties as I did before the war.'

But it meant that he could gather information quite easily. The question was, would he be able to make use of all this activity?

It was dusk, one evening in November, when the butler announced to Marie that there was an elderly French art dealer at the door of the apartment, who had been told she might have some military prints for sale. She at once told him to usher the gentleman in.

The disguise was excellent. Shuffling in, with a low bow, came a man apparently in his seventies. Only when they were alone did he look up sharply, and she saw the face of the English officer.

'Your message was very clever, madame,' he remarked. 'What can I do for you?'

'How did you get here?' she cried.

'I am a *parachutiste*, Madame la Vicomtesse,' he answered with a smile.

She explained quickly that it was Charlie who was anxious to make himself useful, and that it would be best if the two of them met alone. He immediately suggested a spot in the Parc Monceau the following day and departed.

When Charlie met him, and explained what he had to offer, the English officer was impressed, and told him that he'd soon be contacted. 'You're just the sort of man Colonel Rémy needs,' he said.

'Colonel Rémy?' The name meant nothing to Charlie.

'Code name. Safer,' said the Englishman, and left.

Within a week he'd received his first instructions from Colonel Rémy. A list of information needed, and the address of a safe drop where he could leave his reports.

Soon Charlie was making careful notes on all the barracks, the road and rail transport used by the Germans, the places where ammunition and explosives were kept, any information that might come in useful later for sabotage.

It was useful information. He could see that. But he wanted to do more. He was told to be patient. But Charlie wasn't very good at being patient. 'I want the chance of some action,' he confessed to his father. And it was after some weeks of this frustration that his father finally gave him the name of a man who might be able to help him.

'I have no idea if he is in any Resistance movement,' his father said, 'but I have made some inquiries about him. He is a socialist, and I am sure he is not pro-German. He might be able to put you in touch with people. But tell him nothing about your business with Colonel Rémy. Keep the two activities totally separate, or you could compromise security.'

A few days later, the elder Le Sourd had been surprised when, soon after he had left his home in Belleville, an athletic young man, almost as tall as his son, fell into step beside him.

'Monsieur Le Sourd?'

'Perhaps.'

'I am Charlie de Cygne. My father sent me. May we speak alone?'

'Why?'

'My father told me I could trust you.'

'He did? Why?'

'I don't know. He said you were comrades in the Great War.'

'He said that?' Le Sourd considered. 'How do I know you are his son, and that he sent you?'

'He told me that, if he had been killed, he had asked you to send something to me.' Charlie pulled out the little lighter made from a cartridge shell and showed it to Le Sourd.

'What else did he say?'

'That we should not shoot each other until France is liberated.'

Le Sourd nodded slowly.

'There is a little bar along the street, young man,' he said. 'We can talk there.'

When they had finished their talk, Le Sourd had told him that it would be best that he had an operational alias, and asked him what he would choose. After hesitating for a moment, Charlie smiled.

'Call me Monsieur Bon Ami,' he said. A good name, he thought. For that's what he'd like to be: a Good Friend.

When Luc Gascon first met Schmid, he thought the young German wasn't so bad – for a Gestapo man.

It had been an icy day in early December of 1941. News had just come from Russia that the Germans had suffered their first reverse. At first, they had swept through south Russia and taken the city of Kiev. But now, up in the north, they had met such furious resistance in the suburbs of Moscow that they had turned back.

In the Gascon bar that morning, the news had been greeted with pleasure. If the emperor Napoléon himself had been forced to retreat from Moscow, it would have been galling if Hitler had done better. And one of the regulars at the bar had just remarked, 'Hitler's buggered,' when a young man in a black Gestapo uniform entered the bar and ordered a drink.

Luc had happened to be in the bar just then, and he'd moved quickly as an awkward silence fell. Explaining that he was the owner of both the bar and the restaurant next door, he welcomed the

Gestapo man with discreet politeness. Skilfully showing the young German respect, it hadn't taken him long to engage him in conversation. He soon let it be clear both that he was solid for Pétain, and that he might be a useful mine of information about the city. He also learned that the German was named Schmid, that his family were farmers, that he had a married sister and that he worked in the Gestapo headquarters.

Karl Schmid was unremarkable to look at. Were it not for his black uniform, he would be the kind of figure who is immediately lost in any crowd. Medium height, mousy hair. Only his pale blue eyes were at all memorable.

After the German had left, one of the regulars remarked sourly to Luc that he'd been nice to the German. Luc only shrugged.

'Who needs to annoy the Gestapo? I want them to leave us alone.'

But in fact, he had already decided that this young Gestapo officer might be useful to him.

Luc always found ways to make a living. His first task was to ensure there were provisions for the restaurant. Using the black market he managed to keep the restaurant going, despite the wartime food shortages.

But his income was down. Though he could still obtain a little cocaine, many of his clients had left, and the high-ranking German officers who used the drug had their own suppliers. He never saw Louise now, but it enraged him that she must be making a fortune at L'Invitation au Voyage, and was paying him nothing. There wasn't much he could do; but he still vowed that one day he'd make her wish she hadn't treated him like that.

In the meantime, however, he knew how to live by his wits. And it was natural that he had been wondering for some time how he should profit from the German occupation. People like Marc Blanchard and Louise met Germans at the highest levels. He did not. But young Karl Schmid the Gestapo officer might be just the sort of contact he needed.

Two days later, he went to his office.

Karl Schmid sat behind his desk and considered the world. He was twenty-eight years old and remarkably fortunate.

For a start, he was in Paris – a city he'd always wanted to visit, and never dreamed he would live in.

Not only that, his office was spectacular. Not his own, personal office exactly, since that was quite a small room. But the building was spacious and situated on one of the noblest avenues in the world.

After the Great War, the wide, stately avenue that ran down from the Arc de Triomphe to the Bois de Boulogne had been renamed after one of the war's great French generals: avenue Foch. And the Gestapo had chosen well when they took over three houses at the avenue's lower end. 'My office,' he had written to his parents with satisfaction, 'is on the Avenue Foch, which is a very good address.'

He was not entirely surprised when Luc appeared to see him. When he had first encountered him, it had seemed to Schmid that, by his demeanour, the fellow might be a potential informer, and he had been thinking of going by the bar again some day.

He was pleased that Luc didn't waste any time.

'I could not speak in public, Lieutenant Schmid,' Luc said politely, 'but I know many corners of Paris. If I can ever be of service to you . . .'

'Do you expect to be paid?' Schmid asked.

'If my services are useful. One has to live.'

Schmid had no intention of paying without results. It was a good sign that the man wasn't asking for that.

'I can pay a little.' Schmid looked at Luc thoughtfully. 'If you hear of any illegal activity, any terrorist plans . . .'

'I avoid that world myself,' Luc said carefully. 'But I sometimes hear things.' He paused. 'Is there anything else you need?'

'The Wehrmacht has already confiscated some art, as you will be aware, I am sure. But there is so much art in Paris, often in criminal hands. Paintings especially. I take a personal interest in such matters.'

'I understand. The owners have to be arrested. But then the work may be confiscated.' Luc nodded. 'A valuable business.'

'I have said you will be paid.'

Luc inclined his head politely.

'I shall make inquiries,' he said. 'They may take time.'

'Come to see me at the start of every month,' Schmid ordered. 'Meanwhile, I know where to find you.'

Time would tell whether this smooth Frenchman of the streets would produce anything of value.

As Luc went about his business in the months that followed, one thing seemed very clear: his self-interest lay with the Germans.

True, only days after he had first met Schmid, news came that the Japanese had bombed Pearl Harbour, and America had entered the conflict. People were saying that the tide of war would change. It might be so. It might not. But any such change was far over the horizon.

By June 1942, the British were starting to bomb German cities. But that wasn't stopping the Germans from launching a new offensive in Russia that was sweeping towards the mighty River Volga.

And in France, in Paris especially, the German grip was total.

All the same, Luc didn't want to get on the wrong side of the Resistance. Successful or not, the Dalou boys and their friends could be dangerous. He'd be better keeping in with them. Besides, the more he knew about their activities, the more opportunities there might be, if he was careful, to sell information to Schmid.

More than once he'd said to Thomas, 'I was wrong not to have come out with you when you did the job on the Eiffel Tower. Tell the Dalou boys I'd be glad to come another time.'

It was a dangerous line to walk. But he thought he could manage it.

He hadn't yet been able to find an art collector for the German. He'd thought of Marc, naturally. But in the first place, Marc was a long-time customer – and Luc always looked after his customers. Besides, Marc was in high favour with the Germans, and he doubted very much that Marc was involved in any way with any Resistance groups.

But he'd been able to make himself useful to the Gestapo nonetheless. When Schmid had asked him to watch a French engineer who he thought might be running several wireless operators, he had done so, and the engineer had been arrested. Luc had been paid something after that. Once, when he overheard the Dalou boys planning a raid to steal explosives from a store down in Boulogne-Billancourt, he'd waited to make sure that Thomas was not involved, and then gave Schmid the tip-off. The next time he saw Schmid, the

Gestapo man remarked: 'We ignored that tip you gave us about the explosives.'

'And?'

'They stole them. Can you tell me who they were?'

Luc threw up his hands.

'Unfortunately no,' he lied. 'It was two men I overheard, but I'd never seen them before. If I see them again, I'll tell you.'

'Well,' Schmid said, 'I shall listen to you next time. By the way,' he added, 'there is something else I want. If you can find me some.'

'What is that?'

'Jews. But not just any Jews. I want French Jews. Find me a French Jew whom I can arrest, my friend, and I will pay you well.'

It was a hot day that July when Luc Gascon walked along the bank of the Seine past the Eiffel Tower.

He was going there because he made a point of seeing everything that was going on in the city. And this was certainly an unusual occurrence. He was going to take a look at what was going on at the large building that lay just a short distance downstream from the Eiffel Tower.

The old indoor bicycle stadium which had proved such a useful venue for the boxing matches during the '24 Olympics was still in use. The Vélodrome d'hiver, the winter bicycle track, remained its official name. But everyone called it the Vel d'hiv. And for the last few days, the French police had found another use for the old place. It was a holding station for a large number of undesirables they had just rounded up. Several thousand of them. Jews: foreign Jews, mostly.

When Luc got there, he could see a number of police vans outside the stadium, but there didn't seem to be any people going in or out. All the doors of the stadium were closed. In the strange silence, under the harsh sun, the scene reminded him of one of those surrealist paintings he had seen, as though he had walked in upon a dream. But as he got closer, something else struck him that wasn't like a dream at all. It was the smell. Not just a smell, a stink, a terrible, sickening stench of latrines overflowing, of excrement warmed and putrefied. He pulled out a handkerchief and held it over his nose.

Luc didn't especially like or dislike Jews. People who had strong beliefs said they were capitalist bloodsuckers, or Marxist revolutionaries.

And they'd crucified Christ, of course. Personally, Luc never went to church and didn't care whether they'd crucified Christ or not.

Most of the Jews he'd met weren't so bad. He supposed they were mainly French Jews, and they might be rather different from all the foreign Jews who'd been flooding into Paris in the last few years.

And it was the foreign Jews that the police had been rounding up.

He stared at the building with its terrible stench. Whoever those poor devils were inside, he considered, this was a terrible way to treat them.

He'd been standing there for a little while when he noticed another figure, a small, neatly dressed man, also watching the Vel d'hiv from a street corner. The fellow looked vaguely familiar, and he searched his mind, trying to remember where he'd seen him. He saw the man turn and look at him, then walk towards him.

When Jacob had told his wife he was going to see what was going on at the Vel d'hiv, he had felt a secret sense of dread, but he had not told her that. Now, as the art dealer gazed at the big building, he understood exactly what he saw.

The logic was simple: if they would pen all these people up in conditions like this – if they would treat them worse than animals being prepared for slaughter – then there was nothing they would not do.

Perhaps, if he had not known the long history of his people, he might have remained like so many in the Jewish community who refused to believe that a French government could be so evil. Perhaps, if he had not spent all his life in the company of works of art, and known their stories and the characters, sometimes, of the very men who commissioned such beauty, he might have been less keenly aware of the terrible possibilities that lie within the human spirit.

But Jacob knew these things, and foresaw what was to come, and knew he must get out, if he could.

Ever since he had given some of his paintings to Louise, Jacob had been preparing for the worst. If he could have, he'd have gone to England. But escape across the Channel was almost impossible. A few months ago, however, a friend named Abraham had told him of a new opening.

'We're going to organise a route across the Pyrenees into Spain,' Abraham had told him. 'It's not in place yet, and it'll be risky, of course; but we're getting our people together.' He'd promised to keep Jacob informed. Jacob had told his wife about the conversation, and between themselves they referred to this option as 'visiting Cousin Hélène'.

Abraham lived in Montparnasse. If Abraham could just get them to a safe house of some kind out of Paris, Jacob thought, that at least would be a start. He still had money to invest in the enterprise.

And he was so shaken by what he had just seen at the Vel d'hiv, so afraid that any delay might put his little family in danger, that he resolved to go straight to Abraham and, if possible, to flee at once.

He just needed to get a message to his wife. A couple of hundred yards away he could see a telephone kiosk. He glanced towards the police vans. A couple of policemen were standing beside one of them, watching him idly. That was a nuisance. As a Jew, he wasn't allowed to use the public telephones. It would be ridiculous to get arrested for some tiny infraction like that.

But there was another fellow standing not far from the telephone. Perhaps he could be of help. It was worth a try.

Luc gazed down at Jacob. He remembered him now. Their meeting had been very brief. He'd called to see Marc Blanchard at his apartment, a few years ago, just as Jacob was leaving. Marc had introduced him as his dealer. They'd spoken for only a few moments before Jacob had to go.

Evidently Jacob didn't remember him, and he was just debating whether to introduce himself, or whether it might be a bore, when the dealer started speaking.

'A terrible business,' Jacob said, nodding towards the stadium. He looked distressed, and agitated.

'I believe they're all foreign Jews,' said Luc.

'Ah. Yes. Perhaps,' Jacob replied absently. 'I wonder if you could do me a small favour,' he said suddenly. 'I should like to tell my wife that I shall be home late. But you know I can't use the phone over there. If I gave you a number . . .'

'But of course,' Luc spread his hands. 'No problem.'

'Well then, my wife's name is Sarina. If you could just tell her that I am delayed until this evening, but that I have not forgotten we are going to see her cousin Hélène in the morning.' He smiled. 'She thinks I forget everything.'

'All wives think their husbands are forgetful.'

'You are very kind. Here is the number.' Jacob wrote it on a scrap of paper. 'And the price of the call.'

'No payment, monsieur. It's a pleasure. I'll do it right away. If you stand over by that street corner, the police won't see you, but you'll be able to see me make the call.' He smiled.

'You are very kind, monsieur.'

Luc made the call.

'Am I speaking to Sarina?'

'Yes.' The voice sounded cautious.

'Your husband was just here, by the Vel d'hiv. He can't use the public telephone, you understand? He asked me to give you a message.'

'I see.' She still sounded a little doubtful.

'He is delayed. He won't be back until this evening.'

'This evening?' She sounded very surprised.

'That's what he said. And something else. He said to tell you that he hasn't forgotten he is going with you to see your cousin Hélène in the morning.'

'Our cousin Hélène? He said Hélène?'

'*Oui, madame.*'

'Oh my God.' Her voice sounded terrified. 'Oh my God.'

'*Madame?*'

'Nothing. Thank you.' She hung up.

Luc glanced towards Jacob and nodded. He saw the Jew give a grateful nod in return, and hurry away.

Now what, Luc wondered, was that all about?

Sometimes Schmid despaired of the Vichy French. Not that the government of France was being uncooperative. Far from it. Pétain was a splendid figurehead. The respect he'd earned in the Great War meant that the French were glad to follow the old warrior. And it was evident that, as a realist, Pétain had decided the only way to save his country was to become a German satellite. The French police were keen to do Germany's will. Almost too keen, sometimes.

Yet they kept missing the point.

Karl Schmid leaned back in his chair, put his hands behind his head and sighed. 'It's partly our own fault,' he murmured to himself. 'We didn't have a proper plan for the Jews.'

Nobody wanted them in Germany, of course. They were kicked out of there. But there was so much to accomplish that the problem of what to do with them had been rather shelved. And since they had been fleeing there from Eastern Europe anyway, France had, rather by default, become a dumping ground for the Jews of the Third Reich.

But now it was time to tidy things up. At the start of that year, Schmid knew, a final solution to the Jewish question had been secretly agreed, and this very summer the methodology was being perfected. Officially however, the Jews were to be sent as workers to the East, or kept in labour camps.

There was only one problem. The French did not understand the Jewish question. It had been glaringly apparent at the meeting the French police came to in the Gestapo offices here on the avenue Foch just a couple of weeks ago. Though he was only a junior fellow, they had allowed him to sit in on the meeting, and he had watched with fascination.

'We shall conduct the round-up, but we have two stipulations,' the senior Frenchman said.

The first was that they should wait until after the fourteenth of the month. To conduct the round-up on Bastille Day would seem unfortunate. This was easily agreed to. But the second stipulation was more tiresome.

They wanted to round up only foreign Jews. No French ones.

'It might provoke bad feeling in the city,' the French police chief said. 'Stir up trouble. Just what we don't need.'

'But why?' one of the SS men asked him. 'This is not just a question of rounding up troublesome Gypsies who don't belong here. That of course we understand. But the Third Reich does not make a distinction because a man is a German Jew as opposed to a Polish one. That is not the point. What matters is that he is a Jew.'

'We have no objection to the statutes that rightly make Jews into second-class citizens,' the Frenchman answered. 'Eventually, I dare

756

say they may all be removed. But we should at least start with the foreign ones.'

'We make no distinction.'

'In France' – the police chief spread his hands – 'when a man is a Frenchman, even a Jew . . .' It was clear that somehow the French, even now, were so proud of their nationhood that they considered it could somehow mitigate the most fundamental facts about a man.

His boss had turned to Karl.

'What is our capacity at present, Schmid?'

'We could take in a little over thirteen thousand.'

'Good.' The German turned to the French police chief. 'We want thirteen thousand, whoever they are. And no children. Remember, these people are all going east as labourers.'

'Understood.'

But of course, though the French policemen had started at dawn and moved with commendable efficiency, they'd brought in all the children as well. Some people said it was because they couldn't bear to part the children from the parents. It might be so. Schmid suspected it was so they wouldn't have to deal with all these inconvenient children themselves.

Thousands of them were in the Vel d'hiv at this moment. It must be like an oven in there, he thought. Soon they'd be transferred to other holding camps. And then in due course, sent east.

But admirable as this was, it still did nothing to address the question of the French Jews. Some had been arrested, of course. Blum, the former prime minister, was being kept in detention – but a comfortable one. Jew or not, it would be foolish to treat a former prime minister of France without some show of respect. His brother, however, was in a holding camp already.

Patience, thought Schmid, patience would eventually do the rest. When they'd worked through all the foreigners, the French police would be obliged to start rounding up the Jews they so foolishly considered as their own.

In the meantime, any French Jew who broke a regulation or stepped out of line could be taken instantly.

He was just considering this when an orderly told him that Luc Gascon had come to see him.

★   ★   ★

The Frenchman's face was a mask, but Schmid sensed that he was quite excited.

'You have something for me?'

'I am not sure. I have a French Jew. He is an art dealer, so I assume he owns a quantity of paintings. Whether he has broken the law, or is planning to, I am not sure. But let me tell you what happened.'

Schmid listened carefully as Luc described what had taken place at the Vel d'Hiv. When Luc had finished, Schmid asked him what conclusion he drew.

'I think it's possible that Jacob was so shocked by what he saw that he is going to try to escape from Paris, maybe from France. When I used the words "Cousin Hélène," his wife sounded so frightened that I think it may be a code word between them.'

'I agree.' Schmid nodded. 'It is possible. If so, there may be an escape route we know nothing about; and this Jew could lead us to it.'

'Can you arrest him?'

'I can pull him in on suspicion. After that, we shall question him. See what he says.' He smiled. 'Give me the telephone number and leave the rest to me. You have done well.'

The two plain-clothesmen waited outside Jacob's house the next morning. Schmid's instructions to them were simple: they were to observe where the family went.

Early in the morning they saw Jacob leave the apartment block where he lived on the rue La Fayette. One of the men followed him to his small gallery, where he remained until the end of the morning. Meanwhile, his wife went out shopping, and returned home. Late in the afternoon, Jacob returned home. Nothing else happened. 'Watch again tomorrow morning,' Schmid instructed. 'If he goes to the office again, pick him up and bring him in.'

At noon the next day, they brought Jacob in. They didn't take him to the avenue Foch, however, but to a house on the rue des Saussaies, just behind the Élysée Palace. It was well equipped for such encounters.

Schmid conducted the interrogation. As he looked at the small, neatly dressed art dealer, he felt no particular emotion. He asked his questions gently. He could always use other methods if he chose.

So he learned at once that Jacob had a wife and a single child, a little girl. That was easy. What was his business? Jacob explained that he was an art dealer. Schmid asked for the keys to the gallery. Reluctantly, Jacob gave them. Had he any other family?

Not much. He had a cousin named Hélène.

The first setback. Hélène was not an invention. She might still be a code word, of course. He asked for her address, so that he could check the story. How often did he see her? Quite often. He had planned to go around to her house with his family yesterday, but then changed his mind.

Where had he been two days ago? To the Vel d'hiv. Why? To see what was happening. Was he afraid? Yes. Where did he go afterwards? Into Montparnasse. Why? He had a friend whom he hadn't seen for a while named Abraham. He'd been concerned he might have been rounded up and taken to the Vel d'hiv. And had he?

'I don't know,' Jacob said simply. 'When I got to his place, they told me he'd moved a couple of months ago. That's all I could discover. So I went home.'

Schmid guessed that some of this story was probably true. But was it the whole truth? He took Abraham's address.

'We shall talk again,' he told Jacob, and sent him back to a holding cell.

By evening his stories had been checked out. Cousin Hélène turned out to be a plump middle-aged woman of no account. Abraham had moved, but not registered his new address. He might be of interest.

Meanwhile, Schmid had gone to the gallery himself. Its contents were quite intriguing.

If the Third Reich confiscated art collections – especially Jewish ones – Schmid had started acquiring art as well. He believed he was developing an eye. He found many things in Jacob's gallery – some of it degenerate art, which would have to be burned, of course – but many good things as well. No doubt there would be more in Jacob's house. It seemed likely that Jacob's art inventory was of far more interest than was Jacob himself. He stayed there until dusk. Before he left, he took a small sketch by Degas, rolled it carefully and put it in his briefcase. It would never be missed.

On the way back, he called in again at the rue des Saussaies. He had them bring Jacob to an interrogation room and strap him in a chair.

He explained to Jacob that he believed there was an escape route out of France, and he wanted to know about it.

Jacob said that if there was one, he didn't know it.

Then Schmid took a pair of pliers and pulled out one of Jacob's fingernails, which made him scream, and Schmid said: 'It is painful, you see.' He asked him: 'Did your friend Abraham know an escape route? Isn't that why you were looking for him?' Jacob said no. So then Schmid did what he had done before, and Jacob screamed again. And as he was sobbing, Jacob looked up wretchedly and said: 'If I could have escaped, do you think I'd be here now?'

Then Schmid told them to take the art dealer back to his cell and to arrest Jacob's wife for questioning the next morning.

Laïla Jacob was seven years old and a bright little girl. When her father didn't come home from the gallery, her mother went to look for him and came back very frightened. At first she wouldn't tell Laïla what had happened, but then she changed her mind.

A Gestapo man had been in the gallery when she got there, she told Laïla, so she had not gone in. But the people in the store next door said that her husband had been arrested.

'They are coming to take us away to prison,' her mother told her. 'All of us. No Jewish house is safe.' Then she hugged Laïla very close, but she didn't say what they could do about it.

The next day was fine, and Laïla wondered if maybe her father would reappear and everything would be normal again. But at nine in the morning, they heard heavy steps coming up the stairs to the landing where their apartment was, and her mother suddenly told her to hide and not to make a sound.

'Wait a little while. Then go to your cousin Hélène,' she said. 'She'll look after you until I get back.'

So Laïla ran and hid in a closet. She heard the door open and heard the men take her mother away with them. And then there was only silence.

For about an hour, Laïla waited in the apartment. When she opened the door and looked out, the landing was empty. She went down the stairs and out into the rue La Fayette.

She started walking up the street towards the Gare du Nord, because Cousin Hélène lived on a street behind the station. But before she reached the Gare du Nord, she passed a little square with a church, and a few benches; and she sat on one of these and considered what she was about to do.

Although she was only seven, Laïla always thought for herself. She had a logical and practical intelligence. And the more she thought about it, the more the little girl wondered if her mother's instructions were right. If no Jewish house was safe, she reasoned, then Cousin Hélène's house wasn't safe either. The only place she might be safe was a house that was not Jewish. And she tried to think of someone she knew who wasn't Jewish.

Then she remembered, a little while ago, her father pointing out a house to her and telling her: 'There's a very nice lady who lives in there. She's keeping some things for me.'

'Why?' she had asked.

'Because I can trust her. She'll keep them safe. Just remember that. You can always go there to get our things, one day.'

She hadn't known why he said this, but she had remembered the house.

Now she wondered: Was the lady Jewish? Laïla had a feeling that she wasn't.

When the little girl turned up on the doorstep of L'Invitation au Voyage just before noon, Louise was quite astonished. She was just going up to her own apartment nearby to have lunch with Esmé. The little girl said who she was, and did she know her father. Yes, Louise said, she did. Then the child wanted to know if she was Jewish. No, Louise said, she wasn't.

Then Laïla told her what had happened.

Louise had to think quickly, then. Her first impulse had been to take the girl up to have lunch with little Esmé. But Esmé was with his nanny. The fewer people who knew about Laïla the better. So she took the little girl up to her office at the top of the house and closed the door.

She quickly telephoned the nanny to say she'd been delayed, gave Laïla something to eat and sat down to think. After ten minutes, she telephoned Charlie. Fortunately he was in Paris. She asked him to come around. Then she told Laïla to stay where she was and not make a sound, and that she'd be back in an hour. Locking the door behind her, she made her way downstairs and went to see Esmé.

'You can't keep her here, the place is full of Germans,' said Charlie decisively. 'If the parents show up, there's no problem. But . . .' – he made a sad face – 'they may not.'

'I can't keep going around to the parents' apartment or even the gallery. It'll look suspicious,' Louise remarked.

'Don't worry. I have men who can take care of that.' He smiled. Whomoever he worked with in the Resistance, he never gave Louise any details. 'If the parents appear, they'll be told she's safe, and I'll get her back to them. If it's what they want.'

'But where will she go in the meantime?' asked Louise.

'Oh,' – Charlie grinned – 'that's the easy bit. Some country air will do her good. The last place anyone's ever going to look for a little Jewish girl is my father's château on the Loire.'

'But will he agree?'

'He'll do it for me.' Charlie paused. 'I'm busy tonight, though. I can have an alibi all ready by this time tomorrow, and I'll drive her down in the car. But can you keep her until then?'

'I wonder where.'

Charlie considered, made a suggestion and departed.

That evening, Schmid decided to celebrate. The Jacob woman had been panic-stricken. Though she didn't exactly contradict her husband, she became so confused when he cross-questioned her about her cousin Hélène that the truth was obvious. Luc Gascon was right. Jacob had clearly used her name as a code. He'd been terrified by what he saw at the Vel d'hiv, decided that all the Jews were in danger, gone to a fellow who might, or might not, be able to provide an escape route and been unable to find him. The Jacobs didn't know where this Abraham fellow was. Schmid was sure of it. They were of no further interest, therefore.

But they could certainly be sent to Drancy. The big holding camp on the northern outskirts of Paris already contained all sorts of Jews, including some of the ones who'd been herded into the Vel d'hiv. From Drancy, in due course they could be sent on to meet their fate.

He didn't have to concern himself with that. There was a daughter too. He didn't care about her either. But the Paris police had been informed that they should pick her up.

Meanwhile, his chief had been delighted by the art haul. A few more neat operations like this, Schmid thought, and he might be in for a promotion. He also had a Degas sketch now, of his own.

So he decided to pay a visit to L'Invitation au Voyage. He'd always heard so much about it.

Schmid was not entirely pleased by the little interview with Madame Louise in her upstairs office. To be asked such questions was intolerable.

'Do not interrogate me, madame,' he said sharply. He was the interrogator, he thought, not this brothel keeper in an occupied country.

But his anger did not seem to faze her in the least.

'Forgive me,' she replied calmly, 'if I remind you that the Parisian establishments like this are the cleanest in the world, and many senior German officers regard my house as – how shall we say – a second home. Our clientele is very select. We take great care. People trust each other. If by any chance you had some little problem which were to be passed on, causing senior officers discomfort, or worse . . . Well, I'm sure you would not wish such a thing.' She paused. 'Nor to be suspected by them as being the culprit.'

He saw the point of course, at once. He could just imagine a very angry general, and the speedy end of his career. But he hated being obliged to answer to this cursed woman.

'There are no problems,' he said furiously.

He was also staggered by the amount of money she calmly demanded. It was more than a week of his pay. No wonder it was only senior officers who came here. No doubt that was how this infernal woman had been able to acquire the artworks he had noticed on the walls.

Well, he thought, at least he was seeing how the game of life was played. He was more glad than ever that he had taken the Degas sketch from Jacob's gallery. He should have taken more.

An hour later, having enjoyed some refreshments and champagne with a most delightful young woman, and having also caught sight of some very senior officers, he felt somewhat mollified. This was an exclusive club. There was a softness, a scented luxury about the place that he had never experienced before. Whatever the irritations of his introduction, these were the prizes for those who rose high. Schmid had always been ambitious for success, but this was the first time he had ever smelled the fruits. And he knew that he wanted them. He wanted them badly.

It was on the landing that the little incident occurred. His companion was conducting him to a room towards the back of the house. He had asked her about some of the various themed rooms, and passing a door he had asked her what was in there.

'That's the Babylon Room,' she answered.

'I should like to see it,' he said.

'I'm afraid it's closed.'

He would not have given the matter a second thought had he not seen Madame Louise coming up the stairs with an officer he recognised as Colonel Walter.

A chance, perhaps, to put the woman in her place. Bowing politely to the colonel, he addressed Madame Louise.

'I should be interested to see the Babylon Room, madame. I hear it is closed, but perhaps I might be allowed to view it.'

'Ah, that room is a work of art,' Colonel Walter remarked, with a smile.

But Schmid had noticed something else. Had he just seen a tiny flash of fear cross the woman's face? It was gone in an instant, but he could have sworn he had detected it. Schmid already knew a lot about fear. Louise turned to Colonel Walter.

'I thank you for the compliment, *mon colonel*,' she said. 'But I am preparing a new room in there.'

'Really?' Schmid cut in. 'Will you tell me what? It would be interesting to see the work in preparation.'

Again, the woman turned to the colonel.

'You surely would not wish to ruin my surprise?'

Colonel Walter stepped forward gallantly, and took Schmid's arm.

'My dear young man,' he said kindly, but with a trace of admonition, 'one does not interrupt a great artist in the middle of their work.' He turned back to Madame Louise. 'We shall look forward to seeing your next, astounding creation when it is ready.'

So Schmid allowed himself to be conducted along the passage, and soon had other things to think about.

And Louise wondered what on earth she was going to do with that room now.

And, unaware of what had passed outside the door, little Laïla Jacob slept in Babylon that night.

The following day, just after noon, Charlie de Cygne swept up to the guard post in his big car. The guards recognised him at once. Not many Frenchmen had such a car, or a pass to drive up and down from their family château, nor could they possibly get the fuel to put in the car to make the drive.

But this aristocrat, whose family were such firm supporters of the regime, had all these things.

As he pulled up, they noticed a small girl, swaddled in a blanket, huddled in the back of the car. She looked pale.

'Our housekeeper's granddaughter,' Charlie announced calmly, and waved a letter from a fashionable French doctor in front of them. 'Taking her down to the country.'

The young officer glanced at the letter, which Charlie had procured that morning.

'No doubt the country air will do her good,' he remarked politely.

Charlie looked him straight in the eye and made a face the little girl could not see.

'We hope so,' he said quietly.

The officer waved them through.

It wasn't long before the reports came to Charlie. The police had been looking for Laïla. Schmid and his men had taken all the work from Jacob's gallery. The Jacob apartment had been let to someone else. Clearly they weren't coming back.

For a small payment to one of the guards, one of Charlie's men was able to ascertain that the Jacob parents were being held at the big camp at Drancy. Since they were French, they hadn't been shipped east yet, although trainloads of foreign Jews had already gone that way.

Meanwhile, though Roland de Cygne was a little astonished to find a little Jewish girl living at the château, he and Marie kept up the story that she was a granddaughter of the old housekeeper in Paris, and no one was any the wiser. To be on the safe side, she was called Lucie. As for the little girl herself, she understood very well what she must do.

'Have they killed my parents?' she asked Marie, who told her no, not yet.

'Shall we pray for them each night, just you and I?' Marie asked her, and Laïla nodded.

She read with her each day, and Roland would take her for walks and taught her to fish in the stream.

She was an enchanting child: small, very pretty. If she was a little reserved and watchful at first, that was only to be expected, but it was clear that once she learned to trust the inhabitants of the château, she was full of life.

Charlie found a little bicycle he'd had when he was her age, cleaned it up, and asked if she knew how to ride it.

'Oh yes,' she told him. 'Mama and Papa liked to ride together on a Sunday afternoon, all the way to the Bois de Boulogne. I haven't been there yet, but they taught me to ride in the park near where we lived.' And she had taken great pleasure in riding on the paths around the château.

It had taken some time before Charlie had learned for certain, but as winter began, he confided to Marie that the Jacobs were no longer in the holding camp at Drancy. They'd been put on a train that would take them east, along with many others, including the brother of Léon Blum, the former prime minister. When did it happen and where were they sent? Marie had asked.

'September. To Auschwitz.'

The three de Cygnes had discussed for some time whether they should tell Laïla. In the end, no one wanted to.

'Let's wait and see what happens,' said Marie.

The rescue of Laïla had one other, unforeseen effect. Charlie started worrying about his son.

Right at the start, when he had first suggested to Louise that she might pass on information about her German customers, he had realised that there was a risk. Like many operatives, she had taken a code name. 'Let them call me Corinne,' she had said. But in the early months, the sort of material she had been able to give him, though useful, was not sensitive. He knew all the officers who came to her establishment, their duties, and sometimes more. It was all excellent background for the future, and he passed it on to Colonel Rémy's network. Occasionally she had come up with something which could be used locally – for attacks on Germans, or the sabotage of a goods train here and there. This information he passed on to Max Le Sourd and his boys. He did not think any of this information could have been traced to her.

In hiding a Jewish child, however, Louise had crossed a line. Had she been discovered, she would have been arrested. And what would have happened to little Esmé then? Would he have been able to claim him? Perhaps. But doing so, at such a moment, would have invited suspicion. Sooner or later, Louise might place herself in danger again. Despite her earlier insistence on keeping Esmé all to herself, Charlie felt he had to challenge her.

'Don't you think it's time we told my father he has a grandson, and sent Esmé down to the château where he would be safe?' he suggested. But she still wouldn't hear of it.

'I'm not giving away my child,' she told him. 'Never.' And no arguments, however reasonable, would sway her.

Meanwhile, very gradually, news came through that brought hope. Soon after the rescue of little Laïla, a brave Canadian and British force attacked the coastal town of Dieppe in northern France. The attack was a disaster, yet Charlie took comfort from it for two reasons.

'In the first place,' he remarked to his father, 'it proves that the Allies can strike back and rescue France. And secondly, the fact that the hidden German gun emplacements caught them unawares at Dieppe proves to Churchill and de Gaulle that the French Resistance, not just the Free French forces outside the country, but the fellows here on the ground, will be critical to their success.'

In the east, as the weeks went by, word came that the Germans were held at Stalingrad. Then in November, from North Africa, came the wonderful news that Montgomery had smashed the German Afrika Korps at El Alamein, and chased them all the way back to Tunisia. In the Pacific, the Americans had already decisively defeated the Japanese fleet at Midway back in June. By the end of

1942, therefore, on every major front, there seemed to be signs that the tide of war could be turning.

In Paris, Charlie had plenty to occupy his mind. The Resistance movement was growing. In the southern Vichy zone, people were referring to the Resistance as the Maquis – since that was the wild bush terrain in the mountains where the guerrilla groups were forming – and soon Resistance fighters all over France were being called *maquisards*. But what really mattered now, Charlie thought, was that they were being properly organised.

In the spring of 1943, soon after the joyful news that the Germans had finally surrendered at Stalingrad, another important development occurred.

'There's been a big meeting in Paris,' Charlie told his father. 'De Gaulle's right-hand man, Jean Moulin, was there. People came from all over France. They've coordinated all the Resistance networks, and they've pledged allegiance to de Gaulle.' He smiled. 'When, eventually, the Allies come to rescue France, we shall have an entire Resistance army ready to help them.' He grinned. 'You will be glad to know that the network set up by Colonel Rémy took the name the Confrérie Notre-Dame. As good Catholics, we place ourselves under the protection of the Virgin.'

His father smiled.

'I shall pray to the Blessed Virgin to keep watch over you when you are out with our communist friends as well,' he remarked.

'Please do, Father.'

Charlie was always grateful that Max Le Sourd let him take part in his operations. He hated to be doing nothing, and the communist Resistance didn't mind accepting help from any political quarter.

'I've made you an honorary communist,' Max had told him wryly.

Max's men were a loose-knit group, drawn from several parts of the city. Charlie never knew exactly how many men there were. There were the Dalou boys from up on Montmartre. Sometimes old Thomas Gascon came out with them, especially if there was any work that required dismantling bridges or railway couplings. Once or twice he'd brought his brother, Luc.

Twice, agent Corinne had provided information that had led to action. She had heard of a troop train coming in from Reims, and

Max and his group had taken part in a successful attack on it. Another such tip had led, through Colonel Rémy's network, to a train being bombed by British planes.

Charlie had taken part in attacks on guard posts, and a successful raid on an explosives store. But by the summer of 1943, Max and his men had been ordered to hold back a bit.

'We don't want to lose you just now,' Max was told. Radio operators were getting caught all the time because the Germans could track their signals. The large and vicious German reprisals on whole communities where outrages occurred might be having some effect. 'What we need is for you to build up a larger force to prepare for the really big operations in the future,' they promised him.

For it wasn't as if Paris was short of Resistance activity. The group that the Germans feared most was led by a poet.

'They say that poets and intellectuals are the best terrorists,' Roland had remarked to his son. 'I don't know why.'

And certainly there was no one better than the poet Manouchian.

He was Armenian. A few of his group were French, but most were Polish, Armenian, Hungarian, Italian or Spanish, and half of those Jewish. By the late spring of 1943, he and his group had swung into a frenzy of action. All through that summer and into the autumn, the Germans in Paris had been terrorised by Manouchian. Once, thanks to a tip from Louise, Roland had been able to get some information to Manouchian that allowed him to take out one of the most senior Wehrmacht officers in France.

It was fascinating to see the nervousness of German officers and men in the street, after that. Now they know what it feels like to be terrorised, Charlie thought. Anything that was bad for German morale.

Yet, for all these hopeful signs for the future, Charlie's daily life was gradually getting more restricted.

Food had been rationed since early in the occupation, but wood for fuel was hard to find now, and legally one needed a permit to buy it. The cold winters were bleak for Parisians, therefore. And by the summer of 1943, it was almost impossible even for Charlie to get fuel for his car. He had to take a train to reach the château.

Down in the south in the Vichy zone, a force of French-grown Gestapo, the Milice, seemed to be everywhere, eager to arrest enemies of the regime. There had been betrayals within the Resistance, too. Once, when he and Max's men were meeting a couple of new recruits, brave Spanish boys, they found the Germans waiting for them. They'd lost both recruits. They decided in the end that a careless word from one of the recruits might have tipped the Germans off. But one could never be quite sure. 'It's an uncomfortable feeling,' Charlie confessed to Max, who nodded.

'It's the worst part of the job,' he said.

And then, in November, the terrible blow had fallen. Manouchian and his group were arrested. Was it treachery, Charlie wondered?

'No,' said Max. 'Just good police legwork. The Germans know the French police will always be able to do better than they can. After all, they're French, they know the people and the territory. Their special brigade's been tailing a lot of people they suspected. In the end, if you do that long enough, you discover patterns. And they did.' He looked grim. 'They'll all be shot, of course, but not before they've been tortured for information. Let's hope they don't give away too much.'

It was this salutary reminder that caused Charlie to go to see Louise the following day and beg her to let little Esmé stay with his parents.

'We're neither of us safe now, you and I,' he pointed out. 'For the sake of the child, I beg you.'

But still she wouldn't budge. Christmas passed. As the new year of 1944 began, he pressed her again. To no avail.

By the start of February 1944, Luc Gascon was getting worried, and with good reason.

When he'd started working with Schmid, the Allied threats to Germany's grip on Europe had been so distant they could almost be discounted: trumpets unheard, over the horizon.

And so Luc had been able to live the way he'd always preferred, never pinned down, the fixer who was friends with everybody, the wheeler-dealer in the street who balanced risk, operating in the shadowy territory between German masters and French Resistance men, taking profit where he could. But even the cat who walks alone can find fear in the alley.

For gradually, month after month, the gathering Allies had been advancing until they had appeared on the horizon, as Hitler's armies were slowly beaten back – worn down in Russia the year before, kicked out of Africa, and now the Italian army had surrendered, taking heavy losses in Italy as the Allies advanced, slowly but inexorably, northward towards Rome.

Increasingly Hitler looked like a man in a huge trap. He was still mightily dangerous. But as Luc Gascon calculated the odds, the landscape of his own, personal world looked very different.

What would happen, if and when the Germans lost?

In Paris, he suspected, the revenge on those who had cooperated with them would be unpleasant.

Did anyone guess about his cooperation with Schmid? Luc didn't think so. But who knew what there might be in the German files? Or who might guess? Or who might talk? He needed to put more distance between himself and the Gestapo man.

At the same time, as things got worse for them, the Germans would be getting jumpy. Being an informer is not a healthy occupation. Schmid probably didn't trust him either.

It was with these worries in his mind that, on a cold February day, Luc went to the avenue Foch for his usual meeting.

But he found the Gestapo man rather cheerful.

'Have you heard the news, my dear Gascon?' he asked. And seeing Luc uncertain: 'Those Manouchian gangsters have just been sentenced, an hour ago.'

'Ah.'

'They will all be shot. At once. Except the woman. She will be handed over to you French. Women are not shot in the Reich.'

'What will happen to her, then?'

'She will be beheaded.' Schmid seemed to find that quite amusing. 'Which would you prefer, to be shot or beheaded?'

'Shot, I think.'

'Perhaps you will get your wish.' Schmid laughed at this too, watching Luc as he laughed. 'Are you loyal, Gascon, or are you a double agent?'

'My information has been correct. I gave you Jacob. And I gave you those two Spanish lads.'

Two unfortunate Spanish communists, coming to a meeting with the friends of Thomas and the Dalou boys. He'd picked his spot carefully where he knew at least one of the Dalou boys would be watching. The shots that rang out had cut down the two Spaniards at once. He'd asked Schmid to make sure that some shots came in his direction, so that it looked as if he were a target too. Two shots whizzed past him, one right between his feet, the other actually grazing his cap. He suspected that Schmid had ordered this for his private amusement. But it seemed to have kept the suspicion off him, as he'd run down an alley and shown his cap to his brother and his friends.

'True.' Schmid stared at him. 'You have done well, Gascon. But not quite enough to convince me. So I am giving you another task to prove your loyalty.' He looked down at a piece of paper. 'During a recent interrogation, a name came up. A person who is well connected and who passes information. The name appeared in the files once before, but that is all.' He looked pensive. 'A woman's name. Of course, it may be a man using a female name as his alias, but I suspect it's a woman. Now if you can find out who this is, I would pay you well, Gascon. I might even trust you.'

'Just a name? Nothing else?'

'She has access to people in high places.'

'What name?'

'Corinne.'

The name meant nothing to Luc. Maybe he could find something out.

'I'll see what I can do,' he said.

But as he left, he reflected bleakly: he might want to put distance between himself and the Gestapo man, but it was not going to be so easy to do.

On a misty day in early April, no one would have thought anything of the two old men engaged in a game of *boules* in the little square on Montmartre. One was tall, one short, and neither of them could have been under seventy-five.

After finishing their game, they enjoyed a coffee together and a little cognac. Another man joined them. It seemed he was the tall man's son, who perhaps had come to take his father home.

All three men made their way slowly across to Sacré Coeur basilica and stood in front of it gazing over the city. The mist was lifting. The grey bulk of Notre-Dame, like a stern old ark moored in the

Seine, loomed reassuringly in the distance. Across to the right, some miles away, the Eiffel Tower rose gracefully into the sky, as though she were the guardian of the city's spirit. The three men stared at it.

'They still haven't fixed the cables,' Thomas Gascon remarked with satisfaction. He nodded. 'I'll go up and attach the Tricolour to the top of it before long.'

Nobody contradicted him.

Max Le Sourd looked at the two old men affectionately. Despite their age, they were both useful. His father's work on *Le Populaire* had helped drive the illegal paper's circulation to amazing heights. As for Thomas, the indefatigable old man had insisted on coming on sabotage missions whenever it had been physically possible. It was he who had pointed out that instead of blowing up railway lines with explosives, it was far more effective to take the plates off and pry the rails apart where they were joined. He'd invented a simple way of doing it, and it had worked brilliantly.

But now, at last, the day of which they'd all been dreaming was coming. No one knew the day exactly – unless General Eisenhower did – and no one knew the place. But it was coming soon. A huge invasion of Allied troops from the island of Britain. Liberation.

All over France, the networks so long prepared were getting ready. A massive programme of disruption would take place. German troops would find their trains unable to move, electric wires would be down, while a huge bombing of every kind of military target would come from the air. And in Paris, barricades, mayhem, guerrilla warfare.

And something else.

'The timing will be critical,' Max said quietly. 'As the Germans are driven out, we shall need a *fait accompli*, but it can be done.'

'A commune. The workers will take over Paris.' His father smiled.

The National Council of the Resistance had already agreed, in mid-March, that the new French state would be a very different place from the France before the war. The workers and unions would be given power. Women should have equal rights, welfare be hugely increased.

The commune was only a step further, a way to make sure that, this time, the revolution was fixed immutably in place.

'I like it,' said old Thomas.

'But is the FTP solid for this?' Le Sourd inquired. The *Franc-Tireurs et Partisans*, the communist resistance, Max's boys. In the last two years, it was they who had taken the lead in most of the guerrilla attacks on Germans. Their numbers were large.

'Moscow is against our plan,' Max said. 'If Stalin wanted to please Hitler before, now he wants to please Churchill. Who knows? But I don't give a damn. We'll have a commune.'

He paused. There was just one other subject he had to bring up. It was awkward.

'The numbers in the Resistance are swelling dramatically,' he remarked.

'Naturally,' said his father. 'People can see which way the wind's blowing. The rats will start leaving the sinking German ship.'

'True,' Max continued. 'And the Germans are making it worse for themselves. They're so short of manpower that they're trying to force the boys in the countryside into uniform to fight for them. Sooner than get caught in that trap, the country boys are running off into the woods to join the partisans.'

'That's good,' said old Thomas.

'Yes,' Max agreed, 'but there's a danger. We never quite know what we're getting. It's easier for the Germans to plant spies and stooges in the Resistance now. We need to be very careful about who has information.' He had come to the point now. He glanced at his father.

The older Le Sourd took over. Taking Thomas gently by the arm, he said softly: 'Are you sure about your brother, Luc?'

It was an instinct. Just a degree of uncertainty about his character. The Dalou boys didn't trust him. There had been something not quite right, Max had always felt, about the way those two Spanish lads had been killed and Luc had escaped. Nothing one could pin down. But a concern . . .

'He's all right,' said Thomas.

But he said it without the conviction for which Max was listening. Max knew he would trust old Thomas with his life. No question. But did Thomas feel the same way about his own brother? Max suspected he did not.

'Don't tell him anything,' he said. It was an order.

Thomas nodded. He did not say a word.

The previous winter had been a strange time for Marie. Normally, she and Roland would have spent the darkest months in Paris, but this year they had preferred to remain in the quiet of the château.

It was very peaceful. Indeed, with the increasing difficulty of getting gasoline, it was like returning to an earlier time. They walked or rode, or used an old pony trap that had been kept in the stables. Roland would go out into the woods with his gun and return cheerfully with a brace of pheasant, or pigeons, or a rabbit or two. He also enjoyed the gentle exercise of splitting logs, and as winter set in, they would sit in front of the fire, well supplied with firewood from the estate, and taste the pâté that Marie and the cook had made together, with a fine Burgundy that Roland had retrieved from the cellars – 'For we may as well drink them while we are here', as he charmingly put it – and they would read to each other.

In the depth of winter, the old château looked like a medieval scene in the snow.

She missed her daughter. Claire had two children now, both girls, and Marie wished she could see them. While her husband continued his teaching, and she looked after her children, Claire had taken up studying again. In particular, she was studying the history of art, taking courses when she could. Her teachers were impressed with her essays. She might even try to write a monograph one day, she confessed. When the children were older.

Was she happy with her husband? Marie wasn't quite sure. One of her letters, while it had still been possible to receive them, had been slightly ambiguous.

> *Being Mrs. Hadley isn't so bad, I have to say. I wouldn't want to be married to a man I shared everything with, I don't think. I guess we complement each other. The girls are a delight. We share them at least.*

But Marie had another little girl to look after now, in any case. Little Lucie, as they called Laïla. She seemed to regard the château as her home now. She especially liked the old hall where the unicorn tapestry hung. The tapestry itself seemed to fascinate her.

Marie and her husband were sitting by the big fire and gazing at the tapestry one evening shortly before Christmas, when Roland quietly asked Marie if she remembered the day when Colonel Walter had come. She said that of course she did.

'And I told him that my father had bought that tapestry to stop it being bought by a Jew.' Roland nodded thoughtfully. 'It was quite untrue.' He was silent.

'It satisfied our visitor.'

'Yes. But you see, the point is that I had no difficulty saying it. None. It came quite naturally.' He paused. 'And now, with this little girl here.' He shrugged. 'I don't feel the same way.'

'Don't blame yourself. You didn't put her parents on that train.'

'No. But I could have. Perhaps I would have.'

'What matters is what you did do. You saved Laïla.'

'I? I did nothing. I did it because Charlie asked.'

'Are you glad she's here?'

He nodded, but did not speak.

As winter drew to an end, however, Marie could not help feeling a new emotion: impatience. She hadn't enough to do.

She had the château to run, of course, but she had long ago discovered all its mysteries, and the place now ran itself beautifully. The little girl was learning everything the cook and the housekeeper could teach her, and Marie did lessons with her for a couple of hours most afternoons. She looked after her husband, she took exercise. And she liked to read.

Ever since her marriage to Roland, Marc would come down to join them at the château once or twice a year, always bringing something interesting to read. Soon after the arrival of Laïla, he had arrived with various books that had passed the censor, but also an illegal item – a slim volume titled *Le Silence de la mer*.

'It's by a French patriot who has taken the name Vercors,' he explained. 'It's about an old man and his niece who make the German in their house understand the true nature of the occupation by maintaining total silence all the time. Hence the title, *Silence of the Sea*. It's clandestine literature, of course. But it's being read all over France.'

Of all the books she had, Marie found this novella the most moving, and she read it many times.

But there was the problem. Vercors, Charlie, all kinds of brave people were doing something for Free France. As the spring of 1944 began, with Charlie's whereabouts frequently unknown, she could sense that the preparations were becoming large, and urgent. And what was she doing?

Her frustration came to a head in early April. She and Charlie were at the château, walking in the park.

'Why can't you give me something to do?' she demanded crossly. 'Because I'm a woman? If I could run a department store I'm quite sure I'm capable of helping. Are you going to tell me there are no women in the Resistance?'

'Surprisingly few, as it happens,' he replied. 'Even the communists of France are quite conservative when it comes to women.' He looked at her and smiled. 'Of course, they haven't met you.'

'Well then.'

'You're already helping by sheltering a Jewish girl. Remember that. And incurring serious risk by doing so.'

'I doubt anyone's looking for her now,' Marie countered with a shrug.

'You have too much energy,' he said with a shake of the head. 'Truly, the most important thing you can do at the moment is help me maintain my cover. It may not satisfy you, but it's important. I'll let you know if I think of anything else,' he added to pacify her.

But she saw what he was doing, which only made her crosser.

Luc had thought hard about the conundrum of who Corinne could be. His first thought had been that it might be Coco Chanel. She was friendly with the top circles of the German regime. She could be acting for the Resistance as well. That would be clever. Living in the Ritz, she could pass on messages to so many people, from a barman to a friend passing through. But there was no way that he could find out.

Several of the senior officers had mistresses. There was the great actress Arletty, for instance. But the more he thought about it, the more it seemed likely to Luc that Corinne was not a woman at all, but a man. And the first name he thought of was Marc Blanchard.

Marc didn't seem to go out so much, but when he did, he mixed with the highest German circles. With his huge network of contacts, he could be collecting information from dozens of sources.

In the end, Luc made a shortlist of half a dozen names he thought possible, and gave them to Schmid, who looked them over and nodded briefly, but didn't seem much impressed.

'I need information, not guesses,' he said curtly.

After that, Luc gave up on the idea of getting anything from Schmid and concentrated on a matter that was daily becoming more urgent.

How to save himself.

For there was no doubt about which way the wind was blowing now. On every front, the Germans seemed to be in retreat. People were saying that it was only a matter of time before the Allies invaded France. That would mean a huge battle. The Germans might even win it. But with the vast resources of America behind the Allies in Europe now, it could only be a question of time before France was liberated. And what then?

He had few doubts about that. One had only to listen to the muttered conversations at any bar. The open collaborators, in the Milice for instance, would be lucky not to be shot. Even lesser collaborators would be in danger.

Did anyone know about his visits to Schmid? What if someone had seen him? They could have. What if his name was on a list? He shuddered to think of it.

He needed to strengthen his links with the Resistance. Then, even if some person denounced him, he'd be able to claim that any contacts he had with the Germans were only to gather information. He needed to go out on some more missions with them, fast.

'You know, you should tell your friends to make more use of me,' he told his brother, Thomas. 'With all the people I know, maybe I can find things out for them. And when are we going out on another operation? They know I'm not afraid. I already got shot at. They should ask me more.'

But Thomas only shook his head.

'They've got younger people than us,' he said.

Luc was sure his brother was still operating with the FTP boys. Clearly Thomas was keeping him at a distance from their operations. It hurt Luc that his brother didn't trust him. But worse than that, it frightened him. If Thomas didn't trust him, the others didn't either. That suggested some ugly consequences.

Thomas will protect me, he told himself. Hadn't his big brother always protected him? But if his name was on a list of German collaborators, even Thomas mightn't be able to save him.

The month of May arrived. The rumours of an Allied invasion were growing stronger every day. Luc turned many things over in his mind. Should he bluff it out? Should he hide? Was there some way to escape for a while, and if so, who might know of it?

It was in the third week of the month that he went to see Louise.

She received him in her office at L'Invitation au Voyage. She was surprised to see him, but she asked him how he was, and what she could do for him.

'I was thinking about you.' He smiled. 'Perhaps I was worrying about you a little.' He shrugged. 'Whatever may have happened, we are still old friends.'

She made no comment.

'Louise,' he went on with a little show of urgency, 'I make no comment about how you live. Who am I to do so? But I worry because if the Germans are kicked out, I think you could be in danger. Everyone says that half the German senior staff come here. They will call you a collaborator. Then things could get ugly.'

'They find women here. Nothing else.'

'I know that. But down in the street, I can tell you, people may not make such a distinction.' He smiled. 'You are living in a rather protected world, my dear.'

And a rich one, he thought. God knows how much money she must have put by over the years. If anyone had an escape planned and paid for, it must surely be this woman. The question was, if he showed enough concern for her welfare, would she be prepared to save him too?

She nodded thoughtfully.

'I think you may be right. Have you an escape to offer me, Luc?'

'I hoped you might have got one already. I'm sure yours would be better, and safer than anything I can offer.'

'I have no escape route, Luc.'

A silence fell.

Was she playing with him? He had a faint but uncomfortable sense that she was. He stood up, and gazed around the room.

'I shall have to find one then,' he said absently.

'For me, Luc, or for yourself?'

He started, but quickly controlled himself. She was sharp. She knew him too well.

'I was thinking of you,' he answered quietly.

Why was she so calm, though? Did she not understand her danger? Or was there some other reason? Had she already got the protection that he had tried to get for himself? Did she have friends in the Resistance?

He gazed at the portrait that graced the main wall. It wasn't Louise, of course, but it looked quite like her. Clever to have the two sketches for the painting as well. A nice touch. She was rich all right. He was struck by a pang of jealousy.

He stared at the sketches, noticed the name in the corner of one of them, looked more closely.

Corinne.

'Do you know something, Luc?' her voice came from behind him. 'You have never in your life done anything that was not for yourself. Therefore, if you are here now speaking about an escape route, it is because you need one, and you are wondering if I can provide it.'

'Actually, you are wrong,' he said evenly. 'There is no reason for me to escape.'

'Then that is fortunate. Because I am going to let you in on a little secret. I wish you no harm, Luc, none at all. But if I had an escape route, I wouldn't tell you. Because I don't trust you.'

He felt a spasm of rage pass through him. How dare she not believe him? Not only that, she was treating him with scorn – the same scorn she'd used when she had thrown him out before. And though he had kept his resentment most carefully in check when he had arrived at her door, the memory of that event, of his humiliation and impotence, now hit him again, suddenly, with the force of a wave.

She had gone too far. He'd made her what she was, yet she dared to treat him with contempt. Very well. She was going to find out how dangerous that was. This time he would punish her. He would teach her a final lesson, the last she would ever learn.

'If this is how you treat your friends,' he said, in a voice so quiet it was little more than a whisper, 'I shall leave you, Louise.'

★ ★ ★

One hour later, Schmid was surprised to receive a visit from Luc. And still more so when, as soon as he was seated, the Frenchman calmly announced: 'I have news that may interest you. I think I've found Corinne.'

It did not take the Frenchman long to tell his story. After he had finished, Schmid nodded slowly.

'It is possible you are right. I know this woman and her place.'

'She has some good pictures.'

'Yes.'

'You said you would pay well.'

'Oh yes, I will pay.'

'Can you go there and look for yourself? It would preserve my cover.'

'Come back in three days,' said Schmid.

Louise was irritated, two evenings later, that the Gestapo man Schmid had announced that he would pay one of his rare visits. The girls didn't like him. But for all her connections with senior Germans, Louise knew it would be highly unwise to annoy a Gestapo officer.

She had one satisfactory memory of him, however. And that had been his second visit.

She had not forgotten his attempt to see the Babylon room when little Laïla was hiding there. And she had racked her brains for a satisfactory theme for the redecoration of the room that had been forced upon her.

Just as she'd expected, when he had come again, he had insisted on seeing the room, and she had watched his face as he had done so.

For she had turned it into her Nazi room.

She had been subtle. There was nothing for him to complain of. Nothing crude, no hints of viciousness. The carpet was black, the big bed spotless white, with a swastika in the middle of the cover and on the corners of the pillowcases. Everything was simple, geometric, the furniture in a simplified Bauhaus style. On the walls, a painting of Austrian woods and mountains, a portrait of the führer, two prints derived from Leni Riefenstahl's film of the Nuremberg rally and one of a happy group of blonde and athletic Aryan women at a holiday camp, showing a tantalising amount of flesh.

Schmid had stared at it, half-admiring, half-disappointed not to have caught her out.

'Very good, madame,' he'd said.

But this evening, when he'd come, he'd been surprisingly charming. Quite meek, and friendly with the girls. She might have guessed something was up. Sure enough, before going up with the blonde girl he'd selected, he asked very politely if he might have a word with her in her office.

He came straight to the point.

'Madame, your establishment has no equal in Paris. That is why so many senior officers come here. And although a promotion has come my way, I am sure you know that a junior officer like myself can scarcely afford to come here.' He made a sad gesture. 'The trouble is, once he has been here, no man could wish to come anywhere else.'

She gracefully inclined her head at the compliment. What else could she do?

'How can I help you?' she asked.

'I am embarrassed to have to ask, but I confess, madame, that if you could offer me a discount, it would make my life easier.'

She tensed and eyed him coldly. He was going to try to rob her.

'What did you have in mind?' she asked.

'I could manage two-thirds of the normal rate.' He paused. 'I think you know that this is true.'

She'd been expecting something much steeper. He'd still find it expensive. She didn't like it, but thought it wisest to yield.

'I should be glad to accommodate you,' she said. 'But this is for yourself alone.'

'Of course. I thank you, madame.' He stood up, then looked around the room. 'You have wonderful taste. The pictures here are very fine. Can this be one of yourself?'

'No, but people often say it's like me.'

He nodded appreciatively, glanced at a small landscape on another wall intently, and then retired.

The visit could have been worse, she supposed.

Marie always liked to spend the month of May in Paris. She loved to see the tree blossoms on the boulevards and avenues.

She was almost at the end of her stay at the rue Bonaparte when, one morning, she was told that a lady and her son had called to see her. The name on the lady's card was not familiar, but Marie had them shown in all the same.

The lady who entered was about forty, very elegantly dressed, and accompanied by a boy of five. Marie had an idea that she had met the woman before somewhere, but she had met so many people when she was running Joséphine that she couldn't possibly remember them all.

But when she saw the little boy, she started.

Louise had hesitated for so long. Strangely enough, though she had little respect for him, it was Luc who had decided her to come.

If the Germans were driven from Paris, she had no fear of being tried as a collaborator. The Resistance leaders knew Corinne, and what she was doing for them. I'm more likely to get a medal, she thought.

But the final conflict might be quite a different matter. There might be a siege, and bombardment. There could be extensive fighting in the streets. Not a good place for little Esmé to be. And then, assuming that the Germans were driven out, a period of confusion. That, she now realised, was the greatest danger of all. Luc was right. Ordinary people, if they were in a lynching mood, would see the favourite brothel of the German High Command and its madame as a natural target. They might drag her out into the street, stone her . . . There was no knowing.

She knew very well that the time of invasion was approaching. She couldn't put off the decision about Esmé forever. And perhaps the obvious panic that lay behind Luc's visit affected her too.

She would have liked to talk to Charlie, but he had disappeared at the moment, and when he was away on a Resistance mission, there was no way of knowing when he would surface again.

So she had decided it was time to take Esmé to his grandparents. She knew already from Charlie that they would be in Paris for the month of May. Better do it straightaway, therefore, before they went back to the valley of the Loire.

And she'd thought carefully about exactly what she must say.

At her request now, Esmé was taken out of the room to spend a little time with the housekeeper, and she began.

'I see that you noticed something about my son, madame,' she began quietly. 'He looks just like Charlie. That is because Charlie is his father.' She paused. 'You did not know of his existence?'

'No.'

'That was at my request. I had my reasons, though I can assure you that I had no objections to Charlie's father, nor to you, madame. Quite the contrary, in fact. But Charlie is very anxious that Esmé should be taken to a place of safety, and I can no longer deny that he is right. Charlie is engaged in dangerous activities himself, as we both know. And I too run certain risks.'

'Ah.' Marie looked at her. A woman in the Resistance. She had no doubt that Louise was telling her the truth.

'I have brought you documents.' Louise handed across the registration of Esmé's birth. 'As you will see, Charlie is named as the father. As soon as he reappears, he will be able to confirm all this.'

'Why did you avoid us? Because the child is illegitimate?'

'You would have insisted that Charlie take my son away from me. And he is all I have.'

'Why would we have done that?'

'Because I run the best brothel in Paris.'

Marie nodded. 'You are right.'

Louise paused for a few moments.

'There is something else, madame. A secret that even Charlie does not know.' Louise paused for a few moments. 'If anything were to happen to me, I should like to be sure that Esmé has all the love and care that is possible. I have no doubt of your kindness, madame, but there is a particular circumstance that may cause you to take an interest in my son.' She handed Marie a sealed envelope. 'These papers concern my mother. Her name was Corinne Petit. My father, I finally discovered, was Marc. Your brother, madame. He knows nothing about me, and it's better that way. But I wish you to know that Esmé is your nephew.'

Marie stared at her.

'Why did you not tell Marc?'

'I was too embarrassed.' She shrugged. 'I met him once. In professional circumstances.'

'He came to your establishment?'

'No. I went to his house.'

Marie frowned, then understood.

'Oh my God.'

'It could have been worse. For that's where I discovered. I saw the photographs of your wedding, and I recognised your husband. He was my English parents' lawyer. He'd arranged my adoption.'

She and Marie gazed at each other.

'Do you mean that you and Marc . . .'

'No,' said Louise. 'Thank God. I was able to leave, before . . .'

'And after that, you felt you couldn't tell him.'

'I was always proud of my independence, madame, if not of the way I achieved it.' She smiled. 'By the way, I admired the way you ran Joséphine. I tried to model my establishment on it, in a slightly different way, of course.'

'My husband is out, but he will be back in an hour or two. I wonder what he will say.'

'Esmé is his grandson. I think he will take care of him. It should be quite possible for you to check the truth of everything I have told you.'

'I do not disbelieve you.'

'If it were not true, madame, I would hardly be giving you the only treasure I possess.'

As Schmid considered his situation, he felt quite hopeful. On the one hand, of course, things had been going badly for the Wehrmacht. Allied bombing was increasing, so were the Resistance activities. Attacks on guard posts, factories sabotaged, trains derailed. The French, clearly, believed that an invasion was coming soon, and that France would rise up as General Patton led a huge assault across the Channel.

But where? Some said the Allies might land in Normandy, or farther west. But Schmid didn't believe that, nor did intelligence support that idea. The Allies would strike across the narrowest point of the Channel, between Dover and Calais. Why would they do anything else?

And when they did? That would be the test. No one should underestimate the genius of the führer, or of the Wehrmacht. For wherever they struck, the Allies would find the Germans ready for them. The assault would fail. The Allies would be massacred. Eisenhower would lose his command. Quite possibly the Americans would lose heart and give up, and then where would the Allies be?

Europe would belong to Germany.

That, Schmid told himself, as he waited for Luc Gascon to arrive, was how it would be.

It was destiny. It could not be otherwise.

Luc had passed three bad days. Now and then, he had felt remorse for what he had done. But his remorse was not great. Whatever relationship they had once had, Louise had scorned him. Indeed, when she'd said that even if she had an escape route, she wouldn't tell him, it was quite clear that she'd happily leave him to his death. No, he thought, he owed her nothing at all. Nothing. He was just repaying her in kind.

What worried him was something far worse. He had just put himself in greater danger.

What if she told one of her Resistance friends about his visit and their quarrel? And that she already suspected he was a collaborator? When something happened to her, who was going to be at the top of their list of suspects? The fact that Schmid had also been there might provide a partial cover, but it wasn't enough. He should have thought the whole thing through more carefully before he went to see the Gestapo man.

He'd let his feelings get in the way of his judgement – not something he would ever do normally. But he had this time, and he cursed his folly.

Even more than before, it seemed to Luc, he needed a place of safety. A place, at least, where he could hide for a while without being found. A place nobody knew.

He could think of only one. True, his brother, Thomas, knew of it. But nobody else. And Thomas, thank God, was the one person in the world whom he could trust.

There'd be work to do, of course. He'd have to stock it with food and water. Not an easy thing to do with rationing. But he could take canned food, smoked ham, other things that would keep, a little at a time from the restaurant. He told Édith he needed them for a customer, and she only shrugged. After all, it was his restaurant. He'd begun the process the evening after he'd seen Schmid.

And now, here he was again, back in Schmid's office, and Schmid was smiling.

'I looked at the sketch,' the German said pleasantly, 'and I agree with you. I have just given the order that she is to be watched day and night, and followed wherever she goes. With luck, she may lead us to something.' He passed a small wad of francs across the desk to Luc. 'You have earned this. If our suspicion is correct, there will be more.'

'And if she doesn't lead you to anyone?'

Schmid smiled.

'We shall set a trap.'

How peaceful it was at the château. If massive preparations were in motion, across the English Channel, for the greatest amphibious invasion in history, down in the Loire valley there was not a hint of it. Unless, perhaps, one counted the occasional Allied bomber, driven off course after bombing the railway yards around Paris, that droned across the sky.

But Marie had plenty to occupy her mind. She had little Esmé to think about.

There was no doubt about who he was. Within two hours after Louise left, Marc had arrived at the rue Bonaparte. Five minutes of explanation and he confirmed the truth of everything.

'Take a quick look at your grandson,' she commanded. 'Don't try to see Louise. She doesn't want it, and you must respect that. Then go.'

Roland, however, was quite another matter.

She'd never seen him so excited.

'I have a grandson? Let me look at him. *Mon Dieu*, but he's like Charlie.'

'He's illegitimate, of course,' she gently reminded him. She didn't want him to get too happy, and then suffer a reaction, and take against the child. But she needn't have worried.

'Oh, that's nothing.' He shrugged. 'Some of the greatest generals and statesmen, the noblest families in France, descend from the illegitimate children of kings.'

'True.' Marie thought she'd better get everything out of the way, at once. 'But I must tell you that his mother – though she looks and behaves like one of us – is nonetheless the madam of a brothel, and was once a courtesan herself.'

787

This didn't interest Roland either.

'*Ma chérie*, many of the royal mistresses were little better. It's the same in other countries too. At least one of the English dukes is descended from a prostitute.' He thought for a moment. 'You say she's charming?'

'Yes.'

'*Voilà*. That's all that matters.' He glanced at her. 'For a mistress, of course. Not for a wife.'

'So you'll be kind to him?'

'Of course I'll be kind to him. He's my grandson. The only one I have – unless Charlie has others we don't know about.'

'That also would please you.'

'One welcomes proof of the family's vigour.'

And he could hardly be separated from the little boy, took him on his knee, even carried him on his shoulders when they went outside.

The only person needed to complete the family circle was Charlie himself. But of Charlie, so far, there was no sign.

He'd been away so long, Marie wondered if the invasion might be imminent. The first days of June passed. The weather turned poor. Farther north, up by the coast, the seas were stormy. Whenever the Allies were coming, she thought, it clearly wouldn't be just now.

It was mid-morning on the eighth of June when Charlie took the train from the station at Montparnasse. He hadn't wanted to go. He'd been having such an interesting time with Max Le Sourd and his boys to the east of Paris that he hadn't even been back to the apartment for more than two weeks. But this was an emergency.

The last three days had been dramatic. Seizing a small break in the bad weather, the Allies' massive D-day invasion of Normandy had caught the Germans completely by surprise.

But not unprepared. Despite the heavy bombings, the huge bombardment from the sea and the vast sabotage efforts of the coordinated Resistance networks, the beaches had been stoutly defended. The Allies were establishing their beachhead, but the fighting was intense. The Allied advance would be neither easy nor swift. Even assuming all went well, it might be weeks before they could reach Paris.

And the fever of Resistance activity – derailing trains carrying troops to the new front, blowing up arms depots, cutting off German fuel and power – also included one lesser but important task.

Saving Allied airmen.

The message had got to Charlie early that morning, brought by one of his friends in the Confrérie Notre-Dame.

'There's a Canadian airman. One of a bomber crew. They came down in the Loire valley. The rest of them didn't make it, but he got lucky. Our boys down there have got him, but they need help.'

'Can't they send him south?' asked Charlie.

That was the usual procedure. The Resistance had set up quite a good escape route. Passed from group to group, airmen were being smuggled across the Pyrenees into Spain.

'We've just had word of several airmen being betrayed. Some of the southern groups must have been infiltrated.'

This was the trouble with the rapid enlargement of the networks, Charlie thought. Inevitable perhaps, but it still sickened him.

'What do you want me to do?'

'We may have an alternative. Couriers we think we can trust. But we need a week. And a new safe house.'

'Where is he?'

'About three hours' walk from your family's château.'

When Roland de Cygne heard a light tap at his bedroom door in the middle of the night and found Charlie there, he was overjoyed to see him. It took only a brief whispered conversation to discover what was up.

'We came by bicycle,' Charlie told him. 'It's lucky I know all the roads so well. We came here without using any lights.'

'Where is he now?'

'In the old stable. Where I keep the car. If he's discovered, you and Marie can always say you didn't know he was there.'

By now, Marie had joined them. Charlie turned to her.

'You said you wanted to help,' he told her wryly. 'Now you have your wish.'

There was one other thing he had to caution them both about. Security.

'It's best if you don't see him. But if you do, remember that he was brought here at night. He has no idea where he is. Above all, he knows me only by my code name: Monsieur Bon Ami.'

'It sounds very cloak and dagger,' Marie remarked.

'Yes,' Charlie replied, 'but if the airman gets caught, the less he knows about us the better.'

The Canadian's name was Richard Bennett. The arrangements for hiding him worked out well. Nobody went to the old garage where Charlie's beloved Voisin was kept under lock and key, except for Charlie himself; and so there was no need for anyone but the three de Cygnes even to know the airman was there.

'I've always wanted to sleep in a Voisin,' Richard told his host cheerfully. He swore he was perfectly comfortable, and though Charlie had produced two travelling rugs for blankets, he said he hardly needed them during those June nights.

He was certainly well fed. Charlie put far more food on his plate than he really meant to eat, and slipped it into a container when no one was looking. Marie gave Charlie small items from the larder and Roland added an extra bottle from the wine cellar. With these items secreted in a bag, Charlie would go down to the old stable, ostensibly to tinker with his car. No one suspected a thing.

As for keeping himself clean, the Canadian used the hose already in the stable for washing the car. The water was cold, but it was summer. Charlie brought him some of his old clothes to wear. They were a little big on him, but they served well enough. As for his other requirements, Charlie dealt with the chamber pot after dark.

They also made a hiding place. Against one wall in the stable, there was a long, deep stone trough which was used for storage now. With some planks, they made a shelf that fitted over the bottom of the trough, leaving enough space for the Canadian to slide underneath it. Above the shelf, Charlie piled drums of oil, tubing, wrenches and all sorts of mechanical odds and ends. Once Richard was inside, he could pull down a pile of oily rags over the end of the shelf and it was quite impossible to guess that a person was hidden in there.

Charlie would give him the newspaper to read. Sometimes they'd pass the time playing chess together. Charlie was pretty certain that every other game, the Canadian was letting him win.

Roland's feelings were mixed. They must hide the airman, of course. But all the same, he wished the fellow were not there – not so much for his own safety, or even that of Marie, but for that of little Esmé. If the police came looking for the airman and found him, Charlie's story that no one knew he was there might work, but Roland doubted it. More likely, the whole family would be arrested. And what would happen to his grandson then?

With luck, he hoped, the family's conservative reputation would protect them from suspicion. The second day after Charlie's arrival, he decided to walk down to the village. Seeing a police van in the little square, he went over to chat with the officers.

They were friendly enough, and soon told him that an enemy plane had come down a few days ago.

'Ah?' Roland feigned surprise. 'I didn't hear anything.'

'*Non*, Monsieur de Cygne. It was about twenty kilometres away.'

'That would explain it. Any survivors?'

'There might be one or two. But we don't think so.'

'So long as they don't poach my rabbits.'

The policemen laughed.

'Don't worry, Monsieur de Cygne. If the Maquis find any airmen, they won't bring them this way. They take them south, to Spain.'

'So I've heard.' Roland shrugged. 'It's a long way.' And after chatting a few more minutes, he moved on.

So far, so good.

Now he could give his full attention to Charlie and his grandson.

Charlie had been so delighted and relieved when he had discovered that Louise had brought Esmé to them. 'I had no idea,' he explained. 'I hadn't spoken to Louise, because I've hardly been in Paris for three weeks.' He'd smiled at Roland. 'I have wanted Esmé to know his grandfather for a long time.'

They were wonderful days. Strange, but wonderful. Two hundred miles away, day after day, wave after wave of Allied troops were being landed on the secured beaches of Normandy, where huge artificial harbours were being floated in. 'They'll probably bring a million men over before the big breakout,' Charlie told his father.

The Germans were fighting back furiously. Crack panzer divisions were determined to hold the old Norman town of Caen. Still unwilling to believe that the main invasion would not be up at the

Strait of Dover, Hitler was only reluctantly being persuaded to send forces from there to Normandy. 'It's going to be an enormous fight,' Roland judged.

Yet here at the château, everything was so quiet that one could almost forget there was a war taking place at all. It couldn't last, of course. Once the Canadian was safely on his way, Charlie would want to go back to Paris, where there was so much work to be done. Whatever form the battle for Paris took – assuming the Allies succeeded and Paris was in contention – Charlie de Cygne certainly wasn't going to miss it.

'So I suppose,' Roland remarked to Marie, 'I should be grateful to the Canadian for keeping Charlie here.'

What a joy it was to walk in the sun with Charlie and the little boy. Roland realised with a pang that three generations of de Cygnes had never been together since some time before the French Revolution. Dieudonné, born back in those terrible days, had never even seen his father, and had died before Roland was born. His own father had not lived to see Charlie. But now at last, after almost two centuries, a grandfather, son and grandson could all be together. Perhaps it might have been better if the little fellow had been legitimate, he admitted to himself, but one must thank the good Lord for what He gave.

Marie took a photograph of each man standing with Esmé, and then one of the three of them standing in front of the château together. Being of the old school, Roland was reluctant to smile into the camera, but Charlie cracked a joke and Marie caught all three of them smiling in a way that was charming.

Only one thing, like a small dark cloud in an azure sky, briefly caused irritation to Roland de Cygne. They were discussing the Canadian.

'He speaks perfect French, you know,' Charlie told them. 'Occasionally he'll use an expression I'm not familiar with, but the interesting thing is his accent. It's more nasal than mine.'

'What you are hearing,' Roland told him, 'is an accent trapped in time. They say that in Quebec one hears French as it was spoken back in the time of Louis XIV. Curious, but interesting.'

'He told me that's where his mother's family come from. Their name is Dessigne.' He smiled. 'Do you suppose it could be a corruption of de Cygne? I mustn't tell him my name, of course. He knows me only as Monsieur Bon Ami. But perhaps we're related. He says his mother's family is quite numerous.'

Roland was silent. That letter of long ago, and Marie's later discovery. Once again he felt a sense of guilt. He'd behaved badly. But there was nothing to be done about it now.

'It's possible, I suppose,' he said. 'Though any link would be centuries old.'

'Well,' Charlie said cheerfully, 'he's a good fellow in any case, and a brave man.'

And that, Roland comforted himself, was the most important thing, in a world whose secrets no living creature knows.

So he thanked fate for sending this kinsman, if kinsman he was, to grant him these precious days with his son, and which were over all too soon.

Each evening a little after dusk, Charlie walked out on a farm track that led through a wood on the edge of the estate. He had been there a week when, from behind one of the trees, a voice gently called to him: 'Monsieur Bon Ami.'

'Who are you?'

'Gauloise.'

'Where are you going tonight?'

'Toronto.' The password.

'Is it safe now?'

'God knows. The police have picked up dozens of men, all over the place. English, Canadian, airmen from New Zealand. It's a huge mess. But we have a new route now. Men we can trust.'

'I hope he makes it. He's a good fellow.'

'They're all good fellows.'

'Wait here. I'll get him.'

It was a quarter of an hour before Charlie came back with Richard Bennett.

'Good luck, *mon vieux*,' he said, as he embraced the Canadian. 'Monsieur Gauloise will get you to Spain.' He fumbled in his pocket. 'Take this.' He handed him the little lighter his father had given him. 'It brings luck. You can return it to me after the war's over.'

'I can never thank you enough.'

'Go safely.'

Moments later, like shadows, the Canadian and his guide had disappeared into the night.

The next morning, after saying good-bye to his family, Charlie returned to Paris.

It was a pity, Louise thought, that both Colonel Walter and Schmid should be coming. It was the second week of June.

The girls liked Colonel Walter. He was uncomplicated. His needs were those of any normal man, and his manners were excellent. She was a little surprised he didn't keep a mistress. Did he feel it was too time-consuming? Or perhaps he preferred the amusement and variety the establishment could offer. In any case, he was always welcome.

When Schmid turned up, however, even when he was trying to be agreeable, there was tension in the air. She was pretty sure that Colonel Walter didn't like him, either.

But nothing could have prepared her for the scene that took place that evening.

They both of them came rather early, as it happened. She greeted them herself, and joined them in the salon. Two of the girls came in and one, called Catherine, started talking to Schmid. But it seemed that she displeased him in some way, and he told her rudely to go away and send him someone better-looking. The girls were used to handling all kinds of behaviour, but it was obvious that Catherine was offended; and Louise was about to ask Schmid to be a little nicer when Colonel Walter intervened.

'My dear Schmid' – his voice was silky soft, but the rebuke in it was clear – 'I know you have many things on your mind, but you will find it easier to relax if you make an effort to be pleasant.'

'I always have things on my mind, Colonel Walter.'

It was apparently intended to close the conversation, but Walter went on, quite unperturbed.

'My dear Schmid, the word is that you have the honour of conducting a certain visitor to the theatre tomorrow night.' He shrugged. 'Though what our friend Müller will make of *Antigone*, I cannot imagine. But if I were you, I would go home now and get a good night's sleep, rather than exhausting yourself here tonight.'

Müller? Louise's face did not move a muscle. It was a common German name. There were several senior figures in the Reich who bore the name. But the effect on Schmid was remarkable.

'May I ask where you heard this, Colonel?' His voice was icy.

'At least two people said it to me when I was in headquarters today.' For the first time, she caught a hint of nervousness in the colonel's voice.

'I believe you, Colonel, because we are aware that someone has started this rumour. But I can tell you that it is entirely untrue.'

'I understand.'

'I hope you do, Colonel Walter. Because rumours can be dangerous.' Schmid's voice rose. 'Dangerous also for those who spread them.'

'You are the only person to whom I have said it, I assure you.'

'I hope so for your sake.'

And then the mask dropped. The look that Schmid gave Walter was venomous. Gone was the deference to his rank. The Gestapo man looked like a snake about to strike. And Walter shrank with fear.

Schmid stood up.

'I think Colonel Walter is right. I am not good company tonight. I shall return another evening.' He made for the door. A moment later Colonel Walter hurried after him. Standing discreetly in the hall, as the two men went out of the door, Louise heard Schmid hiss to the colonel: 'Are you mad?'

The door closed behind them. There was a long pause. So she did not hear Schmid turn to the colonel when they were twenty yards down the street and remark in a very different tone: 'Thank you. That was perfect. Only one sad duty remains for you, if you would be kind enough.'

When Colonel Walter returned to the house, he looked a little shaken, and asked for a whisky, rather than the usual champagne. A little while later he went upstairs with Chantal, one of the girls he liked best. But it was only half an hour before he came down again and quietly left.

Chantal came down soon after.

'Something's bothering him,' she said. 'He couldn't keep it up tonight, no matter what I did.'

It was ten o'clock the following morning when Charlie reached Max Le Sourd.

'We have a message from Corinne. It came by the usual route this morning.'

The note would be neatly stuck between two banknotes which Catherine, the girl Louise trusted most, would take to her home early in the morning. A little later, going out to her local market, she would use the notes to pay a flower-seller. Within an hour, placed in an envelope, the notes would be dropped through the letter box of a safe house.

'This could be Heinrich Müller himself,' Max said, after reading the message. Heinrich 'Gestapo' Müller, the second most important man in the entire Gestapo. 'It's the first we've ever heard of him coming to France,' he continued, 'but with the Normandy landings, it would be natural for him to pay a visit to Paris. The Germans will be dreading an uprising here.'

'If he were to come,' Charlie took up the theme, 'security would be high. I imagine it would be a secret. But someone like Colonel Walter might hear of it.'

'If it is Gestapo Müller, I'd hate to let him slip through our fingers.' Max considered. 'It might be a trap.'

'Only if Corinne is compromised in some way. We've no reason to think she is.'

'What about the play? What do you make of that?'

'The theatre's always suspect. Anouilh's *Antigone* got through the censors and the Germans have been watching it happily enough, but some people think it's covert anti-German propaganda. He might want to see it for that reason.'

'We haven't much time to get organised,' said Max. 'And it's risky. But I think we have to try.'

'Try what?'

'To kill him, of course.'

Luc told himself that he was worrying unduly. But he couldn't help it. His last visit to Schmid had been very unsatisfactory. When he'd asked whether there was any news about Corinne, the Gestapo man had remarked that she had not led them to anyone yet. Then he had smiled.

'But I am still confident.'

'You had said you would trap her.'

'Perhaps.'

'May I ask how?'

'No. But I will tell you if the outcome is satisfactory.'

It would be a trap then. But what sort of trap? A likely method would be to feed her false information. Information she would pass on to the Resistance and incriminate herself. But what sort of information? Impossible to know. But a false lead of some kind. Something that would lead Resistance men into a trap.

It needn't concern him. Except for one circumstance. What if his brother were caught in the trap?

He knew Thomas was still going out on operations. He was indefatigable. Indeed, it seemed to have given him a new lease on life. Thomas mightn't be as fast as the younger men, but he still had a good eye, and he was reliable.

And every time he did so, of course, Thomas put himself at risk. Common sense told Luc he shouldn't worry about it. That was Thomas's choice, and his own business.

Yet the thought that his informing on Louise could cause his brother's death, or worse, his arrest and torture, preyed upon his mind. Was there some way he could persuade him not to go out any more? Could he warn him off?

He started to spend more time at the restaurant. As the days went by, Thomas seemed quite content minding the bar. The two of them would chat for an hour or two. There was no hint of any other activity.

He was in the restaurant soon after noon one day when he noticed two of the young Dalou men approach the bar and start talking to Thomas. He might not have paid much attention if he hadn't caught sight of Édith. As she stared across at her husband and the two Dalous, her face froze. Lines of anxiety suddenly appeared. Luc went over to her.

'Are you all right? Is something wrong?' he asked.

'Yes. No. It's nothing.'

After a few minutes, the two Dalou men left and he saw Édith go over to Thomas immediately afterwards. She was saying something urgent to him. He was listening, but it was clear that she wasn't getting anywhere. Luc saw Édith take Thomas by the arm, and saw Thomas shake his head.

When Édith came back, he could see she was close to tears.

Luc wondered what to do. He'd like to have intervened, told Thomas some story that he'd heard from one of his contacts that the Germans were going to set up traps to catch Resistance groups. But he couldn't do that. It would have invited further questions, awkward ones. They might ask him, 'How do you know?' Besides, if this was Schmid's trap, and the Resistance failed to take the bait, then Schmid would surely conclude that the leak must have come from him.

No, he couldn't do that. But at least he could try to dissuade his brother from going.

He called to Édith.

'I saw what you saw. The Dalou boys. There's no need to say anything, Édith. Thomas doesn't tell me about what he does, and I accept it. But I'm not a fool.' He paused. 'Do you know why I've been around so much lately? Because I started having nightmares. I don't know why. I never had them before. But I started having night-mares about my brother being caught. They won't go away. I'm afraid for him.'

'Tell him,' she said urgently. 'You have to tell him at once.'

'All right.' He got up. 'He won't thank me, but I'll do it.'

And he did. He told him about the dream that kept returning, and begged his brother: 'I don't want to know what you're up to. That's not my business. But don't go out with the Dalou boys or anyone else. Just enjoy your old age and keep your wife company. She's worried sick about you.'

Thomas looked across to where Édith was standing and nodded thoughtfully.

'You may be right, Luc,' he said. 'Perhaps I should stop.' He shrugged. 'But when one has made commitments, you know . . .'

Luc stared at his brother sadly. Whatever he had agreed to with the Dalous, he was going to do. That was clear.

'Listen,' said Luc. 'I'm going to tell you a secret. I've been worried about you. Do you remember a certain place that we went to years ago? A secret place, under the ground, that nobody knows?'

The cave under Montmartre. Thomas didn't look pleased to be reminded of the incident.

'What of it?' he said.

'I've put provisions in there for you. If ever you need to hide, you could stay in there quite a while.' He might have prepared it for himself, Luc thought, but who should he share it with if not with his brother? 'Don't tell anyone, not the Dalou boys, or any of your friends, or even Édith. If nobody knows, nobody can tell. No one comes by my house, as you know, so I won't lock the door. But if ever you need it, go there at once.'

'All right,' said Thomas.

Schmid was pleased with his arrangements. The key to a successful operation was simplicity. The object of the mission was to discover if Louise and Corinne were one and the same. Everything, therefore, was subordinate to that.

There were three cars, all full of Gestapo men. In the middle car were three men dressed in the uniform of senior Gestapo officers, one as a general. All three were prisoners, due to be shot. They had been told that if they played their parts well, their lives would be spared. The one dressed as a general looked very like Müller.

There would be some police around, of course, but not too many. This was supposed to be a discreet private visit. And he wished to provide the Resistance men with a tempting target. He didn't want to put them off. They must be allowed to make the attempt on the man they thought was Müller. If they did, then he knew the identity of Corinne. He would arrest her. And then he would see what she could tell him.

The efforts of the police were entirely secondary. Only after the attempt was made were they allowed to move. If they could catch some Resistance men, that was a bonus.

'Try to take at least one of them alive,' he instructed. 'I may be able to identify a corpse,' he told the senior police officer, 'but a man we can interrogate is worth a hundred corpses.'

The bait was in the trap. Now all he had to do was see if the bait was taken.

The Théâtre de l'Atelier lay in the section of the city just below the steep slope of the park that led up to the great white basilica of Sacré Coeur upon Montmartre.

It was a modest, rectangular building, suitable for an artistic and intellectual audience rather than the fashionable *beau monde*. At its western end was a three-door entrance under a small columned porch, and in front of that, a cobbled area not even a hundred feet long, dotted with small trees.

Max had been thorough. He and Charlie would stand in the hall-way of an apartment building beside the little café just to the north of the theatre entrance. He'd already spent two hours carefully exploring the small gardens and alleyways behind the building. With windows carefully unlatched, they would be able to run through this little maze and emerge into the next parallel street to the north, which gave directly on to the steep park. From there they could run through the trees and into the tangle of streets on the eastern side of the hill.

At six different vantage points on the streets approaching the theatre, he had a man stationed. The two young Dalous, three other men of his own, and on the street nearest the park, old Thomas Gascon.

There was no question, the old man was very game.

'It's funny how they call us the Maquis these days,' he remarked. 'And they say that's the countryside down in the south of France. But the real Maquis is right here, where these boys and I come from.' He gave the Dalou boys a grin. 'The Maquis up on the hill of Montmartre.'

For all the old man's cheerful resilience, Max was still concerned that Thomas might be too slow. But he'd surprised Max by running down the street and back quite swiftly, and since Max hadn't time to find more men, he'd said a prayer and retained Thomas where he was. Since his station was right beside the park, he should be able to vanish into the trees before any pursuers even reached that street.

Each of these men had a whistle that made a piercing sound. If they saw anything that looked like an ambush, they were to blow hard on their whistle, and vanish.

The Dalous and the other three men had also prepared some rather interesting distractions that might keep the enemy busy.

But all the same, Max was worried. There were several things about this business that he did not like. The short notice. The high risk – for he told Charlie that he thought there was a good chance they'd both be shot when they made the attack – and the complete uncertainty about how Müller would be guarded.

'If at the last moment Charlie and I see that the thing can't be done,' he told the team, 'then we stand down. You hear no shots, and you all vanish.'

One big question had been whether to make the attempt as Müller arrived at the theatre, or when he left. Since it would still be broad daylight when he came, it was decided to try as he departed.

'He'll probably come out before the rest of the audience. That means that we'll be visible, but have a clear shot. If not, then we'll just have to mingle with the crowd and take a shot if we can,' Max said to Charlie. 'It'll be more complex. Frankly,' he confessed, 'if this were for a lesser target than Müller himself, I wouldn't attempt it.'

Charlie carried a small pistol, Max a large Welrod with a silencer. Between them, they also had a Sten gun.

As the time of the theatre opening approached, the audience began to gather on the cobbles among the trees. Gradually they filtered through the doors. There was no sign of any official presence until, just as the last of the audience went through the doors, a police truck rolled up and halted at the end of the cobbles. A dozen police got out, but remained surveying the scene by the bus. A couple of minutes later, three cars drew swiftly into the street on the other side of the theatre. Two Gestapo men got out of the first, another two from the last. The middle vehicle was a larger staff car. Three obviously high-ranking Gestapo officers stepped out. The general in the centre was a dark-haired, middle-aged man with a clear-cut, rather sour-looking face.

'That certainly looks like Müller,' Max whispered. The first two Gestapo men swiftly entered the theatre, presumably to make sure the way was clear. Then the others, moving in a posse with the general in the centre, walked straight in through the doors. The police stayed where they were. After this, there was silence.

Charlie and Max waited over an hour. Charlie wondered if there would be an interval, but as nobody came out through the doors, he assumed not. Dusk fell. The policemen remained by their bus.

'There's only one thing to do,' Max said. 'You'll have to open up on the police with the Sten gun. That'll give me cover, and the noise will alert the others. Give me your pistol. I'll make a dash for the general with that and the Welrod. If I get back, we leave as planned. If I go down, you leave alone. Don't hang about.'

Another half hour passed. It was getting quite dark. They inched the door of the building just ajar and listened carefully for any whistle from the surrounding streets. There was nothing.

And then it all started to happen.

The first two Gestapo men appeared at the theatre doors. Moving swiftly, they went over to the staff car while the driver leaped to open the door. The policemen gazed placidly from in front of their bus. The two Gestapo men looked around to make sure the streets were clear.

And then Müller and his two companions stepped out.

'Now,' said Max.

It happened so fast that the men in front of the theatre hardly knew what hit them. Charlie raked the policemen with the Sten gun and the air filled with noise. He saw half a dozen of them go down. Others were trying to take cover and return his fire. They hardly even noticed Max, his hat pulled down over his face, sprinting towards the Gestapo general.

Before Charlie's first burst of fire was completed, an uproar arose from the streets all around. There were shots, explosions, huge flashes. This was the Dalou boys and their friends putting on a show.

Both the police and the Gestapo men were totally distracted now. Max was face-to-face with Müller.

And then Müller screamed.

'We're French. It's a trap!' And his two companions were shouting as well. And Charlie saw Max stare at them and then swivel, bob his head down and double back towards him. As he came closer, Charlie saw one of the two Gestapo men still in the theatre run around the theatre door and take aim at Max, but he managed to bring the Sten gun around and got him with a short burst.

Then Max was crashing through the doorway, and Charlie smacked it shut and locked it behind him, and then both ran down the passage and out through the window at the back. And they kept running into the narrow alleyway, and got over a garden wall, and burst into the building beyond.

Max was panting as they reached the doorway that gave out into the street beyond. They looked out. There was nobody there except the small form of Thomas Gascon, at the edge of the trees, a hundred yards away, signalling to them that the coast was clear.

They had just caught up with him, and were running up the slope when they heard the sound of boots in the street behind them. Four or five police were on the roadway. They were taking aim. Charlie heard a rattle of fire, felt something thud into him. The next moment he felt Max pulling the Sten gun out of his hands. The Sten gun chattered into life. He heard a scream. Max's arm was under his left arm, Thomas Gascon's under his right. The old man was amazingly strong. He felt himself stumbling forward. Max glanced back.

'They won't follow,' he said. 'But within the hour, they'll be searching house to house. We've got to get Charlie somewhere safe. Can you walk a bit, Charlie, if we help you?'

'I think so.'

'Well,' said Max to Thomas, 'do you know a place we can hide around here?'

'Yes,' said Thomas, 'I do.'

When Luc saw Thomas and his companions at his door, he was horrified.

'We've got to get him out of sight,' Thomas whispered.

'What do you mean?' Luc whispered back.

'You know.' Thomas turned to Max. 'We're going into the garden at the back.'

Luc seized Thomas by the arm and pulled him to one side.

'Are you insane?' he hissed urgently. 'That's my hiding place. That's just for you and me.'

'It was a trap. He's been shot. We have to hide him,' Thomas answered.

Luc moaned.

'You don't understand. They'll know my hiding place.'

'Not if we're quick. We left them back at the bottom of the hill. They've hardly started searching yet. Open the back door, for God's sake.'

'Oh, brother, you've just killed me,' Luc told him.

But Thomas took no further notice.

'We'll need a lamp,' he said.

It was a long night. At about midnight, the police rapped on the door of the house. Luc, half asleep, opened the door. He seemed puzzled, and asked them what it was all about. They searched the house, went into the garden at the back, opened the shed. But Luc had done a good job. There was no sign of people hiding or of any disturbance to the place at all. After searching the other buildings nearby, the police abruptly left.

For Thomas and Max, alone with Charlie in the cave, the hours passed slowly. They hadn't taken Charlie all the way down to the chamber at the end, but found a place around the first bend where there was enough room for him to lie comfortably. Some of the food supplies that Luc had stored were stacked just a few feet away.

Max had looked carefully at the wound in Charlie's back. Charlie was shivering a little.

'Can we get a doctor?' Thomas asked.

'Difficult now. Maybe in the morning,' said Max.

'I just thought . . .'

'I was in the war in Spain,' said Max quietly. 'I saw a lot of people get hit. Just trust me.'

A little after midnight, Charlie's mind seemed to wander. He started murmuring. He said the name of Louise. Then Esmé. Then he grew quiet. He was breathing with difficulty.

'*Mon ami*,' said Max, 'you know who I am?'

'Yes, Max,' said Charlie.

'We were betrayed tonight. Could it have been Corinne?'

'Never. She would never . . .'

'One can never be sure, Charlie. What if the Gestapo threatened her family?'

'She came from England. She's no family here, except for her son, Esmé.'

'Where's he?'

'Down in the country with his grandparents. The Germans think they're Vichy.' He paused. 'Max, I'd better tell you I'm his father.'

'Ah.' Max considered. 'She wouldn't betray the father of her son. No, I don't believe that. But if she didn't betray us deliberately, then she must have been used. Someone planted the information on her.' He nodded. 'I have to warn her, Charlie. I'd better do it fast.'

'Yes. Don't be seen.'

'I'll take care. But remember, Charlie, Corinne's your contact. We just get the messages at the safe house. You'll have to tell me who she really is.'

'Madame Louise. She owns L'Invitation au Voyage.'

'Ah. I know of it, of course. It might have been one of her girls, then.'

'Perhaps . . . Or someone else.'

'Maybe I can find out if I talk to her.'

'Maybe. Can you protect her?'

'Yes, Charlie. I'll protect her. I promise.'

'That's important.'

'Don't worry about a thing.' He gazed at the aristocrat. 'How do you feel now?'

'Cold.'

'All right. Nothing to worry about.'

There was a long pause. Charlie looked strangely grey.

'Max.'

'Yes, Charlie.'

'Would you hold my hand.'

Max took it. A minute later, Charlie gave a shudder, and his head fell to one side. Then Max closed his eyes.

'Did you know he was dying?' Thomas asked, after a long pause.

'Yes.'

'Have you any idea who betrayed us?'

'Not yet,' said Max.

Thomas was thoughtful.

It was a little after one in the morning when Schmid began to question Louise. So far, he thought, things had gone very well.

It was unfortunate, of course, that so many policemen had been wounded. One of them was probably going to die. But that was a police problem, not his. Everything else had been entirely satisfactory.

It amused him that the prisoners dressed in Gestapo uniforms had given the game away. No doubt, thinking that they were about to be shot by the Resistance, they had hoped to help their colleagues by giving the game away. In fact, they had done the Gestapo a favour. It was far more discouraging for the Maquis to know they had been betrayed than to think, however mistakenly, that they had shot Müller. He wouldn't have to keep the three men in prison any longer either. They could all be shot at dawn.

As for the mission, of course, he had already got the information he wanted the moment the attempt had been made.

Madame Louise was Corinne.

They had raided the brothel at midnight. The various officers using the place had been politely asked to leave. The girls had been asked for their papers, then sent home.

And now, at one in the morning, Madame Louise was sitting in an interrogation room in the rue des Saussaies.

He began quite politely.

'Madame, let me save you the tiresome and unpleasant business of denying your identity. The little comedy you witnessed between myself and Colonel Walter the other evening was in order to plant false information with you. You passed the information on to your contacts. As a result, an attempt was made tonight on the life of a man pretending to be Müller. Thanks to this, we know for a certainty that you are Corinne.'

Louise said nothing.

'Perhaps you would like to tell me the names of your associates.'

Louise said nothing.

'Let us start with something easier then. How do you pass on the information?'

'There is a drop.'

'Thank you. And where is that?'

'In the River Seine.'

'Ah, madame. I am afraid it will be necessary for me to persuade you to do a little better than that.'

He worked on her for a while until she fainted.

It was time to turn in. If necessary, he could always bring other forces to bear on her. She had a son somewhere, he knew. Any threat to a child will break most parents. But it irked him professionally to have to resort to those means. He would persuade her. It would be a challenge to break her.

Early that morning, Max Le Sourd stopped in the rue de Montmorency and gazed towards L'Invitation au Voyage. There was a van and a Gestapo car in front of it.

He didn't go any closer, but stopped at a nearby café to ask what had happened.

'They came at midnight last night and arrested Madame Louise,' he was told. 'The place is closed. No one knows anything else.'

*　　*　　*

806

It was nearly ten in the morning when Schmid returned. But when he did, he received a shock.

'Dead? How? You did not leave a blanket or sheet in the cell?'

'No, Lieutenant.'

'A sharp object?'

The fellow looked embarrassed.

'A knife. When the guard brought her breakfast.'

They showed him. She had slit her wrists, in the correct manner. She had bled to death in minutes.

Schmid cursed and cursed, in fury. Then he ordered a car to take him to her house. That must be closed and sealed. At least he'd have her pictures.

As Thomas sat in his usual place by the bar, he supposed that he should be grateful. Luc hadn't much wanted to have Charlie's body in the cave at all, but as Thomas pointed out, it was less likely to be found there than anywhere else they could think of.

After that, he'd made his way home, where Édith had been more than relieved to see him. In the middle of the morning, Michel Dalou had come by to let him know that everyone had got back safely from the operation.

'Do you think anyone was identified?' Thomas asked.

'No. We all had face covering of some sort, and before the police recovered from the racket we made, we'd all run off.'

'That's good.' Thomas didn't tell him about Charlie. He'd have wanted to know what they'd done with the body.

'I heard we were set up,' said Michel Dalou.

'Maybe. Leave that to Max. He'll work it out.'

'Are we safe?'

'Yes. Nobody got captured, and you say no one was seen – so the police and the Gestapo have nothing.'

'That's good,' said Michel Dalou, and left.

But Thomas Gascon was thoughtful. The events of last night were forming a pattern in his mind. And it wasn't a pattern he liked at all.

Corinne was Louise. He knew Louise: the girl that Luc had set up, long ago. She'd paid his brother too, for years, before they'd had a falling-out.

He remembered also how his brother had been so anxious that he should not go on the mission last night.

And what about the cave? He'd said he'd been preparing it as a hiding place for him. Yet he'd never mentioned the fact until last night. Did that make sense?

Stranger still, now that he thought of it, had been Luc's reaction when he and Max had arrived with Charlie. At the time Thomas had been so concerned about Charlie that he hadn't paid much attention. But what had Luc said? 'They'll know my hiding place.' But who? Max; Charlie, if he'd lived. Why was that so terrible? Was he planning to hide from them? And then that final little cry: 'Brother, you've just killed me.' He wasn't just planning to hide from the Resistance. He thought that one day they'd kill him.

He remembered how Max had already been suspicious of his brother. And how he himself had made no comment, because, alas, he knew Luc's character.

Luc had known that last night was a trap.

It was early afternoon when Max stopped at the bar.

'Louise has been arrested. Midnight last night. I think I've figured it out. There are two alternatives. They may have used her to lure us into a raid, so that they could capture us. But I don't think so.'

'Why?'

'Because they failed to catch us. They could have had plain-clothesmen hidden around the place. They didn't. So that wasn't their object.'

'Go on.'

'I believe they set up Louise. Fed her false information that she passed on in good faith. They wanted to know if she was Corinne. By taking the bait, we confirmed it for them, and they arrested her. We just destroyed Louise.'

'So someone must have informed the Gestapo that Louise was Corinne,' Thomas reasoned.

'I think that must be it. One of her girls, perhaps.'

'Perhaps,' said Thomas.

Then he was very sad.

★　　★　　★

Luc was sitting alone in the room that gave on to his garden when Thomas arrived. He looked up a little anxiously when Thomas came in, and seemed relieved when he saw that his brother was alone. Thomas had a knapsack on his back. He put it down and went to sit beside him.

'I have a message from Max. He says thank you.' Thomas reached into his pocket and pulled out a flask of brandy. 'We need a drink.' He poured two glasses. 'What shall we drink to?'

'I don't know.'

'Well then: To us.'

They drank. Thomas waited a little while.

'There is one thing more.' He paused. 'I need you to tell me something.'

'Whatever you want.'

'I've been thinking about last night. I didn't understand at first. Then I remembered how you had tried to stop me from going. You said you'd been having bad dreams. And you reminded me I could hide in the cave.'

Luc said nothing.

'You were trying to save me,' Thomas continued. 'You tried to save your brother. I know it.' He put his arm around Luc. 'Do you remember when I fought Bertrand Dalou after they took your balloon?' He held his brother closer. 'It's always just been you and me. And now you tried to save my life. Do you know what that means to me?'

'You're my brother,' said Luc.

'But you have to tell me one thing. How did you know it was a trap? Who's your contact? Is it one person, or are there many? I need to know so I can protect you.'

'I don't think you can.'

'I can. Didn't I always?'

Luc looked down at the floor. Then he took a deep breath.

'It's just one man. Schmid. He's Gestapo. Works out of the avenue Foch offices.' He still didn't look up.

'Are you with others, or alone?'

'Alone.'

'And Corinne?'

'He asked me who it was. I didn't know. I just made a list of all the possible people I could think of. Coco Chanel, Marc Blanchard . . .

A whole lot. That was all. He didn't seem very interested. But then he told me he was setting a trap. That's all I knew. I didn't even know if yesterday was the trap, but I thought it might be. So I told you not to go.'

Was it the truth? Perhaps. Probably not the whole truth. But it was enough. Luc had informed. He'd let the others walk into a trap, and made an attempt to save his brother. A feeble one. Not enough to blow his own cover.

'I'll take care of Schmid,' Thomas said. 'You don't have anything more to worry about.'

'Really?'

Thomas smiled.

'We have to do something now. We need to move Charlie's body. We can't use the passage with it lying there. It wouldn't be too pleasant. We should take it all the way down into the chamber at the end.'

'Now?'

'I think so. Then we're going to burn it. It won't smell so bad. I brought some petrol.' He indicated the knapsack. 'Enough to get started.'

Luc shrugged.

'As you like.'

So they went into the garden, and Luc carefully opened the entrance into the passageway and lit a lamp, and led Thomas down to where the body was.

Then Thomas put the knapsack down and he took Charlie's body under the shoulders, and Luc took his feet, and they slowly carried Charlie down to the chamber. They stopped twice to rest on the way. It took them nearly a quarter of an hour. Finally Charlie was laid to rest in the centre of the chamber.

'Give me the lamp,' said Thomas, 'and I'll get the petrol.'

He moved swiftly up the passage and found the knapsack. He opened it to check that everything was in order. Then he started back down the passage again.

As he reached the chamber, Luc appeared in the lamplight, looking pale.

Thomas put the lamp down by Charlie's head, then in the shadow, he squatted over the knapsack and began to open it. He looked up at his brother.

'You needn't have worried, you know,' Thomas said quietly. 'I'd never have let them hurt you.'

Luc nodded.

Thomas smiled.

'I love you, little brother.'

'I know.'

Luc never saw the big Welrod with its silencer in his brother's hand. Thomas fired once. The shot went straight into Luc's heart. Thomas stepped over and quickly put a second shot into the back of his head.

The shots made a sound in the cave, but not much. Outside the cave, there was no sound at all.

Fifteen minutes later Thomas met Max and handed him back the knapsack containing the Welrod.

'It was him. It's done,' he said.

'The contact?'

'Gestapo. Schmid.'

If the Allies had hoped they would sweep across northern France, they had been disappointed. All through June the fighting in Normandy was intense. The western port of Cherbourg was taken on the twenty-first, but the Germans left its deep-water harbour almost inoperable. Reinforced, the panzer divisions at the old city of Caen held out, into July. Even a month after Cherbourg fell, the Allies had been able to take only the heights south of Caen. In the last week of July, the Allied forces in the far west began to swing around below the Germans, but the going was still tough.

Then, early in August, news came that General Patton's Third Army had joined this forward swing. One of the divisions serving under him was French. Drawn from the Frenchmen who had managed to get abroad, and by troops from Algeria and other parts of North Africa, General Leclerc's Second Armoured Division had just landed, eager to fight for France.

But where would Patton and his Frenchmen go?

One thing seemed almost certain. They wouldn't be coming to Paris. It made no sense. Eisenhower wouldn't want one of his armies to get bogged down in weeks, perhaps, of bloody street fighting. He would sweep across to the Rhine and beyond, and deal with Paris later.

Meanwhile, for Schmid there was his regular duty to attend to.

There were still huge stores of pictures in Paris that had not been sent back to Germany. But when it came to the confiscations for which Schmid was responsible, he had impressed his superiors very much. On his own initiative he had contrived to get everything crated and sent back into grateful hands in Berlin, and his zeal had been noticed.

Apart from the drawings he had kept for himself, of course. Those he had sent through the mail to his sister to keep for him, together with a note saying that he had bought them in Paris. When he'd found Jacob's pictures stored in Louise's attic he'd done the same thing. That had been a rich personal haul.

And now, on the morning of the nineteenth of August, he stood outside L'Invitation au Voyage and supervised the last of the crates being loaded on to the truck that was to carry them away on their journey eastward.

As the men closed the back of the truck, he signed their papers and the truck left. He watched it to the end of the street, until it turned the corner.

Just then, from somewhere in the distance on his right, he heard a brief rattle of gunfire. Then silence. He wondered what it was.

He turned. A few paces behind him, an old man was standing. Evidently, he'd been curious to watch the truck with its crates of pictures depart. There was a bag of provisions at his feet, and now the old fellow stooped to pick it up. Schmid was just about to walk past him when the old man pulled something out of the bag.

There was a soft thudding sound. Schmid frowned. Something had hit him with huge force in the chest. He stared in surprise. His legs were giving way. The cobbles on the street were rushing at his face in the strangest manner.

Thomas Gascon put the Welrod with its silencer to the back of Schmid's head and pulled the trigger again. Then he turned. No one had seen him. As he started walking down the street, he heard the sound of more shots. Nearer this time.

The Paris Rising had just begun.

*   *   *

The Paris Rising of August 1944 was not unexpected. They had all been preparing for many months. Yet all the same, when it began, Max was taken by surprise – not by the barricades, and the snipers, and the bombings, or the general strike which paralysed the city for several days. What astonished him was the number of Resistance men who had suddenly materialised.

They were easy to distinguish. The uniform was simple. A black beret was all a sniper needed to show which side he was on. Some Max knew, loyal men who'd been helping the Resistance for a long time, and were only waiting for the moment to come out and fight. Many more had joined during the last twelve months. But large numbers, Max strongly suspected, seeing which way the wind was blowing, had hastily added themselves to the insurgency practically overnight.

The Germans were not overwhelmed. They were still formidable. But they were confused.

Soon the city was split into districts, some under German control, others controlled by the Resistance. The situation was fluid, chaotic. Sometimes the Germans were shooting Resistance men by firing squad only two streets away from an area under Resistance control.

Max was engaged all over the city. His father was busy producing the broadsheets that would be distributed when the moment came – though Max found him cheerfully manning a barricade with the younger men in Belleville more than once. But each evening they met in company with several dozen other committed FTP men, communists and socialists, and reviewed the situation. The excitement was palpable. They were taking ground from the Germans all the time. Soon the Maquis would control the city.

Only one development threatened to throw everything in doubt. The Maquis received an urgent message from General von Choltitz, the commander of the city himself.

'The führer has given orders. If we have to evacuate, I'm to blow up the city.'

Frantically, with the help of the neutral Sweden's envoy in Paris, the Maquis negotiated with the general. At last the German commander made his choice.

'He's going to ignore Hitler's orders,' Max reported to his father. 'He knows what'll happen to him if he obeys them.' Then he smiled. 'It seems, Father, that the Paris Commune is about to be reborn.'

And then, on the evening of the sixth day, came the crushing news which put all their calculations at risk and, by the seventh day, destroyed all their hopes.

General Charles de Gaulle arrived to liberate Paris.

To be precise, the advance guard of General Leclerc's Free French Division arrived at the western gates of the city. When Max first heard it, he couldn't believe it.

'Impossible!' he cried. 'Eisenhower's not coming to Paris.'

'Eisenhower isn't,' they told him. 'But de Gaulle is.'

Within an hour, the advance guard had raced into the city, straight up its central axis, and arrived at the Hôtel de Ville behind the Louvre by nine-thirty that night.

When the two Le Sourds met with their usual committee that night, the story was becoming clear.

'It's all de Gaulle's doing. Eisenhower didn't want to go near Paris at all. But once the Rising began, de Gaulle badgered him, told him that if the Germans massacred us, it would be worse than the tragedy of the Warsaw uprising. In the end Eisenhower gave permission for Leclerc's division, together with the US Army Fourth Division, to divert up here. Leclerc actually disobeyed orders to wait and just drove straight through to Paris. He'll enter with his entire force, and the American division as well, in the morning.'

'Then we're screwed,' said Le Sourd bitterly. 'We can't organise the Commune overnight.'

With an entire division of well-armed and well-trained Frenchmen marching in to liberate Paris, not to mention another division of honest American soldiers to whom the very idea of socialism was anathema, the conservative patriot de Gaulle had not only the moral authority, but the naked power, to take the city over and impose his will.

The obstinate, lone officer who'd refused to give in, and gone to England to raise the Cross of Lorraine, had just shown himself to be a ruthless politician as well.

And so it came about. The following day, Lerclerc and the Americans swept into the city. The German general, probably secretly relieved, surrendered. And the following day, the twenty-sixth of August, a huge parade of troops, Resistance fighters and public men marched down the Champs-Élysées.

But it was one figure upon whom all eyes were fixed. Dressed in his general's uniform, towering over his companions, the tall, unyielding figure of Charles de Gaulle moved with a stately stride down the centre of the great avenue, knowing, as all who saw him knew, that he was the man of destiny that France would follow now.

Paris was liberated. The agony was over.

Max Le Sourd also marched, for old Thomas Gascon, and the Dalou boys, and his other comrades in the march would have been disappointed if he had not.

But his father remained at the side of the Champs-Élysées and grimly watched. And as the tall and lonely statesman strode past, Le Sourd could only shake his head.

'*Salaud*,' he muttered sadly. 'You son of a bitch.'

It was the next morning that Thomas Gascon decided to gather all his family together for a celebration at the restaurant. 'At least,' he pointed out, 'we have some extra food stored here.'

During the morning, Édith sent him down on an errand into the Second Arrondissement, and at noon he was already returning up the rue de Clichy.

He was less than a mile from home when he saw the small crowd coming towards him. There were about fifty of them, and they were goading a young woman. Her shirt had been ripped, and they were chanting and taunting her for sleeping with Germans.

Thomas frowned. He'd heard that these attacks were starting to happen. They were absurd, of course. If every Frenchwoman who'd slept with a German in the last four years was going to be hounded like this, there would be no end to it. God knew how many thousands of children had been fathered by lonely German troops in Paris alone.

But the ritual rage of a crowd that feels guilty has a special viciousness.

The wretched girl was the same age as one of his own granddaughters.

They had just drawn level when one of the girls in the crowd ran up to the young woman, pointed at her and screamed: 'German whore. Shave her head!' And she spat in her face.

'Fuck off!' the woman cried back. But the crowd was encircling them.

'Scissors!' someone cried. 'Razors!'

Thomas wasn't afraid to fight, even at his age, but half of them were women, and he wasn't used to fighting women. There were too many people anyway. So he did the only thing he could.

'*Mes camerades,*' he cried, 'I am Thomas Gascon from the Maquis of Montmartre, member of the FTP, Resistance fighter. It was I who cut the cables in the Eiffel Tower. Come with me to Montmartre, if you don't believe me, and I will show you witnesses. Whatever her faults, I ask you to let me take this young woman home, on this day of celebration.'

They looked at him. Could this old man be telling the truth? They decided he was.

'*Vivent les FTP!*' somebody cried. 'Bravo, old man!' And they started to laugh and clap him on the back.

For such is the strange and sudden sense of chivalry of the French mob.

'She's free. She's free,' they cried.

So Thomas Gascon took the girl home, before he went to his family celebration.

For Max Le Sourd, however, there was one duty still to be performed. When he explained to his father what it was, his father agreed to help.

Their first trip was to the cemetery. They needed to break some rules. After a little talk to the guardian, the matter was arranged.

So it was the corpse of Charlie de Cygne that was now placed in a simple casket and taken by Max Le Sourd, Thomas and the Dalou boys in a van to the cemetery of Père Lachaise. There the coffin was lowered into a small plot, pleasantly situated near the grave of Chopin.

Over the grave they placed a wooden cross inscribed with Charlie's name, the description 'Patriot', and the fact that he had died for France.

★　　★　　★

There were no religious obsequies. 'His family can do that,' Max said. But there was something else to be done. 'You're the writer,' Max said to his father. 'I'll give you the information, but you write it.'

The letter was a good one. It made no mention of the betrayal, but stated that Charlie had been wounded in an operation and died without pain. He had shown great bravery and dignity. His compatriots loved and respected him. Before dying he had spoken of his son.

It was simple and respectful.

'Shall we send it in the mail?' asked Max. But his father shook his head.

In early September, Roland de Cygne was surprised to receive a visit from Jacques Le Sourd at the château. Asking to speak with him alone, Le Sourd bowed his head, and told him: 'I have the great sorrow, Monsieur le Vicomte, to bring you the news of the death of your son. But he died bravely.' And he handed him the letter.

Roland read the letter slowly.

'When he disappeared, we feared something might have happened. But one always hopes, you know.'

'I trust it meets with your approval, monsieur, but to honour him as best they could, his comrades buried him in Père Lachaise.'

'Père Lachaise? There are some great names there.'

'His grave is close to that of Chopin. For the moment, it is marked with a wooden cross, very simple, with his name. You may wish a priest . . .'

'Of course.' Roland paused and thought for a moment. 'Was he carrying anything?'

'No papers, monsieur. They preferred not to carry identification, on a mission.'

'I understand. There wasn't perhaps a little lighter, made of a bullet casing?'

'Not that we found, monsieur.'

The letter from Richard Bennett did not arrive until the summer of 1945.

It explained the great difficulties he had encountered in tracing the benefactor he had known only as Monsieur Bon Ami.

But eventually, I was able to discover through a Paris lawyer that the owner of a Voisin C-25 coupé kept at a château in a certain part of the valley of the Loire was a Monsieur Charles de Cygne. I have learned with great sorrow that he died not long after he saved my own life. Please accept my deep condolences for your loss.

More than a hundred and sixty airmen, from Britain, Canada, Australia and New Zealand were betrayed or captured, many being sent to the camp at Buchenwald. Thanks to your son, I was one of the lucky ones to escape.

When I parted from your son, he gave me a little lighter, which I enclose, telling me it would bring me luck, which it certainly did. He told me I could return it after the war. Alas, he is not there to receive it himself, but I believe he leaves a son who, perhaps, might like to have it as a memento of a friendship, and with respectful gratitude from a Canadian airman whose life his father saved.

It was a graceful and charming letter.

'You know what's worst of all,' Roland said. 'If Charlie had kept that lighter, it might have brought him luck instead of the Canadian. He might be alive today.'

The next day they went to Père Lachaise. Roland de Cygne showed the little lighter to Esmé and told him that one day he should have it, as his father had before him. Standing together beside Charlie's gravesite, they let a moment pass in silent remembrance.

CHARLES de CYGNE
PATRIOTE
MORT POUR LA PATRIE
JUIN 1944

Epilogue

1968

If Paris in the spring was romantic, Claire thought, there was a beauty about the city in the autumn season that was just as lovely. And it brought new stirrings too. For after the traditional holiday month of August, when the place is strangely quiet, September marks the beginning of a new school and cultural year. And then, in October, comes the wine harvest.

She stepped out of the funicular and began to walk into Montmartre. She had spent all morning trying to come to a decision, but without success. Perhaps, she thought, if I get a little drunk up here, I shall know what to do.

She loved France. She knew that. All the years she'd been living in America, she'd always followed what was going on there. Not all of it had been happy.

After de Gaulle had brought some stability to the nation as it emerged from the war, Claire had been grateful to see France return to democracy. Given the deep richness of France, its economy would bear fruit under almost any government. It had seemed the French could even afford a generous welfare state. And the new European Community, thank God, had put an end to wars between France and Germany forever. But the internal politics of the Fourth Republic had been embarrassing. The mechanics of the French parliamentary model had been poorly arranged, and in ten years, there had been twenty governments. De Gaulle had refused to have anything to do with them.

The remaining French empire had also crumbled. In northern Africa, Algeria had gone into revolt. With many French colonists wanting to keep the territory, there had been a virtual civil war. In Indo-China, France had been pushed out of her colonies, and in one of those, Vietnam, the problems of communist insurgency had remained to become a nightmare for America too. Then, when Nasser of Egypt had nationalised the Suez Canal, and France and Britain had hatched a plot for military intervention behind America's back, they had been forced into a withdrawal that had destroyed their reputations as world powers, perhaps forever.

It was not until 1958 that the Algerian crisis had brought the Fourth Republic to an end, and that strange, lonely statue of a man, Charles de Gaulle, had finally returned from his retirement to take the reins of power.

Claire had mixed feelings about de Gaulle. His Fifth Republic had been nearer the American, presidential model. His prestige alone had made it possible for France to accept a free Algeria. He'd glorified the French Resistance and promoted the myth that only a handful of Frenchmen had been collaborators. He'd behaved before the world as if France was still a great empire. And France had regained some dignity.

And some glory too. André Malraux, the Resistance fighter and writer whom de Gaulle had made his culture minister, was busy transforming the dirty old buildings of Paris into a gleaming splendour that delighted the whole world. Notre-Dame was looking better than it had since it was built.

Yet for all this glory, it seemed to Claire, something of de Gaulle's personal spirit had also descended upon French society: proud, xenophobic and, socially, deeply conservative. Not that he was without humour, or didn't appreciate the traditional regional chaos of old France. 'How,' he had once famously asked, 'can one govern a country which has 246 kinds of cheese?'

But it was one thing to love France – to visit every year or two – and another to alter her life. The message from Esmé had been outrageous. COME AT ONCE, he'd said. The cheek of the fellow. But then it was easy for Esmé. He was free. He could do whatever he wanted.

She loved Esmé de Cygne. Though they met only when she came over to see her mother, they'd got to know each other well over the years.

They'd always had an easy relationship. He'd been so young when he'd lost his parents that Roland and Marie had been the nearest thing to parents that he'd known. He always called Marie 'Grand-mère', and he'd cared for her so devotedly as she grew older that despite their difference in ages, he and Claire had come to treat each other almost as if she were his older sister and confidante.

It wasn't until his teens that he'd come to know more.

As a child, Esmé had thought of Marc Blanchard as an honorary uncle. Roland had decreed that he should not know more than that. 'The little fellow needs some simplicity in his life, not more compli-cation,' he'd said. And both Marie and Marc had agreed.

But when Esmé was thirteen, and Marc became seriously ill, it was decided that he should learn the truth.

'And so I suddenly acquired another grandfather,' Esmé had told her. 'And learned that I share the same blood with Grand-mère and with you, my dear Claire, which makes me very happy. I think it was then,' he added, 'that I began to realise that all life is mysterious.'

Marc had seen quite a lot of his grandson during the last year of his life. He'd show the boy his paintings, and talk about Aunt Éloise, who'd started the collection, and about the old days when he would visit Monet at Giverny. When Marc died, he'd left Esmé both the art and his considerable fortune.

Roland had lived another five years after that. And after he'd died, very peacefully down at the château one summer, Esmé had inher-ited that as well. As an illegitimate heir, he could not have the title, but he had everything else. Fortune, it seemed, had smiled on him.

But not quite. There were still things that his family had concealed from him.

'I knew that Louise had been the child of Marc and one of his models,' he had told Claire on one of her visits, 'that she'd been brought up by upper-middle-class English parents and left an inherit-ance. I knew that she was a heroine of the Resistance, like my father. But then in my twenties, I began to notice that people would some-times give me a curious look. It was as if they knew something I didn't know.' He'd shaken his head in wry amusement. 'I had a vague memory of my early life, of course. I supposed that my mother had owned a hotel of some kind. It was only after making more inquiries that I discovered my mother ran one of the most famous brothels in Paris!'

'Was it a shock?' Claire had asked.

'Yes. At first. I made Grand-mère give me all the papers she had about me. I discovered everything about my mother, including her own mother's family, who are called Petit.'

'Did you meet them, too?'

'Yes. They had disowned Louise's mother and we had nothing to say to each other. But I'm glad to have known everything. In fact, it's been very useful to me.'

'How's that?'

'It's been a liberation. You know, bastards often feel that they have to make their own way in the world. Especially if there's something shameful in their origins. Would William the Conqueror ever have conquered England if he'd been legitimate, and not the grandson of a tanner who stank of urine? Who knows. Probably not.' He shrugged. 'But up until then, I had always thought of myself as – all right – the bastard son of Charlie de Cygne, but the inheritor of the estate, the son of two Resistance heroes. My place in life was set. Now, suddenly, my identity wasn't so secure. And that was good.' He nodded. 'I can understand those movie stars, you know, who go to Hollywood and reinvent themselves. That's a wonderful freedom, to be able to do that. So I have completely reinvented myself.'

'As what, Esmé?'

'As an outcast. It's wonderful. I come from the backstreets of the Faubourg Saint-Antoine. My mother was a whore and a brothel keeper. And I am also half an aristocrat. It's a revolutionary story. The child of the streets takes over the château. I'm becoming quite famous. I'm the editor of a magazine now. They interview me on television.' He shook his head. 'I feel sorry for aristocrats, actually, because no matter how good they are at what they do, nobody will take them seriously, which is quite unfair. But by being this outsider, I am probably better treated than I deserve.'

He was amusing company – and he had his feet on the ground. She liked that.

And he'd been wonderful to her that spring, when her mother died.

It hadn't been a shock. She'd always encouraged Marie to come to America, despite her age, so that she could see her grandchildren. Last summer, Marie had spent a delightful month with her, but told her frankly: 'I don't think we shall see each other again, my dear. One gets a feeling about these things, you know.'

Her mother had lived with her devoted housekeeper in the apartment on the rue Bonaparte right up to the end. Esmé had called in almost every day. And her departure had been entirely peaceful, in the first week of May, only hours after talking to Claire on the telephone. By the time Claire got to Paris for the funeral, Esmé had taken care of all the arrangements. There had been a large number of her mother's friends and admirers. And then there had been her French family, of course.

She had not often seen the other Blanchards. Ever since the days when she and her mother ran Joséphine, she had always found her cousin Jules well-meaning but rather dull. His son David, instead of following in the family business, had reverted to his ancestor's career as a doctor. Claire found him easier to talk to, and his wife and children were charming. She had found it a surprising comfort to know that her mother's family were still represented in Paris, and in the old house down at Fontainebleau.

After that, she'd stayed another ten days to sort out the estate.

There had been one quite unexpected feature of her stay, however.

That weekend, a simmering dispute over university conditions had suddenly turned into a huge battle in the Latin Quarter. Staying in her mother's apartment on the rue Bonaparte, Claire had been just outside the area of serious trouble, but only a short walk away from the excitement.

The night of her mother's funeral had been the worst. Vast crowds of students hurling *pavés* – the heavy cobblestones they tore up from the old roadways – had fought the police who'd occupied the Sorbonne. There were barricades everywhere, burning cars, and the terrifying CRS riot police swinging their heavy *matraques* had done serious injury to many young demonstrators. Within days, the unions and factory workers of France had joined in. A huge general strike had brought the country to a standstill, and even General de Gaulle himself had seemed about to fall.

But the *Quartier Latin* had been the place to be. The students had been allowed to occupy the university. Night after night, she and Esmé had wandered into the quarter together. They'd gone down the rue Bonaparte to the church of Saint-Germain-des-Prés, and had coffee and cognac in Les Deux Magots, and seen Jean-Paul Sartre coming and going more than once. They'd gone into the Sorbonne, and listened to students, workers and philosophers plan a new Paris Commune, and a new and better world. They might be somewhat Marxist, they were surely idealistic, but they were the eager heirs of the French Revolution, after all. And where else could one see this mixture of rhetoric, philosophy and French wit, except in old Paris?

It was a time to be young. Before long, France would re-elect conservative de Gaulle again. But if the protests against the Vietnam draft had ushered in a social change in America, Claire had a feeling that something similar was likely to take place in France.

She was glad she'd been there to see it.

It had been just as she was about to return to America that Esmé had sprung his idea on her.

'I wish I could see more of you. And it's obvious that you enjoy being here in Paris. Now that Grand-mère is gone, you need an excuse to come over. Why don't you buy a little pied-à-terre here in Paris? You can certainly afford it.'

'It wouldn't make sense to do that if I wasn't going to spend quite a bit of time here. At least two or three months a year,' she pointed out.

'So why don't you? There's nothing to stop you.'

'I really don't think so,' she'd said.

She'd talked to her children about it, back in America. But with their own young families to keep them busy, they didn't think they'd be able to make much use of such a place.

'Just do it if it makes you happy, Mother,' they'd said.

But like most people who've been mothers, Claire didn't find it easy to do things just for herself. So she'd turned to Phil.

After drifting slowly apart from each other, she and Frank had waited until the children were grown before quietly divorcing in the fifties. Frank had married again. She'd had a few discreet affairs, none really satisfactory. She'd concentrated on her own work.

And she'd made a small name for herself. She had written three well-received art books, and two works of fiction based on the lives of artists. Not only had these sold well in America, but to her great delight they had been published to critical acclaim in France.

And then she'd found Phil. Or, he would say, he'd found her.

Phil was her friend. He was her husband now, and she couldn't be happier about that fact, but above all he was her friend. He wasn't tall and handsome like Frank. He was somewhat round. He didn't have eyes that made her go weak at the knees. His eyes were brown, and gentle, and amused. He'd been a doctor, recently retired. Her children liked him. That was important. Just as important, so did her mother. After she'd been with him for a year, but not yet married, Marie had told her: 'I've left Phil a bequest in my will, dear, that I thought you ought to know about. I've decided to leave him that painting of Saint-Lazare in the snow. The one by Norbert Goeneutte.'

'But I always loved that painting!' she'd cried.

'Yes, dear. I know.'

When Claire had asked Phil what he thought about a Parisian pied-à-terre, he'd been unequivocal.

'I think you should do it,' he said. 'You've family there.'

'I don't care too much about Jules's family. And if Esmé wants to see me, he can get on a plane. He's free, and he's got all the money in the world. And I'm pretty much happy staying here with you, you know.'

'You mean you won't take me to Paris?'

'Not for months at a time. You don't speak French.'

'So I can learn. It'll be a project.'

'I'm not going to ask you to do that for me.'

'The offer's open.'

But she'd put the idea out of her mind, and spent a very pleasant summer sailing and seeing her grandchildren, and Phil's.

And then Esmé, with his cheek and sense of humour, had sent her a telegram.

COME AT ONCE.

'This is ridiculous,' she'd said.

'Why don't you go?' said Phil.

It was perfect, of course. It was delicious beyond all words. It was on the Île de la Cité itself, with a quaint living room with old beams, and two bedrooms, and a view over the Seine one way, and a glimpse of the flying buttresses of Notre-Dame the other. It was romantic. It was fun.

'You can be on either the Left Bank or the Right in a five-minute walk,' the agent pointed out, when she and Esmé inspected it.

'It's Friday,' Esmé said. 'I'll give you dinner tonight. Then we can go to the château for the weekend. I've already told them you'll want to see it again on Monday. Then you can make up your mind.'

'You've already planned all this?'

'Yes,' he said.

They had dinner in the Marais quarter. Claire had always found that part of Paris interesting. Since the days when King Henry IV had built the lovely brick square of the Place Royale, the Marais had been home to so many of the great aristocratic *hôtels*, as they were called. But when the court had moved to Versailles, the nobles had little need of their Paris mansions, and many fell into disrepair. The aristocracy had usually gone to the Saint-Germain quarter, after that.

But if the grand old mansions had been split into tenements, and parts of the area had become a thriving Jewish quarter, and other parts had filled with poorer folk from one or other of France's colonial possessions, whose streets, rightly or wrongly, had a bad reputation at night, one old square had retained its magical charm. The old Place Royale was called the Place des Vosges now. Apartments in its quiet brick mansions were favoured by international stars and the artistic rich. It was chic.

And it was in a quiet restaurant under the old colonnades that Esmé and Claire enjoyed a mellow dinner, and talked of the old days when she ran Joséphine, and met Hemingway, and Gertrude Stein, and many others. And Esmé told her that he was thinking of buying an apartment in the Place des Vosges himself, and how André Malraux was cleaning up the whole area, and restoring the old mansions, and how they were planning a huge new cultural centre over in the south-west corner of the Marais that would be like a sort of modernist cathedral when it was built.

But he was careful not to mention the subject of her pied-à-terre at all.

The next day they drove down to the château. Esmé didn't spend as much time there as he should. He was too busy with his life in Paris. But the place had its chatelaine.

Claire had heard about Laïla, the Jewish girl whom they'd rescued in the war, but she'd never met her. She found a delightful woman in her thirties. Laïla had married recently, a local vet, and they had converted one of the stable yards into a delightful office and animal hospital, as well as a large apartment for themselves. It suited everybody.

'Laïla's part of the family,' Esmé explained. 'She knows far more about everything in the château than I do, and she keeps the place in wonderful order.'

When Laïla took Claire around, and explained all the furniture to her, it was clear that she had mastered her subject to an almost professional standard. Indeed, when she showed Claire her favourite unicorn tapestry, one might almost have thought that she owned it herself.

Claire spent a relaxing weekend at the château, enjoying the country air. Then Esmé drove her back to Paris. Upon parting from her, he reminded her that she had an appointment to see the place on the Île de la Cité the following morning, but that he would not accompany her.

'I'll see you for dinner,' he said, 'and you can tell me the verdict.'

Claire left the funicular behind her and went through the streets of Montmartre. She had only once before been up there for the wine festival, and that had been long ago. No doubt it was even busier at the weekend, but there was still plenty of activity. The little vineyard on the back of the hill was looking very charming. Below it, the streets of the old Maquis were looking quite respectable now. But the whole hill still retained a bright, intimate village atmosphere that probably went back to medieval or even Roman times. The wine from the grapes themselves was not too drinkable, but she found space at a table at the Lapin Agile where the men welcomed her very cheerfully and insisted on sharing their bottle of wine with her.

It took only a couple of drinks for her to feel very much at home.

Were they all from Montmartre? she asked.

No, they laughed, they were all from the car works out at Boulogne-Billancourt. But their foreman was from here.

He was a short, sturdy, thickset man, but with a kindly face. His grandfather had lived in the Maquis when he was a boy.

'You had to be tough to live in the Maquis,' one of the men said, and there was a chorus of agreement. Yes, one had to be tough.

She was quite definitely a little drunk by the time she thanked them and went back up the hill. She might be a little drunk, she thought, but it hadn't helped her in the least decide what to do about that pied-à-terre. Did Phil really mean it when he said he wanted to learn French?

It was half an hour later that Marcel Gascon walked out on to the wide steps in front of the great white basilica of Sacré Coeur. It was a lovely afternoon, the light catching the towers of Notre-Dame, the distant dome of Les Invalides and the graceful curve of the Eiffel Tower.

There were quite a few people about, but he noticed one woman sitting alone, staring out over the city. It was the woman who'd shared a drink with the boys a short time ago. She'd been an elegant woman, distinguished.

He'd rather wished the boys hadn't made so much of the toughness of the Maquis. It was true, of course. But they made it sound as if everyone who came from there was crude, stupid, perhaps.

He went over to the woman, and stood beside her. She looked up and smiled.

'I come up here every year, madame, to look at the view.'

'It's beautiful.'

He pointed at the Eiffel Tower.

'It never looks the same, the tower. Changes in the light. Like those Impressionists. You know. They'd paint the same thing in different lights. Different every time.'

'This is true,' said Claire.

'It's made of iron, yet it looks so delicate. It's masculine, but feminine.' He shrugged.

'That is very observant, monsieur. I agree with you.'

'*Oui*,' said Gascon, feeling quite pleased with himself. 'It's indestructible, that tower,' he continued with satisfaction. 'Like a ship, weathers every storm.' He paused. 'My grandfather built that tower,' he couldn't resist adding.

'Really? That's a fine thing. You must be very proud, monsieur.'

'*Oui, madame*. Have a good evening.'

Claire watched him go, then gazed at the view.

Now she knew. She'd better telephone Phil. She'd enjoy teaching him French.

Afterword

P<i>aris</i> is first and foremost a novel. Other than the historical figures – from monarchs and ministers to Claude Monet and Ernest Hemingway – all the characters who make their appearances in its pages are entirely fictional. The names of these fictional families include some of the most common names in France, with two exceptions.

The name of Ney is chosen for reasons that the story will make clear; though Monsieur Ney and his daughter, Hortense, are, of course, entirely fictitious.

And the invented name de Cygne needs a word of technical explanation. The use of the particle 'de', which simply means 'of', is often a sign of a noble family. A man with this sort of name is addressed as 'Monsieur de Cygne', or spoken of as 'Jean de Cygne'. But when using the family name or title by itself, we do not need the particle. Just as in English we may refer to the Duke of Wellington as 'Wellington', we should properly say 'Cygne', rather than 'de Cygne'. In the case of French names, however – except when speaking of the most famous historical figures – it has become common nowadays to add the particle even where it's not needed. And so in this novel I have referred to 'de Cygne' and to the 'de Cygne family', rather than the more technically correct 'Cygne' and 'Cygne family'. I hope that purists will forgive me for this.

A few times in the tale, I have made some tiny adjustments to historical detail where absolute precision would have been confusing to the reader. For instance, the great minister of King Henry IV is called Sully, the name by which he is best known to history, although this was actually a title he gained two years after his appearance in the narrative. Insofar as possible, I have sought to avoid the use of more than one historical name for each given place or street. All named places are real with the sole exception of the little Chapel of Saint-Gilles. The saint is real, but his chapel is invented.

One error, however, I have allowed myself. In this novel, Ernest Hemingway attends the Paris Olympics on July 21, 1924. In fact, ignoring the games, he left for Pamplona on June 25 and did not return to Paris until July 27. But I feel he should have been at the games, even if he wasn't! At other times, he certainly liked to visit the Vélodrome d'hiver, as related in the story.

While I have undertaken extensive research in writing this book, I have also been aided by the fact that, though I am of British origin, I have a large number of French cousins whose homes have been my own, in Paris, Fontainebleau and other places, ever since I was a child. And while none of those cousins, or my many French friends, make any personal appearances in this story, my familiarity with them, and my memory of many stories heard, were a great help to me in imagining the tales of French families interacting through the days of the Belle Époque, the two world wars and the French Resistance.

To thank all these many people would take too much space. But I should like to record my particular debt, both for their hospitality and their cultural advice in the preparation of this book, to Isabelle, Janine and Caroline Brizard, to Jeanne Masoero and to the late Jacques Sarton du Jonchay, whose memories of the interwar years were invaluable.

Similarly, rather than record my thanks to all the curators of the many museums and cultural institutions in Paris I have come to know down the years, I should like to recommend just two that readers might possibly overlook. The Musée Carnavalet in the Marais quarter takes one through the history of Paris magnificently. And the charming Musée de Montmartre is full of fascinating surprises.

Despite the fact that, even nowadays, I always finish each project with an enviable collection of printed books to add to my library, I have never thought it appropriate as a simple storyteller to supply a detailed bibliography for each novel. However, having enjoyed his books ever since I first read *The Fall of Paris*, his masterly account of the Siege and Commune of 1870–71, I could not fail as a reader to record forty years of gratitude to Sir Alistair Horne, whose books on France and on Paris continue to be such a delight.

Once again, my many thanks to Mike Morgenfeld for preparing maps with such exemplary care and patience.

And finally, as always, I thank my agent, Gill Coleridge, for her constant guidance and wisdom, and my two exemplary editors, Oliver Johnson at Hodder and William Thomas at Doubleday, for their vision, unstinting support and creative responses to the many challenges of a complex project of this kind. I also owe great thanks to Coralie Hunter at Doubleday, to Cara Jones at RCW and to Anne Perry at Hodder for their help in guiding the manuscript through its various stages.

About the Author

Edward Rutherfurd is the internationally best-selling author of seven novels, including *London*, *Dublin: Foundation*, *Ireland: Awakening*, and *New York*.